FOR THE ETERNAL GLORY OF ROME

FOR THE ETERNAL GLORY OF ROME

TOM KRATMAN

For the Eternal Glory of Rome

A Baen Books Original

Baen Publishing Enterprises
P.O. Box 1403
Riverdale, NY 10471
www.baen.com

ISBN: 978-1-6680-7307-0

Cover art by Dominic Harman
Photos in Appendix C used by permission of the photographers identified there.
Link for CC-BY-4.0: https://creativecommons.org/licenses/by/4.0/

First printing, January 2026

Distributed by Simon & Schuster
1230 Avenue of the Americas
New York, NY 10020

Library of Congress Cataloging-in-Publication Data

Names: Kratman, Tom author
Title: For the eternal glory of Rome / Tom Kratman.
Description: Riverdale, NY : Baen Publishing Enterprises, 2026.
Identifiers: LCCN 2025043292 (print) | LCCN 2025043293 (ebook) | ISBN 9781668073070 hardcover | ISBN 9781964856490 ebook
Subjects: LCSH: Rome--History--Fiction | LCGFT: Alternative histories (Fiction) | Science fiction
Classification: LCC PS3611.R375 F67 2026 (print) | LCC PS3611.R375 (ebook)
LC record available at https://lccn.loc.gov/2025043292
LC ebook record available at https://lccn.loc.gov/2025043293

Printed in the United States of America

10 9 8 7 6 5 4 3 2 1

For my friend, General Claudio Graziano, of Turin, Italy, and, further, of Italy's fine Alpine Troops.
22 November 1953–17 June 2024

CONTENTS

9 A.D.

FOR THE ETERNAL GLORY OF ROME

406 A.D.

CHAPTER ONE

Who would relinquish Asia, or Africa, or Italy, to
repair to Germany, a region hideous and rude, under
a rigorous climate, dismal to behold or to cultivate,
unless the same were his native country?

— Tacitus

*Northwest Germania, September 9, 762 Ab Urbe Condita
(hereafter AUC)*

Rain poured from a leaden sky onto what had been over twenty
thousand miserable, shivering soldiers of the Roman Empire. The
numbers were fewer now. To add to the misery, a cold north wind
swept around them, finding the holes in their cloaks and the chinks
in their armor, chilling them to the bone. The forest around and
above them did nothing to shield them from either wind or rain.

Two men, a tribune—a junior officer—and what later generations might have called a "regimental sergeant major," stood
in the rain, trying their best to look unworried. The five or six
thousand men with them might collapse if they saw fear on the
faces of their remaining leadership. Five or six thousand? It could
have been more, by now, what with the refugees. Or less, what
with the losses.

"What was the name of that town, Top?" asked the officer.
"The one on the Lupia River, about a week's march east of the
castrum at Vetera? I think it was two days' march before we
went into summer camp on the Visurgis. I'd been thinking I'd

1

liked to have retired there, after my time with the legions was up and Lower Germany pacified and brought into the Empire."

Military Tribune Gaius Pompeius Proculus' face was ashen, though the centurion to whom the question had been addressed thought the boy was doing a commendable job of keeping the panic out of his voice and fear from his dark brown eyes. Which was good because, with the senior tribune butchered by the Germans, early on, the legate—if he was still somehow alive, stuck somewhere out there with Varus—and that newly worthless turd, camp prefect, the *praefectus castrorum,* Ceionius, looking ready to bolt, command would like as not fall on the young tribune's shoulders before nightfall.

Gaius Pompeius was young, just turned twenty-two, and a bit swarthy, like many Romans from the city proper. His nose was Roman, too, which was to say just a bit on the large side. Both hair and eyes were brown and his face unlined. That face was somewhat more triangular than usual. This, with his haircut, tended to make him look a bit like the youthful Julius Caesar, though he lacked the aura of seemingly genial psychopathy Caesar had often exhibited.

By education Gaius was an engineer, though he hadn't had much opportunity to practice since joining the legion. And, though he now carried a shield courtesy of a dead or badly wounded legionary, he wore a very high-end gilded muscle cuirass, partially concealed by a fine quality, red-dyed *sagum,* or cloak. Repelled by the lanolin that had been left saturated in the wool, rainwater ran off in rivulets, gathering at the bottom seam to drip onto the ground in a heavy stream.

In his right hand, Gaius carried an equally high-end short sword, ivory-gripped and made from steel forged in Toledo, Spain, much like the blade of the one carried by the senior centurion he had addressed as "Top." Atop and around his own head the tribune wore a crested officer's helmet; below the muscle cuirass hung a kind of skirt made of strips of white-washed leather, reinforced with small metal plates.

"Do you know how to use that, sir?" asked the first spear, gesturing at the gladius.

"Somewhat surprisingly, I do," answered the young tribune. He then explained, "When I first got my appointment—when my *father* got me my appointment—as tribune, he hired a retired centurion to teach my something about the army and a freed gladiator to teach me to use sword and shield in combination."

For his part, "Top," more formally known as "First Spear Centurion of the Eighteenth Legion, Marcus Caelius Lemonius," wore a similar *sagum,* almost as fine. His armor was a comfortable, if heavy, *lorica hamata,* or chain-mail cuirass. Crossing the mail, on their own rather complex harness, were *phalerae,* decorations for courage in battle. He did not wear—though Gaius Pompeius knew he was entitled to wear it—the *corona civica,* awarded for having at some time saved a citizen's life in battle. All muscles and scars topped by short hair, Caelius looked more as if he'd been carved out of a lightning-blasted oak and then been given life by the God of War, Mars, than like a normal, mortal man.

"Wise man, your father," said Caelius. "In any case, forget that town, sir; it doesn't exist." Caelius was the centurion in charge of the first century, of the first maniple, of the first cohort of the legion, hence of the maniple, of the cohort, and, for many purposes, of the legion.

The first spear removed his transverse-crested helmet from his reddish-blond and gray head to let the sweat evaporate. At over fifty-three years of age, his hair was heavily shot with gray and had gray at the temples. He was, of course, clean-shaven. He continued, "All that exists is that idiot Varus, dying back there with most of the Seventeenth and Nineteenth, and our own commander. And some of the *impedimenta* with a good deal of the army's tents and rations, of course. Oh, and the twenty-five or thirty thousand hairy, smelly barbarians in the process of killing them; they apparently exist, too."

Marcus Caelius pointed with his chin to the east, whence came the sounds of battle—the clash of stone and iron on bronze and steel, the terrified neighing of horses and lowing of oxen, the screams and shrieks of wounded and dying men and men gone mad—clearly, even through the thick, confusing fog. Even at this range and even with the trees, the fog, and the sound-absorbing mud on the ground, it wasn't hard to tell Latin from German. Nor, from the rising inflection and volume of the Germanic war chant, the *barritus,* to grasp that the Romans in the main group were losing. Badly.

But they haven't given up the fight yet, thought Caelius. *That would be a whole different sound.*

Caelius scorned anything resembling a muscle cuirass, thinking them fit largely for fops. Instead, underneath his *lorica hamata*, as with most of the legionaries of the Eighteenth, he wore a *focale*, or scarf, for both warmth and to protect the neck from the armor. Below that was a *subarmalis*, a quilted and padded jacket to reduce or prevent blunt trauma and to provide a bit of standoff for pointed weapon attacks. The *subarmalis* was wet, hence it sucked heat right out of Caelius' body.

A few of the newer men, those in the Second and Seventh cohorts, had those newfangled things, the *loricae* made from face-hardened steel bands around the abdomen and chest and over the shoulders, the whole assembly being held together by leather straps to which the bands were riveted. The men who wore them never ceased their complaints about how beastly uncomfortable they were, even with a scarf around the neck, this despite getting better protection for about half the weight.

Caelius also wore a single bronze greave, on his left, or forward, shin, adding a measure of protection where needed beyond what the *scutum* could provide. He'd bought a pair but had found he didn't need the one for his right leg and that using that one slowed him down more than he liked. He still kept it, for use on parade and such.

On his feet the first spear wore *caligae*, Roman military boots, supplemented by wool *udones*—socks—to protect his feet from the cold and to provide protection from the leather of the *caligae*.

The *caligae* were made from strips of leather, sewn to a thick sole and tied above and to the foot. The sole was reinforced with hobnails, both for wear and traction. On the theory that there is absolutely nothing one can do about water getting into leather footwear, the strips had gaps between them. If these allowed water in, they also allowed it to run out. Further, in the normal environment of the legionary, the hot and dry Mediterranean, the *caligae* allowed the feet to cool nicely.

Socks were expensive, so many troops wore foot wrappings, not different in principle to later Russian Army *portyanki* or German *Fusslappen*. The entire legion might add rabbit skins for warmth, but those were for later in the year. Similarly, most men by this time knew to have trousers, called *braccae*, for when the northern winters grew unbearable.

"Be our turn, too, soon enough." Caelius looked around,

outwardly sneering at the futile efforts of the men of the Eighteenth, along with their own hundred or so cavalry, plus two of the auxiliary cohorts. One of these was of mixed Thracian archers and Rhodian slingers. The other was made up of simple light troops, Germans who had taken the oath to the Emperor seriously and unto death. In addition to these, there were two *alae* of auxiliary cavalry, one of Gauls and one of Palmyrene horse archers. Flavus, the brother of the arch-traitor, Arminius, kept the cohort of German light troops well in hand, aided by an old sub-chieftain of his tribe, Agilulf.

On his own initiative, Marcus Caelius had pulled in the perimeter to form a camp for about seven or eight thousand men, which Legio XIIX might have a chance to build and defend, from the initial one planned, for twenty-plus thousand men and no small number of brats, tarts, and sutlers. Even so, progress, amidst all these trees with their tough and entangling roots, was slow and inadequate. And digging in mud was always slow and miserable.

"Though, even though we started with six thousand men, including the attachments from the Seventeenth and Nineteenth, what with both losses and refugees, I don't know how many we may have now. Fifty-five hundred or so would be my guess. Not counting the *auxilia*."

Not even the legion's own relatively small wagon train, the *impedimenta*, could add much to the defense, though it helped to strengthen the vulnerable corners a bit. And Marcus Caelius was pretty sure he didn't entirely trust the German auxiliaries, Flavus and Agilulf or no.

"Even if we get so much as a half-assed camp built," Caelius continued, "we've got maybe enough food for a week or ten days, on the men's backs and in the wagons. So we'll still have to try to break out. And there are too many of those shitty-assed Germans to have a hope of that. And, no, sir, there aren't any legions close enough to march to our aid."

"But," countered the tribune, "surely these barbarians will starve before we do. They've no logistic skill or foresight; barbarians never do."

"I'm not so sure of that, sir," replied Caelius. "In the fifth place, tell it to the shade of Crassus, who had his ass handed to him by barbarians who most certainly *could* do logistics. In the fourth place, they've been learning from us. In the third place, they've been here for some days. Couldn't have built that wall to the south that's given us so much trouble all that quickly. Probably started stockpiling food here when Varus sent that treacherous bastard Arminius to prepare matters for our arrival on the Visurgis. And *didn't* that son of a bitch prepare matters for our arrival? Maybe even before that. Maybe for the last couple of years; this ambush was *planned*. But in the second place, they couldn't have known when we'd show up so, for something this important, probably brought enough for several weeks, at least. But in the *first* place..."

"Yes?" the tribune prodded.

"In the first place, they're likely going to have captured all—most at least—of our food."

"Fuck," said the tribune.

"Fucked," corrected the centurion.

While outwardly Caelius might have sneered at the men's efforts at building a camp, inwardly he was deeply proud that the men of his beloved Legio XIIX were still trying, that they hadn't given in to the panic clutching at their vitals.

"Is there any—" Gaius' words were cut off by the cry, picked up at one or two points of their irregular perimeter and echoed across the lines: "Here they come again!"

Men who had been digging in their armor dropped their picks, mattocks, and shovels on the spot, retrieving their red-painted shields from where they'd been placed, stripping off the leather covers that protected them from the wet. Still others had gone forward to retrieve previously cast *pila*. These last now scampered back to their own lines, some with four or five heavy javelins in their hands and arms, some with as many as a dozen, and some with only one or two, the one or two shanks still stuck in German shields. Those men had also spent some of their time out in front of the lines usefully finishing off any wounded Germans who hadn't been able to do a convincing job of playing dead. And some who had; this was called "making sure."

The men who had retrieved the javelins hadn't bothered taking back any that looked broken or too bent; no time for that. They passed around what they'd brought back to their comrades. Some of those struggled to extract the still functional *pila* from the shields they'd pierced. Even with the encumbered ones, once freed, there wasn't quite one *pilum* for each man.

"What was that, sir?" asked Caelius, putting his helmet back on and tying the chin cord.

"Nothing, Top."

"Right. Sir, why don't you stay here? I'm going to walk the perimeter. I also want to have a chat with the chiefs of the auxiliary cohorts and the senior centurions trying to organize the escapees and advanced parties from Seventeenth and Nineteenth into something like military formations."

"Sure, thing, Top," the tribune replied, though he was loath to lose the first spear's steadying company. Moreover, he always tried to be honest with himself: "Know thyself"—that's what Menandros, his tutor in philosophy, had tried to drum into his head. So Gaius Pompeius understood perfectly well that he lacked the first spear's presence, charisma, and way with the men. To say nothing of battlefield insight. It's one thing to have read about Nero Claudius Drusus' campaigns in *Germania*, quite another to have been a part of them.

Gaius wasn't stupid, he was pretty sure, so figured he'd learn these things eventually. But for now? Let the experienced noncom handle matters and take his advice when a decision was called for that required an officer.

Well, I would have learned those things, eventually, *he thought. But I'm going to die here and have my corpse dumped in an unmarked grave. Wait, who am I kidding? The Germans aren't going to bury us; they'll just leave us for the wolves and crows. Maybe eventually the army will show up to bury what's left. My family tree has pretty deep roots, but I didn't really expect to get buried deeper here in Germany.*

As Caelius turned to go, one of his freedmen, Thiaminus, also called Caelius, ran up and tugged at the sleeve of his tunic. "Sir, the camp prefect would like a word with you."

"Where is the wretch, Thiaminus?"

The freedman—Caelius had freed both Thiaminus and his other servant, Privatus, largely because he didn't think you could hope to trust an outright slave when the going got tough—made a subtle little gesture with his head, adding for emphasis, "He's hiding in that thicket over there. Next to the legion's eagle."

"Of course he is," Caelius agreed, genially. "What else would he be doing? Lead the way, Thiaminus; I may need a witness."

Even as Caelius turned, a chorus of centurions ordered their men to "loose," which led to a strong volley of *pila*, and a good deal of *most* satisfying and exemplary Germanic screaming. This was followed by the sounds, much closer than where the men with Varus were dying hard, of clashing metal and stone.

The way led past the legion's small battery of scorpions—small torsion-driven artillery capable, under ideal conditions, of throwing a heavy bolt with quite respectable accuracy a distance of as much as two thousand feet. Sadly, in Germany's miserably wet climate, accuracy and range both fell off dramatically. This was so even though the twisted skeins that powered the scorpions were covered in bronze cylinders to protect them from the rain.

Even as Caelius arrived at the battery, several *twangs* sounded as the scorpions loosed their bolts. To the first spear, the sounds seemed *off.*

"Not that it makes much difference, Top, the endless rain," said the chief of the scorpions, a senior centurion named Quintus Junius Fulvius, from Caelius' own cohort. Fulvius was older than most centurions of the legion. He'd been passed over for promotion many times. Nonetheless, gray and old and a bit broken down, he was the legion's expert on artillery.

Scowling, Fulvius said, "Beyond that this damp has the skeins all floppy and as loose as an old whore's vagina, I'm just about out of ammunition. I've got some of the boys out cutting some wood but, you know, without a metal head and fletching, it's probably not worth the effort. And even with the skeins in poor shape, we still shoot farther than I'd care to send any men to retrieve the bolts."

Suppressing a sigh, Caelius answered, "Just do the best you can, Quintus. Nobody can ask more."

Silently, Fulvius nodded, then tramped off to see to the tightening of the skeins on one of the farther scorpions. He felt the skein with his fingers, then flicked his forefinger at it, several times in different places. As he did, he muttered under his breath various curses aimed at certain gods and goddesses, and especially Tempestas, which Caelius feigned not to hear.

The first spear, led by Thiaminus, suppressed a smirk and continued on to the thicket within which cowered the camp prefect, Ceionius.

Without stopping, Caelius saluted the legion's eagle, with its plate underneath reading "XIIX." Even as he did, he wondered,

Should I have a fire built so that we can at least keep it and the imperial images out of the barbarians' hands? Or at least get one ready we can torch off at need and toss the eagle into? Well, first things first.

With an audible sigh, Marcus entered the thicket. He noticed immediately how *old* Ceionius had gotten, so very suddenly. *He'd always seemed like a younger man to me, full of energy. But with all the spirit drained out of him now, only this old husk remains.*

"Sir?" Marcus asked of the camp prefect, inside the thicket. He kept his voice carefully neutral, lest his contempt for the man shine through. This was made slightly easier by the sight of Ceionius' ears, sticking preposterously far out from the sides of his helmet.

"We've got to surrender," said Ceionius. The terror in the man's voice was palpable. "We haven't got a chance, not a chance, Caelius. We don't even have enough food to march to a river."

"Are you out of your fucking mind?" asked the first spear, heatedly. "Don't you remember what the Germans did to Legio Five when they destroyed it twenty-five years ago? They crucified the survivors, the lot of them. We're not surrendering shit."

The words seemed to go in one of Ceionius' ears and out the other. In any case, he acted as if he hadn't heard. "Yes, that's our only chance. Surrender. Then the emperor can ransom us. That's it! That's the only way!"

"The fucking Germans don't care a fig for gold or silver, you idiot," Caelius hissed. "There's nothing much to buy with them, except what our merchants sell...and I don't imagine they'll survive the month. And the emperor is not going to give them what they do want, arms and armor. No, it would be a bad death or slavery for the lot of us if we were stupid enough to surrender."

Now those words, Ceionius *did* hear. And didn't like. "I outrank you, you pissant centurion and you *will* do as I order."

"I will *not*, you overaged and overpromoted coward. We'll stand here and fight. This is the bloody Eighteenth Legion; not a man will obey you."

"They'll obey or they all *will* find themselves decorating a cross, and you, too, you insubordinate son of a whore." At this, the camp prefect drew his gladius, not so much with intent to do harm as a form of punctuation.

No matter, thought Marcus Caelius. He gave Thiaminus a quick glance. The former slave shrugged, as if to say *You know what's best, boss. And, at least, since I'm not a slave anymore, they won't torture me for testimony.*

This is hard, hard, thought the first spear. *I can remember better days with Ceionius. Sharing wine. Telling stories, some of them pretty tall ones. What happened to turn a former first-spear centurion into such a... such a... well, frankly, such a girl? If I let this, this girl out to start giving orders to the troops, some will obey. Others won't know what to do. We'll be weakened and then destroyed without even a decent fight. So...*

Caelius' hand moved to the gladius hanging at his left side, unlike normal legionaries, who wore theirs on the right. In a single, seamless motion the sword then leapt from the scabbard to Ceionius' throat. A quick and deft pull to the prefect's left completed the destruction, slicing neatly through both a carotid and a jugular. Blood gushed to fall to the muck below, the softness of the ground dulling the splash. Ceionius fell equally silent, only the clattering of his armor and the *phalerae* adorning it making any sound. And the wood of the thicket and the mud below absorbed that.

Gently, Caelius took one knee beside the body. He wiped his gladius on Ceionius' tunic, where it showed past his right shoulder, then re-sheathed the blade. Gently, almost reverently, Caelius used the same hand to close the prefect's eyes.

"He was a fine soldier once," the first spear muttered. "Let's see if we can't make sure that that's the part people remember."

"I saw it all, Centurion," said Thiaminus. "He was clearly out of his mind, lunging at you like that. Why, you couldn't help yourself."

Caelius smiled and said, "You're a shitty liar, Thiaminus, but I appreciate the thought. No, if it comes to it, I'll just tell the truth, that he had to be killed to put an end to pusillanimous conduct in the face of the enemy. But I hope the question will never come up. I'd prefer he be remembered for the soldier he was, once upon a time.

"Now come on, we've got a line to troop."

Stepping lightly from the thicket, Caelius told the aquilifer, "The camp prefect is indisposed." *Which is, come to think of it, as true a statement as has ever been.* "Come with me. Let's see if we can't find some opportunity for you to earn your four hundred and fifty denarii."

It was said lightly, with a grin, which prompted the aquilifer, one Gratianus Claudius Taurinus, to likewise grin and answer back, "But however will you earn your thirty times as much, Top?"

Marcus looked about, then seemed seriously to consider the problem. Rubbing his chin, thoughtfully, he answered, "Well, let's see; thirty thousand Germans, give or take...at a denarius apiece, butchered, skinned and cleaned...that's thirteen thousand, five hundred for me to kill and butcher. Meh, all in a day's work. Let's call it another sixteen thousand for the legion and auxiliaries, two and a half each...and so you're going to have to murder nearly five hundred of the bastards, yourself. You up to it, Claudius? I'd hate to have to have your pay docked."

"Fuck, yes, Centurion!" The aquilifer grinned even more broadly under the lion's head draping his helmet; the creature's skin cascaded over his shoulders and down his back, while the arms and paws were tied across his chest.

"Good lad; knew you were." With a hearty clap to the aquilifer's shoulder, Caelius said, "Well, come on then, let's go see to the troops!"

Marcus deliberately steered his little party away from the tribune and toward as assemblage of refugees and the advanced party from the Seventeenth, resting their leather-covered shields while standing in ranks and being harangued by a senior centurion of their own.

Earthy, bragging, and to the point—that's what they need to hear. Caelius headed over to listen for a bit...

"...You pussies are *not* going to embarrass me and the rest of the legion in front of the Eighteenth, d'ya hear? Yeah, we took it in the shorts for a bit, and, sure, you need a moment or two to catch your breath, but we're going to take a piece of the line and give some of the boys from the Eighteenth a little break. We're going to get organized. We're going to scout, and, soon as we can, we're going back to get our comrades and our eagle. Oh, and our tents and our whores. Any fucking questions?"

The centurion from the Seventeenth caught a glimpse of Caelius and the eagle. He ordered a more junior centurion up, then trotted over and reported in: "First Order Centurion Quintus Silvanus, Seventeenth Legion."

Silvanus was both shorter and darker than Caelius, about equally scarred, and possibly a bit broader in the shoulder. He looked like a man not to be trifled with.

"I don't think we're going to be able to go back and save the Seventeenth," said Marcus, leaning in and whispering. "Wish to Hades we could."

Silvanus' voice was full of grief. "I know that. You know that. But the troops *don't* know that, and they need some kind of hope to hang onto. Hell, we're all going to die but we can at least keep fighting until the Germans finish us off rather than being pursued and slaughtered like stampeding cattle. Now where do you want us?"

Before Caelius could answer, Silvanus pointed and said, "By Vulcan's blue balls, that's some of our men. Those are our white shields."

Caelius' blue-eyed gaze followed the other centurion's pointing finger. He saw, staggering out of the woods to the east, several hundred, at least, of the legionaries of the Seventeenth, some likewise with white-painted *scuta*, beset on all sides by Germans content to throw their primitive javelins and whatever rocks they could find, plus the occasional flint axe. More Germans beset the front ranks of the cohorts of the Eighteenth, with the Germans' backs to the new refugees.

Before Silvanus could ask for permission, Caelius said, "They're yours; go get them, as many as you can. Don't get massacred in the getting, though."

"Yes, Top! Thank you, Top!"

To Thiaminus, Caelius said, "Go get a couple of the medical types here to do triage when Silvanus brings his lost sheep home."

"Yes, sir," answered the freedman, who then ran off for the field hospital.

Meanwhile, turning to his ad hoc cohort from the Seventeenth, Silvanus bellowed, "All right, you pussies, you see it yourselves. Those are our men. Forward...march...At the double, follow meeee!"

Meanwhile, Caelius and Claudius bolted ahead of Silvanus for the cohorts that stood between the new refugees and the more organized refugees under Silvanus. When they arrived, Marcus knew there was no time to follow the niceties of the chain of command. Ordinarily, he'd have given the order to the senior centurions of those cohorts to let Silvanus' men pass. But, since there was no time, he just shouted out, "You men know my voice. When I give the order, I want you to shift right, those who are uncovered, to cover down by files. Yeah, it's tough with the Germans on you like a stud on a bitch, but ... no more explanation; Cover ... DOWN!"

Automatically, the men of two cohorts shifted right, leaving about half the Germans facing them a little nonplussed. Almost instantly, a wave from the Seventeenth surged through the gaps, bowling over Germans and not even bothering to finish them off. That didn't matter, though, as the red-shielded men of the Eighteenth were more than happy to stab and slice as much as needed to finish off the discombobulated barbarians.

Caelius took careful note of Silvanus' approach to unruly Germans. He attacked with maybe three overstrength centuries, line abreast, and six ranks deep. They all struck to the right side of the approaching mob of fugitives from the Seventeenth.

The Germans were a brave people; Marcus hated their guts, for the most part, but still could concede the truth of that. But they weren't idiots; absent some signal advantage, they had less than no interest in standing up to a metal wave sporting razor-sharp teeth coming on at the double. Casting whatever javelins and axes they may have had left and to spare, unencumbered by armor, they took to their heels to await a better opportunity.

Silvanus continued driving the Germans back and to the flanks until he reached the rear of the mob. He continued then another fifty paces to make sure the Germans were continuing to run, then had his group execute a smart three-eighths about-face, to charge down on the barbarians besetting the other side of the mob. These took off, too, and perhaps that much faster for having seen their fellows on the other side routed. With the mob now free of harassment by the Germans, Silvanus formed his men on line, in a loose order to allow the mob to pass through. This they did, some running, some limping, and some being helped by their fellows. As the last of them passed, the centurion began giving orders for the centuries to leapfrog back to the safety of the Eighteenth, but moving slowly enough for the mob to keep that one critical step ahead.

The Germans began to cluster and come on, then, but tentatively, as if expecting the legionaries still in good order to charge them or even to hurl some of those frightful heavy javelins they usually carried.

While Silvanus kept his little command in hand, Marcus met the refugees as they filtered through the lines of his own cohorts. He wasn't especially bothered by their wounds, their blood, and the occasional legionary trying to hold his guts in with both hands. No, what he found shocking was how many of them had lost their *scuta*, and how every last one of them had lost their *furcae* and *sarcinae*, their packs and the poles to which those packs and other necessary gear was affixed.

*Bad sign. Very *bad* sign.*

"Sit down, boys," Marcus ordered, "but over there where the medics can see to you." He gestured in the general direction of a cloth standard attached to a pole, the standard showing the medical symbol, the caduceus. Marcus also noticed that the legionary *haruspex*, Appius Calvus, what a much later generation might have called a "chaplain," of sorts, was standing by with the medicos, presumably to lend a hand.

Though Marcus Caelius was too far away to hear it, Calvus muttered as he examined one wounded man, "There is nothing alive more agonized than man / of all that breathe and crawl across the earth."

Samuel Josephus, the legion's chief doctor, or *medicus*, did hear it. "Homer?" he asked of Calvus.

"Even so," the round-faced *haruspex* agreed. "*The Iliad.*"

Watching the triage from a short distance, the first spear thought, *This one isn't bad, for all that he's fat. I've seen some that were just lazy shitheads, but he's willing to pitch in where he can. And the troops are pretty sure he's really got the sight, to boot. After all, he did warn the legate about Arminius, even though he probably got the idea from Segestes.*

Turning back toward Silvanus, he saw the men of that makeshift cohort filtering back through the lines of the Eighteenth.

"You saw," said Silvanus, obviously meaning the wretched, demoralized state of the refugees.

"I saw," agreed Marcus Caelius.

"A day of rest," said Silvanus, "and some reequipping, and they should be fine."

"I agree but..." A murmur from the lines distracted both men. They looked generally eastward, to where Varus and the bulk of the army lay, entrapped, and saw smoke—thick, dense smoke—rising upward and billowing to the south. The setting sun illuminated the smoke in a way that, under the circumstances, was positively creepy.

"Fuck," said Silvanus, "that's not some random bit or arson from the Germans, not in this weather. They're burning the baggage to keep it out of the Germans' hands."

"Fucked," corrected Marcus Caelius.

A German, one-eyed and bright blond, strode up to Caelius and Silvanus. He carried his crested helmet under one arm, letting the rain run down his face and neck. He towered over the two Romans. The German wore Roman armor that hadn't been looted, carried a Roman sword, was clean shaven in the Roman manner, and wore his hair close-cropped like other Romans.

"Hail, Flavus," said Caelius and Silvanus, together. "*Ave*, Flavus."

"*Ave, Primus Pilus*," answered the German. "*Ave*, Centurion." His Latin was flawless and without accent, except that of the upper crust of Rome, the city.

Cutting to the chase, Caelius asked, "Can you tell us what happened?"

The German nodded and sneered, then said, "Well...it all began when my father knocked up my mother and then neglected to strangle my bastard treacherous brother in the crib. Or it could be that he acquired his lust for power from you, when Rome was educating us, as boys. But you mean more recently, yes?"

"Yes." Caelius barely hid a smirk. *Anybody who can keep his sense of humor while this deep in shit is a Roman at heart.*

"I don't know how long my brother's been planning this; years, I think. Maybe ever since he saw how poorly the legions fared in dense woods down in Pannonia. Maybe longer still. He always kept his own counsel.

"In any case, he somehow managed, under the guise of diplomacy on behalf of Varus, to form an alliance of tribes, most of which hate each other's guts but apparently hate Rome and civilization more."

At the mention of Varus' name, both Caelius and Silvanus spat.

"Don't hold the governor too much to account," Flavus said. "If Arminius could fool his own brother, how much chance did a near stranger have to understand him?"

"No excuses," said Caelius. "It wasn't your job to ferret out Arminius' intentions, even if—maybe especially because—he was your brother. It *was* his."

"Maybe," Flavus conceded. He then laughed. "They'll be fighting amongst themselves ten minutes after they finish us off, you know. That's a good deal of why half of my tribe supported Rome from the beginning. The carnage we Germans inflict on each other routinely is just appalling."

Caelius found himself a little warmed by the German's use of "us."

"Maybe not," said Silvanus, "not this time. Maybe they'll all march west and then south, as the Teutons and Cimbri did in the time of Marius."

"True," said Flavus, bitterly. He had learned truly to love Rome during the time when he, like Arminius, had been what amounted to student hostages, since early boyhood. "Hades, that *is* true. What the hell are we going to do? The forces on the frontier must be warned!"

"How reliable is your deputy," asked Marcus Caelius, "the big bruiser with the bear skins over his *lorica*?"

"Agilulf? I wouldn't necessarily trust him to fight Cherusci, men of our own tribe, generally speaking, but he'd happily gut any other Germans. Buuut...he doesn't speak all that much Latin and doesn't know much besides line up and poke the man in front of you. On the plus side he keeps good discipline. Which gets into what you asked me originally: what happened?

"I didn't see it myself, mind," the Romanized Cherusci said. "Got it from some stragglers and runaways. But my brother had command of the German auxiliaries nearest to Varus, a whole cohort of them. Big cohort, too, eight hundred men, maybe. At a signal from him—no, I don't know what the signal was—my countrymen came pouring out of the woods in their thousands. Right after he gave the signal, he gave some orders and, instead of forming up to face north and south, that cohort faced east and west and drove into the legionaries that had been ahead of and behind them. Instant chaos. Instant break in the line. Instant inability for Varus to give any commands to the Nineteenth Legion, too. Varus did manage to escape to the Seventeenth, but they were so distorted by the attack he can't have lasted too very long."

A sudden thought came to the German. "Centurion, have you talked to any of those men from the Seventeenth you saved yet?"

"No, not yet," Silvanus answered.

"Talk to them. I'll bet you that they aren't just some stragglers and runaways, but that they're just about every man that's
still free and alive from the Seventeenth."

"Shit!" the centurion cursed, seeing the truth of what Flavus
had said. "My legion is gone, that smoke is from the baggage
from some fires set by the last survivors."

"Cool men, then," Marcus Caelius said, consolingly. "Brave
ones, too, to keep their heads about them and try to help us as
much as they could.

"Hmmm," Caelius continued. "If the Nineteenth had already
gone under, the Germans would be on us like flies on shit. They
aren't, not yet, so the Nineteenth still stands."

"That seems likely," both Flavus and Silvanus agreed. "So what?"

"So maybe in the morning we can fight our way up over
that hill, flank the Germans, and bring the Nineteenth out to
us. Silvanus, if I leave you three cohorts—both the auxiliary
cohorts, and your own men plus the two hundred or so from
the Nineteenth who were with us—do you think you can hold
this...you should pardon the expression...camp?"

Without hesitation, the centurion answered, "No. The perimeter
is too long, the woods too much in and around, and the camp
itself is much too weak. Leave me five cohorts, plus the others,
and I can. But that won't leave you much, not enough to get
through those Germans behind their wall. Especially when the
ones farther east join them."

"Well," mused Flavus, "what if I disguise myself as one of the
tribesmen? There's plenty of bodies here. Some skins. A round
shield. A little war paint. I do speak the language, too, after all.
So we disguise me up and I make my way to the Nineteenth,
tonight. I tell them to strike southwest, across that hill, to link
up with you. Then, somewhere near the summit, you link up
and march back to here. I can probably scout out the best place
for them to attack, though I doubt I'll get back in time to do
much to help you."

"Fuck it," said Caelius, suddenly. "Fuck the camp, too. It'll
be all of us going over that hill. Yeah, the trees will break us
up some, but at least we won't be strung out in a file of twos
and threes. I saw it when you went out to bring your men in,
Silvanus: the Germans don't like facing legionaries in good order
for beans."

"The wounded?" asked Silvanus.

Marcus Caelius was a hard man but even he balked for a moment at the prospect of leaving their wounded to the tender mercies of the barbarians who would flood the camp once the legions and its attachments marched off. But then...

"Few hundred wounded. Okay, maybe closer to a thousand, but half to two thirds of those are walking wounded and can still fight. On the other hand, five to eight thousand legionaries and auxiliaries to be saved. The five to eight thousand have it. We strike at first light. We'll load the non-walking wounded into whatever wagons we have and the walking wounded can guard them. Best I can do."

"Sun will be in our eyes," Silvanus objected.

"Leaving aside that the trees will shield us from the sun, Flavus, will this rain keep up?"

"This time of year? This part of *Germania*? Nearly certain to."

"All right, then. Flavus, you disguise yourself and slip out after the sun goes down. Find the Nineteenth and ask for *Praefectus Castrorum* Lucius Eggius; he's a good man. Explain what we're going to try, from our end, and tell them where and when to attack. Silvanus, you go get as many of your men as can be used, including the ones you just rescued. I want you to put on a good show, that's all, not to slug it out with the Germans."

"I know Eggius," said Flavus, "A good Roman, brave and true as ever any was."

Briefly, Marcus Caelius thought of Ceionius, lying dead in the mud not all that far from here. *What is it that can make one man, as good as any other, turn a coward when age is upon him? I just can't understand it; it's not as if he had many years left to lose.*

Pushing the question away, Caelius said, "Before you leave, Flavus, get your Agilulf and make him understand to follow Silvanus. Silvanus, I want you to stretch out in as solid a line as you can make it from the swamp to just west of the edge of the Germans' wall, to guard our flank, as it were. Meanwhile, I'm going to go explain to the tribune what his orders will be—oh, he's a good lad, and willing enough, but new—and then see that he gives those orders to the other senior centurions. Or maybe I should do it myself, as if they're coming from him. Finally, Flavus, in case this doesn't work steal a horse and get to Aliso.

When you get there warn the commander there—I think it's Lucius Caedicius—about what's coming. It will be up to him to decide whether to hold the fort or pull back behind the Rhine. If this works, we'll strike for the open agricultural country in the middle of Cherusci land, resupply ourselves by any means necessary, then to the Lupia River."

If there was anything Flavus wanted beyond the glory and safety of Rome, it was that the legions should stay far from Cherusci lands. What he hadn't mentioned to Marcus or Silvanus was that his and Arminius' father, Segimerus, was likely also arrayed against the Romans. If they found that out—and they might—and they found their way to the land of the Cherusci, even these woods might not provide enough wood for all the crosses.

Flavus thought and he thought quickly, then said, "No, the bulk of the enemy are to the east. There is probably another ambush site prepared there, too. Moreover—give my treacherous brother his due—I'd be bloody amazed if there were not more than one, and a like number to the west."

"So, what do you suggest?" asked Caelius.

"South," answered the Roman Cherusci. "South for sixty miles. Yes, you may go hungry for a day or two going that way, but once you reach the river you can cross it, to put it between you and my brother's army. Wait, you do have engineers with the legion, still, right?"

"We do," Caelius answered. "For that matter, the advanced parties from both the other two legions were about a third engineers. And we have the pontoon bridge."

"Right," Flavus enthused. "You can bridge it, burn the bridge after you cross, and then be supplied by water as you march to the Rhine."

"I think he's right," said Silvanus.

Thank you, Odin and Jupiter, thought Flavus.

"Makes enough sense," agreed Caelius. "We'll do that. But first we need to extract the Nineteenth."

From the other side of the camp came the cry, "Here they come again!"

INTERLUDE

Exploratory Spacecraft 67(&%#@, Several Hundred Znargs
Above the Teutoburg Forest, Ergtil of the Martyrs 11216

"Can't you do *anything*?" asked Sweetasthescentofglowblossoms, or "Blossom," for short. "Those poor creatures! And they're all going to die horribly, if you can't or won't." Her language was a series of squeaks, whistles, grunts, and sung notes, punctuated with clicks.

Blossom gestured to the large view screen being fed images from a reconnaissance skimmer, far below. On the screen, some bipedal creatures were having their exoskeletons torn off before being tossed onto fires. The tearers and burners were much larger and seemed rather shaggy. Still others among the insects—for so they appeared to Blossom—were being affixed to trees by some kind of metallic pins, very crude things. The mouths of them all were opened in what appeared to be cries of unbelievable agony.

"I don't know," answered Blossom's mate, Scoutmaster Seetheredglowofmorning, also known as "Red." The languages were completely mutually intelligible, but Red's version had rather more grunts and clicks, rather fewer sung notes. "The places where they're all intermixed, I can't do anything about. If I move the insects, I'll move the insect killers at the same time. Same for the ones forming that oval to the planetary east; I can't help them by anything regulations don't expressly forbid."

"But the group to planetary west?" she asked. "They're not closely beset. Can you help them?"

21

"I'm working on it," answered Red. "I could transport them and, if I had several *ergtils* to do the calculations, I could probably do it harmlessly. As is, given the planetary rotation, the wobble, and the speed at which it orbits its sun, if I am not careful, they could end up a *znarg* or two up in their atmosphere or in the middle of one of the planet's oceans. Or in space. I think they need oxygen, so space is right out. And if they could fly, given their circumstances, I imagine they would."

Blossom focused on where some hundreds of the insects were slowly drowning in the swamp to the planetary north of where the great murder and torture were taking place. Sighing with regret, she said, "I don't think these poor creatures are adapted to deep liquid."

Then she asked, "Could you perhaps whisk away all the shaggy-hairies that beset those poor creatures?"

"Strictly against regulations," Red said.

"Buuut... All right, my dear."

"Well, dearest, give me a half a thousand beats to try to fine-tune matters enough for them to survive. Or at least have a fair chance. If it looks like they're going to be destroyed before that, we'll just push the button and hope for the best."

"As you think best, Red," she agreed, stroking one of his twelve shoulders with a soothing tentacle.

CHAPTER TWO

Even iron is not plentiful among them; as may be inferred from the nature of their weapons. Swords or broad lances are seldom used; but they generally carry a spear (called in their language *framea*), which has an iron blade, short and narrow, but so sharp and manageable, that, as occasion requires, they employ it either in close or distant fighting.

—Tacitus

Northwest Germania, September 9, 762 AUC

The rain still came down in sheets, even as the wind continued to find its way through the rings of the mail and the bands of the newer kind of *loricae*. The was little wood that could be set alight. Thus, there were no sentry fires out beyond the camp's perimeter. Warming and cooking fires were right out.

A small group consisting of the tribune, the first spear, the aquilifer, Silvanus, Flavus, and Caelius' servants stood on the side of the camp nearest the fortified hill held by the Germans, but a good fifty meters inside that perimeter. A single tent, a large one capable of seating a score of men, was erected behind them. Inside the tent, protected from wind and rain, burned half a dozen oil lamps, some with multiple channels and wicks.

"In a way," said Flavus, "it's good, the darkness. I'd have a much harder time getting out unnoticed, if the whole area were lit up like daylight."

They'd used the darkness not just to gather material to disguise Flavus' upcoming adventure, but also to retrieve the bulk of the *pila* already thrown. Many of these were currently under repair within the camp by the century of artificers from First Cohort. They'd also used the darkness to retrieve over two thousand German *framea*. Before sunup, every legionary would have at least two javelins again, all of which—*pila* or *framea*—would be effective against unarmored Germanic tribesmen.

Marcus Caelius couldn't see it, in this pitch darkness, but he couldn't help but hear as, in a desperate bid to keep warm, the legionaries had stripped the bodies of their foes for clothing, skins, furs, heavy woolens. These they now tugged on. Especially prized, though they'd never admit it to civilized folk, had been the Germans' trousers.

There had been a cost to all of that, of course, because the tribesmen under Arminius were loath to cede the no-man's-land to the Romans without a struggle. About forty to fifty legionaries had fallen, thought Marcus, dead or wounded, in close combat, against a probably larger number of Germans. Small parties were still out there fighting, and who won or lost could only be discerned in the darkness by curses and screams and by who finally managed to make it back.

"Ready?" Marcus Caelius asked Flavus.

"As ready as I'm going to be," he answered.

"How about Agilulf? He understand what's going on?"

"We worked out some hand signals to supplement his Latin," said Silvanus. "It'll be okay, though he was pissed not to be going with Flavus."

"He's my father's armsman," explained Flavus. "He sees it as his duty to take care of and watch over me."

"I've been studying German for the last couple of years," offered Tribune Gaius Pompeius. "My accent is somewhere between not good and pretty bad but I've got the grammar and vocabulary down. Would it help if I went with the German cohort to translate?"

"Might at that, sir," admitted Silvanus.

"What do you think, Top?" the tribune asked of Marcus.

"Sure, sir, at least until we come back with the Nineteenth. But for Jupiter's sake, no heroics. Since Ceionius disappeared, you're the only actual officer we've got left. Don't want to lose you. Also, you can't go until you give the senior centurions their marching orders."

"I don't know..." Gaius began.

"Hmmm...no, I suppose not. I'll give the orders, then."

In a way, Caelius was relieved. The troops could use a little pep talk before they marched out of the camp to scale the fortified hill to their south. But the operative word there was *little*. There'd be no need for a long-winded speech, the kind he was pretty sure the kid would have picked up in school over in Greece.

The reincarnation of Cicero is what we don't need. Time and place for everything and this is neither the time nor the place.

"All right then, Flavus, if you're ready to go, every minute here jibber-jawing is a waste."

"Yes, Top," the German agreed. "Hey, just had a thought: In case some of my countrymen have better vision at night than others, or lightning flashes at just the wrong time, can you have a squad give me a short chase once I rise up? That should be enough to give me a cover story. No spears unless they aim to miss. By a lot."

"All the cohorts of the Eighteenth are pretty much fixed. Silvanus?"

"I'll do it myself, Top."

"Fine."

"Privatus? Thiaminus?"

"Here, *Dominus*." "Here."

"I want you two to walk the perimeter; Privatus, you go left, Thiaminus, right. Go to each cohort except First and say that I want the senior centurion of each cohort to come to this tent within an hour. Then, Privatus, you find the commander of the cohort of missile troop, same orders. Thiaminus, you find the commander of the cavalry and then the chief doctor and the senior centurion among the walking wounded. I'll take care of the other four centurions from First Cohort. Silvanus, come back here with Agilulf once you've seen to seeing off Flavus in some style. Claudius?"

"Here, Top."

"Terrain model in the tent, emphasis on the big hill to our south. And see if you can roust out something for better light."

"On it, Top."

✧   ✧   ✧

"Now listen up, you turds," Silvanus ordered the nearest sixty or so legionaries in front of him. They didn't know who he was but, even in a whisper, they knew a centurion's voice when they heard it.

"We're sending a German-speaking messenger to work his way through enemy lines to get a message to the Nineteenth. He looks the part, too. But we can't let him be seen leaving our lines. So here's what we're going to do. I and a dozen men from the Seventeenth are going to filter through you and take a position in the front rank. The messenger is going to get on his belly and crawl"—and here Silvanus interjected to Flavus, "Best you curse in Latin the whole time you're crawling. Some of these guys aren't too bright and some are probably frightened out of their wits"—"to a point about fifty feet in front of us. Then he's going to rise and try to get well to the south, just over the big hill, and find the Nineteenth. If and only if we can see him as he does or there's some light from the lightning, we—and *only* the men from the Seventeenth—will give chase and hurl a couple of *pila* in his general direction, but offset to be sure of missing. We will then return and take position in the front rank, and then filter out. No questions allowed but don't fuck this up.

"Ready, Flavus?"

"As I'll ever be." The German still wore his hauberk of mail, but this was not completely unknown to the Germans. Otherwise, he had a Germanic dagger as well as a Roman *pugio*. His sword was his customary *spatha*, which was similar enough to the sword a well-to-do German might carry. His looted round wooden shield was about two feet in diameter. He carried a single *framea*.

"Okay then, give us half a minute to get in front, then onto your belly and make like a snake. And don't forget to curse in Latin the whole time you've got legionary legs around you."

"Right."

Flavus didn't actually try to count the time; small measures of time were unknown among both his people and the Romans. Instead he waited until he couldn't hear any more metal on metal as the men of the Eighteenth made way for Silvanus and his troops. When that died down, the German sank to his belly, closed one eye against the intermittent flashes of lightning, and began to crawl forward. The whole time he did he muttered, just loud enough for the legionaries nearest him to hear, "Fuck this mud...fuck the lousy fucking Germans, too...fuck all the gods and goddesses who led us to this...Venus, you adulterous slut, fuck you, too...fuck this mud...fuck all the Aesir and fuck all the Vanir...fuck that asshole, Varus, while we're at it..."

This was answered with, "Fuck Varus for us, too," by at least two of the legionaries, who turned their heads to spit on the ground.

The crawling was made especially difficult by the need to hold the shield perpendicular to the ground, to avoid the forest of legionary legs. They were known to be short-tempered.

"...Fuck Mars, too..."

"Yeah, fuck 'em all but nine," said one of the legionaries.

"Six pallbearers, two road guards, and one to count cadence," answered Flavus, then continued with, "And fuck Vali and Thor...but I implore the blessing of Mercury, patron of messengers."

Then he was past the last of the legionary legs. One of them—he suspected it was Silvanus—gave him a gentle toe nudge. And then he was out in the muddy open. The rain had largely slacked off for the moment.

The iron smell told him the mud had a good deal of blood in it. He lowered his stolen shield forward-side down to the mud. This was half for camouflage and half to obscure any individual, family, clan, or tribal decoration that might give it away, if seen.

Darker than three feet up a well digger's ass at midnight, was Flavus' sober judgment. Even so, he kept crawling until he was pretty sure he was a good sixty feet from Silvanus and his detachment.

Flavus began to rise to his feet. Even as he did, a long, drawn-out flash of lightning illuminated him nearly as well as if it had been a sunny day in Italy.

Shit, thought Silvanus. He had the presence of mind to shout out, "There's one of the bastards. After him, boys!"

"Shit," said Flavus aloud. He, conversely, had the presence of mind to say it in German. He also finished rising and turned to bolt in the direction of the big hill to the south.

Unfortunately, one or two of the legionaries from the Eighteenth had been dozing on their feet while Silvanus had been whispering his orders. These joined Silvanus' dozen as they began their fraudulent pursuit. Even more unfortunately, when a couple of them, preselected to hurl a missile, loosed, the dozers did likewise. One landed short but the other flew, unfortunately true, for Flavus' back. It struck him squarely and, while the force was enough to knock him forward and off his feet, it had been a captured *framea*, so lacked the energy to punch through the German's first-class mail.

Flavus lay there, stunned, fully expecting whoever had struck him to come and finish him off.

Fortune in the form of Silvanus came to Flavus' rescue. Though the centurion wanted to strangle both the men of the Eighteenth who had missed his orders and thrown to kill, he recognized that he couldn't bitch them out in case there were a Latin-speaking German besides Flavus nearby. Instead, he had to say, "Well thrown!" as if he actually meant it. He added, "Back to the lines, boys! Hardly a German wears any armor. He might die where he fell or he might make it another couple of hundred feet but die he will all the same. Now both you boys from this century who accompanied me, meet me in the rear. I want to get your names for a commendation." He raised his voice to shout out, "Centurion of this century, this is First Order Centurion Silvanus of the Seventeenth Legion. You meet me in the rear, too, so you can know the quality of some of your men."

The point of the *framea* hadn't been turned by Flavus' mail. Instead, it had penetrated about three quarters of an inch, just to the right of the German's spine between his shoulder blades. Blood ran down his back in a small rivulet. The blood wasn't enough to bother him but where the point had sunk in it hurt like the devil. In the restored darkness, after the lightning flash, he rose to his feet and began to feel his way to the south. As he did, he thought, *I hope Silvanus has whoever wasn't listening to his orders flogged within an inch of his life. The stupid bastard.*

Flavus hadn't gone another hundred feet before he heard, "Hail, friend. Saw the whole thing. You are one lucky bastard."

"Nah," answered Flavus, in the same language, "my parents were married, and to each other, and neither of them were Romans."

That drew a guttural laugh. "Suero of the tribe of Bructeri," Flavus' newfound acquaintance said. Almost the Romanized

German answered with his Latin name. He choked on that and then nearly gave up his birth name. *Oh, no, that would never do.* Quickly he improvised, "Eburwin of the Cherusci. I got separated from my group and ended up here. Pigheaded, I suppose. I should have sat down and waited for daylight."

"A noble pigheadedness, if so," Suero said. "I'm about as forward as anyone. Everything behind me is safe. I don't know where your tribe is but someone on the wall might. You keep traveling and as long as you're headed uphill you should find it."

Suero then took a skin of captured wine off his shoulder, passing it to Flavus. "Help yourself. It will steel you for the climb."

"Thanks muchly, friend," said Flavus, taking the skin and a healthy slug from it. "I will look for you, after the battle, should I survive. An acquaintance so well met deserves the chance to ripen into friendship."

"I agree," said Suero, reaching to take one of Flavus' arms and then clasp it in the German manner. "Now take care. You're safe from the Romans but I can't answer for it if you fall into a ravine and break your neck. We've got some warming fires going back there, they may help you find your way."

"Take care, Suero, and good luck. Remember, those Roman bastards still carry a stinger or two."

The tent was just about well enough lit. Claudius, the aquilifer, had found another half dozen oil lamps and from somewhere had come up with some torches. Too, there was a small fire going that added both warmth and a bit of light.

Can't do much about the sound of the rain on the roof, though, thought the first spear, looking upward at the leather of the tent's roof. *We'll have to shout our way through the orders. At least the son of a bitch isn't dripping.*

The first two senior centurions to arrive were Sextus Albinus, from Second Cohort, who stood on the left of First, and from Seventh Cohort, to the right, Gnaeus Gallus. The former looked too old for the job while the latter looked far too young. The chief of the remaining cavalry, a Gaul who went by the barbaric name of Atrixtos, son of Cotilus, came in next, followed by Agilulf, the German, in company with Tribune Gaius Pompeius. The German was a beefy bear of a man—bearlike, too, in the skins he wore over his armor.

Thereafter, a swarm of them arrived, more or less at once. They all formed up around the terrain model, with Marcus Caelius giving them a few minutes to familiarize themselves with the model and orient it in their minds to the ground as they saw it during the day.

No one had shouted out in alarm from the perimeter for several hours now. Which could mean the Germans had fallen back, or that they were husbanding their strength against a breakout attempt, or—and perhaps most likely—that most of them had fallen asleep.

"Me," said Marcus Caelius, "I think they've mostly fallen asleep. They'll be on us like flies on shit before first light."

He used a *pilum* as a pointer. "Hold your questions to the end. Here's the mission the tribune gave us: Eighteenth Legion, with attachments, are going to form up in an almost standard *acies triplex,* about two hours before sunup. By 'almost standard' I mean that the exterior cohorts of the second and third lines will remain in column formation, to guard our flanks. We will do so as quietly as possible, but let's be serious: with all this rain pouring down we're unlikely to be heard."

Though Caelius had warned him, Gaius Pompeius almost did a double take. *He* certainly hadn't given the first spear any orders. He didn't feel remotely qualified to have done so.

I figure he's probably just trying to build me up in the eyes of the men until he can get some real use out of me. Good for him, if he is. Good for me, too.

Caelius cast a glance at the tribune to see if he'd kept his demeanor. He was pleased to see that the officer had.

Then, "Gallic auxiliary cavalry?" the first spear asked.

"Here, centurion," announced Atrixtos. In the light of torches, lamps, and fire his reddish-blond hair seemed to cast back a golden light. He was civilized enough that he didn't chalk his hair before a battle. Even so, most of his troops did. The Gaul was clean shaven, in the modern Roman fashion. In height, Atrixtos stood somewhere between the Romans and the Germans. His shoulders, too, were relatively slight.

"The tribune wants you to the right of First Cohort, to guard our flank and neutralize any German cavalry they may have been able to come up with. We know they have some because the mixed cohort of German cavalry and foot that had been under that bastard Arminius' command defected to the enemy, en masse, at the very beginning. They made up a big cohort—pretty big men on big horses, too—so if they do come after you, I'll peel off First Cohort to your support."

"Got it," Atrixtos agreed.

"Missile cohort?"

"Here, Top." The commander of the missile cohort, Horatius Jovis, was an equestrian sort from around Campania. He had the swarthy complexion common in that area. After this campaign it had been expected he'd move over to a senior slot in one of the legions his performance with the *auxilia* had earned him. Jovis had never become more than a mediocre slinger or archer, but he knew how to make use of those as well as anybody in the Empire.

"Spread your troops out more or less evenly ahead of the second line. The usual: rush out and pepper them at a distance then run for shelter if they try to close. Then I want you to rush back out and pepper them; if they come on again, fall back. By the way, what's your ammunition status?"

"Javelins are good—we looted the Germans' bodies plus recovered a good many of those they threw at us, and lead sling bullets are all right, fifty-five or so per man, including the store in the carts. We've also got lots of stones, courtesy of the barbarians. Arrows status is great because, in this rain, we've hardly got the power to throw one eighty paces. And you know what? Come tomorrow evening we'll be just as flush, because our bowstrings are useless."

"Yeah," agreed Caelius, "I know. Palmyrene *Ala*?"

"Here, Top."

"Just like the Thracian archers, your bow strings are worthless, right?"

"Near enough, yes. We still carry lances but we're not going to be as good as the Gauls are."

"Right; you stay in the center as a reserve. I . . . will ask the tribune not to use you unless we must; you're worth more as horse archers alive than as light lancers, dead.

"Now Silvanus, have you got a good hold of Agilulf's cohort, the one from Seventeenth, and the couple of centuries from Nineteenth?"

"Yes, and I appreciate the tribune coming to help us."

"What's your strength?"

"Between Seventeenth and Nineteenth, almost two full cohorts, heavier on the former, lighter on the latter. The Germans, under Agilulf, bring us up to about fifteen hundred men."

"*Ja*," the German, Agilulf, growled. He growled like a bear, too. Slowly, as if straining for each word, he said, "Two hundred more, we should have, but some of dem ran away. Some maybe to defect to the enemy. And, *ja*, I trust the ones remaining."

"All right," said Caelius. "That's a halfway decent number to stretch from the northern swamp to where the Eighteenth turns left to go over the hill. After we start upward, close on us and guard the rear. Now, who's the senior centurion from among the wounded . . . ?"

The first fire Flavus came to, he stopped just inside earshot and just listened. After a few minutes he thought, *Not a Cherusci accent among the lot. I ought to be safe enough here.*

He advanced slowly and cautiously. At a distance of maybe forty feet he stopped, placed his *framea* in the hand that also grasped the handgrip of his shield. Advancing with his right hand up and opened, he waited until they'd sensed him coming. There were nine or so men that he could see by the light of the fire.

"Hail, comrades," he said, "Suero of the Bructeri tribe said I should use your fires to guide me back to my own people. I am Eburwin of the Cherusci."

"Come closer," ordered one of the men standing around the fire. "You say you know Suero?"

"Not well. We met when some Romans chased me more or less into him. Fuckers stabbed me in the back, too, as I ran away. I'm trying to find my own people, the Cherusci."

"You sound enough like a Cherusci," said his inquisitor, who gave his name as Kunibert.

"But they are not well known to us," he continued. "Some stand with us, some with the Romans; this much is known." He looked at the youngest among the lot, a boy of perhaps sixteen, and ordered him, "Hrodulf, go find Suero and get the truth of the matter." To Flavus he said, "In the interim, sit, presumed friend, have some beer, and help yourself to the beef on the fire. No sudden moves, though, and leave your spear out of reach."

Flavus realized that it *had* been a while since he'd eaten. He threw his spear about five feet to his left, then dropped the shield. Advancing to the fire, he pulled his German dagger and sliced off a half-pound chunk of well-done beef. "You mentioned 'beer,' I think."

"I did. Wait. Sit. Someone will bring some to you."

It was a long wait, so long that Flavus began to doubt his ability to even get to the Nineteenth Legion in time to do anything.

Hrodulf returned and said, "It is as the Cherusci said. Suero confirms that he was almost caught in an attack on the Romans and that one of them struck him in the back with a spear of some kind."

"Funny," said Kunibert, "whether our spears or one of the Roman heavy javelins, a good strike in the back should have come out your chest."

"Stopped, if barely, by my armor."

"And you got armor from where? It is a rarity among us."

"Ultimately," Flavus answered, "I think it came from the Gauls. But what you really mean is how could I afford it, yes? *I* couldn't have but I am an armsman to Chariomerus. He paid for it for me along with my long Gaulish sword."

"I would see this armor and the wound you took," said Kunibert. "And you didn't mention your sword as you threw down your spear."

"Neither did you ask," Flavus answered, undoing the belt that kept his *lorica* tight and under control, then hoisting the mail overhead. As he did the wound, already partially healed, tore open again, letting blood flow down his back. He turned his back to the fire so that Kunibert could see the wound and the flow of blood.

The other German ignored the back for the moment, but picked up and examined the *lorica* by the light of the fire. Thrusting two fingers through the hole left by the javelin, he whistled. "That was a good throw. I've thrown a *framea* at armored Romans myself and seen my spear not make a tear half this wide. Let me see that wound."

After half a moment's close scrutiny, Kunibert said, "You are a lucky man. That spear was thrown in earnest."

"Tell me about it."

"I think I have. I can tell you that you will find your people well to the east. They invest the eastern half of the trap in which we have bottled up the legion there."

"I thank you, Kunibert, for the advice, the meat, and the beer. And now I must be off."

"Stay here, friend, and walk in the morning. It is dark out there with many pitfalls, some Roman refugees, hence many of us too eager to throw a spear."

"I cannot," pleaded Flavus. "Who knows how many from among Chariomerus' armsmen have fallen? There is no rest nor forgiveness for the armsman who fails his chief, should that chief fall."

"You speak the truth," agreed Kunibert. "Hrodulf will guide you as far as where the Marsi begin. I recommend sneaking through their area without trying to introduce yourself. They hate the Cherusci almost as much as they hate the Romans."

Flavus grunted in the affirmative, adding, "Not a lot of love lost for the Marsi from the Cherusci, either."

"Even so," agreed Kunibert. Clasping Flavus on the shoulder, he said, "Travel with care, friend. And good luck."

There were actually a lot of people individually and in small groups, just lying around all over the hill. At a point in time Hrodulf stopped and said, "Marsi from here on out, Lord. Tread with care."

"I shall," said Flavus. On a sudden impulse he slipped off the baldric holding his Roman *pugio* and handed it to the young man. "For your trouble," he said.

"Lord, I cann—"

"Take it. When the last of the Romans are dead, I'll find another as good."

"Yes, Lord. Thank you, Lord."

Alone now, Flavus crept carefully forward, avoiding fires, avoiding voices, avoiding snoring, too, for that matter.

One very large fire loomed ahead. Flavus wasn't quite sure why, but instead of skirting the fire at a distance, he drew closer to it, walking in half steps to be as silent as possible. He then drew closer still. There was a mass of Marsi dancing around the fire. That wasn't what drew his eye. No, it was what stood well above the dancers.

Jupiter, no. Almost, the Roman in him began to weep. There, ahead of him, illuminated by the fire, was a Roman legion's eagle.

He could read the number on the plaque underneath the eagle: XVII. It was the ultimate shame—to lose an eagle meant shame not merely because of what the emperor might have to do and crawl through to get it back. No, worse, it meant that the legion who had lost it had been caught sleeping—that, or unaware, outfought, outthought, out-soldiered.

Turning and moving away from the fire, he continued on his way, sick at heart but still determined to carry out his mission.

Forming up for battle, while inside a marching camp, in pitch blackness was not something new to Romans. But normally it was done in a full camp, with regular streets, even signposts, in camps that never deviated from night to night.

That wasn't *this* camp. No streets here, no signposts. No regular order. And, perhaps worst of all, no decent night's sleep beforehand. And food was nothing but cold and soggy biscuit.

Still, with an unusual amount of shouting, a more than normal amount of confusion, and more than a few strokes of the centurions' staves of office, their vine staves, enough order emerged.

It was a fair sign of the desperation felt by each legionary that no one so much as attempted to gut the centurion striking him, even in circumstances where getting away with it approached certainty. Not to say that a couple might not have thought about it, but a unit without its centurion to guide and inspire it, as well as to coordinate its actions with others, was a unit ready to be butchered.

On the plus side, it had been some hours since anyone on the perimeter had had to cry out, "Here they come." Oh, there were eyes on the camp, everyone knew that. But it was doubtful any of those eyes could see into the camp any better than the men inside could see out.

In any event, the Eighteenth *did* manage to sort itself out into a formation within the camp, Mostly the cohorts faced toward the south in an *acies triplex*, with only two cohorts facing the east and west flanks and Silvanus and the Germans looking north.

The last remaining tribune, Gaius Pompeius, would join the Germans later. For the moment, his duty lay in overseeing the work of the *haruspex*, Appius Calvus, in sacrificing an animal victim and interpreting.

An ox had been chosen for the sacrifice from among the

dray animals, pure white but for the mud around its lower limbs. There was no formal altar, but a part of a tent there hadn't been time or chance to erect had been laid out. Torches on long poles burned over the tent, to allow the *haruspex* to see to his work.

Appius Calvus' assistant led the ox onto the tent. He'd made an attempt, a half-assed one, to garland the creature with whatever greenery could be found. He'd also given the ox some of the legion's wine to drink, though the animal had shown no interest. Finally, he led the ox forward onto the tent, at which point, Calvus leaned over and threw his knife-holding hand and arm around its neck.

Of all the blades in the camp, none was as fine and sharp as Calvus'. Whispering soothing words, Calvus drew the blade one hundred and eighty degrees around the doomed beast's throat. The animal lowed once, confused, as blood from a nearly painless gash gushed out onto the leather of the tent. The blood stank of hot iron. It lowed once again as unconsciousness took it. Slowly, and with surprising grace, the ox sank to the flattened tent, before rolling onto its side, deeply unconscious and soon dead.

With practiced skill, Calvus sliced the ox open, then reached in with both hands, one still holding the supersharp knife, to seize, detach, and extract the liver. Once out of the ox, the assistant poured water over the liver to clear away the blood.

Calvus peered closely at the liver, with Gaius Pompeius looking, likewise, over his shoulder, rubbing his oversized nose with worry.

"What does it say?" asked the tribune.

"I'm not sure," replied Calvus. "I've never seen one quite like this... or even a little like this. I think it says that we are in no serious danger at the moment. But that is so very much not in accord with the events of the last couple of days, that I find it hard to credit." The *haruspex* turned the liver over to its normally flat side, pointing and saying, "And see this ridge and those lumps there? They don't belong..."

"No matter," said the tribune, with commendable decision. "That we will be in no danger is what the legion wants and needs to hear." He ordered the *cornua* to sound the call. "Senior centurions on me." When they arrived at the trot, he told Calvus, "Announce it."

Calvus did, prefacing his announcement with another quote from Homer, "'Be strong, saith my heart; I am a soldier; I have seen worse sights than this.'"

Marcus Caelius, who had been standing close enough to hear Gaius, even when he whispered, thought, *That's my boy.*

After the senior centurions had taken off back to their cohorts. Marcus Caelius gave his shield to Privatus and Thiaminus, saying, "Hoist me up on this."

Once they had his feet at about shoulder level, the first spear spoke in a voice that had chilled recruits across a thousand camps and parade fields.

"I don't know about you pussies," the first spear shouted out, "but as for me, I'm too fucking *mean* to die here."

The first, faint trace of diffuse light made a sudden appearance as Flavus neared the edge of the oval that was the Nineteenth Legion. That was the upside. The downside was that Cherusci tribesman, many of whom would recognize Flavus on sight, were also coalescing into another assault on the legion.

He'd hoped to be able to arrive in the dark and use his excellent upper-class Latin to talk his way through the Roman perimeter. That wasn't going to be so easy now.

How, in the name of the great, purple-togate Augustus, am I going to get through this without either my own tribesmen gutting me or the legionaries doing so when I get within pilum *range?*

While crouching behind a tree and trying to figure matters out, Flavus heard the whirr of massed slings, punctuated with whiplike cracks and the sounds of *scuta* being struck and, sometimes, of the plywood within them cracking.

He glanced toward the whirring and saw his countrymen brushing leaves off what turned out to be piles of stones. *Clever bastards*, he thought. *We marched and rode right by those and never even noticed. They'll keep up the barrage a good long time with those.*

The Romans had some slingers with them, as well. Moreover, instead of using rocks they had cast lead sling bullets, pointed at both ends, with greater range and greater striking power than the Germans' crude projectiles. To add to their psychological effectiveness, the Romans' cast lead whistled sharply as it flew. In Flavus' view he saw tribesmen fall, heads smashed and brains leaking, or clutching a punctured gut, or hopping away on one leg.

Even so, there were a *lot* more German slingers. Moreover, they had the high ground, which helped. Flavus couldn't see well enough to be certain, but suspected that they'd even cleared fields of fire.

But a German with no better weapon than a sling was a poor German, indeed. The wealthier ones, now forming up in groups of about fifty to two hundred, began to chant their *barritus*. The tone of the battle chant suggested men confident in their coming victory.

Shit! Once the better-armed tribesmen start to close, the Romans won't even remotely be able to distinguish between them and me. I go now or I go never.

Well, on the plus side, at least the Romans' slingers are going to concentrate on the enemy's slingers. They'll assume the pila *can take care of me when I get close enough. Sooo... best put on a brave show until I get close enough.*

Standing fully upright, Flavus drew his sword and, chanting a Cherusci hymn to their god of war he remembered from his childhood, began a calm walk forward. He waved his sword about his head as if he were a man about to enter into a frenzy.

Behind him, and off to his right, he heard someone shout, "There's that bastard traitor brother of Hermann, our leader! After him, boys!"

Flavus didn't turn to count his pursuers. Instead, he ran at full gallop for the legion's lines, shouting the whole time, in his upper-crust Latin, "I am *eques* Flavus! I serve Rome! I carry a critical message for Lucius Eggius! I am *eques*..."

At fifty feet Flavus saw half a dozen legionaries aiming javelins at him, some *pila*, some *framea*. The *framea* held no terrors, despite the wound in his back, but a well-cast *pilum* could go in the front and out his back, right through his shield and his *lorica hamata*.

Time to take a massive *chance.*

Flavus turned his back to the legionaries, looked the nearest pursuing Cherusci right in the eye, and spat.

Hmmm... if I'm not mistaken that's cousin Sigigastiz. Sorry, Aunt Gudagebo, but it's him or me.

The Cherusci had just a *framea* and a round shield. Stepping forward, Flavus knocked his opponent's spear out of the way, then made a short stab with his long sword, ripping to the right and disemboweling his enemy on the spot. A German right behind the one now dying on the ground drew him arm back and hurled his *framea*. Flavus just barely raised his shield in time to deflect the missile from his unarmored throat. That Cherusci, now disarmed, held back, but two more, one with a sword and one with a spear, closed. There were half a dozen more coming close on the heels of those. Flavus took a step back, then another. The whole time he kept up his shouts, "I am *eques* Flavus! I serve Rome! I carry a critical message for Lucius Eggius! Romans, I am one of you!"

The nearest of the two Cherusci, the one with the sword, suddenly spouted the shaft of a *pilum* from his chest. Staggering, he took a step forward. Blood began to pour from his mouth. He took a final step and fell, face forward, to the leaf-strewn ground. In his fall he twisted the *pilum*'s iron shaft in a way that nothing short of an armorer or blacksmith was going to fix.

Just as suddenly there were half a dozen legionaries on Flavus' right, and a like number to his left. He sensed still more on line behind him.

And then a centurion—*Nobody but a centurion has a voice like that*, thought Flavus—gave the order, calling the cadence to fall back. Flavus fell back with them, while his former pursuers hesitated in fear of those deadly *pila*.

"German," said the centurion, "if you're lying, I swear that we will crucify you and then hold on long enough for you to die up there."

"Centurion," Flavus shouted back, "if my former countrymen ever catch me, then crucifixion would be a dawdle by comparison."

Once inside the lines, the centurion took Flavus' sword and shield, gave them to an *optio*, then had him escorted by the *optio* and two legionaries to Lucius Eggius, the *praefectus castrorum* of the Nineteenth, senior officer present, and a former first spear, himself.

"Oh, give him back his bloody sword," said Eggius. "I recognize you, Flavus. How goes it?"

"Pretty badly," the German confessed. "Seventeenth Legion is all but destroyed. Some of the tribes are hunting down the refugees and some of the legionaries made it to the Eighteenth. Some of yours are there, too, over and above your advanced party. The Eighteenth isn't in bad shape yet.

"Which is what I've come about. Eighteenth is going to try

to outflank that hill to the south, then turn east to come and rescue Nineteenth. But their and your best chance will be if you can attack and keep as many Germans as possible pinned here. After you link up, you and the Eighteenth will cut south and leg it for the river. There, you can build a bridge, cross it to the south, burn it behind you, and leave the Germans fuming on the north side. You can be supplied by water."

"Plausible," agreed Eggius, "but tough. The Germans haven't really hit us yet, but they will soon, and from all sides."

"I know. Give some hasty orders and attack now," Flavus suggested. "It's your best chance."

Slowly, Eggius nodded. Then he called for his *cornicen*. "Blow 'senior centurions assemble on this instrument.'

"Now, what's in front of us?"

Flavus answered, "On your right and center they've made a cut in the hill to create the beginnings of a wall. Over that they've driven in a bunch of posts and woven what amounts to wattle to link the posts. Covers them to about chest high. I went around it, to your left. I'm not sure—actually, I doubt—that I could have gotten over it without being recognized and most probably killed."

"Right. We'll march forward at a left oblique, then. Two cohorts can keep them pinned to the wall. Three can outflank it. The rest can guard our flanks and rear."

"Makes sense," agreed Flavus.

"What are you going to do?" Eggius asked, while waiting for the centurions to show up. "If you try to fight on our side one of my boys is likely to see that blond hair and take you for a German. Unhealthy, that would be."

"After I warned you," Flavus replied, "I was supposed to leg it for Aliso and warn the camp prefect there. Don't suppose I could borrow a horse."

"I think we can set you up with a decent equine," agreed Eggius. "And even throw in a set of spurs."

"How do you plan on getting through?" asked Lucius Eggius.

Flavus looked at the legion now forming for the attack, around him. Three cohorts, which looked shockingly understrength, were to guard the rear and fall back. The wounded and walking wounded were south of those and doing their best to keep up.

To the right and left, a single cohort each was on flank guard, and to the front, the five remaining had formed an *acies duplex*, with three cohorts forward, with two gaps between them, and two following in the gaps.

Only the Romans could do this, Flavus thought, in wonder.

Eggius repeated, "How do you plan on getting through?"

"Oh, sorry, Prefect, I was just admiring the legion. Me? I'm going to wait for your first charge to get them moving, then I'm going to cut right—which is to say, to the west—wave hello to the Eighteenth, go south to the river, then follow it to Aliso."

"Good luck then. *Cornicen*?"

"Here, Prefect."

"Sound the attack."

"Good luck, Flavus," the camp prefect said, clasping the German's arm.

Answered Flavus before mounting up, loudly enough for many of the legionaries to hear, "And to you and Rome's gallant Nineteenth!"

The attack was going in. As Flavus expected. Except at their own wall the Germans had no interest in standing up to the walking wall of the Nineteenth. They did harass Eggius' left flank but got as much as they gave or more.

Seated with his horn saddle tightly gripping his thighs, Flavus drew his *spatha*. He saw to the right that the flank guard had done a brief charge and set the Germans besetting it to flight.

Keep up the fright, thought Flavus, *that's the ticket.* He gave his horse a light prodding of his spurs. The equine was, indeed, a good one. He launched himself forward with such power and speed that only the gripping horns of the saddle kept Flavus in his place.

Though he'd done it, and quite recently, Flavus was loath to kill any Cherusci tribesman he could avoid killing, so, instead...

"Run for your lives!" Flavus shouted. "Run for your lives, the legion is out and no one can stop them. They're killing everything in their path. If you ever want to see your mothers and sweethearts again, run, *run*, RUN for your lives!"

After some of that, Flavus halted his horse and turned it around to look at the Nineteenth. He could see Eggius, sword in hand, mounted atop his own steed, urging his legionaries on with laughter and curses. The Romans seemed to be making no progress whatsoever at the wall, but some in the left-side flanking movement. Still, it was only some.

No matter; if they're drawing the tribesmen against them, it means the Eighteenth will have a quicker and easier time of it. I hope.

With that, Flavus pulled on the reins to point his horse west again and, with a little prod from the spurs, took off.

"Run for your lives. Run, run—the Romans are right behind us!"

INTERLUDE

***Exploratory Spacecraft 67(&%#@, Several Hundred Znargs
Above the Teutoburg Forest***

"I wish I could take them out while leaving their exoskeletons behind," Red muttered. "The power drain is going to be enormous."

"I don't think they'd long survive that," trilled Blossom, in sweet notes and sharp whistles, ending with a distinct click. "Imagine being skinned alive, yourself." All twelve of her tentacles shuddered at the thought, right down to their very tips.

He pointed at the view screen. The skimmer was looking down upon a number of the insects below who did not have their exoskeletons. "They seem all right."

"Maybe they shed their exoskeletons at certain points in their lives. You know there are plenty of insects who do. I'd still bet it's painful enough to kill them if they're not naturally ready."

"You're probably right. But that stuff has *so* much mass to move..."

"Are you taking those green upright things, some kind of plant life, I think?" she asked.

"No, though I am—reluctantly—taking their beasts and conveyances. The trees would be just too much. I'm also not going to try to send any of their exoskeletons that are lying around."

"But what if they need to eat them to help them grow another? Please send those, too. And the upright plant life? They may need those to live. Please send some at least."

"Oh, all *right*. Though what insect eats metal I do not know. I am not sending their deceased. Maybe if we had infinite time to study them. But we don't. I'll send two and a half tentacle sets' worth of the large plant life."

"The universe is full of infinite diversity," she intoned. "And I agree, if they've died, poor little things, there's no point in wasting the power. Can you heal their injured?"

"Maybe if I had infinite time to study them. But we don't. I can do something for those with the weakest life signs."

"I am just about ready. I still have to calibrate...oh...oh, damn. Damn!"

"What is it? Tell me, what is it?"

"They're starting to move out of the dodecagon I plotted around them. They're going to destroy all my calculations."

"Can you save them now? Save them well enough?"

"I don't know," he replied, in a high-pitched series of whistles and guttural grunts. "Maybe enough."

"Send them. Send them now."

Fearfully, Red stretched out one tentacle, said a brief prayer to his divinity—sacrificed by having its tentacles staked out on a beach and left to dry and die, a horrible fate for one of his species—and pushed a button.

CHAPTER THREE

You have power over your mind—not outside events.
Realize this, and you will find strength.
                    —Marcus Aurelius, *Meditations*

Northwest Germania, September 10, 762 AUC

First the ground had shaken and erupted upward, almost like
a volcanic eruption, but without the spewing of pumice or the
flow of lava. And then it got infinitely worse.

Gaius Pompeius had never imagined that lightning could be
so bright, so large, and so loud. The brightness blinded him even
as the enormous *bang* deafened him. Then he found himself falling, before slamming chest down onto what seemed to be solid
ground. His head hurt like a thousand of the worst hangovers
ever known to mankind.

I am dead, thought Gaius Pompeius. *The gods themselves
have struck me down. I will never see home, never see my family
or sweetheart again. I am dead. So now I join the roots of my
family tree.*

Though Gaius couldn't hear it, all around him thousands of
men of the Roman Army—Romans, Germans, Gauls, Rhodians,
Thracians, Palmyrenes, and some numbers of Greeks and at
least one Jew with the medical staff—screamed for all they were
worth. Each, like Gaius, was certain he was dead. It didn't help
that, blinded, they couldn't see anyone and, deafened, couldn't
hear anyone. Each man was all alone.

Even some of the centurions screamed in terror, though if asked they'd have lied shamelessly about it. Some of the horses landed well. Some, though, broke legs on the sudden arrival below. These, too, screamed, though in pain more than fear.

Gradually, outstretched on the ground, terrorized beyond reason and with the breath knocked out of him, Gaius began slowly to realize, *My ass is wet. Hell, my whole body is wet. How does someone who is dead feel that he has a wet ass? Or a wet body? How does someone who's dead have the wind knocked out of him? How does he feel the contours of his muscle cuirass digging into the flesh of his chest. Or the grass on his face?*

"I am alive," he finally concluded, though even he could not hear the words, so viciously had the thunder pounded his ear drums. "Whether this is a good thing..."

Slowly, very slowly, Gaius' eyes accustomed themselves to the surrounding darkness. Blinking, and though his vision was slightly blurred, he realized that he could see much better now than he had been able to in the rain-pouring, foggy German forest. He looked up and saw a very large, very bright moon overhead, with the edges a bit fuzzy. The stars and constellations of stars, fainter, gradually made themselves known.

"No, no man who is dead can see the *Septentrio*, nor Virgo, Leo, and the Gemini. I must conclude, therefore, that I am not dead. Yet."

His ears still rang and his head still pounded him mercilessly. Even so, the young tribune was made of pretty stout stuff. It was this, plus a profound sense of duty, a *Roman* sense of duty, that made him force himself to his feet, unsteadily, and look around to get his bearings.

The first thing he saw was that the forest had changed. There were still trees, but they had been uprooted and fallen over. Still, there weren't many of them and they were mostly not too close to the troops. From what he could see by the light of a nearly full moon, none appeared to have fallen on the troops though some of the troops had plainly fallen on the trees. Even with somewhat blurry vision he could see them draped over the now not quite horizontal trunks. The elevation that made them not quite came from the fully exposed root systems, now all aboveground, and their branches.

The hangover he felt—*Sooo unfair for a man to have a hangover without even getting drunk*—abated rapidly. His vision began to clear more, too. He noticed that, while still soaking wet, he was fairly warm. He remained deaf.

Centurion Silvanus trotted up, not all that steadily. Rather than taking a knee next to Gaius Pompeius, he plopped himself down on the shockingly dry ground next to him.

"Sir," he asked, "what the fuck just happened?"

The tribune looked at him without comprehension. Silvanus shouted the same question.

Whether Gaius' shaking head meant "I don't know" or "I can't hear you," none but he could have said.

Marcus Caelius managed to land his body next to a large rock. His head, on the other hand, managed to land *on* the rock. Short version, he was stunned silly and very lucky not to have broken his neck. Not far away, Agilulf lay dead with a broken neck.

At that, he was in better shape than Appius Calvus, the *haruspex* who, though physically unharmed, had drawn up into a fetal position, apparently catatonic.

The Gallic cavalrymen were not in bad shape, but some fifty-nine of their horses had managed to break legs in the unexpected ten-to-twelve-foot fall. The cohort had a couple of veterinaries on hand, and the legion had several more in the medical group, but how many of those horses could be saved was a matter for speculation. Probably they would all die. Meanwhile, the horses cried out piteously for an end to their pain. Some of the horse-man, who, by and large, loved their horses, though deaf for the time, could still recognize equine agony when they saw it, even if by moonlight. Some of those couldn't take it anymore and cut the poor beasts' throats, then wept like babies over their cooling corpses.

The commander of the Gallic cavalry, Atrixtos, son of Cotilus, was one of those who had felt he had to put his horse out of its misery. He was also one of those who wept over the corpse afterward.

Sextus Albinus, of Second Cohort, had a broken arm. Gnaeus Gallus, from Seventh, was fine other than the deafness.

Gratianus Claudius Taurinus, the aquilifer, had saved his eagle but at the cost of landing in a very awkward way. He'd broken several ribs on Marcus Caelius' rock.

Along with the horses, a fair number of legionary mules, donkeys, and oxen had likewise been hurt. And every wagon and cart the legion owned had broken its axles.

Stunning Marcus Caelius was no mean feat. Keeping him stunned for very long was nigh unto impossible. Walking still a bit unsteadily, he wandered the legion telling each senior centurion from each cohort, along with the *praefecti* of the *auxilia,* to start building a camp. *"No, I don't give a shit that's it's dark. No, I don't care that you're tired. Build!"*

All this was done with hand gestures and standard hand and arm signals. Mimicking using a shovel and making a gesture of pounding in stakes was common. For the cavalry, he pointed around three hundred and sixty degrees and held one hand over his eyes, as if shielding them from the daytime sun. Thus the light troops and horse were sent out to screen. With Agilulf dead, command had fallen to a more Romanized German, one Thancrat, something of a world traveler, who spoke fair Latin, albeit with an accent. The first cohort stayed in armor and spread out to guard the men building the camp. The medics...

By the time Caelius reached the medics and the sick and injured in the center, he'd gotten back some of his hearing. So had they. He was pleased to see that the medical detachment had gotten their tents up, though the fracturing of the wagons and the injuries and deaths to the oxen were troubling.

Where are we going to get more? We don't even know where we are, except that it's not that damned German forest. He looked upward, thinking, *Not that I'm complaining, whichever one of you is responsible for this. If you exist.*

"How are your patients?" he shouted at the senior doctor, an unusually tall Jew who had studied medicine in Alexandria, Samuel Josephus. Unlike many Jews his age, Josephus had a full head of hair that he kept close-cropped. The doctor shook his head, not from despair but from wonder. He made a respectful hand motion for the first spear to follow him into one of the tents.

He pointed at one of the patients, lying atop the ruins of a collapsible cot. "This one was a goner," Josephus shouted. "No doubt about it. Nothing I or anyone could have done about it. He took a deep slash across the belly, sliced his intestines all to hell. Shit leaking out everywhere. And with that, infection and a miserable, lingering death. But look at this."

Josephus moved aside the cloths covering the man. There was a red line marking where his belly had been slashed open, but no sign of an actual cut.

"He was burning up with fever already, before that...that event, I suppose we can call it for now...took us. Now?" Here Josephus put a hand to the man's head and once again shook his head with wonder.

"I have ninety-three more or less like that—all very badly injured, all were going to die; all suddenly healed."

Marcus Caelius nodded soberly, then planted a solid kick in the prone man's side, below the ribs. "Get up, you fucking malingerer. Get your weapons and armor and rejoin your century. There's digging to be done and we need every hale man."

The legionary sprang upright and stood at attention. "Yes, First Spear. As you command, First Spear."

"And you, *Medicus*, get those other ninety-two slackers back to duty."

By the time Marcus Caelius returned to where he'd been dropped on a rock, his hearing had pretty much returned—and apparently so had everyone else's—to the point he could hear digging, stakes being pounded, and shouted orders and groans as the legionary corps of centurions applied their vine staves to slackers.

As it should be.

He found Calvus, the *haruspex*, still in his fetal position—upright, arms around bent legs, rocking back and forth and keening piteously. A quick examination showed no wounds. Even so, Caelius called for medical orderlies to bring Calvus to the medics. *Maybe he just needs some time.*

Tents were going up, too, even the legate's big tent, the *Praetorium*. Marcus hadn't looked but was as certain as he was of anything that Privatus and Thiaminus would have found the cart carrying his limited baggage and tent and would have already unloaded it and gotten to work setting the tent up. Tent, cot, little chest with personal items, including his *corona civica*, leather valise with spare clothing and a spare pair of *caligae*—these were all the baggage Caelius permitted himself. His greater comfort, a family, was back near Castra Vetera, on the west bank of the

Rhine. He'd left a will naming his brother, Publius, also a centurion, as executor, and leaving everything to his girl, Dubnia,
a tall, fiery—in all ways—Gallic slave, a dozen years his junior,
whom he'd freed and married.

*I hope to hell Flavus gets through to warn them. I can also
hope, but really doubt, that Nineteenth Legion managed to cut their
way out. Sorry, friends, but it wasn't our fault we abandoned you.*

Gaius Pompeius, having determined for himself that, on the
one hand, Agilulf was most sincerely dead and, on the other,
that his replacement spoke reasonably good Latin, the tribune
showed up half an hour later, going immediately to his own
tent at one side of the large one called the *Praetorium*. Marcus
Caelius intercepted him, en route, saying, "No, sir, you go to the
commander's tent."

"But I'm just a junior trib—"

"Yes, and you look the part, too," said the first spear. "But,
no, sir. You are the senior officer present. You *are* the commander
and, as such, you *must* take your place.

"Sir," the first spear continued, "the men have been through
a lot. We were three legions and close to six thousand *auxilia*.
We're down to one somewhat understrength legion, two legionary
ad hoc cohorts, and maybe a couple of thousand *auxilia*. We were
surrounded by German barbarians in a dense, dank forest, full of
rough terrain. We appear to be alone now, and on some kind of
grassy plain. We had a chance to fight our way free, but it was
never more than a chance and maybe a slimmer one than I let
on to the men. We are now, at least for the time being, safe. But
even being safe, when you expect not to be, is a kind of stress.
And so, once again, the men have had just about enough. So you,
sir, *will* take over the command tent and you, sir, *will* play the
part of a commander to the best of your ability. And, yes, sir,
I and the other centurions will help you and cover for you to
the best of *our* ability while you learn the job. Is that clear, sir?"

Almost Gaius Pompeius stood himself to attention while
answering, "Yes, Top."

Almost letting an unaccustomed smile peek through, Marcus
Caelius said, "Sir, we don't need officers for the routine things—
assuming battle formation, setting up camp, marching hither and
yon. All those things the centurions can do perfectly well and
routinely. We need officers for the things that are *not* routine.

That, and to provide absolute integrity to a business given to corruption. This means you.

"Now get a little rest. I'll wake you before first light and you and I will inspect the camp's defenses. Watch my face. If I frown, you go 'tsk' and say, 'Not quite up to snuff, is it, First Spear?' I will then castigate the cohort responsible for 'embarrassing me in front of the commander.' If I do not frown you will smile, very slightly, and say, 'I suppose it will do. For now.'"

"Got it, Top. I'm a quick learner; my tutors always said so."

"Very good, sir." Caelius stood to attention for a short time, less than a minute, before tilting his head and saying, "Sir, you need to tell me I am dismissed. Loudly, so some of the men can hear and pass the word."

"Oh. Right. Dis . . . *missed.*"

Caelius saluted and prepared to turn about, then remembered one more thing. "And, sir, you are no longer the tribune. Until further notice you are the legate. Wear his tunics with the purple stripe and look through his goods for a spare belt. Best start thinking about your assumption-of-command speech."

The legate's tent, the *Praetorium,* which Gaius now occupied by order of the first spear, was a lot more luxurious than any other tent in the camp—indeed, it *was* large enough to hold an oversized bed, a collapsible desk, a terrain model board with folding legs, and enough space for the legate, his six tribunes, the *praefectus castrorum,* and the first spear and other first order centurions all to attend orders, meetings, and war counsels at the two-and-a-half-foot-high table, which itself was large enough to seat ten on stools arranged around it. In addition, there were three small tables, much lower, and nine collapsible couches, called *lecti,* arranged around them, for when the legate invited his staff to dine.

Overhead, hanging from a hook in the wooden central ridge of the tent, was a bronze eleven-wick *lucerne,* or oil lamp. Other lamps sat in various other spots, with two five-wick terra cotta jobs at the main table and one three-wick lantern at each of the short dining tables.

I hope the legate had enough oil in the impedimenta *to keep all those lamps going.*

Gaius didn't sleep, though he lay down on the thick bed of

furs some of the men—and he supposed some of the actual leg-ate's slaves—had set up for him.

I am so fucked. *The first spear was right that it's my respon-sibility to take command as senior officer present, but, damnation, I was just getting the hang of morning reports, running the duty roster, and inspecting the guards. I don't know how to prepare and give an order. I don't know anything about gathering and analyzing intelligence and scout reports. I am clueless about the quartermaster functions of an army; Ceionius took care of all that. Speaking of which, I wonder where Ceionius is? I suppose the Germans must have gotten him.*

And where am I going to find replacements for the other five tribunes and the camp prefect? I could promote Marcus Caelius to camp prefect, I suppose, but he'd probably turn it down for now, on the theory that a first spear, under our circumstances, is more important than a glorified clerk and tent-peg counter. And he'd probably be right.

Hmmm...I am pretty sure that, somewhere in the six thousand or so citizens with the legion and the refugee cohorts, there are probably at least half a dozen from the equestrian order, gentlemen rankers, whom I could promote up to tribune. But would anybody take orders from them?

Or maybe I could make eight of the centurions—have to find those who would know what they're doing—to include Marcus Caelius, the de facto heads of the various staff functions, and give them each a ranker from the equestrian order to assist, which is to say to do the actual work.

Yes, got to give anybody like that a capable and literate assis-tant. I mean, take the first spear for an example. He is, all at the same time, the commander of the First Century of the First Cohort and the First Maniple of the First Cohort. He is also the commander of the entire First Cohort. He is also the senior centu-rion of the legion and, as such, rides herd on all of the fifty-eight other centurions. If I gave him one more thing to worry about, I don't know that even he could cope.

The legate's thoughts were interrupted by a knock on the tentpole by the entrance and the sound of someone clearing his throat.

"Yes?" Gaius said.

A tall and skinny form, bearded and swarthy, slipped in

through the tent flap. He wore a simple tunic of linen, somewhat dirtied now, and carried a stylus and *tabula cerata*, or wax writing tablet, in his left hand. The *tabula cerata* was often called a *cera* for short. The skinny form looked over Gaius Pompeius and, though he kept his face carefully blank, he thought, *So young.*

"*Dominus*, I am Gisco, freedman and secretary of the presumptively late legate and supervisor of his slaves. They've prepared some food and poured some wine if the legate would care to eat."

Gaius was taken aback. While he'd seen the man about fairly often, he'd never known his position. He suspected that was because Gisco simply kept a very low profile. He also realized he was famished. Even so, he asked, "What food and what kind of wine?"

Tucking his *cera* under his left arm and placing the stylus behind his right ear, Gisco clasped his hands together and made continuous short, rocking bows as he spoke. "The food is mainly a roast rabbit, with a gravy suitable for dipping the *bucellatum* in. The *bucellatum* is fresh, so not so hard to chew. There are some lovely olives as well as some sharp cheese from Gaul. For meat, a rabbit was all we could find, until the veterinarian decides which animals are hopeless from the fall, and we kill and butcher them. The wine is a well-aged Alban, dry in this case, and I ordered it mixed, of course."

"You know, Gisco, that sounds pretty good."

"We aim to please, Trib...err...Legate. My apologies, Legate."

"It's all right," Gaius Pompeius said. "It's not as if I am used to the change yet, either."

Gisco reached one hand out and snapped his fingers. A slave entered, followed by another. Between them they bore the meal and the wine on trays, the wine with a pitcher of water, a small amphora holding the wine, and a filled cup. Soundlessly, with deep bows, they left.

"Sir," began Gisco, resuming his clasped hands rocking motion, "do we have any idea what happened, and where we are?"

"Not a clue, Gisco," replied the legate. "But one thing I am pretty sure of: Wherever we are, it's not surrounded by bloodthirsty barbarians, in the middle of a nearly impenetrable forest, shivering, while being rained on, in Germany."

"Very good point, *Dominus*."

"Tell me, Gisco, what services did you provide for the legate?"

"Well, *Dominus*, as mentioned I supervised his slaves on campaign."

"How many of those are there?"

"There were twelve, including two girls for the legate's sexual use. Now there are seven, and none of those are the girls. Pity, wonderful and lovely creatures they were; they brightened up every place they went. But they were in the middle of the column, with Seventeenth Legion and the heavier baggage. Hopefully the Germans will appreciate them for their beauty and not just slaughter them out of hand.

"I also handled all his personal correspondence in any of a number of languages: Latin, Greek, and Aramaic, but also Phoenician and Egyptian in Demotic. Also, I have some very limited Parthian, or Farsi, in their own tongue, though I cannot read or write that. I have a smattering of German and Gallic, but cannot claim fluency.

"I reviewed and compiled the daily reports, prepared the daily orders—"

"Wait! *You* prepared the orders?"

"Yes, *Dominus*. Also prepared the notes for battle orders."

"So you know what goes into them?"

"Yes, *Dominus*. It's not that complex. I have noticed, over the years serving the legate—the former legate—that everything in the army is very simple, but all the simple things are very hard. I also—"

"Can you make me a list of everything you did and could do?"

"Yes, *Dominus*. Give me a couple of hours and I'll have it for you."

By now the ditch, the *fossa*, was dug, the wall, or *agger*, was raised, and the rampart of stakes, the palisade of *sudes*, was emplaced. All tents were up, not just the legate's, tribunes', and centurions'. Most of the troops not on guard had repaired to their own tents with severe headaches, still. Marcus Caelius could sympathize; his own head still ached, though it was going away.

One century per cohort stood guard on the walls.

While ostensibly watching over latrines being dug under the closer eye of the medical detachment, Marcus Caelius worried over how the legion was going to make good its losses. And these were not especially light.

He wasn't especially concerned with the loss of the troops—a few hundred, more or less, made little difference to the effectiveness of the legion. But at least nine centurions had fallen or been left behind by whatever gods had sent them here. And those were going to be very hard to replace.

Then there was Ceionius. *I don't think I had much choice. Even so, I wish the surly bastard were here now to do the quartermaster work. Where am I going to find another quartermaster? I know that I don't want the job.*

Ceionius. Ceionius... No, if I hadn't offed the son of a bitch, the legion would have fallen apart where we were. I can't regret preventing that, at whatever the cost.

I also know Ceionius' assistant and staff—competent for routine matters but not an ounce of initiative among the lot.

And then there's the legate... the very new *and inexperienced legate. He desperately needs a staff, but they were all killed either with the old legate, alongside Varus, or in the Germans' first attack, when the barbarians sought them out especially.*

Well, actually, our boy was junior, only got here three months ago, so if one of them had survived they'd *be the new legate.*

All right, first things first. I'll move the centurions around but no more than necessary to make sure there are at least five per cohort. Then I'll look into the optios, *and find the best one per cohort, then have the legate promote them up to* hastatus posterior. *After consulting with the senior centurions of that cohort, of course. As for the legate's new staff...*

All right, suppose I find a dozen or two rankers of equestrian rank. I pick the seven who seem most promising, and we make them optios. *No need to rotate them through the various staff functions; we can afford to specialize. Then I assign one first-order centurion, each, to watch over them and give orders that the rest will obey. Meanwhile, without giving up my position as first spear, one of those equestrians can do the quartermaster job under* my *occasional supervision. For now.*

Gonna be a busy day.

Oh, and, note to self, there's no reason for those optios *to have their own tents as if they were real tribunes, they can crowd into one tribune's tent and like it. The other five of those tents? Well, despite the healing of some men who should have died in any sane world, we still have hundreds of injured, far too many for the tents of the* medici. *So they can take over the extra tribunal tents.*

The first spear turned his attention back to the latrines. *No flowing water so no sewer system to carry off the waste. I've got both the legionary cavalry, the Palmyrene horse archers, and the Gauls out scouting the area. Hopefully they'll stumble upon a decent-sized stream. In the interim, I need to put the engineers to digging some wells, well away from the latrines. Can't know how many until we see what the wells can produce.*

If not, if the scouts find no water, we know it takes about nine days, minimum, for maggots to turn into flies, so every week we'll drop a layer of dirt about a foot thick atop the shit. That should keep the flies down.

I suppose I ought to have the troops start depositing their wood ash at a central location to be turned into lye by wetting and evaporation. Helps with the stench.

And then we'd better see to salting and smoking the meat from the dead and soon-to-be dead animals. Then there's the . . .

Atrixtos, the prefect of the Gallic cavalry to which the survivors of the legion's own cavalry had been attached, had separated his not quite four hundred and sixty remaining men—less the ninety-three for whom no horses remained—into four groups, which he thought of as *north, south, east, and west,* and sent them out in those directions with orders to go out ten miles, then turn to their right for five, then return to camp. Tomorrow they'd do the same thing, only oriented northeast, et cetera.

In addition to the Gauls, there were some five hundred and twenty-three Palmyrene mounted *sagittarii,* or horse archers. A larger percentage of their horses had survived unharmed, being a lighter and more nimble breed, carrying lighter men.

He, himself, had gone out with the eastern group toward the mountains that loomed in that direction. Ten miles hadn't brought them to those mountains, not nearly, but it had brought them to a stream, one good enough to keep the legion and its attachments in water, after a move, if the other detachments, or tomorrow's patrols, found none better.

The grass was quite tall, about to the riders' calves.

Like many ethnically non-Roman Gallic aristocrats—at least among those who had survived Julius Caesar's conquest of Gaul—Atrixtos' family had been given Roman citizenship a couple of generations prior, for services rendered.

"Beats being starved at Alesia before being murdered or sold as a slave," his old grandfather used to say. "And Gaul would still have been conquered no matter what other choice my father might have made."

His Roman name was Attius Julianus. His mother still called him "Atrixtos." So did everyone else except the late Varus, who set massive store by Roman citizenship and culture. In keeping with his Roman name, Atrixtos had had a classical education, at home, first, with tutors bought or hired by his father. Later on, he'd been given a better education at Colonia Copia Felix Munatia, later to be known as Lugdunum, and still later as Lyons. He'd never been to Rome and, from the descriptions, never wanted to.

Sometime after the detachment had turned right, Atrixtos' second-in-command, Taurou, cantered up next to him and said, "We're being tracked. Men on foot, I think, though they may have horses they left behind for stealth. Or are walking."

"I know. Spotted them just after we made the turn. Less than half a dozen, I think."

"I counted five. Could've missed one."

"Here's what I want you to do," Atrixtos said. "Take twenty—no, make it at least twenty-five men. Trot ahead and once we're out of your sight find a good ambush position to either side of our route. Hide yourselves in that position. Send the extra five on, raising as much dust as they're able. We'll march through some distance, then spread out and turn round to make a net of men and horses. Our trackers will follow. Capture—and I cannot overemphasize that I mean *capture*—them. We don't want to make enemies we don't need to."

With a curt nod, Taurou trotted to about midway back in the column and ordered one section of about twenty-seven to follow him. He made sure to include a *cornu* man in the groups.

After the detachment had passed and the trackers showed up, Taurou could see they had been six in number, after all. They were small men, those trackers, and a bit dark or even yellowish. They weren't bald, he saw, though they seemed to have shaved their heads, all but for a black topknot. If they had a weapon amongst them beyond knives and what looked to be light hunting bows,

Taurou couldn't see one. Contrary to his expectation, though, they *did* have horses, just very short and shaggy ones.

Ponies? I've never seen a horse that short, thought the Gaul, standing just high enough to see over the grass, and with tufts of grass hastily tied to his head for camouflage. He watched until the trackers broke into a small stream, where he could get a better look at them. *But if their legs are short, they look strong. We shouldn't assume they're not as fast as ours, at least on the long haul. So we cannot give them the chance for a long-distance race.*

Taurou and the other Gallic riders had their horses—and pretty well-trained horses they were—prone in various depressions on either side of where the main body had been expected to pass and had.

Taurou let the strangers pass and continue on for a couple of hundred yards, then told the *cornicen*, "Blow charge."

The brass call blared out. In an instant, the twenty riders Taurou had kept with him burst from cover. Almost as quickly, their wide-eyed, shocked, yellowish prey mounted their short, shaggy ponies and goaded them to a gallop. Their gallop, however, was a good deal slower than that of Taurou's men and their mounts.

As any pursued rabbit might, the locals tried to bolt left. When they did, they could see a thick knot of the strangers' huge horsemen charging for them. Looking behind, they saw even more coming for them. To what was now their left charged the group that had originally set them to flight. And there was nothing more open on their right.

The leader—leader, for the nonce, though he was not especially senior in the tribe—of the half dozen scouts, for that was what they were, was Bat-Erdene. He was known merely as Erdene to his friends.

He was leader because he had the best eyes of any young man in the tribe. His name meant something like "strong gem," though this was given as a baby before his eyes' abilities became known. Bat-Erdene looked desperately for some kind of opening.

There was, Bat-Erdene saw, a small chance, a small weakness, in these strange people's cordon. This was just to the left of the group now to his front, between them and the group that had first charged them after breaking from ambush.

Pointing with his right arm, he twisted his head and torso about, shouting, "That way! That way! It's our only chance!"

From there it was a race between the maneuverable and strong ponies of the locals, and the monstrously large and powerful looking mounts of the strangers. It was a race that Bat-Erdene and his handful were doomed to lose, however; the strangers' horses were not just big, they were at least thirty percent faster.

One of the strangers to the front, like his horse, huge compared to Bat-Erdene, had shocking red hair, something the young local had never seen before. That distraction was partly to blame for his not swerving in time to avoid having his pony hit sideways by the stranger's big horse. This knocked the pony over, sending Erdene flying. He hit hard and rolled.

Before the local could rise to his feet, one of the big redheaded strangers was atop him, stripping away his small utility knife and pinioning his arms. Another bound his hands behind him. When the strangers hoisted Erdene to his feet, he saw that four of his five companions were likewise taken, while their ponies were being joined into a coffle. He did not see Ankhbatar in their number, so had some hope his friend had managed to escape.

Bat-Erdene thought, *Maybe Father or the chief can come up with some kind of bribe to get these fearsome folk to let us go.* Bribery was their only hope; fighting was just not his people's way.

Someone who seemed to be chief of these strange men said something to Bat-Erdene is an inquisitorial tone. The words meant nothing. The captive gave an eloquent shrug, which the foreign leader seemed to understand.

Atrixtos looked over the captives. Short men, they were, and stout. And, though they carried no hand weapons beyond the couple of knives of which they'd been relieved, plus bows, they seemed to be fairly strong. They wore vests of animal hide, fur side in, and trousers of leather. On their feet were short boots with upturned toes. Each man's head sported a fur cap, which seemed a bit much for the weather.

Their bodies were not the only thing that was strong about them, Atrixtos noticed. "Gods, do these people *stink*. How can they live like that? No matter, get them ready to move."

The captives were mounted on their coffled ponies, then the strangers formed up and began to ride in the direction of the setting sun.

✧   ✧   ✧

Marcus Caelius brought the captives, with Atrixtos, to the legate's tent. There were also present the new legate, the senior decurions of the legionary cavalry, and the Palmyrenes, as well as the most senior decurions of the rest of the Gallic cavalry.

As Atrixtos entered the tent, he heard the Palmyrene leader, Tadmor, describing the river and campsite his men had found.

"That sounds better than what we found," he interrupted. "On the other hand, we do have some captives. Five of them, one got away."

Holding a palm up to temporarily silence the Palmyrene, Gaius Pompeius asked the Gaul, "What language do they speak?"

"Not a clue, Trib...er...Legate. Sounds like nothing I've ever heard. They're seated outside the tent."

"Gisco," called the legate.

Instantly, the secretary was there, *cera* under one arm, hands clasped, making his usual short, rocking bows. "Yes, sir?" One of the old legate's slaves stood at Gisco's elbow.

"There are five captured locals seated outside. Make friends with them. Give them food and wine or water or both, mixed, whichever they prefer. You speak more languages than anyone else in the legion; either learn their language, enough to get by, or teach them ours."

With a deeper bow, the Phoenician disappeared.

"Now, Tadmor," the legate continued, "tell me about this stream. Is there a ford nearby? How far from the hill? And the hill, gentle slopes or steep sided...?"

He is, indeed, a pretty quick learner, thought Marcus Caelius, not without some measure of personal pride.

Make friends first, thought Gisco. *And no better way to make friends than over food and wine. I wish they didn't stink so.*

"Quickly," he told his trailing slave, "bring water, wine, and six cups, immediately, then have the cook produce something decent to eat."

Half a dozen of the Gallic cavalry stood around the bound men, standing guard. As soon as Gisco saw that the captives were bound he ordered that the ropes be struck off.

As the captives were unbound, the secretary made gentle little motions with his hands that they should remain seated. Afraid of the towering Gauls, none of the captives attempted to rise. They did look around at the camp's guarded ramparts and the sheer mass of soldiery everywhere on display.

Gauging their chances of an escape, thought Gisco, *and judging those chances poor. Intelligent enough, even if disgustingly filthy.*

The wine came, accompanied by cups and a jug of water. Gisco poured himself, water first, then just enough wine to be sociable.

He passed the cups out to the captives who, he noticed, refused to take a sip until he had.

After the—*no, not the "captives," our* guests—had had their first sip of the watered wine and seemed pleased with it. Gisco began the lesson by pointing at his own chest and saying, "Gisco."

The captive, who was clearly bright but a little misoriented, likewise pointed as his own chest and repeated, "Gisco."

"Well, this is going to be tougher than I'd hoped," muttered Gisco. "Hmmm...I know: let's try different body parts."

He held up one hand and pointed to it, saying, "Hand." Then, lest the guests make the all too easy mistake of thinking that the word for pointing was "hand," stopped pointing while still keeping that hand up, he repeated, "Hand." He then did the same with his other hand.

A sudden light seemed to dawn in one of the captive's eyes. Holding up his own hand, he answered in something completely unpronounceable, then repeated the Latin for hand without too much distortion.

"Right," Gisco said, "teach you boys Latin, it is. To the extent possible, though, let's just stick to first and second declension, and first conjugation."

To clear up the previous confusion, Gisco made a circle around his own chest, then did the same for the bright guest, followed by each of the others. Again, that light came on in the bright guest's eyes. He pointed at his own chest and repeated the Latin word.

Gisco then made gestures encompassing his entire body and said, "Gisco." Rather than repeat "Gisco," the bright one pointed to himself and gave his name, "Bat-Erdene," then, again, in what Gisco took to be a short form, "Erdene."

Bat-Erdene had a surprisingly intelligent face, with the thinnest, wispiest bit of facial hair Gisco had ever seen. Like the others, he was short and stocky. His topknot hair was so black it was almost blue, and very straight and wiry.

To make sure he got that part right, Gisco then pointed to the other four, in turn, and adopted a quizzical look. One by one they said something that was, in the first place, not "Bat-Erdene," and, in the second place, different in each case. He poured them all some more water and wine, then went through the names a dozen times each until he was fairly confident that he could remember all five.

Food arrived in the form of fresh biscuits and some stew with chunks of beef in it. Again, as with the wine, none of the guests would touch theirs until Gisco had first. The Phoenician decided that, since they had no way of telling if the bowls had been poisoned, rather than the food, this was probably a matter of politeness. While they ate he went through the words for cup, wine, water, jug, bowl, spoon, and stew, then the verbs for eat, drink, and finally, to go, as in to go about the camp. The guards accompanied the group.

"Tent," said Gisco, then, sweeping his hand around to cover an area of tentage, he gave the plural.

"*Tabernaculum, tabernacula,*" all five captives repeated.

Gisco then pointed out one legionary and said, "*Romanus.*" He pointed out several more labeling each as Roman. Then he pointed at a group and said, "*Romani.*" He then pointed to several other groups saying the same thing. Finally he swept his hands around, as if to take in the entire camp and repeated, "*Romani.*" Finally, when he thought he had that message across, he held out both arms to encompass the group of captives.

As one they said, "Argippaeans."

"Argippaeans?" said the Legate, that evening. "Herodotus mentioned them. Supposed to live somewhere north—well north—of Persia, I think. Doesn't help with the language lessons, I suppose."

"Five hundred words," Gisco told Gaius Pompeius and Marcus Caelius. "Five hundred words and you can more or less get by in any language. I'm not saying they'll know the difference between first declension singular vocative and third declension neuter plural, or why *Romanes eunt domus* is wrong and *Romani ite domum* is right. But with five hundred words we'll be able to talk. Should take about ten days."

"And, if not," said Marcus Caelius, with deadpan seriousness, "we can always cut their balls off."

✧   ✧   ✧

Though a new campsite had been settled on, the one found by the Palmyrenes, moving wasn't going to be that easy. Little by little, the century of artificers and fabricators was turning trees into wheels to replace the ones broken in the fall that had brought them here. It would have been slow work in the best of circumstances; given the sheer volume of wheels needed, hundreds, as it turned out, it was excruciatingly slow.

"And there's nothing we can do to speed things up," the centurion in charge of the artificers told Marcus Caelius. "Worse, none of this wood is seasoned. Worse still, we've only got so many wheelwrights. The others are all handy with tools, of course, but I'm stretching the wheelwrights parchment-thin with supervising. On the plus side, at least the hubs and most of the axles are all right, and we've lost none of the ironwork, though a lot of it needs repair. But that's more than balanced out by the wagon bodies that broke."

"Let me tell you what worries *me*," said Marcus Caelius. "We are running out of food. If it weren't for the meat the cavalry is bringing back, and the flesh of the dead horses, mules, and oxen, we'd be starting to get hungry in under a week. We've got to find a source of grain and buy or take it, then haul it in."

"Well, that's another thing, Top: do we need to fix all the wagons when we've lost so many draft animals?"

"We do," answered Caelius. "We can take some of the cavalry horses and put them in harness to supplement what we've lost. But we cannot make from scratch everything we might have to leave behind if we don't have drayage."

"I'll keep them to it, then. We'll fix everything that can be fixed."

INTERLUDE

Exploratory Spacecraft 67(&%#@, Several Hundred Znargs Above the Teutoburg Forest

"I'm losing one," said Red to Blossom, his whistles being cut short, a sure sign of desperation among his people.

"What do you mean?" she asked, her notes and clicks indicating deep fear.

"There is some kind of a sensitive among them. His body is going with the rest but his mind is wandering across the centuries of this planet."

406 A.D. somewhere along the Rhine

Appius Calvus, the legionary *haruspex*, screamed and screamed, making not a sound while doing so. He, like the others, had experienced the shock of seeing trees pulled into the air, had been blinded by the sudden light, and deafened by the blast. But his senses had returned to him, in a short moment. The reason that they had returned, he found to his horror, was that his (for lack of a better term) soul, was inhabiting some soldier's body. Looking out from a stranger's eyes, Calvus saw an uncountable mass of barbarians crossing on the far side of a long loop in a frozen river. He felt the soldier tremble, both with cold and maybe with fear. The soldier looked left and right, allowing Calvus to see the general equipment of the troops. They were armed and armored in a way that reminded him of *auxilia*. Moreover, individually, they looked as German as any one of the barbarians who had swarmed the legions under Varus, or who were swarming up the river bank now.

"Eh?" asked that soldier, in his mind. "And just who the fuck are you?"

"Me?" Appius asked, his mind settling down for the nonce, "I'm Appius Calvus, *haruspex* for the Eighteenth Legion." Calvus realized that neither he nor his inquisitor were speaking Latin. *But, then, we're not actually* speaking *at all, are we?*

"Bullshit," said the soldier. "Everyone knows the Eighteenth was destroyed in *Germania* about four hundred years ago. And *haruspex*? What's that?"

"Four hundred years? My gods! Oh, a *haruspex*? It's a kind of minor priest and taker of omens," Calvus answered. "Though I fancy myself a bit of a poet. I also officiate at funerals. And however long ago it may have been, I *was* with the Eighteenth."

"Yeah? Hmmm; you were probably killed back then and so your spirit has wandered until it came upon me. So not a bloody Christian, at least?"

"Umm...no, I don't think so. What's a Christian?"

The soldier then went into a long litany concerning the myriad failings he saw in Christians, from excessive empathy to hypocrisy to cowardice, along with their theology, such as he understood it.

"No, no," insisted the *haruspex*. "I'm certainly not one of them."

"Good," said the soldier. "If I'm going to die today—and I am—I'd rather not be sharing the afterlife with a Christian."

"We're going to die?" asked Calvus.

"Look at 'em," said the soldier. Calvus felt the chin pointing toward the oncoming horde. "Since Stilicho took away most of the troops to deal with the Goths, down south, we're outnumbered eight or ten to one—or maybe worse—and there just aren't enough of us to hold a long enough line."

"How many legions have you got here?"

The soldier replied, "Six legions, nearly five thousand men."

"Eight hundred men per legion? Six legions should be closer to thirty thousand, and a like number of auxiliaries."

"Maybe once upon a time," said the soldier. "Not now. And now, if you'll excuse me, I have to join my mates in giving the *barritus*."

"Sure," agreed Calvus. "I'll try to stay out of your way as we are killed...in my case, apparently, again. But what's your name?"

"Well, I was born Hrodebert, son of Sigifurd, but when I enlisted they gave me the name, Rodius Sigius. My friends call me Rod."

"Rod, it is. I...Rod, I think I'm being pulled away. Good luck to you on this day."

"Wait on the other side, Appius. I'll need someone to show me the ropes when I pass over."

CHAPTER FOUR

As far as the country of these Scythians the whole land
which has been described is level plain and has a deep
soil; but after this point it is stony and rugged. Then
when one has passed through a great extent of this rugged country, there dwell in the skirts of lofty mountains
men who are said to be all bald-headed from their
birth, male and female equally, and who have flat noses
and large chins.... These are injured by no men, for
they are said to be sacred, and they possess no weapon
of war. These are they also who decide the disputes rising among their neighbours; and besides this, whatever
fugitive takes refuge with them is injured by no one:
and they are called Argippaians.
                                    —Herodotus, *The Histories*, Book IV.23
                                                    (Macaulay Translation)

In camp, somewhere in the land of the Argippaeans, date unknown

While the other four Argippaean captives had not quite reached
the five hundred words Gisco had given as a goal, Bat-Erdene
had well exceeded it. He, uniquely, could converse fairly well in
a sort of pidgin Latin, certainly more than well enough to make
Marcus Caelius' threat merely theoretical.

Gisco hadn't tried to count them, but he thought that, while
the captive's Latin accent remained an atrocity, his vocabulary
was something near three times the goal. Though he still didn't
get the *Romanes eunt domus* joke.

On the other hand, all five had been forcibly bathed by legion-aries, been issued new clothing, and had seen their old clothing burnt as an offering to Pluto. Who deserved it. They were much more tolerable to be around now.

"So, *amicus* Gisco," asked Bat-Erdene, "what to become us? We no object to how we treatment, so far, but families know, by now, that we captured by fierce and powerful strangers. They must be out of minds with worry and grief."

"Well, nothing too very bad is going to happen, I think," answered the Phoenician secretary. "But I can understand your concern. I'll tell you what: let me go see the legate and ask that one of you be given his horse back and be let to go tell your people that you are well, and that we would like to parley with your chiefs."

"Would you?"

"Of course, I shall. In fact, I'll go wait in line to see the legate now."

"Yes, Gisco," said the legate, who seemed to be in the middle of rehearsing his assumption-of-command speech. "What is it?"

"It's the...err...our 'guests,' sir. They're concerned that their families—who certainly know they've been taken—will be deeply worried about them. I was thinking we could send one home on his own horse to set their minds at ease and to set our guests' minds at ease, as well. We could invite a party of them, too, to parley. We may find some friends. We may even find some friends who can stop the first spear from continu-ously worrying about the food situation. And the draft-animal situation."

Poor Marcus Caelius, thought Gaius Pompeius Proculus. *Ended up, after all, with the duties of first spear* and *the duties of camp prefect.*

"If they're going to send their leaders to come see us, they're going to want some kind of surety that they won't also be turned into 'guests,' don't you think, Gisco?"

"I agree, Legate, but I am not sure who we can or ought to send."

"Go see the first spear and ask who he thinks would do. Remind him that they must be sober men, of great probity. Now leave me alone; I have to rehearse..."

"One other thing, sir."

"Yes, what?" Gaius asked, impatiently.

"Well, beyond the men to serve as hostages, someone with a little diplomatic experience ought to go along, too. But the only one in camp with anything like that experience is, sad to say, me."

"Right. You go, too."

"Lucius Pullo and Titus Vorenus," mused Marcus Caelius, pondering the newly promoted-to-centurion duo standing at attention before him. They looked almost to be brothers, about equally ruddy-faced, equally tall, and equally broad of shoulder. Blue-eyed and blond-haired was a given, given where they'd enlisted from. "I don't suppose..."

"Yes, First Spear," answered Vorenus. "They were our great-grandfathers. Took their discharges—no, Titus Pullo wasn't killed at Pharsalus, but switched sides once again—anyway, took their discharges and set themselves up as gentleman farmers in Gaul, about half a day's walk from Nemausus. You know Caesar was a great one for forgiving even the greatest wrongs from old friends and comrades. Plus Vorenus-that-was spoke up for Pullo to Caesar's face.

"Next farm neighbors, they were. Married girls from the local aristocracy; citizens, they were. Then, what with being best friends and all, they exchanged sons and daughters for marriage. Became something of a tradition between the two clans. Though, since the numbers weren't usually even, this let some more local blood in. Became something of a tradition between the two clans. At this point, it's not clear which of us is more closely descended from Titus Pullo and which from Lucius Vorenus. Near as we can tell, from trying to figure out the genealogy from family records, we're closer to half brothers than distant cousins. We're also a bit more than half Gaul."

"I suspect I'm about half Gaul, myself," said Caelius. "From Cisalpine Gaul, you see. If, that is, the hair and the blue eyes didn't already tell you that."

"We figured, Top," said Vorenus.

"Plus," added in Lucius Pullo, "first names also get switched for the firstborn boy in every generation. And when my mum died giving birth to my little sister, Ultima, it was Titus' mom who practically raised the lot of us. Naturally, we also followed the other family tradition and enlisted together. You would be amazed at how much land a couple of generations of senior and first spear centurions can acquire in Gaul off their discharge payments. Enlisted? Yes, we're equestrians but tradition is tradition. And, since the Eighteenth was actively recruiting at the time..."

"I see," said the first spear, continuing with: "Well, I have a job for the two of you. You're going to become escorts for the emissary from the legion to whichever tribe of locals the Gallic cavalry took our captives from. And you're going to stay behind as sureties if they elect to send their own emissaries to us."

Both of the new junior centurions gulped.

"Do you know why I chose you two?" asked the first spear.

"No, Top," they answered together.

Marcus Caelius gave the two an icy smile. "I chose you because you are among the only really expendable centurions in the legion."

All the centurions but two were present for Gaius Pompeius' assumption-of-command ceremony and speech. So were the prefects and senior decurions of the auxiliaries, plus the senior medical staff and some few others, to include the gentleman rankers pulled up to be staff. There wasn't room inside the legate's tent for them all, though food and drink—nothing fancy, just fare a bit superior to what was normal in camp—were laid out inside in buffet fashion. The aquilifer, Gratianus Claudius, stood by the entrance to the legate's tent.

Marcus Caelius read off, "Attention to orders." At this, all those present except the new legate stood to attention. Caelius continued: "Pursuant to the customs and traditions of the service, and under the authority of the emperor, the undersigned assumes command: Gaius Pompeius Proculus."

That was Gaius' signal to move to the lectern and order, "At ease."

He took a small sip of watered wine from a cup resting on a shelf on the lectern, as much to cover his nervousness as to wet his throat.

"So far, so good," he began. "Seriously. Odds were fair that we were all going to be killed in Germany. Oh, we had a chance, yes, but not necessarily a great one.

"Now we're safe, properly encamped, and although our supply situation could be better, it could be a good deal worse, too."

Marcus Caelius, when reviewing Gaius' speech, had been adamant. *No, sir, don't explain yourself. Just confirm for them the situation, then tell them what we're going to do and why.*

"Let me give you the downsides, up front. One, we do not know where we are, though, from the constellations, we can be quite sure we haven't been moved by the gods to some other realm. Now, you are very likely thinking that, if we are on a plain, and this kind of grassy plain doesn't exist in *Germania*, Gaul, Hispania, or anyplace we've been told of in Africa, then we cannot be to the west and must be situated somewhere to the east, right?

"Not so fast. We've never explored the western ocean past the Canary Islands. Could be another continent out there. Could be several. Could be that if we marched west we'd eventually come to a place we couldn't hope to cross without building ships. Could be we'd never find enough wood to build those ships. So for now we're going to sit pat while trying to figure out where we are."

Hmmm, hadn't really considered that, thought Marcus Caelius.

"Well, almost sit pat; there's a better campsite to the east so we will be moving there, most likely.

"Two, based on the physical appearance of the captives the Gauls took, who resemble nothing I've ever seen, we are not close to home. In *any* direction.

"Three, we've lost a lot of men and some of them were key.

"Four, every one—every single one—of our wagons and carts were wrecked.

"Five, we lost a lot of dray animals.

"Six, the food situation is not great.

"Seven, the wells the engineers dug are not producing enough water for all our needs, though we can cook and drink just about enough.

"Eight, we've still got a lot of sick and injured, though whichever god or gods sent us here healed at least some of our men whom we should have reasonably expected to die.

"Nine, no women at all. Ten, there's almost no wood growing around here for cooking, long term."

"Had enough doom and gloom yet?" Gaius asked, with a

broad and well-rehearsed smile. "Here's the good news and the plan for the immediate future.

"First, we're going to get the wagons fixed. Whoever sent us here was kind enough to transport enough wood with us for that and for cooking...for now. Then we're going to load up and move to that better campsite—it's got a good hill and a broad river nearby—that the Palmyrene horse archers found for us.

"We can do a lot of hunting for meat, and the cavalry has been doing a fair job of stocking the larder. But we don't have enough wheat for more than another week or ten days with some rationing. And we're so short that we can't afford to set some aside to plant, even if we could be sure it would grow well in the local soil. So we're going to have to either trade for grain or find someone who has what we need and take it.

"Me, I'd prefer trade. Much safer.

"Along those lines, we've sent—rather, this morning are sending—an embassy to treat with the tribe the captives came from. My secretary, Gisco, who has been teaching them Latin with mixed success, says they do not grow much if any wheat but do grow barley—" This was met with a chorus of groans; barley was what the legions issued as punishment rations. "Yes, I'm no happier about it than you. Better than starvation, though, isn't it?

"Hopefully, too, the local barbarians will be able to give us some idea of where we are. But don't count on it; we may be lucky just to get a good idea of our surroundings. And maybe a source of wood for fuel. I say 'maybe' because the locals allegedly cook over dried dung. No, unsavory though it is, this isn't unknown even within the Empire. Note: Start saving animal droppings, effective now."

Gaius took another sip. This one *was* for a dry throat; he found that the more he spoke, the less nervous he became. He pointed at a little knot of men, generally young.

"That lot over there is going to go to making up some of our losses in key personnel. They're all equestrian class and they've all been promoted to the rank of *optio*. Like other *optios*, they can read, write, and do some arithmetic. They're also somewhat schooled in history and literature. Also logic. So they're a little better qualified than most *optios*.

"That's too junior for their responsibilities so they've each had a senior centurion assigned to watch over them. Unlike normal tribunes, they're not going to rotate through the jobs. Instead, they'll specialize in administration and law, scouting, interrogations, and intelligence, planning, engineering, and supply. One of them, too, is from the camp prefect's section—and, no, whatever happened to Ceionius no one seems to know, probably killed by the Germans. He's not here with us. In any case, that one will be working under the first spear to take care of quartermaster functions.

"The first spear is also splitting with me the duties of the *tribune laticlavius*. So don't fucking waste his time. Or mine. We're both going to be busier than a one-legged man at an ass-kicking competition.

"That also all means that you are not to be feeding shit to, nor fucking with, the staff just because they're very junior; they are backed up by some serious rank.

"Now all of you and the troops really have one question I cannot answer, or not yet, anyway: how and when do we get home? No, I cannot tell you either when or how; be lying through my teeth if I did. I can only tell you that, beyond sheer survival, nothing is more important than getting this legion home and reporting to the emperor."

Again, Gaius Pompeius sipped at his watered wine. "Now, some minor instructions. Senior centurions of the vexillations from Seventeenth and Nineteenth: we're putting your names on the roster and payroll of the Eighteenth. No, don't even think about bitching about it, you don't have your eagles, and you need to be under an eagle. We're going to muster most of you as the Eleventh and Twelfth Cohorts, Eighteenth Legion. By most of you, I mean that anyone from your old legions' first cohort is going to be transferred to the appropriate century of the Eighteenth's First Cohort, at least until it's full strength. We also need you, if you haven't already, to start to compile a list of personal equipment shortages. Speaking of that, Top, how's the inventory coming along?"

Marcus Caelius answered, "Still in progress, sir. A quick sight inventory tells me we've got about half enough *scuta* and gladii to provide for the missing ones, but not nearly enough *furcae*, leather haversacks, *pila*, or cooking pots. I've got the fabricators working on tanning the hides of the dead animals and making new *pila* and *furca* with wood from the uprooted trees and the iron from the several thousand *framea* found about the camp. Might be enough. Centurions, have your *optios* escort your people with shortages to the prefectural tent to sign or mark statements of charges on the payroll roster."

"One area where we are in very good shape," said Gaius Pompeius, "even with the vexillations, we've lost enough men that the pay chests are unusually flush. They were flush even before this, but there's more now. As such, and since the men ought to be paid in September, we're going to start payday as soon as the charges on the pay rosters are annotated.

"Any questions?"

The lad's done fairly well, thought Marcus Caelius. *I suspect that it's that proper Roman nose that makes him seem to the men worth listening to, despite his youth.*

"So how do your people live?" asked Lucius Pullo.

Gisco, Bat-Erdene, Titus Vorenus, and Lucius Pullo, guarded by an understrength *turma* from the Palmyrene horse archers, covered the seemingly endless grassy plain on horseback. They had two spares with them, plus three more with the Palmyrenes, and half a dozen pack mules bearing gifts and trade samples, as well as firewood.

Bat-Erdene had been given back his own horse, along with his bow and quiver. He rode what appeared to be a well-made saddle, felt over wood over leather over inch-thick felt to protect the horse. It was very high, fore and aft, but lacked the leg-clenching horns of a Roman saddle. Short-tied broad stirrups helped him take what looked to be a very comfortable seat well up on the high felt and wood rear. A couple of balanced bags were tied off and hung to either side.

The horse, the Romans noticed, had a much steeper, triangular back than their mounts, so that the saddle sat much higher over the beast's backbone.

"We have pattern," Bat-Erdene replied. He glanced as Gisco and asked, "Pattern? Is right word?"

"Routine might be better," the Phoenician replied.

"Routine, then," he corrected. "We keep sheep, generally. And numbers of goats. Also these big things; don't know the name because saw nothing like in camp. Have..." Here Bat-Erdene used his fingers to make horns on his head.

"Ohhhh, cows and bulls," said Pullo.

"Okay, if say so. We call '*ngek*'; more than one '*ngekud*.' Have to keep them from turning land to dust, them and sheep and goats. We move them in great circle, mostly marked by watering holes and rivers. Make circle three times a year; always end up in same place, what we call 'winter camp.' We'll also plant barley and rye at each stop, so have something besides meat to eat. Also collect other things—wild apples, some flavorings like...mmm...wild garlic and chives. Honey, too."

"And you live in...?" Pullo asked.

"We have tents on...ummm...wagons—is that the right word?" At Gisco's nod, Bat-Erdene continued. "We call '*gerud*.' Pretty cramped but, when late fall comes, and early spring, cramped and warm is welcome. Mostly, in good weather, we sleep outside rolled up in a blanket made from wool—that, or skins. At winter camp is more permanent lodges."

"Are," said Gisco.

"*Are* more permanent lodges."

Vorenus glanced down at the odd arrangement for Bat-Erdene's feet, hanging from his saddle. They seemed to allow him to ride securely, somewhat bent-legged, but without needing horns to grip his thighs. Pointing at them, he asked, "What do you call those?"

"*Yobud*," Erdene responded, figuring that the Roman meant his stirrups because he would have zero interest in his feet.

"Hmmm. Where did they come from? Did your people invent them?"

"Nobody really know. Been using that as far back as anyone can remember."

"Them, not that," Gisco corrected.

"I don't know that I'd care to change," said Vorenus, slapping the horns of his own saddle. "Our kind grips the legs and provides a pretty solid platform for fighting from."

"*De gustibus non disputandum*," said Erdene, the use of which raised a solid round of laughter from everyone who could hear.

"You've taught your student well, Gisco," said Pullo.

"He's a very good student," the Phoenician replied. The comment caused Bat-Erdene's chest to swell with pride.

"When will we reach your tribe?" asked Pullo.

"Really good question," Bat-Erdene replied. "I...mmm...'off-set' is right word? Ah, good. I offset our route to the west to come close to where they ought to be. When we reach trail, we will know."

"By the shit left behind?" asked Vorenus.

"No, no; pick all that up for cooking and heating. Set off and pile up to dry. Use on next pass around. No, we will know because almost all grass for miles eaten or trampled down, and soil chopped up by hooves."

"Ah."

"You people don't make war, Gisco tells us," said Pullo.

"No," replied Bat-Erdene. "War most stupid thing I ever hear of. Nobody attack us. Forbidden by them's own customs and laws. We too useful doing what we do. Even Scythians to south no attack, and they attack just about anybody."

"Hmmm...wonder why," mused the Roman.

"Legends say we made war once upon a time. Made whole peoples disappear. So horrible we swore it off. And nobody wants us to start thinking about it again."

"That *would* seem to make a certain sense," observed Gisco. *And neither do we.*

The party reached a large section, many miles across, that seemed almost completely denuded of grass nearly down to ground level. The area had a strong odor of sheep manure, though it looked like most of it had been picked up and moved.

Most, however, was not all. Spying a roughly oval pad of manure, Bat-Erdene dismounted next to it, then bent over and tested it with his fingers.

"Two day ahead," he pronounced, wiping his fingers on the short grass remaining. "Not more than three."

"How fast do they move?" asked Titus Vorenus.

"Speed of sheep and goats, not speed of horse," replied Bat-Erdene.

Vorenus looked at Lucius Pullo, whose family kept sheep in fairly large numbers. The latter thought upon this before saying, "Different kind of grass and maybe different kind of sheep and goat, and we have no idea how *many* sheep and goats, but maybe ten to twenty miles ahead."

"We can catch them," said Gisco.

"Going to be a hard ride, though," Pullo answered.

"Tell my ass about it," said Vorenus.

"We can ride at night," suggested Bat-Erdene.

Gisco asked, "But how will we know where we're going?"

Bat-Erdene looked left at Vorenus, then to the right, at Pullo, before suggesting, "One you two want tell him?"

Vorenus took it up. "Why, by the smell, Gisco, by the soon to be insufferable smell of tons upon tons of sheep, goat and cow shit."

"Let's ride in the daytime," insisted Gisco.

"Wish we had some dogs with us for wolves," pined Bat-Erdene.

"Ummm... wolves?"

"Sure, wolves. Follow herds. Almost only reason we have bows and arrows."

"You not make camp in like other place?" Bat-Erdene asked.

"Like in or as in," corrected Gisco. "'As in' is better."

Lucius looked at Titus to provide an answer.

The latter nodded, and explained, "There are three levels of manning to produce a camp. A whole army of at least two legions and the auxiliaries normally attached can do it in a few hours. Plenty of time left to cook, maintain equipment and animals, and get enough sleep even with pulling guard on the walls.

"A single legion can do it, but it takes longer and so requires that either the march be shortened, or the pace increased, or the ditch and wall—especially the gap between tents and wall that keep the enemy from tossing torches or shooting fire arrows at the tents—be reduced. Or that sleep and maintenance be reduced. Less than a legion and it gets progressively less of a camp, until it's just flat impossible without marching for an hour, building a half-assed camp, then tearing it down in the morning, marching for an hour... You get the idea."

Bat-Erdene nodded as if he did get it, although he didn't, not entirely.

"Sometimes, too, speed gives more security than entrenchments.

"Now we *could* set up the tent carried by one of the pack mules, but that would only insulate us from warning, not from danger. So we'll stay out here, roll up in a blanket just like you, and keep one ear open for the sound of the horses getting frightened. Also, while we won't be pulling guard, the Palmyrenes will keep up a few of men on guard at all times. And out of force of habit, when one of us wakes up, we'll walk the perimeter and check the guards."

"Understand," said Bat-Erdene. Without another word he got up and walked to where the moon showed a short wall of stacked sheep droppings. Kneeling, he felt from top to bottom until he reached some that seemed dry enough to him. He took out a half dozen of them, gathering them up in his arms, and walked back to the little encampment.

Once there, he unceremoniously released the sheep droppings, then plucked a few of the clusters of grass his tribe's sheep had missed. These he twisted and then braided loosely into a rope. Kneeling down on the ground, he coiled the twisted and braided grass rope into a fairly tight mass. Then, using his knife, he dug up three clods of dirt and then a circular ring around those, fairly deep and about a foot in width from the inside of the ring to its outside.

"Uncontrolled fire," he announced, "is thing of dread here on steppe."

Bat-Erdene then went to his own saddle, now resting on the ground, and took from one of the bags a piece each of flint and iron pyrite. "We most lucky have outcropping of these, together, along tribe's route. Friends Pullo and Vorenus, do you have a grating and maybe a cookpot in with the mules?"

"Several cookpots," answered Titus. "One for us and a few for gifts for your tribe's chiefs. Only the one grill, though."

"May I borrow?"

Wordlessly, Vorenus went to where the mule packs lay, selected one and rifled through it until he came up with the iron grill and cookpot. These he turned over to Bat-Erdene, then stood to watch procedures.

Bending low, Erdene stuck the pyrite against the flint, raising sparks with only some of the strikes. After more than one hundred tries, one spark, finally, caught on the loosely twisted grass rope. Blowing gently, he breathed life into that little spark, until the grass went from a smolder to a low blaze.

Around the blaze he broke off and placed chunks of dried sheep droppings, then blew those ablaze.

"Fascinating," said Vorenus.

Bat-Erdene then set the grating on the three mounds of earth. They were high enough that he would be able to feed further dried droppings into the fire, at need.

Finally, with a brisk fire going, Bat-Erdene announced, "I am rotten-horrible-wretched cook, but if one of you cares to..."

"I'm quite a good cook," said Gisco. "I'll handle dinner."

One of the Palmyrenes came over, a decurion, who asked to take some fire for his own group's cook fires. He also asked about borrowing some dried droppings for fuel.

"Help self," said Bat-Erdene. "Always more than need anyway. Shit one thing my people have plenty of. But for fire, see this." And he drew a circle with his finger illustrating the ring around the fire. "Make like or we have big fire and maybe all die in flames." He stopped for a contemplative moment, then added, "Lots of screaming when flames catch. Lots."

It wasn't very long before Gisco had a fair stew, mainly of salt-cured meat, thickened with crumbled *bucellata* and supplemented with some wild onions foraged by Bat-Erdene, simmering in the pot.

"Doesn't smell at all bad," Lucius commented. "Neither does the fire. But, got to say, the idea of eating food cooked with shit ruins my appetite."

"You going be—"

"Going *to* be," interjected Gisco.

"Going to be," corrected Bat-Erdene, "two serious thin men if cooking on sheep droppings bother you. Around here is nothing else *to* cook with. Well, animal crap in general."

"He has a point," said Titus.

"Did you ever look closely at a wood fire?" asked Gisco.

"Not really," said Pullo.

"Not so close as all that," added Vorenus.

"All right, then let me let you in on a secret: the wood doesn't burn. Instead—and you would see this if you looked closely—the fire starts a little distance away from the wood. The heat from the fire does something to the wood to make it give off something we can't see that, itself, burns. Meanwhile, the wood changes in form but does not burn.

"Now one of you please come here and look at the burning shit."

Vorenus did, lying on the ground to allow his face to get as close as possible to the flame. "Hmmm...now that you mention it, yes, there *is* a small gap between the sheep droppings and the flame."

"Right," said Gisco. "Now I'm not going to tell you that there is zero possibility of a speck of crap getting in your food. But I *will* tell you that before it does, it gets completely purified by the flame.

"Do you object to eating bread made from wheat that was fertilized with crap? No? Didn't think so. To eating vegetables grown with manure? No? Didn't think you would object to that, either. Well, this is the same basic thing. For the gods' sake, we've been breathing little bits of crap in the dust in the air ever since we got on this path behind Bat-Erdene's people. Hades, you breathe the same or worse every day in camp and every day you have ever spent in a city.

"In this case, at least, the fire will purify it."

In this case, everyone *did* manage to eat Gisco's stew, Vorenus and Pullo desperately trying not to think about sheep dung, Gisco with some enjoyment, and Bat-Erdene with considerable relish.

"Better than mom's," the short, yellow local insisted. He likewise enjoyed the hard biscuit, the *bucellatum*, which was perhaps a better indicator than most that his tribe lived hard lives, with food other than mutton and goat sometimes hard to come by. And sometimes even those might have run short.

It was actually Bat-Erdene who first sensed the approach of trouble, alerted by the frightened neighing of the horses.

Quickly, he shook Lucius Pullo awake, who mumbled, "What is it?"

"Trouble. Some kind. Horses scared. Think we better get ready."

"Right," Pullo said slowly, shaking his head and wishing someone would come up with some kind of drink or drug to make a man alert on short notice. "Titus, Gisco, time to get up."

Vorenus awakened instantly and almost as quickly said, "Shit, the moon is down. Erdene, can you stoke up the fire again?"

"Working on it, friend Titus."

"I'm going to make sure all the Palmyrenes are up," announced Pullo, then pulled his sword and strode off in the direction of their decurion, Maeonius.

It was a short walk, a matter of a dozen steps or so. "Maeonius?" called Pullo.

"Here, Centurion," answered the horse archer. His Latin was excellent, but for a strong Syrian accent. "I've already got my men up and stringing their bows, all except for two to drive the hor—"

The Palmyrene was interrupted by the sound of a man screaming, and not all that far away, accompanied by terrified horses trying to run directly toward the camp. The horses were hobbled, so their running was pitifully slow.

Then they heard a wolf, baying triumphantly to the east, followed by two or three score more wolves, in accompaniment. A horse screamed in terror and pain.

"We're so screwed," said Maeonius. "Wolves are as smart as we are, twice as mean, braver, and more cooperative with each other. And that's just too many to handle without light."

"Remember, Maeonius," said Pullo, "*opposable thumbs*."

"Well, yes, there is that."

"Light...light..." Having the glimmering of an idea, Pullo trotted to where Bat-Erdene had the fire going again. By the light he could see Vorenus buckling on his armor and Gisco standing clumsily with an unaccustomed sword in his hand.

"How steady are the winds this time of year around here?" Pullo asked.

"Don't change much," Bat-Erdene answered. "Almost always from direction of setting sun. Sometimes blow harder. Sometimes less."

"So if we start a fire, a line of fire, it will push that fire to the east?"

"Yes, friend Lucius. But so dangerous!"

"More dangerous than that many wolves looking for a meal?"

Bat-Erdene considered that before answering, "Maybe not. What you thinking?"

"I'm thinking that we mount up and split into two groups, each group having fire. One goes north, setting the steppe ablaze as they do, while the other rides south, doing the same."

Bat-Erdene wetted a finger and held it up. "Wolves faster than wind," he said.

"That's fine because while they're running we will follow the fire closely on horseback. By the light of that fire the Palmyrenes can shoot the bastards."

"Could work."

Gisco asked, "What will your tribe say if we let an uncontrolled fire loose on the grasslands?"

"Maybe not like it much," answered Bat-Erdene, "but probably understand. Besides, wolves plague on herds. Can always plead greater good."

"Shall we?" asked Vorenus, now fully armed and armored. "It's your call, Gisco."

"Do it," the Phoenician said. "Do it."

"Maeonius!" Pullo called out.

"Here, Centurion." The horse archer had been closer than Pullo had imagined.

"Did you overhear?"

"Well enough. I told my men to get saddled and ready to fight. Should I have?"

"Yes. Absolutely yes," said the centurion. "Now Bat-Erdene, get as many of your sheep droppings burning as possible. Maeonius, I want your men to carry them on the ends of your lances—bend the tips if necessary to keep them there—and to make a fire half a mile across, then pursue the wolves when they turn tail. Do you understand? Can you do that?"

"Yes, and yes, Centurion."

Vorenus cried out, "Watch that one!" then threw a *pilum* that pinned one charging wolf to the ground. The beastie cried out, piteously, writhing on the ground around the cold iron of the *pilum*. The centurion moved around behind the wolf, then plunged his gladius into its neck three times before the wolf stopped struggling with the *pilum* and snapping threateningly at them all.

Inspired by Vorenus' wolf, Lucius Pullo grabbed his shield, no time to put on his armor now, and faced east, with the westerly wind to his back. He and Pullo put Gisco between them and watched out for wolves by the dim light of the fecal fire. Unseen, behind them, Bat-Erdene took his bow and quiver and leapt aboard his horse, bareback. Using only his knees and voice, he directed his short-statured horse to a spot behind the three on foot and nocked an arrow.

In a moment, Bat-Erdene drew and loosed and, in the faint light, missed. Cursing in his own people's tongue, he nocked and drew another arrow, but not before a wolf had Titus backed up on one knee, with the wolf furiously trying to chew the edges of the centurion's *scutum* while, with a desperation equal to the wolf's ferocity, the centurion tried to stab the wolf with his gladius.

"Stab him! Stab him!" Pullo ordered Gisco. The Phoenician stood stock-still in shock. Lucius was just about to pull him out of the way and deal with the wolf himself, when Bat-Erdene loosed again. That arrow flew true, piercing the wolf through its heart and one lung.

"*Gratias*, friend!"

By this time, Maeonius had his Palmyrenes mounted, on line and with burning turds on each lance head. He also had them organized into two groups of ten or eleven.

With a battle cry, the Palmyrenes galloped off, north and south. As they went, they stopped in close-set places to set the grass alight along a rough line. Soon, many of the wolves were fleeing back in the direction whence they'd come. In twos and threes, the Palmyrene horse galloped after them, lances slung and bows drawn, impaling enough to keep the wolves from turning about.

"I just realized the flaw in my plan," Pullo said, in a voice devoid of any emotion but the sense of doom. "Here they come!"

The flaw was that, while there was a tide of fire to the north and south of where the four stood, there was *no* fire directly to the east.

"Oh, shit," said Vorenus, understanding the deadly geometry of the matter. "Bat-Erdene, get some of your flaming shit bricks and hurl them in front of us."

Bat-Erdene started to turn back to the fire, started and then stopped. "Too late for that, Titus."

There might have been as many as nine arrows in Bat-Erdene's quiver. But the quiver was empty in less than a minute with maybe four of the wolves hit. By that time, Vorenus had elbowed Gisco to a safer spot to the rear, then shifted right to almost lock shields with Pullo. "Try to get any that go over us," Titus Vorenus shouted to Gisco, then sank down to one knee to cover his vulnerable legs from the lower-slung wolves.

Having no more arrows, hence nothing physical to contribute to the fight, Bat-Erdene dismounted and ran to the fire. Heart pounding in his chest, holding a half dozen stacked, burning sheep pies in his hands, and burning his hands and arms, he ran back to stand beside Gisco. He dropped them to his feet, knowing that his hands and arms would be a horror story on the morrow.

Rotating to change his direction of aim, one by one he picked up and cast the roughly circular pies to the east. The flight added a good deal to the intensity of the fires, such that, when they hit and scattered, they also scattered flames among the grass. Soon there was another wall of fire, racing east with the wind, behind the other two walls, north and south.

This didn't do anything immediately of use for Pullo, Vorenus, and Gisco, faced with one or two wolves each. And it did less still for Bat-Erdene, who now faced one wolf without either bow or arrow, sword or shield.

"What can I fight with? What can I fight with?"

"Reach over to me," said Vorenus. "There's a dagger on my right side. Better than nothing."

"Fuck that," said Pullo. "Go get the *pilum* Vorenus threw through the first wolf that got through to us."

"Wolf between me and spear," said Bat-Erdene. "I use dagger."

A total of six wolves circled the four now. There may well have been others farther out, waiting for an opening to appear. If so, these were now fleeing from the wind-driven flames. There were certainly a large number being chased by fire and Palmyrene horsemen, and—from the canine screams and pained howling— dying under their bows and lances.

One rushed in suddenly at Pullo, going for the legs. Pullo brought his *scutum* down sharply on the wolf's neck, not breaking it but driving its head down to the ground and then pinning it there long enough for a sword thrust through the back. It wasn't an immediately killing strike; the wolf twisted and turned so vigorously that Pullo could barely hang onto his gladius. On the plus side, the gladius was razor sharp; each twist of the wolf did untold damage to flesh, bones, nerves and arteries. In what seemed an eternity but was probably less than a minute and a half, the wolf shuddered and died.

Another wolf battered its way past Gisco, taking Vorenus in the side. It insisted on trying to chew its way through Vorenus' mail *lorica*. The wolf didn't get through, though the force of its bite caused some damage to Vorenus' ribs. Swinging hard with his *scutum*, Titus managed to hit the wolf with the edge, knocking it several feet away. This gave him enough time to reorient himself to present a shield and sword front to the wolf.

Yet another wolf went after Gisco. The tall Phoenician was no great hand with a sword. The most he could do was to clumsily thrust it out in front, trying to ward the wolf off. The animal wasn't deterred. Rather, it brushed Gisco's blade aside with its muzzle and closed for the kill.

Screaming, "No!" Bat-Erdene threw himself upon the wolf, wrapping an arm about its throat and stabbing it repeatedly with Vorenus' *pugio*.

Sensing the opening, a wolf charged Bat-Erdene. Clumsy still, Gisco lunged forward, point toward the wolf.

The beastie didn't see it or was too convinced of Gisco's harmlessness to even see the gladius as a threat. Or perhaps hunger overcame the normal lupine instincts. Whatever the cause, the wolf leapt onto the outthrust blade. The sword's needle-sharp point first pierced the flesh and then lodged deep in the scapula, too deep for anything the wolf, itself, could do to dislodge it. Though the force of its leap had knocked Gisco to the ground in a sprawl, the wolf lost its interest in Levantine cuisine, instead writhing from side to side in a vain attempt to dislodge the tormenting steel in its skeleton.

Meanwhile, behind where Gisco raised himself on his elbows to half lay, more or less entranced and transfixed at the sight off the struggling wolf, Titus Vorenus was down, trying to pull as much of his body as possible under the *scutum* as two wolves snapped and nosed around its periphery, trying to get around it to tear at flesh. Vorenus had toothmarks on his helmet and his greaves, and at least one bleeding bite on his left leg, while the transverse crest of the helmet was fairly denuded of plumage.

Lucius Pullo, wanting to help Vorenus but unable to do so, shifted shield and sword left then right then left again, fending off first one and then another of his furred assailants. All the while he had a cold and creeping sensation between his shoulder blades that, yes, another wolf might be preparing to leap onto his back and sink its fangs in his neck.

And then, suddenly, one of the wolves attacking Pullo gave off a scream, leapt several feet in the air, and fell in a heap. Another, atop Vorenus' shield, fell over, instantly dead from an arrow sticking out of its side. The one with Gisco's sword in its chest likewise went down, though it was a large beast and took three arrows to fell. The final wolves, aware that the odds had shifted against them and that some humans atop horses had ridden up, dealing out death, turned and ran toward the fire that now receded into the distance, hoping, no doubt, to find some path through it to join their fellows.

"You lot all right?" asked Maeonius.

"Define 'all right'?" asked Vorenus, rising with the help of his *scutum*, with his right hand, while holding insulted ribs with the other arm. His sword lay, for the nonce forgotten, on the ground. Blood trickled down one of his legs.

"Alive? Not ripped halfway to shit? Your entrails still in your bellies where they belong?"

"By those measures," said Pullo, like Vorenus now resting on his shield, "we are probably all right, Maeonius. How are your ribs, Titus?"

"But for the armor and the *subarmalis*, I'd be well and truly screwed. As is, they're sore, maybe bruised, but not too badly damaged. I should be fine."

Gisco, coming out of his quasi-trance, began to curse, mindlessly, in at least seven different languages. Going to the wolf that had beset him, he worked the sword blade loose from the bone that had held it. Then, still cursing and with two hands awkwardly placed on the sword's *capulus*, or hilt, that had room for not much more than one, he went into a frenzy of hacking, slashing, and stabbing the corpse of the huge wolf that had nearly taken his life. All the others present simply watched as the swarthy Phoenician worked out his terror on the corpse of his erstwhile enemy.

Meanwhile, Bat-Erdene stoically felt at the wounds he'd taken, hoping to hell they were not from a rabid wolf.

"How many did you kill?" Pullo asked of Maeonius.

"Hard to say," the latter replied, "but probably more than forty. It was a very large pack; we're all lucky to be alive, those who still are."

"How many did you lose?"

"Including the one taken down before the attack began in earnest, two dead, two more with bites, and another so ripped up he's going to die."

"Shit."

"Shit," the Palmyrene echoed. "We'll get them buried in the morning."

INTERLUDE

Exploratory Spacecraft 67(&%#@, Several Hundred Znargs Above the Teutoburg Forest

"I've confirmed that we've got his body going to where the others are," Red informed Blossom. "At least I think I have. His mind is entirely somewhere else, in space, though not so distant in time. I've never heard of anything like this, Blossom. I wouldn't be able to track his mind, I don't think, if there wasn't still a kind of link between body and mind."

409 A.D. Bethlehem

"Where am I?" asked Calvus. "And who the hell are you?"

The being to whom he spoke now, much like Rod, just a bit earlier, was so accepting of the intrusion of a stranger into his mind that Calvus wondered if, perhaps, he was not speaking to the conscious mind but to some kind of *animus*, something inside a man or woman with an existence independent of the body.

"Who am I? I am Jerome, a humble servant of our Lord, Jesus Christ, and, in good part, a translator of his words. As to where you are: apparently you are with me, and I am in what the Eastern Empire calls Bethlehem, the birthplace of my Lord and God. And you?"

"I am Calvus. As to the whats, whys, and wherefores: too hard to explain," answered Calvus. "I don't even know *how* to explain it. Last I knew I was in a rainy forest in Germany preparing to die. Suffice to say that I mean no one any harm."

Calvus' reticence stemmed from the realization that this "Christ" mentioned by Jerome probably meant that he was a Christian. Despite Rod's earlier mental denunciation of the Christians, Calvus had no desire to offend. Changing the subject, he asked, "What are you doing? Rather, what *were* you doing when I was so rudely thrust upon you?"

"I was writing a letter to a widow, Ageruchia, a wealthy woman of Gaul, advising her not to remarry."

"Kind of a busybody, then, aren't you? And in what language were you writing? What languages can you write in?"

"I wonder, sometimes," answered Jerome, "but in this case, no; the widow asked for my advice. As for languages, I speak, read, and write Latin, Greek, and Hebrew, the language of the Jews. I can sort of get by in Aramaic but my accent is atrocious. This letter is in Latin."

"Sate my curiosity, friend Jerome, and show me."

"How?"

"From experience, I think that if you look at the letter, or read it to yourself aloud, I will see and hear."

"Very well, then."

Calvus paid limited attention to the advice to Ageruchia, but then the tone and message of the letter changed, with Jerome's reading of, "The once noble city of Mogontiacum has been captured and destroyed. In its church many thousands have been massacred. The people of Vangionum after standing a long siege have been extirpated. The powerful city of Remorum, the Ambiani, the Altrebatæ, the Morini on the skirts, Tornacum, the Nemetæ, and Argentoratus have fallen to *Germania*: while the provinces of Aquitaine, and of *Novempopulania*, of Lugdunensis, and Narbonensis are, with the exception of a few cities, one universal scene of desolation. And those which the sword spares without, famine ravages within. I cannot speak without tears of Toulouse, which has been kept from falling hitherto by the merits of its reverend bishop, Exuperius. Even the Spains are on the brink of ruin and tremble daily as they recall the invasion of the Cymry; and while others suffer misfortunes once in actual fact, they suffer them continually in anticipation."

"Gods!" said Calvus, "It is the death of the Empire." Despite being incorporeal, the *haruspex* began to weep. "'Ruin, eldest daughter of Zeus, she blinds us all, that fatal madness—she with those delicate feet of hers, never touching the earth, gliding over the heads of men to trap us all. She entangles one man, now another.'"

"Ah, Homer," said Jerome.

CHAPTER FIVE

It is because the first object of the Romans in the matter of encampment is facility, that they seem to me to differ diametrically from Greek military men in this respect. Greeks, in choosing a place for a camp, think primarily of security from the natural strength of the position: first, because they are averse from the toil of digging a foss, and, secondly, because they think that no artificial defenses are comparable to those afforded by the nature of the ground. Accordingly, they not only have to vary the whole configuration of the camp to suit the nature of the ground, but to change the arrangement of details in all kinds of irregular ways; so that neither soldier nor company has a fixed place in it. The Romans, on the other hand, prefer to undergo the fatigue of digging, and of the other labors of circumvallation, for the sake of the facility in arrangement, and to secure a plan of encampment which shall be one and the same and familiar to all.

—Polybius, *Histories*, 6.42

In camp, somewhere in the land of the Argippaeans, date unknown

When the last of the wagons had been repaired, when the last of the refugees from Seventeenth and Nineteenth legions had their *furcae* replaced, and when the dead horses, mules, and oxen had provided leather for new *sarcinae* to attach to the *furcae*, there was still a good deal of leather and wood to work on other key projects.

There was nothing required to tan those hides that the camp and the dead animals could not provide. Urine there was in plenty to soak the hides in to loosen the hair. Neither was there a shortage of animal dung and brains to mix with water and soak the hides to soften them. Sufficient, if only that, tannin came from the bark of the trees that had been sent with them to...

"Wherever the hell this place is," said Marcus Caelius, "and however the hell we and they got here."

The first replacement shields issued to the refugees came from the men the Eighteenth had lost. These were not quite sufficient, so more were being manufactured. It took time to split wood into strips between a sixteenth and an eighth of an inch thick. More time was required to glue them together in such a way as to create a solid whole, a quarter of an inch thick and curved. Of bronze to create a boss for each shield there just wasn't anything like enough. What there was of bronze was hammered out into strips to wrap around the edges of the *scuta*, to protect the wood from slashes.

Glue came from the same dead animals that had provided the hides.

The *scuta* should have been covered with a hide, over and above the outer protective hide, that was tied on, to protect them from the rain and morning damp, but there just weren't enough hides for the job, not with every other need for leather. Instead, where there wasn't enough hide, they were heavily coated with dyed wax. It would have to do.

"A shield is better than no shield," the first spear had insisted.

One new source of food had been found in the legionary stocks. This was the barley normally fed to draft animals to supplement their foraging. With all the grass around, and with no really hard work being required of them, the animals were doing well enough on a nearly pure grass diet.

The horses, which were in hard use, still required grain. But even after enough was set aside for them, there were still a couple of hundred tons that could be fed to the legionaries, albeit amidst much grumbling.

There were, besides the draft animals and horses, about eight hundred sheep and lambs, more or less evenly divided, which were enough for about eight or ten days' worth of slightly short meat rations from the lambs alone.

Marcus Caelius, not so much filling in for the old *praefectus castrorum*, Ceionius, as supervising the equestrian class *optio*, hastily promoted and put into his place, felt a little more comfortable about the legion's ration status. And, for the little nagging doubts, he was quite sure there was nothing he could do.

Meanwhile, there was training, about which he definitely *could* do something.

Marcus Caelius escorted the legate around the open area east, southeast, and northeast of the camp where the men—half of them—were engaged in weapons drills. These involved repetitive movements of thrusting, parrying, and slashing with their gladii, as well as riposting, blocking, and striking with the *scuta*, plus forward lunges and rearward recoveries.

Individually, for their own centuries, the centurions or their *optios*, called out the commands: "Second. Thrust. Recover. Fourth. Riposte. Advance. Strike. Strike down..."

These commands were different in the details from later forms of swordplay, largely because the *scuta* covered half the possible lines of attack against the individual legionaries.

"I don't really get it, Top," said Gaius Pompeius. "None of those movements strike me as very realistic or practical. Especially since they're fighting ghosts."

"Well, sir," said the first spear, "they're more practical than you might think. For one thing, they've quite good at keeping a man from stabbing or slashing his neighbor. Under the eyes of their centurions, too, they're good for drilling people in economy of motion. But the real reason is that they're the best way we have of keeping the muscles associated with fighting in good condition."

"Ah...so it's more about *exercise* than about exercise."

"Precisely, sir. Also note that we don't have more of the double-weight *scuta* and gladii than about for a century at a time. If we ever settle down long term, I'll try to get it up to enough for a cohort. For now, this is what we have for most men, most of the time."

"I have a lot to learn."

"Wagonloads, sir, if you don't mind my saying, but you *are* learning fairly quickly. Let's go have a look at our new Eleventh

Cohort, shall we? They're working on their *pila* techniques. Hmmm... come to think of it, you could use some training, too, so that you look good in front of the men. Let's get back inside the camp where the legionaries can't see you and we'll work on that; what say you, sir?"

"I've already got at least *some* skill with a *pilum*, Top."

"Hmmm, 'skill,' eh? Sir, look at the men of that cohort."

Whether by luck or just that Quintus Silvanus' men were that good, the next legionary to throw hit the center mark of the target perfectly and drove the point of the *pilum* through an inch and a half of wood.

"Let's go work on my *pilum* technique, Top. And thanks."

Bacchus, my arm is sore, thought the legate, that night at the staff meeting. *When the first spear puts you through your paces, you are going to feel it later on. And, for all my pain, I still have a long way to go to get to be as good as the legionaries.*

The staff meeting consisted of the legate, Gaius Pompeius, himself; all five centurions of the first cohort, including the first spear; the senior centurions of each of the other eleven, including the two new ones; all seven of the equestrian class *optios*, the senior decurion of the legionary cavalry, and the chiefs of the Gallic and Palmyrene cavalry; the two prefects of the auxiliaries; and the senior doctor. Normally, the *haruspex* would be included, but...

"He's still mostly... well, there's no word in Hippocrates to describe it," reported the doctor, Samuel Josephus. "Mostly he does nothing but stare off into space. He screams sometimes, weeps sometimes, and frequently talks to people who are not there. Well, maybe it's talking, nobody can recognize the languages. Not Latin or Greek. Nor even Hebrew. And while some of it sounds a bit like the German spoken by our Germans, it is emphatically *not* that German. Some of it sounds like Latin, too, but not *your* Latin."

"If he's that much dispossessed of his mind," asked Gaius Pompeius, "how are you feeding him?"

"By hand, with difficulty," answered Josephus. "You really don't want to know the details. He is losing weight, but then again, he could afford to lose a few *minae*... or *librae*... or maybe a few dozen."

"How are the others coming along?" asked the legate.

"Shockingly well," answered Josephus. "I've never seen anything like it. You know about the ones who were surely going to die whom the first spear booted out of the *valetudinarium* and back to duty, yes? Well, all of our sick and injured have displayed a resistance to infection I've never seen before. It's like the finger of the One God—or one of your gods, which don't exist—touched each of them and gave them some kind of inner strength."

Only the new *optios* grumbled at that, along with the centurions from cohorts Eleven and Twelve; the rest of the Eighteenth was used to and tolerant enough of Josephus' heresies so long as he continued to be a first-class physician.

"That's really a fine thing, too, since I didn't have anything like enough *opos*, juice of the poppy, for all the wounded I had. Note, though," the Jewish *medicus* continued, "that this is true only for the ones who were already hurt when we came here. I've had several more injured since—one from an axe, for example, who laid open his leg cutting wood. These are healing, or not, as we'd expect.

"In any case, my men are underemployed at the moment, so I've put them to practicing arrow removal, using the spoon of Diocles, from chunks of meat and offal, wound cleaning, suturing, that kind of thing. Tonight they get a lecture on triage and tomorrow another lecture on field sanitation. If all that goes well I'm going to teach a couple of them trepanning."

"Right," agreed the legate, who had a limited idea of what about half of that meant.

Marcus Caelius then ran down the strength of each cohort, plus the attachments. In all, strength was six thousand, three hundred and sixty-three men, no brats, no sutlers, and no tarts. He didn't bother reporting on the few hundred publicly owned slaves with the legion though, privately, he wondered if he ought to have the legate manumit them and enroll them in the legion, to make up for losses to a limited extent. He also listed Gisco, Pullo, and Vorenus as accounted for, which presumed they were still alive.

One by one, Caelius called upon the centurions of the First Cohort to give their status on bringing the legion back into form. He gave each one to the count of one hundred to get their report out, answer any questions from the legate, and then shut up.

The cohort centurions got less time. The *auxilia* and cavalry got no more.

Marcus Caelius *hated* long meetings and hated equally the kind of commander who liked them, as well as the kind of staff officer who wasted time making himself seem important with endless jabber-jabber. Thus, he'd pulled the small plug on the legate's clepsydra, or water clock, at the start of this one, to limit the meeting to no more than a mid-spring or -fall hour, using his own count to divide it up. The legate, being so new, hadn't realized that this was unusual and so had gone along. The *optios* of the staff were equally ignorant, and badly outranked, so couldn't complain. And the centurions, decurions, and *praefecti* were, to a man, grateful to keep the silly thing so short.

Finally, it was the legate's turn and he, again being so new, had little to say. Thus it was with vast relief and immense satisfaction that Marcus Caelius departed the tent with, by his estimate, a good tenth of an hour still remaining on the clock.

And the meeting mercifully over.

En route to the Camp of the Argippaeans, somewhere west of the Sunrise Mountains

By the time they caught up to the roving camp of Bat-Erdene's people, Vorenus' bite wounds had begun to fester, leaving him with a fever and a strong penchant for raving.

"Is it rabies, do you think?" Pullo enquired of Gisco. He prayed to all the gods he knew of, and any whose names might have been skipped over, that it wasn't. Titus was his best friend, his cousin, genetically about a half brother and emotionally a full one. Just as important, he was a comrade in arms within the legion. No one survived rabies; this was common knowledge. And it was a shitty death, almost as shitty as crucifixion, and took even longer to die from. If Vorenus had rabies it would be up to Pullo to put him out of his misery.

"Likely not rabies," said Gisco, in a tone of near absolute certainty. "With rabies people are terrified of liquids. Mind, it can take a while to show up, so he's not yet out of the woods."

Pullo didn't answer, just chewed his lower lip and shook his head.

"No," Gisco continued, "he's not out of the woods, but the

part that worries me are the bite wounds on his leg. They stink and that's never a good sign.

"There is one thing in his favor: wolves are pretty ruthless and particular where the good of the pack in concerned. I think if all of them had been rabid they'd never have been able to mount such a strong attack, on the one hand, and, on the other, if one of them had been rabid they'd have driven it out of the pack and so it never would have been part of the attack."

Maeonius' Palmyrenes were in better shape, all but the one who, as predicted, had died from his wounds and been buried by the side of the broad and bare trail. This had cost the party almost an entire day.

The wounded Palmyrenes, at least, could ride on their own. With Titus Vorenus, he not only depended on the horns gripping his thighs but had to have his torso tied to the horse's bridle and the saddle as well. Even at that, his head flopped from side to side most alarmingly, like a cork at sea in strong waves.

Though the area was, in general, amazingly flat, there were some areas of rolling terrain. They rode up one such and stopped dead, in amazement.

Before them stretched several miles to their right and left and into the distance farther than they could see for all the dust, a moving sea of animals. Some were horses, like Bat-Erdene's, and, like his, bearing riders. Others were sheep and goats. For still others . . .

"Those are the biggest fucking cows I have ever seen," announced Lucius Pullo.

"*Ngekud*," Bat-Erdene said, once again making horns on his head with his fingers.

Indeed, the cattle were monstrous, taller than the horses at the shoulder, taller at the shoulders than men, for that matter, solid as the pyramids of Egypt, and with horns stretching, in some cases, as wide as a man was tall. Pullo whistled as realized the sheer enormity of the beasts.

Though many of them pulled great wagons, others grazed freely or grazed while carrying some substantial wrapped-up loads on their backs.

Dogs, likewise huge though nothing like the *ngekud*, trotted among the animals, keeping them in line and keying off the humans for their general direction. The whole procession moved very slowly, at the speed of grazing sheep and goats.

Admiringly, Pullo said, "Like to get a matched pair of those dogs for the legion, or at least one stud to breed on our bitches."

"They are very fierce but also very loyal," said Bat-Erdene. "Smart, too. We go now?"

"Yes," agreed Gisco, "we go."

Accompanied by the Palmyrene horse, the party trotted down toward the rear of the moving tribe. Very shortly after they'd crested the rise and begun their descent, riders from the rear of the tribe peeled off to intercept. They carried spears but with crosspieces that indicated they were intended for dealing with animal enemies, not human ones. Their bows were encased and hung from their saddles. Quivers of arrows hung across their backs, with the fletching rising a foot above their shoulders.

Upon seeing that the Romans were not disarmed but wore metal armor and carried any number of deadly weapons, and a goodly variety of those, the tribesmen reined their horses to a stop.

"They are frightened," said Bat-Erdene. "May I go to them and calm their fears, Gisco?"

"Do."

Bat-Erdene spurred his horse and trotted up to the locals. They went through a series of greetings, verbal and physical touching, and then several minutes of conversation before he returned to the Roman party. As he did, a pair of the tribesmen galloped off.

"They go inform chiefs prepare welcome."

"Let's hope," said Pullo, "that the welcome is friendly."

It was fully a two-hour ride to get from where the tribe's animals began to where their wagons had been circled for the evening. At that, it wasn't one circle but dozens, some smaller and others very large, indeed. Enormous herds rested in between but, the Romans noticed, the horses and wagon- and load-bearing cattle stayed inside the wagon laagers.

"Can afford to lose a sheep to the wolves, or to the tigers and brown bears that sometimes come off sunrise mountains. Sheep, yes, goats, even, and even untrained *ngek*, though them pretty much defend selves. Cannot lose horse or trained *ngek*."

At what seemed to Gisco to be the largest circle of wagons, Bat-Erdene led the party, to include the Palmyrenes, through a gap which had been opened. People stopped what they were doing and looked on curiously, but no one evinced any hostility.

"Do they know we're the ones who...mmm...invited you to be our guests?" asked Gisco.

"Them know. Ankhbatar, one who escape, tell them."

"They seem remarkably friendly for people who've had some of their own kidnapped," Gisco observed.

"Tell before, no one hurt us. If you take, they figure you got reason other than hurt. And me, I tell you treat us as honored guests. Want talk chiefs."

Titus Vorenus' horse was being led by Pullo. He swayed, senseless and tormented by fever, in the saddle.

They approached a group of seven rather distinguished-looking men and three women, all of basically the same build and face as Bat-Erdene. None were fat.

Gisco asked Bat-Erdene to do the introductions. Except for Vorenus, who was incapable of dismounting on his own, and the Palmyrene horse archers who stayed in the saddle for now, the other three dismounted. Gisco bowed and, after a moment's hesitation, Pullo followed suit.

The center man—also the most distinguished looking—asked Bat-Erdene a question, pointing at Vorenus. Following the answer, he barked some orders and a group of men, plus one of the women in the group of dignitaries, came and gently untied Vorenus from his saddle and lowered him down. Then they picked him up and carried him to one of the *gerud*, their wagon-mounted tents.

"That our chief healer woman," Bat-Erdene said, his voice sounding as if he were very impressed. "She take good care Titus; fix up good as new. That, or he die."

Following introductions—which even Gisco forgot immediately— the central figure in the group of dignitaries beckoned for the Romans to follow him to where a fair-sized fire of sheep dung burned inside a pit. It was surrounded on three sides by cushions. Once there, he clapped and servants or slaves, or maybe even free tribesmen—Gisco and Pullo couldn't guess—came out with more cushions, which they placed on the fourth side. The chief gestured for the Romans and Bat-Erdene to sit, then followed suit himself.

"Your chief," Gisco asked, "what is his name again?"

"Him Qadan."

Gisco smiled warmly in the direction of the chief. "Ah, yes,

Qadan. Please tell noble Qadan that we're sorry for several things. One is arriving in your lands unannounced and without so much as a by-your-leave. The other is taking you and the other four back at camp. You were following us stealthily and we thought you might be hostile. Please remind him that neither you nor the others were hurt or robbed."

Bat-Erdene translated both the opening statement and Qadan's response. "Him say, 'No harm, no foul.' Him also say, 'You came here through will of some god or gods. We no contest with gods.' Finally, him ask, 'What you want?'"

"First and foremost, noble Qadan, we desire your good will," said Gisco, still smiling as sincerely as he was capable of, while Bat-Erdene translated. "Toward that end we have brought some gifts, samples of what we can trade with...Our needs? We need food, both in the form of grain and in the form of meat animals. We eat cheese, too, but Bat-Erdene tells us you don't make that. Olives are probably not in your area but some kind of oil for cooking.... Fish; you may not have enough of to spare any. Leather. We could use horses, too, up to several hundred of them, and maybe some of your great cattle. Dogs or puppies, a few, if you have any to spare.

"Maybe most importantly, we need information. Where to find wood, for example...We've found a place to make a better camp than we have now; we'd like your permission to settle there.... Oh, and if any of your young men want to join up with the legion, a place could be found for them, with good pay, food, and adventure."

Bat-Erdene and Qadan, who had answered none of the requests, had a brief conversation. This, Bat-Erdene translated in sum as, "Qadan and the others need to discuss this. He says, 'In the interim, a small camp has been prepared for you next to this one. Go and rest. Women, drink, and food, also fuel, will be sent to you while we here talk. Your injured friend is already there. We will meet again tomorrow.' Come, I will lead you and the Palmyrenes to your encampment."

"Did we put anyone out to make all this?" Gisco asked, being the first to mount the ladder into the tented wagon.

Bat-Erdene shook his head. "No, we have plenty. Plenty wagons. Plenty cushions and blankets. Plenty food. Had sickness come through two year ago. Not super bad; kill maybe one in fifteen. So have extra wagons and plenty food.

"Some year hard; lose people and animals. Last winter pretty mild or we have lot more wagons though less food."

"I'd like to check on Titus," said Pullo. "He's here?"

"Yes, I take you."

"How will you know which wagon he's in?"

"Sick one always in wagon downwind so not stink up camp. Plus... well, you see women over there?"

"Sure," answered Pullo.

"Them little... ummm... priestesses. 'Little' right word, Gisco?"

"'Minor' would be better."

"Right. Minor priestesses. Make chants drive away fester demons while main priestess do serious work inside."

"Ohhh... hey, when we first captured you, you stank like a week-old dead sheep. But everyone here is pretty clean. How'd that happen?"

Bat-Erdene shrugged. "When out scouting or hunting, do best to smell like animal rather than people. When not, prefer be clean. There's water here, so everybody be clean as can. Come, we go see Titus."

Lucius Pullo followed Bat-Erdene to the easternmost of the seven wagons of the encampment. He nodded at the two women by the base of the ladder, but they paid no attention, keeping up their chanting. Bat-Erdene led the way up, then sat by a cushion a couple of feet away from the ladder, on the wagon's floor. He made a gesture for Lucius to do likewise. The senior priestess paid them no mind, beyond a quick glance, busy as she was with Vorenus' wounds. He lay on what appeared to be a clean set of furs, on his side, propped up by further furs that had been rolled into cylinders.

The cleaning was done by cloths that didn't seem remotely dirty, insofar as they lay in a ceramic bowl filled with something Pullo was pretty sure from the smell was some kind of vinegar, although... "That's made from honey, isn't it?"

"Yes," Bat-Erdene said, "make drink from honey, kind of like you wine, then ferment again to turn into vinegar. Use some from apple drink turned vinegar to start it."

"Bet the boys would like some of that," mused Pullo. "We drink watered-down vinegar more or less routinely.

"Can you ask her how he's doing?"

"Try," said Bat-Erdene, then proceeded to converse with the priestess.

"She say it pretty bad. But she clean wound, scrape away dead stuff, and give him something for pain and to help fight fester demons. All else fail, she use fly babies to eat away dead stuff."

"Fly babies? Fly babies? Maggots! That's disgusting!"

"Maybe so," Bat-Erdene agreed, "but work pretty good. They get cleaned first with same stuff in bowl."

The healing woman's eyes narrowed. She gestured for Bat-Erdene to show her the burns on his hands. Reluctantly, he did.

She said something that sounded very cross, which Bat-Erdene semi-translated as, "She call me big idiot. Now must let treat my hands, too."

When Pullo returned to his own wagon, the one he'd share with Bat-Erdene and Gisco, he found two women—short, somewhat sallow, and almond-eyed but really quite well built and pretty—tidying things up, in the case of one, and cooking over a sheep-shit fire, in the case of the other. There were other women outside each of the other wagons, likewise cooking.

"They take care of you," Bat-Erdene announced. "See to all needs."

"Ummm...please define 'all needs,' my young friend?" Gisco asked.

"What can say more than 'all'? You need food; they cook. You need clothes mend; they mend. You need water for washing or drinking; they get. You need fuck; they fuck. They expect fuck. Now me, have own girl here. She cut throat if fuck. But you? You can."

Gisco asked, with a sinking feeling, "What about the other women at the other wagons?"

"Them, too."

"I foresee problems," said Gisco. "There is only one woman per wagon, except for ours and Maeonius', but more than one man per wagon. Are they expected to provide for more than one man?"

"Not sure. Maybe. Maybe not in same day."

"Pullo, would you be so kind as to fetch Maeonius. He and I need to have a little chat."

"Sure thing."

"Yes, yes, I already know about the women," Maeonius said, when he'd walked across the little circle of wagons to the one shared by Gisco and Pullo. "And, yes, given how sex-starved my boys are going to be, I foresaw no end of knife fights over them. Already have a solution."

"And that would be...?" Gisco asked.

"My first thought was to have a sort of duty roster, matched to the guard roster. Would have worked like this: There's twenty-one of us left. After taking out myself, my exec, and my senior squad leader, there are eighteen in four wagons, but only four girls. That doesn't work out mathematically for shit, on the face of it. But with one of us in the headquarters wagon on guard duty, and six of them, that's still two or three in the tent at any given time. That's fine for the two but awkward for the three. So I explained to them, in my own gentle and genial manner, that it would be one man per girl per night, it would run on a separate roster than the one for guard, and if there was any fighting over it I'd simplify matters by castrating the fighters, personally, and would continue to do so until there were only four men left who even *could* perform with the girls."

"That would still leave you with a problem," said Pullo. "The three men in your wagon?"

"No problem, the senior decurion only likes boys."

"Oh, no," said Bat-Erdene, "no boys. We bury alive people here for that. Nonononono; no boys. Scythians do that. Call 'Anarya.' Mean 'unmanly.' Remember one, came to our camp, name...seem to recall was 'Athene.' Dress like woman. Act like woman on period, too. Bitchy-prissy-obnoxious-arrogant. Stupid, too. Want do things with boys. Scythians bury alive for us. Give better deal on barley for that."

"I shall let him know," said Maeonius. "Note that he's always been pretty restrained about it. Nobody in the *ala*. Nobody in the camp. Makes do with that kind of brothel when he can and just suffers in silence the rest of the time."

Pullo left just before sunset to have a look in on Vorenus. The women who had been chanting had left off their duties for the night and set themselves up to sleep farther forward in the medical wagon. The priestess busied herself with keeping fresh wet cloths on Vorenus' forehead, to keep the fever from killing him. The wounds were bandaged with fresh clean wool. They gave off a scent of corruption, still, but now mixed with the scents of honey and vinegar.

Pullo gave the woman a smile, then left for his own tented wagon, which now glowed faintly from the inside. When there, when he'd climbed up the ladder, he found the area illuminated by lamps not much different from what he was used to at home. From the smell, he thought they used butter for fuel. The Germans did that, too, as did some Gauls.

Glancing forward, he saw a covering fur rise and fall, rhythmically. *Aha, so Bat-Erdene wasn't lying.* He looked a little more carefully and found the other girl watching him, lying on her back with a rolled-up fur behind her for a pillow, propped up on her elbows and with the covering fur successfully failing to cover her breasts. *Not lying at all.*

My, that was nice, was Lucius Pullo's first thought, the next morning. He awakened alone, not because the girl had run off, but because she'd arisen early to prepare breakfast outside.

The girl? "Zaya," she'd indicated her name was, during the inevitable cross-cultural, post-coital language and culture session. Pullo had no idea what it meant.

Probably something mundane like water-bearer, *though to my ear it sounds a good deal more exotic than that. Let's hope we stay here for a while.*

"Up, Pullo," said Gisco, from outside the *ger—Oh, yes, that was another word she taught me.* "We need to go meet with the elders as soon as we've eaten."

"Right," the junior centurion agreed. "Just let me grab something and check on Titus and we can go."

At what he thought of as the medical wagon, Pullo found the priestess busily but gently scraping away at Vorenus' wounds. He sniffed a bit, and, though no expert, thought the wounds smelled less foul than the day before.

Hmmm...maybe this old bitch knows more than I thought.

Pullo looked at the scraper she was using, a narrow bronze handle ending in a silver spoon. He'd been wounded in action before, more than once, and so he'd seen something like that scraper used before. *A fairly standard thing, some places,* he thought. *Some places . . . some places. Pullo, you're an idiot; our places.*

He fairly threw himself into the tent, grabbing the priestess' wooden medical chest and pulling it toward him. She arose to stop him and then stopped herself once it was obvious that he just wanted to see, not to steal. She did slap his hand when he went to pick something up, but the words she uttered conveyed the meaning to Pullo of "Hands off, filthy beast."

Pullo turned his head, shouting for Bat-Erdene, who trotted up briskly. His hands were still bandaged and would be for some days.

"What is, friend Lucius?" Bat-Erdene asked.

"I need to look at these things and I may need to know where they came from."

A brief conversation between the young herder and the priestess ensued. She then passed over an open jug smelling strongly of vinegar and a little of honey. A clean cloth followed.

"She say you wash hands, can then touch."

Pullo did as ordered, paying particular attention to the crud under his fingernails. He held them up for the priestess' inspection. She nodded and gestured toward the chest. One by one Pullo took them out—knives and saws and scalpels, hooks and forceps and needles—and examined them. Some he knew the names for in Latin; others he did not.

That caused him to pick up something previously inspected and returned. *No, no nomenclature on the thing. Did these people make this box, its hinges, and the instruments in it? Color me skeptical. They do fine with wood and bone, horn, hair, and sheep shit, but bronze instruments? I've seen nothing to suggest it. Even their arrow- and spearheads are flint and maybe some other stone. No, no, this all came from elsewhere.*

Then he saw something he did know the use of, because it had been used on him. He picked up a bronze cupping vessel, then asked Bat-Erdene to ask the priestess what it was used for. As it turned out, she hadn't a clue and had never tried to use it for anything.

"Ask her where the set came from. And how it got here."

"'A trader,' she says, coming from the direction of the setting sun."

"Are there many more?"

"Only this one set in our tribe."

Which, yes, probably means it hasn't been traded so much that it could have made the journey here by some random motion. Mercury—I know where home is!

"Give the noble priestess my thanks," said Pullo, who bowed his head before departing the tent and crossing the short space at a run.

"Gisco! I know where *home* is!"

First came the reintroductions and the presentation of the gifts that had not been possible the afternoon before, due to lack of time. These were removed from the pack mule bearing them, one at a time, and personally given to Qadan by Gisco. The Phoenician, descendent of a very long line of clever traders, watched the chief's eyes to measure what he valued most.

The knives he'd kept, with some enthusiasm. The swords, rather less so, though perhaps he saw some value in them for butchery of livestock. The previous legate had been something of a collector of amber, and those dozen pieces Qadan accepted with great enthusiasm. Qadan had fingered the bolt of white silk, likewise procured from the legate's stores and said, "This come from direction of rising sun. Is valuable, must trade much animals and felt."

But the thing that really excited the old chief's attention was the bag of silver coins Gisco presented. *These people are money poor.*

"Noble Qadan," said Gisco, after the rounds of reintroductions, pleasantries, and gift-giving were finished, "my friends and I are, more than anything, desirous of going to our own home. We have examined your healing priestess's medical chest and determined that there is a fair chance it came from our home, or near it, and that our home is in the west, in the direction of the setting sun. But there are other explanations that also could be true. Do you have any other things that you traded for or were gifted that might help us figure out our locations?" *Of course, you telling us that the silk comes from the East already helped us there a good bit.*

Qadan rubbed his jaw, contemplatively, then called over an underling, into whose ear he whispered at considerably length. That man bowed and ran off toward an unusually large and ornate *ger* that Gisco took to be Qadan's own or, perhaps, just one of his own.

The chieftain than spoke some more to Bat-Erdene, who translated, "While servant collecting things, we discuss what said yesterday."

"Food? Food can help with, packloads barley, also sheep, goats, and cattle." He held up a silver denarius and said, "One such, give one sheep, two goat, ten packloads grain." Qadan's finger gestured toward Bat-Erdene. "This one explain cheese. We don't eat. No what you call 'olives'; nothing like around here. Have butter, one coin per three skins. Fish: we catch and eat, big ugly fish, also eggs of fish, from winter lodge camp, but that camp far behind. No fish.

"Have other grain, one called '*ruzh*'; one called '*arhaan*.' *Ruzh* not have much to grow on great circling but grow over winter near winter camp. *Arhaan* good crop for when not so cold. You want some? Same price as barley."

"May I see some?" asked Gisco.

"Sure, send over both grain and bread later," offered Qadan. "You like honey? Not have much to spare, maybe sixty skins. Three silvers a skin.

"Leather: have some but hard make. Can only make at winter camp, where trees for bark. Use up almost all on great circling. Use more felt and save leather. Mostly tan furs, but they are hard to get, except for sheep. But you buy enough sheep, no need any from us. Can trade felt, not leather. *Can* trade tree bark and skins so you make own."

"Is felt rainproof?" Pullo interjected. "If so, we can make the tents the legion still needs from that instead of leather."

"Felt three times same weight as silk," Qadan continued, "one silver piece. Also have something we call 'happy juice.' Come from East, though not as far as silk. Can have one skin for twenty-five silvers up to dozen skins."

"Hmmm..." Pullo whispered to Gisco. "He's going down the same list in the same order as you gave yesterday, only deviating to add something we might be interested in. He must have one hell of a memory. Also, if that 'happy juice' is *opos*, the hospital could surely use some."

"No writing here," Gisco whispered back. "I've asked. Only makes sense that a people who can't keep records any other way would develop excellent memories. And, I agree: there is no limit to how much we should buy."

Qadan harrumphed, then continued, "Can offer to number of five hundred horse. Five silver piece each. Two hundred big cattle, already docked, nine silver apiece. Also have new litter puppies. Those, no charge, gift to you. But must wait fifty days and nights until weaned. If want trade for mother to leave earlier, is possible, but she fine old girl and cost ten silver piece. Same for her mate. Probably want both; then make more puppies.

"You want find wood. Is pretty good forest near great river, sometimes called 'Raha,' south of where our winter camp is. Is maybe six days' direction of rising sun from where Bat-Erdene say your camp sit. Nearest one. Too far for us; we never use. Can settle in that direction, too, if like. Scythians maybe object. Never really know with them; leave us alone but everybody else just sheep to thems wolves."

At that time two men, one of them the original underling, came back carrying a thick rug. This they rolled out, showing multiple goods. Qadan invited the Romans to examine the pieces and see what might help.

Gisco picked up a bronze pot, about a foot high and heavily inscribed. "Parthian," he said. "Since they mostly write in Greek, I never learned to read it, but I can recognize it."

"Come from South," Qadan said, after an inquiry from Bat-Erdene. "Trader, long beard, too much flower stink.

"As for young men join you, we no do war. But you can hire for scouts and guides if like. Pay two piece silver per moon, plus one to tribe. Per moon. For, say, six moons in advance."

Gisco considered the weight of everything he intended to buy for the legion. "Can you lease us extra animals and maybe some wagons to carry what the animals we buy cannot? We'll need them for perhaps half a moon, then can send them back."

"Yes," said Qadan. "We work out prices later, when you know for sure what you need."

Are any of the girls for sale? Pullo wondered but was ashamed to ask.

"I've got sixty thousand denarii," Gisco said to Pullo. "I can figure some of it myself, but military requirements—not ordering them, I can do that; but estimating them—are beyond me."

"Well," said Pullo, "there are about...mmmm...call it something under seven thousand men in camp, seven thousand plus if we include the state slaves. The couple of hundred young Argippaeans Bat-Erdene says want to sign on for pay for six months; call it seven thousand, five hundred to be on the safe side. That's twenty-two thousand pounds a day for grain. No, wait, men lose weight on barley. Better call it about twenty-four thousand pounds per day. They've got to have oil, but I guess butter will have to do. Maybe twelve or thirteen hundred pounds per day. Meat? Looking at their sheep we might get forty pounds out of one of their lambs. That's enough for one hundred and sixty men for one day. But the cavalry can hunt for about as much, so call it one sheep per one hundred and sixty men per two days. Twenty-five or, at the most, thirty for the entire legion, per day."

Gisco did some figuring in his head. *Let's say we have to march for four months. It's as good a guess as any. That means six thousand sheep or six thousand denarii. So for grain...a packload, based on what I've seen, is about one hundred, hundred and ten, pounds. So two hundred and forty packloads a day, times one hundred and twenty days, about twenty-eight or twenty-nine hundred denarii. Call it three thousand. Honey? Why not take what they're offering? Another one hundred and eighty. Butter, yes, we'll take it all, even if the men don't like it. A skin, based on what the old man showed me, is about eight or nine pounds. So for one day we'll need about a hundred and fifty skins. For four months we'll need eighteen thousand skins or nine thousand denarii. Eighteen hundred for the big cattle, twenty-five hundred for horses.*

"We can do this," he announced. "Couldn't in Gaul and not even in Germany, but these people covet silver a good deal more and probably have very little of it."

Overcoming his shyness on the matter, Pullo asked, "Think we could buy some of the girls?"

"I don't know. We can ask Bat-Erdene about the prospects. Still, consider, Pullo, the jealousy of men without women toward one who has one."

"Good point. Well, if I can't buy, I'd like to get a salary advance to set up my girl, Zaya, in case she comes up pregnant."

"Relax, Pullo, it will still be several weeks before Vorenus is healed, at best. And these girls use something—it might be related to *silphium*—to keep from getting pregnant."

INTERLUDE

***Exploratory Spacecraft 67(&%#@, Several Hundred Znargs
Above the Teutoburg Forest***

"Can you find any pattern to what is pulling the poor creature
hither and yon?" asked Blossom of her mate, in clicks, whistles,
and sung notes.

"Not yet," answered Red, frantically turning dials, pushing
buttons, and hammering keys, "but he seems to be heading to
the large city on that peninsula with the points at the end. He
is still getting farther and farther in time from his own people."

556 A.D. Rome

Appius Calvus found himself looking out at what remained of
the city of his youth through the eyes of some kind of beggar.
At least he must be a beggar, he's so poor and dirty.

The beggar, if that was what he was, seemed to think in a
kind of decayed Latin. Decayed or not, Calvus could generally
follow along. He chose, this time, not to reveal himself to his
host.

It was daytime and yet almost no one was to be seen. He
spotted the Mausoleum of Augustus, which had been completed
when Calvus was a boy. It was overgrown with weeds and had
an air of decay about it different from that of a cemetery.

In front of the Mausoleum there had been two bronze pillars, but Calvus could see that only one was standing. He stopped to read, puzzling out the abbreviations:

Below is a copy of the acts of the Deified Augustus by which he placed the whole world under the sovereignty of the Roman people, and of the amounts which he expended upon the state and the Roman people, as engraved upon two bronze columns which have been set up in Rome.

At the age of nineteen, on my own initiative and at my own expense, I raised an army by means of which I restored liberty to the republic, which had been oppressed by the tyranny of a faction. For which service the senate, with complimentary resolutions, enrolled me in its order, in the consulship of Gaius Pansa and Aulus Hirtius, giving me at the same time consular precedence in voting; it also gave me the imperium. . . .

That was all the time the beggar gave Calvus to read.

There was a morning sun on the left side of Calvus' host. This let him know they were moving south. They passed a temple on the right, dedicated to some god Calvus had never heard of, an Aurelius.

His host took a left, leading them toward an area Calvus knew well, the Campus Agrippae, though he didn't remember it being so weed grown and tawdry.

He began to see people then, though no one greeted his beggar. Neither did the beggar greet them. Though they never formed what could have been called a crowd, the numbers grew greater as they continued on to the area of the Forum.

At the Forum there were many sights Calvus did not recognize. One he did recognize was the *Curia Julia*, the Senate House, the very seat of the Roman Empire. It was subtly different in appearance but recognizably the same building.

What was very different was the smell; someone was using the Senate House to house cattle.

CHAPTER SIX

As long as the earth endures, seedtime and harvest,
cold and heat, summer and winter, day and night will
never cease.

—Book of Genesis, 8:22

***Legio XIIX, in camp in the land of the Argippaeans, date
unknown***

From all around the *Praetorium* came the sounds of the camp,
shouted orders, the clash of weapons and armor, the ring of the
blacksmith's hammer, and the steady tramp of marching feet as
details of soldiers marched to this work detail or that.

"You know something, sir?" asked Marcus Caelius, from
a chair in the camp's main tent. The legate sat opposite him.
Between them, on a low table, sat two cups, a water jug, and a
jug of the dwindling store of wine.

"Any number of things, Top," answered Gaius Pompeius. "And
I suspect even more. But I don't know nearly enough. You must
admit, though, that I am learning."

"Clearly," the first spear agreed, "though you need some experience in an actual battle...one that we win rather than being
allowed or made to escape from. You need some lines on your
face and maybe some gray hair. Never fear, command will give
you both before your time.

"That, however, is not what I'm talking about. Think about
this: what season was it when we were plucked out of *Germania*?"

"Late summer, heading into what I gather was going to be a typically miserable Germanic fall."

"Exactly, sir. And what happens when we turn from summer to fall?"

"Rains...temperature drops...leaves turn. Snow soon follows."

"Yes, sir, and what has been happening to the temperature here since we arrived? Has it been dropping?"

"Hmmm...now that you mention it, Top, no; no, it hasn't. Quite the opposite." The legate's eyes widened at the implication. "And that means that whatever god or gods saved us, they not only moved us in space but in time. Holy crap!"

Gaius' face clouded with thought, briefly. "Oh, wait...that doesn't get us as far as we might have thought. Herodotus mentions a Phoenician exploration that circumnavigated Africa, and discovered the sun was reversed down there. If the sun, then, so the seasons. We could, in other words, have been sent far to the south."

Marcus Caelius rubbed the lower half of his face, contemplating that. "I suppose that's possible. Okay, but it doesn't matter for now. What does matter is that we're in the beginning of spring, and we'd better plant some barley and some wheat, a *lot* of barley because we have more of it, and quickly, if we're not going to starve here.

"And, yes, sir, even though most of them enlisted to escape from farming, the boys generally know their way around a plow and a team of oxen."

"When you're right, Top, you're right. Though I think step one has to be making plows and plowshares, as well as training some of our oxen to the plow. Also, I need to figure out how much we can even afford to plant. I know from studies that spring barley takes about two months to grow and that it doesn't do well in winter. For winter we need to nose around for some rye."

"Pretty good for a city boy, sir, yes. I'll get to work on it. Also, with barley, we can usually get in two crops before the temperature turns.

"By the way, sir, I think you're ready for a lone walking inspection of the camp. I suggest starting with the *valetudinarium*. Check the ill and injured, enquire as to their health, improving or worsening. Then drag the *medicus*, Samuel Josephus, for a tour of the latrines, then stop by the animal pens and check on them with their *veterinarius*. Finally, take a walk along the walls where you will look at the solidity of the palisade, shaking it where it looks iffy."

Smiling wryly, Gaius Pompeius said, "Your suggestion is my command, Top."

"Stout lad, sir. Now, while you're at it, give a lot of thought as to whether we want to move to the better campsite. I think we do but I, of course, am not a highfalutin gentleman officer, so what do I know?"

"Right. So brief me in about three hours on why you think we should."

"Yes, sir." *Good lad, learning to make use of the tools of his trade, which is to say his subordinates, and doing so at fair speed.*

At the *valetudinarium*, Gaius Pompeius wasn't really sure how to act. So he simply told Josephus, "Show me."

Josephus, for his part, clapped for a slave—the medical establishment was a place where there was a calling for state slaves—to follow along with a camp stool.

"We've sent back to duty everyone who was already in bad shape when we came from Germany," Josephus explained. "These are all fairly new."

"How many cases?" asked the legate. "And what kind?"

"Fifty-seven," the *medicus* replied, "a fairly light load. As to what kind..." Josephus shouted for the wax tablet, the *cera*, of the morning report.

"I've got eleven cases of the squirts," Josephus said. "They're in their own tent under mild quarantine in case it's worse than eating out of a dirty bowl, which is the most likely explanation. I honestly think that's all it was but better safe than sorry. I've got three fractured limbs, two of which are healing nicely, but one of which seems to have become infected. We are treating that, of course, but I may have to amputate the leg."

"Do you have enough *opos* in case you do have to amputate?" Gaius asked.

"To dull the pain while I saw away, yes. To keep him sedated while he's recovering, technically yes, but I think I have to save that for the inevitable even worse cases.

"Then there's one centurion suffering from an old case of malaria. Not a lot to be done there; he has to come in periodically and has, so far, always managed to get through it. We help a little by dosing him with *silphium* and keeping him covered in wet cloth, when the fever's at its worst, and changing the cloths, or drying him and covering him with blankets when he gets the shivers, but that's the limit of our abilities. Well, that and restraining him when he gets delirious.

"The remaining forty-two are fairly minor: cuts and scrapes, the occasional superficial sword wound from training. Most of those will be discharged by tomorrow with a prescription for light duty for a few days or a week."

After a short reflection, Gaius Pompeius said, "Bring me to the one who might need his leg amputated."

When they arrived in the ward for the unfortunate, Josephus introduced them by saying, "This is Mucius Tursidius, Legate. Mucius, this is the commanding officer."

Tursidius looked to be about nineteen years old. And very, very ill, his face pale and covered with sweat, even though he was now shivering.

"What happened to you, Tursidius?" asked Gaius, taking a seat next to the hurt soldier's cot, on the stool placed by the medical slave. He couldn't help but notice the smell of putrefaction.

"Sheer bad luck, sir," said the legionary, still obviously full of pluck. He also smelt of unwatered wine, which likely helped. "We were loading logs onto a wagon when the horses bucked and a pile of the logs rolled onto me. Broke my leg in a few spots, and some bone came sticking through the skin. Hurt like...well...I don't know what it hurt like. Still does, but duller now. It's gettin' worse now; I can tell. Stinks more."

Suddenly, pluck disappeared and Tursidius grabbed Gaius Pompeius' arm with the desperation of a drowning man. "Sir? Sir?" he begged. "They think I can't hear but I can. I know the surgeon is thinking about cutting my leg off. Don't let them, sir, I beg you. If I could get up I'd beg you on a bended knee. Don't let them. Do anything—drown me in one of the latrines; *anything*, but don't let them cut my leg off."

Tursidius let go the legate's arm, let his head fall back, and began to sob, "Don't take my leg...don't take my leg..."

Later, on their way to check out the latrines, Gaius Pompeius asked, "What do you think, *medicus*—is there anything you can do for the boy?" The legate laughed at himself, "I say 'boy,' but I'm not much older."

Josephus shook his head. "We're doing everything we know to do, keeping it clean, disinfecting with vinegar. There's an old method I learned that came from somewhere in the original land of Abraham about washing with hot water, and I'm trying that, too. We drain the wound and apply poultices." Josephus clenched fists, looked skyward, and just barely suppressed a scream of frustration. He let his chin sink onto his chest and said, "Nothing works; it just keeps getting worse.

"Not even my God is listening."

Gaius Pompeius placed a gripping hand on the Jew's shoulder. "Look, Samuel, you can only do what you can do. Nobody, not even your god, expects more." *Which,* thought Gaius, *is not, come to think of it, especially bad advice to give myself.*

Later, at the latrines, Gaius noted the dearth of flies. "Some, of course, only to be expected, but fewer than I expected. Less stink, too."

"Well," said Josephus, "as far as the stench goes, we make lye with the ash from the wood fires. Doesn't fix it all but helps a little. Mind, there just isn't that much wood for burning so we're making it slowly, via evaporation. As for the few flies, if you dug down about a foot you would find a mass of maggots, feasting on shit. But they will never get out to be an annoyance.

"In this temperature, about weekly, we cover them with a foot or so of dirt. That buries them before they can hatch into flies.

"This isn't a bit of arcane *materia medica,* by the way. This is all centurion knowledge, gained and passed on over centuries of campaigning. For the Jews, we have religious instruction for the disposal of human waste, but it's entirely for individuals and completely impossible with the kinds of camps you Romans generally put up. This may explain why you are ruling us rather than us ruling you, despite our having the one and only true God on our side."

Josephus continued, "We Jews might not like the Empire, and most of us don't, but we've got to admit we owe you Romans a lot for the clean, flowing water, the sewer systems, roads for commerce, even if you didn't intend them for that. Plus, of course, irrigation, which is only possible because of the aqueduct. Oh, and public order and public baths."

"Don't forget the wine," Gaius added. "And peace."

✧   ✧   ✧

Gaius decided to hit the veterinary before the walls. He'd never really thought about how many animals there were accompanying the legion and its attachments. He was shocked to discover literally thousands of them, for the most part, barring the food animals, penned in and munching grass that had been cut outside and brought to them.

These ranged from the legion's own cavalry horses to those of the Gallic *auxilia*, the Palmyrene horse archers, and the legate's own string, now the inherited property of one Gaius Pompeius. At that, they were short horses because of the fall when they'd first arrived here.

Beyond that was the mule and donkey train, numbering over a thousand, plus oxen for the wagons and carts.

Beyond those, outside the wall and under guard by foot, horse, and canine, were the sheep and some goats for food. Gaius wasn't sure how many of those there were, only that Marcus Caelius never stopped worrying about the inadequate numbers of them.

From behind a row of tents came a steady sound of hammering iron. Above the tents thin smoke billowed upward.

A wagon passed through the lines of the animal area. Details of state slaves carefully and thoroughly shoveled crap by the wagonload, slinging it onto the wagon for transport to the latrines. They didn't seem especially upset with their lot, which made Gaius wonder a bit about their treatment. It was probably better than most would have to endure, across the Empire. He wondered, once again, as Marcus Caelius had subtly suggested, if they should be manumitted and enlisted as legionaries. It was not, after all, unheard of. Rome had purchased and then enlisted four full legions of slaves after the disaster at Cannae, a couple of hundred years prior, promising them freedom and citizenship upon discharge.

Maybe I should, mused Gaius Pompeius, *but I don't know if I should, nor how the legionaries will take it to have to share a tent with slaves. Maybe if I make an offer to a few select ones and see how the troops react to that . . . maybe. Maybe some could come to staff, releasing Romans to fight.*

Gaius asked one of the slaves, the one who seemed to be in charge, from the manure detail, "Where can I find the chief *veterinarius*?"

The slave took one look at the tunic's broad purple stripe,

another at the ornate belt, and said, "Just wait one little second, sir, I'll fetch him for you. The legate, ain't you, sir? Yes, sir, right away, sir."

The hammering suddenly ceased. Moments later, the *veterinarius*, a grizzled old soldier, perhaps a centurion who had shown talent and interest, came out from behind the row of tents, rubbing dirty hands on his leather apron.

"I was just making some *soleae ferreae* for the horses, sir. Decimus Vitelius at your service, sir. How can I help you?"

"Just show me around...ummm...Centurion?"

"Yes, sir, centurion of the fabricators, doing double duty at the veterinary, since we lost our regular one back in Germany. I dabble a bit in blacksmithing, too, since my dad was a blacksmith.

"So, this way, sir."

"Before we walk through, tell me, Centurion," Gaius asked. "If you were inspecting, say, the veterinary service and animal train for, say, the Seventeenth Legion, what would you be looking for?"

Vitelius repressed a smile. "Well, sir, if it were the Seventeenth Legion, I'd be looking for a way out of Hades. But let's say some other legion? The Eighteenth, say?"

"Yes, some other legion," agreed Gaius, figuratively kicking himself over his poor choice.

"All right, sir. Well, first thing, I'd look for a heavy saturation of flies. That would mean nobody was policing up the manure, which is bad for us all, man and beast both. As you can see, sir..."

"Yes, I see the detail at work and I see very damned few flies. All right, what next?"

"Next, sir, I'd demand to see the number of animals, sick and injured, and the types of sickness or injury. That can tell you a lot, sir, not just about the animals but also about the discipline of the legion. Lots of the men don't know, for example, how to take care of their donkeys and mules—not feeding them the right grasses, not currycombing their hides, then overloading them until their hooves split and their backs give out. Even if it doesn't get that bad, saddle sores are a distinct problem. Why? Because if you let them, the men will put their personal equipment on the donkeys. Those sores can get infected, too. And since every donkey and mule is assigned to a specific *contubernium* by number, you can find out which centurions need their butts chewed, so they can go chew out some legionaries.

"Now, let me save you a spot of trouble, sir.... Felix!"

"Yes, master," answered the slave on crap detail.

"Fetch us the tablets for the animals."

"Yes, master. Immediately, master."

While the slave was running, Gaius asked, "*Felix?*"

"Sure, sir, just go ask him if he's happy. He was on his way to a lead mine when the legion bought him. I assure you, sir, he is very happy not to be in a lead mine."

"Yes, one imagines. And imagine that, being sentenced to a short life at hard labor, underground, for a crime you never committed."

"We didn't make the world, sir."

"No, I suppose..."

"Here are the tablets, master," said a breathless Felix, "all thirty-seven of them." He departed immediately back to his manure detail.

"He can count?" asked Gaius Pompeius, tactfully waiting until the slave was out of earshot.

"Yes, sir," replied Decimus. "Reads, too. Won't say how he learned and I'm not curious enough to beat him over it. I suspect he was a house slave who annoyed the master...or mistress. That would also tend to explain the lead-mine gambit."

"I see. All right, explain to me what these tablets mean."

"Right, sir," Decimus' finger ran along the top of the first one. "These are the animals by cohort. They show the number for full strength, by type. So, for a regular cohort of infantry, you can see that full strength is seventy donkeys. That's one per *contubernium*, plus one per junior centurion, another two per senior centurion, and another three for the centurion of the cohort. Plus there are five spares kept by us that can be loaned out if one of the donkeys comes up lame or ill through no fault of the *contubernium*."

Gaius had to ask, even though he was pretty sure he knew the answer, "And if it *is* the fault of the *contubernium*?"

Decimus smiled wickedly, "Then they can carry all their shit—tents, cookpots, and everything else—on their backs. Or, if that's impossible because of the difficulty of the march, they turn in their tent, which is carried on a spare, and they do without a tent."

"I see," said the legate. "What if the cohorts are understrength?"

"Makes no real difference, sir, since the equipment is still going to be on the legion's rolls and has to be moved with the legion. Now, we *do* require more state slaves to guide and care for the spare animals, but we don't have to pay *them*.

"So, sir, you can go over each cohort's tablet pretty much the same way. Number understrength tells you what has to be requisitioned from depot or locally purchased. Whether the cost of that is taken from legion funds or from the pay of the troops depends on whether you find that the loss of the animal is the legionaries' fault. It isn't, always; the enemy will have his say, of course."

Decimus shuffled the wax tablets, settling on the injury and sickness report. "Now, here, sir, you can see the numbers of ill and injured animals. It used to be a lot higher, just after we came here, but most of the difference died or was slaughtered for food and leather. Wouldn't have been so bad but we'd already loaded them up for a march. That extra weight broke a lot of legs. And we haven't been marching since getting here, so none of them have come up with saddle sores or hoof issues."

Marching? Marching? thought Gaius. *We don't have enough animals to move the entire legion in one group to the new camp. Let's hope the first spear has a solution to this, when he briefs me—which is to say, tells me what I really ought to do.*

"Sir? Sir?"

"Oh, sorry, Centurion, I was musing on just how in Hades we move from here."

"It *will* be a toughie, sir, I agree. Now, if the sir will follow along, these last tablets are individual animals under care, their problems, and the treatment."

Gaius read the first of these, then the second. One thing caught his eye. "Centurion, I see *vermes*. Do some of our animals have an infection of maggots?"

"Ummmm . . . no, sir, not exactly. Best you see, for yourself, sir. This way, if you will, Legate."

Decimus led Gaius Pompeius down the lines of animals to a gap, then through the gap to a separate corral. There, several dray animals stood separate from the others, with bandages covering them in places. One slave was feeding them one at a time, some from freshly cut grass and others from a barley mush. On the ground, by one of the stakes, were two bronze urns with close-fitting tops on them, one large and one fairly small.

Leading Gaius into the corral, Decimus gently lifted one of

the bandages off a dray ox. Gaius took one look and almost gagged for there, in an open and deep wound, were a fair mass of maggots squirming amidst blood and pus.

"That's disgusting!" the legate exclaimed. "Get those vile things cleaned them out of the poor beast at *once*."

"Hold on, sir," said the *veterinarius*, wagging a scolding finger. "This is a trick the previous veterinary taught me when I was filling in, doing some blacksmithing. Those maggots are doing nothing but good, no harm at all. They're eating all the dead and diseased flesh and leaving only healthy flesh behind. May be leaving something else behind, too, that fights infection. Don't know for sure, but I suspect so. Animals with open wounds that get treated this way are much more likely to heal and get fully well than from any other treatment we have."

"But ... gods, flies lay their eggs in filth, rotten flesh, and shit. How can those maggots be clean enough to let into an open wound?"

"We don't 'let' them; we place them. Works like this: You need, in the first place, either the blue or the green bottle fly, in some numbers; never hard to find a few around a stable. Blue's a little better. You can usually scrounge up one or the other, but we keep our own supply. Anyway, you keep a sealed jar with a goodly helping of rotten meat with maybe some shit mixed in. That's jar one, the big one, and in it you keep the flies. Matter of fact jar one is that big bronze thing over there. The flies lay their eggs in the meat and shit and, in no very long time, maggots appear. Then, and this part is tricky, you cover the top of the jar with a cloth mesh with one hole in it to keep the flies in—don't want the nasty little bastards getting loose in camp, after all—and use forceps through a narrow hole in the mesh to grab the maggots, take them out through the hole, and drop them into a jar about a quarter to the third full of wine and vinegar, mixed. Then you cover that jar again, give it several dozen vigorous shakes, and extract the maggots, again, one at a time. You put those maggots on the wound, cover it up, and let them get to work.

"Finally, when they've done their work—and you can tell they've done it because the wound doesn't stink anymore—you pick the maggots out and put them back in the big jar to metamorphize, mate, lay some eggs, and ultimately die."

Decimus gave a wry smile. "Is it, as you say, disgusting? Sure.

But is it as disgusting as a poor animal dying slowly, by inches, over weeks? I'd say not, not nearly."

After seeing the maggot circus, Gaius Pompeius felt a desperate need for fresh air. To that end, he walked to and mounted the *agger* on the northern side, where the westerly winds didn't blow the stink from the latrines; limited lye could only do so much. From there, he began to walk to the northwest corner, where the latrines' stench couldn't reach him at all. As he did, he stopped every few steps to grab and shake the *sudes* to confirm they were well-placed and still solid. The *sudes* were also bound together, so he tugged at those ropes to make sure they were tight and not fraying or rotting. Looking through and over the palisade, he saw over a thousand of the legionary food animals grazing contentedly.

Looking up, Gaius saw a cloud to the northwest, huge, dark, and thick. Briefly, he considered racing for his tent for his *sagum*, then decided that, in the second place, he was unlikely to melt while, in the first place, the first spear would think he was acting like a girl.

And then he noticed two things. One was that the drivers and guards of the food animals had begun to frantically urge their charges back to the safety of the camp. The other was that, *Wind from the west...cloud to the northwest getting closer...clouds don't go against the wind...Fuck.*

"To arms! To arms!"

Word passed quickly, accelerated by the brass musical instruments. In what seemed like mere moments, the *agger* was thick with men, fully armed but some still tugging on armor, their *scuta* resting on the *sudes* and effectively making the defensive wall almost as high as a man's head and much stronger than the palisade alone.

Meanwhile, teams of legionaries were closing the gates with wagons, one side of each of which likewise had a wooden wall, facing to the outside. Men, armored or armoring up, clambered into the beds of the wagons and faced out.

And still the menacing cloud—dust, Gaius now saw—grew closer.

From somewhere off to his right, Gaius heard the steadying, stentorious voice of Marcus Caelius. "Stand firm...don't loose your *pila* without the command...fight until your arm starts to get tired, then tell the man behind you to relieve you for a bit...stand firm..."

With about five heartbeats' worth of reflection, Gaius Pompeius decided that's what he should be doing, too. So, trying his best to copy the tone of the first spear's command voice, he walked counterclockwise, speaking with a calm he hadn't really known he could possess. "We're the Eighteenth Legion and nobody can beat us...we're the favored of all the gods, who saved us from a bad spot in Germany...stand firm...fear nothing...We're the bloody Eighteenth...the gods stand with us..."

He was pleased to hear, after he'd passed, some of the centurions taking up the same themes he had been addressing, often with a good deal of cursing interwoven.

And then came the real shocker: three men, flanked by a score or so of Palmyrene horse archers, rode out of the cloud. Then one of the legionaries, with better eyesight than most, apparently, exclaimed, "Bloody hell, it's the legate's secretary, Gisco, and the two new centurions we sent out!"

Gaius Pompeius, having only normal eyesight, had to wait several minutes to ensure that this was true. By that time, the cloud, unreinforced by further dust, had blown to his right, revealing what looked to be a couple of hundred horsemen and an ungodly number of animals, some of them cattle so big, compared to the horses, as to beggar belief.

"Well, I'll be damned," said Marcus Caelius, still loud enough to hear across half a camp. "It's our long-lost centurions, Pullo and Vorenus, along with Gisco. And they've come bearing gifts." Caelius paused, probably to draw in enough air to burst eardrums, then belted out, "Cheer, boys, cheer! No short rations for us for a while!"

Gaius Pompeius, Marcus Caelius, Gisco, Vorenus and Pullo, and Bat-Erdene sat on stools around the collapsible banquet table in the legate's tent. Servants poured wine mixed with water into silver cups.

"Yes, sir," said Gisco, "I spent nearly all of the sixty thousand denarii you sent me out with." He passed over three wax tablets. "Here's the accounting."

Gaius looked down the tablets at the lists of what had been bought for what price and whistled. He turned the tablets over to the first spear, who did likewise. "Just wait until the chief *medicus* sees how much *opos* you've brought back...Josephus...Josephus? Now what was it? And Vitelius! Damn me for an idiot!"

Gaius turned to one of the messengers who stood by the *Praetorium,* and said, "Run and get me the chief surgeon, Samuel Josephus."

"You've solved just about every logistic problem we had," Marcus Caelius congratulated the Phoenician, "at least for a while. How the hell did you manage all this with only sixty thousand denarii?"

"I'd like to be able to say that it's because my ancestors were the greatest traders in human history, but the fact is that Bat-Erdene's people, the Argippaeans, are animal and grain rich and silver poor. If we got a good deal, by our lights, I'm not sure that they aren't laughing their butts off over cheating the yokel Romans."

A quick glance at Bat-Erdene showed him nodding enthusiastically. "They figure you dumber than dirt, give up so much silver for just so few animals."

"So few?" Marcus Caelius said. "There are thousands of them, and the kind we need, too."

"Yep," said Bat-Erdene, continuing to nod vigorously, "so few. You just yokels. Rubes. Not just Romans, *gullible* Romans. From now on my people have new word: say 'roman' when mean 'gullible.'"

"And that," Gisco said, "is the essence of fair trading: everyone involved being certain he cheated the others."

"Sir," said the first spear, "everything I was going to brief you on concerning a move to the new camp? All obsolete now. I was going to tell you we'd need to move in two separate parties, with all the insecurity that means with regards to building a new camp. No more; we can march in one group, with only an advanced party—I'll command that—and flankers out, and build our camp the proper way."

"Well," said Pullo, "as to marching to a new camp, we've got some news that might change that some. We know where we are, and it's not as far as we might have thought."

"Explain that one," said the first spear.

Gisco let them in on the information they'd gained from the Argippaeans. "The short version is that we are east of the Empire, west of the Land of Silk, and north of the Scythians, who are north of some related tribes who are north of the Parthians. My best guess is that we're somewhere between fifteen hundred and two thousand miles east of home. Could be a little more; Persia is a big place."

"On the plus side at least we're not at the bottom of Africa," said the first spear.

"No shit," replied the legate.

"So do the calculations, Top," said Gaius. "With the food we had, the food these men brought us, can we make it to home in ... what, five months?"

"Not a chance, sir," Marcus Caelius said. "No roads. No telling what obstacles we'll face. Five months of food might get us halfway there, but then we'd be gods know where, no food, and no certainty of finding any. No, we're going to have to march the distance we can and still leave a growing season for the barley. Maybe march about eight hundred miles, in two or, more likely, three months. Plant barley. Let it grow for two months. Harvest it and move on. Except winter's going to hit us ... Wait a minute, sir; remember what I was saying about this being spring?"

"Sure." The legate nodded. "And you're right, the gods not only moved us in space but in time. Scary thought, that they can do this."

"Very," Caelius agreed. "We're going to have to do it like this, sir. Plant now; plant a lot, at the new camp. Harvest in two months. Harvest again two months after that. Then spend a winter in the new camp. I'd say plant rye over the winter, but we don't have any."

"We've brought back a good deal of rye, First Spear," said Gisco.

"No joke? Well, excellent, then. So it's two growing seasons of barley and some wheat, then one winter growing season for rye. And only *then* do we start the march home.

"Then march for two months, stop, plant again, and harvest another crop. And again. Then we build a more permanent camp for the winter, eat up one of those two harvests, and march another two months. You get the idea."

"And," added Vorenus, still a bit pale from his injuries, "at the end of it we're going to have to fight our way through *Germania*, to get home."

"Maybe not," said Pullo. "I know I'd rather not. Might be able to find enough wood near that sea north of the Germans to go to Gaul, by water, then south."

"We can consider making the last legs by sea, when we get to the area and see the feasibility," said the legate. "In the interim, let it be as you say, Top. But I think we ought still to move to the new campsite. It's got wood and water, both of which are in pretty short supply here."

"Yes, sir; no argument. When we're done here I'll start preparing the move."

Gaius turned to Bat-Erdene and said, "And, so, young man, I understand you are now in charge of some of your people who have signed on with us as scouts."

"Two hundred and forty-three," said Gisco, "each with his own horse and two spares. But, sir, there is an issue."

"What's that?"

"They can't fight; it's a prohibition among them amounting to the religious."

"Long story," said Bat-Erdene, in a tone that said he was not interested in telling that long story. "Can scout for you. Hunt animals. Watch over and guard new and old flocks. Cannot make war. Just cannot."

Gaius saw that the first spear was about to explode at both the apparent cowardice and the sheer affrontery of men being unwilling to fight. He showed a restraining palm and said, "Top, at two denarii a month we're not really paying them enough to fight, either."

"I suppose that's fair," agreed Marcus Caelius, grudgingly. "Are you at least willing to help build our camps when we stop for the night."

"Even eager help and learn build," said Bat-Erdene.

"Well...that's *something*, then. Now what about the remaining four 'guests' from your people, Bat-Erdene?"

"I ask later if want join. Think they want go to tribe, see families, first."

"One other thing, Legate," said Gisco. "Life is hard on the plains and harder on men than women. The Argippaeans have a surplus of girls. They do what other peoples do when there are too many women and not enough men. Some become second wives or priestesses or nuns. Others become meretrices. We've brought along six wagonloads of the latter, seventy-two redundant girls. Most of them—maybe all, taste depending—rather pretty and reasonably well built."

"Hmmm," mused the first spear, "that's enough for each man to get a piece of ass about three times a month, without wearing out the girls. But what the hell should they be paid? A denarius?

That would pay a *lupa* back home for a full day's work, ten or fifteen clients, and out of which she'd have to give some to her pimp or owner, some for food, and some for shelter. She'd be lucky to save an *as* a day."

Gaius Pompeius, who, like most free young men of the city, had made some use of prostitutes from the age of fifteen on, was not unsympathetic. "All right, put them on the strength as far as rations go; they'll have deducted from their pay one half of what the men pay, and will be issued rations accordingly. They've already got their own shelter, apparently, so we can deduct that from their normal price."

"There are not all that many *asses* in the legion's chests," said Gisco. "Surely not enough to keep this commerce going."

"You have any suggestions?"

"As mentioned," said Gisco, "these people are cattle rich and silver poor. Bat-Erdene?"

"Yes, friend Gisco."

"Your women who turn to this kind of work, what's their aim?"

"Make enough money and other goods attract decent mate."

"And this doesn't bother those mates?"

"No. Usually end up as *second* or even third wife, but no."

I can't believe I'm doing this, thought Gaius Pompeius, *setting a whore's rightful wages. But we've got to be careful that, in the first place, we don't insult the scouts Gisco's brought us, and, in the second, that the men aren't fleeced of all their pay.*

"Bat-Erdene," the legate asked, "how much money, how many silver coins, would it take for the girls to attract good mates?"

The Argippaean flashed all the fingers of both hands twice, and then on his right hand once.

"So they need to earn twenty-five denarii over six months, if you and they are going to be with us for six months. Okay, fine. If every girl—my father would not believe what I am using my mathematics for—services ten legionaries and auxiliaries per day, for six months, then each servicing must be worth about one seventh of an *as*. Call it a fifth so they have money for food."

"Wait," said Bat-Erdene, "we have pay for food from pay."

"No," said Marcus Caelius. "Auxiliaries, although paid less, are also issued their rations for free. But legionaries and camp followers must pay out of pocket, unless we get lucky and can loot some. Looted food is free."

"Whew, that good thing."

"Anyway, the coinage just won't support that at all," said Gisco. "There is no such coin."

"Right," agreed the legate, "so maybe we do it on paper. Or wax tablets. With chits. The men buy fifty chits with one denarius withheld from their pay. They buy the services of a girl with one chit. The girl brings her chits, once she has fifty of them, and is given a credit of one denarius in the legionary bank. When we're about home and their tour is up, they get paid in silver and can leave with all of our blessings."

"I think," said Marcus Caelius, "that we'd better start figuring out how to make *spintriae* for the legionaries to show the girls what they want."

"No need, Top," said Pullo. "Just put up signs showing all the variations that the men can point to."

Pullo was thinking longingly of seeing Zaya once more. She suited him.

"Easier than making detailed tokens, sure. Good thought, Pullo. But sir, I don't think the fifty chits at a time will work. The girls can only do so much in a day. Some of these horny dogs would try to knock off all fifty . . . well, all right, ten of the fifty, in a day. And that means fights and worn-out girls and blood in the streets."

"Then what do you suggest, Top?"

"A get-laid roster by unit, sir. Two cohorts a day, balancing the numbers as evenly as possible, and withholding of a fifth of an *as* from each man in a cohort every time the cohort's number comes up. The centurions can keep order. No fights. Especially no cross-unit fights as everyone tries to crowd into the same holes, so to speak. Very much simpler, sir."

"All right, we'll do it your way," agreed the legate. "Now let's get the word out: orders to march tomorrow morning, break camp and march out the next day."

Josephus appeared at the *Praetorium* door. "You sent for me, Legate?"

"Yes. Tell me, have you taken off that boy's leg yet?"

"No. I was going to, but he got ahold of a sword and swears he'll kill anyone who comes near him."

"Great!" exclaimed the legate. "Let's you and I walk over to the *veterinarius* and have a little chat with Decimus Vitelius."

INTERLUDE

*Exploratory Spacecraft 67(&%#@, Several Hundred Znargs
Above the Teutoburg Forest*

Red used four of his twelve tentacles to massage the crown of
his mantle. He seemed visibly deflated.

"Worse?" trilled Blossom.

"Worse; the creature had jumped ahead roughly seven hundred
circuits of this planet around its sun."

Of course, being a twelve-limbed species, Red's seven hundred
was not the same as a human seven hundred.

"What is drawing him on?" Blossom wondered, aloud, her
high note at the end indicating deep puzzlement over impos-
sibilities come to realties.

"He seems to be hitting his people's slow slide to oblivion."

"Can you do anything at all?" she enquired.

"I've got the artificial intelligence working on it. I'm hoping
that if we can get ahead of him along the temporal wave he's
riding, we might be able to catch him and return him to his
own body."

City of Constantine, May 29, 1453 A.D.

"Where am I?" Calvus asked of his current host, though he was
afraid of the answer.

"Who the hell are you?" asked his host.

135

"People keep asking me that," Calvus replied. "Sometimes I wonder myself. My best guess, in any case, is that I am probably the *animus* of one Appius Calvus, a Roman probably killed in Germany in the year of the consulship of Sabinus and Camerinus, or the year 762 from the founding of the city."

"Then what the hell are you doing here," asked his host, "if you died in Germany over fourteen centuries ago?"

"Being punished, I suspect, though for what sins I know not."

"Fair," said the host. "If you're not in Hell, then this is Purgatory for you, I suppose, which means your soul is not damned. And if you came for punishment, you came to the right place."

"And this place would be?" Calvus asked.

"The City of Constantine, sometimes called Byzantium, the capital of the Empire—what there is of it."

"The...Empire? But the Empire fell. I know it did. I saw the results."

"Reborn here, but Greek-speaking. Politically and culturally pretty much Roman, though. We were able to hold on when the Western Empire fell. We were even able to reconquer most of the old Empire. But we couldn't hold it...and then a plague hit. We never really recovered from that plague. Maybe we might have, but then the Mohammedans showed up, and from them there was no recovering."

Calvus suddenly realized he couldn't see a damned thing. "Can I ask you to open your eyes, friend? I can't see what's going on, though I hear a commotion somewhere to your...our front. By the way, who are you?"

The host opened his eyes and announced his name as, "I...I am the Emperor Constantine XI Palaiologos. For the next hour or two, I am, anyway. Maybe a little longer if we can turn back the assault coming for us."

"Hour or two?"

"Look, friend, at our mighty walls. See you not the great gap in them, smashed through by the Mohammedans, using artillery provided them by so-called Christians?"

Calvus didn't really want to get involved in another discussion of religion. Instead, he asked, "What kind of artillery can have smashed through such strong walls?"

Involuntarily, Constantine brought forth a memory for Calvus to share, a memory of a great bronze tube: "It's called a 'gun.'"

The scale of men around it indicated it was between twenty-seven and thirty feet long. Suddenly, flame belched forth from one end, trailing a great stone ball. The ball left the flame and smoke behind, to fly through the air and smash into a great wall, inflicting considerable damage on that wall.

"That kind," said Constantine.

"Gods!" Calvus uttered. "What army could hope to stand against something like that?"

"Actually," answered Constantine, "those things are not of much use against armies. Too hard to aim at moving targets. Too slow to reload. Impossible to move quickly. And the targeted troops can duck or hide. But walls cannot move, cannot duck, and cannot hide...but at least we have the satisfaction of knowing that Orban, the faithless pseudo-Christian Hungarian bastard who cast their cannon for them, died from an explosion of one of his own faulty guns. That, and that he's currently roasting on a spit in Hell."

"Why aren't you more upset at my being here, and what awaits you?" asked Calvus, even though most of his hosts had been similarly calm and detached.

"Perhaps because we are conversing *anima ad animum*."

"That could be it." Calvus thought back, then asked, "What's going to happen, now?"

"In a few minutes, they're going to come pouring through the breach...Oh...no...not in a few minutes; there they are."

Calvus looked through Constantine XI's eyes to see a horde of swarthy men, in strange barbarian costume, pouring through the breach and engaging a thin line of defenders.

"We'll try to hold them, but they outnumber us a little better than ten to one, maybe as much as twelve to one, so we're probably not going to succeed. At some point in time, four or five thousand survivors will break and run for the ports and the ships. Some may even make it.

"And then there will be lamentations and weeping in every house, as barbarians force their way through the doors to slaughter the elderly and useless, and smash the skulls of babies against the walls. There will be screaming at every crossroads, as women and girls down to the age of ten or even nine are thrown to the pavement, have their legs forced apart, and then find themselves painfully and repetitively violated. The priests will be slaughtered around their own altars. Everything not nailed down will be instantly stolen, and anything that *is* nailed down will see the nails pried up.

"The Mohammedans will stalk through the town, stealing, disrobing, pillaging, killing, and raping. They'll take captive men, women, children, old men, young men, monks, priests, people of all sorts and conditions. Virgins will awaken from nightmarish sleep to find clouds of those brigands standing over them with bloody hands and faces full of abject fury. And lust. Then the mass of the survivors will be auctioned off, and few or none will ever see their homes again."

"How can you stand to live to see it?" asked Calvus.

"Why, I cannot stand to live to see it." Constantine drew his sword and began to stride forward, shouting imprecations at his enemies and daring them to face him. "The city fallen and I still live? No, not for long.

"You need not stay here to feel my death," said Constantine.

Replied Calvus, "I cannot leave you to shun it. This is my civilization, too, that is dying."

CHAPTER SEVEN

I must tell, too, of the hardy farmers' weapons, without
which the crops could be neither sown nor raised. First
the share and the curved plough's heavy frame, the
slow-rolling wains of the Mother of Eleusis, sledges and
drags, and hoes of cruel weight; further, the common
wicker ware of Celeus, arbute hurdles and the mystic
fan of Iacchus. All of these you will remember to provide and store away long beforehand, if the glory the
divine country gives is to be yours in worthy measure.
                                    —Virgil, Book 2, the *Georgics*

*In the land of the Argippaeans and the Scythians, date
unknown*

It was the seventh day of marching, which was also, therefore, the
seventh day of new camp construction. If the legion had lost any
skill of camp construction, they'd picked it up again under the
lashing tongues and vine staves of the centurions. Also, if reports
were accurate, tomorrow would be the last day, and that a light
one, and they would find themselves in position at the new camp.

The way had been, and was, broad, meaning that, in the first
place, the column didn't have to be even remotely so strung out as
the legion had been in *Germania*; in the second, that there were
few places for an enemy to hide for an ambush; and that, in the
third, having eleven cohorts of heavy infantry in the main body,
less some people assigned to the advance party that would lay

out the camp, they were able to march in four columns, one each forward, left, right, and rear, with the *impedimenta* in the center.

Ahead of the forward column, the cohort of German *auxilia* acted the part of *extraordinarii*. Mixed task forces of the Palmyrene horse archers and Gallic cavalry guarded the flanks and rear. Farther out, half the new *ala* of Argippaean scouts kept watch while the rest, on the inside or the near outside, herded the animals. They likewise had the wagons of the tarts and their own wagons, many now drawn by huge *ngekud*, mixed in with the herds.

Every now and again one of the legionaries on the flanks would glance inward at the *ngekud*, shaking their heads and plainly wondering how such beasts could be and yet have neither tusks nor trunks.

Far out ahead by a good seven miles, having left before first light, Marcus Caelius and one of the staff *optios*, accompanied by the century of engineers and a guard made up of mixed cavalry and the first cohort of the legion, had the job of laying out the camp. It would be a winter camp, so some thought could be given to more space for shelter, heating arrangements, a better hospital, and—blessedly—a bathhouse.

The first spear, the legate, that staff *optio*, and the centurion in charge of the engineers had spent late into the night before the march commenced racking their brains, working up the dimensions and the spacing for a legionary camp that was two infantry cohorts larger than normal, plus had many more *auxilia* that any single legion could normally expect, plus would require two rooms, each the size of a standard tent, per *contubernium*.

And then there's that huge damned contingent of animals of all kinds. The intervallum *isn't going to be enough space to hold them all. And for those big cattle, I am thinking entire tree trunks for the horizontal beams of the corrals. And those may not be strong enough. And then there's the perimeter...*

"What was that, Top?" asked the staff *optio*, a young gentleman ranker by the name of Junius Rubelius. He was a bright-looking lad, dark of hair and eye, but unusually fit for a gentleman. Much of that was probably due to the physical training he'd received as a gentleman ranker.

"What? Was I thinking out loud?"

"Yes, Top. Not loud but muttering about something."

"Well, I'll tell you what's bugging me, Rubelius. This camp, because of all the animals and the extra huge *horreum* for the harvests—oh, and let's not forget the tarts; mustn't ever forget the tarts—is going to be a little too large in the perimeter to comfortably defend. We're going to have to put up a lot more additional defenses."

"Like Caesar at Alesia, Top?"

Marcus Caelius nodded, "Yes, very much like that—lily pads, spurs, sharpened abatis aboveground and more sharpened abatis in ditches. And more than four corner towers and a tower on each gate."

"And stone walls?"

The first spear sneered. "You see much stone since we arrived in this place, Rubelius?"

"Now that you mention it, Top, I don't know if I've seen *any*. Maybe mudbrick, then?"

"Mudbrick, sun dried, is pretty weak, Rubelius. But it does have the advantage of being fireproof. So maybe that in front of a stout palisade of logs. And, also, maybe mudbrick for the *horreum* to protect the grain from mice and rats. Also, I need to actually see the ground before I decide, but I think we may need parallel walls down to the river the scouts found. That's more work to build and more to guard."

Caelius could almost see Rubelius search his brain for where he'd heard or read of something like that before. "The Athenians, during their war with Sparta, were able to keep going because they had parallel walls down to the water."

"The sea, Rubelius, the sea. And they didn't use it for drinking water but to import food. Worked, too, until they lost a naval battle and the Spartans were able to cut imports."

Marcus Caelius gave Rubelius a smile that was at least half sneer. "What, you think career soldiers who can read in Latin and Greek don't, *optio*? I was reading Thucydides long before you were a gleam in your father's eye."

Rubelius half wilted under the first spear's glance.

"And the real bitch is that all that is too much to do over a single day, so we're going to have to build a regular marching camp, except considerably bigger than normal, then improve it day by day until it's a regular winter camp. While farming."

Trying to regain whatever favor he may have lost to the first spear's apparent sensitivity, Rubelius said, "You know, Top, if we do have to build parallels down to the river, that's probably where you want to put the bathhouse."

"Good point. I don't know why everyone says that all gentlemen rankers are idiots, Rubelius."

The bulk of the advanced party stretched out behind Caelius and a few others, which few included Rubelius.

The Palmyrenes told us, but I didn't quite believe it, thought Marcus Caelius, standing on a hill at a bend in the river the width of which he found incredible. *A mile wide to the north and two miles to the east. Even the Rhine doesn't compare. Hell, the Rhine doesn't* remotely *compare.*

Meanwhile, Rubelius said aloud, "Shit. I was thinking we should call this after the Argippaean name, but 'great river' is a hell of a lot more accurate."

"Indeed," agreed the first spear. "And, now, decision time: Do we put the camp here in the low ground, to the west on the high ground, or to the east on the not quite so high ground? What say you, Rubelius?"

"West, Top."

"Why?"

"Well, First Spear, in the first place because it's higher than where we are and higher than that rise to the east. That means more defensible and more warning, right?"

"It does," Marcus Caelius replied, with a serious, even pedantic, nod of his head.

"But in the second place, it's got a stream—doesn't look to be seasonal, either—we can use for sewerage runoff and as an obstacle. And the stream pours into that huge river downstream from where we can draw water for the camp. But in the third place...this area right around us? We're going to want it for grazing or raising crops, no? Between it and the land to the south and the west, it looks to be an easy ten or twelve thousand *jugera*, more than enough permanent grazing for all the sheep we have. I don't know about those big bastard cattle, but it can probably feed them, plus the goats, and the horses, too. We probably don't want to dump sewage in the upstream part; the animals will need that for watering, but lower down we can."

Marcus graced Rubelius with a rare smile. "I am impressed,

young gentleman ranker. You have done well. Let's go pick out the spot for the *Praetorium*."

Caelius turned his head, shouted a command, and directed his horse to the east.

When they'd reach the summit, the first spear looked all around, then went to a spot that was not quite at the summit, but from which the standard layout for a camp could be paced off and surveyed. There he ordered a marker emplaced, oriented in such a way as to show the lengthwise orientation of the camp. *Metatores,* standing by, immediately began using their chains and rods and precisely cut ropes, along with the *gromatici,* with their surveying instruments, to begin the process of marking out the camp. A team of troops drove a cart up. From the cart they unloaded a much larger-than-normal tent, the *Praetorium.* This they began to set up, assembling poles, pacing off the spots for the stakes, and spreading out the leather tent over the crossbeam for later raising with the uprights.

Meanwhile, some *metatores,* a part of the engineer contingent, with survey instruments marked off the square that would be in front of the *Praetorium,* two hundred by two hundred feet, which was enough for every man to assemble to hear the legate speak or to witness religious ceremonies and divinations.

Still other engineers and regular troops of the advanced party, under the guidance of the *metatores,* set up aligned and numbered stakes to guide the rest of the legion.

Marcus Caelius had a sudden idea, looking east at the shape of the creek. He trotted over and told the engineers laying out the line of the eastern *fossa* and *agger,* "Julius Caesar had no issue with following advantageous terrain when laying out his walls at Alesia. I want you to change our northeastern wall to a wedge, to take advantage of that creek. Keep it about *pilum* range from the creek. Don't change anything else and don't put anything in that wedge, except for laying out a bathhouse and main latrine. Understand?"

"Yes, First Spear."

"Good. In case it wasn't clear from the orientation of the *Praetorium* marker, I also want the camp oriented to take advantage of the same stream, to the south."

"It was clear, Top," replied the senior of the *metatores.*

"Good." With that, Caelius spurred his horse up to where the *Praetorium* was being raised. Likewise the medical tents were going up. His own tent and those of the other centurions of the first cohort and the accompanying cavalry decurions were likewise being raised, his by his freedmen, Privatus and Thiaminus. Rubelius, too, was kicking in to help raise the one oversized tent given over to the new *optios* filling in for missing tribunes.

Next to the *Praetorium* a tent rather smaller than that was being raised for the officially vacant spot of camp prefect, as well as one of the same size as the camp prefect's for the missing *tribune laticlavius.*

I've been avoiding accepting the promotion, as well I should, since I'm the one that killed Ceionius. But I am beginning to suspect that the good of the legion demands I take it over officially. Do ghosts of the murdered haunt tents as well as houses? I wish Calvus were here to guide me ... well, here and not apparently insane.

It was just after noon when the advanced party began to hear the sound of singing, coming from the west, accompanied by the axe's ring as logging teams finished the clearing of trees from inside the future camp. It grew steadily louder, the songs interspersed with purely instrumental pieces, and the songs themselves changing. By the time the main body turned north in the plain, below, and marched through the southern gate, they were singing:

> When I left home for the Empire's sake
> Up the *Via Aurelia* to *Pisae*
> I thought my mother's heart would break
> When we hugged and both said our goodbyes
> Just before I left home for *Pisae.*
>> And I've tramped Spain
>> And I've tramped Gaul
>> And *Pannonia*
>> Where the snowflakes fall ...

As this was the seventh camp built since leaving the first camp, the one where the legion had been dropped without warning, no one from the advanced party needed to meet their cohort to guide them to their new tenting ground. Tenting ground here or tenting ground there, it was all the same. Everything stood in precisely the same relationship to everything else. And every man, by now, knew exactly where that everything else was.

Oh, yes, certainly, it had been strange at first when the overcrowded Camp One had given way to the more properly spaced Camp Two. Then, indeed, ground guides had had to lead every cohort and maniple, every *turma* of cavalry, as well as the specialty shops, to include the wagons of the tarts, from the gate to where they belonged.

Soon the camp was filled with the sounds of stakes being pounded, of the orders and chants that propelled men to raise the tents, the creak of wagon wheels turning, and the bleating and *maa*ing of goats, the *baa*ing and bleating of sheep, the neighing of horses, and the deep, resonant lowing of the huge *ngekud*.

Smells followed sounds quickly enough: smells of unwashed, sweaty legionaries, of the horses and other animals, and—most welcome—the aroma of food being cooked over wood fires.

Having turned his horse over to the stables, Caelius strode to the *Praetorium* to wait for the legate. He didn't have to wait long.

"Quiz time, sir," Caelius said.

"Must we, Top? Well, I suppose we must. Lead on, O illustrious pedagogue."

Immediately, Caelius strode to the east, slowing just enough for Gaius Pompeius to catch up, and subtly shifting left to push the legate to take the right.

When they reached the military crest, below which troops were already hard at work carving out the *fossa* and building up the *agger*, Gaius Pompeius exclaimed, "The Palmyrenes weren't lying. That river is practically an inland sea. It makes the Tiber look like Jupiter is taking a piss."

The first spear raised an inquisitorial eyebrow, causing the legate to say, "Yes, Top. Sorry, Top."

Caelius gave a curt nod and said, "The selection of campsites for a marching camp isn't that hard, sir, especially in a place as flat and treeless as this area is, in general. But here we've got some terrain and resource issues to deal with. So, for one point, why this hill as opposed to the one to the east or the plain down below us?"

Gaius' face scrunched as he thought on it. "Well, Top, just from here it looks like we're a higher hill, with a steeper slope on three sides, so better defense and better visibility."

"Yes, sir; very good. But why not the plain?"

"I don't know beyond what I've already...oh...we need it for agriculture, don't we?"

"One point, sir. Now, for your second point, why isn't the wall going up on this side straight? Why is it a wedge?"

Gaius rubbed his jaw, thinking hard. "Well, it's not because the crest of this hill is down there...Let me guess: it's either that you determined that we need the extra space, or there's some kind of terrain feature down there that aids defense."

Caelius gave Gaius a wintery shadow of a smile. "Not quite enough, sir. Yes, we could use the space and, yes, there is a feature down there, an all-season creek, that we can cover, but there's something else..."

"A creek? A creek? Why would we... Aha! Sewerage runs off; that's it, isn't it? Bathhouse? Maybe latrine, too?"

"Full point, sir.

"Now, sir, what are we going to use for building materials for the wall? This is, after all, a winter camp..."

"Good enough, sir—eight points out of ten. Let's tour the camp now, shall we?"

Gaius nodded, then said, "Yes, let's, but as we walk let us talk, too."

"Anything in particular in mind, sir?"

"Yes, you need to become the *praefectus castrorum*."

"I know..."

"And the reasons you need to... What did you say?"

"I said I know. And the reasons are that we're not fighting, right now—and as far as we know are not all that likely to be, any time soon—that what we've got going now is largely a logistic effort, and that is a camp prefect's job. Moreover, we've got a fair number of senior centurions who could be first spear. Moreover, though you don't know it, most likely, my term as first spear should have been coming to an end soon, anyway, so I *have* to become the camp prefect if I'm to stay in the army at all."

"Well...under the circumstances I think the emperor would forgive us for not driving you from the army, especially since we desperately need you, and all."

Caelius smiled at the compliment. "Maybe so, sir, but somewhere in the legion is someone—several someones as a matter of fact—who deserve to be considered for the position of *primus pilus* and who might get a little resentful if I keep holding it down."

Gaius Pompeius twisted his face off to one side, answering, "Yes, I suppose that must be true. Well, who to replace you, then?"

"I've thought on it," Caelius replied. "My first choice would be Quintus Silvanus, from the Seventeenth Legion, but it's not clear that the corps of centurions of the Eighteenth would accept him, or not yet, anyway. Moreover, the Eleventh Cohort, which is what remains of the Seventeenth, while a little overstrength in manpower, for a line cohort, is weak in centurions, having only four experienced ones. They need Silvanus more than we do, at least for now."

"So who, then?" asked Gaius Pompeius.

Caelius removed his helmet and scratched at sweat-soaked hair and scalp. "Got to be my former number two from the First Cohort, Faustus Metilius, meaner than weasel shit and smart, too."

"All right, I approve," said Gaius. "How much more shaking up will we have to do?"

"Not sure, yet, sir, but... well... if we do have to shake things up now's the time to do it, while we're growing food, and not in the future when we're marching through hostile territory or fighting. We also need to promote a couple... mmm... no, three more men to the centurionate."

"I'm still going to call you 'Top,' you know."

"That will be fine," agreed Marcus Caelius. "Only you're going to have to call Metilius 'Top,' too, or he'll be insulted. And when we're all together... well, fuck, first names will have to do. Well, I suppose I'm effectively an equestrian now, too."

"Done."

"And, sir, there's one other thing. You are the legate but you're ending up pulling officer of the day, every day, because we don't have any tribunes. You can't command when you're bogged down in that much minutiae. And the *optios*, even backed up by first-order centurions, just don't have the clout."

"So what do you suggest, Top?"

"Those seven gentlemen rankers have to be promoted to tribune."

"Do I have the authority?"

"Do you see anyone around here who outranks you?"

"Good point."

"And speaking of soon-to-be tribunes..."

Rubelius, still atop his horse, came trotting up. "Hey, Top," he said, "lots of stone down by the river. Also the troops digging the *fossa* are running into it. Good sign, no?"

Unseen by anyone in the camp, nor by anyone in the Roman Army, there were eyes watching in puzzlement from the shelter of the wooded hill to the east.

Skyles of the Skolotoi—the name the Scythians used for themselves—watched in wonder at the town growing before his eyes. He'd neither seen nor even heard of anything like it. It was not the existence of the town that surprised him; his people frequently raided towns along the southern border of his people and even unto the land of the Parthians. They raided for slaves, especially female ones, gold, weapons, and prisoners to sacrifice to their gods. Also they raided for scalps, for scalping their enemies was something of a competitive activity among the Skolotoi. Indeed, so much were scalps prized that some warriors had collected enough of them to make entire garments.

But what *was* surprising was the speed with which the town was going up and the disciplined order on display as it did. Skolotoi were tough, everyone knew it, and brave, yes, that, too. What they were not, especially, was disciplined.

"It is a strange and frightening thing to see."

When Skyles had seen enough he went over the hill and down to the southeast, to where his men and his horses waited. He told one of them, Artames, "Stay here with your two brothers. Keep watch on those strangers. Don't be seen. Don't get caught."

"I'll tell you on the way," he told the rest of his warriors. "For now, we must ride like the wind to get back to camp to tell the chief that we have strangers on our land."

"It's not exactly ours," said one of the underlings. "We just take wood from it every year to reraise the wooden platform for worship and prisoner sacrifice."

"Yes...and those strangers are already cutting down a good deal of the wood."

The amount of wood needed for winter quarters could not be procured in one fell swoop. Even though the men were available, the pioneer tools were not. Thus the changeover from leather tents to split-log cabins would be a gradual one, and that only after palisades were put up and towers built. And before that happened there would be bridges over the creek fronting the *Porta Principalis Sinestra* and the *Porta Decumana*.

The actual sleeping room size was to be just slightly larger than that for the tents, but there was considerably more effective room inside one, since the legionaries would also build bunk beds, as many as three bunks high. In front of that was a shallower communal room for arms and equipment storage, and cooking, the fireplace for the latter also serving to heat both spaces in winter.

Cavalry barracks would be built to similar dimensions, except with a loft above for a state slave to help care for the horses and pull guard while the troopers were training or patrolling, and with the horses housed in one of the two rooms for a three-man team. The cavalry lived much more comfortably than the infantry, a point of some bitter contention between the branches.

Horses were to be sheltered from the weather. Sheep, on the other hand, carried their own insulation with them. For them, sheds would be built, unheated but with a shingle roof overhead and walls on three sides, to block the wind. Much the same was true of goats, although they were not nearly so well insulated as the sheep.

The great *ngekud*, so Bat-Erdene assured them, would be fine in the worst weather and, moreover, hated being closely confined. "Strong corral...well, very strong corral...be enough. Them huddle for warm. Also fuck a lot for warm. Have new *ngekud* in spring."

Mucius Tursidius, the boy with the formerly nearly gangrenous leg, the leg having been saved by maggot therapy, stood at attention in front of Gaius Pompeius, flanked by the new camp prefect, Marcus Caelius, and the new first spear, Faustus Metilius. Besides Metilius was Tursidius' own centurion, Caius Gabinius. Caelius, Metilius, and Gabinius, all three, looked like they could have been carved, not from the same block of marble, but from the same gnarled, old, lightning-blasted oak...except that they all looked a good deal tougher than oak. Of the three, Metilius bore the most and worst visible scars. One of these was particularly horrific, running from the senior centurion's forehead then all the way down his cheek to his jawline. Off to one side stood Samuel Josephus, slouching as befit one not actually a soldier and not interested in soldierly games. The legionary aquilifer, Gratianus Claudius, stood by to record any monetary punishment, as did the signifer for Tursidius' maniple, as these were the treasurers, the bankers, for the unit.

Tursidius was a pale and ghastly white, and it wasn't because of his recent brush with gangrenous death. No, Tursidius had committed a terrible crime, taking up arms against a legally superior officer, Josephus, who had the privileges of a centurion, if no command authority except over the medical establishment, and a senior noncom, the chief of the medical orderlies who ranked with a *tesserarius,* or corporal, in modern terms. He was facing a potentially severe punishment. It was the possibility of severe punishment that had him standing stiff before the legate. Had the offenses called for a mere beating or extra labor... or literally shitty labor, cleaning used sponges, for example... his own centurion would have handled matters.

The new *praefectus castrorum,* had already drilled the legate in how to administer punishment. "First and foremost, look mean. Then be aware in your own mind what you're going to do. Then rehearse it until it comes out like the judgment of Caesar, himself. Bring the guilty bastard in along with his chain of command. Tell him the charges and the possible punishment. Get him to plead—they almost always plead guilty—and anything he might say in mitigation. Get the description of the commission of the offense from the one offended against. Ask the boy's centurion, the first spear, and then myself for our recommendations. Ask the *medicus* what he thinks. Then do what you were going to do anyway, possibly modifying it for the benefit of the centurions."

And so, looking over Tursidius, and glad beyond measure that the boy didn't lose either his leg or his life, Gaius Pompeius wore an insincerely severe face.

"Mucius Tursidius," said the legate, "you stand here accused of disobedience to a superior officer and a superior noncommissioned officer, and threatening the same with death or grievous bodily harm. The potential penalties range from a bad flogging to death. Although some lesser penalty or penalties are also possible. How do you plead?"

"Plead, sir?" asked the terrified boy.

"Yes, did you do it or did you not?"

Tursidius gulped, screwed his courage up, and answered, "I did it, sir."

"We take this as an admission of guilt. Is there anything you can say in mitigation?"

"Just that I was out of my mind with fear and despair, sir. And that I'm sorry, sir."

Gaius turned to Josephus for a description of the incident. This the surgeon gave, but added in of his own accord, "I think the boy was delirious, suffering hallucinations. I don't believe he knew he was threatening me or my chief of the medical orderlies. And I am a *medicus,* trained as such in Alexandria, Egypt, and thus a vastly better judge of his mental state than Tursidius, himself, is."

The boy cast an infinitely grateful glance at the legion's chief doctor.

Both Caelius and the legate suppressed smiles; the plea for mercy for the boy, coming from Josephus, was so very predictable.

"Centurion Caius Gabinius, what is your judgment of Tursidius' worth to the legion?"

"Well, sir," said the centurion, snapping to attention, "he's fairly new; came to us only a few months before we marched into Germany with Varus."

At the mention of the name, all present barring Josephus and Tursidius turned their heads and spat on the ground. It had become a legionary tradition over the preceding weeks.

"But he's been a good lad, sir. Always cheerful. Never slacks off. Trains hard. Trains in his limited off time, too, and of his own accord. I think, sir, that with time, he'll become a real asset."

Gabinius summed up with his own judgment. "Sir, left up to myself I'd have knocked him over the head with my *vitis,* called him a 'very naughty boy,' and told him not to do it again." Gabinius relaxed to a position of parade rest, hands clasped behind his back and feet spread shoulders' width apart.

Gaius nodded soberly. "I see. *Primus Pilus* Metilius, what is your opinion? Note that Centurion Gabinius has told me what he would have done, not what he thinks I should do."

The first spear likewise stood to attention. "I'm inclined to listen to the *medicus*, sir, and just let the boy off. He was surely just out of his mind. We are Romans, after all, sir, and don't hold people accountable for their acts when insane."

"Camp Prefect?"

Marcus Caelius, as an officer and newly minted member of the equestrian class, said, "No excuses or defenses I've heard here fully persuade me, sir. Discipline ought to be used. That said, sir, death is extreme. So would be a severe flogging. The rest I leave up to you, sir."

Gaius took a long moment staring severely at Tursidius. Finally, he said, "Mucius Tursidius, I find you guilty. I sentence you to forty lashes with the *flagellum*, the withholding of one month's pay, next payday, one month of additional hard duty to be decided by your centurion, and loss of privileges to visit the camp tarts with your cohort for three months."

Tursidius began to sway, so much so that both Gabinius and Metilius reached over to hold him up.

"However," said Gaius Pompeius, "based on the recommendations of your chain of command and the chief *medicus*, I am suspending the flogging for six months, contingent on your good behavior. If you have been a model soldier for that time, the sentence will be removed from your record as if it were never imposed. All other punishments remain. Any questions, Tursidius?"

Color began coming back to the boy's face as soon as he understood that his back was not going to be turned into strips of torn skin and raped muscle. His swaying stopped enough that the flanking centurions let him go, to stand fully under his own power.

"No questions, sir,. And thank you, sir. For this and for my leg, sir. I won't disappoint you, sir."

Gaius said, simply, "These proceedings are finished. Dis...MISSED."

Instantly, the new first spear gave the command, "A-bout...FACE. Forward...MARCH. Left-right-left-right-left-right..." Until he, Gabinius, and a much-relieved Mucius Tursidius were out of the *Praetorium*.

"So how was that, Top?" asked Gaius Pompeius.

"Almost perfect, sir," Caelius answered. "It would have *been* perfect if you had managed fully to hide your absolute disgust to be called on to punish a boy you really didn't think deserved punishment."

Bat-Erdene went to see his friend, Gisco, to arrange an appointment with the legate. Based on what he had to say, Gisco cleared half a morning and arranged for the far more militarily knowledgeable Marcus Caelius to be present as well.

Bat-Erdene showed up with two of his men.

"Scythians here," Bat-Erdene said, simply. "Two scouts find traces, maybe so many." Here he held up both hands, fingers spread, twice. "Follow tracks carefully off to one side. Three still here, watching. Only three."

"What does it mean?" asked Caelius.

"Only mean two things for sure," answered Bat-Erdene, whose Latin was definitely getting a bit better. "One is they know you here. Other is they are looking to see what you do. Could be they come attack you. Could be they afraid you attack them. No more can say."

"'No more can say,'" repeated Gaius Pompeius. "About the ones watching us?"

"Right; thems."

Gaius pondered a bit on the difficulty of translation, then asked, "What can you tell me about the Scythians, in general? One of our historians, our storytellers, talked about them a lot, but that was several hundred years ago."

Bat-Erdene paused, collecting his thoughts, then answered, "My peoples not know all that much. Do know used to be very powerful. Many, many. And much rich. Now, not so much powerful. Don't know about rich. Just leftover, staying out of way of more powerful ones. Group called Huns came through, beat them, took some their women. Huns, last I hear, down mouth of great river. Other group, Sarmatians, also beat. Couple more beatings and they fled most of homeland, set up south of here. Not so many. Not so powerful. Still mean and dangerous."

Bat-Erdene continued, "Also gots womens fight. Mean, too.

All use poison arrows. Also, arrows barbed. Really hard pull out. Very bad. Whole people mean. Blind slaves. Use scalps for hand rags. Sacrifice slaves and prisoners. Burn alive sometimes. Use people skin for leather."

"Yeah, that would be the very definition of mean," agreed Gaius. "How many are they?"

"Maybe as many as you, just warriors, plus more womens, plus many slaves. That true hundred years ago. Could be many more now."

"Women?" asked Gaius Pompeius, incredulously. "You mean the legends are *real*?"

"Not know nothing about no legends, but women on horses with bows real. Seen. Use light bows because cannot draw heavy ones. That why must use poison arrows. Shoot-shoot; then run away on horse while poison kill. No womens with people my scouts find."

"Do you think we can capture them? Those three, I mean," asked Gaius Pompeius.

"Hard," answered Bat-Erdene. "*We* could maybe capture but not allowed. You all pretty noisy. Best chance, probably use Palmyrenes. Or use them and legion, stripped down, no armor, just swords and shields. Maybe heavy throwing spear. But remember: poison arrows."

There was another problem nagging at Marcus Caelius. "Hmmm...what language do they speak?"

"Close mine," replied Bat-Erdene. "Some difference. Can talk. Can trade."

"Ah, good," the camp prefect said. "No sense in capturing them to interrogate if we can't understand each other."

Instead of a map, some of the troops from First Cohort, in conjunction with various infantry and cavalry patrols, had built a terrain model for the fifteen miles around the camp, but without anything for the opposite shore, across the great river. Patrols to the other bank were planned, but for the future.

The three-dimensional map resided on the floor of the *Praetorium*, in a place where neither tiles nor rugs had been laid. Gaius led Bat-Erdene and Caelius to the terrain model, handed Bat-Erdene a long, thin wooden pointer and said, "Show us exactly where they are."

The Argippaean spoke to one of the two scouts, then handed

over the pointer. The scout examined the terrain model carefully, as if not understanding. Then, upon recognizing the bend in the great river, a sudden light came to his eyes. He traced out what had happened, with Bat-Erdene translating.

"How would you handle it, Prefect?" Gaius Pompeius asked.

"No time to make more boats, or at least we can't count on there being time," replied Caelius. "We've got an even twenty-four for making pontoon bridges. We can probably stuff eighteen or twenty legionaries in each, with shields and a *pilum* or two each, but no armor, without actually sinking them. Call it four hundred and fifty men. I think we should use Twelfth Cohort, their morale has been low since they came to us. A victory, even a small one, would do them a world of good. Add in the engineer century from First Cohort to manage the boats. Anyway, they carry the boats to the river down the twin parallel walls, load up and float downstream with very minimal paddling. They land south of that hill mass to the east, assemble quietly, and spread out, three feet between men. They take ropes with them to tie together with *pila* to trip the Scythians' horses. This is all done at night.

"We also send the German *auxilia* out via the western gate, likewise stripped down. The Germans are light, fast, and used to being sneaky. Witness our humiliation under Varus." Every man present but the Argippaeans automatically spat at the mention. "They swing wide around, spread out and advance quietly to seal off the southwest. They also carry ropes to trip the horses.

"Then we send Gallic cavalry out with each man bearing a torch. They make like they're heading south, but once they're spread out, they charge the hill with the Scythians on it, scream-ing their battle cry the whole way.

"With any luck at all the Scythians panic and run into either the Germans or the Twelfth Cohort."

"Timing's going to be tricky," Gaius observed.

"I know," agreed Caelius, "not least because we want to set up before moonrise, then charge with the Gauls to panic them after the moon comes up."

"Three-quarter waning moon tonight," said Gisco, who had taken over the duty of keeping track from Appius Calvus, still indisposed. "Right around midnight."

"Any way to call it off if it all goes to crap?" asked Gaius Pompeius.

Caelius just shook his head. "And not a lot of time to rehearse it in advance so it doesn't go to crap, either. And no way to control things by shouting orders, either, for that matter. Or with *cornicines*. Or drums."

"Which makes me think we ought to delay a few days, both to rehearse as much as we can and to let the Gauls establish a pattern of leaving the camp at night with torches to go off and do something somewhere else. Keep our targets from panicking and running off before we're in position.

"On the plus side, there are only three of them. The worst that happens is that they escape, not that our troops are in any serious danger."

INTERLUDE

*Exploratory Spacecraft 67(&%#@, Several Hundred Znargs
Above the Teutoburg Forest*

Blossom brought Red his late shift repast, a brace of large crus-
taceans, accompanied by a mild liquid euphoric, carrying it with
two tentacles on a red lacquer tray while swaying gently in a
way Red found extremely appealing, and sliding along the deck
of the command module on her other ten.

"Any luck?" she chirped.

"Don't confuse luck with planning and decision factors," Red
replied, adding a whistle at the end to indicate humor. "But, yes,
I've caught him almost exactly eleven hundred and twenty-four
journeys of this planet around its sun in the future. His mind, if
that's exactly what's traveling, is on an island well to the west of
where we plucked his people out of. He's touched on a hundred
and five times and places so far."

Tapping a screen lightly with a tentacle, Red told Blossom,
"He's roughly here."

London, England, 1908 A.D.

Calvus, on his long journey, had acquired, he found, something
of an ability to sense the form of whoever he was intruding
upon. It was, thus, upon the semiconsciousness of a man almost
preposterously large—and large in all dimensions, immensely tall

and rotund, both—that a profoundly distressed and depressed Appius Calvus intruded.

"Why, who is this?" asked the mind or soul of that very large man.

"The unhappiest spirit in all the world," answered Calvus, "for I have seen the destruction of my army, my civilization, and even the last remnant of my civilization. And who are you?"

"Oh, me? Nobody important. Some call me 'the apostle of common sense,' though, and in my vanity I admit to taking a certain pleasure in the name. More formally, I am called Gilbert Chesterton, an Englishman. But why so glum, chum? For I sense that you are even more depressed than your words."

"I am," said Calvus, "the last somewhat living representative of the glory that was Rome. I am a poor representative of it, of that I am sure. But the last one, nonetheless. I was killed, I think, by the Germans of Arminius. I do not remember my passing. Since then I have wandered the Earth, seeing much, understanding little, and what little I understood showed increasing ruin and decay."

"Fascinating," said the soul of the large man. "Do you flit around, present to past to future to present again?"

"So far," replied Calvus, "it has all been one way, past to increasing future. When is it now and where am I?"

"Why, it is the year of our Lord, Nineteen Hundred and Eight and you are in London, arguably the greatest city in the world. There is one with more people, New York, over in America, but it, while great, doesn't really have the depth yet that London has."

"There cannot be a greater city than Rome," said Calvus.

"Ah, but there can. Our population—I speak of the city's—is six times greater than Rome's. And we, the British, rule an empire greater in extent than Rome's by a similar factor. We rule it badly, in many cases, and for base motives, in still more, but rule it we do. There is also a place west of here, across the ocean, with a city even bigger and similar land."

"And do you love it, this city?" asked Calvus.

"Most of us do, though it is my and my wife's ambition to move to a smaller and quieter place in the country. Why do you ask?"

"Because Rome was not loved because she was great. She became great because men loved her."

"May I steal that? I am writing this book, you see, which I've tentatively entitled *Orthodoxy*."

"Of course," replied Calvus, "and welcome to it since I no longer have a use for it. When last I saw Rome, and that through the eyes of a beggar, I don't think anybody loved her."

"Well, on that score be at peace; Rome is loved again. So tell me, how's this sound to you: 'Go back to the darkest roots of civilization and you will find them knotted round some sacred stone or encircling some sacred well. People first paid honor to a spot and afterwards gained glory for it.' And this is where your line fits: 'Men did not love Rome because she was great. She was great because they had loved her.'"

"I like it," said Calvus.

"I would give you credit for it, friend, except that I think I'll be doing well to remember even the line. I am asleep now, you see, and this will all be a faintly remembered dream to me in the morning."

"I feel my time with you is almost up," said Calvus. "Good luck with publication. Have you many slaves to copy it out?"

Before Chesterton could explain how things were published in his time, rolling presses and all that, and in codices rather than scrolls, his visitor was gone.

CHAPTER EIGHT

As to war, these are their customs. A Scythian drinks
the blood of the first man whom he has taken down.
He carries the heads of all whom he has slain in the
battle to his king; for if he brings a head, he receives a
share of the booty taken, but not otherwise. He scalps
the head by making a cut around it by the ears, then
grasping the scalp and shaking the head off. Then he
scrapes out the flesh with the rib of a steer, and kneads
the skin with his hands, and having made it supple he
keeps it for a hand towel, fastening it to the bridle of
the horse which he himself rides, and taking pride in
it; for he who has most scalps for hand towels is judged
the best man. Many Scythians even make garments
to wear out of these scalps, sewing them together like
coats of skin. Many too take off the skin, nails and all,
from their dead enemies' right hands, and make cover-
ings for their quivers; the human skin was, as it turned
out, thick and shining, the brightest and whitest skin of
all, one might say. Many flay the skin from the whole
body, too, and carry it about on horseback stretched on
a wooden frame.

—Herodotus, 4.64.1–4

Land of the Scythians, date unknown

Standing on the bank of the great river, with the waters lapping around his *caligae*, Marcus Caelius just shook his head in

161

disgust. The Twelfth Cohort, made up of the former advanced party of the Nineteenth Legion combined with about a hundred and twenty refugees, was just hopeless. They could not load the boats properly. They could not or would not keep quiet.

Marcus Caelius called over the first-order centurion, Sextus Sattius, and used a torch to look at the man's face and, especially, his eyes.

He's lost his spark, along with his will and, therefore, his ability to lead or control.

"I'm sorry, Prefect," said Sextus Sattius. "I've...I guess I've lost my touch."

The important thing is to get him away from the troops before he ruins them, thought Caelius. *This cohort is short centurions but a bad centurion is worse than none.*

Gently, he said to Sattius, "I think you may have caught some kind of a fever. Go report to the chief *medicus*, Samuel Josephus, and tell him I want him to examine you. Go on now; it will be all right."

As soon as Sattius was out of earshot, Caelius told his freedman, Privatus, "Race like the wind to Josephus. Tell him I want him to judge Sattius as temporarily unfit for his duties for medical reasons. He can make up something plausible sounding. Then run to the first-order centurion of Ninth Cohort and tell him I want Lucius Pullo and Titus Vorenus to report to me here. Then find the first-order centurion of Eleventh Cohort, Quintus Silvanus, and have him likewise report here to me."

And Eleventh is short, too. Never enough; never enough.

As Thiaminus raced off, Caelius turned his attention to the men of the Twelfth Cohort. "You pussies are a disgrace to the entire Roman Army. Worse, you're a disgrace to your dead comrades, back in *Germania*. But still worse than that, you've fucking pissed off *me*, beyond which there is no worse disgrace. So get your little girls' asses out of the water. Drag the boats with you. We're going to have a little training session before we continue..."

Silvanus, Pullo, and Vorenus met at the entrance to the staggered wall, leading from the northern point of the camp down to the river's edge. They could hear Caelius' stentorious voice, commanding some set of victims in seemingly endless repetitions of physical exercises: "One hundred and six...one hundred and seven...one hundred and eight...one hundred and nine..."

He finished with, "One hundred and twenty-five," then told the men to rest. Fully a fifth of them were puking and all were covered in sweat.

"Who's your second-in-command and how good is he?" Caelius asked Silvanus.

"Caepo Ignius and quite good. Maybe a little too harsh, a little too often, but quite good nonetheless."

"Good," said Caelius. "He's the new chief of Eleventh Cohort. Meanwhile, you're taking over this mob. Even with you, this gaggle is short two centurions." Caelius pointed his finger as Vorenus, first, and then Pullo. "These two are them.

"Now I want you to take control of these—and I am using the term loosely—people, plus the engineers, whose fault this clusterfuck is *not*, and get them ready to board boats tomorrow night and move to the south of that hill mass east of here, to block off anyone's escape. Clear enough?"

The question was addressed to all three and all three answered it, "Clear, Prefect."

"Good. Now get to work unfucking this mob."

Two hours later, Caelius briefed the legate on what he'd done and why, ending with, "And we're still short some centurions, only it's four now, not three."

"What are we going to do with Sextus Sattius?" asked Gaius.

"Josephus says he had a really bad time in Germany, and feels unbearable guilt for living when almost all his friends died. I think he could use a stint in agriculture, nice relaxing agriculture, working for me in my capacity as chief quartermaster. Besides, go far enough back and he's a farm boy from generations of farm boys."

Gaius gave that half a second's thought before agreeing. "But we're still short centurions."

At about that time, Gratianus Claudius Taurinus knocked on the upright pole by the main entrance to the *Praetorium*, and requested permission to retire the eagle for the day. Gaius gave that permission but before the aquilifer could leave the tent, Caelius motioned him over with a beckoning finger.

"Here's one candidate," the camp prefect said. "Tell me,

Claudius: if you were promoted to the centurionate, who would you recommend for the position of aquilifer?"

Without hesitation, Gratianus replied, "The imaginifer, Titus Atidius Porcio. He'd protect the eagle with his corpse. And to replace him, the *vexillarius*."

"And to replace *him*?" asked Gaius.

"Sir, once his punishment is over I think you should consider Tursidius for the job, new or not. He's got the spark of someone you could trust to the death."

"Maybe," said Caelius.

The moon was well down. On the banks of the river, lit by a very few torches, Silvanus gave the orders for Twelfth Cohort and the engineers to embark. Quietly now, after countless rehearsals, in groups of eighteen to twenty they picked up their boats and marched into the river. As the water picked up the weight of the forward pair of men, they eased themselves over the gunnels and into the boats. Others followed the same pattern, until the boats were fully supported by water and were carrying their entire complement plus the engineers who would do the paddling and steering.

Atrixtos, son of Cotilus, waited impatiently on the *agger* by the southern gate for the first hints of moonrise. He'd already seen off the German light troops by the western gate, before returning to his own men on the *via Principalis*, the main street, by that southern gate. In this case, with the *Praetorium* facing to the west, the gate in question was the Porta Principalis Sinistra.

Atrixtos had a new horse, from the remount section. His own horse, the one he'd had in Germany, he'd had to put out of its misery. The new mount was held by his orderly, below on the street. Most of his men still had their old horses.

We've got a lot of them, though, riding the horses acquired by Gisco from the Argippaeans. All of them awarded the new horseflesh started out pretty skeptical of both the size of the horse and their saddles, which are quite different from the horn saddles used by Romans and ourselves. But our saddles are completely impossible to use with the Argippaean horses, because of the structure of the backs of the latter and the prominence of their spines.

The speed of the smaller horses was a surprise, and a pleasant one. So was the fact that they can do better on just grass than our horses, though a little grain doesn't hurt matters. But the real shocker had been stirrups. These were not just shocking but took a lot of practice with the Argippaeans to get used to. Some of the boys still grumble about them. And, frankly, I've not gotten used to them yet, even though I've tried.

The German light foot have been out for hours now. It ought to be about...

Atrixtos looked eastward. Yes, there it was, a tiny faint sliver of moonlight, just revealing itself. He bounded down the grass-covered side of the *agger*, grass-covered because the Romans invariably lifted off the sod first, when building a camp, expressly to reuse it on the top and near sides to provide firm footing, to reduce erosion, and to cut down on the mud dragged off.

"Mount up!" Atrixtos shouted. The command was echoed up the street by his underlings. "Light torches." The command didn't have to be echoed as slaves ran from horseman to horseman setting their torches alight. Torchlight flickered off copper-red and blond hair all along the column, Atrixtos' not least. "Open the gate," he ordered, and the legionaries on duty sprang to lift the crossbar and pull it open.

The Gaul raised his right up to give the hand signal to march, remembered it was too dark for anyone to see him, then gave it anyway but also the verbal order, "Forwarrrrd at the wallllk...MARCH."

Under his breath, Quintus Silvanis cursed the darkness. The river bank to his right was barely discernable under the starlight. Even the hill they were skirting was almost undiscernible in the darkness. As for his cohort and their boats, they couldn't even hear each other as the river's current sufficed to move them. Only the faint gurgling of the steering oars helped mark their relative position.

If a good third of them don't end up ten miles downstream with never a clue where they are, I'll be shocked silly.

With the first hint of moonlight, Silvanus could see that they were about a quarter of a mile past where he wanted them to land. He ordered his engineer on the steering oar to turn to starboard. Likewise the engineers on the oars began to give way, pushing the boat to the bank. Behind him he heard the number two boat's commander, Titus Vorenus, giving the same command. Faintly, he could hear that boats oars churning the water.

A slight nudge followed by a sudden stop said they'd reached the bank. Without a command Silvanus jumped over into thigh-deep water. A splash from the port side told him the other forward man had done as well. Both men, as they'd rehearsed, turned inward and grasped the boat, lifting it against the bank. The engineer took a spike, connected to the boat by a stout rope, and climbed up the bank. He stretched the rope out tautly, then drove the spike into the soft ground.

As rehearsed, the men farther to the rear moved carefully forward, leaping from boat to bank when they were the men in front. The stern of the boat lifted as the center of gravity shifted and water buoyed it up. With their left hands and arms occupied with holding their *scuta* and a torch, each, they used the *pila*, held in their right hands for balance. Silvanus formed them up on the flat.

The boat holding Vorenus nudged in, just a few inches port-side of the first boat. His crew, too, spiked the boat down, then walked forward to debark from the flat prow. As soon as Vorenus had his men formed up ashore, he hunted down Silvanus.

"I wish I'd thought to connect all the boats with ropes," whispered Silvanus. "As is, I'm afraid a lot of them will go astray."

"Could happen," agreed the junior centurion. "But if you had connected them with ropes, odds are fair they'd have gotten tangled up and half of us would drown out in the river."

"Point," agreed the first order centurion.

That two more boats had safely landed was evidenced by twin lines of men, one to the north and the other to the south, filing by to form up on the left.

With half an hour, Silvanis was reasonably sure he could account for twenty-one of the twenty-four pontoons. "If the rest show up, we'll shift left. Do you have the fire, Vorenus?"

Titus tapped a small bronze vessel from which a faint glow came. "Right here," he said.

"Don't let it go out. All right, First Century, First Maniple, Twelfth Cohort...Lefffft FACE. Single file from the right, Forrrwaarrrd at the trotttt...March. Follow me."

Mentally, Silvanus counted off the pace for the full half mile his reinforced cohort was supposed to stretch. When he neared the end point he passed back over his shoulder, "Prepare to halt." When he reached it, someone said, in pretty fair Latin with a German accent, "You Romans make too much noise."

"That's because we're not rabbits, sneaking through the forest. That you, Thancrat?"

"Me, yes. How did your journey go?"

"When I left the bank to stretch out in your direction, I was missing three boats. Maybe they'll show up."

Both men looked toward the camp, where a double row of bright torches showed that the Gauls were coming out.

"Atrixtos' orientation is pretty good," said Thancrat, after watching the Gauls veer toward them at what they were pretty sure was the bridge. "Should be fine, so far."

Pullo came up, breathless from running from the bank. "Those last...three...boats showed up, Quintus Silvanus...seems they...went too far and...had to...fight...the current...to come back. All present...or accounted for."

Silvanus waited until he heard the Gallic cavalry sounding their battle cry, and saw the line of torches turn eastward. He told Vorenus and Thancrat, "Light the torches."

The first two lit were Vorenus' and Pullo's, followed by Silvanus' and Thancrat's. With the Germans the flame leapt from man to man, torch to torch, reaching generally to the northwest. Eastward, though, the pattern was a little different, as Pullo ran to the bank faster than the flame could be passed. Once there he lit a torch, then stood back to watch the flame from the bank race westward to meet the flame from the juncture racing to the east.

When he was reasonably certain that every torch had been lit, Silvanus gave the command, "Post torches." This was echoed down the line, the echoes making time with the running forward of the legionaries and their driving the safe ends of their torches into the ground, about fifty paces to their front. Once the torches were driven in, the men returned to their previous line at the double. When he sensed that they had returned to the line, Silvanus order the men to jab their light *pila* into the ground, and began connecting them with short pieces of rope carried by each man. They then retreated twenty paces, took a single knee, grasped their heavy *pila* in their throwing hands, and made themselves as small as possible behind their *scuta*.

✧　　✧　　✧

Artames, the Scythian scout, hadn't trusted either of his brothers to stay awake on the middle watch, though he just barely trusted them to stay awake for the first and last watch. Thus it was that he'd seen that procession of torches leaving the strangers' camp. He'd seen it before, for the previous two nights, and so saw nothing strange in the procession.

The gentle lapping of the river against its banks made staying awake and alert most difficult. Still, Artames had some self-discipline. He wet his fingers and moistened his eyelids. That helped. When he felt that even this wasn't working he drew his dagger and stuck his own leg with the point, not deeply but just enough to encourage alertness. And the alertness was sufficient to let the Scythian sense the approaching enemy.

"Get up! Get up! GET UP!" Artames shouted at his brothers. "The strangers are coming for us. Their scouts must have spotted us!" Briefly, Artames considered letting them all be caught. Skyles was not noted for mercy or forgiveness of those who failed his command. Still, Skyles was a known threat; the strangers were very strange, indeed. *Better the demon you know.*

There was no time for saddling the horses. As one man, the three Scythians unhobbled their horses, leapt upon them bareback, aimed their noses to the south, and spurred them on, with Artames in the lead. They broke out of the woods to the south just as the lead Gauls were climbing the hill to the east.

Artames saw the line of torches sticking in the ground to his front. His eyes searched in that light and by moonlight for the enemies who had placed them there. He thought he saw them, crouching low. Muttering repetitive curses under his breath, Artames drew an arrow from his quiver, mounted by his side. He contemplated opening his little bronze jar of poison to contaminate an arrowhead but decided there wasn't time and, without the stability of a proper saddle and stirrups, wasn't much point anyway. Gods knew, he didn't want to spill that nasty crap on himself. *Might not kill me but I don't want to find out what it will do.*

There were three main advantages that stirrups gave the horse archer. These were the ability to elevate oneself above the horse, hence to see better; the ability to avoid being jarred by the movement of the horse, because the archer's legs could handle all the movement; and the ability to turn in the saddle to fire while running away.

None of these applied here. Artames took a shot at a lump near the ground he thought might be a man. Where his arrow went he didn't know, as he heard neither a scream nor the sound of it hitting something solid. He drew another one and, just as he passed the line of upright torches, saw that those lumps were shields with parts of men protruding from them. He saw a head and tried to take aim. At that point he felt his horse's head going down at its hindquarters arose. In a tangle of rope and javelin, amidst the sound of its terrified neighing, the horse pitched Artames forward onto his face. He hit and skidded for several yards, being knocked so silly that he barely registered the flights of his brothers' arrows, the screams of their horses, and the agonized scream of one brother as a heavy javelin punched through his leg, pinning him to his tumbling horse.

Artames tried to sit up and draw his sword. A heavy shield smashing into his face knocked him flat on his back again. Next thing he knew, practiced hands were flipping him over and lashing his hands together behind his back. He felt his sword being taken from him, along with his dagger, his bow, his quiver, and his little vial of poison.

Between the slamming of his head onto the ground and the slamming of a heavy shield onto his head, Artames was pretty badly concussed. Sick at the stomach, he vomited, with some of the vomit landing on one of his captors. That earned him a swift kick in the ribs along with several punches to the face, his head being held by the hair for the punches.

One groaning brother was dumped beside Artames. He hoped the other one had gotten away. That is to say he hoped it until he was dragged to his feet by his hair and had a chance to see his youngest brother, pinned both to and under his horse, with his neck twisted at an obviously fatal angle.

Artames and the next younger brother were roped together by the neck and prodded forward with the points and butts of heavy *pila*, forcing them to the northwest. After a couple of hours of walking and, as often, when concussive nausea struck, staggering in the moonlight, they and over a thousand horse and foot passed over the bridge and through the stout log gates of the strangers' city. Ominously, those massive gates creaked shut behind them.

Bat-Erdene was dressed as a Roman. He'd been redressed so that, on the off chance one of the Scythians escaped, or even was let go, they wouldn't be able to report to their tribe that there were Argippaeans among their enemies.

The two prisoners were bound, wrists and ankles, and gagged, to prevent them from talking with each other to collaborate on a story. Roman guards stood to either side of each and two Roman torturers from the First Cohort stood by with a collection of instruments, to include some irons heating up in the coals of a brazier. One of the torturers took an iron from the coals and touched it to a fresh piece of mutton. It sizzled in a most attention-getting way, filling the small log building with the smell of burnt meat.

However stunted his Latin could sometimes be, Bat-Erdene was perfectly eloquent in his own tongue. He'd also been briefed by the senior of the two torturers on how to act, what to say, and what to expect. Gisco had also, long before, briefed him on a bit of Roman history. Bat-Erdene didn't like any of it, but he could see the value, given the kind of rough neighborhood in which the Romans lived.

He nodded his readiness to begin. At that nod, the torturers slapped each of the Scythian captives across the face, five or six times.

"Now that we have your attention," Bat-Erdene began, "I am your translator. If you're curious, I picked up your tongue in Thrace.

"The people who hold you are called 'Romans.' You Scythians pride yourselves on your cruelty. Let me assure you, compared to the Romans you are rank amateurs. There is nothing so outright disgusting that you can imagine that they haven't done, and sometimes to entire peoples. Cities huge beyond comprehension, well-fortified beyond your capacity to understand, and wealthy beyond your wildest dreams of avarice have been completely obliterated from the surface of the Earth, along with their people. They are truly merciless."

Bat-Erdene believed all that was true, at one level, but at another had a hard time imagining it, himself, of the Romans of the legion, who had shown themselves to be friendly, even comradely, and generally virtuous and upright.

"However, unlike your people, the Romans are not wantonly cruel. Cooperate and they can be quite...well, nice, frankly. It's only when balked that they turn nasty.

"Part of that niceness involves giving the peoples they encounter all the information those people need to reach the correct decisions on how they wish to deal with Romans. To that end..."

One of the Romans produced a wickedly sharp, curved-bladed cutting knife, explaining its use.

Bat-Erdene translated, "This is used for skinning. They will, if you balk them, flay the skin from your face, your hands, and your feet, then pour salty water over it to both increase your pain and insure you do not die, but are sent back to your people as abominable freaks. The knife has a secondary usage in taking out tongues, in conjunction with these..."

One of the torturers held up a stout pair of rough iron forceps.

The senior torturer pointed upward, to where a hook hung from the ceiling, with a rope passed over it.

"That," said the Argippaean, "has three uses. One, the lightest of the three, is that you are suspended it from it in a cage and then spun. This will make you feel very ill. And it will not end, that feeling, until you cooperate fully. Another is to suspend you by your wrists with your arms behind you. It is very painful. The third is to just hold you above the ground until it becomes difficult to breathe. It takes about an hour to die that way, but the Romans won't *let* you die. Instead, they'll make you suffer all the pains of dying, over and over and over, without any final release..."

The Romans held up a strange box, bigger than a foot but with an opening at the top of one end.

"Now this one is curious. Looks like a shoe, doesn't it? Well, indeed, it is for your feet. This is placed over one foot—but note that there are two of them—and then wedges are driven in with hammers, crushing your foot completely, leaving you a cripple, unable to walk for the rest of your life, dragging yourself about like a snake or a worm...

"And this one is shoved up your anus, then opened by twisting this handle. It is worse than any anal rape...

"And this is a *flagellum*. Note the little pieces of bone and metal wound into it. They can take the skin right off your back..."

With each explanation, the two Scythians grew paler even as their eyes grew wider.

Finally, Bat-Erdene explained, "The two of you are going to be separated now. Once this is done, I will ask one of you a question and get an answer. If you don't answer you end up hanging with your wrists behind you from that hook until you do answer. Once I have an answer, I will then go to the other hut and ask the same question. As long as the answers match perfectly, we can just move on to the next. But if they do not match then these men will inflict pain upon you for about an hour. I will then ask the question again. If the answers match, we can move on to the next question. If they don't, then the torture increases, not in duration but in intensity. Do not try to second-guess the other. If he and you both have the same information, then the only way to stop the pain will be to keep to the truth. I truly pity you two if there is a question one of you does not know the answer to..."

Once the prisoners had been separated, Bat-Erdene asked his first, rather innocent, questions: "What is your name? What is the name of the other man? And what is the relationship between you?"

By that evening, the intermittent screaming and outright shrieking had stopped and Bat-Erdene had every bit of information Gaius Pompeius and Marcus Caelius had asked for, from the strength and location of the tribe—and the strength was much greater than Bat-Erdene had thought—to the leadership to the composition of the poison used in their arrows. That last the *medicus* Josephus had asked for, in the hope of perhaps finding an antidote.

Artames and his brother were still alive, though rather the worse for wear. At that, their feet were uncrushed, their skin was whole, barring a half dozen or so burns from hot irons, and they each still had both eyes. It could have been a good deal worse. Both smelled of vomit, where they'd been spun until sick. And the shoulder sockets of both still ached abominably from near dislocation while hanging from their wrists.

✧   ✧   ✧

"But," said Caelius, "the problems with using our slingers against these poison-arrow-wielding barbarians is that, on the one hand, the Rhodians aren't all that armored to begin with, and, on the other, that they're so badly outnumbered. Not saying we can't use them. I am saying that they won't last very long in a heads-up throwing match."

"We've got the archers, too," said Gaius Pompeius. "And their bowstrings are dry now."

"Same problem, really," answered Caelius. "Only delays the time between initial engagement and not having anyone to engage them with. Yes, our slingers will outrange them and our bows *might* outrange them, but the Scythians will just close the distance."

"If you Romans will forgive a foreign medical mercenary?" interjected Samuel Josephus.

"Go on, *medicus*," said Gaius Pompeius.

"In my holy books, there is a story of one of our early kings, before he became the king, a shepherd by the name of David. He killed an enormous giant of our enemies, the Philistines. Some—indeed, most—think he used a regular shepherd's sling, not different in principle to the one used by your Rhodian mercenaries. But there are at least ten good reasons to think he was using a very different kind of sling, a staff sling."

"All right. And?" queried Gaius.

Josephus replied, "Well, the thing is that, unlike the Rhodians' slings, a staff sling is ridiculously easy to learn to use. Also, they throw a heavier—a *much* heavier—projectile as far as or even farther than an arrow with a bow. Or you can put four of five standard projectiles in the cup at the cost of some range. And, since they don't need a wind-up throw, you can mass the slingers in a way that's impossible with the Rhodian sling. Not worth a damn at close range, mind you.

"Some say they're as accurate as a shepherd's sling. I used both as a boy, before I went off to Alexandria, and I can't say that's true. Maybe with a huge amount of practice and industrial manufacture of precision ammunition . . . maybe. But the range is impressive, almost as good as the Rhodians', and the power when you hit with a half-pound rock just astonishing."

"A half-pound projectile?" scoffed Hermagoras, the chief of the Rhodian slingers, standing next to his chief, Horatius Jovis. The chief of the archers, Zalmoxis, a Thracian—in some ways resembling a Greek or Macedonian, equally clever but rougher edged, with the right side of his torso overdeveloped from drawing a stout bow—stood on the other side. "Almost as far? That would be astonishing, indeed. But color me a skeptic. I'll need to be shown."

For the moment, Josephus ignored him. "So picture this," the Jew continued. "You use your Rhodians to inflict some damage and bait the Scythians to come closer to have a chance of hitting the Rhodians. Then suddenly your staff slingers pop up on a wall or from behind a line of legionaries and just *deluge* the Scythians with a torrent of fist-sized rocks moving fast."

Silvanus cleared his throat and asked, "Are these...these 'staff slings,' did you call them?...hard to make?"

"Easy as porridge," replied the *medicus*. "Bring me a stick about shoulder height in length, an inch and a half across, a piece of leather and some heavy string, and loan me a sharp dagger and I'll make you one right here as you watch." Here he looked directly at the Rhodian, saying, "Bring me a rock or three and we can go up to the *agger* and I'll show you."

"Well, I will be dipped in shit," explained Hermagoras, standing on the *agger* next to Josephus. "Do it again!"

With a shrug, Josephus loaded another fist-sized rock from the river bank into the pouch of his staff sling. With his left side pointed downrange, the *medicus* rocked back onto a slightly bent right leg, twisting his torso to the right as he did so. He held the staff slightly below the middle point with his skilled hand, and near the base with his left one. Then suddenly, with explosive force, he whipped the staff forward with his hands at the same time he pushed off with his right leg and bent his torso to his left.

Almost too quickly for the eye to follow, the sling swung forward, the upper loop slipping off a sort of hook Josephus had carved at the end. The rock sailed off, accompanied by a whip-like crack as the now released loop end broke the sound barrier.

For about a fast count of three the rock flew, before crashing to the ground five hundred or so feet away.

"And I'm not especially strong," said Josephus. "Put one of these in the hands of your legionaries and you will see a better range. Also, different length slings and different weight projectiles give different results. Shape can matter, too. Experiment a little."

Marcus Caelius whispered to Silvanus, "What do you think?"

"I think I want to volunteer my new cohort to learn this... this staff sling. Attach the missile cohort to me for us to train together and we can do this thing the Jew suggested: bait the Scythians in and then pound them silly with big damned rocks."

"You're it, then," Caelius agreed. "I'll clear it with the legate. *Medicus* Josephus?"

"Yes?"

"I'd like you to talk the Twelfth Cohort through making their own and get them started on training. Can the hospital spare you for a day or two?"

"Should be able to. Everything's pretty routine at the moment."

Smoke from a score of fires told of baking ceramic *glandes*—the area had huge deposits of excellent clay—for both the Rhodian slings and the staff slings. Wagons creaked up from the riverbank, fully loaded with round or ovoid fist-sized rocks from the rivers. Still other wagons brought in cut grass to feed the animals once a siege commenced, if it would.

Farther out, the animals were moved from pasture to pasture, under those of the Argippaeans not detailed to distant scouting. They were intended to denude any area of grass that might have fed the Scythians' horses or kine. Caelius didn't expect the Scythians to starve. What he did expect was that they'd have to disperse to keep their animals fed and that in that dispersion there *might* be an opportunity for the legion to strike.

Though most of the men and facilities were still under leather tents, the stockade and towers would be complete within two days, composed of stout twelve- to fifteen-inch logs. A fortnight longer would see them faced with mudbrick that was brought up from the river in a steady stream. Inside the stockade, a walkway had been erected, broad enough for a line of soldiers two deep to stand, backed up by another two-deep line of staff slingers. Ladders ran from the ground to the walkway.

At the corners, at the gates, and spaced out a bowshot in between, arose towers on earthen platforms jutting out slightly ahead of the main *agger*. Mudbrick could not be used on these to any good effect, so the wood had been covered with animal skins, to be kept wetted down against fire. Some of the towers held scorpions from First Cohort. Others were set up for archers to fire from loops cut through the walls. Bolts for the scorpions were massed by each piece of artillery. All of the scorpions were under leather tarps, partly for camouflage but mostly to protect the twisted skeins that powered them.

Spaced out inside the camp, in the *intervallum*, on raised earthen platforms, were larger and more powerful legionary artillery, stone- and incendiary-throwing *tormenta*, assembled from trees cut down locally and iron parts carried in the *impedimenta*. Large stones, somewhat shaped by hand, were piled in rough pyramids to feed the *tormenta*.

Stone circles, already piled with wood, above which stood cauldrons on tripods, were positioned at regular intervals on the walkway. Some of the cauldrons were filled with water, still others with sand. None contained oil as, even with the butter brought back by Gisco, there just wasn't more than enough for minimal culinary purposes.

From the walls, outward, a series of traps and obstacles were laid out. Their purpose was not to stop the enemy, but to slow him down to make him an easier target for ranged weapons, to damage his order, hence his discipline and morale, while also making it extremely difficult to carry a scaling ladder up to the wall. Any one of Caesar's legionaries from the Siege of Alesia would have recognized the form and the purpose of the various obstacles and traps.

These included, looking from the walls, outward, long poles driven into the *agger*, spaced at less width than a man's, which would make getting to the walls difficult, while the gaps in the line of those poles would leave the attackers open to missile fire from the walls and towers. Past those was the *fossa*, the ditch. It had been modified, however, to have sharpened stakes—*cippi*, in the Roman slang—at the bottom and along the friendly side. More *cippi*, in belts, ranged past the *fossa*. Beyond the *cippi* were *lilia*, hidden and camouflaged from plain view but with sharpened stakes to impale the unwary. There were arranged in a belt eight deep, in a quincunx formation.

Spurs, *spinae*, defended the *lilia*. And beyond that was a field of mixed chevaux-de-frise and sundry other obstacles and traps.

From the gates, however, zigzag paths through the obstacles were left bare. Though easy to see from the walls and towers, or once someone was in them, they were considerably harder to see from ground level outside of them. These were especially well covered by artillery.

The only thing Marcus Caelius had wanted that could not be produced were caltrops, because there simply wasn't enough iron in the camp left over for any. *But if ever we get near a source of iron...*

"The problem is, though," said Caelius to the legate, the two of them standing atop a tower and looking south, "the problem is that we don't really know how horse nomads conduct a siege. Will they even try to assault the walls or will they simply make it impossible for us to go outside to forage? Given that they live off their horses and their flocks, for which the grass provides all they need, is there any possibility of our limiting their provisioning in the slightest? We've got discipline, so we probably won't get sick to any great extent. But they're nomads who usually move before disease can start. If they hunker down for a siege, will disease catch up to them?"

"Top," said Gaius Pompeius, "I wish to fuck I knew."

Twelfth Cohort and the senior surgeon were all well outside the western wall of the camp, past the hundred and fifty or so double paces of the obstacles and traps.

"All right," said Josephus to the ranks of the Twelfth Cohort, "now you're going to use your daggers to cut a hook in the top just like the one I'm passing around."

The men had already cut their staffs to about shoulder height, and trimmed them down to the minimum thickness that could still be counted on not to break under the strain. In addition, one end of a sling was attached about a handsbreadth down from the business end. That attachment cord went to a leather cup, no larger than required to hold a half pound stone. From the cup ran a slightly longer length of cord, ending in a loop.

With that, he gave his staff sling over to Silvanus, who gave it to the right front man of the cohort. He looked at it from a couple of angles, passed it on, and began carving on the end of his staff with his *pugio*.

For the while it took for his sling to pass down the ranks, Josephus flitted from soldier to soldier, offering hints and guidance wherever needed. It was over an hour before the last hook had been carved.

"All right," repeated the *medicus*. "Now, I need a volunteer."

"I'll volunteer," said the junior centurion, Titus Vorenus.

"You sure, Centurion?" Josephus asked. "You were on light duty not so long ago."

"Yes, *medicus*, I am sure, because if these pussies can't out-shoot a sick man they'll deserve to be decimated."

That got a pretty enthusiastic round of laughter from the men.

"As you wish, then. Come on up."

When Vorenus had made his way up from his previous position behind the rear rank, Josephus did a quick inspection of the staff sling. He then showed the centurion the proper position, returned the staff, and talked him into that position.

Picking up a smooth, spherical rock of a little under three inches in diameter, Josephus announced, quite loudly, "Until we can find a goodly deposit of lead, or until the ceramic *glandes* are ready, or, for that matter, after the *glandes* run out, you're going to have to be able to use rocks. That means judging both the weight and the resistance of the air to the shape of the rock. Here, Centurion, hold this."

With that, Josephus passed over the rock. "Weigh it in your hand. Feel around the surface to see how smooth it is. Once you've done this three or four thousand times, you'll know without even thinking about it how to judge how far any given rock will go, and how much to increase or decrease the power of your cast.

"Now lift the butt end of the staff while you let the business end go down. Now, when I tell you to, I want you to pull down on the butt and rotate the end with the sling as hard and as fast as you possibly can. Ready?"

Vorenus shifted his body around, almost catlike, as if loosening and readying his muscles for a major effort.

"Ready," he said.

"LOOSE!" commanded Josephus.

The staff made a distinct whooshing sound, following by the whipcrack of the sling as it tore through the air. Centrifugal force pinned the rock into the pouch until, at apogee, the loop slipped off the hook. At that point, the rock flew loose of the pouch, continuing on down range at a speed much greater than that of any bow-launched arrow in the legion.

Josephus, Vorenus, and every man in the cohort strained to follow the path of the rock. They'd have lost it completely except that, after hitting the ground, it bounced up a dozen feet into the air some fifty double paces downrange.

"Not at all bad, Centurion," congratulated Josephus. To Silvanus, he said, "That wagonload of rocks is all for you. I'd suggest you just work on range for the rest of today. We can start off improving accuracy tomorrow."

Twelfth Cohort was lined up in two ranks. Each man standing in the front rank held his staff sling. Those in the back rank had placed their staff slings on the ground, holding in their arms and hands a dozen rocks each. It was their job both to pass rocks to the forward ranks and to coach them on their accuracy in hitting the logs.

At various ranges from twenty-five double paces to one hundred and twenty, logs of man-height stood upright, held by crosspieces nailed to their bases.

"Slingers," commanded Silvanus, "load your slings...assume position. At the seventy-five double-pace targets...Ready...LOOSE!"

The air was filled with both the whooshing of the staves and the crack of the slings, over which was added the somewhat muted displacement of the air as over a hundred and fifty deadly stones flew downrange. Not all reached the hundred-and-twenty-five-yards-distant targets and some, a lesser number, overflew them.

There were not many hits, maybe five from that whole half of a cohort, but, equally important, there were still a lot of near misses.

"And, boys," encouraged Silvanus, "don't be discouraged. Remember that your targets are going to be a lot more than man-sized, so a near miss is actually a probable hit on *somebody*. Now reload."

INTERLUDE

Exploratory Spacecraft 67(&%#@, Several Hundred Znargs Above the Teutoburg Forest

"Annnd...caught him!" clicked Red to Blossom. "Now to reel him in." In this, Red was alluding to a game popular among the young males of his species, involving cast javelins on stout lines, and large predatory fish. It was not a game without its risks, though the ultimate risks to the fish were greater.

"This is more fun than *zingfurging*!" he admitted, with an exclamatory whistle.

"Will you be able to return his mind to his body in one go?" trilled Blossom.

"Nooo...no, I don't think so. I'm going to try short pulls, or at least one short pull, first."

Burwash, East Sussex, England, May 1906

The strange thing was that the room was lit up as bright as day while, looking through the *fenestra*, it was obviously pitch-black outside. Someone in the room was singing, but he couldn't see the singer despite the light. The song mentioned:

I wish the queen of England

Whoever that is.

Would write to me in time
And place me in some regiment...

By now, Calvus was fairly well prepared for any mental state, from dead asleep to wide awake, from hopeful to filled with a sense of doom. What he hadn't up to now encountered was someone so fully concentrated on the job at hand that, though wide awake, he had no idea Calvus was there. Calvus was thus privileged to hear a long litany of cursing—mild cursing, yes, but cursing all the same. He could sense his new host's frustration.

Looking through his host's eyes, the *haruspex* read:

When I left home for Lalage's sake
By the Legion's road to Rimini.

After reading a few more lines, Calvus couldn't help himself. "This just doesn't work," he said, into his host's mind. "No, not at all. In the first place, by using Rimini you are misplacing the accent on the second syllable, but we Romans place it on the first. And then this whole notion of a girl waiting for a soldier of the legions? No, no; no girl waits for twenty or twenty-five years and no boy enlisting into the legions is stupid enough to think she will."

The poet brushed off the *haruspex* with, "Poetic license. I want my people to have some feel for the lot of the soldiers on the far-flung limits of *our* Empire, and our troops come back, as the Nightingale song says, after 'seven long years.' And, now you've ruined my concentration and JUST WHO THE HELL ARE YOU?"

"Calvus," replied the *haruspex*, while thinking, *How many times have I made this introduction?* "Calvus Appius, seconded to Eighteenth Legion."

"Well, if you don't know how many times, how am I supposed to?"

"You could hear that?" asked Calvus.

"After a fashion. Why shouldn't I be able to? After all, you're hearing me when I'm not actually *saying* a bloody word."

"It's just that I thought it was different, speaking to the mind, or the *animus,* and thinking to myself. And I apologize for disturbing you. I don't seem to have any choice in who I disturb, but I should have seen from what you were doing that you were busy. Again, sincerely, I apologize."

"Oh, never mind; it wasn't like I was making any progress. And for just the reasons you said. I *know* that the accent goes on the first syllable and I know that legionaries enlisted, near enough, for the huge and overwhelming bulk of their adult lives."

"Well, as you say, poetic license will carry you a good ways. Maybe I can help. There *was* a legionary marching song something like this. Let me see if I can remember. Ah, here we go."

In his host's mind Calvus began to sing:

When I left home for the Empire's sake
Up the *Via Aurelia* to *Pisae*
I thought my mother's heart would break
When we hugged and both said our goodbyes
Just before I left home for *Pisae*.
    And I've tramped Spain
    And I've tramped Gaul
    And *Pannonia*
    Where the snowflakes fall...

"Hmmm...I might be able to use a good deal of that, with modifications. Different language and all. Oh, my manners; I am Gigger."

"What are you people, Gigger?"

"We're called English or, if male, Englishmen."

"Oh, that's funny. I was just visiting another Englishman. Said his name was Gilbert...umm...Chester-something. Good fellow."

Calvus looked through Gigger's eyes at the objects scattered about his writing table. One item, carelessly placed, was some kind of a machine, with a handle and a fluted cylinder. It was sufficiently outside of Calvus' experience that he didn't even think to ask about it. Instead...

"What's that?" he asked.

"What's what?"

"That thing that looks like a box with a hinged cover."

The Englishman tapped a book. "This?" he asked.

"Yes, that."

"It's a book...Let me think: you're used to scrolls that roll up, right?"

"Yes. Only those. Well . . . we *do* write—really only keep notes—on wax tablets that are sometimes bound together at one side. And some say that Caesar—Julius, not Augustus—made a similar notebook of papyrus bound on one side. But . . . could you hold it up and show it to me?"

"Surely." Gigger took up the book and showed the spine, bearing faint letters and a single number, embossed, apparently, in gold.

"I see the letters through your eyes," said Calvus, then admitted, "but the words mean nothing to me. Could you . . . ?"

"They say, *The History of the Decline and Fall of the Roman Empire*."

"Oh. How depressing. Or it would be if I hadn't seen so much of it myself. There are individual sheets inside that thing?"

"Yes," said Gigger, then turned the book around, opened it, and shuffled a hundred or so pages.

"The slave scribes must be very skilled around here to have made such tiny and easy to read letters. So much information that book must contain, hundreds of scrolls' worth."

"Thousands in the entire set, but we don't use slaves anymore. Thank God. It's done by machine."

"Could you show me?"

"I wish I could; I've never seen them close up. I understand they're very complex, though this one, a first edition, was done on a simpler machine.

"And then there are the money presses."

"Money presses?" asked Calvus. "You mean mints where coins are struck?"

"Oh, we do that, too, of course. But most of our money is printed like . . . hmmm . . . wait a second."

Gigger took a thin leather container from his pocket and pulled from it a ten-pound note, holding it up in front of his own eyes so that Calvus could see.

"This is a ten-pound note," Gigger explained. "In theory you might think it's worth an actual ten pounds of silver. In fact, it is not. It's actually worth . . . mmm . . . maybe two and a half pounds of silver. And it has one great virtue: carefully done, and with restraint, it increases the money supply so that people can conduct more commerce."

"Oh, dear," said the *animus* of Calvus, suddenly very faint.

"I sense you are leaving," said Gigger.

"Yes, I never get to stay long." That last was said in what amounted to a whisper.

"Would you mind if I used you in a story? I'd have to change your name to Puck..."

CHAPTER NINE

About the Sauromatae, the story is as follows. When
the Greeks were at war with the Amazons (whom
the Scythians call Oiorpata, a name signifying in our
tongue "killers of men," for in Scythian a man is "*oior*"
and to kill is "*pata*"), the story runs that after their
victory on the Thermodon they sailed away carrying
in three ships as many Amazons as they had been able
to take alive; and out at sea the Amazons attacked the
crews and killed them. But they knew nothing about
ships, or how to use rudder or sail or oar; and with the
men dead, they were at the mercy of waves and winds,
until they came to the Cliffs by the Maeetian lake;
this place is in the country of the free Scythians. The
Amazons landed there, and set out on their journey
to the inhabited country, and seizing the first troop of
horses they met, they mounted them and raided the
Scythian lands.

—Herodotus, *The Histories*, 4.110

In camp in the land of the Scythians, date unknown

Maeonius fretted impatiently at the edge of a copse on a bit of
ground rising slightly above the endless plain. When the dark
cloud had first appeared on the southern horizon he'd thought it
had been just another storm on the steppe. When it got closer,
even moving against the wind, he'd dispatched two of his best
scouts to investigate. That had been early the day before yesterday. They were now overdue. At the same time he'd sent back

two messengers to the camp, to warn them of what he suspected was coming.

The Palmyrene horse were spread out in small detachments along the hundred-degree arc defined by the great river, centered on the camp, and at a distance of about a hundred miles from the camp.

Given the number of remounts the Scythians were said to keep, there was essentially no chance that the pickets could outrun them if they were allowed to get very close. For this reason, those Argippaeans not on herding duty were stationed in echelons closer to the camp, each echelon with enough remounts for the cavalry pickets. When pressed, they'd ride back to the next remount station, change horses, and gallop on.

The pickets and the remount stations had two big advantages. One was that they could be pretty sure of what was, hence of what was not, behind them, while the Scythians could not be sure of what was in front of them. The other was that they'd be galloping for their lives, while the Scythians would only be chasing them to kill them.

In addition, the Gallic and legionary horse, in three groups of about one hundred and twenty, lay in ambush in three different positions. The positions were widely spaced—indeed, the steppe didn't offer all that many good ambush positions—so it was incumbent upon the Palmyrenes to lead the Scythians into ambush if the pursuing groups were small enough for one hundred and twenty cavalry to destroy. And, if they were not that small, the Palmyrenes were to send warning messengers to the Gallic and legionary cavalry to bug out, then continue running for the camp.

Maeonius' first large hint of the fate of the two scouts he'd sent out came in the form of a barrage of arrows, whistling through the air with malevolent intent. Some bounced off the trees of the copse. Others bounced off the armor of the cavalrymen. Still others buried themselves harmlessly in the ground. But five found the bodies of unarmored horses while two more found their marks through chinks in the armor and into the bodies of Maeonius' men.

Of the two men who were hit, one took an arrow to the throat. He sank in a gurgling mess to the ground. The other had his arm sliced, drawing a gasp and a curse but not much blood.

Not a lot of time to think. Where did they...oh, that dry streambed. Didn't think it would hide much. What does it mean...what...oh, they left their horses behind. Gives us a minute or two to build up a lead.

He briefly considered the man with the arrow in his throat. "Leonidas is a goner," Maeonius said. "But...we can't leave him for the Scythians. Pick him up and run for your lives!" he shouted.

Then Maeonius saw two men trying to remove arrows from their horses. "Forget it," he told them. "Those arrows are barbed with dull barbs. You try to remove them and you'll hurt your horse worse than the arrow did. Worse, you'll just spread the poison. Now run!"

Bursting from the north side of the copse, the Palmyrenes galloped for the remount station. Dust and clods of dirt and grass kicked up behind them. This far out the grass was still lush enough, rising calf high, for animals to subsist on.

Before reaching the remounts, first one horse, then another, and then all five that had been hit voiced vast pain. After this they crumpled to the ground, shaking and writing like human epileptics.

At that time, Maeonius decided that Leonidas, who had since died, was too much of a burden to bear, given that they were going to have to double up on some horses. While shuffling riders around, Maeonius looked behind.

Ah, shit, more than a hundred of them. That's too large a target to risk ambushing without a lot more advantages than we have. And if they're anything like us, they'll just shoot and run, shoot and run.

He told off two pairs to ride to the ambush positions to their left and right front and tell the Gauls and the legionary cavalry to leg it for the camp. While they were galloping off, the one wounded Palmyrene grasped his slightly wounded arm and then began to shriek in agony. He fell to the ground and began to convulse like the wounded horses.

With the Scythians closing and the wounded man begging for help when there was no help to give, Maeonius dismounted and, following a gentle whisper, cut the man's throat.

To the rest he ordered: "Now RUN!"

❖   ❖   ❖

Both Marcus Caelius and Gaius Pompeius stood on the right-most tower by the southern gate as the cavalry screen cantered in, leading a mass of worn-out horses and with a number of both horses and men sporting arrows lodged in bodies. Each commander, in turn, climbed the tower to report in. The gist was that none of the ambushes had worked, all of the pickets on screen duty had been engaged, and, in Maeonius' words, "They kicked our asses."

Caelius said, "It's not like we expected to be able to deal with five or ten times our numbers in cavalry and worse than that in horse archers. At least we got the food animals, horses, and *ngekud* back into camp before the Scythians showed up. And it could have been a lot worse."

"It's still pretty bad. And remember, all of those men and horses shot with arrows? They're probably going to die."

"Tell me something I don't know, sir."

"How long before their main body arrives, do you think?" asked Gaius Pompeius.

"A hundred miles? Being pulled by their version of the *ngekud*? A week, easily. But their forward parties, the ones that trounced our cavalry screen? They'll be here within two to four hours."

"Be interesting to see," said Gaius, "their reaction to our having removed, eaten, or destroyed all the grass within ten to fifteen miles."

"I think what we're going to see is a lot of pissed-off Scythians."

Atrixtos climbed the ladder and reported in. He'd been on the westernmost ambush site and, like the other two, had been pulled in because they were faced with just too many Scythians.

"It was them," Atrixtos announced, "the women Bat-Erdene warned us about. About three hundred of them, would be my guess. No body armor. Nothing above the waist, as a matter of fact. And never did three hundred sets of tits—no, they all had both tits—look less appealing.

"They're faster on their horses than even the Scythian men are, probably because they're lighter than the men. Their bows don't range as far, which is a damned good thing because they almost caught up to us."

In summation, Atrixtos said, "Mean bitches, too. One of my men had his horse break a leg in some kind of animal burrow, it must have been. We couldn't go back for him. *Him* the women caught up to. They shot him up with arrows, in his extremities, then scalped him alive. Then they started skinning him alive, too. We could hear him screaming for a mile. We ever catch one of those cunts and I'm going to personally oversee her getting raped by one of the *ngekud*. And after that, we Gauls are going to do a fair imitation of you Romans and we're going to nail the bitch to a cross and watch her die by inches over days."

"What," asked Marcus Caelius, "you're not going to put her in a wicker man and light it on fire?"

"Too easy," Atrixtos replied, without hesitation. "And besides, we don't have any druids to officiate."

"I can see where that might be a problem," said Caelius. "Tell you what, we'll lend you a good, experienced *optio* to assist with the crucifixion."

The Scythians appeared outside the defenses in three columns. Whether this was just an artifact of there being three objective stations, left, right, and center, or whether they'd scouted out and pegged the cavalry screen before committing, none on the legion's side could say.

As soon as they arrived, the Scythians charged the defenses, trying to get within bowshot.

"Sound 'Hold your fire,'" ordered Caelius to the *cornice* standing by. Gaius Pompeius gave him a quizzical glance.

"We want them to commit to a major attack before opening up on them so we can really hurt them when they do."

"They're going to run into the obstacle belt and figure out what that means pretty quickly, then," Gaius said.

"Hmmm...fair point. Thiaminus?"

"Here, *Dominus*," said Caelius' freedman.

"Go and bring us the leaders of the missile cohort and the archer maniple within it."

On the southern and western walls, about a score of the Scythians had managed to run their horses into one or more of the obstacles. The beasts writhed in pain. The Romans didn't care about that one way or the other, most of them. They were definitely interested, however, in the ones thrown from their horses onto the *cippi*, the stakes, the hooks, and the chevaux-de-frise.

Zalmoxis and his commander, Horatius Jovis, clambered up

the ladder to the tower's platform. Zalmoxis wore a *linothorax* reinforced with some metal whereas Jovis wore mail.

"You sent for us, sir?" asked Jovis.

Gaius gestured toward Caelius, who answered, "The legate would like you to use archery to make it as difficult as possible for the Scythians to clear the obstacles or even lanes through the obstacles. Can you do this?"

Zalmoxis answered, "We can make it difficult and dangerous. We cannot make it impossible."

"Okay, go do that, then. In doing it, do everything you can to avoid being struck by their arrows. They're all poisoned."

"Didn't we capture some poison from the three we captured or killed?" asked Jovis.

"Yes," said Caelius. "Three little jars. They're at the *valetudinarium* being studied by Josephus."

"He doesn't need three to study," said Zalmoxis. "Let us have two."

"Why, in particular?" asked the legate.

"Several reasons," answered the archer. "One is simple revenge. Another is seeing how well they work. But a third, and this may be the most important one, is that if we can hit one with a poisoned arrow and then see that one's face again, we can be pretty sure that there at least *is* an antidote."

"Do it," said Gaius. "Use it on the Amazons at the western boundary of obstacles."

Josephus scowled. "Do not, I repeat do NOT, get this stuff on your skin. Even small amounts will probably make you sick."

"Understood, *medicus*," agreed Zalmoxis. "Hold it in a spare scrap of leather, do you think, as the boys file by and dip their arrows?"

"Double the leather and position yourself so that they cannot drip it on your hands, arms, or feet. Or theirs."

"That bad, huh?"

"It might be. Do you want to take the chance?"

"No. Hey, is this jar gold?" Zalmoxis asked.

"Yes," the surgeon answered. "Now ask yourself: what kind of crap is so toxic that it has to be kept in a jar even any acid but *aqua regia* won't eat through?"

"Right. Got it. I'll be careful."

"One more reminder to be careful," said the *medicus*. He opened the jar and held it under Zalmoxis' nose.

"Gods, that's awful!"

The stockade around the camp was crenellated, with some logs sticking up a man's height over the walkway and others low enough to allow the hurling of a *pilum*.

Zalmoxis stood with his back to a section of wall, under the walkway. That section consisted of three stout logs, a foot and a quarter across, each, with mud chinking the inevitable gaps between them. Outside the quantity of mudbricks had never been enough to make them reach high enough to do much good.

Zalmoxis' arms were covered with thick leather. Likewise the hands, grasping one of the poison pots, wore winter gloves and held the pot in an additional two-foot-square piece of leather. His assistant, Ajax, was likewise shielded. Like the men, both wore *linothoraxes*, torso armor made of multiple glued or sewn together pieces of linen. Also like the men, both had their right sides distorted by the mass of muscle required for archery with strong bows. Some of the *linothoraxes* had some metal scale reinforcement over part of their surface. The thick linen—over four tenths of an inch thick—provided as much protection as a tenth of an inch of bronze, at about a third of the weight, and for a small fraction of the price. The only real disadvantage over bronze was that the armor needed beeswaxing every six weeks or so. And it was not very effective against extremely sharp points and blades, on higher end metal.

In front of them, two overstrength centuries of archers stood in ranks. Behind them, very occasional arrows *thunk*ed into the upright logs. It didn't sound as if the arrows that managed to strike the palisade had much power.

Zalmoxis addressed both centuries. "Boys, here's what we're going to do. You are going to walk by either myself or Ajax and carefully, and I mean *very* carefully, dip one arrow, and then another into these jars. The jars are poisonous... and I mean really poisonous, so do not get any on your skin and do not, oh, nonononono, accidentally prick yourselves with the points or cut yourselves with the sides.

"After you poison two arrows, and let them dry—no, do NOT shake them dry—you are going to mount the walkway and, bending over and keeping your bows horizontal so nobody sees you, take positions on either side of the gaps. Then, at command, you are going to expose yourself no more than absolutely necessary, draw, aim, and put some of these half-dressed women into the cemetery. Indeed, I want you to do your level best to put them *all* into the cemetery.

"The women supposedly use weak bows, so you're going to have range and power on them. You're armored, so, while a wound, even a small one, to wherever on your body is exposed, might kill you, you're going to be invulnerable anywhere you are armored. They're not invulnerable at all.

"Also, I want you to go for the females actually trying to use their bows, first."

Zalmoxis continued, "Now you're going to take some fair hits on your *linothoraxes*. Get those arrows out of your armor and drop them on the ground on this side of the palisade, so we can reuse them. Look down before you do it. And do it before you inadvertently scratch yourselves. Now, if everybody is ready, start filing by."

Atrixtos joined Zalmoxis, just as the latter was about to climb to the walkway. "I owe these bitches," the Gaul explained. The archer nodded his understanding, then commenced the short climb.

Once he had come abreast of the first of his men, which is to say the last one to have mounted the walkway, Zalmoxis filled his lungs. "Prepare to looossse! LOOSE!"

Almost two hundred and forty archers popped up around the crenellations, finished drawing their bows, picked their marks, and let their arrows fly. While those were still in the air, they nocked their other poisoned arrows, picked more targets, and let those fly. Then they all ducked back, except for one young fool who stayed out to see the results and got an arrow in the eye for his trouble. He fell backward, toppled off the walkway, and plummeted to the ground.

The immediate cessation of covering fire from the Amazons, coupled with intense shrieking from many female throats, said that the outgoing fire had been quite effective. Zalmoxis risked taking a fatal hit to look halfway around the edge of the merlon, the raised portion of the crenellation. About a score of the women lay on the ground, apparently dead, and this without the poison having been remotely necessary. Farther out, about sixty or seventy double paces away, still more sat or lay screaming their agonies to an unfeeling Heaven. Others could be seen sporting arrows and running for their horses.

"Ninety of them, give or take, I think," said Atrixtos, peering out around Zalmoxis. "Not bad. Puts us ahead—in numbers, anyway. Though we have a debt to settle in terms of pain that they'll never forget once we settle it."

"Hmmm; I wonder why they didn't extract the arrows before the poison could take full hold of them."

"Barbs," answered Atrixtos. "All of their arrows are barbed. Probably can't imagine the existence of arrows that aren't barbed."

"That might just be it," the archer agreed.

"I wonder," mused the Gaul, "if any of them will be alive long enough for us to grab them and crucify them."

A steady drum-drum-drumming came from three camps ranging across the front of the Roman camp and well away from it. Whether this was intended to unnerve the defenders, to buck up the attackers, or to propitiate their gods none, not even Bat-Erdene, could say.

Looking for a captive on whom to vent their hatred, Atrixtos and fifty of his Gauls crept through the narrowly cracked gate after sunset and before moonrise. They'd all covered their red or blond hair with soot from the fires.

"Remember," he told them before venturing out, "we want a captive, yes, but we also want their bows, their arrows, and any of those little pots of poison they might have. Gold would be nice, too, but don't risk your lives over it."

Walking very carefully to avoid the traps, the Gauls went in small parties from one to another of the Amazons. They didn't find any alive, but did recover forty-two little gold pots full of poison, a like number of quivers with, typically, between forty and fifty poisoned arrows each, and seventy-six bows that were really too light to be of much use to anybody but women, girls, and barely pubescent boys. They took these anyway; maybe the tarts would find some use for them.

Briefly, Atrixtos considered skinning the Amazons and leaving those flayed corpses on the edge of the obstacle field for their sisters to find.

Ah, but what would be the point? These little shits wouldn't feel a thing and any leather we made from them would likely be accursed.

Instead, he had the corpses carried to the edge of the obstacle field and dumped in a heap. *Let the Scythians worry about them.*

Then, with a signaling whistle, Atrixtos counted his men, one by one, back through the gate. A faint light emerged from the crack, coming from a number of much brighter torches on the friendly side. These were to identify each man by face and to kill any enemies who tried to infiltrate with them.

"No live ones?" asked Marcus Caelius, after the last of the patrol had been counted back through.

"Sadly not," answered Atrixtos. "We did get some useful booty, though."

"And the gold?"

"They'll be piling it in Privatus' cart," replied the Gaul. "Yes, I reminded them of the penalty for private looting, and emphasized it by saying I'd stake any man found guilty outside the camp and leave him for the Scythians.

"Also, I'm not sure what to do with the bows we captured. They're pretty light."

Caelius considered this for a moment, then said, "Maybe we'll issue one or two per maniple, along with some arrows. After all, any bow is better than no bow."

The bodies of the Amazons disappeared the following night. Somewhat distantly, Zalmoxis wished he'd thought of ambushing the pile of corpses but, ultimately? *There just aren't that many competent archers here with the legion, while the Scythians have no shortage. Besides, the shits did us a favor by removing those bitches before the flies could start breeding on the bodies. Doubt they realized that, though.*

The main Scythian camp, when it finally showed up, dwarfed the Roman fort by an order of magnitude. Unlike the Romans, though, it wasn't very dense on the ground and, instead of a ditch and wall, made do with a wagon laager.

As for people, even the sharpest-eyed legionaries couldn't make out that kind of detail. Meanwhile, the Scythians began continuous parades outside the fort—outside of bowshot, too, for that matter—while drums beat incessantly in what by now was clearly a pretty obvious attempt to try to intimidate the Roman occupants.

"I know we should wait," moaned Quintus Junius Fulvius, the chief of the light artillery, standing atop a tower with Caelius and the legate, "but you cannot imagine how much I'd like to wipe the certain smirks off those barbarian faces."

"I understand," said Gaius Pompeius, "but we need to keep our little surprises for when they try to rush us."

"And they *will* try to rush us," Marcus Caelius said, with total confidence.

"How do you know, Top?" asked Fulvius.

"Because they've stopped shooting arrows at us. In other words, they've figured out that shooting arrows at us is only arming us better against them, while few of them have much armor to ward off an arrow. So, it's starve us out, and that's a race they can't be sure to win; kill us with thirst, but with the river at our backs and a walled pathway down to it, that's not going to happen; *or* try to take the walls."

"You sure they've never heard of artillery?" asked Junius.

"Well," replied Caelius, "they might have heard of it. But the knowledge to build it? The skill to use it? Color me very skeptical. Fulvius?"

"Yeah," answered the artilleryman, "it is something of a dark art. And, yeah, I agree: they're not likely to know how to build it or use it. It's not like any of us have been teaching them."

Not long into the siege, with a south wind blowing from the Scythian camp, an unusual smell washed over the Roman fort. It had some of the attributes of polecat scent, coupled to unburied latrine pit and rotting corpse.

"What is that crap?" asked Marcus Caelius, during the nightly command and staff meeting.

"Cannabis," replied Josephus.

"And that would be?"

"It's a drug, something like *opos*, though not as strong. Almost impossible to kill yourself with it, whereas with *opos* it's pretty easy. Induces a strong euphoria. Also had some interesting side effects. For example, if you have a patient who cannot or will not eat, put them in a closed room and burn some of the cannabis. Their appetite usually gets restored because their pain fades but, beyond that, they just get ravenously hungry afterward. No, we don't know why."

"That's the Scythian name for it," said Bat-Erdene, "'cannabis.' Them heat up rocks, take into sealed tents, and throw seeds onto hot stones. Seeds smolder. Usually in the course of a funeral. Them probably mourning those women fighters you killed. My people use less seed, more stems and leaves."

"How...hmm...what's the word?" wondered Gaius Pompeius. "How strong is the effect, *medicus*?"

"Really hard to say," replied Josephus. "There are different cultivars of different strengths, so I've been told. As far as I know, nobody really has a good idea of which ones are stronger and which weaker, except by reference to a given plant. And then you don't know until it affects you or your patient."

Gaius Pompeius held up one finger. "*Praefectus Castrorum?*"

"Sir?" responded Caelius.

"All exterior patrols are cancelled."

Caelius sounded incredulous. "Sir?"

"I'll explain later."

"So why end exterior patrolling?" asked Marcus Caelius, after the meeting had broken up. "Not questioning your right to do so, Legate, but deeply curious as to why."

"Because when they try to rush us, we're going to kill a lot of them, right?"

"Well, we certainly hope to, sir. But, yes, we're going to murder the bastards in job lots."

"And if we kill enough of them *and* manage to hang onto the camp, they're all going to dope themselves to the gills, right?"

"Yesss..." Caelius was doubtful but... "That seems to be what Bat-Erdene suggests."

"And then, that very night, we can attack their camp, but only if we've let them get so overconfident that they're not putting out pickets to watch our gates—or us, generally. Oh, no, we're going to be placid, unambitious rubes. Right up until they dope themselves insensate."

"You think we can cross the three miles to the edge of their camp without being detected?" asked Caelius.

"I think we've got a pretty fair chance. German cohort out front to screen—sneaky bastards, as I believe you've said more than once—wear cloaks to help deaden the noise . . . maybe make a special effort to dampen all the things that make noise, too. Yes, a pretty fair chance."

"There is a downside, though," said the camp prefect. "If we're not doing any aggressive patrolling, they're going to come right up to the obstacles and start clearing paths."

"We can still make them pay a price for that."

The Romans could hear the Scythian preparations for an assault.

It was, as it turned out, a lot worse than just clearing paths. Not that the Scythians didn't do that. But they also moved up log shelters—*plutei*, in the Latin—to allow the archers to snipe while being at no serious disadvantage to the Romans on the walls. Maybe worse, they put drummers into those shelters to pound the Romans' eardrums.

Meanwhile, every night there were probes, attempts to get ladders up on the walls. Attempts to set fire to the walls, that happened, too.

"On the bright side of life, though," said Marcus Caelius, "the arrogant fucks haven't tried either to camouflage those things, neither have they fireproofed them. So tell me, Fulvius, how do we deal with that when the time comes?"

"Well, Prefect," said Quintus Fulvius, "there's a technique for it. Doesn't have a name, so far as I know, but like a lot of our arcane knowledge, it gets passed down as if from father to son. That's how I learned it.

"Basically, someone gets up on the walls and gets himself in perfect alignment between the *tormentum* and the target. The *tormentum* crew then aims at him. He also has to make an estimate of range, and also pace off the range from the wall to the *tormentum*. It's not exactly precision work, but we ought to be able to silence most of those shelters when the assault comes."

"Rocks, ceramics, or incendiaries?"

Fulvius considered that. "We don't have too many incendiaries, basically just what we could get from boiling down pine sap. Wouldn't even have those except that the chief *medicus* and the *veterinarius,* both, asked for some, independently, for medicinal use. And then you demanded a few hundred *congii* for lamp fuel. Since we had it all set up, we went ahead and boiled down enough for one hundred and twenty shots and had the ceramic kiln make us some one-*congius* pots. We've really got no other use for the incendiaries, so may as well use them.

"And before you ask, we'll make some test shots before we really open up to make sure we've got the slings right and won't hit our own people on the wall."

"Or burn the fucking wall down," said Caelius.

"Goes without saying, doesn't it? Thing is, though, sir, that sometimes shit just goes wrong."

"Tell me about it. But you make sure nothing is allowed to go wrong."

"Best I can," agreed Fulvius, "but some things are in the gods' hands, and some of them are outright bastards."

It was the darkest of hours on a dark, dark night. None of the usual clientele were waiting for entrance outside, nor grunting their exertions inside, the compound; all were on guard or in reserve. Wrapped in a legionary cloak Lucius Pullo had acquired for her, Zaya popped her head out of the separate gate that opened into the small compound for the *meretrices*. Seeing nobody watching, she slipped out and closed the gate behind her.

Flitting from shadow to shadow, she found her way to the tent belonging to Pullo. He wasn't there but she sat down on his cot to wait.

She didn't have all that long to wait; she'd told Pullo she'd come to his tent for a good-luck screw before the coming fight. She'd come before and had every intention of coming again.

Zaya loathed the thought of money being taken from Pullo's account every time Twelfth Cohort's turn came at the field brothel. She kept careful count and every time she determined he'd had a full denarius withheld from his pay, she paid him a visit and left a coin to make up for it. The first time Pullo had tried to give the coin back. Accordingly, she'd turned on the tears and tried to make him understand in her poor Latin that only in this way could she show him he wasn't just a client.

I had never imagined what it meant to be in love, thought the girl. *Now I know: it is almost all pain and the little that isn't is madness.*

Pullo showed up about half an hour later. Though the tent was even darker than the open, outside, he sensed her presence and held his arms open for her.

"There's no time, love. The Twelfth is having to position itself close to the southwest corner, where we expect the Scythians to attack."

Understanding, she started to drop to her knees.

"Not even time for that, Zaya," he said, putting hands under her armpits and lifting her to her feet. "Though I wish..."

"What happens we lose?" she asked.

"That would be very bad," he said. "I'll be dead but what the Scythians would do to the women...doesn't bear thinking about."

"Give something kill self?" she pleaded. Without hesitation, Pullo slipped off the baldric that bore his *pugio*, and passed it over. Then he turned her toward the tent flap, swatted her on the posterior, and ordered, "Back to your compound, you; it's the safest place for you to be."

"These people could really amount to something with some group discipline," commented the *praefectus castrorum* to the legate.

Answered Gaius Pompeius, "They are, I admit, pretty good at coming up with practical solutions for the problems they can see."

Both men stood on the tower by the southern gate, the Porta Principalis Sinistra, taking turns peering through a vision slit in the tower walls. Just to be safe, the vision slit had its own dark wall behind it, to prevent anyone on the outside from knowing that someone was looking out, by the change in contrast.

What they saw were squads of Scythian riders, galloping back and forth across the plain, each dragging small cut-down trees behind them, and raising clouds of dust sufficient to choke camels. Beyond those clouds nobody in the camp could see what was going on. They could, however, all hear redoubled pounding from the drums.

Between the dust clouds and the obstacle belt, now sadly compromised where not outright cleared, the *plutei* were busy with archers, popping up and taking a shot, then ducking down again before return fire could find them.

For their part the Romans were saving their arrows—saving their archers, too, for that matter—and letting normal legionaries, who were in more plentiful supply, take the risks of glancing out to see what the Scythians were up to.

There were two rows of legionaries seated on the walkway, pressed up close enough to the crenellated wall to leave ample space for a man to walk. Centurions and *optios* glancing out kept up a running narrative to keep the men informed: "Just a dust cloud now...Watch out!...Those nasty archers are at it again..."

Cauldrons of boiling water and heated sand stood at intervals along the battlement.

Well behind the wall were eight of the legion's dozen *tormenta,* each crewed by ten men, including a noncom. There were fifteen incendiary pots by each, baked clay covered in some of the thick felt gained by trade with the Argippaeans. A goodly measure of turpentine stood ready to be poured onto the felt, as soon as they were ready to be launched. Also nearby was a small brazier with a fire going. Each *tormentum* had two spare crosspieces, to make replacements when, as would inevitably happen, the firing arm striking the crosspieces on the engines broke them. Finally, there was a barrel of water to douse the cup of the sling on which the turpentine-filled pots would sit.

Up on the wall, for each *tormentum* back in the *intervallum,* one legionary got himself as precisely as possible between his *tormentum* and one of the Scythians' *plutei.* It was on these men that the artillery pieces were aligned.

For their parts, collectively under the command of Quintus Silvanus, the Rhodian slingers, Thracian archers and Twelfth Cohort, the latter bearing their staff slings, were down at ground level waiting to be sent to wherever it looked like the Scythians would throw in their main effort.

"Remember the order of engagement," Silvanus intoned. "Slingers hurt them and bait them into coming closer. When they do, the slingers fall back behind cover. Then Twelfth Cohort rises up and drenches them with big rocks, once they are close enough. Finally, the archers shoot them in the ass as they run away."

One reason for making the archers shoot last was that nothing was as dangerous as a man who knew he was doomed to die, and in agony. That man would seek out death and seek out revenge as he was doing it. But hit them on their unarmored and unshielded backs as they run away? Those men would die out there, in despair, with no prospect of finding any easier death except through suicide.

"I wish to Hades we could see through smoke," cursed Marcus Caelius, backing away from the vision slit.

The legate pointed with one finger off to the right and high. "Maybe we can," he said.

"What? What are you talking...Oh. Oh, I see."

What Gaius Pompeius had seen, and the camp prefect was a bit late in seeing, was another cloud of dust, rising much higher than that called forth by the galloping riders.

"Are they going to hit the corner, the western wall, the western part of the southern wall, or all of the above?"

"I think 'all of the above,'" replied Gaius.

"Hmm...no, after the Amazons got their asses handed to them, they've never made an attempt on the western wall's obstacles. I think not that. I think the corner and the western part of the southern wall."

"All right," Gaius agreed, "makes sense. What now?"

"Now, sir, I think we have Quintus Fulvius start firing on the *plutei*, on that end of the wall and get Silvanus to bring his herd over there, too."

In the *valetudinarium*, Josephus used his spoon of Diocles to try to remove a presumptively poisoned arrow from the face of one of the legionaries, wounded on the wall by a Scythian archer firing from behind one of the *plutei*. The boy was thoroughly drugged with *opos*.

That legionary was not the only arrow casualty from the walls—half a dozen others awaited care. He was the worst, though.

The thing would have gone into this boy's brain, had it a little more power behind it...or he a less dense skull.

Making two small incisions, he used a probe to determine the dimensions of the arrowhead. Once he found them, he almost gave up in disgust.

The barbs exceed the width of my spoon of Diocles. It won't be of the slightest help in getting the head out. I wonder, am I doing this boy any favor to get it out, or will the poison he's already taken give him a worse death? No matter, my oath is to do what I can. So, what can I do to get the arrow out?

One thing Josephus realized, the arrow had been shifted once it entered the skull. And unlike flesh, the bone would not close around it—or, at least, not very quickly—to make extraction more difficult and damaging, both.

He started to twist the arrow's shaft, to realign the head with the wound, then stopped himself. *Oh, no, nonononono. If I detach the shaft from the head, I'll have no end of trouble getting it out.*

"Get me the stoutest, strongest pair of forceps we own!"

After a brief delay caused by one of the medical orderlies sorting through the main medical chest, that orderly returned with some fairly stout-looking forceps. Josephus took these and tried to reach in through the wound channel to grasp the arrowhead.

"No, these damned things won't do. They're just too damned big. Find me something a little more delicate. Maybe the curved set."

In fact, he still couldn't get in to twist the arrowhead. *Hmmm...what if I try to lever it around?*

The curved head helped there. He managed to get it to one side of the arrowhead and, bracing the forceps on bone, to rotate it to be once more in line with the wound.

I still don't trust the shaft not to come loose. Hmmm...I wonder if...

Reaching in again with the forceps, Josephus felt around— there was too much blood welling to see much of anything—until he was pretty sure he had the forceps around the socket of the arrowhead. This he squeezed for all he was worth, feeling a slight resistance—*Well, an arrowhead has to be light, after all*—that then yielded. With one hand on the shaft and the other gripping the forceps, the *medicus* began to twist...twist...twist...

"Aha! Take that you damned barbarian, heathen, pagan, bastard arrow!"

At that point, something funny occurred to Josephus. "It doesn't stink. Every other sample I've checked of the Scythian poison reeks to Heaven." He sniffed at the still-open wound. "Doesn't stink, either."

Josephus trotted from one arrow-wounded patient to the next, sniffing at the wounds of each. In one case, one of his assistant surgeons had managed to extract an arrow. He sniffed at that, too. Still no stink.

"Orderly," the chief *medicus* called. "Orderly, run and find the legate or the camp prefect. My compliments and tell them that the Scythians are not, for now, at least, using poisoned arrows."

INTERLUDE

Exploratory Spacecraft 67(&%#@, Several Hundred Znargs Above the Teutoburg Forest

Blossom rested on her usual pedestal, nervously chewing on two of her tentacles. Red had never seen her so worked up, not in one hundred and seventy-four *z)p$#la^ths* of lawfully and divinely sanctioned juncture.

"Don't worry, dearest," he chirped, itself a sign of his complete confidence now, "our creature will be back in his own body very soon. I've got his spirit speared now and I'm ready to reel him in."

Mainz, Germany, 1458 A.D.

Through his new host's eyes, Calvus saw a machine that made him think of nothing so much as an implement of torture. He decided, again, to remain perfectly quiet until he had a question he thought could be answered.

First, he saw his host's hands spread out on a large piece of flat stone some kind of blackish substance, thicker than water but not so thick as gruel. Onto this, those hands pushed soft— *Leather-covered, I think*—pads, stuffed with something and with vertical grips imbedded in them; pushed and rotated them until they were fairly saturated with the blackish stuff. Calvus wanted to ask desperately, but still decided to wait.

Those leather pads were then moved to the torture machine

205

and rubbed, rotated, and lightly pounded down on several rectangular flat pieces of *something*, with irregularities in them, until those somethings were covered in the black stuff.

After this, Calvus saw a flat screen holding a sheet of yet another something. The screen was rotated over those same somethings. Then—*Aha! I knew it was an instrument of torture!* The host reached up and pulled on a long wooden bar, which rotated an enormous looking screw, forcing another flat plate down onto the screen. The bar was held in place, very briefly, then pushed in the other direction, lifting the flat plate off the screen.

When the screen was then rotated away, Calvus saw—*mirabile visu*—four pages printed where it had all been blank before.

"Sir," asked Calvus, "did you invent this? And before you ask, I am no longer sure of what I am. I have no body that I can see or feel, but someone or something is sending me to converse with the minds, the *animi*, of very learned men. I mean no harm to anyone."

"Fair enough," said the host back. "Have you a name, spirit?"

"I do, or, at least, I did. Appius Calvus, at your service. And I have the honor of addressing?"

"Johannes Gensfleisch zur Laden zum Gutenberg."

"That's a mouthful," said Calvus. "Or would be, if I still had a mouth."

"Tell me about it. I go by Johann or Johannes Gutenberg, for short."

"Perfectly understandable," agreed Calvus. "So please tell me about this wonderful machine."

"In the first place, Appius, I must be honest: I didn't invent it. These things have been around for a while, used carved wood blocks to print material on pages of parchment, paper, or vellum. Why, I am quite certain that the origin of the press can be found in the wine and olive presses of Romans and Greeks!"

"You know, Johannes, you are right. I can see the origin of this machine in the olive and wine presses of my own day!"

"What, out of curiosity, was your day, Appius?"

"The year seven hundred and sixty-two from the founding of the city," replied the *haruspex*. "What year is it now?"

Gutenberg did some mental figuring, then answered, "Twenty-two eleven *ad urbe condita*."

"Gods!"

"A long time, I am sure. As to what I did invent"—Gutenberg's finger pointed down at the still black-stained plates—"this ink. Rather, I changed it from water based to oil based. It works a lot better."

The host picked up a piece of silvery metal, square on the sides but tapering down. "This was my chief invention, though: moveable type. They're made of an alloy of lead, tin, and antimony..."

By the time Gutenberg was finished showing the process, Calvus thought he had a pretty fair handle on how those "books" shown him by Gigger and Gilbert had been made. Likewise, too, he knew how to make the ink, though not the detailed process. Paper remained something of a mystery, though he gathered it was made from fibers—flax or hemp or something like that— pulped in water, left to ferment, then spread out in boxes with fine wire screens on the bottom, and finally purged of the water, and with some kind of starch used to help hold them together and smooth them out. He gathered that some kind of light polishing was required and that some kind of waxing was useful for at least some purposes. But it was all so much, so quickly to try to absorb.

"What a shame my own people will never know this," wailed Calvus, "that they will fall to barbarism before...Ooops...goodbye, Johannes. And thank you!"

CHAPTER TEN

The battle was being fought in full view of everyone, and it was impossible for any brave deed or act of cowardice to escape notice. Men on both sides were spurred on to acts of valor by their desire for glory and their fear of disgrace.

—Julius Caesar, *De Bello Gallico*, 7.80.5

In camp, in the land of the Scythians, date unknown

While the Rhodian slingers climbed the towers along the southern wall, the Twelfth Cohort with their staff slings took their places along the walkway behind the cover of the crenellations. The Thracian archers, likewise formed along the walkway, but kept out of the way of the Twelfth. The legionaries on that portions of the wall made themselves scarce to make room for the missile troops.

Behind them, four of the *tormenta* crews cranked down the arms of their engines, hooked the slings to the spurs coming from the very ends, loaded eight-pound rocks, and pulled the lanyards to fire.

True to their name, the backs of the *tormenta* rose up like a donkey trying to kick someone. The sound of the arms hitting the crosspieces resounded through the camp, despite the thick padding placed where the firing arms would strike them.

The men whose job it was to serve as aiming points took their chances and exposed their heads and eyes to follow the solid projectiles all the way down to the ground. Using their hands to signal, they indicated whether the crews needed to manhandle their machines left or right, and whether the slings needed to be adjusted for the range. In each case, there was little adjustment required.

Reloading was brisk. The chief of the piece attached a hook to the firing arm, then two men cranked the windlass to tighten the rope and haul the arm down. Another man held the incendiary projectile while yet another doused the partially covering felt with turpentine. A fifth man doused the cup of the sling with water. It was rather stout leather, so it could deal with flame briefly. Finally, the chief of the crew gave the command "Light," followed by "Loose!" as soon as the felt was well lit.

Sproing-whoosh-wham! The firing arms swung, slamming with almost incredible force against the crosspiece.

The burning jars were already on their way at that point, sailing over the wall and another nearly quarter of a mile before striking down, shattering, and spreading a sheet of flame in the direction of the enemy.

Only one of the four shots actually landed exactly where desired. This spread a gallon of liquid flame onto the material of the Scythian *plutei*, setting it alight and forcing the archers behind it to retreat.

The men serving as aiming points made hand signals to their *tormenta*, fist pumped upward to adjust the sling to increase range in increments of ten double places, and down to decrease it by the same distance. In one case, the aiming point man moved to his left as he faced the enemy to bring his *tormentum* into better alignment. Already the release hooks were attached to the firing arms.

As fast as thought the windlass men sprang to their duty: insert a bar, lean into it, crank down, crank down, crank down. Withdraw. Reinsert. *Crank-crank-crank.* A ratchet kept the windlass from going back.

Up on the walls and towers the Rhodian slingers spun their slings two or three times, each, then released them. Hundreds of lead *glandes*, spinning furiously, and whistling like the devil, sailed outward to strike the mass of dismounts approaching the walls.

"Give 'em absolute hell, boys!" shouted Hermagoras, caught up in the excitement. Certainly few of his men could hear him over the sounds of smashing *tormenta*, the cries of the Scythians, or the whirring of their own slings. "Give the fuckers HELL!"

The mass of Scythian foot milled about with fear and confusion under the hurricane of lead. Shouted orders saw the advance of a large mass of archers on foot. These the Rhodians took particular joy in striking down.

A few of the slingers—unlucky men!—fell to the Scythians' arrows. Most of those arrows, however, fell substantially short, burying their heads in the dirt or at the base of the *agger*.

The wounded were hustled off to the *valetudinarium*. The dead were likewise carried off, lest their presence adversely affect morale.

A dozen more arrows hit the slingers, proof enough that the Scythian archers had closed the range. As if more proof were needed, their arrows began to bury themselves, en masse, in the logs of the palisade.

Sproing-whoosh-wham! Another volley of incendiaries flew out, trailing smoke, sparks, and bits of burning felt behind them. Screams erupted from the mass of disorganized but still thick-on-the-ground Scythian foot as numbers of them were engulfed in flame.

Per prearrangement, the Rhodians took cover behind the logs. Immediately as they did, the Twelfth Cohort drew back their staff slings and released a volley at the archers, followed by another. Admittedly, most missed. But those which hit, perhaps a hundred and fifty to one hundred and sixty half-pound ceramic projectiles, laid the Scythian archers low in droves, with smashed skulls, cracked ribs, and broken arms and legs. One unfortunate even took one to the throat, the damage from which caused his throat to swell up, starting the slow process of strangulation.

Another volley followed. It could not be said that this one was any more accurate, as it was near enough to impossible for the men of the Twelfth to even tell which *glandes* were theirs. At the fourth volley, enough Scythian archers had been laid low to put the remainder on the knife's edge of rout.

Sproing-whoosh-wham! With the falling amongst them of another four incendiaries, the Scythian archers toppled off the edge of the knife. They began to run, only to encounter the mass of spear- and sword-armed, ladder-bearing foot troops waiting for the archers to have cleared the way.

"Zalmoxis!" called Silvanus, through cupped hands. "Get your archers up here to hit them in their backsides! Hermagoras, give them more lead!"

Up, up the ladders on that part of the wall clambered the Thracians.

Sproing-whoosh-wham!

If the Scythians had stopped using poisoned arrows, perhaps to avoid becoming armorers to the Romans, the Thracians had no such compunctions. Bows were aimed high. Poisoned arrows sailed high. And then poisoned points arced down gracefully to bury themselves in the mass of unarmored, unshielded backs of the Scythian archers. And again. And again.

Sproing-whoosh-wham!

Overlooking the scene from the protected tower near the southern gate, the Porta Principalis Sinestra, Gaius Pompeius watched the mayhem created by several hundred heavy rocks slamming into heads, arms, and torsos, and wondered aloud, "We're slaughtering them. Why don't they run?"

"They can't," replied Marcus Caelius. "The mass of the ones in the rear see no reason to move, since nothing we've got can hit them. As long as they won't, the ones in the front that we can hit can't escape.

"Give them a few minutes, though," Caelius continued. "Someone in that mass is going to figure out that a missile duel is a losing proposition for them. When he does—or they do—they're going to charge for the wall."

"They've got the ladders for it."

Sproingoingoingoing-whooshooshooshoosh-whammamNING!

"Ah, shit," cursed Fulvius, as the wound and tightened cords of sinew on one side of one *tormentum* gave way, splitting into scores of individual, disjointed threads. "Oh, fuck!" he added, when his experienced eye saw the trajectory and probable point of impact of the incendiary projectile flung forth by that *tormentum.*

"Cease fire! Cease fire!"

"Oh, bloody hell!" exclaimed Marcus Caelius. His battle- and siege-trained ear had heard the parting of the torsion cords as readily as had Quintus Junius Fulvius. His eyes were in an even better position to see the arc of the flaming projectile.

"Sir," he said to Gaius Pompeius, "we'd better double-time two cohorts—at least two—to isolate that section of wall in case the defenders have to fall back."

"Will they?"

"Tough call, sir. But battle's a funny and tricky business, and men are funnier still. That—Ooh, shit!"

"Send for those two cohorts, Top. Send for them now!"

A little better luck and the incendiary just might have sailed through the low point in the battlements, one of the embrasures. As it was, it achieved a solid hit on a high point, the merlon, and broke apart. Liquid flame scattered over the men defending a good twenty-five feet worth of the wall. The legionaries were affected, but their discipline held them in place even as their armor gave them a modicum of protection from the burning turpentine.

The Rhodians and Thracians lacked both the same level of discipline and the same level of armor. Indeed, with some effort the glue and linen of their armor could burn, a fate which befell two of the men on the wall. They were also from a culture that tended to see treachery even when there was none on offer. Some screaming in pain, others in fear, and yet others in anger, they began jumping off the walkway en masse and falling to the interior portion of the *agger*, fifteen feet below.

Panic is infectious; others, likewise in full panic mode, raced for the flanks. The legionaries, however, held firm for the nonce.

Someone among the Scythians must have seen the flames and grasped some sense of the partial panic on the Roman side. Whatever he said to rally the troops will never be known, but whatever it was, it was enough to turn the demoralized archers back to supporting the assault and enough to get the mass of infantry running forward, despite the continuing barrage of ceramic *glandes* and simple fist-sized rocks from the Twelfth Cohort.

Silvanus ordered the recall of the Twelfth, partly because at close range the staff slings were fairly useless, but even more because he intended to use them to restore order among the slingers and archers, at sword point if necessary. With a good deal more order and discipline than that shown by the Rhodians and Thracians, the Twelfth clambered down the ladders and even jumped from the battlements to roll along the earthen *agger*.

On order, they formed ranks again quickly, there in the *intervallum*. In those ranks, at the double. Silvanus led them to form a sort of corral to hem in the panicked archers and slingers.

It didn't work. The onslaught of the Scythian foot resembled nothing so much as the tide rolling in, except that onrushing waters never pitched a mass of ladders to surmount sea walls. The Scythian tide, however, did.

"Let them through; let the slingers and archers through," Silvanus ordered, followed by, "Toss the staff slings as far back as you can. Prepare *pila*."

It was his hope, a desperate hope, that once the light missile troops had passed through to relative—and probably temporary—safety, their own leadership would be able to rally them . . . for as long as Twelfth held firm.

To cover the space with the three hundred-plus men of the Twelfth, at anything like normal depth, was a sheer impossibility. Silvanus spread them out two deep and just barely covered the area of the breakthrough.

We can't hold them for long, he thought. *Not the slightest prayer of that.*

To his men he said, "Hold them, boys, help is on the way!"

I hope.

The infantry still on the walls, under Centurion Caius Gabinius, popped up and threw their heavy *pila*. They could hardly miss, so closely were the Scythians packed, despite having near enough to no time to pick a target and despite having to duck down again as soon as they'd thrown to avoid incoming archer fire.

The numbers, though, were too great. Scythians poured through the low embrasures and leapt over the high merlons, coming down upon hapless legionaries from above. Soon the walkway was covered with the dead and dying, even as more Scythians jumped down from the walkway to the *agger*, looking for more Romans to kill.

In full view of Mucius Tursidius, Gabinius took a blow to the head and a stab to the side. The stab probably didn't penetrate, Tursidius thought, but the helmet blow staggered Gabinius, knocking him to the walkway. At that, at the loss of leadership, panic began to set in among the men of the century. They threw whatever they had to throw at the Scythians, but stopped trying to push back the ladders. Instead, they turned, threw their *scuta* to the *agger*, fifteen feet below, and jumped for safety.

Tursidius, standing at the flank of the Scythian breakthrough, screamed something unintelligible even to himself, then hurled his *pila* at first one, then another member of the howling barbarian horde standing over Gabinius and preparing to strike downward with blows powerful enough to penetrate mail.

The first *pilum* passed though both shield and body of the target, pinning them together. Screaming in pain, that Scythian sank to the walkway where he stood, both hands gripping the staff of the *pilum*. The second Scythian target was made of better stuff. Seeing the *pilum* coming, instead of trying to block it, he subtly deflected it with his shield, while dodging, causing it to fall harmlessly into the *intervallum*. The distraction was enough to save Gabinius for the time being.

Meanwhile, Tursidius drew his sword downward and then whipped it up to point out from beside his *scutum*. Then the young legionary charged.

The bodies layered on the walkway made for poor footing. Nonetheless, Tursidius hit the barbarian preparing to kill his centurion like an avalanche, smashing outward with his shield to add to the force striking his enemy. The Scythian was bowled over.

"Run, Centurion, run!" Tursidius shouted. "I'll hold them."

Gabinius was in no state to run at the moment, but he did manage to crawl.

"Keep going, Centurion!" Tursidius traded space for time, backtracking himself but always keeping between his centurion and the barbarians.

Then they reached a point where the legionaries of the sister century of the maniple were holding their own, forcing away ladders and slaughtering any barbarians who managed to make it to the top.

"We can't go back any farther, boy," Gabinius said, weakly, "not without letting them start to roll up the whole wall."

Grimly, Tursidius nodded his understanding. Looking ahead, he spat over his shield, daring the Scythians to come on.

Four of them took him up on his challenge.

Tursidius charged, charged and rebounded, off the mass of Scythians coming for him.

Behind him, Gabinius scrambled to pick up a *scutum* and gladius from one of the men fallen at the wall.

✦   ✦   ✦

The men of Gabinius' century, fleeing from the wall, were still legionaries. They hadn't lost their swords and they picked up their shields from the *agger* where they'd thrown them. At the sight of Twelfth Cohort standing ready to receive the barbarian onslaught, they rallied on their own, taking places among the men of the Twelfth by threes and fours and five. It didn't make for a solid defense, just one a little less mushy.

At the moment the barbarians reached the fifty-foot mark, Silvanis ordered, "Loose!"

The single volley of *pila* the Twelfth Cohort loosed upon the Scythians wasn't enough. At best it gave a moment's respite, and then the barbarian mass, sometimes tripping over their own fallen and even each other, was upon them.

The Romans fought back furiously, making a low but rising wall of the Scythian dead and dying. It wasn't enough. The sheer mass of Scythians pressing on the thin line of the Twelfth Cohort pushed them inexorably back across the *intervallum*. A man steps back to avoid or deflect a spear thrust? So, too, does the man behind him and so, too, do the men to either side. Enough of those and the entire line had moved back half a pace. Still more and they've retreated ten paces, or twenty. Or more.

Neither was it one-sided; Romans fell too, to spears to the face, or had to limp off with leg wounds gushing blood. The wounded were on their own unless an ambulance found them; Twelfth Cohort, even reinforced with the men from the wall, had nobody to spare to help them off.

As gaps were created by losses, the men filled in, moving up or shifting left and right to cover the space as best they could.

The four cohorts of the first line in the *acies triplex* had been kept out of the battle for a hoped-for attack that evening. That idea was pretty much moot at this point. Under Faustus Metilius, the new *primus pilus*, vice Marcus Caelius, the roughly nine hundred men of those two cohorts double-timed from their previous post, near the Porta Principalis Dextra.

With them, close on Metilius' heels and bearing the legionary eagle, came Gratianus Claudius Taurinus, whose impending promotion to junior centurion had had to be put on hold for a time.

Metilius picked a spot, just in front of the double line of the Twelfth. "Claudius, post yourself there."

"Aye, Top."

Turning about, Metilius ordered the commander of the cohort immediately following him, Second Cohort, under Sextus Albinus, "Form line of battle from just to the right of the eagle to the western wall."

"Right, Top," answered Albinus, then led his men to form that line. Albinus' arm was still in a modified sling, modified enough to let him carry his *scutum* at the cost of some pain.

Following Second Cohort was the Seventh, under Gnaeus Gallus. Without a word, using only his hands, Metilius sent the Seventh to form up to the left of the eagle.

Metilius trotted up to where stood Silvanus. The new first spear's facial scar seemed to pulse red. To Silvanus, he said, "On order, I want your men to run like hell and form up behind us. Leave room for the Thracians and Rhodians to form up. Get some fire on the part of the wall we've lost. Try not to hit any of our men but I'll understand if it happens."

"On it, Top."

Metilius headed back to where the eagle stood. Seeing the missile troops milling about, unsure of what to do, he shouted, "Hermagoras? Zalmoxis? Get your rabble behind these two cohorts. You'll be fucking *safe* there. Pussies. And then get some fire on the Scythians coming over the wall."

The four Scythians besetting him forced Tursidius back and then back and then back some more. His sword was just enough to parry their spear thrusts, but not enough to get past their guard. That was bad enough, but worse, he could see that there were a seemingly infinite number of barbarians surging over the wall where there were no living Romans in place to guard it.

He barely managed to parry one spear thrust with his gladius, to block another with his *scutum*, and to duck a third that was aimed for his unarmored face. A fourth forced him back another step.

At that point, Tursidius found himself parallel to one of the cauldrons of boiling water. Without hesitation, the Roman pushed the cauldron over with his *scutum*, sending the boiling water rolling down the planks of the walkway.

Screaming over their parboiled feet, the Scythians didn't so much fall back as collapse back. Once again, Tursidius charged.

The planks were warm, still, but the water no longer dangerous. This time the barbarians had too much distracting them to put up a solid front, much less attack. Tursidius lunged forward with his left leg ahead, pushing with his right, and knocked one Scythian off his feet. The Roman advanced over the man, then did a sort of lengthened half squat, lowering himself just enough to drive his gladius into the barbarian's midsection. He twisted the blade, letting air in and freeing both it and a scream of utter agony from the Scythian.

From behind Tursidius came a familiar voice. "Just keep moving ahead, boy. I'll finish off the wounded for you."

"Yes, Centurion."

In an instant, Tursidius was again in a nearly erect fighting position. The next strike with his shield failed to knock his intended target off his feet. Instead, it knocked the man's shield away, leaving an opening for the gladius, quick as a scorpion, to strike. With a despairing, pain-filled cry, the barbarian tumbled off the walkway.

The next two actually had their backs to the Roman as they tried to escape. There was no pity in Tursidius; he knew, as did the entire legion, of Atrixtos' flayed cavalryman. One Scythian felt the gladius—a weapon for thrusting, true, but a fine chopper, as well—slice into his neck, not enough to sever the spine, let alone the entire neck, but enough to let his life's blood gush out as if from a fountain.

The other clutched at his eyes as salty blood bathed them and his face. This barbarian's discomfort from his eyes was short-lived, as Tursidius drove the point of his sword directly into the barbarian's kidneys. This was a wound so incredibly painful that even a scream wasn't possible.

Between them, Metilius and Silvanus had brought a measure of order out of chaos. And just in time, it was, too, as a mass of Scythians, having surmounted and then conquered that portion of the wall, began another charge.

The barbarians really didn't have a choice. As soon as they crossed over to the Roman side of the wall they were beset by a hornet's nest of flying two-ounce *glandes* from the Rhodians, a stinging rain from the Thracians' poisoned arrows, and, perhaps worst of all, a deadly hailstorm of half-pound rocks from the staff slings, after Twelfth Cohort had recovered theirs.

At that range and in those numbers, against the kinds of soft, unarmored targets presented by the Scythians, it's not clear that a half dozen modern machine guns, firing sustained rate, would have been a bit more effective.

Meanwhile, from the towers, the scorpion crews threw bolt after heavy bolt with terrifying accuracy at the Scythian horse, waiting beyond archery range for a decision to be made and a breach created or a gate unbarred. The scorpions took particular care to target the better-dressed and horsed, the barbarians with swords, and the ones who looked to be wearing armor.

With the missile troops continuing to rain down hell on the Scythians standing atop or still trying to come over the wall, Metilius marched the Second and Seventh forward to something like optimum *pilum* range, about fifty feet. This was, basically, point-blank range for a mass hurling.

On command, the men of those two cohorts drew their arms back, en masse, and launched, en masse. Up and up, too, the *pila* flew, en masse, and crashed down on the stymied Scythian mob, still en masse. One volley might have been enough to break them. Two was overkill. The Scythians began to run for the ladders to escape over the wall.

"Oh, no, my fine fellows," whispered Metilius, "there'll be none of that for you." The first spear's voice changed to a bellow: "Drawww...SWORDS. No fucking prisoners. Forwarrrd...KILL 'EM ALL...CHARRRRGGGGE!"

With bloodthirsty cries and howls, the Second and Seventh Cohorts of Rome's—still Rome's, always Rome's—Eighteenth Legion charged forward to slash, stab, hack, and work enough slaughter on the barbarians to give their multi-great-grandchildren, if any, nightmares.

At the *valetudinarium*, the wounded trickled in by ones and twos, or gushed in in knots of eight or ten as the ambulances galloped in.

As was often the case, Josephus saw that there were those crying over a few scratches or the loss of a finger or two, while others, with gut wounds they and everyone else knew to be fatal, would be full of fight yet.

The *medicus* divided the wounded into three groups. Those

with light wounds that were just serious enough that they'd be at a severe disadvantage, and probably be killed, if they stayed in the fight, were put on low priority. If he'd had any, he'd have issued each man a cup of undiluted wine. What he did have, mead from the Argippaeans, he gave out.

The next group were the ones he fully expected to die, men holding in their guts with their hand, men with cracked skulls and brains exposed. There were not too many of these, fortunately. Full of fight or not, they were taken off to a couple of the tents and given mead laced with opium. When they were sufficiently doped up against the pain—an unusual kind of case where a man under the influence of narcotics might well make a more rational decision than a completely sober one—an orderly would come by and offer them a lethal dose. It was entirely up to them whether or not they took it but failure to do so amounted to self-condemnation to a lingering and agonizing death, a stinking, shitting yourself, writhing, sweating, begging, pleading, delirious death, a death devoid of any semblance of dignity.

The final group, and the group to which Josephus and his skilled surgeons would devote all their efforts, were those who had a fighting chance.

There were a lot more of those than the medical establishment could really care for, but they had to try.

And then Josephus noted the presence of over seventy of the Argippaean tarts—all seventy-two, it turned out, once he could count them—standing expectantly outside his surgical tent. It had to be them; they were the only women in the camp. One stepped forward, oddly enough, wearing a legionary cloak and with a *pugio* hanging from a baldric. "Me Zaya. We come help. Speak little Latin now. Tell us what do."

Still up on the protected tower by the gate, Gaius Pompeius and Marcus Caelius kept low with most of their bodies protected by thick logs. In their sight, a scorpion snapped out its bolt. Their eyes watched the bolt fly and pass completely through some Scythian chief, then continue on to impale itself on an underling directly behind. The chief seemed for a moment unharmed, but then toppled forward and right off his horse. At that, a hundred or more of the Scythian horse galloped off, leaving their dead chief's body behind.

"If we could set their cavalry to running I'd almost risk a pursuit," said the legate, "even abandoning my idea for a night attack."

"No, no," replied Caelius. "Those *yobud* things the Scythians and our Argippaeans use? Allows the riders to turn completely around in the saddle and shoot arrows, in this case quite possibly poisoned arrows, at you. You can't catch them, too many remounts, and every pace farther you lose men to their arrows."

"Right. Got it. No pursuit. Night attack is on, then."

Both men turned their eyes back to the carnage being enacted at the southwestern corner of the camp. There, some two thousand, maybe even twenty-five hundred, Scythian foot were trapped between a wall they couldn't scale and about nine hundred first-class legionary infantry, backed up by a like number of excellent missile troops. And they couldn't respond to the missile troops because all of their living archers were on the other side of the wall.

Two flights of *pila* lanced out, and the effect on the Scythians was devastating. Nearly every *pilum* found a target to perforate. Some few even managed to take down two. The Scythians inside the camp were, for the most part, trapped.

Oh, there were ladders aplenty for them to use to climb up, but so great was their terror at the complete reversal of their fortunes once the reinforcements showed up, that they only fought each other over the only way to escape. And then, worse still, as the reaping machine that was the front of the Second and Seventh Cohorts slammed into their undefended backs, the barbarians became so compressed that even using their weapons was impossible. They were trapped and squashed together *ut in vasculo sardinae*—like sardines in a vessel. This also made it impossible to climb the ladders to escape.

And then the slaughter began in earnest.

"Back up, son," said Centurion Gabinius. "Those missiles are as dangerous to you as to the enemy."

Mucius Tursidius was surprised suddenly to find himself standing at the ready with no enemy to face him. The whistling of Rhodian *glandes* just past his face was enough to get him to back up to where the fire still burned next to an overturned cauldron. He placed his body on the friendly side of a merlon, then raised his shield to rest it on the open top of a crenellation. He even let his exhausted sword arm dip, though he retained his grip on his gladius.

One of Tursidius' *pila* projected upright from the Scythian body in which it was buried. A quick glance told Tursidius that it had been so bent by the barbarian's falling backward that he hadn't a prayer of pulling it out for the moment.

And, at that, more than likely I'll have to chop it out before I can take it to the blacksmith for restraightening. Nasty job that will be.

Had Tursidius been able to see himself as he was at that moment, covered in gore and filth, blood everywhere, he'd have laughed at his own squeamishness.

"Well done, son," said Gabinius, from behind. "Very well done."

A nice little pile of gold taken off barbarian bodies was growing in front of the *Praetorium*, under the watchful eye of one of the newly promoted tribunes, Junius Rubelius.

"What we gonna do with the gold, sir?" asked one of the centurions assisting Rubelius.

"That's a good question." Rubelius bent and picked up a golden comb—simple teeth but surmounted by a lovely hunting scene. "It would have artistic value in Rome, so if we could auction it we'd have a lot more for the legionary accounts and the legion's treasury. As is, though, the gold will probably be weighed and melted down, most of it, then banked. But portions of it will be credited to the accounts of every man in and with the legion, in accordance with rank. Perhaps even the tarts might get some, 'for services rendered.' There's a rumor I heard that the services now include more than the sexual."

"Heard the same thing, sir," replied the centurion. "Many's a man went off to the underworld a little bit happier because there was a pretty girl there to hold his hand as he passed through. They did more than that, too, I heard from a friend works the *valetudinarium*. Cleaning off the wounded for surgery. Sewing up wounds. I won't object to the girls getting a fair share. For that matter, I don't think there's a man in the legion that would. Nice girls, they are, if not the kind you'd want to take home to meet Mother."

"What about that pile of shields, sir?" asked another centurion, pointing.

Rubelius considered. "The Scythian shields are near enough to worthless, and their armor scant, but what there is of it we may send off to the Argippaeans as trade goods. Same with any clothing we don't want."

The looted Scythian clothing formed a growing pile, alongside other piles of cloaks and shoes and any leather than didn't look to be made of human skin. Much of the gear was bloodstained. Swords were being collected, as well, along with spears. These latter were inferior to the Romans' *pila*, but Quintus Junius Fulvius thought they had good points, strong and sharp, and that the scorpions could get some use out of them.

Also the Roman dead were being collected and brought to the open assembly area in front of the *Praetorium*. Parties of soldiers detailed from each century that had lost men carried water up from the river and took care of the delicate business of stripping off the armor for potential reissue, washing the bodies and redressing them in any better tunics they might have had. The various signifers stood by to credit the reclaimed armor and weapons against the dead legionaries' accounts. Most of the dead would have left their personal property to somebody, often enough a girl and a kid or two back in *Germania*, and the legion would owe those somebodies the equitable value of the equipment, once the legion returned. Personal items, if small enough, would be brought back, too. Some would be auctioned off with the proceeds deposited in the bank, credited, likewise, to the dead legionaries' accounts.

Wood pyres would be assembled, soon, once more pressing business was taken care of. The legion lacked a *haruspex* to officiate on the religious aspects of the ceremony, but someone could be found to fill in. The funerary chants might not be in Latin so archaic that nobody outside the temples, and not all of those, understood it, but the gods would just have to deal with that.

Carts creaked continuously, as wagons carried piles of naked Scythian dead down to the river to dump them.

Just like the ones inside, the corpses of the Scythians outside were being stripped of anything remotely valuable. These bodies were also taken off by the wagonload and dumped in the stream. The cavalry and the missile troops guarded the legionaries who had stripped off their armor and laid aside their weapons for the hard and grim work of moving bodies.

From the Scythian camp, a few miles away and upwind, came the unmistakable smell of cannabis being burnt. The smell was vastly stronger than it had been when the Amazons had been beaten off.

In the *valetudinarium,* Appius Calvus, the *haruspex,* sat bolt upright and gave off a scream both heartrending and earsplitting.

Calvus began patting himself all over, from the top of his bald head through his now much reduced torso and down his legs.

"I'm back," he whispered with wonder, "really back. I'm not dead and haven't been converted into a wandering ghost after all."

Unsteadily, on legs long unused to standing, Calvus arose. Hearing the sounds of moaning, sawing, and the occasional barely suppressed screaming, he staggered out of the tent in which he'd found himself.

"How in Hades...no, *where* in Hades am I?" wondered the restored *haruspex.* "I've never seen any place in Germany as flat as this." He glanced at the walls, where he could see them, and then the towers. While most of the camp was still in tents, he also noticed more permanent log cabins standing in a number of places. "And how much time has passed that the troops set up a winter or a permanent camp?"

Calvus felt his thin stomach again and said, "Quite a while would be my guess."

INTERLUDE

Teutoburg Forest, September 21, 762 AUC

A tall German, blond, well built, strode among corpses and trees. He wore skins over his Roman muscle cuirass. His weapons, too, were Roman. In his heart, however, he was pure German.

Arminius, known as Hermann among his own people, and known, too, for being very bad-tempered, was furious with frustration. It was impossible, just impossible, for the Eighteenth Legion to have simply vanished without a trace, with no tracks leading away from where they'd tried to make camp to make a stand.

Well, no tracks but for those allegedly left by my ungrateful, treacherous, Rome-loving so-called brother, Flavus. I will not even think of his German name; he's unworthy to bear it. And to think of all the fights I got into on his behalf, back in that vile, overcrowded sewer of a city. Tracks? Well, a few of course, the occasional deserter, but not the legion as a whole.

And I don't have the proof of absolute victory to show the naysayers. I need three eagles and we only have two. And enough of my people have seen them to know there should be three.

Quietly, Arminius walked about the camp, a handful of bodyguards in attendance. He nudged with his toe an abandoned *pilum* here, a gladius there. Once he kicked a cast-off *galea* with enough force that he thought he might have broken a toe.

And that's another thing: this area is nearly bare. Just a comparative few bodies, and the only one of note? That's probably

Ceionius, the camp prefect of the Eighteenth. Funny how he got killed; he was so far from the front. And no framea *made that wound in his neck. No idea what to make of that. Well, to be honest, though I met him many times, I can't even be sure it's him, the body's so badly rotted at this point, and I think the wolves have been at him.*

Then Arminius remembered something. Just before giving his cohort the order to attack both forward and to the rear, the attack that split Seventeenth Legion from Nineteenth, he reached up and ripped off the *signaculum* held in the little leather pouch on a cord about his neck. The *signaculum*, for military purposes, served as a means of identifying the dead. Tearing his off and throwing it to the ground was his statement that his loyalty to Rome, rather his pretense of loyalty, was at an end.

But whoever this corpse was, he presumably kept his.

Arminius bent over the corpse, barely keeping himself for heaving, and found the leather cord around the neck. He yanked it off, roughly, and then took the contaminated little pouch in hand. Opening it, he pulled out a small lead tablet. He read it and laughed.

"Aha, so it is you, Ceionius. What a pity—you'd have made a fine entertainment, nailed to one of our grand German oaks. You got off far too lightly, old comrade."

Dropping the *signaculum*, contemptuously, Arminius continued his perusal of the camp.

In any case, very few weapons, no tents, no carts, a minimum of dead bodies—and most of those were ours. But I don't care about any of that. What I want—what I need—is the third eagle.

I must have that third eagle, but how...?

Oh, yes, that would work well enough to fool my countrymen. We've got the two in hand to serve as masters to copy. We've got the pay chests of two legions and enough gold to plate the silver, even after some hefty bonuses to the tribes.

Yes, yes, yes—that's it! We'll make a false eagle and present it as the eagle of Legio XVIII!

CHAPTER ELEVEN

The Syracusans and the allies, and Gylippus with the
troops under his command, advanced to the rescue
from the outworks, but engaged in some consternation
(a night attack being a piece of audacity which they had
never expected), and were at first compelled to retreat.
But while the Athenians, flushed with their victory,
now advanced with less order, wishing to make their
way as quickly as possible through the whole force
of the enemy not yet engaged, without relaxing their
attack or giving them time to rally, the Boeotians made
the first stand against them, attacked them, routed
them, and put them to flight.

The Athenians now fell into great disorder and
perplexity, so that it was not easy to get from one side
or the other any detailed account of the affair.

—Thucydides, *The History of the Peloponnesian War*,
7.43.6–7.44.1

In camp, in the land of the Scythians, date unknown

Torches burned in the *intervallum*. Near to the torches, bathed in
their light, Gaius Pompeius stood at the Porta Principalis Dextra,
the port nearest the great river, just ahead of First Cohort. With
him were Caelius, Metilius, and the aquilifer, Gratianus Claudius
Taurinius. The German commanding the cohort of German
auxilia, Thancrat, likewise stood by. Also a quartet of *cornicines*
followed along. These would signal the attack once the cohorts
were spread out in line abreast.

Ahead of the command party skulked Thancrat's Germans, all of whom were thoroughly pissed to have been left out of the day's fighting. Behind First came Second, Seventh, and Ninth Cohorts, the middle pair of which were only somewhat tired from their slaughter of the Scythians, earlier in the day. Behind them were some of the missile troops, the Thracians and Twelfth Cohort.

The entire body of combatant cavalry, Gauls, legionaries, and Palmyrenes were stationed on the opposite gate. The Argippaeans were to be left behind. The rest wouldn't sortie until the barbarian camp was well and truly aflame. Ambulances, inherently rather noisy, would only come out when the cavalry did.

The first-order centurions of each of the cohorts, along with the prefects of the auxiliaries, had inspected each man for muffled equipment. Thracian quivers were stuffed not just with arrows, but with grass to keep the arrowheads and shafts from clattering against each other. Those arrowheads were a mix of poisoned and incendiaries.

Those legionaries wearing the newfangled *lorica segmentata* had stuffed felt between the iron bands to keep them from rattling against each other. Helmets, too, had any buckles and loose metal attachments tightened down to the point of pain or stuffed or covered with some softer material to muffle sound.

The troops chosen for this adventure were set up to be as quiet as humanly possible. Fire was being carried by the Thracians in the same arrangement as used by Silvanus in the downriver operation to capture the Scythian scouts.

Special care had been taken to pour melted fat into the crude hinges of the gate to cut down on noise. Moreover, because navigating on a moonless night was a sheer bitch, the rocks that had supported the fires for heated sand and boiling water had been moved up to the towers facing south. Already beacon fires were lit. The legionaries would skirt these, as they swung wide to take the Scythian camp from the west. But they would still see them and could, to a degree, judge their direction from them.

Both Gaius Pompeius and Marcus Caelius looked east to see if there was any trace of a rising moon yet. There was not.

Gaius looked to Caelius for assurance. The camp prefect looked back and gave an almost imperceptible nod.

"Thancrat?" said Gaius.

"Yes, sir? We're ready, sir."

"Lead out, then, and make sure there are no living Scythians along our route to give warning."

"Sir."

Gods, that crap stinks, thought Caelius, probably along with every man in the column. *Makes me want to puke. If what Josephus and Bat-Erdene say is correct, nearly every man in that camp is going to be higher than a hawk. And maybe some of the women, too. Might make them fearless but it's also going to make them uncoordinated and stupid, just as if they'd all fallen into a barrel of wine.*

To their right, the men of the cohorts could hear the murmuring of the great river to their north. They'd parallel that for a mile and a half, before turning south.

The expedition turned to the left at the point where the Germans judged it to be one and a half miles from the western edge of the fort. They continued on in column until all the beacon fires atop the towers pretty much lined up. At that point the German cohort began to spread out by little knots of *contubernia*. Those sixty knots of men covered about half a mile, at full extension. The *decanus* of each counted off the paces or used a knotted bit of rope for the innumerate ones. As soon as they reached the assigned pace count to cover the total front, they turned left or right depending on whether they were on the right or left of the release point, and continued moving to south.

Behind the German cohort, the rest of the troops stayed in a column of fours, albeit more spread out than they would have been for square-bashing in broad daylight.

Gaius stepped aside for a minute and just listened. *Yes, I can hear the men, here, very faintly. Not much talk, only a little. Shutting them up will be noisier than letting them whisper. No metal on metal. No groaning. Better than good chance the Scythians won't hear a thing until it's too late.*

So far, so good.

Meanwhile, Marcus Caelius, listening to the same column at the same time, thought, *If I can identify them I am going to skin those motherfuckers if I hear so much as one more little whisper.*

I swear, I'll kill them on the spot. Well, if I can find the bastards responsible I will.

Fortunately, the Scythians are too overcome with their drugs...

The cohorts continued the march south, the troops getting progressively quieter as they neared the enemy camp and the safety of their own fell behind. They frequently looked back longingly at the tower fires.

Caelius and Metilius looked back frequently, too, but in their cases they were trying to keep their bearings and their direction. Between the raucous camp of the Scythians, growing closer on their left front, and the extreme fires from their own camp, coupled with long experience in the army, they were both fair hands at that kind of thing.

Metilius sensed that the column was beginning to accordion. Usually, that problem stemmed from the leading elements of a column marching too fast, then slowing too much. Then the one farther back had to hurry to catch up, and the ones beyond them...with everyone behind eventually slamming into those ahead.

"Faustus," Caelius whispered.

"I'm on it, Marcus. My cohort now, after all." The first spear then trotted carefully to the front of the column and ordered, again at a whisper, "You stupid fucks either slow down or I cut your balls off. This isn't a race." He then turned around and began marching at the pace he wanted the first rank to assume.

There was some jostling from the middle as the men who had been trying to catch up ran into the ones now being held back. Every little sound that came from the jostling set both Caelius and Metilius to the warming thought of floggings and other forms of physical correction.

One of the Germans appeared in front of Metilius, still keeping the pace, now joined by Caelius and Gaius.

The German spoke a little bad Latin. "Us find two horsey limp-wrist boys, butt-fucking by small bush. Kill both. Quick kill. Chop-chop. Stab-stab."

"Are we compromised?" asked Gaius Pompeius, who spoke fair German.

"No, no," the German responded, in a tight whisper, using

the same language. "They were too engrossed in each other to pay any attention to us as we crept up on them. Half a breath and they were never going to breathe again."

"Well done, soldier. Now back to your unit."

"Sir."

We really don't deserve all the luck we've had, thought Caelius.

Ten minutes or so later, Thancrat showed up, whispering, "I'm starting my cohort's wheel toward the camp."

"Understood," agreed Gaius. "We'll march ahead another five minutes and turn the column to the left."

"Understood."

The moon was up now, though still low in the sky. The point of the column, the *triumviri* of Pompeius, Caelius, and Metilius in the lead, was headed almost straight for the Scythian camp now. That camp was lit up inside nearly as bright as day, with thousands of cook fires and fifty or sixty enormous bonfires burning. The aquilifer, Gratianus Claudius, marched just behind the three leaders. At a point Gaius counted as being about one hundred double paces short of the Scythian camp, he raised a hand, easily visible in the moonlight.

Able to see now, the troops halted without the crashing into each other from behind that one might have expected on a completely dark night.

"First Spear, go," Gaius said to Metilius. The latter turned around and gestured for the four on-hand centuries of the First Cohort, currently about six hundred legionaries, to follow him. Off he led them at a right angle to the line of march. Metilius kept a pace count as they marched. At three hundred and seventy double paces he'd signal a halt.

Behind First Cohort came Second under Sextus Albinus. His cohort wasn't quite as strong as the four double centuries of the First. Hence, he paced off only two hundred and forty double paces. Seventh came up and turned right, while Ninth, when it was its turn, veered left.

Zalmoxis of the Thracian archers reported in, quietly. "Spreading my men out now, sir."

Last up was Silvanus, with his Twelfth Cohort. "Twelfth, ready to rock them in a few minutes."

There were gaps left between the line cohorts wide enough to hold the three maniples of the German cohort, though they only had to contain two. At this point, these were no great distance ahead, though still spread out.

"*Cornicines*?" asked the legate. He and Caelius had gone through the necessary commands in the necessary sequence until Gaius had them down cold.

"Here, sir."

"Blow '*auxilia fall back.*'"

The piercing call of the Roman brass set the Germans to racing back to the gaps and the flanks. It also created an immediate hubbub inside the Scythian camp.

"Zalmoxis?"

"Here, sir!"

"Burn me those tents."

"Light the fire arrows!" Zalmoxis called. "Fire as lit."

Two men bearing vessels containing glowing coals fed in some sap-filled wood chips and blew the coals to life. Then they paced down the line of archers, lighting off their incendiary arrows, the incendiary part being a thick lump of pine resin, residue from the turpentine manufacture. As his arrow was lit, each Thracian nocked his arrow, drew back, and let fly. By twos emanating from the center, outward, the arrows flew up and impacted onto the tented wagons of the Scythians, fundamentally the same as the ones of the Argippaeans. A reversal of the procedure sent arrows from the flanks out, with the pairs coming inward.

What was a hubbub before became a panic-stricken riot as the Scythians realized they were under attack and that its first wave was fire.

All plains nomads feared fire above all else.

"Centurion Silvanus," ordered Gaius, this time at a shout, "start pounding anyone who might try to fight those fires."

"Sir!" Almost instantly the whipcrack of staff slings was added to the snapping of bows and the whooshing of fire arrows.

Ahead, in the Scythian camp, cries of pain were added to the cries of alarm.

"At the double, the Eighteenth Legion will advance to the burning wagons. Prepare to ADVANCE!" This preparatory command was echoed down the line.

"Advance!"

With a shout, the six and a half cohorts in the operation charged for the burning wagons. There were people among them. They didn't last long. The legionaries didn't go out of their way to slaughter women and children—after all, those would have value as slaves, which value would be shared out among the men—but neither, given the Scythian Amazons' treatment of Atrixtos' man, were they interested in taking any chances. Women, children, and the men who had been trying to beat down the fires ran off screaming in terror as warning to the center of the camp.

"Zalmoxis!"

"Sir."

"Fires on the wagons ahead of us and to both flanks."

"Sir!"

This time the Thracians didn't need coal pots to light their incendiaries; there was plenty of fire to hand.

The wind was at the Romans' backs and had been since they'd turned toward the Scythian camp. Flaming bits of cloth, carried on that wind, began to supplement the Thracians' arrows.

A group of what were quite obviously women, shrieking like harpies, began racing for the Roman line. None bore bows but, rather, carried spears, axes, and a few swords.

"Why no bows?" Gaius wondered aloud.

"Takes time to string them," answered Marcus Caelius. "And it isn't that easy."

"Ah."

The Amazons reached a point about fifty feet shy of Second Cohort. With no obvious sound of regret, Sextus Albinus ordered, "Loose!" Then "Loose!" again.

Two flights of about four hundred *pila* each were launched out, to fall among the Amazons so thickly that few were left standing. Credit where due, those few—or, rather, about fifty—without hesitation threw themselves upon the Romans.

And promptly bounced off, as large, manly *scuta* smashed little feminine faces and bodies. The woman and girls were slammed back and down as if they were not even there. Thereafter, the men marching forward bent their forward knees almost as if to lunge. But the bending wasn't to lunge; it was to treat the Scythian Amazons to a little stab-hack-chop. Female screams arose over the camp for a short space, and then were forever silent.

Some of the *pila* were bent while others were straight enough.

Bent or straight, the legionaries ripped them out of their Amazon targets, brutally and ruthlessly. Tangled guts sometimes followed the *pila* heads out. A few of the Amazons turned out to be not as dead as all that. In those cases, the *pila* were stuck in again and again, as many times as needed until the screaming stopped.

The forward men kept one or two of the best, while the rest of the *pila*, generally rather bent, were passed back to the rear ranks to try to straighten.

Gaius saw one tent flap fly open. It was a large tent and out of it staggered fourteen or fifteen giggling, dull-eyed, slack-jawed ruffians. A flaming arrow ignited the tent—like many or perhaps most leather tents, waterproofing was helped a good deal by regular oiling or nearly as flammable waxing—and the staggering fools pointed at the flames shooting up one side and laughed.

"Cut 'em down," shouted Sextus Albinus. "Don't waste your *pila* on them."

A third of the camp was in flames and three or four thousand Scythian corpses lay behind the Romans. There were, at this point, no prisoners. On the other hand, there were Roman dead as well and, worse, Roman wounded. Wounded were worse because each man had to be carried or guarded in place. Thus, while a dead man left a gap, a wounded one might leave three or four, at least until they could be collected at what a later age would have called a "casualty collection point," where a common guard could cover the lot with lesser numbers.

"We can't advance any farther without spreading out, sir," Caelius told the legate.

"Spread the Germans out," said Gaius Pompeius, without more than a moment's hesitation. "The Scythians won't want to come up against the Germans and face being taken in flank by our own cohorts. Also split the archers and Twelfth Cohort up to provide support to the entire front."

"Got it, sir!" Marcus Caelius ran off to give the necessary orders while congratulating himself on the military education of the legate, which had been mostly supplied by himself.

The wind came from the west, or from Atrixtos' right. He stood on the same tower the legate and camp prefect had, during the defensive battle for the camp. His eyes were still good; he had little trouble making out the twin arcs of incendiary arrows, launched from not far to the west of the Scythian camp, and landing along a number of the tents.

"Wait," the Gaul told himself. "A few fires don't make a conflagration."

Between the height of the tower and the hill mass on which the Roman camp had been built, it wasn't hard to follow the course of the battle. Indeed, it was well illuminated by the course of the tide of flames, burning steadily from west to east.

The light wasn't enough to make out much in the way of detail. Nonetheless, Atrixtos had the sense of a tide of people fleeing those flames and the soldiers who followed them.

The wind picked up a bit, from the speed of a walking man to the speed of a trotting horse. It lessened, briefly, but then kicked in again. It occurred to the Gaul that, while "a few fires don't make a conflagration," a few fires steadily reinforced and coupled to a stiff wind just might.

"Maybe I shouldn't wait. Maybe I should start moving now."

Making his way by the firelight, the legate had moved off to the right to confer with the first spear. Caelius and he had both known this wasn't militarily necessary. It was, however, politically necessary, to let Metilius, still living to some extent, under the shadow of the *praefectus castrorum*, see that his counsel was valued.

The fire came from other things than grass. There really wasn't anything to burn on the ground; the steady tramp of human beings, horses, and kine had ground all the grass into the dirt, even as it churned the dirt into muck. The whole camp, for that matter, had an air of piss and shit about it, something the Romans couldn't smell over the smoke of the cannabis until they got well inside it.

But the tents and the wagons, those were another story. As the things burned, embers and bits of burning cloth and oiled leather were cast off to be picked up by the wind. Most of these ended up on the ground where they tumbled along, wind-borne. Others, however, flew high initially, and then came down on still more burnable material.

And then there were the tents atop the wagons. When those burned, more often than not they took the wagons with them.

The latter were made of old, seasoned wood in most cases and went up with a will.

"We're going to be spending days just sifting through the ashes for gold and silver," said Marcus Caelius.

"How about that?" replied Claudius, the aquilifer. "Make for a tidy nest egg when we reach home. There's a girl in Vetera I've had my eye on for some time now."

"German or Gaul?" asked Caelius.

The aquilifer couldn't answer, as a trio of Scythian men charged out from behind a wagon that hadn't caught fire yet.

One fell to the arrow through the throat from a sharp-eyed Thracian. The other two were on Caelius and Claudius with all the ferocity their people were justly noted for.

Claudius and Caelius both whipped around to face their foes. The former had no shield. Instead, the stout wood bearing the legion's eagle had to do for defense. Caelius, on the other hand, had a good, solid *scutum*, which he got between himself and a Scythian sword barely in the nick of time.

The barbarian hacked at the metal rimmed edge of the shield, bending his own sword in the process. With a snarl, he threw the useless sword away and threw himself on Caelius' *scutum*, trying to rip it out of his possession, preparatory to ripping out the Roman's throat with his teeth.

Caelius stabbed the Scythian once, twice, three times in the belly. Each time he gave his gladius a vicious twist, to let air in to make the gripping flesh release the blade. The Scythian hardly seemed to feel any of them. With his guts beginning to slither out onto the ground, still he tried to get his hands past the shield to throttle the life from the camp prefect.

Finally, Caelius managed to get a blow in with his shield that rocked the Scythian back. In that small gap in space and time, the Roman drove the point of his gladius up and up, under the Scythian's chin and then further into his brain. The barbarian's eyes rolled up as he fell, finally, though with his jawbone and his hands holding the gladius tightly, dragging it and the camp prefect's arm to the ground.

Dropping his grip on the sword, Caelius drew his dagger—his *pugio*—and, shield still on his arm, went to help the aquilifer.

Both the aquilifer and the barbarian, Caelius saw, had a grip on the staff, with each taking turns blocking or hacking at the other.

Two steps forward and Caelius slammed the barbarian with his shield. That was enough respite for Claudius to knock the barbarian's blade out of the way with his own, and then to drive the point home.

"Some of both," the aquilifer answered, between breaths.

"What?"

"The girl in Vetera. She's pretty like a Gaul and blond and tall like a German."

"Oh."

"How much do I owe you for the assist on the Scythian, sir?"

"Well... ordinarily, I'd dock you three sesterces for inefficiency but since you did manage to hang on to the eagle, I'll let it go for now."

"Bloody generous of you, sir."

"Isn't it just? Now wait while I retrieve my gladius."

Atrixtos mounted up, thinking, *Now here would be a good use for those* yobud *things. Much easier to mount up with armor.*

Tadmor was standing by, mounted on his own horse. He was one of those who had taken to the *yobud*, as, indeed, had many of the Palmyrene horse archers. In the shadow of the tower, despite the moonlight, facial expressions couldn't be well seen. Thus, rather than a quizzical look, Tadmor asked what was going on.

"So far," replied the Gaul, "the camp appears to be falling rapidly. And burning just as fast."

"And so?"

Atrixtos looked up, judging the moonlight. "So I think we need to get in position to hit them in the ass or pursue the fugitives."

Tadmor, likewise, looked up. "Just enough light. Maybe."

"Yeah, maybe. You ready?"

"Lead on."

"*Medicus* Josephus?"

"Here, Atrixtos."

"Follow us as closely as the ambulances can."

"Well, it had to happen, sir, eventually," said Metilius to the legate.

The thing that had to happen eventually was that the cannabis would wear off, the Scythians would rally, and there'd be a hard fight to finish matters, one way or the other.

"Yes," said Gaius Pompeius, "I suppose it had to, though, frankly, I didn't personally see the need. What we...I...hadn't expected was quite so big of an 'it.'"

The size of the "it," roughly five thousand dismounted Scythians, backed up by what looked to be two thousand or so who had managed to find their horses, was intimidating, to say the least. Mind, it was hard to tell the numbers, both from the smoke and from the number of wagons sitting in the way. And it was possible that some of the depth was false, the result of the disarmed, the non-Amazon women, and children taking shelter behind.

Maybe worse, their chiefs and priests seemed to be working them into a frenzy.

"Recommendations, Top?"

Metilius didn't answer immediately. *But then Caelius says this lad's got a good head on his shoulders, asks the right questions, and is learning quickly.*

"Halt, sir. Pull the flank cohorts, First and Ninth, back to form at right angles or, better, right angles but with the corners softened. Put the Germans in the rear. Hope Atrixtos has some initiative and moves now so he can hit them in the ass once they charge us."

"Right. Concur. First Spear, I want you to pull the four centuries of the First Cohort back, to form at right angles..."

And a sense of humor, thought Metilius.

It was all harder than that. Once Caelius had seen First Cohort pulling in, he'd sent messengers to Ninth and the Germans to do what only made sense. But then, with the Germans going to guard the rear, the Second and Seventh Cohorts had had to fill in the gaps. This, in turn, required First and Ninth to backstep to join up with the flanks of Second and Seventh. In turn, since an actual corner was extremely vulnerable, Metilius had detailed one of his centuries to close the gap at a forty-five-degree angle, next to Second, and the same, but opposite, where the Germans were going to be. But the Germans were a little slow, so...

"Fucking headache," said Marcus Caelius, desperately trying to get the flanks closed, on the one hand, and to close the broad gap where the Germans were falling back to be the rear guard, on the other.

"Zalmoxis, Silvanus, what's your ammunition status?" Caelius demanded.

"Dozen arrows per man," the Thracian said. "One of the downsides of fire arrows is that there's really no recovering them. And though the Scythians use arrows a lot, most of those burned in the wagons."

"About three times that in *glandes*," said Silvanus. "They don't burn and can be recycled."

"All right," said Caelius. "Better than nothing. We ought to be able to hold off the Scythian foot; they've got little armor and less training in fighting as infantry. What I am concerned about is the ones who've found their horses. Fair chance—no, it's a near certainty—that they've also strung their bows and have their arrows already poisoned. So I want your men to keep those horses at bay, out of range. Hmmm...*cornicines*?"

"Here, sir," answered the chief of the *cornicines*.

"Stand by. But I think we're going to need a short conference of the first-order centurions."

Well, *that* didn't happen. Before the first-order centurions could be assembled, the Scythian cavalry galloped through the mass of infantry being worked into a frenzy, and began to swirl around the elongated lozenge that was the six and a half cohorts. Their attack lacked a certain something in terms of both mass and velocity, largely because of having to dodge around wagons, burning and otherwise, as well as a great deal of horse-leg-threatening detritus lying on the ground.

But as they closed—and they closed a lot closer than the theoretical range of the bow suggested, roughly *pilum* range or a bit less—they stood in their stirrups and loosed arrows at the legionaries.

"They probably should have learned from their assault yesterday," Marcus Caelius said, "that arrows are a lot less effective on heavily armored men with good shields."

"Suspect the log palisade fooled them about that," said Gaius Pompeius.

As he said it, one legionary in their view fell back with a bloodcurdling cry, an arrow embedded in his brain above the bridge of his nose.

"I'm starting to get an idea," said Gaius.

"What's that?"

"Well, I know what they say above junior tribunes and maps,

or junior tribunes citing their vast experience, but suppose we have all the troops form *testudo*—what happens then? The command party can join Twelfth Cohort in the center."

"They lose any good targets…"

Another legionary's cry caused them to glance toward Seventh Cohort, where the man staggered out of formation and dropped, an arrow in his throat and blood gushing from the wound.

"Yes, they do," the young legate agreed. "And then what? I think they think we're cowards and try to get among us…"

Catching the spirit of the thing, Caelius exclaimed, "And then we blow the signal to come out of the *testudo* and to attack! But we can't do it yet. They'll smell a trap unless we've suffered a good deal more loss than two—"

There came another scream, based on the direction it had to be from a German auxiliary.

"—rather, three of us," Caelius continued. "These are our men but I think we need to let the Scythians take down about a hundred of them—yes, even knowing that we'll get not a single man back because of the poison—before we form *testudo*."

"Desperate times," said the legate.

"Desperate measures; I agree. Besides, it's not like we're not taking out a few of them, too."

To punctuate that came the mass whipcrack of a squad of staff slingers from the Twelfth, followed by the screaming of a horse and the falling of a man.

"One problem, though, sir," said Caelius. "If that mass of foot hits us in *testudo* formation, we'll be overwhelmed. And they may start to charge—it may be the signal for them—when they see us get down."

"Take them a few minutes to get here. If we can kill the ones on horseback, bet you a whole amphora of the former legate's best Falernian that the mob takes to their heels."

"In your experience?" asked Caelius, a little bit sarcastically.

"In my reading, because, you know, Top, some of us equestrian shitheads read a lot, too."

"All right, sir, let's try it. I don't see a lot of other choice. I'll get the word passed to the cohorts."

The horde of Scythian riders kept circling the cohorts, darting in to fire an arrow here and there, then darting right back out again. Most arrows missed their targets or impacted harmlessly on the legionaries' *scuta* or *loricae*. Some of the barbarians fell to *pila*, some to the staff slings, and still others to the Thracians' arrows.

And casualties kept mounting.

"I don't understand why that mass of foot is still hanging back," Caelius said.

"I don't either, Top, but I figure it's just about time. *Cornicines*, blow 'form *testudo*.'"

Instantly, the musicians raised their *cornua* to their lips and gave the signal. Just as instantly and with a minimum of confusion, the legionaries and auxiliaries maneuvered their shields to form a complete defense—front, rear, sides, and top—to the barbarians' arrow fire. As the command party did, the Thracian archers, who lacked shields, ran inside the ranks of the Twelfth, making an altogether too tight mass under the protection of the *scuta*.

For some time, several minutes, anyway, the Scythians continued their circuit, trying to fire arrows into the small open areas within the *testudo*. These were notably ineffective.

Eventually one of the Scythians, either bolder than the rest or still under the influence of the *cannabis* more than the rest, rode his horse right up to the edge of *testudo*—Third Maniple, Second Cohort, as it happened—and leapt onto it.

Though none of the Romans saw it, the expression on that Scythian's face was one of wonder, for the *testudo* gave not more than an inch under his weight. Laughing—which gave a certain degree of support to the "still doped to the gills" thesis—he started to jump up and down on it. He could shake it but he couldn't break it.

Other Scythians then brought their horses to a halt, drew swords or brandished spears, and walked right up to the outer tortoise shapes and began to try to strike inward through the small openings or to pry the thing apart.

At the change in sound, Gaius Pompeius had a legionary from the Twelfth raise his shield to get a look.

Dear gods, they've all dismounted, every one. This is going to be like drowning puppies... not that I ever have.

"*Cornicines*?"

"Ready, sir."

"Blow 'out of the *testudo*' and then 'free attack.'"

✧　　✧　　✧

The first Scythian, the most likely still doped-up giggler, was most surprised when the shield on which he stood suddenly was twisted, allowing him to fall inside the *testudo*. His surprise at that was as nothing, though, compared to when three different gladii plunged into his abdomen, lungs, and neck. Twice. Each.

Indeed, a *lot* of Scythians were caught off guard at the sudden change in the Romans' formations. Their surprise, too, for many of them, ended with a *pilum* in the gut from the legionaries, or a spear from the German *auxilia*.

Many more tried to run to get back to their horses. But a foot soldier trained to run is almost always going to be faster on his own feet than a horseman on foot but trained to ride. The fleeing Scythians, many more of them, were cut down from behind as they ran. Some managed to get to horses, their own or somebody else's, and fled, all pretense at fighting this inhuman machine likewise fled.

Oh, and didn't the Thracian archers have a fine time, shooting at the unarmored backs of the routed Scythian horsemen. Twelfth Cohort, too, launched projectiles, a good many of which hit home.

Gaius noted the mass of Scythian foot bearing down on them. "*Cornicines*, blow 'recall' and 'form line of battle.'"

"Damn," said Gaius to Caelius, "there's no way to form a properly spaced line. And I owe you a jug of Falernian."

"We'll just have to take them on as we are. I wish that fucker Atrixtos would ride up and hit these bastards in the rear!"

"Here they come!"

Atrixtos, in fact, was not so far from the battle site. He had seen the Scythian horse riding around the cohorts. He'd seen, too, the cohorts falling into *testudo* formation to defeat the horse archery. He'd laughed, not quite along with the Scythians, at what they were letting themselves in for by dismounting in no particular order to try to pry apart the *testudo*. And he'd slammed his right fist into his left hand as the Romans mushroomed out from their defensive formations to wreak slaughter upon the unwary barbarians.

"Tadmor?" he called for the commander of the Palmyrene horse archers.

"Yes, Atrixtos."

"I want you to pursue the fleeing Scythian horse—keep them on the run or annihilate them if you can."

"I'll go for annihilation," said the Palmyrene. "My men's horses are fresh, where theirs are not. And their usual strings of remounts do not really appear to be available."

"Go, then. Kill them all."

"Legionary cavalry."

The decurion in charge of the Eighteenth's normal complement, now rather understrength, answered, "Here."

"You're not really armed or equipped for this. Follow us in reserve, ready to pursue the Scythian foot when they break."

"Will they break?" asked the Roman.

Atrixtos ran a finger under his nose, then answered, "Well, when they run themselves onto the immovable wall that is Roman infantry, and then find several hundred Gauls fucking them in the ass, yes, I think they'll break and run."

"Good hunting to you then, Prefect. We'll keep close and ready to pursue."

In Atrixtos' distant view, the mob of Scythian foot—brave, clearly, but without much in the way of discipline and order—hit the first two cohorts, sort of bounced off, then came on again while lapping around the flanks.

If I can rout the ones on the nearest short side, the Roman cavalry can pursue and that cohort can roll up a flank.

Coming to a decision, Atrixtos drew his *spatha*, raised it overhead so that at least the men nearest to him could see, and then brought it down in the direction of the Scythian foot, besetting the flank cohort. "Charrrrge!"

With the Scythian horse repelled or destroyed, Twelfth Cohort and the Thracians could come out from behind their shields, as could the command party.

Caelius breathed a sigh of relief to see the enemy foot more or less bounce off Second and Seventh cohorts. His breathing became a little more constrained when he saw them come back and their flanks begin to lap around the flanks. True, the flanks were secured by First Cohort and Ninth, as the rear was by the Germans, but Romans had become rather sensitive to being enveloped ever since a very unfortunate August day, by the River Aufidus, in Italy.

And then he heard the sound of pounding hooves heading

for the left flank and noticed that Gaius Pompeius, the legate, was legging it at high speed for that flank.

Barring that jug of Falernian he owes me, the boy's done rather well over the last twenty-four hours. Even acquired a couple of gray hairs. Let's give him his head now, unsupervised and unadvised, and see what he makes of it.

Atrixtos couldn't help but thank his gods for the horns gripping his thighs as the Gallic horse went from a canter to a trot, to a gallop.

Some of the Scythians in the rear on that flank turned around, wide-eyed with shock and despair to see the Gauls bearing down on them. A few, initially, made to fight but, as the mass panicked, joined in that mass panic.

Then the Gauls were on them, stabbing with lances, slashing down with their *spathae*, and knocking men over with their horses. There might have been a thousand men besetting the Ninth before the Gauls intervened but within seconds there was nothing but a fleeing horde of demoralized individuals, running full-out in an attempt to save their own skins.

Of course, a couple hundred of them were left lying on the ground, stabbed, slashed, and trampled by the horses.

Without being told to, the legionary cavalry—under one hundred men—took off after the fugitives, running them down in droves, stabbing them in the back all the way.

"Ho, Atrixtos!" called the legate, through cupped hands. Atrixtos looked to see him standing just inside the perimeter.

Paying very little attention to the bodies underneath his horse's hooves, some of whom cried out, the Gaul moved up to the edge of the Roman line.

"I want you to swing wide around the rear and take the Scythians on the other flank in the rear, just like you did this one."

"Should not be a problem, Legate," the Gaul replied.

"Good. Now I'm going to direct the Ninth Cohort to wheel wide and take the enemy in the flank. After you rout the ones on the other flank, tell Metilius, the first spear, to do the same thing, to wheel around and then inward. Then I want you to pursue but not more than a mile, turn around and hit the Scythians in the rear. Got that?"

"Got it."

"Then run, run, run like the wind."

Gaius looked around frantically for the first-order centurion of Ninth Cohort. He knew he'd be off to the right... *Aha, there he is.*

Again, the legate took off at a brisk run. "Centurion Camillus!" he called. "Centurion Camillus!"

Camillus looked around until, seeing the legate, he called his second forward and ran to meet him.

"Sir?"

Gesturing with one finger, Gaius squatted down and began to trace on the ground what he wanted done. "Can you do that?"

"If nobody attacks us while we're swinging, yes, sir, no problem."

"Do it, then!"

In point of fact, Camillus couldn't quite do what the legate wanted, or at least not immediately. This was because the First Maniple of the cohort was already somewhat engaged on the cohort's right flank. Instead, he maneuvered the Second and Third Maniples, about three hundred men or a bit fewer, at this point, to line them up perpendicular to the line of battle. Then, once they were in position on the enemy's open flank, he charged them forward to smash into that flank. Once the enemy reeled back, First Maniple was able to wheel to take up their position.

Camillus noticed that the enemy was so compressed he was having a little trouble using his weapons. For that matter, the shock of the cohort's charge had been transmitted through his ranks, knocking a number of men over.

Though the horses moved faster, Gaius had a shorter trip. Thus, despite stopping midway to confer with the camp prefect, he managed to reach Metilius several minutes before the Gauls reached the rear of the Scythians on that flank. While he ran, he noticed that Thancrat, the prefect of the German *auxilia*, had stretched his men out to provide a rear guard to Ninth Cohort, while maintaining a rear guard for the Second and Seventh.

Caelius noticed it, too. "We've got a good man in Thancrat. You would never guess he was a German."

Gaius arrived at the First Cohort almost out of breath. Thus, it took several minutes for him to explain to Metilius exactly what he wanted done, which was basically a mirror of the maneuver pulled off by the Ninth. He was just finishing up when they both heard the dreadful pounding of the Gallic horse, moving from a trot to a gallop.

Then came the crash, neighing, frightened horses, screaming, perforated, terrorized men, and the sound of steel on steel and steel on flesh as the Scythians went under.

For reasons unknown, the barbarians were thicker on this flank and perhaps a bit stouter of heart. Oh, the panic was still there, to be sure, but more of them didn't panic, even when most of their fellows did.

Atrixtos found himself trading blows from above with a Scythian on foot until that Scythian drove the point of his spear into the Gaul's horse. The horse reared up and brought both hooves down on the Scythian's shield, driving him to the ground. But then the horse sank and began to roll. Atrixtos jumped free just in time, hit and rolled...and then found his former foe back upon him, stabbing down again and again as the Gaul writhed frantically to avoid the wickedly sharp point of his spear.

The Scythian might have killed the prefect of the Gallic cavalry except that Metilius, leading from the front, drove his gladius all the way to the hilt through the Scythian's body. Dropping his spear, the dying barbarian brought both hands to his wound. Unseen, his eyes rolled back. Per routine, the first spear gave his short sword a vicious twist and withdrew it. The Scythian, gasping and sobbing with his agony, sank to the ground.

Metilius reached out one hand to help Atrixtos up. After a warm "Thanks, Top," the Gaul ran the few steps to his wounded horse. Seeing there was no hope, Atrixtos patted the horse, gently, whispering, "Goodbye, my friend." Then, as quickly as he could, he cut the horse's throat.

I've had to do this too often, thought the Gaul.

The double-strength centuries of the First Cohort maneuvered around the Gaul, paused to dress their lines when parallel to the Second Cohort, then continued to wheel inward, somewhat raggedly at this point.

Ragged or not, they hit the Scythians at the run, smashing into them with the force of several runaway elephants, knocking more than a few off their feet. Already compressed, the Scythians foot was now pressed together, *ut in vasculo sardinae.*

"Best find another horse and pursue the fugitives for that mile the legate told you to," suggested Metilius.

"No need to find one," said the Gaul, as he caught sight of his second-in-command, Taurou, leading a replacement to him.

"Cease fire! Cease fire!" Caelius ordered Silvanus.

"If I may ask, why, sir?" asked the chief of the Twelfth, after ordering his cohort to stop slinging their half-pound projectiles into the writhing mass of Scythian infantry ahead.

"Because your fire is quite effective at that big interlocked mob over there. And I don't want you creating any spaces for them to use their weapons or to run away."

"Ah."

The Gauls' horses were a long way from fresh. Fresh or not, though, they were a good deal faster than the fleeing, demoralized Scythians.

Atrixtos, still angry over both his near death in front of the First Cohort *and* the skinning alive of one of his men, rode and slaughtered without pity.

A weaponless Scythian, beardlessly young, ran before him, repeatedly looking over his shoulder and crying something that sounded a lot like a request for quarter.

It didn't matter—Atrixtos brought his sword down on the boy's skull, splitting it in two. He didn't even look back or slow down, but rode onward, roughly pulling the blade from between the two halves of skull.

It wasn't very long before Atrixtos realized that there were horseman ahead of him. He called for his *ala* of cavalry to halt and to prepare to engage enemy horse. And then he heard the cry in good Latin:

"Great hunting, my red-haired friend. Shall we go and help finish the enemy off?"

"Yes, let us. Have you seen the Palmyrenes?"

"Indeed we have. They've surrounded and are guarding a great bloody mass of slaves awaiting the coffle, mostly women and children but there are some men there, too."

"Dammit, *dammit,* DAMMIT," cursed Marcus Caelius. What had the *praefectus castrorum* so angry was the steady stream of

Scythians managing to disentangle themselves from the mass and go fleeing off, generally toward the east. "If enough of these bastards get away, there'll be no end of trouble."

"Take another look, Marcus," said the legate, using his mentor's and subordinate's *praenomen* for the very first time. What he saw that the camp prefect had not was a different steady stream, of panicked Scythians, running back into the mass from which they'd fled. And then they both saw the cavalry, legionary and Gallic both, driving those fugitives back to their doom.

And then the final slaughter began, because taking prisoners in those circumstances was just madness. All had to die.

INTERLUDE

Aliso, Germania, September 14, 762 AUC

Flavus thanked his gods, Roman and German both, for his very narrow escape. *And I might not have, except that, traveling with the legions, I knew the ground a little better than the men my swine of a brother sent after me.*

"And you and your men are for it, too, Lucius Caedicius," Flavus told the commander of the fortress. "By now the Germans are on their way here in their thousands."

"We're set up well for rations," said the *praefectus castrorum* of the fortress. "And have enough men to hold the walls, at least for a while, long enough for relief to reach us. And, as you escaped, I am sure some others will get away to join us."

"It could be," admitted Flavus. "And I pray to all gods that it will be."

"Now tell me what happened," demanded Caedicius, though gently. Something in Flavus' eyes told the Roman that he'd seen horrors almost beyond comprehension.

"It was my treacherous rat of a brother," said Flavus. "He enticed Varus into moving off route to put down a rebellion I am certain was spurious. Along the route he allowed my brother to lead him into, there was a large ambush prepared, good terrain for light German infantry, bad for heavily armored Romans. At a signal, my brother—no, Arminius; I shall never call him a brother of mine again—had his own cohort of German *auxilia* break the line of march between Seventeenth and Nineteenth Legions. Then, while smaller numbers held the Eighteenth and Nineteenth in place, they'd simply piled on and overrun the Seventeenth. Those men held on as well as they could have, for as long as they could have, long enough in any case, to burn their *impedimenta* to keep the food out of the chance of the enemy."

"And how did you escape?"

Briefly, Flavus told of the plan for Eighteenth and Nineteenth to attack the hill and link up on it. And his twin missions to bring the word to Lucius Eggius and then the warning to Vetera and Aliso.

"It was a close thing, at that," answered Flavus. "From my departure from Lucius Eggius and the Nineteenth Legion, I passed through the field of slaughter that was the site of the Seventeenth's last stand. There were some hundreds of legionaries, stripped of their armor, sitting in the rain under guard. But for every living legionary bound, I have no doubt, for a life of the harshest slavery, that, or a very hard death as sacrifices to the Germans' bloodthirsty gods, I saw then there ten stretched out lifeless on the ground. And for every two such legionaries there'd been the corpse of an auxiliary. And for every legionary and auxiliary combined there had been a slave, or a sutler, or a woman...or a child, done to death without mercy by German tribesmen enraged beyond reason.

"Most of the dray animals and horses had, likewise, been slaughtered.

"The bodies hadn't been there long enough to really rot, yet, but twenty thousand or so voided bowels had a stink of their own, you know?"

"I know," agreed Caedicius. "I've been there. And death almost always has a stench of its own."

"Yes," said Flavus. "And overlaying the stink of death and shit was the smell of burnt wagons and carts, and the stores they contained.

"I saw parties of tribesmen, Lucius, walking among the dead, looting cloaks and armor, swords, and *pila*. Those...and making sure the dead were, indeed, dead.

"It made me sick to have to bluff my way through that ghastly display by cheering on the victors. And then I arrived at the place where Eighteenth Legion had been, where they'd been preparing for their own assault on the hill to the south, to fight their way to a linkup with the Nineteenth.

"And there should have been fighting. There should *still* have been fighting, on my left. But nothing. All was quiet. And every trace of the Eighteenth was gone but for a small number, maybe two or three hundred, of the dead."

Caedicius saw tears come to the German's eyes. "Oh, poor, brave Nineteenth," he said, almost sobbing. "No help, I fear, ever came to you."

Wordlessly, Caedicius lifted a jug to pour the German more unwatered wine.

"And then, while I was sitting there atop my horse, in deepest despair, some mounted pursuers, no doubt sent by that wretch Arminius, spotted me.

"I wanted to go back, Lucius, to just draw my sword and exact what little revenge I could for the Germans' treachery. Almost, I did. And then I remembered my word, to do my best to bring word to you."

"Well done that you did," said Caedicius. "And, you know, maybe Eighteenth managed to cut their way out, but Nineteenth failed to meet them. It could be that the Eighteenth is already coming to reinforce us here."

"Yes . . . yes, I suppose that could be true, Lucius Caedicius." In his heart, though, Flavus didn't believe it.

"So we're going to hang on. But you? After you've had a good meal and some wine, maybe even a few hours' sleep, you must exchange horses and ride like the wind for Vetera. For it is possible that the Eighteenth will not come, that we will fall. And so Vetera must be warned."

"I will do it," said Flavus, firmly.

CHAPTER TWELVE

Vae Victis!
—Brennus the Gaul, inside the walls of Rome, 390 B.C.

Former Scythian camp, three miles south of the Roman camp—land now of Rome's Eighteenth Legion, date unknown

Gaius stood by the southern edge of a roughly four-hundred-by-eight-hundred-foot site of massacre. The Scythian dead, who had not yet begun to stink, were piled four deep in places. In no place was it necessary to set foot upon the ground to walk; little of that ground wasn't covered by bodies.

Off to the right, under the guard of the Palmyrenes and both the Gallic and legionary cavalries, was a horde of what must have been twenty thousand or more weeping captives, mostly women and children but also those who had been enslaved by the Scythians, themselves. Some of these were led forward by others because their previous masters had put their eyes out.

Almost every wagon in the legion, as well as some of those captured by the legion, were involved in carting off the bodies to dump in the great river, downstream from the camp. About forty of them, however, with *ngekud* standing in the traces, sat around the massacre site. Into these were dumped the gold, the silver, the weapons, the armor, the shields, the leather and clothing, and the bows and arrows of the dead. There were a good many—thousands—of the little gold stoppered pots containing the Scythian poison. From somewhere, too, the Scythians had acquired an impressive assortment and quantity of mainly Greek wine. That was all Roman property now.

And, Gaius thought, *Marcus Caelius tells me I'd be well advised not to stint the men, but issue each man a quarter of a* congius, *once the cleanup is done.*

Parties of legionaries dug through the places where wagons had burnt, looking for metal of any kind, but especially gold and silver. Still more searched diligently in the open areas.

The take in horses, oxen, and meat animals was simply immense. Every legionary and auxiliary could be put on horseback now, with a remount for every man and plenty more to haul the *impedimenta*.

Rubelius, along with every man of the *quaestor* department but for the *praefectus castrorum*, reinforced by the other new tribunes, took precise inventories of everything. He couldn't believe the wealth the legion had acquired. None of them could.

Bat-Erdene and Gisco rode up to Gaius and dismounted. "What you do with captives?" he asked.

"I suppose they're slaves now," the legate said. "That's the usual process, anyway. Well, after the paperwork is done, it is."

"Well, I tell you, my people no want. You take Scythian slave womens, they have kids. You end up with Scythian kids. That mean war, because womens raise to be Scythians, not Argippaeans. So you have feed or you have kill . . . or you have let go. Up to me, I let go."

A broadly smiling Gisco chimed in, "My Argippaean friend lacks imagination, sometimes. Those captives are our ticket to a much faster, albeit more indirect, march home. Especially in conjunction with all the horses and drayage we've acquired."

"How's that?" asked Gaius Pompeius.

"Think back to what the camp prefect said, how we'd have to march for a while, then grow food for a while, then march for a while. Well, we're still going to have to grow a lot of food, and start quickly, to keep those slaves alive. But once we start to march we don't march west, as we were planning, but southwest to the Euxine, to where the farming Scythians are . . . or were."

Gisco shot a glance at Bat-Erdene, who said, "They still there, but not alone . . . ummm . . . intermixed with others—Sarmatians, Huns, and who know what. Think still farm."

"So we get among them—or at least along their outskirts—and

we trade the captives for more food. The whole while our food stocks grow, even as our need to use food decreases. We follow the north coast of the Euxine to Hellas, then across to the Adriatic, then maybe sail to Italy. Or maybe we get to the Danubius and follow it back to upper *Germania*. Yeah, that latter, I think; Phoenician or not, the idea of sailing makes me ill. In either case, we may get back to civilization in a year or less. Well, a year or less after we get in a couple of crops."

Bat-Erdene shrugged. It seemed possible to him—hopelessly cruel, yes, but possible. "One other thing," he said. "Thems new slaves got a lot of useless mouths, but almost all skilled work Scythians get come from them's slaves. You wants metal? Them's slaves. You wants leather? Them's slaves. So some you maybe want keep. Some you maybe want free. Some maybe you put to work with the Argippaean working girls. Also some young ones orphans now. Mama kill. Father kill. If young enough, maybe you adopt. Maybe even we Argippaeans adopt. Maybe. But no womens or older girls."

Gaius thought about all this, pointed, and then said, "All right; Bat-Erdene, I would like you and Gisco to go report to that very frustrated-looking young man standing in that wagon, Tribune Rubelius. Tell him to give you another tribune and some clerks to keep count. Then I want you to go to the captives—the cavalry is going to march them into the low ground east of the camp—and start sorting them. I'll leave it up to you two to figure out what classes they should be sorted into, but Bat-Erdene's thoughts on the subject sound like a good beginning to me."

Before the Praetorium

All the cohorts, all the *auxilia*, too, were formed in a C around three sides of the assembly area in front of the *Praetorium*. On the fourth side, standing on a raised dais, stood the command group, Gaius Pompeius in front. He'd just finished a short congratulatory speech to the legion, with emphasis on victory, loot, bravery, dead Scythian bodies, captives, loot, and loot.

"The men like loot," Marcus Caelius had advised. Because he had that kind of sense of humor, Caelius had also had a whipping post erected in front of the dais.

Speeches over, it was time for awards. These included *phalerae*, especially for some of the centurions and a couple of *optios*. Finally, the normal awards having been given, Caelius called out, "Legionary Mucius Tursidius, Centurion Caius Gabinius: front and center."

"What? Why me, Centurion? What did I do?"

"Not sure, son," replied Gabinius, who was in on the joke, "but all you can do is take it like a man."

Steeling himself for the coming ordeal—they'd all seen that whipping post—Tursidius nodded, stepped back out of ranks, then faced right and marched around to join his centurion.

"All...all right, I'm ready."

"Forward...march," Gabinius whispered, then followed up with a quietly called cadency, "Left-right-left-right-left-right."

"Centurion Caius Gabinius and Legionary Mucius Tursidius, reporting as ordered, sir."

"Legionary Mucius Tursidius," the legate began, "some short time ago you were sentenced to a flogging, which sentence was suspended pending your good behavior."

Oh, gods, it looks like he's ready to faint.

"That suspended sentence is now put aside."

"Wha...what?"

"Just shut up for a bit, won't you, son?" intoned Gabinius. "No, he said you were *not* going to be flogged."

Pitching his voice high, to make it carry, Gaius spoke to the legion. "When we were under attack in our own camp, and the Scythians in their thousands came baying over the wall; when our own defense was nearly collapsed by a short incendiary projectile, falling among our own men, Centurion Gabinius charged on his own to try to seal up that impossible gap. For this, Centurion Gabinius is awarded a *phalera*, in silver. Centurion Gabinius, step forward."

Gabinius did, and was handed the silver *phalera*, a disc displaying a martial scene taken from the late legate's store of such things.

Again turning to the legion, Gaius continued, "When Centurion Gabinius was struck down, as was inevitable given the forlorn nature of his self-imposed mission, one of his soldiers, Mucius Tursidius, drove the Scythians from him and then stepped over his fallen and insensate body. Tursidius then proceeded to shield Centurion Gabinius with his own sword, his own *scutum*, and his own life, fighting off something between four and, by some accounts, a dozen Scythians in face-to-face combat, and killing all or nearly all of them. For this gallantry in action, in the face of an armed enemy, Legionary Mucius Tursidius is promoted to the grade of *tesserarius*. In addition, he is awarded two gold *armillae*. Finally, for saving the life of a citizen in battle, *Tesserarius* Mucius Tursidius is award the *corona civica*, the second highest decoration for valor available to the legions.

"Given recent custom, this award will have to be approved by the emperor, once we get home. Until then, on my own authority, it stands. Mucius Tursidius, come forward to receive your awards..."

The legate and camp prefect, in the process of splitting the amphora of Falernian Gaius Pompeius owed over his questionable call in the battle—that, and laughing over the look on Tursidius' face as he halted in front of the dais—were interrupted by a knock on the upright pole by the door. It was, as it turned out, Josephus and Appius Calvus.

"Come in! Come in!" said the legate. "It's good to see you up and around, *Haruspex*, especially with the funerals we have to conduct, hundreds of them, and more still to come as men succumb to the Scythians' poison." The wine had gone a long way toward making Gaius take the losses philosophically.

Both men walked in and took seats around the table.

Without a word, Marcus Caelius stood up and went to one of the *Praetorium* chests. He rummaged around in this until he came up with two more silver cups to match the ones in use, plain things, as befit an army camp, but of an admirably heavy gauge of nearly pure silver.

"Help yourself," he said, placing a cup in front of each. "The wine's free, after all."

Not knowing the story, both of the newcomers just showed quizzical looks.

"A bet, of sorts, that I lost," Gaius explained. Looking at Caelius he asked, "And I suppose you've never made a mistake."

"Many," the camp prefect said, "just not that kind."

"Harrumph. So, in any case, the *medicus* tells me that you have a strange tale to tell, Appius Calvus."

"Very," the *haruspex*, repeating, more softly, "very."

"Well, tell it, then," said Caelius, impatiently.

"I confess," said Calvus, "that I am still trying to understand what I experienced. I wouldn't know what I had fallen into now, but that the good *medicus* explained to me what's happened so far.

"But what happened to me physically—though 'physical' may not be quite the right word—was this: When the legion was snatched from probable doom in Germany, my body stayed with the legion. My mind or my spirit or my soul, however, did not travel with my body. Instead, it wandered. A lot.

"My first trip was to a place along the Rhine, about four hundred years from now, I think. I inhabited—coinhabited—the body of a German soldier, in the service of Rome. He and his comrades, who were true to Rome, stood overlooking the Rhine as a horde, an uncountable horde, of Germanic barbarians crossed on thick ice. I didn't see the battle, but he was quite certain that they couldn't stop them, that they were all going to die. Blamed the lack of numbers on somebody else...Now *what* was that name? What...oh, he was called Stilicho, and he denuded the Rhine frontier to deal with some other group of barbarians, nearer to Italy."

"Barbarians across the Rhine?" said Caelius. "That would be the Teutons and the Cimbri, all over again."

"Worse than that, sir," said Calvus, "for the auxiliary in whose body I dwelt mentioned no Gaius Marius. And the legions were tiny, not as good as ours, and overmatched.

"From there I traveled to some holy man, but of a strange, non-Roman religion. He was writing of all the cities destroyed by the barbarians who crossed the Rhine and the ones who followed them. I'm not sure I remember all of them but I do remember his having listed Mogontiacum, Vangionum, Remorum, Ambiani, Altrebatæ, Morini, Tornacum, Nemetæ, Argentoratus, along with the provinces of Aquitaine, *Novempopulania*, Lugdunensis, and Narbonensis. The barbarians were also moving into Spain."

"That..." said Gaius Pompeius, in a voice replete with nausea. "That would be the end of the empire."

"Even so, sir," Calvus agreed. "It gets worse—are you sure you want me to continue?"

"Yes," said Gaius, "we must know the worst."

With a regretful sigh, Calvus said, "The next part *is* the

worst. At least it seemed so to me. I was back in Rome—oh, yes, I know the city well, it *was* Rome. And yet it was a horrid version of our Rome, depopulated, filthy, unmaintained... well, falling apart, frankly. But that wasn't the worst. The worst was the Senate House; it was being used as a stable."

Even Caelius, hard-bitten and cynical almost beyond measure, gasped at that sacrilege.

"The next part was, in a way, almost as bad. It seemed that some kind of rump of the empire continued to live, but Greek speaking. Where it existed in fact I cannot say. Has anyone here heard of Byzantium?"

"Yes," said Caelius. "Thucydides mentions it. It's a city on the eastern side of Thrace, on a peninsula, opposite Anatolia. Good defensive position, I gather."

And I am the one with the classical education, thought Gaius, *yet his self-teaching coupled to his experience makes him the military master I can only, so far, aspire to be.*

"Well, it was a great city that I visited, almost as great as Rome, and with the most impressive walls I've ever seen, but some new engines of war had smashed gaps in those walls like kicking a child's sand castle. It was being done by the minions of yet another non-Roman religion. I have none of the details on that, though.

"And that was the final end of our world.

"Or so I thought. I should probably mention that I made stops in scores of places. But the next stop on my weird sojourn was to a city in Britannia, of all places, that was a city that dwarfed Rome and the seat of an empire that dwarfed ours, too. I saw there strange and wonderful things, none of which I really understood."

Calvus stopped speaking, briefly, to wet his throat with some of that fine Falernian being shared out by Caelius.

"There were more wonderful things at the next stop, which was still in Britannia. There I saw light come from little...mmm...globes, more or less—bright as day, too, nothing like what we get from our poor oil lamps. And the room I was in was filled with singing, and yet not a singer in sight.

"There was just one more stop, and it was to a city called Mainz, somewhere in Germany. There was a man there and he was making books—precise letters, not copied out by hand, but being made en masse on a machine. And so quickly. In the time

I take to tell of it, I saw him print out as much material as might be found on a thick scroll."

"How?" asked Gaius.

"The machine was something like an olive press, and it used metal letters to force...well, 'paper' was what he called it, like parchment but so much cheaper to make. Think of it: hundreds of copies of the longest and most important works known to us, cranked out—yes, literally cranked out—in a matter of days."

"A fever dream," was Caelius' judgment. "Nothing more."

"I wondered about that, too, To...err...Prefect," Calvus answered. "But I have to reject it. Why? Why because I saw things I had never a clue to, never heard of, never imagined. And I saw one thing I did understand, one big important thing, but in a way I had never imagined. Between those two boundaries, my mind tells me that what I saw was real."

"That does lend your experience a certain credence," admitted Caelius.

"I'll see to those funerals now," Calvus finished, then stood to leave. At the door to the tent he turned about and said, "There is one other thing. Not something I saw but something I felt. We need to get back home as quickly as possible; the empire needs us. Badly. Even now."

It was two more days before Rubelius could report to the legate and camp prefect on the loot taken. He found them over dinner in the *Praetorium*. Most of it was pretty obvious and surprised nobody. But the sheer amount of gold...

"Trying to measure it as coinage, or in terms of silver weights, just won't do," Rubelius said. "It's at least one hundred and sixty talents of gold or, if you really insist on a value in silver, a fine female pubic hair over nineteen *million* denarii. Mind, haven't weighed it all. Could be two hundred talents."

"Gods!" exclaimed Gaius. His family tree not only had deep roots but was unusually rich for the equestrian class, besides. But nineteen million denarii was, if not quite getting into Crassus-like levels of wealth, let alone Gold of Tolosa, still enough to qualify for nineteen senatorial seats, or to bribe a much larger number of senators.

As if reading the legate's thoughts, Rubelius added, "If that's not quite up to Crassus levels of wealth, it would still be enough to get the old pirate to start thinking about how to steal it from us. Also, that's not counting the silver, which is about as much in value or maybe a little more. Moreover, a lot of the gold is in the form of some very fine art that would certainly fetch more at auction in Rome than the mere weight of gold suggests."

Rubelius picked up and opened a cloth bundle he'd previously set on the floor. Inside were all manner of rather intricate Scythian gold objects, from an extraordinary pectoral showing herds of cattle above and mythical animals locked in battle below, to golden horsemen and infantry, locked in battle, to plaques of hunt scenes, to ornate kitchen implements, jewelry boxes, plus half a dozen fibulae. There was even a forest scene on a belt plaque, with horses, hounds, and harts, inset with semiprecious green stones for leaves. Also set with gems were two golden deer, pulled from a shield, one of them more than a foot across.

"This is fairly typical work," Rubelius said. He held up the pectoral, adding, "The patrician ladies of Rome will browbeat their husbands into paying any price for items like this."

"It's all very nice, yes," said Caelius, "but I've got a question. Where did all that gold and silver come from?"

"It's an interesting question, too, sir," said Rubelius. "I asked a couple of them who could more or less get by in Greek. You know that the Scythians used to be quite mighty, maybe a hundred times more so than the ones we defeated. But they kept getting pushed off their land and shrinking in numbers. They made a habit, however, of making sure that none of their precious metal was ever left behind, except in tombs. So as they shrank, the quantity of gold and silver didn't. Instead, it just concentrated. And they'd had maybe as much as eight hundred or a thousand years, looting all their neighbors, to accumulate it."

"Fair explanation," said Caelius.

"As for the human wealth," Rubelius continued, "Gisco and Bat-Erdene finished the classification of the new slaves. There are twenty-two thousand, seven hundred and two of them. Unless there have been some recent births and deaths. Of that number there were an even dozen Amazons we gave over to Atrixtos to crucify in repayment for the flaying of his man."

Gaius winced. He understood the Gauls' need for revenge but, even so, nailing women to a cross just rubbed him the wrong way. *And, if we didn't permit it, the Gauls would probably mutiny, while the Palmyrenes might just join them.*

Rubelius continued, "There are, in that number, also eighty-seven metal workers, already enslaved by the Scythians, and one hundred and sixty-two leather workers, same. There are also seventy-six skilled wagonwrights, same. All of these have been turned over to the various departments of the legion to make use of.

"There were, as it turned out, one hundred and twelve girl orphans under the age of twelve and ninety-six boy orphans likewise young.

"There were four hundred and fifty-three blind slaves, used for milking. Also two thousand, one hundred and fifty-three old previously freedmen and -women, of no particular value to anyone.

"There are two thousand and fourteen farmer slaves, none of them blinded, who will be of use.

"There are thirteen hundred and seventy-six young men, all of an age to bear arms and all of whom were certainly trained to arms. I would not trust a one of them enough to turn my back on them and recommend they be killed."

"Seems a bit harsh," said Marcus Caelius. "Rome's been enslaving enemy warriors since almost the founding."

"Those were not Scythians," said Rubelius. "Trust me, Prefect, we'll all sleep a lot more soundly when they're dead. Guarding them will eat up manpower like you wouldn't believe. And we'll never tame them. I've taken the liberty of both separating them from the others and having them bound."

Caelius gave Gaius Pompeius a long inquisitive look. "If you need an excuse," he said, "you can always look at the poisoned arrows. Yes, we used them, too, but they used them first."

Finally the legate nodded his assent, then said, "Kill them as mercifully as possible. But save out a dozen likely candidates for interrogation."

"The remainder, some sixteen thousand, one hundred and seventy-two, are a mix of women with their children, plus adolescent girls, all of whom will have market value along the Euxine and none of whom apparently know a damned thing about growing their own food. Some of them claim they can cook. Might even be true.

"Oh, and we put those two Scythians we captured earlier in

with the slaves. They're included in the number of young men I think we need to kill.

"On the plus side, however, we captured a very large amount of grain and obscene quantities of butter, about twelve thousand *congii*. Much of the grain was burned, yes, but much was saved, enough to feed the slaves a decent, if not lavish, ration for about four months and to allow the Germans to start brewing the beer they favor for the entire legion. And then there are the kine, and the horses, they're still being counted. All of the stinky burning drug the Scythians use has been turned over to the *valetudinarium*..."

"One correction," said Gaius, "or, rather, two. The former Scythian slaves are now free. As for the others...I have to say that their legal status isn't settled yet. Until the paperwork is done, let us call them 'captives,' rather than slaves.'"

Atrixtos and his Gauls had erected a dozen poles on the slope leading from the camp's stockade down to the low ground, on the eastern side of the camp. The poles were in full view of the gaggle of slaves. The tops of the poles had been carved down to allow the fitting of crosspieces. There was a crosspiece in front of every pole, each crosspiece being hollowed out in the center to allow it to be placed firmly upon the uprights. To either side of one of the poles were stepped platforms.

An *optio* on loan from First Cohort had supervised the erection of the poles, the *stipes*, and the hollowing out of the crosspieces, the *patibula*.

Atrixtos had Bat-Erdene standing by to translate. He wanted these dozen bitches to know exactly *why* they were going to die in the most appalling, painful, lingering, undignified, and disgraceful way possible.

The Amazons were marched out under guard, with their hands bound behind their backs and their ankles coffled to allow a less than full step. One tripped while marching and was set back on her feet by the expedient of lifting her by her hair. She screamed with pain and then cursed the one doing the lifting. He simply prodded her forward with his sword.

When they arrived at their execution site, and with roughly twenty thousand pairs of eyes watching, Atrixtos had Bat-Erdene translate.

"Some days ago when one of my men fell into your hands, yours or your sisters, you skinned him alive. No doubt you thought that was a just sentence of agonized death. That, or you were just having fun. Well, what you are about to experience will show you that you are just bloody amateurs when it comes to inflicting a horrible death.

"Watch now as, one by one, you are all affixed to these crosses, upon which you will be your own torturers, and from which you will beg for death one thousand times, and not find it until the last bit of pain has been extracted from your bodies. You think you are tough? No matter; affixed to these you will beg for release."

Without bothering to translate, he told the *optio*, who had a body of five Gauls to assist, "Begin."

They grabbed the youngest looking of the Amazons, a woman of perhaps nineteen years, and roughly cut and tore away her garments, leaving her ashamed and naked before the gaze of that twenty thousand pairs of distant eyes, and several hundred closer Gauls.

With the Amazon kicking, writhing, and trying to bite, they half carried, half dragged her to the first *patibulum*. There they threw her face down and untied her hands, taking special care to control her arms and lashing fingernails. Roughly she was pulled to the *patibulum* and had her arms outstretched. Ropes then were tightened to hold her wrists in place. The experienced *optio*, a specialist in this sort of thing, knelt next to her. He felt with the point of a rough iron spike for the special spot in the wrist, the one replete with nerves and with a partial hole just right for driving a spike through. The spike passed through a wooden disc to prevent the victim from forcing her arm over it and thus escaping her punishment. All the spikes were like that.

Two whacks with the hammer and the Amazon let out a scream of pure agony unlike any the Scythians had ever heard. Though the Scythians were too far away to see, the Gauls were close enough to see a stream of urine shooting up from between her legs before splashing to the ground.

The *optio* went to the other side and repeated the process, getting another piercing shriek though not another stream of urine.

Watching the process, Bat-Erdene wanted to throw up. It was only by the smallest margin that his will overcame that desire.

With the Amazon already sobbing, begging, and pleading, two of the Gauls picked up the *patibulum* and carried it to the upright. There they mounted the steps up to the platforms, dragging the *patibulum* with them. With a mighty heave, they lifted it up, aligned its central hole with the narrowed part of the *stirps*, then let it slam down.

Again, the Amazon shrieked her agony.

"Now this part is a little tricky," said the *optio*. "Bend her legs to forty-five degrees and tie them in place to either side of the *stirps*." He waited for the tying to be done, then went to the left side, placed the point of another spike against the heel, and gave it three good whacks to drive it through the flesh, through the bone, and into the rough wood.

Once again the Amazon screamed. She screamed a fourth time when the other heel was affixed to the wood. After that, screaming gave way to sobbing.

Watching tears roll down her face in a continuous stream, Atrixtos said, through Bat-Erdene, "You should be happy that this is all you will suffer. I'd have made it worse but I couldn't figure out a way to get you bitches gang-raped by the *ngekud*."

"Let's see who's next," said the *optio*.

All twelve of the condemned Amazons, naked and exposed to the world, were mounted on their crosses. Already, they were learning of the true wickedness of crucifixion, as their weight on their out- and upstretched arms made breathing difficult, forcing them to push up to gain a breath. This caused extra agony in their heels, grating and then resting on the crude spikes that affixed them, which ended—briefly—when they let themselves down again, causing extra agony in their forearms.

Through the pain the reality began to dawn on them that this would only get worse, and that they really would be the architects of their own deaths by torture.

It was at about that time for most—a few, one should pardon the expression, hung tough a bit longer—that the begging began.

Less the dozen saved out for later interrogation, the shuffling young male Scythian captives were herded at spear, sword, and arrow point to the river, northeast of the camp. There, backed up by the Palmyrene horse archers, Fifth Cohort was detailed to handle the massacre. In addition to the Fifth, every *contubernium* that had lost a comrade, or had one still dying, to the poisoned arrows had been invited to send men to participate.

Though the Romans took some pains not to divulge their intentions, the women left behind, most of them, set up a miserable keening as the young men were prodded away.

Even the dozen Amazons dying on crosses seemed to understand what was happening, that this was the true end of the Scythians as a people. Hard though it was to credit, this understanding seemed to redouble their misery even beyond what the nails and gravity were doing to them. Briefly, they ceased begging for death and sent up a keening parallel to those of the women and girls still under guard.

The legate had ordered that the young males be killed mercifully. On the off chance that he might be watching, this was done. Generally speaking, the process was to drag the bound captives to the water, force them to their knees, cut their throats, and then push them off. A few Romans stood by with long poles to push the bodies out into the current.

It was disquieting, really, how little resistance was put up, once it was obvious all was lost. It was even more disquieting for the Romans when they thought about their comrades, back in *Germania,* and their hopeless situation.

In the space of an hour and a half it was done, with the last male Scythian body floating down the river, staining the waters around him an even deeper red. Out in the river a more or less solid raft of freshly killed bodies had collected, floating south with the current and rolling a bit with the waves of the river.

Autumn was in the air, with winter following her closely. Nights were growing cold with the wind shifting to come from the north.

The agricultural enterprise had thrived, with each of the Scythian farmer slaves being freed, put on the same salary basis as the Argippaeans, and made a supervisor for about fifty of the formerly free Scythians. These former slaves were given a lash to get the women and old men to put out a maximum effort to growing grain. A good deal more of that grain would be wheat, too, since the Scythian wagons had held quite a bit of wheat, as well as admirable quantities of rye.

Now the harvest of barley and wheat was hurriedly being gathered from the thousands of acres planted by Roman soldiers and Scythian slaves. Even as that was being done, new granaries were going up to secure it, while seed for winter crops—wheat, oats, and rye—replaced the seed for fall.

The slaves of the Scythians, all free men now, understandably, given their treatment at the hands of their former masters, had little or no sympathy for the enslaved women and children of those masters.

Those women and children, along with their old folks, were housed in sheds. These had been made by themselves from wood cut and brought in by the legionaries. They lived inside a guarded stockade about two thousand feet on a side down in the low ground east of camp. Their cooking and heating fires were all animal dung, the wood and charcoal being reserved for the legion. A not especially generous portion of the metal cooking vessels salvaged by the Romans from the former Scythian camp was provided to them.

On the slope west of the stockade stood a dozen upright poles, narrowed at the top. The Amazons who had once decorated those uprights, and the bars that made them crosses, were long dead and their bodies dumped. The uprights of the crosses remained to remind the rest of the captives what awaited them should they disobey or try to escape.

The *Praetorium* tent was long since washed, oiled, and turned in to the quartermaster's office for safekeeping. Now the legionary headquarters—divided into staff offices, conference room, treasury, safe room for the eagle and related standards, etc.—was a one-story log building with a hypocaust for warmth. Details of legionaries and slaves were tasked with keeping the fires going.

Gaius Pompeius had his own quarters, behind the *Principia*, and heated by the same hypocaust. An enclosed passageway connected the two, with doors hung on hinges generated by the blacksmith's shop. There wasn't any extensive decoration of either, just clay and whitewash.

Though glass was beginning to be used for windows and skylights back in the Empire, the best the legion could do was stretch on frames very thin sheets of leather—thin enough, in fact, to let a diffuse light through—and then place the frames in spaces left for windows, mudding the gaps.

Everything was actually quite comfortable for the legate barring only the one serious shortage.

"He needs to get laid," said Marcus Caelius to Gisco, as the two of them watched Gaius lose his temper at an imprecise figure for German beer production, followed by seeing his eyes glaze over with what looked like sheer frustration. "Needs to...but he can't."

"Why not? Ohhhh."

"That's right: his position doesn't allow him to use the same women being used by the rank and file and his fundamental decency doesn't let him corner for himself what is actually a fairly rare commodity."

"Not so rare," said Gisco. "Sure, the meretrices are still only seventy-two in number, but there are thousands of Scythian girls, most of whom would be only too eager to volunteer if it meant more and better food and a warm place to sleep, to say nothing of avoiding the beatings by their former slaves."

They weren't bothering to whisper, which meant also that Gaius heard every word.

"No doubt I have my flaws," the legate said, "but a rapist I am not. And abusing a slave girl is nearer to rape than I have ever come and nearer than I ever care to."

"No one said anything about abuse or force," said Caelius. "We're just talking about making a decent offer that they're almost certain to desperately want to take. And it's not just you, you know. Myself, the tribunes, the prefects of the auxiliaries, we're all in the same boat: can't screw the Argippaean girls and can't commandeer one for ourselves. For that matter, the other first-order centurions are suffering, too."

"I'll have Bat-Erdene see if any of them want to take the offer," said Gisco. "Can we hold out the prospect of manumission and perhaps a stipend to start life somewhere else when our journey is over?"

"Make mine between thirty-five and forty-five," said Caelius. "I'm too old to deal with children; junior centurions and *optios* are bad enough."

For his part, Gaius didn't answer immediately. Instead he drummed his finger on the conference table, kneading his temples, and looked upward before finally answering, "Yesss. But how in Hades am I supposed to communicate with her? And until we do the paperwork to enslave them, manumission would be premature."

"Oh, some of the upper-class ones—well, some of the *really* upper-class ones—speak some Greek. It's a trade language and commonly spoken by the Parthians. It may be a little debased from the glory days of Scythia, but it's something to work with."

Gisco, Caelius, and Bat-Erdene were the escorts, the latter because he was necessary and the camp prefect because he just couldn't wait to see the expression on his officer's face when he saw the girl.

For her part, the girl curtsied and said, in some dialect of Greek, which dialect Gaius could faintly recognize but had never actually heard and couldn't really comprehend, "My name is Zaranaia, Lord. I am yours, forever or for as long as you will have me."

"This one spoke it the best of those I interviewed," said Gisco, after Bat-Erdene was finished translating. "It leaves something to be desired, even if she does not. Her name derives from a word that means golden and, as you can see, she is golden, indeed."

That much was true. Zaranaia was nearly as tall as Gaius, and he was tall for a Roman. Her golden hair was long, braided and piled upon her head in an extremely complex coiffure. Large blue eyes set off a nose straight and neither too long nor too short. Her eyes were at a slight cant while high cheekbones told of a measure of eastern ancestry. While her jaw was perhaps a teensy bit strong, her chin remained somehow still delicate. Her white neck was almost swanlike in both dimensions and implied grace. In short, she lacked nothing in the three measures of beauty: symmetry, proportionality, and harmony. And that was even before one's eyes strayed below her neck.

"Sir? Sir?"

"Oh, sorry," said Gaius to Gisco. "I was..."

"I'm sure you were, sir," said the Phoenician, causing Caelius to have to suppress what surely would have been a hearty laugh. "She is also very clean. I marched her, plus the one for the camp prefect, the six for the tribunes, and the four for the prefects of the *auxilia,* through the quartermaster's warehouse for clothes and then down to the bathhouse at the hour set aside for the

Argippaean girls. The Argippaeans fussed all over them, washed and combed and brushed and did their hair, et cetera, but the clean part they already knew. Apparently the Scythians use soap; the Argippaeans use soap; and so...

"She is, by the way, very willing. Girls of her class from her people are used to arranged marriages, political marriages, dynastic marriages, and not a whole lot of personal choice in marriages. She's a slave—or thinks she is; she doesn't know that no one's ever done the paperwork for enslavement hence that it's more fair to call them captives than slaves—and so is sure she isn't fit for marriage anymore. Still, some approximation would do. But she has some conditions. She says she couldn't live in luxury while her family—I gather that means mother and sisters and little brother—languish in durance vile. The other girls have similar conditions."

"I don't know..."

"Didn't think you would, sir, so I visited the camp prefect, here, and he said he'd been thinking about establishing a centurions' mess where he could set the tone for the reinforced legion's corps of centurions and decurions. The fifty-two women and children ought to be just about enough for that."

"Knives?" asked Gaius Pompeius. "Poisons?"

"Hostages," answered Caelius, "and they'll eat samples of all the food before the centurions do. Plus they'll take oaths to their gods of such seriousness that we can probably trust them."

"But," objected the legate, while hoping desperately that Gisco or Caelius would have an answer for this, too, "we butchered just about every remaining adult male in their tribe, fathers, sons, husbands, sweethearts...we murdered the lot."

"*Serious* oaths to their gods," said Gisco. "The Scythians were vicious, mean, spiteful, vindictive, and all-around nasty. But Bat-Erdene assures me that they are not treacherous where their gods are concerned and take their oaths seriously. Note, here, the many centuries they have not attacked the Argippaeans. Also... women...well...women follow the strong horse willingly. The strong horse, here and now, is us.

"And then, too, those dozen crosses remain on display. In fact, I marched the lot by the crosses—you should have seen their near panic before we continued on through the gate—to make that point."

Gaius' face wrinkled. He understood the need for occasional exemplary measures. He still didn't like it.

"She *is* very beautiful," Gaius said wistfully. "I will never want to let her go, never want to let her out of my sight, until the sun goes out."

Zaranaia hadn't understood the words. Nonetheless she fully understood the tone and the meaning. She gave Gaius a smile that lit up the otherwise dim room in which they stood like the rising of the sun.

"Deal," said the legate. "*Praefectus Castrorum,* I'd like you to have built an officers' mess off of the main kitchen. Make it big enough to seat twenty-four, or maybe thirty if we have guests to entertain someday. And you, Gisco: Latin lessons for the twelve girls and their families working in the mess."

"I shall see to it, sir."

Mucius Tursidius had exterior guard, which is to say the thin guard mounted on the Scythian compound. Being a *tesserarius*, he didn't have to pull guard, but one of the other men in his century had asked him to do so as a special favor, and he'd agreed.

Shortly after passing through the gate of the compound, on his way to his post, he heard feminine weeping. His initial thought was to ignore it, but, after trying to force himself away, he found that he could not.

And why not? Because it sounds just like my little sister, that's why not.

He had a little time before he was due at his post, and so he followed the sound to a little shed built against a wall. The Scythian women and children around him all shuddered and hid as he passed.

Well, I suppose seeing your daughters and nieces crucified will do that. I am sorry for those women, but they did flay one of ours alive so I cannot say that their punishment was unjust. Just nasty.

His arrival at the shed caused a series of screams from four Scythian children and one teenaged girl. The children cowered behind the girl and all pressed themselves against the back of the shed, as far from Tursidius as they could get except that the teenager made sure to keep herself between the little ones and the Roman. All were filthy and poorly dressed, especially against the nighttime cold. They had no fire and, as far as Tursidius could see, no food to cook on it.

He asked the girl, first in Latin and then in his crude German, what the problem was. She didn't understand the words, but she did understand the tone. She said something in reply that the Roman had no clue to, but then pointed to her stomach, and to that of one of the children, and hung her head.

"You don't have anything to eat—that's it, isn't it? But why not? It's not like we're not feeding you. Hmmm...let me guess: you're small and slight and someone here is taking your food from you. I'll bet that's it."

In his haversack, the Roman had half his day's rations: about a pound of bread, some cheese, and some sausage. No olive oil, sadly, but there was some of the Argippaean butter wrapped up in a bit of thin leather.

Without hesitation, Tursidius dug the food out of his haversack and tried to pass it to the girl. She looked on him without understanding, keeping her hands to herself.

"Go on and take it," said the Roman. "I can miss a meal without collapsing." Again, he tried to give the girl the food. Again she didn't seem to understand. Finally, Tursidius broke off a small piece of bread and a smaller one of cheese, took a very tiny nibble of each, and then held the remainder up to the girl's lips. She took the food, then started to take off her ragged garments.

"No, no, no," said the Roman, waving his hand in the negative. "Not that there aren't plenty in the legion who would take you up on the offer. But I'm not them; my mom and dad raised me right." He bent and began to tug the girl's clothing back on her. "It's a shitty world when a young girl thinks she had to spread her legs over a simple gift."

He pointed at himself, saying, "Mucius." Then he pointed at the girl, who answered, "Leimeie."

In the end, Tursidius simply left the food on the little quasi-family's blanket, patted the girl, Leimeie, on the top of her head, and went away. As he walked he heard something that sounded a good deal like a prepubescent feeding frenzy going on behind him.

The next morning, though tired beyond words and ravenous, to boot, Tursidius stopped off at the little shed. The children and the girl looked up at him, hopefully. He made a gesture to Leimeie to follow him. Hesitantly, at first, she did.

They came, at length, to one of the places where rations were passed out to the captives. All the other Scythians backed away from the Roman, lest they end up on crosses like the Amazons had. This also stopped the handing out of their daily rations.

The Roman beckoned Leimeie forward, unmolested by any of the others. His gesture said she should take what food she needed for herself and the children. This she did, and she may have been a bit greedy about it.

But given that they've probably been keeping her from the food for days now, that is probably justice and need, not greed.

Tursidius directed Leimeie to return to her shed. Then he folded his arms and glared at the throng of Scythians. The message was clear, *This girl and her charges are under my protection. Do not harass her.*

Spring came and with it came eleven pregnant Scythian girls. It probably would have been twelve but that Marcus Caelius' forty-two-year-old, Tabiti, was almost certainly past child bearing age. Since, as Gaius Pompeius made a point to emphasize, the mothers were only captives, not slaves—"We are *Romans*, gentlemen; nothing is official until the legal paperwork is done!"—then the children would, likewise, be born free. Gaius was surprised at how relieved the former gentleman ranker tribunes and the prefects were at having this pointed out.

Marcus Caelius, who understood young men better, wasn't remotely surprised. "Women," he said, "are magic spells crafted to capture the hearts of men." *And it isn't as if Tabiti isn't well on her way to half capturing mine.*

With the coming of spring also came the preparations to leave their home for the last year, the great camp by the river. These preparations were extensive. There were about three thousand wagons to pack, most of them the enormous Scythian versions. There were tents to take out, inspect, and oil, thousands of them. Many, indeed most, of these were newly manufactured, for the Scythian captives, for there was no room for them on the wagons, what with the loot, the grain, and the enormous barrels of beer. Room was, however, found for the eight mistresses of the officers and the four of the auxiliary prefects, eleven of them great with child, while the Argippaean meretrices had their own wagons, as well as new tents for conducting "business."

Junius Rubelius raised a key point during one of the nightly—and mercifully brief; Caelius still used the legate's clepsydra to keep them that way—command and staff meetings. Rubelius still had—and would likely retain forever—the quartermaster responsibilities, under Marcus Caelius.

Caelius had also introduced a new rule to help keep things short: every staff officer with something to say had to stand while doing so. Thus it was that Rubelius stood, under the turpentine lamps, to speak.

"Building a proper camp nightly is going to be physically impossible for the men," Rubelius announced. "We're having to put in a wall for a camp big enough to hold five full-strength legions. The men cannot do it."

"He's quite right, you know," Caelius said. "I haven't done the calculations but we'll be having to build a camp with three or so times the perimeter, near enough, and the men can't do it—not and make any decent forward progress each day. And if we don't make progress, we run out of food."

"It's even worse than that," said Rubelius. "We've got such an enormous herd—well, herds of herds—of horses, goats, sheep, cattle and oxen, *ngekud*, and now a fair number of puppies, too, that we cannot fit them all inside any conceivable perimeter, not the way we do it.

"And if we try to leave most of the animals outside, dogs and Argippaeans or not, we'll have packs of wolves following us like sharks following a leaking boat that throws the garbage overboard. Only there will be a lot more wolves than sharks. And the...ummm...captives? They'll fade away, many or most of them, unless housed and guarded inside the walls.

"As far as guarding a camp of that size goes, forget it. We don't have enough men to guard it, especially at night and *most* especially if we're attacked."

Caelius gave Gaius the usual glance that said *Ask if he's got a solution.*

"Do you have a solution?" asked the legate.

"Maybe," the tribune said. "It requires a certain change of mindset, but I think it's workable."

Meaningfully, and noisily, Caelius tapped the water clock. *Get on with it, Rubelius.*

"Right," agreed the tribune for logistics. "Think of our camp, as we shall build it, as a base for the legion, but also an emergency shelter against danger for the rest. It houses what our camps have always housed: men, absolutely essential supplies and animals, the official camp followers, and so forth.

"Outside that camp, we put together a laager, a wall of wagons. Sometimes it would be evenly spaced around the central camp, sometimes off to one side or two sides or maybe even three, if we find ourselves next to a major river. That's where the herds stay and that's where the captives stay, both under guard.

"Now this requires very aggressive patrolling, and at a good distance from camp, enough of a distance to provide warning to bring in the captives and drive the key animals into the *intervallum*. The wagons are going to have to be close enough to keep the animals in, and delay any attackers, but far enough apart to prevent fire from spreading."

"Tough set of requirements to meet," said the legate.

"Depends on the wind, sir," replied Rubelius. "But we can make it better by building a load of those movable obstacles we used to defend the camp. We'd need to build and take with us maybe six thousand of them, having two strapped on each wagon and placing those two between each wagon, once the laager is set up, for one, and under each wagon, for the other.

"Further, sir, if we were attacked, we'd have a choice: pull everything critical inside the central camp and hang tough, or go out and meet the raiders in the space between the central camp and the wagon wall. We'd have the advantages of scorpion fire from the walls and the outer wagon wall rationing any horse archers into the in-between areas, too. I think, sir, that we've proven that good infantry can beat horse archers under similar circumstances."

"One problem," said Bat-Erdene, whose Latin had gotten to be rather good over the winter. "Well, two. Most of my men want to go home to the tribe. And I believe all the girls do. After all, the girls have twenty-five denarii now...well, actually probably twice that, because a lot of the legionaries give them tips from time to time. That's more than enough to buy themselves a place with a good man."

"Can you recruit more?" asked Marcus Caelius.

"Men, yes. Girls, probably not. You're going so far away that they'd never get back, which pretty much defeats the purpose of earning silver."

Caelius nodded his understanding. "What if we paid the men we have a substantial bonus to reenlist, so to speak?"

"Might get a few more, but most just want to go home to tribe. Have mothers. Have girlfriends and wives. Fathers, brothers, and sisters. They want to go home," he repeated.

"Fine," said the legate. "Draw a bag of silver from the treasurer...how much would you need?"

"Maybe two thousand denarii. Once they find out how far we're going, and how long we'll be gone, two denarii a month isn't going to cut it."

"Fine. Draw two thousand denarii from the treasurer and bring us back as many men as you can get."

"What are we going to do for meretrices for the men?" wondered Caelius, aloud.

"Gisco?"

"Yes, sir. Bat-Erdene, you and I need to do some more interviews of the captive women. Same conditions as for the Argippaean girls, sir? The Scythians were not nearly so money poor, so I think we're going to have to pay a good deal more."

"That's fine," answered the legate.

"One minor matter," said Caelius. "The men have grown *really* fond of the Argippaean girls. Sir, you had better prepare a nice *ave atque vale*, a speech for their departure. It's a morale matter, sir."

I really cannot believe the silly shit I am called upon to do sometimes.

The *medicus* piped in with, "And they really deserve a nice bonus for their help at the hospital during and after the battle with the Scythians. Maybe another dozen denarii. Maybe even twenty."

"Speaking of things that get ridden hard," Caelius said, "I'm going to make a recommendation that really tears at my foot soldier's soul, especially since I despise cavalry on principle."

Caelius looked over at Atrixtos and said, "No offense, of course."

"None taken."

"And that would be?" asked the legate.

"We need to mount every man in the legions on horseback. Go ahead and ask me why; the answer may surprise you."

"Okay, I'll bite: why?"

"Logistics," said Caelius. "Just logistics, and the simplest but most important aspect of it: food.

"Yes, I know, none of you get it. What do our horses eat? What do our men eat?"

Rubelius took up the challenge. "Our men eat meat and grain while our horses eat grain and grass."

"Yes," agreed Caelius, with a broad smile. "Now tell us, O overpromoted gentleman ranker, what the locals horses eat."

"Just grass."

"Now, for extra credit, do men riding need to eat as much for a given mile as men walking with heavy loads?"

"Well . . . no."

"So, do the math in your head, young Rubelius: if the men ride horses will the horses need grain and will the men need less grain?"

"By the gods, Legate," the tribune said, "the camp prefect is right. We can move faster and stretch the food out more if we put the men on horseback. And the grass is an infinite resource, easily found, that doesn't have to be carried, while the meat and grain are, mostly, none of those things."

"How do we fight?" asked Gaius Pompeius.

"We dismount," said Caelius.

"Then what happens to the horses?"

"We add two Scythian freedman, the former farmers, to every *contubernium* as horse holders and servants."

"There aren't nearly enough of them for that," Rubelius objected. "Not even if we use the old men. Why not? Because we're also using them to guard the laager and the Scythian women."

"Does someone need to be able to see to hold a horse?" asked the camp prefect.

Rubelius considered this briefly, then answered, "Well, no, I suppose not, not if there's someone to tell them to follow them. But that's still not enough. You need over seventeen hundred of them. There are only a bit over two thousand farmers, and maybe half a thousand old men not too frail to do the job."

"And that's where those orphans come in," finished Marcus Caelius.

✧   ✧   ✧

The entire force was once again lined up in the shape of a C, less only those on the towers, the walls, or on patrol, as the caravan of Argippaean meretrices, the scouts taking their discharge, and the recruiting party, all under Bat-Erdene, made their departure. The girls and their escorts were leaving with a message for Qadan, their chief. That message, memorized by Bat-Erdene, was that the fort would be left intact for the Argippaeans to use, if they cared to, and, if they did not, it was a ready source of firewood. They were also leaving with a crash course on how to keep up and use the fort, from the baths, to the hypocausts, to waste management.

Gaius Pompeius made a short but eloquent speech about their contributions to the legion, ranging from morale maintenance to medical assistance, and summing up with, "But for you lovely girls, I think that for most of us, life here would not have been worth living."

From a front rank, Junior Centurion Lucious Pullo waved sadly at Zaya as the wagon carrying her and eleven others began to roll. For her part, she waved back, just as sadly. She knew for a fact that Pullo had never taken any of the other girls. And as far as she went, she had always counted the days between visits by the Twelfth Cohort. Furthermore, on Twelfth Cohort nights, she'd invariably taken Pullo to her own group's wagon, made love, then went back to work, after which she cleaned herself thoroughly before returning to sleep with Pullo for a few hours before he had to go to what the Romans called "stand to."

Zaya's face was a sculpture in despair, a despair mirrored on Pullo's. Suddenly, though, as if coming to a welcome decision, her face changed. She spoke a few words to her mates, riding in the front of the wagon, and, at their understanding nods, got up and disappeared inside. A few moments later she reappeared at the rear, bearing a bag of her clothing and a smaller bag of silver.

Bearing both she walked determinedly to Lucius Pullo. She threw her parcel of clothing at his feet and handed him the bag of silver.

"Lucius," she said, and clearly, for her Latin, too, had become quite fluent over the winter, "I realized when I saw you standing here that I don't want to leave. I *can't* leave. I don't want anyone but you. Take my money and take me as your woman, to be yours alone, until one of us dies. I will stop taking the herbs that prevent babies and bear you as many good sons and daughters as I can. If you want another wife sometime, I will understand."

Standing next to Pullo, Titus Vorenus said, "I'd take her up on it. For one thing, once we get home, our clans—really, our clan, if we're being honest about it—could use some new blood. For another thing, she is very unlikely ever to cheat on you; she knows men altogether too well for that. And for a third and final, she must truly love you if she's willing to give up her people and her way of life for you."

Shouted Marcus Caelius, who was not all that far away, "Centurion Lucius Pullo!"

"Sir!"

"Two-day pass, commencing now."

Said Gaius Pompeius, sotto voce, "You are *such* an old softy."

"Nothing of the kind," replied Caelius. "Rather, I am a cynic who understands that most men are not as cynical as myself. Most—and soldiers are even worse than most—are romantics. They all dream of finding a true love and most of the time rejoice when they see that someone else has. So young Pullo gets his pass for *their* morale, not his."

"But she's a . . ."

"Yes, sir, she's a whore. Now tell us in what way she sells her body that's more obscene or for a more obscene purpose than us selling ours?"

At that, Gaius was at a loss for words.

Tursidius had made a habit the last several months of stopping by to see Leimeie and the children about every two or three days. Sometimes he brought them little gifts, often enough serviceable clothing, obtained from the quartermaster's shop. He made sure they had enough firewood, as well. More often he gave Latin lessons and picked up some Scythian. He was a little surprised to see Leimeie filling out very quickly under a regime of decent and plentiful food. He'd thought her to be perhaps twelve, and an underdeveloped twelve at that. After three months she appeared to be at least fifteen, and perhaps even a slender sixteen.

"How did you end up in such bad circumstances?" he asked the girl, once she had enough Latin to make conversation possible.

"Father was king," she answered, "killed in the battle. The people cannot blame him or punish him for disaster, since he dead, so they blame me and brothers and sisters."

"King?" Tursidius asked, swallowing at being in the presence of royalty. "That's means you're a princess?"

"Suppose so. Means nothing." Leimeie reached out to stroke the Roman's bare cheek. "You more a prince than I ever a princess."

INTERLUDE

Domus Augusti, Palatine Hill, Rome, December 762 AUC

The cry "*Quintili Vare, legiones redde!*"—"Quintilius Varus, give me back my legions!"—echoed through the fairly austere "palace" of Augustus Caesar. More often than not, the cry was accompanied by one or more heavy thumps as the emperor of the greatest empire the world had ever known, up to this date, pounded the wall with his fists or even beat his head against it.

Augustus had been in mourning ever since receiving word of the disaster in Germany. His hair, nails, and beard were uncut and, though quite fastidious normally, his bathing had become rather haphazard and infrequent, as well. His tunic was torn and dirty.

Once upon a time, some two hundred and twenty-five years earlier, Rome had lost approximately a third of all the military age manpower in Italy to Hannibal the Carthaginian, and all in an afternoon. This represented sixteen overstrength legions plus a great many cavalrymen. Rome had still gone on to win the war and, fifty years later, to destroy their Punic rival.

Now, when fathers were cutting the thumbs off their sons to render them unfit for military service, when the fertility rate of Roman women had dropped through the floor? Now the loss of three legions was an unmitigated disaster that might never fully be made up.

Indeed, so great was the reluctance of Romans to report to the eagles to make up for the loss that Augustus had been forced to

281

enroll freedmen and enact conscription and recall of the already discharged. These measures were backed up by capital punishment. And as for the father who cut his sons' thumbs off, all of his property was seized and made forfeit to the state.

And even with all those measures, there was no ready fix for the loss of three legions and a goodly number of *auxilia*.

"*Quintili Vare, legiones redde!*" Thump. Thump. Thump.

Some had escaped, of course, either from fortuitous and wise early desertion—though none would admit to that—or even by escaping after capture. The tale these told was one of unadulterated woe, centurions crucified, or nailed through their skulls to trees, intestines cut out as sacrifice to the barbaric Germanic gods, men hanged and left hanging on the Germans' sacred oaks. Even men burnt alive. There was no end to the list of horrors done to Rome's soldiers.

But the very worst thing of all? Eagles, three of them, lost to shame and barbarian capture. And Augustus took massive pride in getting back the eagles lost at Carrhae by Crassus, too. Now all that pride was nullified by Varus' stupidity and gullibility.

"*Quintili Vare, legiones redde!*" Thump. Thump. Thump.

CHAPTER THIRTEEN

When, after this, they are gone out of their camp, they
all march without noise, and in a decent manner, and
everyone keeps his own rank, as if they were going to
war. The footmen are armed with breast-plates, and
head-pieces, and have swords on each side, but the
sword which is upon their left side is much longer than
the other, for that on the right side is not longer than
a span. Those footmen also that are chosen out from
the rest to be about the general himself, have a lance
and a buckler, but the rest of the foot soldiers have a
spear, and a long buckler, besides a saw and a basket,
a pickaxe, and an axe, a thong of leather, and a hook,
with provisions for three days, so that a footman hath
no great need of a mule to carry his burdens.
—Flavius Josephus, *The War of the Jews*, III.5.5

In camp, land of Rome's Eighteenth Legion, date unknown

The Argippaeans left camp first, about a hundred old hands,
now reinforced by about three hundred and twenty new, and all
at standard auxiliary pay scales, for infantry, plus a substantial
stipend for their horses. Half went forward; it was their job to
scout for danger and opportunities, both, as well as for obstacles.
The other half, and all of the dogs, moved to secure the huge
herds of animals the legion now owned.

After leaving camp, they all also had to pass through one of
the gates in the wall of wagons. This had been set up and torn

down half a dozen times, for practice, before the legion left the fort on the banks of the great river.

As the Argippaean scouts passed through the second set of gates, the German *auxilia* cohort emerged from the Porta Principalis Sinistra, in a single column of horse, two men across. They continued in this form until passing the line of wagons, already dissolving into columns themselves, at which point the Germans first spread out, by widely spaced centuries, then peeling off half the strength of those centuries to form lines of skirmishers between them. All of them were mounted.

Following the Germans, and likewise mounted—although in their case they actually knew how to ride a horse—came the Gallic, which included the legionary cavalry, and the Palmyrene cavalry. They had the horse archers, cross attached, sending half their subordinate formations to the Gauls and the Gauls approximately returning the favor. These passed out and peeled off right and left at a sharp angle to provide left and right flank security.

Next came the command party: Gaius Pompeius, Marcus Caelius, the seven tribunes, the aquilifer, signifers, and imaginifers, plus runners and guards.

Following the command party came First Cohort, like others also in column of four but covering a great deal more ground to account for the horses. Twelfth Cohort, with their invaluable staff slings, followed the First Cohort, and the mixed cohort of Thracian slingers and Rhodian archers followed them.

The next eight cohorts peeled off, staggering left and right, though neither so far nor at such a steep angle as the Gauls and Palmyrenes. Just as in the marching camps planned, the legion and its *auxilia* were to provide a refuge at the center, not an impossible defense of everything.

Behind those, and forming in the space defined by the left flank, the right flank, the command group, and the rear guard came the more usual and utterly necessary legionary *impedimenta*, the carts and wagons, as well as the donkeys and horses carrying the tents and mess gear of the *contubernia*, a month's worth of rations for the legionaries and *auxilia* alone, siege parts, tool kits, et cetera.

Eleventh Cohort brought up the rear. It was under the returned-to-duty First-Order Centurion Sextus Sattius, now much the better from his long stint working agriculture, though it was Caelius' opinion that Sattius, while still useful, ought never be put in charge of anything critical...

Well to either flank of the legion, but still inside the cavalry's screen, the immense Scythian and Argippaean wagons formed up in two sections of widely spaced lines.

Danapris River, also known as the Borysthenes, date unknown

On horseback, making upward of twenty-five miles a day across the steppe, the legion reached a river after some forty-seven days of movement.

Gaius and Caelius sat on their horses, on Scythian saddles modified to use the Argippaeans' stirrups. In front of them stretched a broad river, not so wide as the great river, left behind them, but more than they could hope to bridge.

"Besides," said the *praefectus castrorum*, "there's no damned wood here to make a bridge."

"You know," said the legate, "it's funny—I was assigned to the legion as an 'expert' in engineering. And I haven't done any of that since arrival. Might be interesting to take it up again."

"I've got scouting parties to our north and south," said Caelius. "Maybe they'll find some wood, or a place we can hope to ford, or some people who have boats big enough to ferry the Scythian wagons. In the unlikely event that such boats exist outside of the grain ships from Alexandria... Oh, that's another thing."

"What's that?" asked the legate.

"We should have... *I* should have known that there was going to be a problem with the Scythian women."

"What problem?"

Caelius sighed, wistfully. "It was my girl, Tabiti, who first brought it to my attention. Just about every legionary has found himself a Scythian girl. Some of them have found more than one. The ones who haven't appear to be looking."

"In other words," said Gaius, "we can't sell them anymore?"

"Pretty much," Caelius agreed. "*O tempora, O mores.* Everybody's got himself a Scythian girl, near enough, and every girl has relatives. Tabiti says the young ones who haven't found a member of the legion or an auxiliary are being pressured by their families to do so before those families get sold."

"Mutiny if we tried to sell them now," said Gaius.

"That's my read on it, too."

"It's not like I'm sorry," said Gaius, "I didn't want to sell them, anyway, not really. We'll have to spend from our obscenely flush treasury to buy grain now. Ho-hum; it's not like we don't have the money. As for Romano-Scythian...ummm...*relations*, my Zaranaia has been pestering me for weeks about it. So, no, it doesn't come as a complete surprise. Not a surprise at all, really; the Scythian girls...it's not like they're not attractive."

"Tough," agreed Caelius, "brave, hardworking, and pretty, most of them. Thing is, what are we going to do to both make this work and keep up discipline?"

"I don't know," Gaius admitted. "Haven't even the tiniest glimmering of a clue, really."

"Well," said Caelius, "on the plus side and at least so far, the men have been decent about it, not visiting their girls until after the camp is built, staying away no longer than it takes for a decent screw, or just a meal with their girls' families, then returning to their *contubernium*. It could be a *lot* worse. And, though one hates to admit it of a gentleman ranker, that young upstart Rubelius was right about the main camp as refuge. The men are happy enough securing that, knowing the cavalry are out on patrol for early warning and so their girls and their families can scramble to safety if we're attacked."

"Speaking of which," said Gaius, "it's funny we haven't been attacked since we began our march."

"We look too tough," said Caelius. "Three or four times more powerful than we really are. However, maybe that will change." Caelius pointed with his chin at a party of horsemen, riding hard from the southeast. "Did we send any patrols in that direction?"

"Nope. Privatus?"

"Sir?"

"Go find Metilius. Two cohorts to stand to under arms, mixed force of Gallic and Palmyrene cavalry, half a dozen *turmae* each. Keep the slingers, staff slingers, and archers under wraps. All here in a hurry."

"Why no foot missile troops?" asked Gaius after Privatus had trotted off.

"We want them to know we're too dangerous to attack, but not just how dangerous we are in case they do attack."

✧　　✧　　✧

The newcomers, who introduced themselves as "Goths," might not have been interested in attacking, anyway, but the presence of about nine hundred well-armed and armored Romans, supported by a few hundred cavalry, probably didn't hurt matters.

Caelius directed that the bulk of the party be brought to the centurions' mess tent and be fed, watered, and given beer there. The three obvious chiefs—obvious because of the richness of dress and the amount of gold and silver about their persons—were brought to the adjacent officers' mess for those purposes, as well as discussions.

For the Romans, those in attendance included the command group, including all the tribunes, the prefects of the *auxilia*, the chief *medicus*, the *haruspex*, and the *primus pilus*.

The senior among the Goths, who gave his name as Wulfila, spoke for them.

"They speak something that's pretty clearly *related* to the German that I know," said Gaius to the camp prefect, "but it most definitely is *not* the German I know. I can maybe grasp about one sentence in five. Maybe."

Gisco, likewise in attendance, simply shrugged his narrow shoulders, as if to say *Don't look at me, boss.* Bat-Erdene was similarly useless.

"Hmmmm, I wonder," said Marcus Caelius, then sent his man Thiaminus to find his woman, Tabiti, and ask if any of the Scythian girls or women could understand them. As it turned out there were three former slaves of the Scythians, all now freed, who had been taken in raids long ago, and who spoke a version of the language of the Goths.

Once the former slaves were found and brought in, and after tongues had been pretty well lubricated by beer, communication could commence.

"What you do here?" was the first question from the Goths.

"Passing through on our way home to Rome. Set up a series of camps. Graze our animals."

"What else you want?"

"To cut trees to make a bridge somewhere over this river. To buy grain if you have any to sell. We could use information, too, about what lies ahead, what dangers lurk."

"You no attack us?"

"Wouldn't dream of it, old boy."

"What you pay for grain? Weez gots wheat, rye, barley."

"What you...How much do you want?"

That took some figuring but, as it turned out, the Goths would sell wheat, for example, at three *modii* per denarius. This was a much better price than in Rome, and even a better price than in the provinces.

"We've gone through about three hundred and sixty thousand *modii*," said Rubelius, "since leaving the old fort. Thus, we have room on the wagons for another three hundred and sixty thousand. One hundred and twenty thousand denarii, from a treasury the size of ours, would be—well, frankly, and no pun intended, albeit recognized—chicken feed.

"What else have you got to trade?" Rubelius asked through the interpreters.

"Gots beer, maybe better than yours. Maybe. Eggs. Chickens. Gots wine. Trade for wine from Greeks..."

"Wait a minute," said Gaius. "You trade with Greeks? You *speak* Greek?"

Wulfila looked surprised, then answered in that language, "Some do. I do. Koine, not pure Attic." Koine, a dialect of Greek, was the lingua franca of the Hellenistic world.

"Well, fuck me to tears," said Marcus Caelius. In Greek, he asked about the wine. "And the cheese?"

"Well, I personally doubt that the little boy buggerers sell us their best, but it's certainly drinkable. Has a funny piney kind of taste. The traders say that's necessary to keep it from going bad. As for cheese, we make some lovely ghastly, stinky cheese on our own. Also some more bland varieties."

"How much wine can you sell?" asked Rudelius. "How much cheese and sausage? Umm...pork sausage."

"Maybe a thousand amphorae," answered Wulfila, "but if you care to wait, we can get a great deal more. Thirty denarii per amphora, delivered. Cheese, the price varies, but it is unlikely you people can exhaust our stores. Yes, pork. Well, some is a mix of pork and beef, but pork predominates. Our supply borders the unlimited."

"Wish we could wait," said Gaius Pompeius, "but we really can't. Still, we'd be happy to take your thousand, or any above that you think you can spare, for thirty thousand denarii. Or, if you prefer gold, equivalent weight of twenty-five hundred coin."

"Is the gold in coin form or bars?" asked Wulfila.

"Mostly jewelry, to be honest," answered Gaius. "Pretty stuff; I'm sure you will like it. Also very pure. How long will it take you to assemble the grain and wine?"

"A week or so, and another to transport it. Can you wait that long?"

"We can wait two weeks," said Marcus Caelius, who was getting heartily sick of water and beer alone, and not enough of the latter. Even so, he asked, "Have to put up a bridge. And beer—a lot of the men have developed some taste for beer."

"Beer's a lot cheaper than even pine-tasting wine," answered Wulfila, frankly. "But it's hard to transport in quantity. We can barge it up the river, but it will take longer. We might be able to get another thousand amphorae of wine faster than that."

Gaius and Calius both looked at Thancrat, who said, "Not worth the wait, for the beer. After all, we can make what we need in the barrels and on the move. More wine might be good."

"Fine, no beer," said Wulfila. "I'll work on the extra thousand of wine. That pretty much exhausts our extras. But you said you wanted information ..."

Before anyone else could answer, Appius Calvus, the *haruspex*, had a question, spurred by his time coinhabiting with Jerome. "You speak Greek. In my ... mmm ... travels, I found that the language, some places and times, went with a particular religion. What's yours?"

"We are Christians, most of us," answered Wulfila, "followers of the teachings of Arius. We have been ever since our women converted to it. And our women were converted by a number of Christian woman whom some of us captured in a raid, one of whom gave birth to the mother of Ulfilas, our former bishop. Yes, Ulfilas is something pronounced 'Wulfila.' No, we are not related.

"We do have a pagan group under a chief named Radagaisius, some of our people, plus some Vandals, and some Alans. If I were Roman, Romans being almost entirely Christian now, I wouldn't trust him.

"By the way, I see some fine-looking animals in your herds. Also some fine-looking women. Would you be willing to sell any?"

"Maybe," said Gaius. "What are grazing rights going to cost us?"

"Not sure. Up north is a different clan ... well, clans. Would you like for me to go see them and negotiate a decent price? For a price?"

"Please," agreed Gaius.

A new marching camp was built, right on the banks of the Danapris River, with the animal-enclosing wagon laager stretching on three sides around the camp. Life settled down nicely for a bit and, as Caelius said, "The boys could use a break."

Part of the break was that the Scythian women, now picking up Roman ways, were performing stand-to on their own, without guidance, to make sure no raiders—four-legged wolves or two-legged men—entered the laager area unchallenged. A surprising number of previously hidden bows and quivers of arrows materialized to this end.

The wine and grain came, the gold was paid over, and then a goodly amount of it paid back for some fine Scythian horses, some sheep, and some cattle. Wulfila was especially interested in getting some *ngekud*, so Gisco soaked him for a bull and six heifers. The dogs all stayed with the legion, as it would have been as much a cause of mutiny among the men to sell off their beloved puppies as if someone tried to take away their Scythian girlfriends.

That said, there were some Scythian women who had not been able to find mates among the Romans or, bitter about both their defeat and the massacre of their remaining young men, were simply unwilling to. Instead of selling these off—"We are, by the gods, *Romans*, and nothing is official until the paperwork is done!"—they were let go to the Goths, and with dowries, to boot.

Gaius took his woman Zaranaia, now waddling like a duck, and still beautiful, or maybe more beautiful, still, to speak to one third of the departing women, while Gisco and Bat-Erdene took another group each.

The legate saw that there was a mixed group of about thirteen hundred women, children, and oldsters seated on the ground and waiting for him to speak. He spoke through Zaranaia.

"We understand that you hate us," he began, "and we understand why. I will not ask you for forgiveness because, in the first place, the Scythians attacked us first, without parley and using poisoned arrows. That last was sufficient reason to have gotten rid of your remaining young men—that, and that we could never have trusted them.

"However, *we* do not hate *you*. Indeed, we rather like you and will be very sorry to see you go.

"Now, I understand that most of you think you have been enslaved, because you were captured and put to work. No. We are Romans and we do not just declare someone to be a slave. Or, at least, we do not necessarily and universally do so. We prefer that things be formal, with titles and bills of sale; records, in any case. We did none of this with you and so, while you were, again, captives, no, you were never slaves. You are free, as free as you were before we took you. So, yes, you are entitled to hold your heads as high as any freeborn woman, now and forever."

Many of the now no longer captive women began to weep at this bit of enlightenment. Four women got up and left the group, trailed by a dozen children, apparently deciding to stay on with the Romans.

"We don't really know enough about the Goths to advise you about them beyond a little bit gleaned during our business dealings. Women are apparently pretty free there, and those with some wealth and position of their own do quite well. So we're going to send you all off with dowries. I've worked out with one of my officers what we can afford to give you, or give you back. This will include to each a wagon, though not of the biggest, with animals to haul it, Some of these will be horses or mules, or sometimes oxen, but no *ngekud*. We'll also give you a small mixed herd of goats and sheep, about fifteen head per adult woman. You'll also get a modest—in both senses—wardrobe. On top of this we'll give you a cash present of a hundred denarii. If you take with you some of the oldsters or older couples, especially those for whom the rigors of the trek were becoming life threatening, we'll add in another fifty denarii. You will also take with you one good horse, each, with a Scythian saddle, the better to attract a local mate.

"Your children will go with you unless they want, of their own volition, to stay with us."

The numbers of women who chose to settle among the Goths were above two thousand; with the oldsters and children, almost five thousand mouths were removed from straining the legion's logistics.

That said, exceptionally speaking, there were two hundred

and twenty-seven Scythian boys, too young to be included in the massacre but old enough, now, for the romance of military life to have taken hold. These, reluctantly, said goodbye to their mothers and grandmothers and presented themselves, via a group of representatives, to Gaius Pompeius. With similarly aged boys from women who had taken up with the legionaries, the total came to six hundred and twelve. None were old enough for enlistment, but that was no reason not to make them auxiliary cadets and commence their training as the "Fifth *Ala* of *Auxilia*, Scythica."

"Who are you going to put in charge?" asked Caelius, when told by Gaius.

"No idea. Any suggestions?"

"Well, the boys are young. Probably could use a gentler hand than most. And Sextus Sattius' Eleventh Cohort has a fire eater who could take his place. How about Sattius?"

"Works for me, at least for their basic training. Now what have the scouts found?"

"They found what Wulfila had told us of, that about one hundred and fifty miles north of here there is a bend in the River Danapris with islands dividing the river on both sides of the bend. They didn't go past that on the theory that if he'd told us the truth about the river, he'd probably also told us the truth that not far north of that bend the steppe ended and great forests began. We can float the trees that we'll need down the river.

"I'm leading out the advance party tomorrow a couple of hours before dawn."

"Right," said Centurion Sattius to his new charges, most of them under thirteen. "Time for us to get acquainted a bit. I am Sextus Sattius, your new *ala* commander. Standing behind me are your centurions, Titus Vorenus, Gratianus Claudius, Aelius Nerva, Ovidius Paulus, and Publius Rufinus. We are your training cadre, though Vorenus will be the only one staying on after you are trained and most of your new leadership selected from among your own ranks. The rest of us have regular jobs to get back to.

"Now what we are going to do is divide you all into five maniples, just because we're all infantry and are used to maniples. Your names will be taken and a description written down. After this, you will be given a course in rudimentary close order drill, the same things you have seen the regular legionaries engaged in, when not mounted atop horses.

"We will practice this for two hours every evening when the legion stops to build camp. On the march, you will ride in the wagons with your mothers and, for some two hundred and twenty-seven of you, your assigned foster mothers. These will also be measuring you for linen armor, cutting the linen, and building it up with thread and glue to fit you. Any questions, so far?"

One of the boys, taller and probably a bit older than the rest, stood announced himself as, "Ishkapaia, sir," and asked, "Weapons training, sir?"

"Ishkapaia, you are assigned to the first maniple under Centurion Titus Vorenus. Further, you will henceforward be known as Ishkapaius, in keeping with your position as a future soldier of Rome. As for weapons, that will come. Right now we are thinking that your best use will be to serve as horse archers. How many of you know how to ride?"

Instantly, all six hundred and twelve right hands went up.

"Do you have any experience with bows?"

"Light bows, yes, sir," Ishkapaius answered. "Won't get much use out of us unless we use poison arrows. Not, at least, until we've grown a good deal."

"We'll see, Ishkapaius."

The steady scrape of the pioneer tools and the pounding of stakes, were all overlaid by the neighing, baaing, whinnying and all around complaining of the animals... the *tens of thousands* of animals. To this was added the cursing of men discovering—as they discovered anew at every attempt at setting up the tents— just how uncooperative a tent can be. Farther out, the Scythian women were setting up their laager under the stern rule of the *gromatici* and the *metatores*.

Not far from the camp but right on the banks of the Danapris, Gaius Pompeius asked, "Here, you think?" The legate sounded dubious. Here or, rather, to their front were two islands, one much larger than the other, set in the river.

"Well," said Marcus Caelius, "I'm not an engineer, but I've seen a lot of rivers bridged and took part in my share of the bridging. I think that it's easier to build three bridges of three hundred, eight hundred, and thirteen hundred feet than one bridge of twenty-four hundred. I also think it will be quicker, since we can be building all three at the same time."

"How deep is it?" asked Gaius.

"Twenty-seven feet was the deepest we found, more or less dead center in the longer stretch. The engineers are assembling a list of depths at the distance between pilings, to send on to the cohorts on forestry duty, which happen to be the Sixth and Eighth cohorts, guarded by a mix of Gallic and Palmyrene *auxilia*."

Based on reports of the forest to the north, there were more than sufficient trees of more than sufficient height for the piles. He asked, "Will the islands support our heavy wagons?"

Shaking his head, Caelius answered, "Not a chance in Hades. We're going to have to put in corduroy roads across the islands to support the wagons. To support the *ngekud*, for that matter; it's *really* marshy out there."

Twelve rafts were arrayed in three of the channels that had to be bridged, two on the shortest span, four on the middle one, and six on the long stretch. Atop each was a pyramidal framework, designed to hold sharpened pilings at an angle and to raise and then drop a heavy weight, stones collected from the area, onto those pilings, to drive them into the riverbed. The stones were enclosed in a wooden framework, raised by winch and released by metal hooks scrounged from the iron implements used to construct siege engines. It had, in fact, been the number of release hooks available that had limited the number of rafts to twelve.

For every barge with a pile driver, there was another with a crane, used to lift and emplace the crosspieces and maneuver the reinforcing pieces of the frame, as well as the timbers laid from crosspiece to crosspiece.

The moon was three quarters, and waxing, with a moonrise about midway between sundown and midnight. What this meant, in practice, was Marcus Caelius complaining of the incessant and random, hence unpredictable, racket. "I understand this is considered a form of torture, in some places."

"I know," admitted Gaius, holding his head in his hands while seated at his field desk. "I know. It never ends but goes on and on. I tried to sleep, but couldn't."

"I went and looked over the works," said Caelius. "The three-hundred-footer is ready, for pilings, crosspieces and bracing, framework, and stringers. They're laying the top now. Almost done, matter of fact. You want to take a look?"

"Let's," agreed Gaius. "It's not like I'm going to sleep with this racket."

They didn't need a torchlight, the moon was bright enough to guide their steps, just as it was bright enough to illuminate the work with the rafts and the bridges.

Leaving the *Praetorium*, they walked on a corduroy road that ran through the camp and then to the edge of the river, then down between the double walls protecting the way down to the water. Every step drew them closer to the pounding.

At the beginning of the bridge were two pairs of turpentine-fed lamps, burning brightly in the night. There were two more on the opposite side, all of them having been laid in by the surveyors to keep the work aligned. Red flags took the place of the torches in the daytime.

The nearest pounding stopped at the same time as they reached the near bank. "Gods be praised," said Marcus Caelius.

The walkway was awkward, enough so for the centurion in charge to caution them, "Watch your step, sirs, you can twist an ankle on this kind of surface. We're going to put in a mix of gravel and clay for the animals' hooves."

"Not that I'm complaining, but why did the bloody pounding stop?" asked Gaius.

"Put in the last pilings, sir, the ones in threes to protect the bridge from things floating downstream. We'll be moving the rafts around to the middle stretch in the morning. It's not really light enough to do so safely at night, even with the moon. Probably get them grounded in some way that will take days to fix if we tried."

"Right. Well done."

"You and the *praefectus castrorum* can cross all the way over, sir, if you've a mind to. The timbers linking crosspieces are all in place. Just watch your step, sirs."

Wulfila showed up with a barge of beer, shortly before the final span was finished. He took one look and gave a long, admiring whistle. "I am impressed," he told Gaius. "Oh, and since I was coming anyway I figured to find a market for the beer."

"Damned well ought to be impressed," said Marcus Caelius.

"We did more than Caesar, faster than Caesar, with a lot fewer men. And beer would be a fair reward for the men, too. See Rubelius for payment."

"To be fair," corrected Gaius, "Caesar didn't have *ngekud* to haul logs, nor seventeen thousand Scythians—mostly women, to be sure, but still tough and strong—to sharpen them. By the way, Wulfila, how are the Scythian girls getting along with your people?"

"Most have already received proposals of marriage. Maybe a fifth have accepted so far."

"Ah, good. But none of them speak your language and you don't have anyone who speaks theirs, nor enough Greek speakers on either side."

"My father," said the Goth, "always held that when men and women are interested in each other, there's a language they speak between them that has no words but conveys the message perfectly."

"It may be so," said the legate, thinking of how few words had to pass between him and his Zaranaia, even though her Latin was coming along nicely.

Caelius looked at the Goth's face before saying, "Something is troubling you. What?"

"Two things, actually," admitted the Goth. "One is that Radagaisius has left our lands for an invasion of Italy. The other is that, though the remainder are Christian, most support him and some have even accompanied him because the Huns are pressing on our eastern border. The Huns, if you didn't know, are ferocious and vicious, both."

"We've heard," said Caelius.

"We're going to have to flee," said Wulfila. "We're no match for the Huns, not out here in the open. And I don't see the Empire letting us in peacefully, not after Adrianople. And, mind you, that war and the battle were not entirely our cousins' fault. The Empire promised to let them in and give them land, also to feed them until they could get their own crops in. But they let the Visigoths starve."

Something in the Goth's tone raised the figurative hackles on Caelius' back. *We didn't leave so long ago for this much history to have passed. We knew the Gods moved us in time, but how much time was it?*

"What was Adrianople?" he asked, keeping a neutral tone in his voice.

"Big battle between the Visigoths—my people are Ostrogoths, if I didn't mention it—and Rome. Rome...lost. Emperor killed..."

"What? Augustus killed?"

"No, no," said Wulfila, "Emperor Valens was killed, and about ten thousand good infantry destroyed."

"Emperor...ummmm...Valens?"

"Well, co-emperor. His brother, Valentinian, the original emperor, appointed him..."

"Co-emperors...What year is it?" asked Gaius, suddenly. "Seriously, what year is it? In Roman years?"

"Roman years? Well, my Lord, you know I'm not sure. Let me think a minute. Christ was crucified in the year 33, so the holy fathers say. And he was born in the year one or three or four or five or six years before that, depending on which holy father you ask, which was somewhere between seven hundred and forty-seven and seven hundred and fifty-three years after the founding of Rome. And now it is something between the year three hundred and ninety-nine and four hundred and five from whenever it was we started counting. So the Roman year would be...oh...something between one thousand, one hundred and fifty-two and one thousand, one hundred and fifty-nine. Give or take."

Both Caelius and Gaius found themselves feeling slightly faint, as the ramifications of this washed over them.

They spoke in Latin to keep the Goth from understanding. "I had a family at Vetera," Caelius said. "Wife, three sons, two daughters. Two grandchildren, at least two, on the way. All gone."

"I promised my mother that I'd be home for her forty-fifth birthday," said Gaius. "No mother now. No father. No sister or brother. No friends from home. All gone...gone. Even my fiancé...gone."

"What the fuck are we going to tell the men?" asked Caelius. This was an officer question and it was up to the only original officer of the legion to answer it.

"I have no idea."

To Wulfila, Gaius turned and asked, in Greek, "How much history do you know? Is there someone in your clan or tribe who knows most or all of it for the last four hundred years?"

"Well," answered Wulfila, "I am probably as knowledgeable as any Goth, but that's not going to be all that knowledgeable. What may be more important to you is that I have a history of the last three centuries or so in book format—codex form, not scrolls—as well as a copy of what I am told are the lives of the first twelve Caesars, plus a history from someone named Tacitus. I bought them but cannot read them. I was hoping to find a Latin-speaking slave to help me learn Latin. Maybe if Radagaisius' expedition prospers."

"The first *twelve* Caesars. Twelve. HAHAHAHAHA. *TWELVE!*"

Gaius Pompeius had never heard the camp prefect sound anything like hysterical before, not even in Germany when they all believed they were going to die. He certainly sounded close to it now, though.

"Top!"

"Yes, sir. Sorry, sir."

"Two hundred denarii for the trio," offered Gaius, without hesitation.

"Three hundred," was Wulfila's counteroffer. The Goth didn't know why this was so important to the Romans, but from their nearly fainting in public and the sound of the older man's laughter, he sensed he could extract a better price.

"Three hundred," agreed Gaius, still without the slightest hesitation.

"Sold," said Wulfila and then, sensing he could have squeezed still more, added, "And since you're going to have to wait for delivery, can I interest you in another barge's worth of beer?"

As it actually happened, Wulfila didn't own any of the books he had offered, but he did know someone who owned them. Moreover, while modern Roman silver coinage was badly—even preposterously—debased, Wulfila knew that *these* Romans' coins were good silver, as near to pure as one might ask.

"Twenty *tremissis*," was Wulfila's offer for all three books, a sum equivalent to roughly old style ninety denarii.

"Thirty," said the owner of the books.

"Done," agreed Wulfila. *Damn, but I will miss the Romans when they've moved on. Such easy marks. Well, not that Gisco fellow; he's as sharp as they come.*

✦   ✦   ✦

The books arrived about the same time the first of the babies did. This was convenient—or divinely planned, Gaius Pompeius couldn't be sure anymore—for providing an excuse to stay in place so that he and Caelius could read the books provided by Wulfila. What they found was appalling, enough so that they felt they had to keep it from the troops, at least for now. For this reason, they could only discuss it while out on "scouting expeditions," and those with their guards ordered to keep out of earshot.

"In what way," asked Marcus Caelius, "is the Empire even Roman? Everyone who isn't a slave is a citizen, while being a citizen means just about nothing. Like citizenship, the money is mostly worthless." Caelius barked a bitter laugh. "Why, *we* may be sitting on more actual cash than the Empire can come up with. Even both halves of it—did you hear me say that? 'Halves!'—of it. The old religion is gone, replaced by this newfangled superstition out of Judea. And Rome, *our Rome*, isn't even the capital anymore."

"It's worse than that, Marcus," Gaius added. "Emperors murdered left and right. We thought the civil wars were behind us; how naïve we were. And rival fragmentary empires springing up all over the place, Palmyra, Britannia, Gaul and the Rhine. Emperors—well, one emperor—captured and held by the Persians or Parthians or Sassanians; take your pick, they're all bloody orientals. It's almost two hundred years of one disaster after another. And the two hundred years before that weren't any great shakes, either."

Caelius sighed. "I do wish that Julian fellow, the pagan restorationist, had not been killed in Mesopotamia."

"But he was."

"Yes, he was. And the question before us is, what are we going to do?"

"Well, the three basic options are that we stay here to help, ally with the Goths, and do our damnedest to keep the Huns from crossing this river—that's one."

"We could make this impregnable and be fed across the bridge we just put up," suggested Caelius. "Secure our animals and women on the other side."

"Yes," said Gaius, "it's conceivable...until you look at it closely. But even on horseback and moving at the speed of cavalry, and even allied with the Goths, I don't think we can patrol enough of the river well enough to keep the Huns on this side of it. So let's consider option two: we make our best guess of where safety

might lay and run like Hades for it, then fight whoever we have
to fight to keep our own people and our families safe."

"Tempting," said Caelius, "but I don't think it will work. The
only place that's far enough off the beaten track is Britannia,
but it's an island. If we cannot hope to secure this river line,
even allied with the Goths, what hope to secure the shores of
an island that big?"

"So that leaves us option three: we do what we'd planned,
run like hell for the Rhine, and be there when the barbarians
try to come across."

"Concur," said Caelius. "What are we going to tell the men?"

"I think we're going to tell the centurions first," Gaius said,
"then the tribunes, the decurions, and the auxiliary prefects.
Also some of the medical and specialist staff. And the *optios*."

"Yeah...I can hardly wait."

Command, for the purpose of maintaining the security of
the camp, was effectively turned over to the junior noncoms,
various signifers, and Junius Rubelius, whom Gaius had read in
on the issue already, but only after drawing bloodcurdling oaths
of silence until the rest of the legion could be told.

Everyone else in a leadership position, except the cadets of
the Fifth Scythian Auxiliary *Ala*, was present in front of the
Praetorium, with everyone else barred from being anywhere near
it. Beer had already been served, and enough remained on site
to get fairly well tipsy, if not staggeringly drunk. There was a
good deal more beer available and Gaius intended to pass out
quite a bit of it to the men, once the leadership was dismissed
to inform them.

In what was just possibly the very first rendition of what
would eventually become a nearly universal joke, Gaius Pompeius
began riffing off his first speech as commander, "I have some
good news and some bad news. Bad news doesn't get any better
with time, so I'm going to start there."

And he's getting some lines on that all-too-young face, finally,
thought Caelius. *All to the good.*

The joke fell flat. Under other circumstances, perhaps, the
leadership might have laughed. Now? Now the expressions and
intonations of the legate and *praefectus castrorum* forbade mirth.

"No sense in dilly-dallying around. We are not where we

thought we were. Or, rather, we are exactly where we thought we were in space, but very much displaced in time.

"We had surmised before, and made no secret of it, that the gods sent us a bit forward in time. Yeah...no. Instead of the gods having sent us a little bit forward, we were sent about four centuries forward.

"Yes, that means that any of you who had parents? You are now orphans. Your sweethearts, children, business partners? All those are dust now. In short, we are—none of us—ever going back to the homes and the people we knew."

Well, thought Caelius, *other than the mass draining of blood from now pale faces, they're taking it fairly well. For now.*

"And the Empire?" Gaius went down the list of things that had changed, and none of them for the better, along with giving a synopsis of the treason, ruin, and betrayal, of all the troops had held dear. "Not least among these is that the Empire has abandoned its old religion and adopted a new one. According to one of the historians of three of the last four centuries, this religion is a good one, but the people who adhere to it are no better than people ever are.

"It gets worse," said the legate. "The Huns are coming. Huns? Think Scythians, only more ferocious and very, very ugly. They are coming and they're driving before them the very people who, when they break into the Empire, will conquer it, rape it, and then partition it into any number of petty kingdoms."

At that point, Gaius listed the three basic options. Finally, he said, "We are not a democracy. I will make the final decision. But I want each of you—or at least as many of you as care to give an opinion—to speak your mind on what you think we should do. We will do this by rank by cohort. First Spear Metilius?"

"We still have taken the *sacramentum,* legate. Our duty, even to this husk of an Empire, remains. I think we should drive for the Rhine and take up our duty there, no matter what."

And from that opinion, there was not a great deal of dissent. There was weeping, yes, even from strong men, at the loss of wives and parents and children. But there still wasn't much dissent.

"Fine, then," said Gaius. "Go tell your people. There is plenty of beer to soften the news. But tell them anyway that we are Romans, soldiers of the Empire, and we are going to march to the Rhine to defend the Empire!"

✥   ✥   ✥

The Scythian boys were extremely proud of their new linen armor, light and strong, and with small and thin bronze plates sewn on by their mothers and foster mothers. And, though the legionaries found it all highly amusing, they were also men who remembered being boys, who remembered the first call to military life and the sheer romance of military life. No one ridiculed the boys, for those reasons and because they were so damnably *earnest*.

Most of the boys had been issued an Amazon's bow, from captured stocks. There were not quite enough of these to go around, so nineteen or twenty from each grouping of four *turmae* had received slings and several pounds of lead to cast bullets. "Better than nothing," Sattius had told them. "Moreover, as you all get bigger we'll be issuing full power bows and passing the women's ones down, until you're all bearing full-power arrow tossers. It's not like we don't have about fifteen thousand extra bows, after all."

Thereafter, every time the legion stopped for the night, targets were set up and the boys put to work with their missile implements. They didn't have the range and power of fully grown men yet, but their accuracy wasn't bad.

INTERLUDE

Temple of Mars Ultor, Forum of Augustus, Rome, 795 AUC

A guard—a composite maniple under one of the tribunes—was sent by Faustus Gabinius, nephew of Caius Gabinius and a centurion, himself, to escort the recaptured eagle of the Eighteenth Legion, first to Italy, then to Rome, and then finally to the Temple of Mars the Avenger, where it would remain in perpetual repose. It was intended that the eagle would join there its brother eagles from the Seventeenth and Nineteenth Legions, forever.

The vexillation had presented the eagle first to the new emperor, Claudius. He, now fifty-one years old and not looking especially healthy, had stutteringly thanked the men and reached out to pat the eagle's head, as if it were a pet bird or even a dog, then directed that it be taken to the place set aside for it, as token to Mars that the loss of three legions had finally been avenged.

Though Rome had spent the last thirty-three years raiding into Germany, in part to bury the fallen, in part to exact revenge, and in part to recover the eagles, there was no question of ever going back to recolonize the area between the Rhine and the Elbe. Three legions lost was three legions too many, and nothing that could ever be extracted from Germany in taxes was going to repay the cost of extraction. The emperor ordered that the Rhine would be the frontier forever.

The eagle, itself, looked like it had seen better days, as no doubt it had. Indeed, enough damage had been done to it, whether in

the battle in which it had been lost or in damage willfully done
to it by vengeful Germans, that it looked old and tired and worn.
Or, as one of the centurions on the escort had said, "Damned
thing looks crude to me."

Crude or not, the maniple had stopped at the Temple of Mars
Ultor, with the eagle centered on the broad and shallow steps
and one century ahead of and one behind it. There the tribune
in charge had given the order, "Right . . . face!" followed by "Place
the eagle."

The first century had then faced right and filed from the left
to enter the temple, while the second century had faced left and
filed from the right. The three men holding the eagle had simply
marched forward into the temple.

Inside, though it was dimly lit, the bearer and his immediate
two guards could see two eagles and under them plaques bearing
the letters: SPQR, "The Senate and People of Rome," and below
those the numbers, XVII and XIX. Both were held up by stands.
An empty stand stood between them.

Two priests of Mars stood by the stand, one to either side. It
would be their job to purify and re-sanctify the eagle from the
shame of barbarian captivity.

On command, the trio marched forward to the empty stand.
There, the bearer reverently placed the newly reacquired eagle,
so that now three numbers could be read, left to right, XVII,
XVIII, and XIX.

The tribute then ordered a mass salute. Thereafter, they filed
out of the temple and sortied off by ones and twos, fives and
tens to see families and friends or just wallow in wine and filth,
as the spirit moved them.

CHAPTER FOURTEEN

The story of its ruin is simple and obvious; and, instead
of inquiring why the Roman empire was destroyed, we
should rather be surprised that it had subsisted so long.
The victorious legions, who, in distant wars, acquired
the vices of strangers and mercenaries, first oppressed
the freedom of the republic, and afterwards violated
the majesty of the purple. The emperors, anxious
for their personal safety and the public peace, were
reduced to the base expedient of corrupting the discipline which rendered them alike formidable to their
sovereign and to the enemy; the vigour of the military
government was relaxed, and finally dissolved, by the
partial institutions of Constantine; and the Roman
world was overwhelmed by a deluge of Barbarians.
  —Edward Gibbon, *The Decline and Fall of the Roman
Empire*, Chapter 38

Viadrus River, Germany

Between the need to follow rivers, for water, and the channel-
ing effect of mountain ranges and rough terrain, to which was
added the necessity of finding lumber both for bridging and for
firewood, the legion ended up a good deal north of where they'd
hoped and planned to be.

No matter. Thancrat, who had traveled a bit in his youth
before joining the *auxilia,* pronounced it to be the "Viadrus"
and, further, that "We're maybe four hundred to four hundred

and fifty miles from the Rhine. That's straight line, of course. No telling what kind of route we'll have to take."

"But you've been here," objected Caelius.

"Came by sea and then sailed up the river. Only thing is, this area has been devastated by something...or someone."

That was obvious from the unburied, half-decomposed bodies of men, women, and children, the burnt villages, slaughtered animals, and unploughed, unsown fields.

Even with all that ruin and destruction, though, Caelius noted that this *Germania* bore little relation to the one from which the gods had carried the legion forward in time and to a distant place.

"No," said Thancrat. "No, I agree. This Germany has actual towns, not just scattered farmsteads. This Germany has a lot more land cleared, land that probably would have been under cultivation but for the massacre of the people."

"Any idea who might have done this?" asked Caelius.

"Other Germans? Huns? Slavs? Unless we can find some witnesses, there's no telling."

"No. No, I suppose not. Any idea how far to the Albis?"

Thancrat did a little arithmetic in his head. "One hundred and fifty to two hundred; it doesn't flow perpendicularly to either the Rhine or the Viadrus. Neither is it parallel. There is one thing I can tell you: if the rest of Germany looks like this then there are a lot, an awful lot, more Germans than there used to be."

And isn't that *an unsettling thought,* mused Caelius.

Back from a leader's recon, Gaius Pompeius dismounted, considering. Finally, he pointed at a spot nearer to the river and ordered, "Camp here; bridge there."

Instantly, the legion's leadership and specialists sprang into action. *Gromatici* dismounted their surveying instruments and marker flags from the carts, set them up, and began laying out the basis of the camp. *Metatores* with their measuring ropes and rods worked from the markers of the *gromatici* to lay out the lines of the camp.

Outside the boundaries of the camp-to-be, the Scythian women and their children—many of them Roman children now—took one look at the ground, another at the location of the camp, and began driving their wagons to form the laager the layout on the ground suggested. Argippaean scouts herded the animals to the best grazing to be found; after all, there were no local people to object. In the evening, when foraging was done and the laager finished, the herds would be driven into the area between the laager and the river.

By this time, the legion had set up so many camps and bridged so many rivers that the worst and broadest were all to be taken in stride. And the Viadrus was not especially deep, especially strong, nor especially wide.

Already Gaius Pompeius and Marcus Caelius could hear the chopping of the axes and the buzzing of the saws, as yet another forest was plundered to provide material for the bridge and the camp.

Albis River, Germany

"I can't understand a word they're saying," said Gaius Pompeius. "Send for Thancrat."

Holding up his palm to indicate that the small party of rather civilized-looking barbarians should be patient, Gaius sent for wine and beer, along with some bread, Gothic cheese, and sausages.

When Thancrat showed up, he tried to speak to the visitors. "Not a word, not one damned word," he said, at hearing their tongue.

Finally, one of the visitors smiled around a piece of sausage, chewed, swallowed, and said, "You could, you know, try Latin."

The accent was appalling, with *V* pronounced like a kind of hard *F*, instead of a proper *U* sound, and diphthongs where no diphthongs ought ever be permitted, but it was still recognizably Latin.

"I see," said Gaius. "And you chose to reveal this just now because...?"

"Because we wanted to see what you might reveal when you thought we couldn't understand. Oh, my name is Berchar. Don't bother with yours; you've already revealed them."

The speaker, who identified himself and his half dozen com- patriots as Franks, was of middling height, quite stocky and with a fair padding of fat around his midsection. He was mostly blond of hair and mostly gray of beard. He had put down the shield that he bore along with a long sword, while his broad leather belt bore two fairly heavy-looking but short-handled, hence throwing, axes.

"Now who are you?" Berchar asked. "You speak Latin but you don't look like any Roman soldiers I ever saw. But then most of the Roman soldiers I have seen looked like a younger version of me."

"We *are* Roman," Gaius said, "but we have been gone a very long time."

"Indeed? And so where are you going?"

"To the Rhine, to cross over and take our position defending the Empire."

"Good that somebody's going to do it. We are 'Friends and Allies' of Rome and were supposed to stop the Vandals from crossing the Rhine. We tried and thought we had it won. Indeed, we *did* have it won. And then the Alans and their heavy cavalry—armored head to foot and their horses armored, too—decided to join in on the game with the Vandals. We could not stand against the Alan heavies. Hardly a Frankish family isn't in mourning. On the other hand, the bastards didn't get across the Rhine here."

"I thank you, then, for your trying," said Gaius. "What are you going to do, try to shelter west of the Rhine?"

"Oh, we're already on the other side of the Rhine," said Berchar, "on lands granted us to support us while we guarded the river. But we can't feed all of us on those lands, so many are our mouths even after the loss to the Vandals and Alans. So here we must stay for here we must hold."

"What about your cousins on the western side of the Rhine?" Gaius asked. "Will they join in in defending the frontier?"

"You'll have to ask them, but I wouldn't expect too much, and nothing very far from Frankish lands. Six or seven thousand of our dead came from there."

"So there isn't much to hold back the Vandals?" asked Caelius.

"I'm not sure there's *anything* to hold back the Vandals but the river itself and the limited garrisons on the near or far sides of the bridges. And it's not just the Vandals coming. I mentioned the Alans. Add to them the Suebi. And some Goths, the ones whom the Romans drove out of Italy not so long ago. Most of those, however, defected to Stilicho."

"How do they fight, these Vandals, Suebi, and Alans?" asked Marcus Caelius. "We've seen the Goths."

"Well," said Berchar, "the Vandals have some horse, mostly small ones, but fight mostly as infantry. Use swords and spears. Also axes. Some javelins. Not much armor and most of that lamellar. Not much mail, nothing like I saw some of your boys wearing, the stuff that looks like a lobster. Not many archers. Those are mostly non-Vandals. Fight mostly in a shield wall, like us and like the Romans.

"The Suebi—you can tell which ones they are by the knot they tie their hair into on one side—also fight in a shield wall." Berchar twisted his own hair up on one side, to illustrate. "Some bows. Mostly sword, shield, spear, axe, and javelin. Some cavalry, mostly light. Armor is hit or miss. Like us, nobles have it and foot troops not so much.

"Now the Alans," Berchar continued, "they're not all on horseback. In fact, they have a pretty good mix of light infantry, heavy infantry, archers, light cavalry, and heavy cavalry. The cavalry, light and heavy, all seem to use bows, too. They are very good, which is to say very dangerous, as we Franks have good cause to know. And their alliance with the Vandals seems to go way back to when they were all pretty far south of here."

"Numbers?" asked Caelius.

"Hard to say," said Berchar. "Vandals, maybe twenty thousand. There used to be a lot more of them but we managed to get about half. What that means, though, is as many as two hundred thousand in their total population. Alans, somewhat less than that, call it fifteen thousand. Goths, maybe four or five thousand. Suebi? Well, they can put between twenty and thirty thousand men in the field, from the army they have south of here. Total numbers? Might as well try counting the stars."

Caelius wiped his hand across his forehead. "Sixty to seventy thousand?" He turned to the legate and said, "You know, running like Hades for Britannia is looking better and better."

"It's not as bad as you think," said Gaius Pompeius. "They can't get their wagons and families across unless they get a bridge, so all we have to do is keep them from grabbing the western side of one of the Rhine bridges." He turned back to Berchar and asked, "How many Rhine bridges are there now?"

"Four," replied the Frank. "From south to north: Mogontiacum, Confluentes, Colonia, and then the one nearest to here, Vetera. Vetera is just a good—at least, it used to be good—wooden bridge, while all the others are stone."

Rubelius piped in with, "How big a wagon can the bridge at Vetera take?"

Berchar looked around, taking in the huge Scythian wagons, and said, "I don't see anything it can't handle, though you may want to reduce the loads on some of those big ones, especially the ones being pulled by the monster cattle. I mean, sure, the bridge *might* take those but I've never seen anyone try to take anything that heavy-looking across it."

Caelius, still focused on the enemy, asked, "Any of those groups any good at sieges?"

"They can surround a place, build a wall, and try to starve it out. I've never *heard* of them doing much to assault a well-defended city or fortress."

"So, what's on our side?" asked Caelius.

Berchar considered, then said, "Maybe ten thousand men, between the four garrison towns. No real field army unless you denude those garrisons. Also the *Classis Germanica*, the Rhine Fleet, which is plenty to keep them from crossing in boats."

"Hmmm...that *is* a bit of good news, isn't it," Caelius admitted.

"See?" said Gaius. "I told you it wasn't as dark as all that."

"There is one thing, though," offered Berchar. "When the Vandals and such drove us out, they captured a lot of food. But they did *not* capture anything like enough to feed the two hundred thousand or so mouths in their horde. They don't have a lot of choice—though they may not realize that yet—but to get to the western side of the Rhine and take what's there if they're to avoid starvation. They left nothing behind them; they must flee forward if they're not to become extinct."

"But, on the other hand," said Marcus Caelius, "if we can keep them from crossing, then starvation may just end the problem for us. Who's in charge and what can you tell us about him?"

"Nobody's in charge," answered Berchar. "Not so far as I know. But the king of the Suebi, Hermeric, may be first among equals. Or may not, because he's pretty new to the job. Hermeric is a pagan. I'd have given the honors to the king of the Vandals, except that we managed to kill the old king, Godigisel, in battle. His son, Gunderic, has taken over the tribe, but he's probably still trying to assert control over his own people, so isn't in a position to control the others. The Alans are led by Respendial. Beyond the name I know nothing about him except that he kicked our asses—which is, you know, probably enough to know about him. I don't know who's in charge of the Goths. Not many of them anyway.

"I have heard, but cannot swear, that there is another group of Alans, somewhere farther east, maybe, under a chief named Goar. And even that may not be true."

The column was long and the road none too good. In many places the legion had to stop to let the engineers of the First Cohort, often aided by another cohort, fell trees to make a corduroy road.

At one point, with a substantial hill to the left, and a swamp to the right, Marcus Caelius blurted out, "I wonder if old Flavus made it."

"What's that?" asked Gaius Pompeius. "Who do you...?"

And then Gaius saw what Caelius was alluding to. They were there: there at the same spot where the gods whisked the legion so far to the east and so forward in time; there where the Seventeenth and Nineteenth Legions were destroyed; there where Varus committed suicide; there where the current dubious fate of the Empire was set in motion.

"By the gods, you're right," said Gaius. "It was here. *We* were here."

"Trees are new, of course," said Caelius. "The swamp may have receded a bit. Less forest and more farmland. But if you look at the base of that hill on the left you can see where the Germans excavated and built their defensive works."

Then they heard the murmuring of the ranks behind them.

"We're not the only ones to have seen this," said Gaius.

Replied Caelius, "I should think not. You had better prepare a speech for this evening's camp, one with heavy emphasis on the hands of the gods and our special providence."

"I think...I think you're right."

Vetera, Germania Inferior

Gaius wondered, *Reduce the wagons' loads and ferry them across in stages or reinforce the bridge? Or would it be quicker to just build another bridge?*

"I see no end of administrative problems with reducing the loads and ferrying them across in stages," said Caelius. "Yes, there are ways to do it, but when you figure the time to unload, to cross, to unload the rest, to recross, reload and finally cross again, we're talking four times longer, maybe five, than it would take us to cross on a reinforced bridge. We could probably build a whole new bridge—we've gotten quite good at it—faster than trying to stage across, one small group of wagons at a time."

"How do you do that?" asked Gaius.

"Do what?"

"Read my mind."

Caelius laughed. "No mind reading involved, young legate, it's an obvious problem and two people just happened to see it at about the same time. So I recommend that you, with your training as an engineer, figure out how to reinforce it. And at least there are plenty of trees about."

"Problem is," observed the legate, "we can't drive piles angling away from the bridge, as we usually do. And even straight down won't be easy."

"Actually," observed Caelius, "before we start worrying about reinforcing the bridge, we probably ought to talk with those people"—here he referred to a small party approaching from the fort fronting the bridge, a fort which didn't look remotely familiar—"about whether they'll insist on fighting us over it."

Out of politeness, Gaius and Caelius dismounted. The aquilifer, one Titus Atidius Porcio, a large and immensely strong Italian, of Sabine stock, was about to do so when Caelius ordered, "No, stay there. Let these people see that, while we are civilized and polite, our politeness and degree of civilization are finite. And, sir, something tells me you should go formal."

"*Ave*," said the trousered but clean-shaven sort emerging from the eastern side of the fort. "Waldalenus, son of Remaclus, Roman Army, at your service."

The vulgate pronunciation, the *V*-sound in place of the *U*, was still there. Likewise the unaccountable diphthongs. But otherwise the Latin was clear and crisp.

"Gaius Pompeius Proculus. And this is my *praefectus castrorum*, Marcus Caelius Lemonius. Behind me is the Eighteenth Legion."

"Right," said the Frank, Waldalenus. "I come out here in good faith and you decide to mock me. Everyone, and I mean *everyone*, knows that the Eighteenth was destroyed by Arminius nearly four centuries ago. And you still—"

"Be quiet," said Caelius. "Yes, we've been gone a long time, but we *are* the Eighteenth Legion. You want maybe to walk the line and touch our armor to make sure we're not just playing dress up?"

"Well," admitted Waldalenus, "I admit that the armor some of your men wear is of an unusual design. Likewise the shields. And I admit I've not seen spears like you're carrying. And, yes, your swords are uniquely archaic. But, once again, the Eighteenth was destroyed. There's plenty of proof of that in and around town. Moreover, everyone I see is on a wagon or on horseback, while the real Eighteenth would have marched on foot. Where did you get all the horses?"

"Scythians," answered Gaius. "About fifteen to eighteen thousand dead Scythians. Killed by us. That's where all the women came from, too."

"So how..."

"We don't know, Waldalenus," said Caelius. "There we were standing in the rain, and waiting for a howling mob of bloodthirsty barbarians to come and finish us off—all right, that's not exactly true, but there we were, about to try to break out from a mob of howling bloodthirsty barbarians and then, *wham*, we were hit by lightning and moved two thousand miles east and four hundred years forward. And that's all we know about it. After getting our affairs in order there, we've spent the last year and a half marching and skirmishing our way back to... well, not to home, our homes are lost... but at least to the Empire. What remains of it.

"You want proof?" Caelius took the leather pouch containing his *signaculum* from around his neck. "When's the last time you saw one of these? Ever? I think never."

Caelius drew his gladius from his left side. "Now who do you know who carries these? I've seen your Frankish swords and I see what you're wearing. Do they look anything like this? 'Course they don't."

He indicated the shields of the Roman foot. "Who uses those anymore? Anybody? Nobody." He pointed at the first rank of the following troops. "Somebody bring me a *pilum*. Have you even heard of these, Waldalenus, son of Remarchus?"

"I've heard of them," the Romano-Frank admitted.

"Now look at me," Caelius demanded. "Look at us. Do any of us—outside of those Scythian women and the Gallic cavalry, a little farther back—look like Franks? Or Goths? Or Vandals? Or Huns? Or anything but Italians? You are all Christian now, yes?"

"Yes," Waldalenus said proudly.

"Go walk down the ranks, if you like. See if you can find so much as a single Christian among us."

Waldalenus shook his head. "No need. I've come to believe you. Indeed, I don't understand it, but I believe you."

"We don't understand it either, friend. It just is and we have to live with it."

The Frank sighed, then offered, "How can I help you?"

"You can start," said Rubelius, "with telling us how heavy a load this bridge can take. Then, if it's too light, you can help us reinforce it."

"The bridge is old. It's only wood and the wood itself is old. I've never seen anything heavier than a one-horse cart cross it. As for help, I've got four hundred men, many of them too old to bear arms, and some of them ill. I might have two hundred and fifty to help. But I have no idea how to reinforce the bridge."

"That's where I come in," said Gaius Pompeius. "But I think we need a new bridge, based on what you've said."

There had been too much soil in the water to see, but the legion had sent good swimmers, hyperventilating and holding their breath, to feel their way down the pilings of the Vetera bridge.

In came the commentary: "Half-rotten, cracking wood coming out in lumps. About a third of the pilings don't even touch the bottom anymore."

"Well," said Gaius, "that settles that—not only a new bridge but we probably need to pitch in and help the locals reorient their fort a little bit to cover the new bridge. I am thinking a shallow C-shape to allow cross fire on the bridge."

"I'll send out scouting parties to find us some more wood," announced Marcus Caelius. "With the increases in settlement and farming, the old forests of *Germania* are sadly depleted. Though, you know, with most of the forests gone, the old Roman Army would have an easier time retaking it."

"And maybe a drawbridge on the friendly side," Gaius continued, either not hearing Caelius' comment or just assuming he'd take care of the details. "Or, simpler, just a panel that can be dragged off and put back into position. On rollers, maybe."

✧   ✧   ✧

In the end, yes, rollers it had to be. This didn't eliminate the ability of some hostile group to cross on the stringers, one at a time, but it did mean that, on the one hand, since the stringers were greased, their passing would be treacherous, while on the other, they'd be rationed into the area below the fort at a rate the defenders could at least hope to kill before they grew too numerous.

They also demolished the old bridge as something useful only to migrating barbarians and the very unwary. The demolition took under half a day and commenced the minute the sliding section was moved to the nearest section of the new bridge, allowing passage.

Thus it was that on the twelfth day after meeting Waldalenus, the legion, still entirely mounted or wagon-borne, began its march across the Rhine.

The Romano-Frank had watched the erection of the camp, the extension of his own fort, and the building of the bridge with some wonder. *This,* he thought, *this is what kept the Germans on their side of the Rhine for so long. How sad that, but for this band, their like doesn't exist anymore.*

After letting the Palmyrenes and Thancrat's German *auxilia* pass, Waldalenus met the command party at the near side of the bridge. To Marcus Caelius, he said, "It took me a while to remember, but your father's name was Titus and your brother's was Publius, weren't they?"

"Yes," answered Caelius, warily. "How did you know?"

Waldalenus' smile was inscrutable. "I didn't, friend, until a few days ago. Had to go look up some public records, after a fashion. Good luck to you on your passage and good luck, great good luck, in securing the upper Rhine."

Just past the expanded fort, they turned left, to follow the still passable Roman road to the south. They'd followed the Roman road no great distance when the column came to a sudden, grinding halt, accompanied by the mass clattering of armor and *scuta*, as troops ran into the ones ahead of them.

"What in the name of...?" asked Caelius, followed by a not uncommon string of curses. "I'll see about this."

With that he spurred his horse off the road and then forward, using his vine staff on any troopers who dallied in getting out of his way. Finally, he came to a thick knot of

German and Palmyrene auxiliaries, intermixed with legionaries of the First Cohort. He saw Metilius, standing slightly apart from his men.

"First Spear, what is this bullshit?" Caelius demanded.

Metilius just covered his mouth with one hand while pointing with the other. His facial scar was its normal pasty-white. Almost, Caelius thought he was suppressing a laugh, but that just couldn't be the Metilius he knew.

Dismounting, Caelius, leading his horse, forced his way through the knot of soldiers and came face-to-face with a large rectangular stone. The colors were worn but the letters quite legible. There were three figures carved on the stone and some words, mostly in standard Latin abbreviations. He read:

To Marcus Caelius, son of Titus, of the Lemonian district,
from *Bologna*,
first centurion of the eighteenth legion. 53½ years old.
He fell in the Varian War.
Their bones may be interred here. Publius Caelius, son of Titus,
of the Lemonian district, his brother, erected this.

Feelings of both warmth and loss warred with Marcus. *Never mind that, I can sort out feelings later, and alone. For now, though . . .*

Marcus Caelius used his horse to leverage himself atop his own four-foot memorial stone. Standing there, his face bearing a ferocious scowl, he said, "I *told* you pussies I was too mean to die. Now get back in formation. Forward . . . MARCH."

And thank you, brother. I won't even critique the poor likeness of myself, let alone my freedmen, Privatus and Thiaminus. I trust you took care of my family. My best to Father and Mother, assuming you're together now in the wherever. And I wonder which multi-great-grandchildren I have floating around here, in Vetera. Someday, if I can, I'll come back and see who owns the farmstead I bought north of town to settle down on. Might still be in the family, after all. And I might be able, then, to visit the grave of my fiery Dubnia. And that is all I can stand to think about now. Later . . . later.

✧   ✧   ✧

The march south continued, aided by the Roman road where that road was still in good repair, but bogged down a bit where it wasn't and where the legion had to stop to fell trees to put in some corduroy. The horses and food animals ate a good many farmers out of house and home, but the legion made that good from its still very flush treasury.

About a thousand veterans along the line of march, knowing full well what was at stake, signed up to join. These had to march on foot, not because there were no horses available but because they simply didn't know how to ride. This slowed things down to something less than fifteen miles a day, since many of those veterans were in their fifties and a few in their sixties and, while still strong, they hadn't the feet they'd once had.

Along the road they passed fort after fort for the *limitanei*, which forces were where their reenlisted veterans had, for the most part, come from.

"They're us," said Metilius, one night over wine. For wine was now available for purchase in bulk, grown on grapes from Gaul and from the Rhine's own fertile banks.

"What do you mean, 'us'?" asked Caelius while pouring himself another. "They don't look like, are not equipped and trained, for that matter, anything like us."

"I mean these '*limitanei*'; I've been talking to some of the brighter ones. They're what's left of the legions. Or some of them are. Others are *auxilia* formations, though badly reduced. You can ask them; they'll tell you who their legionary ancestors are and when they ended up stationed here on the Rhine in little fortlets."

"Are they willing to learn to do things our way?" Caelius asked.

"Yes. Not only have they never seen anything as militarily impressive-looking as us, but they have a firm grasp of the desperation of the hour. Rumor seems to travel as fast as we do, or maybe faster."

Caelius asked, "What are they asking to be paid?"

"Nothing; the money they used to be paid is near enough to worthless. Almost no silver in the things. I think we should pay them, mind, a solid auxiliary's wage. Except for one thing."

"And that would be?"

"The legal basis for auxiliaries doesn't exist. Everyone in the Empire who isn't '*foederati*' or a slave is a citizen. And *foederati* are just barbarians who browbeat the Empire into granting them land inside the Empire, where they live under their tribal chiefs, and from which they pay little or nothing in taxes."

Caelius stroked his own chin, thinking about the implications of that news. Finally, he said, "So if they're all citizens, and our *auxilia* are already citizens, then they're entitled to the same pay as legionaries."

"Yes."

"Well, we've got the money for that, anyway."

"I suspect, old friend," said Metilius, "that we have more money, more silver and gold, than the imperial coffers do. And based on the conditions of the roads and the army, I suspect further that, were we to share with the Empire, most of it would disappear into the ravenous maws of senators and bureaucrats."

"Fuck," said Marcus Caelius.

"Fuck," agreed Metilius.

Colonia, Rhine Frontier

The legion stopped to build an overnight camp fourteen times on the road from Vetera to Mogontiacum. Two of these were at the major cities of Colonia and Confluentes. At each of those they stayed two extra days. At the others there was usually a small detachment, under a hundred, of *limitanei* left to try to hold things down when the bulk of their comrades had been marched off to join Stilicho, in Italy.

Colonia and Confluentes, however, had something they called a "full legion," each.

Gaius and Caelius decided to look closely at just what a "full legion" was. To this end they rode across the stone bridge at Colonia to the other side of the Rhine, then pounded on the west-facing gate for admission. The gate was guarded by two flanking towers, while the entire fortress had sixteen.

"Good centurion-bad centurion, sir?" asked Caelius.

"Yes, and since you're a lot better at it, you get to play the bad centurion."

Caelius smiled and said, "Wouldn't have it any other way."

Once the gate was, to all appearances most reluctantly, opened, they strode in.

"I am Gaius Pompeius, of Rome's Eighteenth Legion," said the legate to the fat and elderly prefect of the castle on the eastern side of the river, "and I am here to inspect and, if I deem it wise, make personnel changes."

"By whose authority?" demanded the prefect, leaning out from the right-hand gate guard, who gave his name as Christianus Vibianus.

Caelius thought, *The kid's too nice for what must be said.* Accordingly, he responded with, "By the authority of the Senate and People of Rome. By the authority of the divine emperor. And, most importantly from your point of view, you lardy muffin, by the authority of the army on the other side of the Rhine who will, on command, reduce this fortress and execute everyone found inside it for mutiny."

"Sorry, sorry," Vibianus hastened to say. "I didn't know. It's just that, so far out here..."

"Never mind," said Gaius, in his conciliatory fashion. "We are marching to the upper Rhine to contest a probable attempt at crossing by some barbarians from around the Danube. We are going to inspect your troops and take with us...hmm...how many do you have?"

"About nine hundred, sir."

"About?" demanded Caelius, fully playing his part in the good centurion-bad centurion game. "A-fucking-bout? You're the commander of this gaggle and you don't know?" He turned around and shouted to one of the half dozen escorts, "Ride back and tell the legionary executioner to prepare a cross. We have someone—"

"Now, now, Marcus," said the legate. "I'm sure that won't be necessary." Turning back to Vibianus, he said, "I'm sure it's just our sudden appearance here that has you confused. So now think really hard and tell us how many men you have."

"May I send for the morning report?" asked Vibianus.

"Yes, by all means." Gaius looked around, saw the poor and slovenly dress of the men on the walls, and asked, "When was the last time your command was paid?"

"Define 'paid,' sir. They send us food. They send us some clothing. And they send us something they call 'money' that is essentially worthless."

"Do you have the ability to coin money here?" asked Caelius, more gently since the local commander seemed cowed.

"In Colonia they do."

"Fine," said Gaius. "We're going to provide enough silver to mint enough silver coins, of near enough to complete purity, to pay your men about four months wages. Yes, in actual silver. Oh, and you, too, of course, along with your officers."

Vibianus' eyes widened at *that* announcement.

"However," said Gaius, "we are going to inspect your fortifications, inspect your troops, and take about half of them with us. We will be providing a one-for-one exchange with men a bit old for long, hard campaigning, but certainly adequate to defend a place like this. Naturally, though, we do not want to disrupt things so will leave you and most of your officers here to see to the defense. When the threat is over, your men will be returned to you and the men we'll be giving you will be discharged back to their farms and families."

In Colonia's mint, Gaius and Rubelius held coins in their hands, marveling that anyone would accept them in exchange for anything except, perhaps, equally wretched coinage.

"I mean, seriously, sir," asked Rubelius, "what self-respecting whore would take these for any service more intimate than a passing sneer?"

The mint master said, "I know, good sirs, I know. But what choice have I? The emperor, or his appointed representatives, issue me a certain amount of silver or gold, and an invariably much larger amount of copper or brass, and tell me how much precious metal I can put into each coin. Right now, it stands at one part of silver in fifty. The other forty-nine being dross.

"That's for silver. The gold solidus is a better bet, at one seventy-second of a pound each and being nearly pure."

"Exchange rate between gold and silver still about twelve to one?" asked Gaius.

"Yes, sir," said the mint master, "and also, sir, it means that solidi that ought to be worth, say, thirteen or so old-fashioned denarii cannot be had for less than about six hundred and fifty."

"What is a soldier's pay, these days?" asked Rubelius.

"Why, I think it's a thousand antoniniani; that's two thousand denarii, equivalent. Per year."

"Gods!" exclaimed Rubelius. "At two percent purity, that's only forty real denarii a year!"

"No wonder they look slovenly," said Gaius. "Mint master, how long to cut some dies and strike, oh, say, one hundred thousand effectively pure gold *solidi*?"

The mint master's face went through serious contortions as he calculated. "Depends on what you want on it, sir?"

"Can you do a likeness of Caesar Augustus?"

"I think we may already have some back in the archives, denarius dimensions."

"That should work. I'll have fourteen talents of gold delivered. From that I want one hundred thousand *solidi*."

"Dear God," said the mint master, who was apparently a Christian, "to have real materials to work with again!"

INTERLUDE

Vandal camp, east bank of the Rhine, 406 A.D.

Gunderic, king of the Vandals, listened to the reports. Three boats they'd sent across the Rhine, all packed with fine men. Three boats had gone out to raid the other side and three boats had been found by the Romans and mercilessly destroyed.

As king, Gunderic wore the best armor available to the Vandals, silvered and gilded in places, and altogether too heavy for comfort. His helmet likewise was gilded, and bore ornate wings on the sides. His sword was a long *spatha*. All three had come from Byzantium, though none bore maker's marks.

Under the armor and helmet, the king was actually of average height among his people, but unusually heavyset. His bearded face was a bit long, and framed by hair almost white. His deep-set eyes were a sort of icy blue, which was also common among his people.

Tomorrow, thought Gunderic, *we'll double down and try six. We only need one to get across. One can kill and rape and steal and burn enough to make the Romans spread out.*

But the more I try, the more I lose. It is a depressing situation. I wish my father were still here to take charge. Damned Franks.

Gunderic's father, called Godigisel, had been killed when the Vandals had fought the Roman-allied Franks and been defeated. They'd later won and driven off the Franks, thanks to the intervention of their own allied Alan-heavy cavalry. But that hadn't brought the old king back.

I need to think long on this. Maybe sending out six more boats in the hope of getting one across is silly. Maybe I should send twelve ... or another three ... or one.

But I have to do something. We took everything there was to eat, near enough, tortured the local farmers ruthlessly to get what was left. And it isn't enough. We are going to starve over the winter. Already some of us, those who have lost husbands and so cannot get a full share of the food, are going hungry.

And I cannot decide whether I hate more the Romans, who refuse to let us into the Empire, or the Huns, who've driven us out of our old place to the border of the Empire.

CHAPTER FIFTEEN

After a diligent inquiry, I can discern four principal causes of the ruin of Rome, which continued to operate in a period of more than a thousand years. I. The injuries of time and nature. II. The hostile attacks of the Barbarians and Christians. III. The use and abuse of the materials. And, IV. The domestic quarrels of the Romans.
—Edward Gibbon, *The Decline and Fall of the Roman Empire*, Chapter 71

Mogontiacum, Germania *Superior, 406 A.D.*

There was a base at Mogontiacum, just west of the town. The walls of the one and the walls of the other joined along the southwest side of the town. Perhaps better said, the town had grown northeast of the base, then spread around to its flanks, and now the base jutted into the town.

It was by no means a small base, having housing sufficient for two whole legions of the old-fashioned variety, and at this point, a bit run-down. It could also house a decent complement of *auxilia*, to include a couple of *alae* of cavalry, as well as warehousing, granaries, mess halls, a large *valetudinarium*, baths, and housing for the officers and centurions. The baths were fed by an aqueduct that entered the base on the southern corner, then drained via a sewer that ran under the town, emptying into the Rhine, downstream from the town. The sewer drained several other public baths and lavatories.

In addition to the main base, there was a smaller one south-east of the town and a naval base to the northeast.

A bridge ran from the town, across the Rhine, to a castle, a very strong-looking fortress, made of stone, on the other side. This was Castellum Mattiacorum. It was possible to go around the castle to get to the bridge, but various artillery engines on the walls suggested that this would be a very bad idea. There had once been a village around the castle, but the inhabitants had fled with the arrival of the barbarian horde and all the buildings had been torn down, lest they provide cover for the invaders. The wood from the town had been piled up between the castle and the Rhine.

From the castle's crenellated walls, Gaius could see the hundreds of thousands of barbarians camped and laagered on three sides. Even though he knew they were mostly noncombatants, and hungry ones at that, it was a frightful sight. Adding to the fright was the scores of ladders cast down from the walls to litter the ground around them, as well as the scores of barbarian bodies lying outside the walls that hadn't been reclaimed yet. That those bodies didn't stink much, yet, was a good indicator of how recently the assault had been repelled.

Let them get over the border and start feeding and breeding and we'll be fully in Calvus' nightmare.

"Why should I listen to you, youngster?" asked the commander of the local garrisons, especially the garrison on the east bank of the river, at the end of the stone bridge. The commander had given his name as Metrovius, son of Engelram. He looked very Germanic, indeed, but his accent was pure Gallic-influenced Latin.

"There are several reasons," said Gaius, turning his attention away from the barbarian corpses. "One is that no matter what rank you think you are, mine is higher. Moreover, even if you imagine your rank is equal, I have four hundred years' worth of date of rank on you.

"The third reason is that I have the only army worth mentioning for several hundred miles, and Stilicho isn't going to get here any time soon to contest it. Finally, and this is key, I am paying your men, and if I tell them that I will no longer pay until I see your dangling corpse strung up by its own guts, then that is what I will see within the hour. Do you dispute any of this?"

"N-n-n-no, sir," said a deeply chastened Metrovius.

That's my boy, thought Marcus Caelius. *My, but how far you've come along.*

Gaius glanced away from Metrovius and at the commander of the *Classis Germanica*, the German Fleet or Rhine Fleet.

"Oh, I'm willing enough to obey, sir," said the *praefectus classis*, Benedictus Candidus. "The problem is that I don't have much to obey *with*. Yes, there was a day when we had hundreds of ships, to include serious warships like triremes and liburnians. Now what I've got is a couple of dozen *naves lusoriae*. And not all of those are sea- or even river-worthy. Though they're more maneuverable, they don't really give us any huge advantage over the barbarians except that we know what we're doing and they, once in boats, really don't."

"Could you build some more triremes or even liburnians?" Caelius asked.

"No," answered the naval prefect. "Once upon a time it would just have been a matter of money. Now? No, the skills are lost. Maybe if you brought up some shipwrights from Misena or Ravena. But we don't know how anymore. Yes, it's bloody sad, I agree."

"All right," said Gaius. "I understand. Can you keep the barbarians from crossing?"

"Depends," answered Candidus, not especially helpfully. "So far they've only tried to slip across small raiding parties. The regular patrols we send out have, so far, proven sufficient to deal with most of these. And, if they try to come over in a larger group, we can spot them coming. For that a series of signals would get the fleet into the water in minutes. Then we just massacre them, hit their boats, capsize them, and spear them like fish in the water. We can do that forever so long as the raiding parties are not huge. If they ever get as many as eighty boats in the water at once, maybe as few as fifty, they'll swamp us. Note that I never have more than a dozen boats ready to attack; the rest are always out patrolling the river and have to be."

Gaius nodded. It was probably the best the river sailors could do. Turning back to Metrovius, he asked, "Can you hold this castle?"

"Food is not a problem, sir," a much-chastened Metrovius replied, "not so long as the bridge stands. And water? Well, obviously water isn't. Even besides the Rhine, we've got two good wells inside our walls. The factory in Mogontiacum has been able to keep us in ammunition for the artillery. But the last attack almost overwhelmed us. I've got under five hundred men and this castle can really hold and use up to two thousand."

Gaius looked at Caelius, who said, "We could give them the rest of the discharged veterans that joined us on the march down from Vetera. It's a bit over a thousand men. And they haven't really been successfully integrated with the legion, though some of them, a hundred and twenty-five, I think it was, fit right in with Thancrat's *auxilia*, once they had some language lessons."

Nodding, Gaius ordered, "Leave the ones that are with Thancrat where they are. Put the rest under the command of one of our centurions, and him with but not under Merovius, who will be *attached* to that centurion, and under the authority of the legion."

"I know just the man," said Caelius.

"Why me, sir?" asked Lucius Pullo, standing at attention while Marcus Caelius inspected him and his outfit from every side.

"Several reasons, young centurion," answered the *praefectus castrorum*, in an even, conversational voice. "One is that the recalled and returned veterans adore the very name of 'Roman Army,' at least insofar as they imagine that army to have been, back in our day. This is even more true since we seem to have returned from the dead. Another is that command requires a certain social difference and, while yours, in the legion, is nothing special, despite your great-grandfathers, yours, with regard to them, is vast.

"Then, too, you have a sort of earnest pigheadedness about you, Pullo. This is precisely what is needed in a fortress under siege or assault, and you will see both of these.

"We are sending you, too, because I think it's funny. And I have one more reason, but you will have to figure it out for yourself. Telling you would ruin the joke. Any questions?"

Pullo sighed, answering, "No questions, sir."

"Now," Caelius continued, "we're having more scorpions built for you, an even dozen, and I am sending over Quintus Junius Fulvius to spend a couple of days training some of your men on them. Ammunition is also being assembled. We'd have sent *tormenta*, too, but don't think the walls can handle them."

"No questions, sir, but one objection. I can maneuver my century within a cohort. I can order relief of the front line. I can train them on arms and inspect. But I don't know the first damned thing about commanding an overstrength cohort of over eight hundred men."

"Yes, yes, I know, Pullo. Relax; you're not going to have to do fancy maneuvers. You're going to have to supervise guard mount, inspect nightly, train—rather, retrain—the men in their weapons, and lead, at most, one or two centuries at a time in repelling any breakthroughs. I believe you have just admitted you can do that."

"Yes, sir."

"One other thing, Pullo: you can have your Argippaean girl and your baby in the fort with you. On the one hand, I think it will motivate you greatly to defend that fort to the death. On the other, I am pretty sure that getting your little tail wet nightly will do wonders for your morale."

"Yes, sir! Thank you, sir!"

Caelius just frowned and said, "Your ten centuries of reenlisted veterans are waiting under the south wall of Mogontiacum. There's been an *optio* appointed to each one. Go take command, young Pullo. It's your castle."

Though there was a pier a short distance from the stone bridge that crossed the river to the castle, the main naval base at Mogontiacum was a stockade forty *jugera* downstream from the town. Inside the stockade were a few barracks, several warehouses, sundry slipways, and a couple of dozen *lusoriae*, three of them drawn up on land for maintenance. Into this, Gaius Pompeius walked, with a half dozen legionaries from First Cohort for escort.

"Room for one or two more?" asked Gaius, as he walked the pier up to Benedictus Candidus.

"Know your way around boats, sir?" asked Candidus.

"Somewhat; my family had a small galley the slaves would row us around on."

Candidus seemed to consider this. Then he asked, "Know your way around a boat in a fight?"

"Not remotely," said Gaius, cheerfully. "I'm hoping to learn."

"Fine. Let's get you familiarized, then, with procedures. And also, I'm going to need you to sit on the rear platform and just stay there, without much moving. Further, pick one man from your escort to sit on the other side of the rear platform to balance things out. These are not, after all, infinitely stable craft."

✧　　✧　　✧

It was a new moon over the Rhine, hence darker than the lowest pit in the deepest mine in the empire. Benedictus Candidus had fourteen of his currently twenty-one serviceable *lusoriae* rowing upstream with the prevailing wind, spaced about half an hour apart. They kept to the friendly side of the river, moving against the current. At the apogee of their racetrack they would then ship oars and take in the sail to float silently down the middle of the river, listening for the invariably confused and stressful sounds of a barbarian boat, trying to make way through the current of the Rhine.

Gaius could smell something burning, but could see no flames.

The typical *lusoria* was carvel-built entirely of oak, some seventy Roman feet long, and a bit under ten across. The draft was about two feet while the gunwales rose above the water about three. On each side of the boat and above the gunwales, round shields were hung to provide an additional measure of protection for the soldier-rowers. Torches, unlit ones, stood above the shields, plunged into the same uprights that held the shields. The oaken planks were under an inch thick, but still capable of taking a shock. Besides being light and of shallow draft, the double steering oar, aft, made the boats nimble, indeed. Total crews ran from about thirty-three to as much as forty, each.

The Rhine was fairly broad here, leading to a current of about two to three knots. Thus, with a fair following wind and sails and oars in play, the *lusoriae* could make twenty or so miles up the Rhine in about two hours. Oars and current, together, would bring it back to Mogontiacum in a bit under two and to twenty miles below the city in another two. The return to Mogontiacum, with the north wind being useless on this largely east-west course of the Rhine, took a bit over three. The total racetrack-like journey took roughly nine hours, at which point the crew of the *lusoria* would pull into the harbor slashed out of the western bank, then grab a meal and some sleep, while another boat took its place.

Benedictus Candidus, with Gaius and his single escort, had taken out the first boat, leading from the front, as it were. On the boat sailed and rowed, until the smells and the flickering lights told him that he had reached the town of Vangionum.

"Lower the sail," Candidus whispered to the two sailors aboard.

There the boat made a fairly wide sweep to come about and

out into the center of the Rhine, bow to the north. The men automatically leaned a bit to starboard to balance the boat against the current.

Leaning down, Candidus whispered to Gaius, "This is life in the *classis*, unbearable boredom, and frequent agonizing fatigue, occasionally punctuated by stark terror."

"Terror tonight or boredom?" asked Gaius.

"Hard to say, but, given the new moon, I'd put my money on terror. Get ready for some instability as we enter the cross-current from the Moenis."

"Let it run, boys," Candidus whispered. "And just listen." The rowers lifted their oars from the water. Briefly, there was a sound of multiple dripping as each oar shed the water it had taken from the river.

Downstream the *lusoria* traveled, with partially lit towns and farmhouses to port, and nothing but the smell of smoke and occasional rotting bodies to starboard. Beyond the smells, there were female screams and female sobs, as women and girls who had not been able to escape the hordes gathered on the eastern side were repeatedly violated.

Gently, the steersman tapped Candidus on the shoulder, then plied his steering oars to adjust his direction a bit. The prefect strained to listen then sent forward the whisper, "Last six men, ship oars... quietly."

With minimal sound, those men passed their oars inward and across. They then took up a number of light javelins, each, and waited.

Gaius tapped Candidus' leg. When the prefect bent down, he said, "My *praefectus castrorum* put me through a thorough course in *pilum*. Can I help with the spear tossing?"

Unseen, Candidus nodded and said, "Pass him one of your javelins, each, boys." Gaius split the take with his solitary legionary escort.

It's so damned dark I can't see a thing, grumbled Candidus, mentally. *Fortunately, those fuckers are noisy.*

Sensing the minor changes of direction applied automatically by the steersman, Candidus waited... waited... waited.

"Ready oars! Javelins free. Now stroke... stroke... stroke... stroke."

The *lusoria* lunged forward like a bird of prey. Ahead, the dimly sensed presence of the barbarian boat guided the steersman. Ahead, too, the barbarian crew seemed suddenly overcome with panic, with men shouting and sounds of swords being drawn.

"Hold water," commanded Candidus, not bothering to whisper at this point. All the men not bearing javelins dropped their oars in and then held onto the grips. The boat slowed, slowed, and then hit the barbarian boat on the side. The curved prow of the *lusoria* served as a guide, lifting the other boat up, up, and then capsizing it.

"Ship oars!"

With a terrified shout, a score or so barbarians found themselves plunged into the dark, cold water. The *lusoria* passed by, twisting the other boat out of the way.

From a firepot kept hidden under the rear platform, Candidus lit two small torches and passed them forward. Suddenly, the *lusoria* became an island of light on a midnight-dark sea. But the light wasn't restricted to the island. Instead, it passed out over the waters, illuminating a sea of twenty or more barbarians, some of them struggling with the weight of armor, trying to save their lives by swimming.

"There's not a lot of room for mercy on the water," said Candidus. "And usually none for prisoners on one of these things. We occasionally grab one for interrogation, but only if they appear to be half drowned already."

"Port side, back water," the prefect commanded. "Starboard side, all ahead full."

Like the kind of graceful dancer for which it was named, the *lusoria* turned about on its own axis, to face the struggling barbarian mob.

"All ahead, slow."

As they neared the capsized enemy boat, Gaius could see as many as a dozen men clinging to the sides. Uncommanded, the steersman brought the *lusoria* to pass the barbarians to their starboard. Also without command, the last three men on the starboard side cast their javelins at range so point blank that not a one missed. Mortally wounded and agonized men lost their grip on the capsized boat, some to float on the surface, others to sink beneath the rippling waves.

Another series of commands and the *lusoria* twisted about again to sweep down and rake the other side. Once again, javelins flew with considerable force but without a trace of pity.

"Now watch this," said Candidus, as the *lusoria* came about once again. "There are almost always one or two..."

This time the steersman struck the boat to bring one side up above the water. There were more sounds of panicked men as the couple who had tried to hide under it lost their grips. Again the javelins flew.

"Back water! Back water!"

And Gaius realized, with a degree of shame, that despite his bold words, he hadn't thrown a single one.

"If we hadn't capsized it," Candidus said, "I'd try to drag it to the bank and recover it tomorrow to sell. As is, too much drag."

Then he told the steersman, "Bring us alongside," and to some undefined crewman, "Axes."

In a few minutes, holes had been chopped in the hull, letting the air out and allowing the water to rise.

"It'll be no use to the barbarians now."

"It's of no use to the dead ones, even without holing it," said Gaius. This raised a laugh from the entire crew.

"Zigzag," ordered Candidus. "There were more men in that tub than I saw punctured."

"How do we know that the ones trying to cross are barbarians?" Gaius asked.

"It's actually pretty easy," Candidus replied. "The ones we want to accept in—and there have been some though not any for several weeks now—cross in the daytime. Raiders and reconnaissance cross at night."

Mogontiacum

"And so how was our little fishing expedition?" asked Marcus Caelius, waiting at the port like a mother hen, for Gaius' return.

Exhausted after the sleepless circuit of the Mogontiacum to Vangionum to Bingium, Gaius sat down heavily and said, "Different, interesting, and more than a little scary. All things considered, I'm glad I didn't settle on a naval career. Also, all things considered, the sailors more than earn what we're paying them. And while I was gone?"

"No matter," said Caelius, "we're paying them what we can. Besides, unlike in the old days, these men are almost all married with families. They're fighting for those more than for the money. Or even for the Empire. And it was dull in your absence."

Castellum Mattiacorum

Zaya and her baby, as it turned out, were not going to be the only civilians living inside the east bank castle, her man's castle, defending the bridge from Mogontiacum. Indeed, as Pullo's oversized cohort marched in, several hundred women, their children, and two sutlers, turned out to watch.

This just seems so wrong, Pullo thought. *Soldiering and families don't mix. But then, what kind of hypocrite am I, given Zaya and the kid?*

"Left-right-left-right, one-two-three-four," called the newly minted, though generally rather old and gray, *optios* of Pullo's cohort.

Marching out in front, with the cohort's newly created red madder-dyed *vexillum* being carried behind him and to his left, Pullo marched the cohort right at the gate, then left at the southeastern corner, left again at the northeastern corner, and halted the lot when the leading century was at the gate leading into the German interior, now overrun with Vandals, Goths, Suebi, and Alans. The column of recalled, reenlisted soldiery was followed in by a dozen scorpions, with only drivers for the mules, and some carts bringing in necessary supplies, plus Zaya and child, whose name was, per clan tradition, Titus.

Under the northern wall, Metrovius and roughly three of his five hundred stood in ranks. The remainder? On the walls or on labor detail or on sick call.

The mules stopped stomping when halted. The troops took up marching in place until Pullo called them to a "halt" and a "center face." The commands echoed off the walls of the castle's central courtyard, itself stone held together with that excellent Roman concrete, and mostly covered with ivy.

Pullo smiled across the courtyard at Metrovius, who gave a cold smile back.

Surly and bitter bastard, thought Pullo. *No matter, provided he follows orders. And the bitterness is understandable, besides.*

"*Optios,*" Pullo ordered, "fall in on me."

At the same time, ten men from Metrovius' garrison trotted over. Pullo had already worked out between them and Metrovius where the newcomers would be billeted. It was just a matter now of linking the guides up with his subordinates and having them lead off the troops to their billets.

As for himself and Zaya, who came to stand next to her man once the troops were dismissed to settle in...

"There's a smaller set of quarters off the *principia*," Pullo told her. "There are two, one bigger than the other. If you don't mind I'd prefer to leave the bigger one to Metrovius, even though he is junior."

"Why?" Zaya asked.

"He's got a wife and several children." Pullo shrugged. "He just needs more room."

"Show me," she demanded.

Pullo took Zaya through the *principia* to the smaller one. Zaya, expecting something awful, clapped her hands at seeing the apartment had frescoed walls, something she'd never imagined before. It also had two beds, a reception room, and a kitchen with space enough to eat in.

"It's a little cramped," Pullo admitted.

"Oh, no," Zaya replied, "It's perfect. Room for us. Room for the little one. I've never before had so much indoor space to myself and my family, not even in the winter camp!"

Pullo smiled. *She is* such *a reasonable girl.*

The whole setup of the castle was mostly outside Pullo's experience. For one thing, cooking for the troops was done by twenty-three of the wives, acting together, and served out in a mess hall on the bottom floor. Another crew washed the dishes.

These were all unpaid. Pullo resolved to see about maybe paying them a small wage, maybe a solidus a month, for their efforts.

Have to discuss this with the legate, he thought. *Also going to have to take on more women. Twenty-three could cook for four or five hundred, but it's going to take more like seventy to cook for my boys, too.*

Off to one side of the mess was a small dining room for leaders. It was here that Pullo met his *optios*, the leaders of the troops already here, and Metrovius, who still looked like a man sucking on a lemon.

Metrovius asked, "Are you, perchance, any relation to the Pullo mentioned by Julius Caesar?"

"My great-grandfather. I'm also descended in about equal measure from the same Vorenus who was a mutual rival with Pullo, and later his best friend."

"And so your class would be?" Metrovius continued.

"Equestrian."

"Sir!" said Metrovius, and seemed to mean it. "Pardon my previous attitude and manner. I did not know you came from such an illustrious and worthy background. I and my men are yours to command, and willingly."

And this is something I need to discuss with the praefectus castrorum, *because I don't understand it at all.*

"Fine, then. This is my intent as far as defending the castle goes. Metrovius, your group has the eastern wall and all the artillery you previously used: put most of it on the corner towers to support at least two of the walls. I want one man in five on that wall at all times, I'm going to use one of my centuries to man the twelve scorpions and split that twelve, six to the north wall and six to the south.

"I'm also going to put three centuries on the north wall, three on the south, and one facing the river. The remaining two, the youngest and most recently discharged, are my reserve, charged with reinforcing walls in the greatest danger and kicking out any barbs that make it in.

"Medical?" Pullo continued. "Is there a surgeon in the castle?"

A tall, slender, and largely bald Judaean-looking man raised one hand. "Ruvaine ben Aharon ben Solomon, at your service."

The Judaean surgeon carried an air of competence about him, and spoke with a sunny, optimistic manner, unusual for men in his grisly line of work.

"*Medicus*, make an inventory of what you have, supply-wise, what you need, and then go see Josephus and do some horse-trading. How are you set for staff?"

"I'm the only surgeon," Solomon replied. "I've got two male orderlies who can sew up a cut, and I've been training two dozen of the women in the fort as nurses and fourteen of the biggest and strongest among them to evacuate the wounded to me."

"Where's your hospital?"

"Southern corner of the fort. It's marked on the inside wall."

"Very good, *Medicus*; thank you. My wife may join your medical women; she has some experience with our own surgeon, from some time back. Quartermaster?"

"Here, sir. Beatus Vitalianus."

"Much the same for you as for the doctor. List all supplies on hand and needed, then go find Tribune Junius Rubelius and do some horse-trading. Note that while I won't claim to be able to judge the surgeon's medical needs, I can judge the command's, so report to me both before and after you go to see Rubelius."

"Yes, sir."

"Can your artillery, once reconstructed, reach the other side of the Rhine from this side?" asked Gaius of Quintus Junius Fulvius, the chief of the legion's artillery.

Fulvius looked over the Rhine. His face twisted as he did some mental calculations. "Yes," he said, "the *tormenta* will reach, sir, but with a definite *but* to the matter."

"'But'?"

"Yes, sir, 'but.' The but is that it will have to be on a very high parabola. That means that, sure, it will flatten the one barbarian who happens to be unlucky enough to be under it when it lands, if any one of them is, and might wing the one next to the flat one, on the upward bounce, but that's about it.

"You see, sir, we prefer to have our projectiles fly at a low angle, to take out entire lines of the buggers. At that range, we just can't."

"Incendiaries?"

Fulvius winced at the sudden recall of a particular incendiary short round that hit among their own troops during the fight against the Scythians.

"You *have* fixed the skein that snapped by the great river, haven't you?"

"Oh, yes, sir, long since. And since we wouldn't be shooting over anyone's heads, a short round wouldn't mean anything. I just shudder every time I remember that incident back there."

"I understand," Gaius said. "So the effect of using incendiaries would be...?"

"Short version, sir, less death but more damage. Just about everybody is afraid of being burnt, so when the barbs see fire raining down on them they'll start to try to move away, to not cluster, and to disorder themselves. Really fuck up an assault on the castle walls, sir."

"All right, then. Good," Gaius said. "I want every *tormentum* we can assemble—twelve, yes? Good—on both sides of the bridge, six per, to support the castle walls, north and south. And—and I cannot emphasize this enough—*without shooting over the heads of our own men*. Now how quickly can they be ready to fire?"

"Two days, sir," answered Quintus, "but we need permission to put some of the brickmakers and stone masons in Mogontiacum to work, making ammunition. Oh, and we'll need more turpentine."

"You have it. Get a quote from them for the charge and bring it to Tribune Rubelius to settle."

Gaius Pompeius and Marcus Caelius sat by the east bank of the Rhine, facing the castle on the opposite side. Outside those castle walls, teams of men were pacing off and carefully placing small cairns of stones, range markers for the artillery on the walls. Not far away, Quintus Junius Fulvius was busy inspecting each *tormentum*, to include tapping the skeins that powered them with a small hammer and listening to the sounds they made. Below them, in the river, floated a number of mostly naked male bodies, sporting long blond hair. These were victims of the *Classis Germanica*, sometime in the last few days.

"What am I missing, Top?" asked Gaius. "I can't think of anything and that just makes me worry more."

Gaius Pompeius only called the camp prefect "Top" when they were alone, lest Metilius be offended.

Marcus Caelius replied, with a shake of his head, "I honestly don't know, Gaius."

Much the same rule applied to Caelius' use of the legate's first name: only when they were alone.

Caelius continued, "The castle looks impregnable; young Pullo's doing a creditable job over there. The barbs can't cut it off from food, water, or reinforcement. We can support it with *tormenta* fire from here and they've got plenty of scorpions on their own walls.

"Even if they could take the castle, though, that doesn't get them much. They've still got to cross the bridge under fire and at this end they run into real Roman soldiers of the kind that gave their multi-great-grandfathers nightmares, and with us having every advantage.

"The fleet here, and the naval squadrons south and north of here, are doing a good job—to be fair, a nearly perfect job—of stopping infiltration. And if the barbs could somehow manage to get five hundred boats and swamp the *classis*, and then somehow land ten thousand men on this side? Well, so what? They'd not have a single horse and out in the open we can handle any ten thousand barbs that ever lived. And that's without even using the five thousand German *auxilia* we've assembled here.

"Hmmm...speaking of the Germans and of the 'Roman'—for some highly expansive values of 'Roman'—troops here, I admit there are three things that bother me."

"And those would be?" Gaius asked.

"Well, I say 'three things,' but it's really just one thing, one thing that shows up in three forms. 'What's that?' you ask. *Spathae*, *plumbatae*, and spears. 'What's wrong with those?' you ask. After all, isn't their steel better than ours? Their steel is better, yes, but what's wrong is only this: they're all an attempt to try to keep the enemy away, not to close with him and rip his guts out."

Caelius drew his own gladius. "Now *this* is a weapon for men willing to get in there and finish the job quickly. It's a difference in attitude that just manifests itself in the armaments. We, when we fight, fight to conquer. Them, when they fight? They fight to live. We live, usually, because we do conquer. Them? They all too often neither conquer nor live.

"And I don't know how to break them of that."

Across the Rhine the near gate for the castle opened, briefly, letting a single man, unarmed and unarmored, slip out. That man then began to race on foot across the bridge.

"Deserter or messenger, do you think, Top?"

"Messenger; someone, after all, closed the gate behind him."

"Point. He's quite fast, isn't he, Top?"

"Very."

They both went silent for a while, waiting for the messenger, if that was what he was, to arrive.

"Sirs! Sirs!" the messenger managed to get out, bent over and panting. "Centurion Pullo sent me to tell you that three of the chiefs of the barbarians are waiting outside the western gate and have asked for a parley."

Castellum Mattiacorum

As a gesture of good faith, and without being asked to do so, the barbarian chiefs had sent their escorts a third of a mile back. They, themselves, however, were only about two hundred feet from the gate, well within light javelin or plumbata range from the walls. They'd also sent their personal weapons back with their escorts, and bore only shields.

Said Marcus Caelius, as the gate opened in front of him, "If I didn't think they'd elevate new chiefs or kings or whatever within something between hours and days, I'd have given the order to the men on the walls to kill them."

Replied Gaius Pompeius, "But, of course, that's just how long it would take them. So let's see what they want. Who knows; it could mean peace."

"My ass," said Caelius. "Even so, yes, it's worth a try."

Their horses' hooves made a clattering sound as they moved across the last bit of stone courtyard to the gate, and for some short distance thereafter. Then the road turned to dirt and the hooves went silent.

When they arrived at a point very close to the barbarians, the lightest of the three, a heavyset and bearded man with very light, almost white hair, raised one open palm and said, in passable Latin, "I am Gunderic, son of Godigisel, king of the Vandals. My Alan colleague, here"—and here Gunderic indicated a much swarthier man, in very heavy scale armor, on a nearly as well-armored horse—"is Respendial, chief of his band of Alans. He doesn't speak Latin but authorizes me to speak for him." At that point Gunderic spoke to Respendial, who in answer to the Romans made signs—thumb to his own chest, fingers to his own mouth, and then pointing at the Vandal—to indicate that, yes, the Vandal could speak for him. "Lastly, this gentleman is Hermeric, king of the Suebi. Hermeric can understand a bit of Latin but speaks almost none."

"*Ja*, understand good," said the Suebi. He had his helmet under his arm, exposing a surprisingly genial face, his blond beard close-cropped. His eyes were a lighter blue than Gunderic's. His hair was tied up to one side in an ornate knot that must have taken hours to create.

In return, Gaius introduced himself and Caelius as, "I am

Gaius Pompeius, legate of Rome's Eighteenth Legion. My colleague is *Praefectus Castrorum* Marcus Caelius. How can we help you?"

"You can let us pass, Roman, to settle in your Empire."

"That we cannot do," answered Gaius. "I lack the authority and, even if I had the authority, I would not cede the Empire's land to a people who will always retain their true loyalty to their own people and chiefs, and none to Rome; a people who will farm but not pay taxes; and a people whose customs are alien to our own. Finally, a people to whom our own people will be hostile, which means atrocity against your people and then reprisal against ours. There is no place for you within the Empire."

"Roman, a place *must* be found for us. The Huns are pressing behind us; we've lost our home; and we are beginning to go hungry. Since we have no choice, we *will* get in. How we act when we do depends on whether we are welcomed or resisted."

"You are…Germans, are you not?" asked Caelius.

"We are. The Suebi are. The Alans started in the vicinity of Persia. Why do you ask?"

"Oh, I was just thinking that, combined, we probably could defeat the Huns. But the last time we trusted Germans they turned on us without provocation, and massacred two Roman legions. So, no, the troops would never tolerate trusting you again."

"You have Germans with you," objected Gunderic. "Have they not proven trustworthy?"

"They," answered Caelius, "are assimilated to us. You are not."

Thought the camp prefect, too, *Which doesn't mean that I trust any of them in the slightest, barring only the German auxilia under Thancrat, who have stuck with us through thick and thin. Them, and good old Flavus, who is long gone now.*

"You can bluster all you like," said Gaius, "but the fact remains that you cannot get in unless we let you, not until you and your horses can walk on water. And we will not let you. You can march up and down the length of the Rhine and we will follow, faster than you can march."

"The Alans, here, are not on foot," said Gunderic.

"We are *all* mounted," said Gaius, "And we can fight on horseback or on foot."

"Roman, we have no choice; we must get in."

"Vandal, *I* have no choice; I cannot let you."

"If you leave us here the Huns will force us into alliance with them. We will become doubly dangerous, then."

"If the Huns join you or you them, you will all just starve that much sooner."

"Attack tonight, do you think?" asked Gaius, as the heavy wooden gate closed behind them. Pullo was there to meet them at the gate and so overheard the question.

"No, sir; they'll assemble tonight," replied Caelius, "attack first thing in the morning."

"Do you gentlemen feel up to lunch?" asked Pullo. "The ladies of the fort have put in a special effort."

"Sure, Centurion Pullo," Gaius agreed. "Prefect?"

"I'm up for it," agreed Caelius.

Lunch—which was long over for the troops and the leadership—began with bread and epityrum, a kind of olive-based relish, then moved on to a roasted duck stuffed with a mix of stale bread, leeks, and coriander. There was a sauce for the duck made with enough of the drippings to be considered a gravy. Bread with additional olive oil, for dipping, was served throughout, as was a very decent local wine, white, light, and sweet. For dessert there was *savillum*, a flattish cheesecake sweetened with honey and sprinkled with poppy seeds.

While the women of the troop mess did the cooking, Zaya took upon herself the serving of the table, then went to sit with the women in the main mess and chat.

As the final bites of *savillum* were being downed, Gaius remarked, "A glorious meal, Pullo, my compliments to the mess."

"Thanks, sir. The ladies will be pleased. I confess, I've not eaten so well since I joined the Army as I have here. Which brings up another subject: these women are not slaves. They're working their asses off to keep the men of the garrison fed, which is not their duty. Can we pay them something, maybe a gold coin a month?"

"That's why you wanted to feed us and pour some wine into us, isn't it?" Caelius said. "To get some pay for these women?"

"Yes, sir, and also for my surgeon's medical staff. Like I said, sirs, it needn't be much, the equivalent of a dozen denarii a month? Surely we can afford it? And isn't the cooking worthy of it?"

"It's quite good, Pullo," said Caelius, who then cautioned, "Don't let yourself get fat."

"One solidus and four denarii every three months," said Gaius, "and Tribune Rubelius will be intolerable in his whining about the expense."

"Fair deal," said Caelius. "It's most of the pay for *auxilia,* or what we were paying the *auxilia* before we came home and found out everyone was a citizen, so had to up their pay to keep peace."

The camp prefect then swirled the remaining wine in his cup and said, "You know, I'm a little surprised that they serve wine here, and such good wine, rather than beer."

"I asked about that," said Pullo. "Seems the Germans and Gauls have been growing wine in this area for about four hundred years. Mind, they brew beer, too, but wine is the big thing. Oh, and they also have a good deal of hard cider. We have a stockpile here if you want to try it. It's really quite refreshing." Without waiting for an answer Pullo summoned one of the women and asked for a jug.

The conversation ended for a bit until Pullo asked, "Something's been bugging me: these people, and especially Metrovius, were outright surly until Metrovius asked if I were descended from the Pullo mentioned by Caesar. I said that I was, and from Vorenus, too, and that I was also an equestrian. After that, everybody was all smiles and more than eager to listen and obey. It's practically been easy to command this place, ever since. Why, if either of you understand it, could this be?"

Caelius waited for the legate to answer and when he did not, began to explain. "This is my take on it; take it for what you will. It has to do with the nature of men and soldiers, Pullo. A man, a soldier, who is just eager to obey for its own sake? Probably doesn't have enough self-respect to be worth much in a fight. No, we want men who are confident in themselves, proud of themselves. It's the self-pride that makes them worthwhile.

"So you take a man like that; he does not *want* to obey or, if he does, still needs an excuse to do so. That excuse is what we might call 'legitimacy' or 'legitimacy of command.'

"Now, legitimacy can come from a lot of different things. You can, in the legion, get legitimacy by promotions, if the promotions were given because of brains and bravery. Or by decorations, but those tend to go with bravery. Or you might get legitimacy by your class; note the centurions who are, or at least were, directly appointed to the office. They came from a higher class than the run of the mill of the soldiery, a class that the troops themselves think of as entitled to give orders. And that's the excuse the men need.

"There's a third way, and that's where you come in—Titus Vorenus, too, for that matter: family background. Characters like your famous great-grandfathers, storied characters, richly portrayed in our history, give you legitimacy, and reasonably so, because we presume that they impressed their experience, wisdom, values and character on their sons, who did the same to your fathers, who did the same to you. This is true even though you both resemble bloody Gauls.

"Now let me tell you what does not give legitimacy." Caelius held up his vine staff. "If you think that the legal ability to beat a soldier senseless gives legitimacy—and I've known centurions who did—then you'll find out differently, with a knife or a gladius slipped into your belly, your back, or your neck, some dark night or darker day of battle. The vine staff only serves to support legitimacy you already have, and that only if used with restraint. It can never grant it, on its own."

"Funny," said Pullo, "my grandfathers, both of them, and father, too, used to say something somewhat like that. Though they used to append to that, 'So I'm not beating you as an act of legitimacy, but because you were a very naughty boy,' which, I must admit, I often was. Titus was better behaved."

"Case in point about the value of upbringing and family culture," said Caelius, with a curt nod of his head.

"Thanks, sir. Now, to more important matters: you think the barbs are going to hit us tomorrow?"

"Most likely, yes, but they *are* barbarians, so it may take them an extra day or even two to prepare."

"They won't succeed," said Pullo, with vast confidence.

"The enemy gets a vote, young Pullo; don't ever forget that. And my reading of the Vandal king is that he's going to make his vote count. And, you know, in his shoes, I can't say I'd do anything different than trying to escape the Huns by getting behind *our* walls."

"No," Gaius agreed, "and neither would I. But what would happen if we let his people in as anything but disarmed slaves is exactly what I said. So, sympathy or not, they must be stopped."

"'The enemy gets a vote,'" quoted Pullo, "doesn't mean we don't get to keep ours. I was thinking about the bridge. You may need to send reinforcements. I will need to evacuate some of the wounded and even the dead. As is, anyone trying to cross is going to come under enemy fire, bows, slingers, maybe even light artillery; my people say that the enemy has some inferior scorpions. So I think we need to put up a protective wall raised from halfway across it all the way to the western gate of the castle. That will cover our people going to and from, but leave the barbarians open to every kind of fire if somehow they manage to take the castle and try to storm across."

"You get that from your grandfathers, too, Pullo?" asked Caelius.

"No, sir; it was Vorenus' dad who used to lecture us on the shape of things in war."

"Good. Then he probably told you shit goes wrong in war; put up that protective screen almost all the way across. Leave open only the last fifty or so feet."

Mogontiacum

Appius Calvus had, with Gaius' permission, drawn a substantial advance on his salary and rented quarters and some warehouse space almost exactly one thousand feet and almost exactly due south of the western terminus of the stone bridge. He'd also, so to speak, passed the hat and gotten about three times that in loans, mainly from the officers and centurion. *Medicus* Josephus, in particular, had been generous, commenting on the advances to medicine could there but be standard texts produced to spread medical knowledge far and wide. Even the *medicus* in the castle, ben Solomon, had kicked in.

For this was Calvus' self-imposed task, or, rather, set of tasks: to develop a printing press, moveable type, a decent ink, and cheap paper. Failure in any one, he knew, would mean failure overall, and expensive failure, to boot.

Step one was making type. Calvus had seen the process in the mind of Johannes. The first step was to make a series of punches, one for every letter in Latin. These had to be made from the hardest material known, which could still be cut and formed. This material was steel. They also had to be cut in mirror image.

The steel was then used to punch the letters into a softer metal; copper sheeting did nicely. The letters were then surrounded by two L-shaped pieces to form a mold. Then a mix of lead, tin, and antimony was melted down and poured into the molds, one letter at a time, until enough of that letter was produced.

I am lucky, thought Calvus, *that our Latin letters are so much simpler than those strange German ones I saw in the printing shop.*

The next step was ink. Calvus had seen the ingredients—lamp black, linseed oil, walnut oil, turpentine, pine resin, cinnabar and some few other substances—but hadn't seen them being made, so could only guess at and experiment with the measurements. He'd hired a literate and numerate boy from a local merchant who normally traded for wine and other merchandise across the Rhine to Germany. With that trade shut down, for the time being, the boy had become redundant, hence available. He hadn't cost Calvus much beyond room and board.

"Keep careful records," Calvus had ordered the boy, "of just how much of each ingredient went into each different mix. There are one hundred different bottles for you to use; label them and make the record reflect each label. Once we get one that will work decently, we then expand on the recipe for it, until we approach perfection."

The most expensive part, and perhaps the most complex, was the printing machine itself. Oh, it was easy enough to come up with a wine press, especially so close to one of the premier wine regions of Gaul and Germany, but there were modifications needed that took a good deal of explaining to the carpenter Calvus took on.

And then there was the paper. Johannes had had only a glimmering of how that was made: flax or linen chopped up and soaked into a mash, then left to ferment, briefly. Whether the mash was poured out over a fine mesh screen, or the screen was dipped into a tank of the stuff, Johannes hadn't known. He also didn't know for a fact, but reasonably assumed, that the stuff on the screen must not only be allowed to drain but also to be pressed.

And Johannes thought that something else was needed in paper, something that was called "filler" or "sizing." But he wasn't sure what that was, only what it was intended to do. And what kind of wire am I going to use to make the screen? Gold is too soft, even if I could afford it. Bronze is too hard. Maybe brass. Or maybe just pure copper . . .

South of Mogontiacum

Marcus Caelius watched the Germanic shield wall advance across the open field, eight ranks deep and about one hundred and ten or twenty across. Except that the shields were much lighter, the armor less encompassing, and the men taller and blonder, it might have been a phalanx from Hellas, nine centuries prior . . . or the Roman Army from before Caudine Forks, slightly more recently.

Slightly to the west, a different Germanic formation was taking turns, half practicing with their *plumbata*, while the other half engaged in mock duels with their long swords.

Since the Eighteenth Legion's treasury was supplementing the pay of the more modern "legions," and with—wonder of wonders—actual *money*, the Eighteenth's command group was the command group for the entire army, now of about thirteen thousand men and boys.

And that means, thought Caelius, *that these amateurs are also my responsibility. But how to convince them of the error of their ways? That turd, Cicero, might have been an effeminate fop, but that doesn't mean he was uniformly wrong: "Nothing is more enduring than custom."*

Caelius had a sudden idea. He *hated* that idea for a number of reasons but it still seemed workable enough to try.

"Thiaminus?"

"Yes, Lord?"

"Take my horse and go back to camp. Fetch me my *scutum* and three—no, four—*pila*. Also my greaves; yes, both of them."

"At once, Lord."

Impatiently, Caelius waited for his freedman servant to return. With each minute of watching the German mercenaries hired by the Empire practice his interior rage grew.

Finally, when Thiaminus had returned. Caelius put on the greaves, ran his arm through the shield's loop, grasped the hand grip, and ordered, "Follow me."

They went immediately to where the Germans were throwing *plumbatae*. Caelius stopped and watched for a few minutes to find that one German who seemed most skilled with the weighted darts. Once he had, he walked over and asked, "Do you speak Latin?"

"Fair, sir," the German replied, in a deep and resonant baritone.

"You are the best in your unit with these little dart things?"

The German shrugged. "Maybe not best, maybe in top ten. Pretty good, anyway."

"Excellent," said Caelius. "You will certainly do. What's your name, soldier?"

"Hrodebert, son of Sigifurd, but my army name is Rodius Sigius."

"Very good, Sigius. Now here's what I want. I am going to march down the field with my *scutum*. When I reach a distance you think is ideal, shout out and let me know. Then I am going to turn around and get behind my shield. Once I've done that, I want you to try your very best to hit me with three of those darts. Do you understand?"

Shocked silly, the German's mouth opened like a fish out of water. Finally, after several failed attempts at speech, he said, "I cannot do that, sir."

Caelius ignored him for a moment, while scanning the line of Germans with their darts. "Where is this man's commander? This man's commander: I want him to report to me instantly!"

After a moment's hesitation another German—obviously German, from the size, the eye color, and the hair color—trotted up and asked what the problem was. Caelius explained what he wanted, then pointed to one of the *pila*, carried by Thiaminus.

"And the reason I am going to do this is that I want you to see the advantages of those over these little *plumbatae*."

"Sir," said the German commander, whose Latin seemed perfect, "I think you may get hurt or even killed, but you are my superior officer and, over my protest, this man will obey."

"Excellent." With that, Caelius began striding downrange, until the German dart thrower called out, "There; that is a good range for me."

"Very good," said Caelius, turning about, crouching a bit low and positioning his *scutum* so that there was only a narrow slit for his eyes between his helmet and the top of the shield. "Now throw, and no slacking off about it. And *don't miss!*"

With something of the air about him of a condemned man

told to lay his head on the chopping block, Sigius took one of his *plumbata* in hand and drew back for an overhand throw. Like a scorpion's tail his arm lashed up and forward, propelling his dart at a modest arc and an immodest velocity.

Caelius' eyes followed the dart until it began to descend. At that point he made a slight movement of his *scutum*, to make the dart hit the metal boss. It made a dent but did not penetrate, instead deflecting off to hit the ground.

"Again."

Once again, Sigius drew back and let fly. Caelius, who had a good deal of experience with things being thrown at him, judged that this one could not be deflected by the boss and was going to hit a bit low. At the last second he crouched lower, dropping the *scutum* nearly to the ground.

The *plumbata* hit low, rocking the shield. The very point just barely made it through the thick plywood of the shield, though the barbs of the dart actually helped prevent penetration.

"Again!"

By this point Sigius was getting embarrassed. The third one he put his whole heart and soul into, nearly knocking himself over with the force of his own throw.

Caelius tried, once again, to bounce the dart with the boss of his shield. He didn't quite make it. Rather, the *plumbata* struck the wood on the left side of the shield and, once again, only barely penetrated the plywood.

"Excellent, Sigius," Caelius shouted from where he stood. He began to walk back to where Sigius and his officer stood. "Now, Commander, I want you to get the strongest shield in your command and the best armor available and put them fifty feet in front of young Sigius, there. Get some hay or lumber to hold the shield upright and fill out the armor."

Doing this took the better part of an hour. While waiting, Caelius asked the German commander to nominate the best swordsman in his unit.

When this worthy was presented, Caelius said, "Get your shield and your sword. I'm going to show you the advantages of both speed and leverage. I am not going to try to kill you but I want you to try to kill me."

The German swordsman looked at his commander doubtfully.

The commander just shrugged, saying, in German, "The man

is obviously crazy. But he not only outranks us, he and his are paying our salaries. We'll humor him. But try not to kill him."

Caelius drew his gladius and said to his opponent, and by extension the hundred or so German mercenaries within earshot, "The shield is as much an offensive weapon as the spear or the sword."

With that, Caelius tapped the flat of his gladius against the bronze rim of his *scutum*, and shuffled forward, left leg leading. The German raised his sword overhead for a downward slash, intending to split the *scutum*...

And found himself lying flat on his back, gasping for breath, his sword lost somewhere unknown. Caelius gave the German a few minutes to catch his breath and retrieve his sword, then said, "Now, in slow motion, let me show you what happened. Go ahead and raise your sword as if to slash down. Do *not* slash down, however, because I am going to be showing you what happened very slowly."

With that, as if immersed in water, Caelius shuffled forward, then slowly knocked the German's light shield side with his own and shoved the shield toward his chest.

"All right, now do you understand what happened?"

"Think so," said the German. "Uncovered self and so allowed you to get in close. Got to keep sword pointed at you, yes?"

"Almost right," Caelius said. "Let's try it again, but you keep your point toward me, to try to fend me off. That's what a long sword is for, isn't it?"

"*Ja*," the German said, though his tone said he might have had his doubts.

This time, when Caelius shuffled forward, he didn't try to pound the German's chest with his boss. Instead, he crossed blades, then slid his own gladius up until the near point of the German's was just above his own handguard. At that point, with the leverage all on his side, the Roman simply swept the German's blade out of the way, stepped in closer again, again knocked the lighter shield out of the way, and finally tapped the German's mail twice with the tip of his gladius.

"Can you show my men, all of them, how to do that?" the German commander asked.

"Not with those swords; they're just too long. You shorten them to something close to this"—he held up his gladius—"maybe a little longer to account for your size, and we can work something out. Is the shield and armor ready?"

"Yes." The German commander stepped out of the way to let Caelius see the setup, some fifty feet away.

At that, the *praefectus castrorum* said to his servant, "Thiaminus, toss me one *pilum*, please."

Thiaminus tossed the *pilum,* as commanded. Caelius caught it one-handed and, without wind up, without taking a single step forward, casually threw it right through the shield, and right through the mail armor, both sides.

"You'll want to learn that, too," said Marcus Caelius to the German commander. "I'll send over a century of regular troops to help you learn it."

"What about our *plumbatae*?"

"How many do you normally carry?"

"Five per man."

"Turn in two of every five to the legionary quartermaster, Tribune Rubelius. I'll have him have *pila* made for your men. I think there's a *fabrica* at Augusta Trevorarum. That will give you three shots at distance, because, yes, I can see *some* point to the darts, especially when facing horse archers, and one killer shot, close up."

INTERLUDE

River Moenis, beside the Vandal camp, 406 A.D.

There would be nearly a quarter moon tonight, but it would rise in the daytime and set quite early in the evening. Tomorrow night would be much the same. King Gunderic stood on the bank watching twenty-one of his finest, noblest warriors moving a boat around with their oars.

It's been a week they've been working on this. I don't expect them to be as good as the Romans, but they've definitely improved.

Along the bank, another seven boats of similar size bobbed in the water, tied off to the trees that lined the riverbank.

Coming across the water, Gunderic heard the boat crew being given commands. Those commands were clear enough. Someone listening carefully could also have heard the crying of hungry children, coming from the camp.

I should have realized before, thought the king, *that trying to get men across was an exercise in futility. Those light Roman boats are too fast and maneuverable, and the men that crew them too skilled. My problem is* those *boats. So those boats must go.*

And, who knows, maybe the Romans will be more reasonable when they don't have a fleet to patrol the river anymore. At least, I can hope they will.

So, in the morning, I am going to expend maybe five hundred men . . . or a thousand . . . or two thousand. These are five hundred men—or four times that—I can ill afford to lose after my father's early disaster with the Franks, just to tire out the Romans on both shores. And in that fatigue there is a gap where maybe a score of men might get to the Roman harbor and burn their boats. Maybe. I've had these men practicing for a week. They're not as good as the Roman rowers, not nearly, but they just may be good enough to launch from this river, unseen, then use the current to get through one of the twenty-two gaps between the bridge's pylons, unseen, and then maneuver just enough to get to the mouth of the Roman harbor, unseen, and then dash in, unseen.

And then the Romans can see their ships burn.

Gunderic's own son was the commander of this expedition. He bore the name of his grandfather, Godigisel. He was a good boy, not Gunderic's eldest—indeed, not old enough to really have a beard yet—but still his favorite, and his father prayed to his gods that he wouldn't lose him.

The boy favored his late mother in looks, which was to say that he was a good deal better looking than his father.

If I can burn the boats at the nearby Roman base, then I'll have a chance to burn the next set down, the flotilla at the town that the Romans call Confluentes. That's the most I can hope for, though; the same trick might work twice but not three times.

But twice will be enough. Twice means that any Roman ships that survive will be too few to patrol adequately, too few to stop me from sending raiders across. And let me start launching some successful raids and the Romans will have to start spreading out to secure this little town and that. Spread them out enough and the five hundred rafts I'm having built can carry enough men over to storm the town. Storm the town and I can starve the fort. Starve out the fort—I'll offer good terms if they surrender early—and we can all cross over. Moreover, the town's granaries will feed my people long enough for us to live until we cross over. And then we can feed on the corpse of their rotten empire in Gaul.

CHAPTER SIXTEEN

Regard your soldiers as your children, and they will
follow you into the deepest valleys; look upon them
as your own beloved sons, and they will stand by you
even unto death.

—Sun Tzu, *The Art of War*

Castellum Mattiacorum (Pullo's Castle), opposite Mogontiacum, 406 A.D.

All night, the surrounding enemy had "entertained" the troops
of the empire with the sound of drums, continuously beating.
Accompanying that were the war cries and, more troublingly, the
vast and rolling cheers that seemed to move from the south, to
the east, to the north. Lucius Pullo stood on the tower to the
left side of the eastern gate, the one farthest from the river, just
staring out at the unseen horizon. There were four more men up
on the top of the tower with him, but he'd told them to go to
sleep, that he would keep watch, himself.

That, thought Pullo, *was him, their king, moving from group
to group, and whipping them into a frenzy for the assault.*

Gonna be a hot day tomorrow.

"Lucius?" asked a soft and sweet feminine voice, accented
but clear enough.

"Yes, Zaya. And before you say another word, however much I
appreciate it, it was silly of you to climb those stairs in the dark."

"I leaned against the wall and kept away from the edge," she said. "The women in the mess are making up packages of rations for the men on the wall, nothing fancy, little jugs of wine, bread, cheese, sausage, and butter, all wrapped up in cloth and tied in a bundle. I didn't want yours getting delivered by anyone but me, so here I am."

"Where's young Titus?" Pullo asked.

"I carried his crib to the mess; one of the girls is watching him for me. I cannot see very well but we're not alone up here, are we?"

"No, love, not alone."

"What a shame," she said. "I've never made love in a tower. But if you can manage to tear yourself away and come back to our apartment for a bit, I'd like to give you another good reason not to get yourself killed."

Without another word to his woman, Pullo used the toe of one *caliga* to nudge one of the men napping. "Take over here," he ordered. "I have some business to attend to."

Zaya stopped on the way to retrieve young Titus, then, once she was home, bared her breasts to feed him. By the time the baby was finished, Pullo was out of his armor, his subarmalis, his tunic, and his caligae. An all too short hour after that, she was finished with him. Pullo napped, himself, while she stayed awake to get him up, into his clothing, boots, and armor, and back on the walls well before stand to. She kept a small, oil-fed lamp burning with several more ready but unlit, the better to get him into his armor quickly.

Pullo arrived back atop the tower before the first line of dawn showed in the east. Fortunately, it was still dark enough for him not to have seen the knowing smirks on the faces of his troops. And when it was light enough? Then they had a lot more on their minds than an officer and his lady knocking out a quickie before a battle. Along with Pullo trudged hundreds of more men. None looked eager, though most looked at least determined and willing.

The just rising sun illuminated scenes, silent scenes, from Hades on the north, south, and east. There, in all those directions, as far as the eye could see were barbarians. The numbers were staggering, but what was truly frightening was that they were not a mob. Rather, they were formed up in neat blocks, with what appeared to be some uniformity of equipment, and a certain amount of task organization. Notably, three of the first blocks—more broad rectangles really—carried ladders and those ladders appeared to be the right length, six-fifths the height, for scaling the castle walls. And then there were the scorpions, dozens of scorpions, with crews ready to wheel them into range.

"Where in the hell...?" wondered Pullo.

The junior noncom assigned to the tower, part of the original garrison, said, "From us, centurion; the barbs learned it from us. Their young men come over and sign up for the army. In the army they learn all kinds of useful things. Then they take their retirement grant, money or, if it's land, they sell the land, and then they go home. Once home, they teach their own people. Bet you anything you like that leading each of those very regular looking blocks are anything up to half a dozen Germans trained by nobody but us."

"You're likely right," admitted Pullo. *It's not that they have them that surprises me, but that they have so many of them.*

"No 'likely' about it," said the soldier. "Last assault we beat off, when we went over the enemy dead we found two who were not only in the army at one time but had served in this castle. Boon companions they were at the time, too. But a German is going to stay a German; it runs deeper than a mere twenty years in the Roman Army is going to fix."

"Right. Seeing the change from the last group of hostile Germans I saw, yes, these are bloody well trained and organized."

Pullo looked over some of the defensive arrangements atop the tower. Besides the scorpion, there was a movable pipe jutting out toward the area in front of the eastern gate. A leather hose led from the pipe to a barrel. A valve by the barrel kept the fluid therein from leaking. Inside was a mix of turpentine, oil, and dissolved resin. It was not Greek fire. Neither was it a flame thrower. Instead, it was a flammables projector, a means of getting burnable stuff down to the ground around both enemy soldiers and any machinery they might have brought up to assault the walls or gates. Fire would be provided once the burnables had reached their targets.

That fire currently rested in firepots in each tower and along the walls. There were other fires, though. Along the walls, hanging on cranes, were pots being heated by fires built underneath. These contained water, or sand. Chains ran from the bottoms of the pots, up to the cranes, and then to the interior of the walls. The chains were to allow the hot stuff to be dumped without any danger to the defenders.

Which is damned bloody good, thought Pullo, *given all those scorpions and the massed archers.*

The silence ended with the pounding of the drums. It began in the center, on the east, then spread to either side and around to the forces arrayed to the north and south. The massed enemy formations began a slow march forward to the beat.

"Gentlemen," Pullo announced, "you know what to do here. I'm going to the northeastern tower, where I can see what's going on, on two sides. Metrovius is on the southeast tower. Good luck to you and the gods watch over you."

"God watch over you, too, Centurion. When this is over, see you in the mess hall, the hospital, or in Hell."

"Well, if it's the mess, save me some of Melissa's honeyrolls, would you?"

In a set of targets arrayed so densely, it wasn't a question of the scorpions hitting or missing so much as it was a question of hitting how many. In Pullo's view four scorpion bolts fired in short order managed to take out eleven Suebi and Vandal men, creating four human shish kebabs of screaming, twisting, writhing men, most of them dying in agony.

Which would be most comforting, thought Pullo, *except that there are about forty thousand more of the bastards.*

"Duck!"

Pullo wasn't sure who had shouted out the warning. It didn't matter, anyway; he dropped instantly below the edge of the stone battlements of the castle. A small fraction of a second later, hundreds of arrows either flew overhead or rattled against the stone of the castle.

Not everyone did duck. On one of the scorpion crews, one man fell with three arrows in his torso while another screamed, clutched one eye, and staggered off the inside edge of the walkway. That one fell on the stone courtyard. His head smashed like a dropped piece of overripe fruit.

From farther out, the Vandals' and Suebi's scorpions sent up regular bolts at the only partially protected defending artillery. They scored fewer hits, but the numbers they did score foretold of a loss of defending artillery in the not too terribly distant future.

Pullo grabbed two nearby messengers and ordered, "Go to each of the scorpion crews—yes, I mean ours, you idiot—and tell them to concentrate on the enemy scorpions." To a third, he said, "Run back across the causeway. Find the commander of the *tormenta* there and tell him, also, to fire on the scorpions. Incendiary would work best. Then go find the commander of the legion, Gaius Pompeius, and tell him that this is dicier than we'd figured. I still think we can hold, but the odds are pretty formidable."

Mogontiacum

Not that the barbarians didn't try; they did. But the bolts from their scorpions, in every case, landed in the Rhine, well short of the Roman artillery on the west bank. After some minutes of this, they gave up trying to silence the Roman medium artillery on that bank, and turned their fire back on the scorpions mounted on the walls of Pullo's castle.

Fulvius' *tormenta* crews jeered at the opponents across the river. That is, they jeered until Fulvius reminded them, "You idiots! Back to the work that actually helps, rather than just making you feel good!"

Instantly the crews got back to the serious business of flinging fire and death across the water. They didn't kill or burn all that many, really, but they frightened and disordered the barbarians in great numbers with their steady drumbeat of both eight-pound rocks and flaming jars full of turpentine.

Fulvius had been letting his men fire at will. He had a second thought. "Boys," he shouted, "we're going to see how volleys work. Everybody crank your arms back, then set the range on your slings to fifteen hundred feet. I want One, Three, and Five to load incendiaries. Two, Four, and Six, I want rocks. Let me know when you're ready to shoot."

There's always one who is just slow, Fulvius mentally cursed. "Number Four, do I have to send into town for some little old ladies to take your places? They couldn't possibly be any slower."

"Sorry, Centurion. We'll try better, Centurion."

Finally, all six on the left-hand side were ready. Fulvius raised his right hand and shouted, "Light your incendiaries. One through Six, ready…FIRE!"

Six lanyards were pulled, six hooks released the arms of the *tormenta,* and six projectiles swung up at impressive speed. The slings slipped off the hooks at the ends of the arms, sending projectiles both solid and burning on a high arc over the river. The rear ends of the *tormenta* leapt up several feet from the arms striking the padded crosspieces.

After that, the crews quickly doused out any lingering flame on the sling cups. One men per hooked the lanyards to the arms, then two men began the laborious task of cranking the arms back to firing position.

Squinting his eyes, Fulvius watched to see the effect on the enemy.

Pullo's Castle

The enemy fire was having an effect on the defenders. Two carts emerged from the western gate, hauled by the women working for the *medicus,* ben Solomon. One of them was loaded with half a dozen wounded, being brought back to Josephus for treatment beyond the stabilization brought on by ben Solomon. A dozen women maneuvered the cart with the wounded. Eight struggled with the cart of the dead.

That other cart contained four dead. One of the women, head down, wept continuously as she pulled the cart containing the dead. Her husband lay on it.

There were more loads waiting, but only the two carts. *Medicus* ben Solomon hoped that the Romans on the other side would take the hint and send more of their own ambulance carts across. *Always something you forget to coordinate for. Damnit.*

From his position on the northwest tower, Pullo saw both the carts crossing the bridge and several—he thought probably six—projectiles flying the other way. The stones were hard to follow in their arcs, but the flamers absolutely captured the eye.

One of the rocks presumably missed—at least Pullo saw none of the barbs fall from it. One took out a German at the juncture of neck and shoulder. He fell and probably wouldn't rise again. One came down on a knee, breaking it and severing the muscle beneath it, then hit the ground and bounced, hitting another man in the jaw and smashing it.

Good enough, thought Lucius Pullo.

The flaming projectiles, on the other hand, those had a more horrid effect. One hit a German's helmet, breaking open and scattering down his body flaming turpentine. He became a human torch, running in a tight circle and screaming. The others backed away from him.

Two other incendiaries hit the ground, broke open, and cast their burning contents generally upward, partially dousing up to four men with lit turpentine. These began to run while desperately beating at the flames.

That company of barbarians stopped in place, then took to its heels in unfeigned panic.

From his tower Pullo heard the drawn out *whummp* of *tormenta* arms hitting padded crosspieces. He looked south to see three more flaming projectiles arcing up, up, up, before being lost in the shadow of the southern wall. He fancied that he heard screams but could see nothing.

One company, maybe two, taken out of play for a while. Every little bit helps.

That thought was fleeting, in good part because the first barbarian ladders were going up on the walls. The men defending had short, forked poles to push the ladders away but, since the six-fifth ratio of length of ladder to height of wall kept the top of the ladder below the battlements, the defenders had to lean out, exposing themselves, in order to push the ladders away. This, given both the masses of archers and the javelins in the hands of climbing men, was a very risky proposition.

In Pullo's view, one of his men, leaning out to push a ladder away, staggered back with a javelin in his throat. Another ended up as a human pincushion, as a score or more of the enemy archers let fly at him.

But it's not one-sided, Pullo thought as one ladder and then another was pushed away, each with men nearly at the top of their climb. For the men on the lower rungs, this wasn't usually that much of a problem. For those at or near the top, however, the long arcing flight back to ground level built up enough momentum to cause permanent and serious injury, in many and perhaps most cases.

The point of greatest vulnerability for the attackers, though, came when they reached the top of the ladder and tried to crawl in between the merlons over the crenels. At that time, they had one hand trying to maintain a shield, another trying to maintain a sword or spear, while on the unsteady rungs of a ladder, and one of those two hands also trying to grasp a merlon to help themselves over. Moreover, trying to come across alone, they were in almost every case required to come up against two to three armed enemies, none of whom had their disadvantages.

In one case—at least one that Pullo could see—a very large barbarian, in just that position of maximum vulnerability, trying to surmount the western wall, was transfixed by two spears at the same time. His howl of agony was audible, even up on the tower and even over the general din of battle. When the spears were withdrawn, he fell straight down the ladder, knocking another five men off. Of those five, one didn't rise again.

But then sometimes the bastards will get lucky, Pullo thought as one barbarian on the southern wall, quick or lucky or skilled or all three, managed to leap over the crenel, then block one spear thrust with his round flat shield while using a sword to stab another defender in the leg. Blood gushed and the wounded defender fell, crying with pain. A quick slash and the cries stopped.

That barb then turned on the one he'd blocked and drove him back, away from the gap of the crenel. This allowed another barbarian to cross over, and soon four more had come over, four who were proving very difficult to kill. Those six managed to clear another crenel and soon the barbarians were starting to come across that, too.

Briefly, Pullo considered committing one or both of the centuries he'd kept in reserve.

But, no, if we need to commit the reserve this soon, we'll be screwed later on. Let the men on that wall handle it.

That penetration was on Metrovius' wall. In Pullo's view, that worthy gathered up a dozen men and charged along the walkway to close the gap before it could become a yawning chasm.

Satisfied that everything that could be done was being done, Pullo turned his attention back to the east. From off in the distance, outside of scorpion range, came an apparition of dread: a battering ram on a wheeled frame was being pushed up to tackle the western gate.

A quick glance to Pullo's left told him that there was another ram coming from the north. *I wonder if the artillery can range it? I wonder, too, if their eight-pound stones can break it or the one-congius incendiaries can set it alight.*

Fulvius, over on the west bank, wondered the same. He had his six eight-pounders aim for the ram, still firing a mix of solid rocks and incendiary amphorae. The rocks just bounced off when they hit. Likewise most of the inflammables were useless against the wet hides covering the frame.

All right, then, Fulvius thought. *If I can't get the thing to burn from the outside, I wonder if I can get some of the liquid stuff to slip under the edge of the framework.*

"Cease fire. Cease fire. Unload rocks and load incendiary. Adjust slings to lower the range a *little*...let me know when ready."

This time Number Four was ready on time.

"Light your projectiles. Fire!"

Of the six, two hit the wet hides protecting the frame. They did no damage. Another two sailed past the ram, raining fire down on some barbarians keeping up with it. That did some good. Two hit short. One of these was too short but another was just about right for the bulk of the flaming turpentive mix to roll under the edge of the frame like a wave. Fulvius couldn't hear it, though Pullo and the men on the west wall could, if barely: shouts of alarm and pain came through the hides, as a torrent of frightened men poured out the back of the ram's frame.

Another volley of incendiaries, to similar result, flew. Soon the ram and its frame were blazing away merrily.

Seeing success against the northern threat, Fulvius trotted south to where the other half of his battery lay. He considered firing again in the same way but... *Too late. Too late. Oh, far too late. I could toss rocks but they're useless against the frame. I could toss fire and risk hitting the men on the wall. And that I will not risk again.*

As the barbarians fought their way along the wall, they freed up crenellations over which more barbarians crossed. Metrovius and his band closed these off, a couple of bodies on each side at a time. Yet they never managed to close one off before two or three more barbarians crossed over.

At length, the barbarians reached the flammables projectors above the southern gate. What barrels there were of the stuff were thrown into the courtyard, as far out of the way as possible, while some others among the barbs went for the tanks and the connecting leather hose with their hand axes. From this, a steady stream of the turpentine-based mix gushed out and spread along the walkway.

Some quick-thinking Roman defender took a burning stick from one of the fires heating up a cauldron of sand, and tossed it onto the walkway where the turpentine flowed freely. The effect was almost instantaneous: where there had been slippery essence of pine sap was replaced by a scene from Hell, with a mass shriek from barbarians now engulfed in flames.

Unfortunately, that also meant that there was now nothing effective with which to tackle the approaching ram.

"Shit! Shit! Shit!" Pullo exclaimed when he saw the flames rising on the walkway above the southern gate. This wasn't made any better by seeing that the ram facing the western gate had almost reached the walls.

Ducking low and raising his shield for protection from arrows as he reached each crenel, Pullo got himself to the western gate. Pointing at the ram, he told the men above the gate, "Burn that damned thing as soon as it reaches the gate."

Following this, he went back to the tower he was using as a command post. At each crenel, arrows struck and often stuck in the face of his *scutum*. Others flew over, ahead of, or behind.

Fuckers seem to have my number, all right.

At the tower he followed the staircase down before emerging into the courtyard. An even four messengers followed him. There he whistled for the *optios* in charge of his two reserve centuries.

As Pullo emerged into the courtyard, there came a gushing sound from the eastern gate, followed by the sounds of several dozen panic-stricken men abandoning their ram and its wheeled shed posthaste. The roar of flames soon followed.

Pointing at half a dozen wagons containing provisions that hadn't been stored along with a good deal of water in barrels, he ordered, "Drag those and form a *V* at the southern gate. Tip them over to form a wall, point of the *V* facing inward. Then get behind that makeshift wall and prepare to fight for your lives."

As the troops began unloading the water and provisions, Pullo nearly lost his temper.

"No, no, NO, you idiots! No time for that. Drag them and dump them."

As the men of those two centuries hastened to comply, Pullo sent a messenger to the men over the north gate. The message was, "Get a few casks of turpentine over to the southern gate and dump them." He then sent another to Gaius Pompeius, on the Rhine's west bank: "Issue in doubt. Could use anything up to a cohort's worth of reinforcements, and maybe the cohort of missile troops, too." That last was prompted by a quick glance around the battlements, where the garrison was contending with what seemed to be half a dozen minor break-ins. Finally, he sent a third messenger to the castle's armorer, ordering that another five hundred javelins be passed out amongst the courtyard defenders of the south gate.

Then he and the rest settled down to wait for the inevitable, as the steady *wham-wham-wham* of the enemy ram began pounding on the stout oaken gate.

Both heart rates and blood pressure rose with each stroke of the ram. When the first crack appeared in the crossbeam holding the gate closed, they both surged. They dropped a little with the arrival of those five hundred javelins, then lurched upward again as the upper hinge on the right section of the gate gave way amidst a spray of concrete bits and dust.

Wham-wham-wham-sproing! That was the hinge giving way.

Wham-wham-wham-crack! That was another crack in the crosspiece.

Then, finally, with a cracking sound that could be heard across the castle, both sides of the gate sprang open as the crosspiece gave up the ghost. Initially, none of the barbarians surged through.

"The crew of the ram is just getting out of the way," Pullo announced. "The follow-ons will be here in . . . and there they are! Ready to loose javelins . . . LOOSE!"

Now where the fuck is that turpentine I ordered dumped outside the southern gate?

The wave of barbarians poured through the gate in a way reminiscent of the sea surging through a burst dike at high tide. At Pullo's command, over a hundred and fifty javelins flew, followed in an instant by one hundred and fifty more. This exhausted the ones initially carried by the two centuries, but were immediately followed by *plumbatae*, almost five hundred in total.

Faced with missiles coming from both sides, the incoming barbarians, using their shields to defend one side, left themselves vulnerable to fire from the other. Moreover, the range was so short that the missiles tended to hit with great and lethal power. Even the *plumbatae,* which had nothing like the short-range penetrative power of a *pilum*, managed to get through shields to ruin arms. Mere mail hadn't a chance of stopping them.

The first wave rolled in and under the relentless and merciless missile barrage tried to surge right back out again, too. There at the gate, the survivors of the first wave ran head-on into the fresh troops of the second. This not only created something of a traffic jam, but left the backs of the first wave largely undefended such that more missiles found and penetrated targets.

So far, so good. Pullo looked up and thought, *Finally!,* as the casks of turpentine arrived and were tossed in front of the southern gate. These mostly broke open or at least began to leak heavily. Fire soon followed, tossed from the battlements above. Screams quickly followed the fire while an apparent stampede of flame engulfed men from the second wave followed that.

Pullo ordered, "Draw gladii," followed by, "No prisoners! Charrrge!"

He and his hundred and fifty men charged out over the wagons and through the gaps, then racing to strike undefended backs.

One barbarian, sensing what was happening behind him, whipped around to face Pullo. Barbarian or not, the German's stance shouted to Pullo "former legionary." Despite his words of a moment before, Pullo was almost inclined to grant mercy. No matter, the borderer on Pullo's left shoved his sword through the German's belly, then viciously ripped it out through clutching hands. In the process, three of the German's fingers were severed, falling to the pavement even before the dying German did.

Relieved at not having to kill someone who, in other circumstances, might have been a comrade in arms, Pullo lashed into the fleeing Germans, stabbing this one through the back of the neck, that one in a howl-inducing kidney, hamstringing this one, chopping down that.

And then Pullo found himself, along with a tight little knot of other Roman defenders, at the remnants of the gate. *We can try to repair it tonight, if we're alive. For now, though . . .*

There were a couple of dead Romans lying on the ground, and a half dozen non-walking wounded, but on the whole the butcher's bill had been remarkably light.

"Block the gate with the enemy dead before the fire goes out," Pullo ordered. "Put a wagon behind the corpses and then more corpses behind the wagon. Make sure the dead really are dead. Then collect up the javelins and *plumbatae*. Lastly, recover the food and water we had to dump."

With that, Pullo ordered over the senior of the two *optios*, Cornelius Eustachius—and this one really was senior, since he'd been an *optio* at the time of his original discharge—and said, "Take charge here. I'm going back up to the tower."

The old veteran seemed quite capable and still physically fit. Pullo wondered why he'd never made centurion.

"Yes, sir," answered Eustachius. "I'll have the men intertwine the arms and legs of the bodies to make it harder to pull them out through the gate."

"Excellent idea, Eustachius. Do it."

Crossing the courtyard, one of Pullo's runners gasped, screamed, and fell to the pavement. A quick glance showed one thigh and the opposite calf bleeding profusely around a spear that transfixed them both.

Gods, thought Pullo, *what kind of monster threw that?*

"Get him to the *medicus*," Pullo said from under a shield raised to ward off further missiles from above. Two of the messengers grabbed the wounded man by both arms, then ran at an all-out pace for the shelter of the *valetudinarium*. The stricken soldier screamed again and again as his heels bounced on the cobblestones, the screams finally subsiding into low, exhausted moans.

Pullo continued his race for the tower. Fortunately, whatever Germanic monster had thrown a spear through his messenger hadn't decided to donate one to him. *That, or he only had the one spear.*

At the tower, and safe for the nonce from any more enemy spears, Pullo and his remaining messenger raced to the top. They arrived there to find the barrage of arrows from the German archers and bolts from their scorpions undiminished.

A quick glance to the east gave the satisfying view of a totally incinerated ram, with some scorched bodies around it. It also showed at least three penetrations over the battlements of knots of Germans, so far holding off any attempts to dislodge them, and keeping the way open for trickles of reinforcements from their fellows' to join them.

Bad, very damned bad.

The north side was better, with the only remaining penetration being contained by two centuries, pressing on it from either side. Meanwhile, most of the Germans on that side had drawn back out of scorpion range.

The southern wall was actually in the best shape, with many of the men there looking over their shoulders with worry at the events on the north and especially the east walls.

Now why should that . . . Ohhhh, the ones who would have been scaling the walls elected, instead, to come through the broken gate. Defeat and demoralize those—and we did—and the rest who haven't run lack the heart to fight much more. That's one threat down, two to go.

Pullo had another sudden and not entirely welcome thought. *And that's also why my men are fighting so hard; their families are here. But, by the same token, if things start to go to crap anywhere their first concern is going to be their families and then there'll be a mad rush for the western gate and the bridge.*

Maybe I should have evacuated the families right off, but so many of them have become key to both the medical effort and the logistics on the place.

All right, the north wall is mostly good. The south wall is good. Only the eastern wall, then . . .

Of the chief of the scorpion crew on the northeast tower, Pullo asked, after pulling him down to look through the same gap Pullo was looking through, "So just how accurate is this thing?"

"Accurate enough to hit some random unfortunate in a massed cohort out to about two thousand feet. Yes, Centurion, as a matter of fact ours *are* considerably better than the ones the Germans ginned up. Accurate enough to hit an individual at maybe half to two thirds of that."

Interrupting, Pullo asked, "Accurate enough to hit a man's head at two hundred feet, while making sure to miss our own man, three feet away?"

"Tougher, but if we're really careful..."

"Okay, here's what I want," Pullo said. "You see that place nearest to us where Germans keep popping up over the parapet to reinforce their fellows?"

"Sure, Centurion."

"Forget engaging their scorpions for now. I want you to put one right through the head or neck or shoulders of any German who pops up."

The chief of the scorpion looked carefully, considered carefully, then said, "We can do that."

"Do it, then."

That should do for the near penetration, Pullo thought. He looked farther out and saw Metrovius still leading a century to attack one of the penetrations. *He'll at least keep them in place, keep them from expanding via other ladders.*

I'm missing something. What is it? What... Ohhh, those two centuries that defended the southern gate. The gate's nearly blocked now with piled up German bodies. I can leave one on guard and use the other to... to do what? Aha! Five hundred extra javelins.

To one of the remaining messenger, Pullo said, "Go find *Optio* Eustachius. Tell him one century is to remain working on blocking the gate, and defending it at need. He need not stay with that. The other one is to become javelin men in the courtyard to engage the Germans who've penetrated onto the battlement of the eastern wall. Got that?"

"Yes, sir."

"No, 'sir,' son, I'm a centurion. I fight for a living."

Now I wonder how things are going in the medical establishment...

Valetudinarium, *Pullo's Castle*

The place was fairly dim, on its own, much too dim for delicate surgery. Barred gaps let air in, but the amount of natural light was minimal. Even the doors were closed and mostly barred, except that they were opened occasionally to load carts for evacuation across the bridge.

So there were lamps burning, more or less everywhere, and more lamps being held by the women auxiliaries to the hospital to light up *Medicus* ben Solomon's way.

Zaya held one of the lamps for ben Solomon, watching and also learning as he cleaned out a wound with a mixture of wine, honey, and vinegar, followed by a bit of cloth on a twig dipped in the same solution. He then began filling the wound with clean lint to stop the bleeding. The wounded soldier had already been drugged with some poppy juice, *opos,* but still bit at a piece of leather while groaning almost continuously with pain.

Following the cleaning, ben Solomon put in a minimal number of stitches to hold things together and then called for a medical orderly to bandage the wound. He told the orderly, "Give him some more wine with *opos,* in it, half a standard dose, then get him on the next cart going across the river. *Medicus* Josephus' techniques may be old-fashioned but they're competent enough, even so, and his facilities are greater."

So many questions, Zaya thought. *So many things I want to learn about.*

While the evacuation crew were busied with bundling the wounded man off to one of the carts, ben Solomon called, "Next!"

A group of six female orderlies picked up a wounded man lying on a litter, and rushed him to the surgeon's table.

Eustachius left the other century to do the scut work of piling up bodies in a tangle. He had better things on his mind. He split the century he took with him into four groups of sixteen to eighteen, then spread them out with each one facing one of the penetrations, the one on the north wall and the three to the east. Two of the *contubernia* had to be split up for the purpose. Before he sent them on their way, he told them, "Our men are closely mixed up with theirs. Accuracy counts a lot more than mass in a case like this. Be fucking careful. Now, go."

Although to be fair, if you can hit five of them for one of ours, I'll call it a win.

Eustachius himself took the center group of the three facing the eastern wall. He also took first shot, tossing a javelin from about eighty feet right through the left thigh of a German trading sword strikes and shield blows with a Roman defender. The German went down with a scream, which was cut short by the *spatha* of his erstwhile opponent.

"See, boys?" Eustachius said. "Do it just like that."

On the right side of the penetration—the right side as

Eustachius faced it—the Germans had a much tougher time from the repurposed troops. This was because their shields, on their own left, faced the eastern wall while their sword arms, with no right-side defense, faced the courtyard.

"Well done," Eustachius congratulated a particular good throw, one that went right through a barbarian's neck. "Cup of wine on me for that one, Firmus."

In Pullo's view, the eleventh German warrior popped his head over the crenel, then arose a foot, only to have a bolt driven through his sternum. He, like the other ten, fell back to the ground. Unseen by Pullo, the illiterate and innumerate German next down on the ladder could still calculate the odds.

Fuck that shit, the German thought, *I am* not *sticking my head up there.* Instead, the German began to slide down the ladder, knocking his fellows off and quite sure he was doing them a favor by doing so.

"Good shooting, crew," Pullo called. "Cup of wine on me for the lot of you, once this is over." The crew was already cranking on the windlass, and was half ready to shoot again.

Farther out, Pullo saw that the middle penetration was beginning to shrink under the triple pressure of attacks from right and left, as well as javelins thrown from the courtyard. There were more Germans going down and being kicked to the courtyard than there were coming over the wall. The penetration on the north wall had been sealed up, though the Roman bodies littering the walkway said it hadn't come cheap. All the way over on the southern portion of the eastern wall, Metrovius seemed to have reestablished the defense.

Then, for a moment, Pullo's heart dropped. The western gate was being opened, and it wasn't to permit one of the medical carts to bring out casualties.

The gate opened a bit more. Pullo thought, *Probably the first, last, and only time I'd be happy to see that unsmiling face.*

In through the gates stepped Marcus Caelius, wearing the smile he only wore when he was extremely unhappy.

"Pullo, you pussy!" Caelius called.

Pullo almost stood at attention. But then those German archers were still active. Instead, he called out, "Here, sir."

Unerringly, Caelius' eyes found the tower from which Pullo

had answered. "I understand you weren't capable of holding this castle on your own."

"Well, sir, that's a bit of a long story..."

On the eastern wall, the twenty or so Germans remaining took a look at the opened western gate, at the cohort of heavily armed Roman legionaries of the type who had given their ancestors nightmares, and, deciding that discretion was the better part of valor, began slipping over the battlements and down the ladders that had brought them up.

Not one of the exhausted Roman defenders raised a hand to stop them from going. They might just have turned around.

INTERLUDE

Imperial Palace, Ravenna, 406 A.D.

Honorius, emperor of the Western Empire—at least in name—looked incredulous. He also looked young. After all, he was only recently turned twenty-two. Scraggly sideburns ran down his cheeks, never quite meeting either in space or in mass well enough to form a beard. Arms and legs were thin and, though young, he had already developed an unseemly paunch. Too, Honorius looked to be not especially bright, but with a kind of low craftiness about him.

"They claim to be *what?*"

Honorius' regent and, for the nonce, still the *effective* ruler of the western half of the Roman Empire, Stilicho, answered, "They claim to be the same Eighteenth Legion that was destroyed in the Varian Disaster."

Stilicho, himself a half Vandal but thoroughly Roman for all that, had been Honorius' regent since the death of Theodosius, some eleven years prior. Though Honorius had come of age, it was unclear whether Stilicho had yet relinquished the imperial power to him. Where the emperor had less than a beard, Stilicho's was both full and shot with gray. The half-Vandal general towered over his so far nominal ruler.

"That's absurd," Honorius insisted.

"So said I, Majesty, at least initially, but the report of several spies in Gaul and along the Rhine have convinced me. Specifically,

373

they insist that these men speak an old-fashioned Latin, one and all, barring only some Gallic, German, Palmyrene, Thracian, Rhodian, and—if you can credit it—very young Scythian *auxilia*. Oh, and another group called Argippaeans. They also, some of them, wear armor not to be found outside the carvings on the Column of Trajan or the Arch of Constantine, stolen from the Arch of Marcus Aurelius. Yes, lobsterback armor; imagine that, Majesty. They have, apparently, an absolutely ferocious discipline, such as the Empire hasn't seen since the disaster at Adrianople, and probably not for a hundred years before then. They carry rectangular, curved shields and use short swords, like a classic legion, and they hurl *pila*, not *plumbatae* or javelins, like a classic legion. They build camps like a classic legion and can throw a bridge even over the Rhine as quickly as, or perhaps more quickly than, Caesar's legions could. They also have in company with them women by the thousands who say they are Scythians and that this legion came into their lands apparently from nowhere. Finally, they are pagan to a man."

Honorius frowned. "But I've seen the eagle of the Eighteenth in the old Temple of Mars in Rome. So, for that matter, have you."

"Yes, Majesty, we both have. Do you remember how the number was spelled out?"

"XVIII, wasn't it?"

"Yes, it was. But the number of this legion's eagle is XIIX, the same way, my spies inform me, as it is spelled on a particular cenotaph in Vetera, way to the north, where the Eighteenth was apparently once stationed. And that's a final thing: the commander and second-in-command of this legion are named Gaius Pompeius Proculus and Marcus Caelius Lemonius. The cenotaph with the number, XIIX, is to one Marcus Caelius Lemonius. There is another one in the same general area to one Gaius Pompeius Proculus. As for the eagle, I strongly suspect that Arminius, of damnable memory, created or had created a false eagle to make his victory seem more complete."

"I suppose that's possible," Honorius conceded. "And it would be just like that treacherous but clever German bastard. But this legion? What do you think, Stilicho?"

Stilicho hesitated, briefly, then blurted out, "Majesty, given that I had to denude the Rhine of most of its garrisons, if I was to have any chance of stopping Radagaisius' Visigoths, I think that it was the hand of God, stretching out and twisting the universe around to save our Christian empire."

"Where are they now?" asked Honorius.

"Mogontiacum, Majesty, facing off against a very large, and very hungry group of Vandals, Suebi, and Alans."

Honorius considered this, then nodded sagely. "Send to them, Stilicho, to send an embassy to us, explaining their present and their past. Oh, and their presence."

"At once, Your Majesty."

"And I'll want them to swear an oath to me, personally."

"I think, Majesty, that we need to think about that one. What if they won't?"

"Then they won't get paid," said Honorius.

Stilicho was tactful enough to mention that the pay really didn't amount to much, anymore, there was so little actual silver in it. He did, however, say, "That's another thing, Majesty. These people are extremely flush, so much so that they've undertaken to pay the rest of the Rhine garrison at old legionary wages, in real silver and gold."

"How presumptuous!" Honorius huffed.

CHAPTER SEVENTEEN

No man ever steps in the same river twice. For it is not
the same river and he is not the same man.

—Heraclitus

River Moenis, Year 406 A.D.

The boy had his face blackened with the soot from camp fires,
mixed with a little grease to make it stick. The rest of the expedition, waiting at or in the boat nearby, was covered in the same way.

Gunderic's son, Godigisel, assured his father, "Yes, Da, I've
looked across the river and counted the lights. We'll know when
to turn into the river port where the Roman bastards keep their
war boats."

"And after you get in there?" Gunderic asked.

With a deep and frustrated sigh—*We've been over this a
hundred times or more, Da*—Godigisel answered, "We kill the
guard, quietly if possible, and outpost the doors and gates. Then
we light our resin torches from one of the firepots and burn as
many of their boats as we can before the serious infantry show
up. Then we get the hell out of there."

"And where do you go from there?"

"We go downstream with the river's current using minimal
oars and steering, then land on our side of the river. We save
and hide the boat, if possible, but it's not that important. Then
we come south on foot until we link up with the horses you'll
have posted for us. Then we report in to you."

Gunderic looked up at the sky. The moon still shone, but he knew there would be no moon very soon. "Then gods be with you, my son. Go and remember that the fate of our people rests on your young shoulders."

"I know, Father. We all know. We won't fail you."

Godigisel stepped off the bank and then let himself be hauled aboard. He had to accept this, because he and the other seven men who would kill any guards and then hold the gates and doors were as well armored as any Vandal in his father's horde. The others, those who would burn ships but would hopefully not have to fight, wore nothing but their tunics and trousers, and carried nothing but a few torches each, plus a sword and shield.

"Let's go," ordered Godigisel.

An unarmored Vandal ashore untied a rope and then jumped into the water, grasped the gunnels, and hauled himself aboard. Another man, this one already in the back, pushed away from the bank with an oar. Gently, half guided by the current, the boat began to move to the northwest.

"Out with the oars," Godigisel commanded. He waited until the sound of wood sliding over wood ended, then began to call off the strokes.

It was near enough to pitch black—so dark, in fact, that the banks of the Moenis couldn't be seen but only sensed. Thus, the two forward oars were not rowed, but were held out to the sides to ward off those banks. It didn't matter; most of the motive power came from the river itself, not from the oars.

It was the conflicting, eddying, *fighting* currents that told Godigisel they were out in the Rhine, not any visual cues. He could feel the man on the steering oar struggling to keep the boat pointed downstream. Once they were out of that unstable current, he ordered, "Pull in the oars, lie down, and be quiet."

After that it was a case of watch and count the *reliable* lights before the stone bridge. There were three of these, one on the town's southeastern tower, one on the gate that fronted the bridge, and one on a watchtower half a mile before the town even began.

Light one, the watchtower, passed to port. Then came light two, the southeastern tower. Finally, the gate light shone.

The bridge itself wasn't lit. It was impossible to see any of the twenty-two gaps between the twenty-one stone pylons on which the Romans had erected the bridge. No, it couldn't be seen.

But it could be heard. Listening carefully, Godigisel gave commands to the steersman in the faintest and tiniest of whispers, "A little left...hold steady...a little right...a little more right...steady."

As the boat approached the bridge, Godigisel could hear carts moving back and forth. The rumbling sound was faint, however, owing to the barriers erected by the Romans against missile fire. There were also men talking, and maybe some women; he couldn't be sure.

One thing I am sure of, though: if they'd taken those barriers down and erected torches, they'd have seen us for certain.

Keeping, as it was, mostly to the east bank, the boat slipped between the last and next to last pylon supporting the bridge. It took only a moment before they emerged again, the sudden reappearance of stars enough to show that.

The reappearance of the stars and an odd sound coming from the port side caused Godigisel to look to his left. The sound carried but faintly over the water. Still, it was unmistakable, the steady stroke of well-practiced oars, driving a barely seen Roman warcraft, not forty feet away.

Gods, please do not let them sense us now, less still light torches to see us as plain as day.

The steersman sensed the Romans, too, stiffening like a board, himself, and letting the steering oar have its own way to keep down the sound. Indeed, Godigisel was pretty sure he'd lifted the oar completely off the boat's stern to keep there from being any sound of wood on wood.

In any case, the Romans didn't notice them but moved forward at two and a half to three times the speed of the Vandal's boat, blissfully oblivious.

And the best part of that warship passing us, thought Godigisel, *is that we know roughly how far apart they send them out in the pitch black. There won't be another one close to us. And we can soon afford to make a little noise ourselves.*

The Rhine was split by an island, perhaps fifteen or sixteen hundred feet from the bridge. This was where Godigisel had determined that risk must be accepted, because, *If we miss the split, and end up on the eastern side of the island, I am not sure*

we can row our way back to the river port. On the other hand,
I am sure that, even if we can, we cannot possibly do so quietly.
So we're going to have to get out in the middle of the stream now,
to make sure we don't end up east of the island. Gods help us if
there's a Roman warship out in the middle of the river, west of
the island.

As it turned out, there was not. Better, the fleet base was lit
up well. Godigisel didn't know why but suspected the Romans
were working around the clock to keep their ships in trim and
to feed crews setting out for or returning from late night patrols.

"Steer for the base," he told the steersman, who leaned against
his oar, pushing it to the right, hence the boat to the left.

Godigisel waited until he was pretty sure that he could see the
mouth of the river port, then told his men, "Rise up. Oars out.
On my command, pull for all you're worth. Annnnddd . . . stroke!
Stroke! Stroke!"

Moving with the current and under oars, the normally sluggish boat practically leapt for the opening that led to the river
port. "Hard left. Hard left," he told the steersman.

There was a Roman on guard. He called out something in
Latin that sounded to the Vandals like a welcome. The lead
man, one who was not pulling an oar, donated that guard
a good javelin that pierced his unarmored belly, eliciting an
ululating shriek.

And then the boat was through and past the mouth, sliding
hard up on a Roman ship.

"Armored men, debark," Godigisel ordered. "Follow me!"

Behind him, the rest of the party opened up the firepot the
boat had carried and began lighting their torches. As soon as this
was done they began racing off, looking for boats to set alight.
It wasn't very long before they found the first of these, a long
and narrow *lusoria*, drawn up on land and flipped over to have
the hull worked on. Most of the arsonists moved on at the run,
while two put torches under the unturned gunnels.

Soon enough, the seasoned wood was alight. The duo who
had seen to torching it moved off in search of more game. At
length, they came upon a barrel of pitch. *Oh, this will help.*

Meanwhile, Godigisel and his armored men ran into the
first resistance. But these were Roman marines, men who were
not issued armor and, as a general rule, preferred to take their

chances without it. They began to fall to the heavier weapons of the Vandals.

Behind the fighting men, the harbor began to light up. Godigisel risked a quick look behind and was pleased to see half a dozen fires raging among the boats, both those drawn up on land and those still in the water.

Unarmored and lightly armed the Roman marines may have been, but there was nothing wrong with their throwing arms. The Vandal to Godigisel's left gave off a gurgling cry, then sank to the ground with a javelin right through his throat.

"We've got to hold them off until the last boat is burning!"

Again Godigisel risked a look behind. By the firelight he saw two of his men carrying a cask and using their swords to scoop out some of the contents onto the unburnt boats, one after another. These, when flame was applied, began to burn with a vengeance.

A javelin bounced off Godigisel's helmet, stunning him for a moment. It wasn't exactly helping that the more ships his men set alight, the easier it was for the Romans to see their targets and aim true.

A quick count told the Vandal that nearly twenty of the Roman ships were burning. *And that's enough.*

"Torchmen, back to our boat. Armored men, begin to fall back after the torchmen pass you."

Even for the armored men, the Vandal shields were fairly small and their mail hauberks reached only to a bit below crotch level. They had no greaves.

At that unarmored space a Roman marine threw a javelin at Godigisel. The missile flew true, piercing the Vandal boy all the way through his thigh. Barely, he kept himself from screaming with the pain as he fell to the stone pavement around the harbor. One of his armored men stooped and broke the shaft of the javelin off, just above the entrance wound. He then heaved the boy across his own shoulders. Two more used their shields to cover him on the way back to the boat. The remainder, reminding their fellow of their duty to their king, to get his boy home safely, threw all caution to the winds and attacked the Romans in a fine display of the *Furor Teutonicus*. The Roman marines scattered, but also closed in around the Vandals from the flanks, casting their javelins at wherever they looked vulnerable. Even with spears protruding from their bodies, the Vandals refused to give up.

At the boat, the firepot was dumped into the water, likewise the torches. The steersman, who had remained behind with the boat, gave the orders to the oarsmen. The boat, moving more slowly than had it been going forward, backed water and began to turn to face the port's entrance.

Once it was aligned the steersman ordered the rowers to put their oars into the water. By the time he gave the order to begin rowing, javelins were already falling around the boat. The remaining three armored men held up shields to ward off the javelins, while the steersman hung his own shield across his back, but a couple slipped through, even so, wounding the rowers.

Pain was better than death; wounded or not the rowers put their backs into it, propelling the boat out of the harbor's mouth and away from the stinging javelins. Fire burned so fiercely now—and who managed to set two of the boatsheds on fire, or was that just the fire spreading on its own?—that the way ahead was clearly lit.

"Stroke . . . stroke . . . stroke . . . stroke."

And then they were in open water, still rowing for all they were worth. It wasn't until the boat was out of javelin range that the steersman ordered "up oars" and "be quiet." Even then, there was still a great deal of light to see by.

After floating downstream with the current for some minutes, the light wasn't great enough to easily make out the gap between the two islands in the Rhine just downstream from Mogontiacum.

The steersman made his best guess on the matter, hugging the shore of the first island as closely as possible, then letting the current drag the boat along.

It was as well that he did. From the west came the sounds of one of the narrow Roman warships, its crew fighting hard against the current. Was it the one that had passed them earlier, just past the bridge? A new one, returning from patrol? There was no way to know; all they could know was that, if it spotted them, they were all dead men.

Either luck was with them or the gods were; the Romans never saw them. And then they were into and through the channel between the islands, with the steersman looking for some place they could make landfall.

Mogontiacum Naval Base

Benedictus Candidus, the *praefectus classis*, looked like a corpse. This was only partly because of the blood lost along with the sword wound he'd taken, a wound already disinfected and stitched up by Josephus, currently working on other Roman wounded. Appius Calvus was already on site to see to setting up the funerals for the dead.

Around Candidus was debris-filled water, the charred remains of buildings, and boats burnt to, or, often enough, past the waterline. Oh, and corpses, of which there were a great many more Roman than Vandal.

"What in the name of the Great Purple-togaed Augustus happened here?" demanded Marcus Caelius.

Candidus just shook his head, weakly. He really should have been lying in the bed in the *valetudinarium*, but had to see the ruin or his force and his base with his own eyes, in the daylight.

"Beyond that they slipped through our patrols and trashed us, I can't say. Give the Vandal bastards credit, though, it was damnably well done, as well done as anything I've ever even heard of."

"What does it mean to our holding the Rhine?" Gaius Pompeius demanded.

"It means," said Candidus, "that I can't stop them now from sending raiding parties across the Rhine. Think about it: fifty men here, eighty men there, slipping across and burning a farmstead or a village, carrying off women and young girls and boys, cutting the throats of everyone else."

"And that means," said Caelius, "that we're going to have to spread out into little penny packets to stop them. Otherwise, the granaries are burnt, the farmers take their families and head for someplace safe, so nobody will be harvesting this year's crops or growing food for next. And that means that, ultimately, we can't stay here.

"If we had three times the force, three real legions, plus three times the *auxilia* and the legion's worth of Germanic mercenaries we've got," Caelius continued, "I'd say we should cross over into *Germania* and take them on. But we don't. We've got maybe twelve and a half thousand men, fit at any given time, only a third, plus a bit, real legionaries. At those odds the enemy will just swamp us. And then there's nothing to stop them."

"Can you rebuild your fleet?" Gaius asked Candidus.

"Yes, eventually," the naval prefect answered. "And I can start rounding up non-warcraft to fight with. I've got the men to man them, though if we use something less than *lusoriae*, we'll be trading lives at something like one to one. The enemy can afford that; in the long run, we can't. As is, I've sent a *lusoria* to Confluentes and Colonia, to order them to send us three of the eight boats I left them each with. That will bring us here up to eleven. This is not—and I cannot emphasize this enough—enough for us to do the job. The most I can do is inflict some fear on the enemy, so that they only try to get across to raid under circumstances most advantageous to them."

"Well, there's one other thing I can do," Candidus said. "I'll have eleven *lusoriae*, but crews enough for twenty-nine or thirty.

"No rest for the boats and not much maintenance, but as soon as one comes back I can put a new crew in and launch. Won't make up for the losses in hulls, not entirely, but it may help some."

"You sent for me, sirs?" asked Titus Vorenus, now commanding the cohort of Scythian boys. Vorenus wore his *sagum* against the mid-autumn chill. The fire in the *principia* was warm enough to allow him to slip the cloak back off of his shoulders.

"Yes, Vorenus," Gaius said. "Sit. Some wine?"

Vorenus sat but refused the wine. "I'm taking my boys out on an exercise tonight and would prefer a fully clear head, if you don't mind, sir."

"Tell us about your command," Caelius said. "I know they're only boys but..."

"Status of my command? Well, they're good boys, eager and smart and meaner than weasel shit. They're as good horsemen as any of our *auxilia* or our legionary cavalry. Actually, they're a bit faster, riding full-size Scythian horses but not weighing much themselves. They're also as good with their bows as they can be, given their age, their strength, and the fact that they're using girls' bows, which is the most they can draw yet. Well, most of them. There are maybe twenty or even thirty who can draw a man's Scythian bow. The armory has turned out enough weaker bows that they each have one, and a fair number are pretty good with a sling, too. They are extremely fascinated with the legion's collective order and discipline, something they never found in their own people. This may be precisely because they're boys."

"Can they kill a man?" Caelius asked.

Vorenus didn't hesitate. "Yes, without question. I can give them discipline and order and have, but they were raised Scythian. They can kill without compunction."

"Can they use poison arrows?" Gaius asked.

"Same answer, sir. But if I may ask, why?"

Briefly, Gaius Pompeius explained the problems caused by the burning of most of the fleet, then continued with, "We can't really afford to parcel out the infantry, either our own or the Germanic mercenaries we've been supporting. We need to keep them together in case the Vandals and their friends manage to make a major push. The same is true for the *auxilia*. So we're going to parcel out your boys along the river in little detachments to the south, and the Palmyrenes to the north. At the same time, we're going to send some of the engineers to help the locals prepare warning beacons. Your boys see a beacon, they ride to the rescue. They intercept the Vandals at a distance and pepper them with poisoned arrows. Let the Vandals escape and get back to their side of the Rhine..."

"And then slowly die where their friends can see it happen," Vorenus finished. "You intend to hold the Rhine with terror. Why not crucify any captives we take?"

"We will," said Marcus Caelius, "if we manage to catch any. But we just don't think we'll take enough to make much difference. But if every raid they send over goes back with half its members dying of poison and stinking green fester, *that*, we think, will make a difference."

"But only for a while," Gaius said. "Their hunger will eventually make them willing to risk anything. Our hope is for their terror to buy us enough time to rebuild the Rhine *classis*."

"*Medicus* Josephus still in charge of the Scythian poison?" Vorenus asked.

"Yes," answered Caelius, "and I've told him that if his sense of medical ethics makes him think about dumping it, there's a cross waiting even for a valued surgeon."

Gisco popped his head into the tent without bothering to knock. "Sir," the Phoenician said, "there's a messenger come to us from the Imperial Palace."

Gaius Pompeius and Marcus Caelius exchanged "I've been dreading this" looks.

"Show him in," Gaius said. "Vorenus, get your boys picketed as far south as you can, consistent with both mutual support and rapid response. Dismissed."

Gisco showed the imperial messenger into the *principia* right on Vorenus' boot heels.

The messenger came in, covered with dust from the road, and decidedly skinny and undeveloped. He sat down without either introducing himself or being invited to sit. When Caelius appeared ready and eager to teach the messenger a very sharp lesson on customs and courtesies, Gaius Pompeius raised a restraining hand.

"*Praefectus Castrorum,*" Gaius asked, mildly, "how long would it take to get a cross ready?"

"Few minutes at most, sir. But this one looks too soft to last long on the cross."

"Ah, well, probably true but good that we're ready."

The byplay went completely over the messenger's head. This was unsurprising, insofar as Constantine I had outlawed crucifixion within the Empire nearly a century prior, but the drift of Latin over the last four centuries might have had more to do with it.

"And your name would be...?" Gaius Pompeius asked.

"Justus Liberius," answered the messenger.

"Let me just have him flogged for his arrogance and impudence," pleaded Caelius. The camp prefect made an effort to speak in the more modern vernacular used by the locals.

"What? What's that? I'll have you know—"

In a trice, Marcus Caelius was out of his seat and holding Justus Liberius by his hair, with only his toes touching the ground, and those but barely. In this posture, Caelius gave a brief lecture on good manners, customs and courtesies of the service, and the deference due to superior officers, which he took—or rather gave—some pains to explain, both he and the legate were. It seemed that being shaken by the hair served to concentrate Liberius' mind wonderfully.

"Now I am going to let go of your hair, you wretch, and let your feet rest on the ground. Then you are going to stand at attention, announce your name and rank, and beg permission to address the commanding officer of the Eighteenth Legion. Is this clear?"

"Y-y-yes, sir."

Caelius opened his hand, releasing the hair and letting the messenger fall to the *principia* floor.

"Do I have to explain things to you again?" Caelius asked, genially.

"No, sir," replied Justus Liberius, who scrambled up, assumed a position of attention, announced himself, and begged permission to address the commanding officer of the Eighteenth.

"Good. Now the legate is a busy man. Explain to him just what it is you want and do it quickly."

Liberius swallowed, then said, "I am sent by the mighty general, Stilicho. Stilicho, in turn, sends me on behalf of His Imperial Majesty, Honorius. Honorius orders that you send to him an embassy, to report, and that your force here swear an oath of allegiance to him, and, further, that you turn over your treasury to the Imperial Treasury."

"Oh, he does, does he?" asked Gaius Pompeius. "How presumptuous of him. Camp Prefect?"

"Sir?"

"I don't believe this man comes from Honorius or Stilicho at all. Place him under arrest and confine him under guard. And prepare that cross but do not crucify him just yet."

As the blood drained from Liberius' face, Caelius asked, "And a rigorous interrogation to get to the truth of the matter, sir?"

"Oh, by all means, a rigorous interrogation."

Caelius turned his attention to the door, shouting, "Guards!"

"All right," said Caelius, once Liberius had been carted off to the brig, "That was a fair bit of playacting on both our parts. Sufficient, anyway, for a line of defense if we ever allow ourselves to fall under Honorius' control. But what are we actually going to do?"

"We're not going to give them our treasury, nor any part of it," said Gaius. "That's first and foremost. They'd convert it into their worthless coinage—and too much of that—or pay it out in pure form to buy a little time from the barbarians. That, or to hire more barbarian mercenaries. We're not going to leave here and leave Gaul defenseless, again; it's too important to Rome and Italy. And I suspect that doing just that is somewhere in the back of Stilicho's mind. His story, such as

I've been able to glean, suggests that concentrating as much military power in his own hands as possible is what generally drives him."

"So much for what we're not going to do," Caelius said, drily. "But that isn't what I asked, sir. Now, once again, what *are* we going to do?"

"Shall we go ahead and send an embassy?" Gaius asked.

"Perhaps," Caelius agreed. "But we can't spare either of my previous go-tos for shitty jobs, Vorenus or Pullo, not anymore. We need Vorenus to run the southern screen with his boys and Pullo to guard the castle that is now, without question, his.

"I'm not sure, for that matter," Caelius continued, "if we can spare any of the centurions. They're all too busy drilling the shit out of German mercenaries and recalled veterans. For that matter, I'm not sure any of them are competent for dealing with the forms of this new empire. We could send Gisco, again, but I don't think he carries with him the hint of deadly ferocity we would want to convey should this Honorius person decide to try to fuck with us.

"The thing is, though, that I'm not sure we can do *anything* with this wretched, degraded, and corrupt excuse for an empire. Everything I've heard about it screams 'rotten to the core' to me. And I'm equally uncertain that we're enough, in ourselves, to stand on our own."

"Well," said Gaius, "if we can't spare any of the centurions, I am sure we cannot spare you."

"Actually, I think we can, at least for a few weeks, which is what it should take us. Metilius can run the legion and the *auxilia* perfectly well, along with the Germanic 'legions' we're paying for. Rubelius has a real knack for the quartermaster function.

"Speaking of Rubelius, I think you ought to put him to moving some of the weapons makers from the nearby armories and depots—Augusta Trevorarum, Argentoratum, Matisco, and Augustodunum—and set up our own *fabrica*, right here."

"I think you're right," the legate agreed. "And stop trying to change the subject."

"What? Me? Never. But as long as we're on the subject, the other tribunes have all the necessary functions down: personnel administration and recruiting, intelligence and scouting, operations, and engineering. So, yes, I do think that Gisco and I can make a decent embassy. And I'm senior enough that Honorius and Stilicho won't feel slighted. Finally, we really do need to understand this world we find ourselves in. And that, all on its own, demands an expedition to the imperial capital."

"It's nigh unto winter," Gaius said. "You might get trapped on the other side of the Alps."

"If that happens, we'll take the more westerly route through Gaul. Hmmm...now that you mention it, we probably ought to take a string of half a dozen horses, each, if we're to make time."

"That, and we can send you with some Scythian baubles as gifts. After all, Honorius is alleged to be not much past boyhood."

Calius gave Gaius an odd look, accompanied by a sardonically raised eyebrow.

"Oh, all *right*," the legate conceded. "I know, I know, I'm not much past boyhood myself. But while no doubt spoiled as a boy, I've been growing up a lot and fast ever since Varus led us into the German swamps."

"That's a statement fair and true," Caelius agreed.

"So, assuming I don't change my mind, when will you go?"

"I'll want to wring out that popinjay, Liberius, for everything he knows," Caelius answered. "Shouldn't take long; just showing him the instruments should be enough. While I'm doing that, Privatus and Thiaminus can be getting the packing done. Don't think I'll take my woman, Tabiti. She can ride a horse, of course, or drive a wagon, all the Scythian women can, but we'll be moving a lot faster than will be comfortable."

"Does she care for you?" asked Gaius.

Caelius considered the question, then somewhat surprised at his own answer, said, "You know, yes, I believe she does."

"Then take her with you. Besides, you may run into wolves and she's likely better with a bow than you or Gisco."

"Perhaps you're right," Caelius half conceded.

"And if you don't take her, if she's remotely like my Zaranaia, you'll pay for leaving her behind in ways that don't bear thinking about."

"Point," said Marcus Caelius. "Right, the wench comes with me."

"Before you go, though," Gaius said, "I wanted to ask you about the ultimate solution to the Vandals, Alan, and Suebi."

"Well," began Caelius, "taking a leaf from you and how we

deal with the Empire, and our mutual conversation with Gunderic, we cannot let them in and turn over a portion of the Empire to them. Ultimately, that reduces tax revenue and makes the Empire weaker. And that's not even counting when their population expands and they start expanding to suit. We cannot buy them off because they won't stay bought. We could let them all starve to death but they won't *all* starve to death.

"Letting the Huns take them over only makes the Huns stronger, at least for a while, and they're not going to be a bit better neighbors than are the current enemy across the Rhine.

"As we've discussed, taking the fight to them and exterminating them and making Germany east of the Rhine completely uninhabitable would be ideal but neither we nor Stilicho nor all of us together have the power to do that. It's not clear to me that if we had both Julius Caesar's army and Caesar to lead that we could do that, and Caesar was no slouch when it came to killing people who needed it.

"So were it up to me, I'd try to kill all the men in that horde...well, all but maybe a few percent we could recruit to fill our own ranks, and then sell the women and children as slaves. That way we get the labor and the reproduction of labor, eventual citizens, after a few generations, keep the tax base in imperial hands, and eliminate the threat. It also keeps the Huns, when they show up, from getting stronger by taking over the tribes. And we can work on making that part of Germany uninhabitable once we've eliminated the horde."

"The Huns are more horse archers, like the Scythians, aren't they?" Gaius asked.

"Hmmm...now that you mention it, yes, I believe they are, though they have a lot of German infantry, forced into alliance, in their ranks."

"Then we can make it uninhabitable by them by killing or evacuating the farmers who have grown up in Germany and letting the trees grow. But that can't be done quickly enough to matter."

"Then you attack it the other way: get rid of or capture and enslave the farmers and then the Hunnish people can't eat. Or at least not much."

"All right," Gaius finished, "that's our goal, then: destroy the Vandal men, enslave their women and children, and capture and deport the Germans on the other side of the Rhine. But I've got to tell you, I'm not really keen on selling all the Vandal, Suebi, and Alan women and children as slaves, either. I've got to hold out a little hope, if only for my own self-respect, that we can find another way.

"Or at least make them an offer they can't refuse. I'll do what I can to put us in the position to do this while you're gone. It may not be much. It may be all I can do to hold the line.

"Speaking of which, I wonder if we could recruit some likely prospects in Italy."

"Probably. But there's another bureaucratic aspect you're not considering," said Caelius.

"What's that?"

"If we're not going to enslave the Germans on the other side who, after all, haven't done us any harm, we still don't want them settling down as a group somewhere where they'll form a cohesive tribe that may eventually find that their interests and the Empire's aren't quite the same."

"And so?"

Caelius answered, "So, we need to do a survey of all of Gaul and Spain and find family-sized plots, widely spaced from each other, buy or confiscate those—if they're abandoned just take them; if the upper classes have taken them illegally, then take them back—and move the German farmers to those farms."

"If we're going to move them places, then we probably want to make sure they learn the language, too," Gaius observed.

"The language and the culture," Caelius added. "But that means they need to learn this new religion, Christianity, too, as apparently almost the entire Empire has adopted it."

"Which leads to another potential headache," Gaius said. "What was it that Ostrogoth, Wulfila, said? Something about his whole people's conversion starting with one Christian woman captured, carried off, and enslaved? We've got a lot more of that now. Our Scythian women are all listening to the Christian women married to Christian soldiers of the current Empire. Even my Zaranaia is listening to the ones I hired to take care of our house. So, what the hell are we going to do about that?"

"Nothing," said Caelius. "Nothing we can do. The Empire—the entire Empire, not just one legion with some *auxilia*—tried to stamp it out on numerous occasions over the last four centuries. They tried massacre, public spectacle atrocities, and even subtler methods to keep the Christians from educating the young. Know how much good it did?"

"Less than none," Gaius said, resignedly. "The Christians only grew stronger."

"Exactly. So far as I know, none of the men have converted yet, not even the boys of Vorenus' cohort who one would expect to be under the influence of their mothers and foster mothers. But it's only a matter of time."

"It's also pretty complex," Gaius said. "There are at least half a dozen Christian sects that utterly loathe each other. I don't want to see the legion—probably the only really worthwhile military formation in the Empire—fractured over something like this."

"No," Marcus Caelius agreed. "If they're going to convert, as seems inevitable now that I think on it, they need to all convert to whichever sect or philosophy of the Christians that is least objectionable to the others, and most able to get along with the others. I mean, sure, one of us could lie and say we were the nearest thing to whatever the Christian we were talking to claimed to be, but about eight thousand of us cannot. It might also help if whatever sect we choose can adopt our old gods as some kind of lesser gods or...what's that term they use?"

"There are two of them," Gaius answered immediately. "Two terms, angels and saints. Yes, yes, Zaranaia has been lecturing me."

"Send Appius Calvus," Caelius said. "Have him do the investigation. Oh, and Josephus if he has the time. He's at least conversant in the superstition that Christianity sprang from."

There were larger churches in Mogontiacum, but a few inquiries of his workers by Calvus had suggested the pastor of this one as having both wisdom and a good deal of knowledge. It sat within the walls of the town and right across the street from some public baths.

"Welcome! Welcome, friends!" said the Christian priest, standing in the doorway of what Calvus was pretty sure had begun life as a pagan temple, but from which all pagan traces had been thoroughly scrubbed. "How can I help you?"

The priest wore a simple robe; perhaps silk vestments and clerical collars lay in the further Catholic future, as Catholicism predictably adopted more and more of the accoutrements of Roman paganism. He was beefy enough, but with a kind smile that showed he still had at least most of his teeth. The smile extended to the priest's brown eyes. His hair, likewise brown although heavily shot with white, was cut short.

Josephus, who remained a Jew, looked over the priest, from genial face, with its reddish nose, to the long gray beard, to the brown tunic, bound round with simple cords, to his bare and dirty feet.

"You're on your own," Josephus told Calvus. "I'll chime in if I think of anything useful."

"Ummm..." Calvus began, not especially usefully, "I'm Appius Calvus. My friend, here, is Samuel Josephus. We're looking for information."

"Well," said the priest, "among all the Lord's servants I am perhaps the most ignorant, but what I can tell you is yours for the asking. Would you like to come in? Some wine perhaps? I think there's some bread and cheese in the cupboard, as well."

They followed the priest in, passing through an open area, mostly covered by a mosaic that had seen better days, past a rough stone altar. The walls were plastered white. On one wall, past the altar, was a simple wooden cross, though the shape was not one Calvus would have expected. He decided not to make a big thing out of it.

And, I have to admit, that shape is somehow more moving than the shape of those that really are used to execute people. A simple T *shape, without anything sticking up above the* patibulum, *wouldn't seem so... eye-catching.*

The old priest finally let the pagan and the Jew into his own simple quarters. "Sit, sit," he said, indicating two of the four stools that graced each side of the table.

To one side of the room was a thin cot, with not much of a mattress. On the other was a cupboard. There, the priest rummaged around until he'd found three simple terra-cotta cups. These he placed on the table. A jug of wine followed, and was followed in turn by a loaf of bread and the promised cheese.

As if in a ceremony, the purpose of which neither Josephus nor Calvus had a clue to, the priest first set aside the larger portion of the bread, then raised up the smaller, and a cup of the wine, in turn, muttering a prayer that sounded like and was Latin but with the accent they'd come to expect from all the moderns.

Finished, the priest broke and passed out rest of the bread, poured the wine, and finally introduced himself as "Alban."

"You're a Greek," Josephus said, finally. "Your Latin accent isn't quite the same as what the locals have."

"Very good," Alban agreed. "I'm from Naxos. How did you know?"

"I went to medical training in Alexandria."

"Alexandria?" the priest mused. "Why, there hasn't been a real medical school in Alexandria since . . . Wait, I know you. Well, I know *of* you. You're some of the pagan but by all reports potentially Christianizing legionaries the hand of the Almighty cast across time to save us in our hour of need!"

"Close," said Calvus. "We are, indeed and as you surmise, of the group that was sent into what was then our future. However, neither of us are soldiers, though we each get the privileges of military officers. My friend Samuel, here, is our chief surgeon, while I am the pagan—for lack of a better term—chaplain of the legion."

Alban, who was no dummy, put two and two together and said, "*Medicus* . . . Josephus . . . Samuel . . . Alexandria. You're a Jew, aren't you?"

"I am, indeed."

"You, at least, will be familiar with monotheism."

"I am," Josephus conceded, "but I have a hard time reconciling what I understand of Christianity with what I know of monotheism."

"Many of us do," Alban likewise conceded, "though I myself do not."

"We," said Josephus, "since we find ourselves living in this new world, are trying to understand the various streams of Christian thought, the better to navigate what appear to us to be some very rocky waters."

"Rocky waters, indeed," Alban agreed. "Witness myself, exiled from Naxos by Arians, who are ordinarily very tolerant of other views, especially in their Gothic incarnations."

"Perhaps because you were both a priest and an eloquent one," Josephus offered.

Alban shrugged. "It's possible. But you want to know about the various sects? We may as well begin with the Arians, I suppose."

For a moment, Alban seemed to be thinking, or trying to remember something. Shortly, he said, "Arianism began about a hundred years ago, more or less, in Alexandria. The big divergence is that they believe that God existed before Christ, and created Christ before the beginning of time. This is different from my own Catholic faith, which holds that they existed before time, yes, but also came into being at the same time. Though 'time' is a poor word, since there was no time at that time."

Alban laughed at himself, then added, "We are stuck using our terms for things that simply do not fit. Why? Why because we are not the Almighty.

"In any case, the Arians have got some reason on their side," Alban admitted, "enough to be tempting, anyway. In the first place, they hold that scripture clearly shows that Christ is subordinate to God, indeed, makes himself subordinate to God. And we Catholics also call Christ 'the son of God,' while no son can be born at the same time as his father.

"However, where I think Arianism went astray is in this: God exists out of time. He was before time and will be after. He looks down upon us as we would look down upon a road map, except that he sees us in four—or, who knows, maybe more—dimensions: length, width, depth, and duration. Thus, if you are 'seated at the right hand of the Father,' you always were and always will be. In short, Arianism injects time into the dimension of the timeless and imposes a limit upon the limitless."

Alban continued, "I would suggest—suggest without knowing because, in the first place, I wasn't there and, in the second, because God never consults with me on these matters—that the entire duration of Christ's ministry on Earth took place while He, Jesus Christ, was also watching from on high. Because time does not exist there. And to the fairly obvious objection of 'You can't be in two places at once,' I can only say, 'Why not?' It's part and parcel of omnipotence to be able to do anything that is in your nature. A more philosophical approach might be to say that Christ was not in two places at once, but in one place at once and in another where the very idea of 'at once,' which is a matter of time, is meaningless in a place which exists out of time."

Alban smiled at the disquieted looks on his guests' faces.

"But you want to know about the other schools, too."

"Yes . . ." Calvus said. "But a god who exists out of time?"

"It's a necessary aspect of omnipotence. Your gods, all of them, had their powers constrained by either other supernatural entities—I am thinking here especially of the Fates—by time, or by simple lack of power. They were created, or born, and were not the authors of the universe.

"Our God, on the other hand, created, so we believe, everything that is or was or ever shall be, whether you can see it or not. This means that He also created time. The God who can create time cannot be bounded by it."

Alban looked to Josephus for confirmation and support. "Yes, that's it exactly," the Jew said.

"Now as for other schools of Christianity, even Arianism is split into different approaches; the Pneumatomachi, for example, deny the divinity of the Holy Spirit. I am not conversant enough with them to give you details, but be careful what you say to an Arian because, in their less tolerant forms, they can be just as sensitive to and hateful of each other as they can be to any other denomination. Or any other denomination to any other denomination, for that matter.

"Then we have Marcionism, which holds that the God who created the universe was fundamentally wicked, and that Christ was created by a superior god who also created the God that created the universe. I think that the inspiration for Marcion just may have been the faith of the Persians. There may still be some Marcionists around, but I confess I've never met one."

Alban then discoursed on Gnosticism, Montanism, Sabellianism, Docetism, Donatism—which was related to Novatianism—and Adoptionism. "But few of those have any significant number of followers left. And, to me, there seems to be a Persian influence in most of them. I have wondered, from time to time, if the Persians didn't send some of their holy men to us to preach the philosophy behind their faith to fracture us."

"So, what do you believe?" asked Josephus.

"Me? I believe what all Catholics believe, to wit:

"We believe in one God, the Father Almighty, the maker of heaven and earth, of things visible and invisible.
"And in one Lord Jesus Christ, the Son of God, the begotten of God the Father, the Only-begotten, that is of the substance of the Father.
"God of God, Light of Light, true God of true God, begotten and not made; of the very same nature of the Father,

by Whom all things came into being, in Heaven and on Earth, visible and invisible.

"Who for us humanity and for our salvation came down from Heaven, was incarnate, became human, was born perfectly of the holy virgin Mary by the Holy Spirit.

"By whom He took body, soul, and mind, and everything that is in man, truly and not in semblance.

"He suffered, was crucified, was buried, rose again on the third day, ascended into Heaven with the same body, and sat at the right hand of the Father.

"He is to come with the same body and with the glory of the Father, to judge the living and the dead; of His kingdom there is no end.

"We believe in the Holy Spirit, the uncreate and the perfect; Who spoke through the Law, the prophets, and the Gospels; Who came down upon the Jordan, preached through the apostles, and lived in the saints.

"We believe also in only One, Universal, Apostolic, and Holy Church; in one baptism with repentance for the remission and forgiveness of sins; and in the resurrection of the dead, in the everlasting judgment of souls and bodies, in the Kingdom of Heaven and in the everlasting life."

"That is a *lot* to believe," said Calvus. "I am tempted, if asked, to tell the asker, 'I'm a *haruspex*,' which is the nearest thing to Catholicism-Arianism-what have you-ism we had where I came from."

"That might be wise," Alban agreed. "And it might even be true."

INTERLUDE

Imperial Palace, Ravenna, 406 A.D.

Stilicho told Honorius over a light lunch, "My spies inform me that this old legion is holding my messenger as a fraud but has still dispatched a small embassy to us. The embassy left with a string of horses sufficient to move almost as fast as the Imperial Post, so I'd expect them any day now. I suppose those two items are not mutually exclusive. Well, not *necessarily* so, anyway. Still, rather strange. Also, it seems that they held the castle that guarded the bridge to Mogontiacum against a ferocious Vandal and Suebi assault. However, the barbarians managed to get a raiding party over the Rhine and burnt our fleet, most of it, out of existence."

"Who was responsible for that disaster?" Honorius demanded. "I want his name and I want him executed for treason to the Empire."

"Let us not be hasty, Majesty," Stilicho said. "In the first place, these things happen in war. The enemy always gets a vote. But in the second place, we don't actually have a qualified replacement. And, in the third and final place, the commander is reported to be doing a pretty good job of making good the losses in boats, funded by, once again, the old Eighteenth Legion."

"Where are these people getting all this gold and silver?"

"We don't really know how much it is, though I have little doubt but that they know down to the denarius. My chief spy in Mogontiacum spoke to some of the Scythian...mmm...I suppose 'concubines' might be the best term. It seems that when the Scythians were driven out of their old haunts around the northern shore of the Euxine, a large party of them escaped north with what amounts to their royal treasury, while each of their clans likewise sent some of their members into exile with their own treasuries. The Eighteenth Legion destroyed the Scythians, captured their women and children, and took every scrap of gold and silver they could find. They sent a thousand pounds of that gold to the mint in Mogontiacum to have it coined into solidi."

"Just out of curiosity," asked Honorius, "whose name and image appears on those coins?"

"Caesar Augustus', Majesty."

Chapter Eighteen

If anyone causes harm to an envoy of a hostile country,
it should be treated as a violation of the law of nations,
because the envoys are considered holy.
—*Enchiridion* of Sextus Pomponius

Ravenna, the Imperial Capitol, 406 A.D.

Caelius' woman, Tabiti, was truly impressed. "I have never even imagined a fixed place with so many people," she said.

She'd impressed him since he'd met her, when she'd been recruited to be his woman, and this was not merely in looks, though she had kept those rather well: big eyes, shiny hair, prominent cheekbones, full lips, narrow waist, well-rounded posterior, and rather large but not pendulous breasts.

No, far more impressive had been her practicality and common sense, as well as a kind of toughness he could sense that mirrored his own. She'd impressed him still more on the ride over the Alps, when she'd been the only member of the small party—himself, Gisco, Tabiti, Privatus, and a dozen *auxilia* from Atrixtos' Gauls, along with a couple of state slaves to cook and put up the tents—who actually knew how to manage a team of horses.

"I don't know what it's like now, dear," he told her, "but the Rome of the Empire I came from was perhaps twenty times larger."

"No!"

"Yes."

"How could they stand it?"

"Now *that* is a very good question."

"We're expected," Gisco said, as they passed through a fortified gate framed by water on each side.

"How can you tell?" Caelius asked.

Gisco answered, "Well, besides that someone just rode off at breakneck speed to inform some party or parties, unnamed, of our arrival, if an armed party of strangers, who looked totally different from anything in your experience, were trying to gain admittance to Mogontiacum, and if that town were under threat by barbarians on the west side of the Rhine, would your men just wave them through?"

"Now that's a good point."

"It means something else, too," the Phoenician said. "They've got spies there reporting on us through the Imperial Post or perhaps an underground postal system. That's the only thing that could have gotten a message here faster than we were moving."

"We need to get word back to the tribune in charge of intelligence to infiltrate and break that spy network."

"Infiltrate, yes. Break? Not so fast. If we break it, it will be replaced by an organization we have not infiltrated and, moreover, it will be seen as a hostile move. If we can infiltrate and suborn it, though, we can feed the capital whatever we want to feed them."

Caelius called a halt just past the gate that guarded the town. He motioned for the senior of the Gauls to come forward and told him, in a whisper, to take three other men, to ride back to the legion, and to pass on to the legate the gist of the conversation between himself and Gisco. Finally, Caelius added, "And take a different road."

Once the four Gauls had passed back through the gate, the remaining members of the party continued south into the town. Tabiti was wide-eyed at the complex of canals, surmounted by stone bridges, dividing the city.

The first order of business was to find a stable capable of handling upward of eighty horses. A few inquiries sent them down a side road, nearer the sea. There, a midsize civil stable that didn't appear to see much business appeared on their left hand. Caelius let Gisco do the haggling.

The horses were turned over. The remaining party, on one horse apiece and three more carrying the tents, rations, and other equipment, started to move back to the main road. They found their way blocked by a tall, half-Germanic-looking sort, sitting a large horse, accompanied by half a dozen armed and armored men on foot.

None of the men blocking the way drew their swords. Caelius thought back to the description, one of several, given by Justus Liberius.

"General Stilicho, is it?" Caelius asked.

"The same," Stilicho answered. "*Praefectus Castrorum* Marcus Caelius, is it not?"

"The same. We were just going to go look for a suitable inn, General. Have you a recommendation?"

Stilicho's face split in a broad grin, while he waved one hand, dismissively. "I can recommend you drop that notion this instant. You're all staying at my house. Oh, yes, there's more than enough room for you, your party, and these horses. And you won't wake up with fleas or bedbugs at my place."

Shops framed the heavy, guarded door leading into Stilicho's *domus*. One of these was a bakery, emitting the heavenly smell of freshly baked bread, the other a cobbler giving off an almost equally enticing aroma of well-tanned leather. Past the door and the two armed guards, a long corridor led from the street to the atrium. Centered in the atrium was the *impluvium*, a small pool for catching and cooling rainwater. Above the *impluvium*, the *compluvium* let in an abundance of light to illuminate the frescoes on the atrium walls.

"Serena," Stilicho called for his wife, once inside the atrium. "Eucherius! Galla Placidia, most noble girl! Come, we have guests from our distant past, delivered by the Almighty to save Gaul for us and from the barbarians."

Eucherius was first to appear, like his father a tall boy, though only looking to be about seventeen years of age and with a beard still trying to assert his manhood. Following Eucherius, the girl, Galla Placidia made her appearance, thirteen or fourteen and somewhat awkward. There was a possibility, at least, that she would eventually grow into a great beauty. Finally came Serena, Stilicho's wife, well and modestly dressed, with a necklace of archaic manufacture about her neck. Serena appeared to be in her late thirties or even early forties, and still quite striking: large brown eyes set in an unlined face, and with only a few thin streaks of gray to betray her age. Stilicho made the introductions, all around.

"You *really* escaped from the Varian Disaster?" Eucherius asked.

"Not so much escaped as were saved," Caelius answered. "But, yes, we were there and then, suddenly, we were somewhere else. And no, we have no idea how, though the who and the why may be much as your father said."

"You're really pagans?" asked Serena, who apparently detested pagans and paganism. Indeed, the archaic necklace about her neck she'd allegedly taken from the statue of Rhea Silvia, the mother of Romulus and Remus, in Rome, largely to show her contempt.

"Yes," Caelius said.

"And you, too?" Serena asked of Tabiti. "Are you a Christian?"

"I'm working on it," the Scythian woman replied. "There is much we women who accompany the legion find of merit in it. But, no, I have not yet converted."

"Then for your sake," said Serena, "I won't just turn my back and walk out. We must have some long talks in the near future. And I *must* introduce you to my priest."

To her husband Serena said, "Lunch will be ready in a few minutes. And in the guard rooms for their guards and slaves."

Lunch was uneventful, though Eucherius was full of questions about old Rome, about the old legions, and about the legion's journey to Germany and then south along the Rhine. Stilicho listened to those questions intently. Why, one might almost have thought he'd put the boy up to them.

I *certainly think so*, thought both Caelius and Gisco. Gisco's thoughts continued with, *But, on the other hand, he's an intelligent boy, very, and just might have come up with them on his own.*

As the staff cleared away the platters and dishes while leaving the cups, Serena stood, begged to be excused, and then took Tabiti in hand, disappearing with her off into the peristyle. Galla Placidia followed along without being asked, while Eucherius made himself scarce at a meaningful glance from his father.

"I'd like to thank you," said Caelius, "for not requiring us to lay down to eat. I'm a simple soldier and we just don't do that much."

For this and other reasons, Caelius found himself liking Stilicho enormously. *But that doesn't mean I trust him. He's too smooth, too political, for that.*

"Hardly anyone does anymore," said Stilicho. "As near as I can tell, the preference for eating from chairs, stools, and benches came from the church. And I, too, bless the fathers for it."

Continuing, Stilicho said, "I've set up an appointment for you to meet with His Imperial Majesty, Honorius, but that is largely a formality. He's just past boyhood and leaves the running of things mainly to me. Which is, perhaps, just as well."

He took a glance at his fingernails, which is to say avoided the eyes of his guests. "I did want to get some feel for the size of your force, your logistics, your finances."

Caelius started to speak before Gisco nudged his leg, an easier matter to perform when seated on chairs than when lying on *lecti*. He let the Phoenician speak, keeping his own peace.

"Our finances are barely sufficient to needs," Gisco said, "now that we have undertaken to pay the entire field army near Mogontiacum, as well as the *classis* and the fortification troops."

What Gisco didn't say was, *And assuming we have to do so for the next fifteen or twenty years.*

"I see," Stilicho said. "That's too bad. I was hoping you might be able to help us come up with some of the four thousand pounds of gold I've promised the Visigoths to go away."

"I see no way that this would be possible," Gisco said, then added the half lie, "I am intimately familiar with the legion's finances and the money just isn't there."

"It makes no sense to pay off barbarians," Caelius said. "It just whets their greed."

"That may be," said Stilicho, "but I lack the means to fight them at the moment."

"But we hear," said Gisco, "that you recruited another twelve thousand men from the remnants of the army of Radagaisius, after you defeated him."

"And indeed I did," he admitted. "And I trust none of them, especially not against their fellow Visigoths. They give the appearance of military power, only, while actually being next to worthless for my purposes or for the Empire's. They're little beyond a financial and logistic burden to me."

"Hmmm…" mused Caelius. "Would you trust them to fight Vandals and Suebi—oh, and Alans? Our money isn't infinite but we're in pretty fair logistic shape up around Mogontiacum. I think we could support five or six thousand of them."

"And their families?" asked Stilicho. "They almost all have families. I enlisted twelve thousand on condition of taking on their families, too. The ones I sold as slaves were mainly pagans. Some, however, were Arian Christians and either had no male to enlist or had one or more that I didn't want. In any case, you're talking probably more than thirty thousand mouths, though many of those are children and some are even nursing children. Call it the equivalent of maybe eighteen thousand adult mouths. If you can do that, and if you can peg their families' continued survival to them fighting well, and if they don't have to face their own people, then, yes, I think you can trust them."

"If you don't have to pay or feed that six thousand," asked Gisco, "how much will that help you raise the money to buy off the Visigoths?"

"A fair amount," Stilicho admitted.

"Good. Now let me make a suggestion. Tell the Visigoths...hmmm, what was the name of their king?"

"Alaric."

"Ah, thanks," Gisco said. "Tell this Alaric that you cannot come up with the money all at once. Delay paying anything as long as possible and, when you must, tell him you can come up with, say, eight hundred pounds a month for the five months."

"What good will that do?"

"It will," said Caelius, "give us up north the chance to finish off the barbarians facing us, then march south. Then, together, we destroy Alaric."

"Not...that simple," said Stilicho. "And there's also a rebellion going on north of you, in Britannia, that is dangerous and will have to be dealt with."

"What makes it complex?" asked Gisco. "I mean the situation with the Goths, not the one in Britannia." *Which we should have known about but didn't. He must have a very nice system of spies and informers, indeed.*

Said Stilicho, "It's the eastern half of the Empire, those damned tricky Greeks. They can't be trusted at all. They're the ones who sicced Alaric on us in the first place. As long as Alaric and his army are a force in being, they can be used as a threat against Constantinople, just as Constantinople has been using them against us."

"I see."

"And what makes you think you can destroy the Vandals, Suebi, and Alans?" Stilicho asked.

"We probably won't," answered Caelius. "But starvation will. And then, unless we can think of something more useful, we're going to make Germany east of the Rhine uninhabitable by any beast more sophisticated than a rat. And then we can leave your Goths on guard and march south."

"It bears some thinking upon," said Stilicho. "And I'll do that, this evening. For now, let's get you both ready for your audience with the emperor."

"I can't do it," Caelius said, shaking with fury, when he and Tabiti were alone in their room. "Can't and won't. I'm a soldier, not a slave; a man, not a dog."

"A hothead, Marcus, not a man of wisdom," Tabiti said, though she was smiling when she said it. "It's the thing about you that most reminds me of my own people and, yes, I love you for it. But love you or not, what happens if you don't get on your belly for this boy called an 'emperor'?"

Tabiti was actually half a head taller than he was, blond and blue-eyed, and though she had borne children, she had kept the shape of a late teenaged girl. Like most of the Scythian women, her breasts were on the larger side, a fact more in accord with Caelius' standards of feminine pulchritude than broader Roman.

"I don't know," he admitted. "Stilicho said it's never happened before, not for the last century." Caelius sneered. "These people who call themselves 'Romans' are just circus freaks, performing dogs, parading around wearing the flayed skin of Rome. Yes, sure, we lived under a dictatorship under Augustus, but he kept the forms, he kept the law, and he made us feel like we were all citizens of a republic. This lot are just slaves."

"Tell me, man who is my husband in all but name, could you restore this thing you call a 'republic'? Could you and all your allies and the Eighteenth Legion together restore it?"

Regretfully, Caelius shook his head. "No, things are too far gone. There's hardly a man alive, worthy of the name, outside of the legion who even knows what a republic is, not really. They're all slaves, even the highest, and no more fit for self-rule than slaves are."

"Then live in the world in which you find yourself, Marcus,

or figure out a way to change it, or defy it and, like the man you are, take the consequences. I will share them with you, whatever they are."

"It's a pity," he said, "that you and Dubnia never met. Other than that whole having-to-share thing, I think you two would have gotten along splendidly."

Imperial Palace, Ravenna

Stilicho, who owed his position as much to his political and social acumen as he did to his undoubted military ability, had left before breakfast for the palace. There, he had engaged Honorius in some deep conversation, careful appraisal, and one serious warning.

"No, Majesty, these are Roman soldiers of the old school. If you jail their second-in-command they will abandon the Rhine and leave Gaul to the barbarians. They will march here as fast as cavalry might get here. They will chew through any army we might put in their path and hardly break a sweat. These are the men who conquered the Empire we are barely hanging on to.

"These swamps and streams hereabouts, that so impress the barbarians, will be as nothing to them. They conquer rivers and oceans as much as they conquer men and cities of men. They will come here to free their leader. And they are unlikely to leave one stone upon another if they do. Neither will they leave one emperor's head upon his shoulders. And that's if they're feeling generous. They don't give a fig about Constantine's ban on crucifixion.

"And if you kill him? Have him killed? They also won't care a fig for plausible deniability. They'll do the same as I've already said except that then there will be no doubt of the crucifixion.

"Majesty, have you any idea of how much crucifixion *hurts*? Or how long it takes to die on the cross?"

Honorius blanched, but came back with, "But this is the capital! Surely they'd respect the capital."

"Their capital is Rome, not Ravenna," Stilicho said. "They care nothing for Ravenna."

"But I'll lose all credibility if they won't do *proskynesis*," Honorius said. "It's expected."

"It won't happen. Oh, the Phoenician would go along with it, but the Roman? Never in a million years."

"But what am I going to *do*?" Honorius wailed.

"I do have a suggestion," Stilicho said, "if Your Majesty will agree."

"Suggest, then."

"Let's say the Roman bows his head and makes as if he is going to prostrate himself on the floor. No, he won't actually prostrate himself, but maybe he can go through the initial motions. You then put up a restraining hand and order, 'Hold, *Praefectus Castrorum*. I cannot let one touched by the hand of God, shifted across space and time, prostrate himself before me. Come, instead, and shake my hand. It would be my honor to do so with one who has come so far, from so long ago.' This way appearances are served, your honor is saved, and so is his. And we don't get that legion marching down from the Rhine to butcher us all."

"How about money?" Honorius asked.

"They're willing to take off our hands half of the former troops of Radagaisius. They'll take on paying them and feeding them, *and* their families. Long term, that's probably as valuable to us as giving us money, and a lot less likely to stick to the fingers of bureaucrats."

"But can you hold off Alaric with six thousand or so fewer men?"

"With four thousand pounds of gold for him to buy off his own people, I can...for a while. There was never any long-term prospect of buying off him and his Goths, only a temporary one. And with the Romans taking on our Gothic troops, that money just became a lot more available."

"All right, then, Stilicho. Show the old Romans in."

"It will be a few minutes, Majesty; they're waiting in the peristyle, off the far anteroom."

They were leaving the palace, on foot, with a signed agreement in hand and no obvious hard feelings on any side. Money wasn't going to imperial coffers but troops were heading to the Rhine. The legion would swear allegiance to Honorius, in his person as emperor of the Western Empire, but not to Honorius by name. And two skilled shipwrights would be going north to Mogontiacum.

"That was," said Gisco, "very smoothly done, Stilicho."

"From you, my Phoenician friend, I will take that as a compliment." Stilicho smiled broadly, then said, "But look at our soldierly comrade, Marcus—he's still trying to figure out how it was all done."

"Relax; I'll explain it to him later."

"Fuck that," said Caelius. "If I need to do something like that again, I'll hire one of you two for the job. Now tell me, Stilicho, is there much of an armaments industry in this town?"

"Some, not much. You can have some high-end specialty work done here, but that's about it. If you want arms, you pretty much have to look around. I've got a list of the thirty-five *fabricae* back at home. What are you looking for?"

"Depends on what your six thousand Goths already have. In general, we'll want each man to have a helmet, a mail hauberk or *lorica segmentata*, a *scutum*, one *pila*, one gladius, three *plumbatae*, and one *pugnio*."

"Well," began Stilicho, "Luca is the place for swords. As to whether they can turn out a decent gladius anymore...I don't know. Probably, though, on the theory that shorter is easier than longer. Still, not much of a market for short swords. Cremona makes shields, but unless you have an example for them to copy, I wouldn't expect a real *scutum*. Maybe not even with an example, for that matter. And the Goths wouldn't know how to use one, anyway. Mantua would be your place for hauberks and helmets. Or you could try Verona for shields, helmets, and armor, all three. Archery equipment comes from Ticinum."

Asked Stilicho, "You want some advice, Marcus?"

"Sure."

"You are thinking of making legionaries—your kind of legionaries—from them, aren't you? Now, you may find some who wouldn't mind joining your ranks and learning. I would not trust them, necessarily, but they likely exist. Most of the Goths, though—and it doesn't matter whether they're eastern or western—are far too pigheaded and undisciplined ever to make legionaries. So I'd advise you to use them in a shield wall—they're pretty good at that—where you can line them up six or eight deep, point them in a particular direction, and let them go. Anything fancier and they'll break your heart with frustration."

"How many of them will speak Latin?" Caelius asked.

"One or two percent, at most, and those will be the chiefs and nobles—who, by the way, are going to have to be your subordinate leaders because the Goths won't listen to anybody who isn't in their own nobility."

"Fuck."

"Speaking of which," said Stilicho, "you'll have to pay their chiefs and let the chiefs pay the men. They'll cheat in a heartbeat, too, so you'll need a paymaster to do the head count for every clan, and to check that they're all properly equipped men. As opposed to completely unequipped women, because they might try that, too. Never trust a Goth."

"Fuck," cursed Caelius. "But I'll tell you, other than the Germans who stayed true to us in the Varian Disaster, I don't trust Germans. And the Goths are still Germans. And—no, don't take offense—because you're only half a Vandal."

"No offense taken, but I have a request."

"Which is?" Caelius asked.

"You mentioned in our discussions that your legion was short officers, specifically one tribune. I was hoping you could take my son—leave me to deal with his mother—to the Rhine with you as a new tribune. He won't be a burden; I've been training him to be a soldier and leader since he turned three."

"Other than as a spy, Stilicho, which I would understand completely, why?"

"Besides for his own experience, I . . . well, I have enemies at court, and some of them are quite vicious and ruthless. I fear for the boy's life, as I do for my wife's and, frankly, for my own."

"We'll take him," Caelius said. *Because if you're gaining a spy we're also gaining a hostage.*

"Excellent. I thank you. I shall have Honorius appoint him as a tribune—"

"Long story," interjected Caelius, "but make him an equestrian tribune. He's young enough to learn but too young to put in charge of our existing tribunes, who are all equestrians."

"Fair. He's a levelheaded boy so should understand the rationale. Also, in a similar vein, I am going to pressure Honorius to elevate your leader—Gaius Pompeius Proculus, wasn't it?—to the high nobility and appoint him commander plenipotentiary for *Germania*, Gaul, and the Rhine, but with the proviso that he is under no circumstances to let the barbarians over the Rhine. Expect a letter to that effect before you leave."

Tabiti was somewhat surprised to find that she liked Serena, even if her Marcus called her "that old harridan." Part of this was that they were within a year in age of each other. Still more was that once you crossed the threshold from pagan beliefs to Christian, Serena became vastly less condemnatory and vastly more charming. She also became very helpful. This very minute, for example, Serena was touring the shops of Ravenna with Tabiti and a number of her own servants in tow, shopping for necessities and some luxuries for the trip back up north.

"Father Cyrenus is agreed," Serena said. "Your conversion will be taken in two days, and you and that pagan will be married immediately thereafter."

"I wouldn't be too critical, Serena," Tabiti said. "Your Empire needs Marcus a great deal more than the Christian faith does."

"Fair point," Serena conceded. "And my husband likes your Marcus enormously. He told me in confidence that, but for the miraculous arrival of the Eighteenth Legion, he didn't think the Rhine could be held—the Goths have him and his army fixed here defending Italy—and all our lives might have been in danger had it fallen."

Muster Field, West of Ravenna

Gisco was off hammering out some details with Honorius' staff. Tabiti was busy learning Christianity, and hinting rather strongly that either Caelius must marry her or she could no longer share his bed. He was considering it, too, not that he was in love— *Well, maybe a* little—so much as that he liked her so thoroughly. Children? She was probably past that. *And she takes such good care of me, in all ways. As well as my lost Dubnia, to be honest. I think I could face being married again.*

Stilicho, Caelius, and a dozen clerks the former had loaned the latter to prepare enlistment rosters all sat under canopies, distinguishable from tents by the lack of walls. Eucherius, Stilicho's son, stood nearby to watch the proceedings.

"Can you communicate with the Goths in their own language?" Marcus Caelius asked of Stilicho.

"Not exactly," Stilicho admitted. "I can communicate in Vandal, which is related, and with good will on both sides we can get the message across. Again, though, that's not usually necessary, because the upper one or two percent of the Goths will speak Latin, at least somewhat. That's that group of one hundred or so coming here to meet us, the nobles who speak Latin and must be left in command."

"And you think getting an oath of allegiance to the Eighteenth Legion from these nobles will be sufficient to ensure their loyalty and that of their men."

"No," answered Stilicho, "not in my wildest dreams. I only think that it's better than nothing. They're still going to be out for themselves, will only tolerate so many casualties, and cannot be trusted to fight their fellow Goths. Oh, and if you ever figure out how to get them to build a proper camp, let me know, would you? So, shall we take their oaths now?"

Though they couldn't be discerned with the naked eye, six staggered wagon laagers, of four to five hundred wagons each, straddled the road south from Ravenna. The sun was not yet up, though the people were. Torchlight had taken over from the recently set full moon.

"All roads lead to Rome," mentally quoted Marcus Caelius, seated atop one of his horses. *Conversely, no roads lead to Ravenna.*

This wasn't exactly true. What was true, however, was that no roads led from Ravenna to Mogontiacum that didn't involve either passes over the Alps that either were or very soon would be blocked by snow, or wide detours through either Gaul- or barbarian-infested lands to the east. *And those eastern areas are probably snowed in, too.*

This also wasn't exactly true. There *was* a road from Ravenna, southwest to the Via Aemilia, which then ran to the northwest to Augusta Praetoria, itself situated in an Alpine pass... *That's going to be snowed in, too.*

Instead, Caelius was going to lead his Goths south, to Ariminum, then northwest skirting the Apennines, along the Via Aemilia to Placentia, then to Genua and the coast along the Via Postumia. There was, in fact, a more direct road from Ravenna to the Via Aemilia, but in Caelius' opinion, it just wasn't up to the amount or weight of the traffic.

From Genua, at least, he wouldn't have to worry about snow, following the Via Aurelia to Arelate, in Gaul. Then it would be north to Lugdunum, then northeast to Mogontiacum.

Eleven or twelve hundred miles, I suppose. Going to take two and a half to three months to make it. Assuming the wagons hold out. Assuming the Goths don't mutiny. Assuming I don't throw myself off a bridge in sheer frustration. I didn't plan on this much delay when I talked with Gaius about me being an ambassador.

One good thing and one only: though I'll never get these turds to build a proper camp, they will *laager their wagons without being told, quickly and, though I hate to admit it, fairly well. Saves about two hours a day, which I can turn either into more miles or more training.*

Wagons... wagons... over three fucking thousand *wagons. Can't possibly march a single column of three thousand wagons. No way to laager anything that long. So they'll be setting out in columns of four to five hundred wagons each, average, one hour apart, and each under one of the more senior Goth chieftains. Who maybe understood my lectures on field sanitation, march discipline, and timing. Maybe... but probably not. Or maybe understood them perfectly and will just ignore me out of pure barbarian spite. Bastards.*

Marcus had purchased a wagon and dray team for himself and Tabiti, who certainly knew how to drive her own, as well as a couple to carry Gisco and the *impedimenta* for his Gallic guards, along with two shipwrights hired from the fleet base at Ravenna. Eucherius would ride with Tabiti and Privatus.

Tabiti... Tabiti. She certainly seems happier since she became a Christian. Or is it that I married her and made an honest woman of her? Or both? Maybe both... probably both. It was, I confess, a joy to see her decorating her own wagon in her own way.

She wants me to join her in this but whatever flaws I might have—and there are, no doubt, many—hypocrisy is not among them. I never believed in our gods; how can I believe in someone else's?

On the other hand, something moved us out of that ambush four centuries ago. And it wasn't just wishful thinking. So, who knows, maybe... and though I am too old and cynical ever to fall completely in love again, I confess that I am still very fond of the wench.

The lead wagon of the lead serial was his and Tabiti's. He exchanged a warm smile with her, just as the sun peaked over the Adriatic, and gave a nod. She gave a broad smile back, flicked the reins and brought her team into action, beginning the great trek to the Rhine.

South of Mogontiacum

There were already a great many lookout towers facing the Rhine. Not all of these were manned and few, after the withdrawal of troops by Stilicho, were fully manned.

Vorenus had put some of his command into the empty towers. He'd stretched out most of his boys, in *turmae* of roughly thirty or so, each, with small bases and a couple of women, mothers and foster mothers, each, to cook, approximately seven miles apart, more if there was a place to see for eight or ten miles along the river and a couple of miles into the other side, less if there wasn't. He knew that he couldn't cover all the possible landing places, so opted to cover what he could while making it risky for the barbarians to use any of them, while, further, aggressively patrolling to catch any who slipped through before they could do much harm or escape with much value.

For each two to three *turmae* he'd stretched out—which is to say for each two thirds to three fourths of a maniple—he'd put one *turma* in reserve. What that meant, in practice, was that only about a quarter of the entire *ala* were actually on outpost duty, and the rest in reserve with a well worked out system of messengers to bring help if the barbarians tried to cross with something more than ten mounted boys with light bows and poisoned arrows could handle.

Of the three overstrength *contubernia* in each forward group of thirty—which did not include the ones in reserve, farther back, while one was on lookout duty, one was patrolling to the south and then returning, and another was resting and waiting to take on lookout duty.

It would be weeks before the *classis* would be able to begin to take up the slack, and possibly as long as two or even three more months to do so fully. And even then, the cavalry screen of Scythian boys would have to continue, as would the screen of Palmyrene horse archers to the north of Mogontiacum, if only to keep watch to warn the *lusoriae* of naval ambushes.

Ishkapaius, leader of the First Maniple, First *Turma*, of the Fifth *Ala* of *Auxilia*, Scythica, with Centurion Vorenus' permission, took first post on lookout duty with his *contubernium* of his *turma* of First Maniple. This was at a spot not all that far south of Mogontiacum, perhaps ten or twelve miles, where the Rhine took a deep bend and from which it was possible to see about eight miles of the river. A line drawn through the shoulders of the bend would have run approximately through the middle of a collection of farm buildings that didn't quite arise to the dignity of a village. Even so, the farmers and their families did their best to make the boys on rest comfortable, delivering fresh eggs and milk, as well as freshly baked bread, a fair ration of the local wine, and the occasional stew. Ishkapaius, who spoke the vernacular Latin of the legion but not yet the vulgate Latin of the commoners, had a very hard time understanding them. Their well wishes, however, as well as the moon eyes of some of the younger teenaged girls, were unmistakable.

A few miles farther south on the Rhine Valley Road was a privately owned *taberna*, while another eight miles past that was a government *mansio*. Ishkapaius, who yet retained the instincts of the nomadic raider, thought that those would be prime targets of the Vandals across the Rhine.

There was also an island, rather a large one, mainly on the other side of the river. He'd been here for three nights, so far, and every night he'd heard sounds of straining men coming from its direction. Even so, every morning there had been absolutely nothing to be seen.

Vorenus came by the on the third day, to check. To him, Ishkapaius had told of his suspicions, "I think it's a major raid being planned and prepared, Centurion. And I think they're hiding boats behind that island just east of here and maybe in that two-mile loop to the southeast. With your permission I'd like to try to swim it tonight and see for myself."

"Permission denied," Vorenus said. "The Rhine's not the river for swimming in, too cold and too fast. And I would not care to lose you. But what I will do is shift a couple of the reserve *turmae*, maybe even three, to the vicinity of the *taberna* and the *mansio*. I'll also suggest to the *classis* that they put their entire remaining force upstream and hide out, in anticipation of a raid. They won't do it, of course, because that big loop is way too dangerous for them, but I can still suggest it."

"Do I have the centurion's permission to bring my entire maniple into the fight if there is a raid?"

"You do."

"Also request permission to build some bonfires down by the river, heavy on the resin and with a bucket of turpentine to help torch them off. We'll set them off if we find out they're really crossing. We can engage them when they're still in the water."

"Good idea. I think I'll have the others do the same, so

that the barbs behind that island—because yes, son, I trust your instincts here—don't take it as a warning."

The raid Ishkapaius sensed did not come that night. It didn't come the next night or the night after that, either. But still, every night the boys on that outpost heard the sounds of many men straining and heavy objects being moved.

He and his group of ten had already been relieved, gone on patrol to the south nightly for five nights, been in reserve for five nights, back at the farmsteads, and then were in their second day of their second shift of outpost duty when the Vandals and Suebi struck out across in the river, carried on forty-four boats bearing nearly a thousand barbarians.

The barbarians didn't seem to be concerned about any ships of the *classis* being on station. There were enough of them that they could overwhelm any likely collection of *lusoriae*. There was one ship, a bit downstream, Ishkapaius knew, but it didn't seem to be interested in taking on forty-four boats, each chock full of hairy, smelly, but quite possibly capable barbarians.

Their leader was asleep when one of the boys on watch shook him awake. "Ish, there are a load of those Vandals trying to come across the river."

Ishkapaius had already considered, carefully and at length, what he'd do in these circumstances. He sent one of his boys riding back to bring up the rest of the *turma*, assuming the nightly patrol hadn't left yet, or whatever was available if it had. He sent another riding south to tell the maniple there, and another one toward Mogontiacum to the same purpose. Finally, he sent a boy to find the centurion and tell him. Vorenus would know what to do.

And until he gets here, I'll just have to do my best.

With the remaining six, plus Ishkapaius, they quickly saddled their horses, lit torches, and rode for the bonfires prepared by the river bank. These they set alight quickly.

Then they collected at about the center of the row of bonfires where Ishkapaius said, "Poison your arrows. Prepare to loose at my command."

The boys pulled out the stoppers from their little gold flasks and began to dip their arrows into the liquid with extreme care. Likewise did they place the arrows in their quivers—which were not human skin; the Romans had burnt all of those as inherently accursed—most carefully. Finally, judging by the light of the bonfires and the rising moon that the barbarian boats had come in range, Ishkapaius had the Scythian *auxilia* boys stand in their stirrups and engage the nearest boats. Seven arrows flew, but five were blocked by barbarian shields and one by their armor. Only one man cried out, and that was with a curse of anger rather than a scream of agony.

Thought Ishkapaius, *You will curse a good deal more when you discover what we have done to you.*

Three times more the arrows flew, but all the boys got for their trouble were another four hits. Not a single boat slowed in the slightest.

And then came the barbarians' javelins and throwing axes. They didn't reach any of the boys or their horses, but they soon would.

"Back," ordered Ishkapaius. "We'll harass them from the flank as they move inland."

The rider sent to the farmsteads rode around the open space between the houses where the wagon with the foster mothers stood, where the campfire burned low, around which the tents were pitched. One ten-man group was saddling their horses for the nightly patrol to the south while another lounged around, being flirting with by the farmers' daughters as the latter passed out some fresh bread and cheese.

In their native Scythian, the messenger shouted, "Turn out! Turn out! The enemy have crossed the river in numbers and our leader needs every boy!"

The patrol hesitated not a moment. With a mass chorus of "Yes! Finally!" they mounted their horses and headed toward the Rhine. One of the others, those for whom it was to be a rest night, translated for the girls, who ran off to their own homes to tell their mothers and fathers and to begin the evacuation. One of the Scythian boys shouted after them, "Leave the barbarians no horses. They're dangerous to you as it is but much more so if they're faster than you are!" This served mainly to set the girls to running still faster, though when the farmers' families began to move to the west they did take their horses with them.

Vorenus had drilled them well—the resting group were armed,

saddled up, and moving less than ten minutes after the patrol group.

After peppering the invaders to no immediate effect, though a number of them now sported arrows they couldn't get out because of the barbs, Ishkapaius led his boys back to stand between them and the farmsteads. He was met there by the group whose patrol was cancelled.

"All right," said the boy-leader, "here's what I want until Centurion Vorenus shows up to tell me different. I want this group to ride to the left and harass the invaders continuously. Don't get closely engaged. *Don't* let them get within javelin- or axe-throwing range. But if you have to run off, come back and hit them again. I'll do the same thing from in front. When the group that was on rest and reserve shows up, I'll sent them to the right as we're facing. When more *turmae* show up, same deal: first stays with me, next goes to you, and next goes to the right. Now go! And good hunting."

By the time Vorenus showed up, there were two full maniples of the Scythian boys in action. They'd managed to inflict maybe two hundred-plus casualties on the barbarians but hadn't gotten away scot-free, either. Ishkapaius' *turma* and maniple had taken about fifty, of which twenty were known dead and the rest being collected back by the farmstead. Before morning they would be en route to Mogontiacum and Josephus' *valetudinarium*. Casualties in the other maniples were unknown but believed not to be as heavy.

Maybe worse than the casualties was that the boys were nearly out of arrows.

The moon was still up, too, a nearly full moon, by the time Vorenus climbed to Ishkapaius' lookout point. There, he saw something he'd hoped never to see: another hundred or so boats, carrying thousands of barbarians, coming out of the long loop in the Rhine, heading for the western bank.

"Shit. Ishkapaius?"

"Here, Centurion."

"Take your *turma*, whatever's left of it, and ride like hell for Mogontiacum. Find Legate Pompeius. Tell him that this incursion cannot be stopped short of bringing the entire legion and all the *auxilia* here at the double."

INTERLUDE

Ravenna, 406 A.D.

Said Senator Lampadius, "I do not trust that Vandal son of a bitch. It's only that legion sent to us from ancient times by God that's kept Gaul from being overrun. And if Gaul went, so would Spain and, who knows, possibly Africa, too. How we would pay for the army, hence the Empire, without the tax revenues from those places I don't know."

Lampadius was a bit on the corpulent side, balding, with no beard. He had, even so, the look of brave determination about him.

Anicius Petronius Probus, the consul, looked not at all well. He shook his head. "It might almost have been worth the loss of Gaul to get rid of him. That man has imperial ambitions, whether for the eastern Empire or the western, and whether for himself or his son."

Scowling, Lampadius continued, "And if he's been looting our coffers for his barbarian friends, now, now when he lacks absolute power, how much more would he loot were he emperor?"

"Everything there is," answered Anicius, "though that would be little after every barbarian in the world had been given a grant of land, which land would never again produce any taxes. But what are we to do?"

Here Lampadius smiled. "I am sending one of my people to Britannia, to stir up trouble, if possible or, at least, to make contacts and gather information. At least they can nose about and see if there's a better candidate than they have so far, that dotard Marcus, to persuade the army there, whatever little bit Stilicho left to them, to rise up and declare him emperor. That would help undermine the bastard's authority."

"The Goths he's already settled among us are none too popular with the people of Italy, either," Anicius said. "I think a few of my people might be able to rouse up a spirit of resistance among the northern Italians. Maybe enough to riot against the Goths and cause a break between Stilicho and the Goth, Alaric."

"Let us do so."

"Let us further hope that, despite the old legion the Almighty sent us, the Vandals can get into Gaul. Then we could get rid of Stilicho permanently."

"Hope and pray," answered Anicius.

CHAPTER NINETEEN

Who can be braver than the Germans? Who charge
more boldly? Who have more love of arms, among
which they are born and bred, for which alone they
care, to the neglect of everything else? Who can be
more hardened to undergo every hardship, since a
large part of them have no store of clothing for the
body, no shelter from the continual rigor of the climate: yet Spaniards and Gauls, and even the unwarlike
races of Asia and Syria cut them down before the main
legion comes within sight, nothing but their own iras-
cibility exposing them to death. Give but intelligence
to those minds, and discipline to those bodies of theirs,
which now are ignorant of vicious refinements, luxury,
and wealth—to say nothing more, we should certainly
be obliged to go back to the ancient Roman habits of
life.

— Seneca, *De Ira*, I, xi, 3–4

East bank of the Rhine, 406 A.D.

King Gunderic had refrained from making a speech before the
crossing. *The troops would only cheer and that would give the
damned Romans more warning than I want them to have. And had
I been honest about the purpose of this crossing, someone who will
be captured would have spilled his guts. So I merely wished them
success. Besides, if weeks' worth of rehearsals were not enough, a
few hundred words would make no difference.*

Instead, he told the commander of this first flotilla of boats—carrying, half and half, nearly a thousand Vandals and their Suebi confederates—to go, and they began to race for the *larger* flotilla, carrying almost two thousand men, hidden in woods next to a loop of the Rhine. The boats, as with those that had been hidden behind the island, had been brought up at night, over the course of many days, then camouflaged.

As soon as he arrived, the king told the commander of this second flotilla to launch. The second group had not been practiced as had the first, but wouldn't have to fight the Rhine's current nearly so much, either.

Mogontiacum

"Sir? Sir?" The tribune of the watch, Gnaeus Marianus, tried to shake Gaius Pompeius awake without disturbing either his Scythian beauty or their child. It didn't work.

Zaranaia awakened, made sure her breasts were covered, then told the tribune, "I'll awaken him, Gnaeus. Wait in the anteroom, please."

"What is it?" asked Gaius as he crossed the threshold of the anteroom to the *Praetorium*. He saw there the tribune and a boy from the Scythian cohort.

"Sir, the Vandals and other barbarians are crossing the Rhine in mass. Centurion Vorenus sends that there are at least three thousand of them on this side of the Rhine and maybe more coming. The Scythian boys haven't been able to hold them though they've tried. He says the legion must come. And quickly."

"Send the runners to awaken the other tribunes, and all the first-order centurions, and summon them to the *principia*. Troops to be ready to march within the half hour. No...not march, ride, to include with the horse holders."

"And the castle, sir?"

Gaius considered. "No, send to Centurion Pullo to go on high alert but stay put and hold on. Oh, and make very sure that *Primus Pilus* Metilius is the first one awakened or he's likely to cut your balls off. Send someone to tell Prefect Tadmor of the Palmyrene to also go on high alert. And get me the prefect of the *Classis*."

✧   ✧   ✧

As it happened, one third of the legion was on conjugal visitation to their women in the Scythian laager. Naturally, they had their personal equipment with them, but getting them up, getting them to their own horses, saddling those... they were going to be a lot harder to muster, though runners, drummers, and *cornicines* were doing their damnedest to hurry matters along.

"We can't wait," Gaius finally decided. "Gnaeus, have them force-march to catch up to us. Top?"

"Here, sir," replied *Primus Pilus* Faustus Metilius.

"Head the eight cohorts we've got out at the trot."

Things had settled down quite a bit on the western side of the Rhine. The Vandals and Suebi had formed up into a crescent while most of the boys of the Scythian cohort who had been able to join the fight, so far, had no more arrows. A few *turmae*, of the thirteen who had been able to get to the fight, still had some arrows, but the barbarian shield wall defeated most of those.

Thought Vorenus, watching from Ishkapaius' outpost, *My boys would try to take these guys on with their lances... or with rocks if I let them, but the size and strength differential is just too great, and there are plenty of barbarian slingers and archers out there, too. No, better to keep them formed up and looking threatening, but out of range until the legion gets here.*

Still, I'm proud of my boys and what they've been able to do. And, win or lose here, a whole bunch of barbarians are soon going to discover what it means to take a poisoned Scythian arrow.

Wait... what's this?

The moonlight still shone, though it would soon fade away. Sounds of fighting, roughly three thousand of his own men against what were alleged to be two or three hundred horse archers, in practice indistinguishable from the Huns. According to a messenger sent across, they were only about as big as Huns, too.

Could the Romans have hired Huns? Gods know they both hate us and want to destroy or enslave us.

A messenger arrived to the king from an observation post he'd set up opposite Mogontiacum, the granary of which was all that stood between his people and starvation in the late winter.

"Sire! Sire!" exclaimed the messenger. "The enemy has taken the bait. They are moving from their base to confront us here."

Soberly, the king nodded, then told and aide, "Light the beacon now."

On the western bank of the Rhine, the leaders of the Vandals and their Suebi allies saw the light from the beacon. As per prearrangement, one third of their bands broke from the crescent and began to run for the boats, carrying the wounded. The rest, keeping their shields up, fell back roughly two hundred feet and reformed. The Scythian boys who still had some ammunition pressed closer, though without any better effect.

Already, Vorenus saw, fifty or more of the barbarians' boats were in the Rhine and rowing hard for the opposite shore. The current was carrying them downstream, to the north, but he had little doubt that those boats could be dragged or carried from wherever they landed to wherever the barbarians wanted to launch another attack.

Even as he watched, half the remaining barbarians bolted from the reduced perimeter. Again, in a few minutes a stream of barbarian boats began to crawl across the Rhine.

And then, with a frightening lack of any confusion on display, the last barbarians charged to their own rear and the waiting boats.

If we had a decent supply of arrows we could reap pretty large now, thought Vorenus. *Note to self: not only collect all the arrows we can—carefully!—we need a triple supply, at least one hundred and twenty per boy. Now how to get those made...?*

His thoughts were interrupted by the sound of thousands of horses' hooves, pounding on the stone-paved road.

Best go meet the legate.

"Neatest thing you ever saw, sir," said Vorenus, ruefully. "And damned dangerous, too. If they can feint us like that, I see no end of trouble."

"What was the butcher's bill?" asked Gaius Pompeius.

"I'm guessing about theirs, but I'd say about three hundred of them either have died or will soon sicken and die. Could be as many as three hundred and fifty. And the easy cost of that was nearly every arrow my boys had, though we'll be able to recover many, maybe most of them.

"As for ours, the tougher cost, I count eighty-seven known

dead, plus roughly twice that whom I think have been evacuated to Mogontiacum and the *valetudinarium*. Or need to be. Think, not sure, because some of my boys are probably hiding serious wounds."

"Why so badly hurt?" Gaius asked.

"We thought that the linen armor would be enough. Apparently, metallurgy has gotten a lot better in these times than it used to be. Steel is stronger, sharper, and more common. And that sharp steel can penetrate a *linothorax* without fairly heavy metal reinforcement."

"Fuck," said Gaius.

"Fucked," corrected Vorenus.

"You've been understudying Marcus Caelius," the legate accused.

"I cannot deny it," admitted Vorenus.

"More importantly, are you strong enough to continue to guard this portion of the Rhine?" Gaius asked.

Vorenus shook his head. "No, sir, not anymore. I think you need to put a cohort right here and shift us south or move the Palmyrenes down here and move us and a cohort north. Sending a cohort here is probably wiser. And I need better armor for my boys, but even on horseback, they're not strong enough for mail. Also, sir, we need to start sending patrols across the Rhine routinely and regularly. We can't afford to get taken by surprise like this again."

Gaius nodded absent-mindedly, while thinking, *I wish to Hades that I had Marcus Caelius here to advise me.*

Via Aemilia, just before Bononia

This close to home—*to my real home, the place where I was a boy, where my mother and father lie buried*—Marcus Caelius felt his heart pound and his blood race. *I must see the old place, whatever may be left of it. And I will do so, before we leave.*

The road paralleled the northern Apennines along the southern edge of the North Italian Plain. From a small hill Caelius, accompanied by a couple of his Gothic guards, watched the first wagon serial pass by below, to his north. Even while they passed, a group of Gothic cavalry rode past behind him. The Gothic leader raised his spear in salute when Caelius glanced over his shoulder. There were other groups of cavalry some distance behind that one. Still others were farther north on the plain. An advanced guard preceded the first wagon, which happened to hold his woman, Tabiti.

While, as with Tabiti, women tended to drive the wagons, men either rode or marched on the flanks to secure their families.

They're not contemptible, Caelius thought. *Different, yes, but not contemptible. We had one way of encampment, when we were legions alone, with no women. We developed a different way, rather, modified our old way, when we picked up women and families. They just started in a different position. Hmmm . . . they do bear some study since* auxilia, *for now or not, there's near enough to zero chance we won't have to fight them at some point in time.*

Caelius pulled his horse's reins to the left, and trotted to catch up to the group of Gothic cavalry behind him. The leader of the Goths, the same man who had raised his spear in salute seeing the Roman riding up, turned over command to his second and veered to meet the Roman halfway. They'd never met but the Roman who had hired them had been pointed out to the Goth and his name given.

"Hail, Camp Prefect," said the Goth. "Hail, Marcus Caelius." The Goth's Latin bore an accent, but was quite correct in all other ways.

That one or two percent Stilicho spoke of, thought the Roman.

"I'm afraid you have the advantage of me, friend," said Caelius, reining his horse in.

"Theodomir, son of Odovacar, at your service," the Goth returned. He was gray-eyed and bearded, his hair and beard about as iron gray as Caelius', himself, and quite tall and broad shouldered.

"Are you senior among your people?" asked Caelius.

"Senior, yes, but not the most senior. I am . . . oh, I suppose third in this group."

"Third isn't bad," Caelius assured the Goth. "I'm curious about the people who will be fighting at our side. I wonder if you can't tell me something of your military style and history."

"History might be better," said Theodomir. "I lack examples enough to contrast our military styles. To me, it's all a case of what is, not why is it."

Caelius spurred his horse to a walk, following the Goths but off to one side. Theodomir mimicked this.

"Fair enough. Were you at the battle against the easterners, the one called Adrianople?"

Theodomir nodded. "I was a young men, then, and yes."

"What happened?" Caelius asked.

"The short version would be bad luck on the part of the eastern Empire, good luck on ours, all coupled to an emperor who lacked patience. You almost had us dead to rights, you know. And you should have won. But that doesn't tell you what happened, does it?"

"Sadly not."

"Well, the background first, then," Theodomir said. He sighed. "We were, as we seem to have been since forever, fleeing the Huns. We called ourselves Thervingi then, but what were then the Thervingi are pretty much the Visigoths now.

"We were looking for safety behind secure borders and an army that, by and large, terrified us enough we could hope it would scare off the Huns, too. The emperor in the east, Valens, let us in, in the hope—and at that time it was a mutual hope— that we'd become soldiers and farmers, increasing imperial tax revenues and helping to fend off the Huns.

"I'm not sure but I think Valens was sincere in this hope. I know I thought he was, as did my people, when we crossed the Danubius. Certainly he promised to feed us until we could get crops in. And we needed the food, too, we'd been driven off our own lands to the east with just about enough to get by.

"Enter the local provincial governors, Maximus and Lupicinus. They had the food they were supposed to give us, but refused to give it. They slaughtered dogs and offered those to us in exchange for one of our boys as a slave. They sold us grain that was already ours by right, by treaty, for all the gold and silver we had. They began demanding our weapons for food. Then, at a peace and provisions conference between him and our co-kings, Alavivus and Fritigern, Lupicinus tried to assassinate both. His big mistake was missing Fritigern but he did manage to get rid of Alavivus."

"And that's when you rebelled?" asked Caelius. At Theodomir's deep nod, Caelius said, "In all honesty, I can't blame you."

"I was detached on a foraging expedition at the time, so I can't tell you what happened exactly, but there was a battle between us and Lupicinus. We won. Some say he was killed in the battle. Others that he was executed by Valens. Me, I don't know; as I said, I wasn't there.

"What I do believe is that none of us really wanted war. We just wanted safety. Valens just wanted peace and taxes and some support. But once the fighting starts..."

"Yes," Caelius agreed, "I know."

Theodomir continued, "So we skirmished and fought all over Thrace, to nobody's clear advantage. And then there were the atrocities, and we were as guilty as anyone there: rape, murder, robbery, arson, all of it. Once those started any chance at peace flew out the window; we knew it and Valens knew it, too."

"Now Valens collected a good-sized army and sent for further help from the west. How many men had he? How many had we? I think we had about twenty thousand. The eastern Romans may have numbered about as many, or maybe a couple of thousand more. We also had about eighty thousand women and children in our wagon laager. It was reasonable to expect that the women would fight to defend their children and themselves from slavery, though, however fiercely, not to any great effect."

"Fairly even odds, then," Caelius judged.

"Yes," Theodomir agreed. "But the odds were about to turn against us when the Roman army from the west showed up. And this is why our king, Fritigern, first tried to make peace—yes, yes, of course at a price—and then, when that failed, sent us out to forage and plunder far and wide, to entice Valens into attacking us before the western army showed up, so that we'd have a chance. I was out foraging when Valens attacked.

"Fritigern had messengers ready for when this happened, to bring the foragers back at the double. My group got back just as the Roman left was lapping around one part of our wagon laager. They were already having a hard enough time of it, but we waited until they were fully committed then hit them in the back. After that was rout, pursuit, and slaughter.

"I didn't count the bodies myself," Theodomir said, "but I've heard that ten or twelve thousand Romans fell. It was worse than that, though; it was the flower of the eastern Roman army. On our part, we probably lost four thousand, or a bit more. Hardly a Gothic family wasn't in mourning."

"A solid victory," Caelius congratulated. "Your people have a right to be proud." *And my people have cause to remember that, just because they don't fight in legions, it doesn't mean that barbarians are stupid. Just like the way they laager and the way they provide defense in depth to their noncombatants; they have their ways and those ways have been well thought out over the centuries. More to learn here, though.*

"Theodomir," Caelius said, "my woman's wagon is the first one in this serial. Why don't you join us for dinner tonight. Bring your wife and...hmmm...have you children?"

"Seven, two of them boys already under arms, and we would be pleased to."

"Couple of hours after we're done laagering, then. Can you find us?"

"Your wagon isn't hard to find. There is only one decorated like it among all the hundreds in this column."

Caelius knew the roads, at least, though many markers and reminders were missing now. *I know old man Celsus' farmhouse was here, not far from the intersection, but there isn't a sign of it.*

The prefect dismounted to walk up the road. *The hills all look familiar enough. And there, there, that olive tree: I played in it as a boy, myself and Publius. So veer right a little and . . .*

And there was nothing to be seen. His family's own farmhouse was gone, as well. He tied off his horse and wandered the unkept yard looking for something, anything, that might be left of his old life. He found some old stones and cleared them away. Underneath was a well. *Now that is familiar. And from the well . . . let me think. About twenty paces to the house, I think, to the east.*

Caelius followed that direction, keeping count of his steps. The ground didn't look much different but "much" isn't the same as "completely." *There was a stone floor. It's probably still down there.*

Unsheathing his sword he slid it into the dirt . . . in . . . in . . . in . . . a little farther. And then, voilà, there was resistance. It wasn't a random rock, too smooth for that. *Home.*

And that means Grandfather and Grandmother's grave is . . . five hundred feet in that direction. "That direction" was, in this case, to the north. He paced this off, too.

Then he found it, half buried, but the exposed part the same as he remembered, his paternal grandparents' grave marker. *No need to dig; it's the same.*

There was another one a dozen feet from that. This one he did kneel to dig out a bit. He dug only until he reached a carven name, "TCAELIOFM." Titus Caelius, the son of Marcus.

And Mother would never have left your side. She's here, too. I always said I'd come home, Mama, Papa. And here, finally, I am. Sorry it took so long. There was a considerable delay I had no hand in.

At that point, for the first time in nearly forty years, *praefectus castrorum* and former *primus pilus* of Legio XIIX, Marcus Caelius, felt his eyes beginning to moisten.

Vandal camp, east bank of the Rhine

The king barely restrained himself from throwing up at the stench. With some muttered words about enduring and getting better, he backed out of the wagon in which one of the wounded from the raid across the Rhine lay, moaning and delirious.

Gunderic didn't understand it. Nobody in his tribe, nor the Suebi, nor the Alans understood it. Sure, getting those nasty barbed arrows out had done more damage than they'd caused when they went in. But then came the shaking, the difficulty breathing, the convulsions... and death for many. But even those who didn't die developed infections, stinking green and black fester, that nothing would cure. A few still lived, delirious and delusional. Most had died. Some had died begging to be killed to put an end to their agony.

How am I going to get the people to do this again? I had planned to cross the Rhine five or six times more, getting the Romans to spread themselves thinner and thinner, until I could get four thousand or so warriors on the other side to drive deep into Gaul, plundering and burning, to pull most of the Romans in pursuit. Then I'd swarm the castle on this side at whatever cost. Then it would be break into Mogontiacum and, for a change, eat well.

Now? How will I ever get them to face whatever black magic the Romans are using that kills everyone who's even slightly hurt? I doubt I can. So, I guess it's back to small raids and quick escapes.

Downcast, Gunderic went to his family laager. His son, Godigisel, seemed to be on the mend, finally. He needed to check on progress.

Mogontiacum

The sound of hammers was as deafening as the smoke of the fires was overwhelming.

Gaius Pompeius, Junius Rubelius, and Faustus Metilius walked through the factory just recently set up using workers enticed to come forward from Augusta Trevorarum, Argentoratum, Matisco, and Augustodunum. Already they could make everything needed, in terms of weapons, armor, and munitions, locally. They were even turning out more scorpions and *tormenta*, albeit slowly. Piles of oiled caltrops grew under sheds.

"The question, though, Tribune," said Gaius, "is: do we continue with making mail or do we switch to the lobsterback, the *lorica segmentata*, that was new back when we were new, too?"

"Well," replied Rubelius, "it's lighter, cheaper, and better protection, but the troops just hate it—too hard to keep rust free and damned uncomfortable. So that's a command decision, not a staff one."

"Recommendations are a staff function," Gaius replied, "and maybe we can do something about the lack of comfort."

"Fair enough. I'd recommend it if the armorers can do it. And maybe they can."

"Top?" Gaius asked.

"Sir, the troops hate it. Just as you say, they hate it for the difficulty in keeping it rust free and for the way it chafes their necks. Now, personally, I think they're just whining bitches, where these *loricae* are concerned. Hades, the things weigh less than half of what a mail coat does and gives better protection. But it's all academic unless the armorers can turn them out."

Gaius nodded. "Let's go find out."

"Wait, sir," said Metilius. "Let me send a messenger to have one brought to the armor shop."

"Do so."

Within a moment, one of the escorts was racing off on foot, to find and bring one set of *lorica segmentata*.

On the way they passed the archery sub-factory. Arrows by the thousands were already piled up, with more in process, though not many bows were in evidence. When asked about it, the chief bowyer said, "Sir, we have to store them a long time under just the right conditions to get the glue to bind the pieces, to make the composite bows stand up to the strain and provide the power."

"What are we going to do for poison?" Rubelius asked. "The cohort of Scythian boys can't be useful to us without poison."

"I know," Gaius agreed. "There's still quite a lot, but I've sent my woman, Zaranaia, to get some of the Scythian women to catch snakes and make more. Should be about two weeks before we start replacing what we've used."

"Nasty business," Rubelius said, "but I don't see much of a choice."

"Neither do I."

They had to leave the archery building and step into the brisk autumn weather to get to the armor shop. Before Gaius could ask,

Rubelius answered, "Supplies of *udones* are increasing. Should be enough for every man to have two pair before the first snows. We already have enough *braccae*. *Digitabulum* are adequate. Each man has a *sagum*."

"Are we charging for the clothing?" Gaius asked.

"Definitely."

Gaius shook his head. "If I had the Empire's tax base, I think I'd arrange to provide everything the troops needed without charge unless lost or destroyed through negligence."

"Well, sir," said Metilius, "the Empire is largely doing that now, because they don't have the money to pay in cash."

"Point."

By the time they arrived at the armor shop, the *lorica segmentata* had arrived. On examining it, the chief armorer said, "Not really hard to make, but the pieces will mostly have to be made for or at least fitted from a selection for each individual soldier. I think we could improve it and their lives, too, by painting or tinning it against rust. And the really uncomfortable part..." The armorer indicated the iron on the edges of the inner shoulder bands. "Well, what do they use now?"

"A scarf, wrapped around their necks," Metilius replied.

"That strikes me as adequate."

"It is," Gaius said, "but the complaints nonetheless remain loud and unceasing. They also complain about the work of keeping it rust free."

Said the chief armorer, "I can imagine but now that I think of it, I don't believe any paint we have would do any good. Just flake off in a matter of days. How about the tinning, then? It would cost rather more."

"First figure out exactly how much more," said Gaius.

"For how many sets?" asked the armorer. "Setting everything up to do tinning would be costly, too, and the unit cost would drop as the volume went up."

"I'm thinking," said Gaius Pompeius, "that we're going to need something like ten thousand sets."

"That will help a good deal," said the chief armorer, "but that also means we must retain Britannia for the tin. And we'll need some huge cauldrons."

"Screw the tinning, sir," interjected Metilius. "Those lazy-as-dirt legionaries are best kept busy, digging when not marching, eating when not digging, cleaning when not eating, and sleeping or guarding when not cleaning."

"Well, yes, Top, I suppose so, but I want to reward the Scythian boys; they fought like Hades."

"Why so worried about making *lorica segmentata,* sir?" asked the first spear, Metilius.

"Again, it's the Scythian boys, Top, at least for starters. They fought really hard and really well, but the linen armor we had made for them just wasn't up to stopping modern spear and javelin points. Nor throwing axes, either. We will probably end up having lost fifty or so boys just because their armor wasn't up to the job.

"Beyond that, we're going to have to spread out some cohorts, I figure at least five of them, three south and two north, and the rest are going to have to move even faster than horseback allows. So we need to take weight off the horses. Every ounce we can lift gives us a little more time to stop the next incursion."

"Enough time to make a difference?" asked Metilius.

The legate shrugged. "I don't know. You don't know. *Nobody* knows. But we all know this: we have to do our best and grab onto every advantage we can."

"Fair point," agreed the first spear.

"And, finally, while we're not beginning to run low on money, not nearly, that day will eventually come, unless we can establish a tax base of our own. And we need to raise a second legion. Maybe even a third. And that second and third legion will need to be properly equipped. Lobsterback, even tinned, is cheaper than mail. And as you say, we really don't have to tin it. That will help, too."

"Also a fair point," Metilius conceded.

"How's the language and accent program coming, to send patrols from Thancrat's cohort of *auxilia* over to the other side?"

"Not especially well," answered the first spear, scowling and shaking his head. "There's just not that much similarity in the languages after four centuries. The modern Germans say no one would be fooled. I'd normally say that we need to send across patrols of the Germans working for us *other* than Thancrat's, but can we trust them not to desert? Not to come back with plans to support an attack from the ones over the Rhine?"

"Arminius again," Gaius said. "Others may forget but we who suffered for it will never forget his treachery."

"No, sir, not for a second."

"Such a shame," said Gaius. "If we could trust them I'd be willing to march across the Rhine and help the Vandals beat off the Huns when they show up."

Metilius shook his head. "But we can't or, even if we could, the troops never would. They'd mutiny before letting themselves be put in that circumstance again."

"There really ought to be a way."

Via Aemilia, Laager I, Gothic column, before the Caelius' tented wagon

Caelius, Tabiti, Gisco, Theodomir, and Eucherius sat with Theodomir and his family, seated on cushions around a large blanket laid upon the ground and holding platters of food. Wine there was, as well, while, as a gift, Theodomir and his sons had rolled over a barrel of good beer. The weather was still fine with no rain or high, cold winds on offer.

Theodomir's wife, Alodia, was a few years younger than her husband, not yet gray, but a bit plump. Still, she was a lively and pleasant woman, and spent the dinner, with much laughing and many gestures, picking up Latin vocabulary from Tabiti. One could glimpse her as a younger woman by her absolutely stunning—and, indeed, Eucherius seemed completely stunned— tall, blond, and slender daughter, Gailawera.

The attraction was mutual enough and so plainly obvious that Theodomir's next to eldest son, Fredenandus, pointed it out, to much laughter and even more embarrassment on the part of the young people. Still, Gailawera was a strong and defiant girl. Instead of wilting under her brother's prodding she stood up, walked deliberately to stand by Eucherius, then sat down by his side.

Privatus did the serving, helped out spontaneously by Theodomir's two youngest girls. They, not entirely surprising, could speak in half-decent Latin, enough to get by.

All the Goths present were polite enough to sample the wine, but quickly reverted to the beer they were more used to and much preferred.

Said Caelius, politely following his guests' lead, "You know, this is pretty good beer. Our own German *auxilia* have undertaken to brew beer for the legion, but I think yours is rather better."

"Well, as everyone knows," said Theodomir, "we Germans are

very pigheaded, but I'd be glad, once we arrive at Mogontiacum, to show your Germans our process. Who knows, they might even pay attention."

"The legion will surely thank you," said Gisco. "The last really good beer we got was from an Ostrogoth named Wulfila. He never offered to show us how it was done."

At length, dinner over, Tabiti summoned all the women and girls to the tent, to talk about woman things, leaving the men and boys to discuss serious matters. Gailawera sought to object but a few stern words from her mother dragged her along, too. The men moved to around the fire, taking their cushions, cups, and mugs along with them.

"How old is Gailawera?" asked Eucherius.

"Not yet old enough to marry of her own volition," answered Theodomir. "She turned sixteen two moons ago. And you, son: will your father, Stilicho, permit you a marriage of love, or only of state?"

"How did you know...?"

"We Goths are a rude and rustic people," said Theodomir, "but we're not stupid. We saw you standing behind him and to one side at the muster and the family resemblance shone through clearly."

"Speaking of rude and rustic, but not stupid," asked Gisco, "what are the hopes and dreams of the Gothic people?"

Theodomir, who had perhaps had a little too much beer, answered forthrightly. "Safety, first; yes, that clearly. Land to farm, that, too. Independence, our own kingdom and our own laws and customs, if at all possible."

"And, see," said Marcus Caelius, "that's at the core of the problem. The Empire cannot safely give you your own kingdom, not inside itself. Safety we can give. Even land to farm, in some places, though not all in the same place. But an independent kingdom..."

"No, wait," said Gisco, "that's not strictly true. Half the Empire, near enough, consists of former independent kingdoms that were assimilated and then amalgamated to Rome."

"We were on the offense then," said Caelius. "Big difference between that and giving over a chunk of your land to a foreign people."

"We would be unlikely ever to let ourselves be assimilated," said Theodomir. "And besides, all those lands around the great inland sea shared much culture, did they not?"

"They did," the Phoenician conceded.

"We do not share that culture. Witness the olive oil for dipping your bread, over dinner, which you used, and which we were polite enough to try, compared to the butter that we mostly ate."

"Hmmm...yes, I suppose that's so."

"Ideally," said Caelius, "we'd set you up as an independent kingdom outside the Empire, sign a treaty of alliance, and then help you—you and the Franks and maybe even the Vandals—to keep the Huns at bay. But the problem always goes back to the last time we trusted a German, Arminius, and the way he betrayed us."

"I've heard of this betrayal," said Theodomir. "Indeed, who has not? So, I understand the problem. And I have no good solution."

"Hostages?" Eucherius suggested. "I mean, sure, I'm a guest of Prefect Marcus Caelius and his household, but I'm under no illusions but that I am also a token of good faith and a hostage...and maybe even an offer of alliance, too; my father didn't say."

Caelius considered this, then said, "The number of hostages would have to be immense to make the legion forget about Arminius. A son per household might be enough."

"That *is* pretty immense," said Theodomir. "But what do you have in mind, assuming former betrayals could be forgotten?"

"Right now, we plan on holding the Vandals at bay until they starve. Then we're going to cross the Rhine and move all the German farmers there and any Vandals who survive to the west bank. There, we'll sell the Vandals as slaves and settle the farmers down on land we'll buy for them. Then we will turn southern Germany into a wasteland that cannot support horse nomads.

"But if there were a way, I wouldn't mind seeing us set up a client state, or a series of them, on the eastern bank, allied with us and just strong enough to keep the Huns at bay with—and I cannot emphasize this enough, *only* with—our help.

"If, if, *if* we could find a way to trust them completely."

"Given history," said Theodomir, "we'd have to learn to trust you, too. There is a great litany of wrongs on both sides."

Caelius sighed. "That, my friend, is so."

Theodomir stopped and seemed to consider something. "There is one thing greater than trust, and that is necessity. We would need you to stop the Huns...or any of the other horse nomads who pour from the eastern steppe with such regular profusion. Perhaps you might need us, too. They *are* fearsome."

"It bears some thinking upon, doesn't it?"

Mogontiacum

It was definitely getting colder—both the *haruspex* and the legate, as well as their brace of guards, were tightly wrapped in their wool cloaks as they walked through the mostly bare, cobblestoned streets of Mogontiacum, heading for a particular church. There were a few flakes of snow on the air.

Appius Calvus, who had a lot more time in Germany than did Gaius Pompeius, said, "We'll be up to our necks in the stuff soon enough."

Calvus returned, this time accompanied by Gaius Pompeius, to the Catholic church overseen by the priest, Alban. The priest, as usual, was the very font of hospitality, welcoming the pair profusely and ushering them through the church, en route to his own humble quarters. The guards he asked to wait in the church, proper, "Since my quarters are so cramped. Go ahead and build yourselves a fire; it would be un-Christian of me to let you freeze."

On the way, Gaius stopped in front of the main crucifix and said, "It doesn't look like that. I've seen it done many times—too many times—and that's not the kind of cross that's used."

Alban looked at it, too, and asked, "Why not?"

"Ease and efficiency," Gaius replied. "When crucifixion is commonly used, it's a lot easier and quicker to have the upright more or less permanently in place, then nail or tie the condemned to the *patibulum*. Tying is worse, by the way. The *patibulum* is then lifted by the execution party and more or less impaled on the upright. Then the ankles are tied to the upright and more nails driven in—if you're going to use nails—before the ties are removed. It's disgusting. It's supposed to be disgusting. It's also supposed to be terrifying, and I guarantee that it is. Rome, in the old days, had one servile insurrection after another, right up until Crassus crucified over six thousand rebellious slaves along the Appian Way. After that? No more slave uprisings. Think about that for a moment: a manner of life so awful that death is to be preferred, and yet death on the cross is so fearful that even slavery is better. Day upon day, writhing up there in utter agony and shame, asking, pleading, begging for death, and being the instrument of your own death by torture... eventually."

Alban's face lost color. His brown eyes looked distinctly troubled and, at the same time, decidedly grateful. "I'd never really thought about it in those terms. How much, then, do we owe Christ for enduring it on our behalf?"

Gaius shrugged. "I don't know, myself. Though I came here to discuss it with you."

"Well, come on, then. I can at least offer you some bread and wine." The allusion was completely lost on Gaius, though Appius had some clue as to what the priest meant. "And the same for your followers waiting outside."

After the bread and wine were served out, and portions sent to the two guards, Alban asked, "How can I help you, then?"

"My wife has become a Christian," Gaius said. "And, as such, she wants to become formally married. I am a pagan, though not a devout one. I don't know if anybody in the legion is devout, really, though they have a deep reverence for the legion and its symbols."

Alban nodded. "A lot of your people, and many, many of the Scythian women that accompany you, grapple with this. So, you want to know if you can be married?"

"Yes," Gaius said. "And without making a liar of myself by proclaiming I am something I am not."

"We," said Alban, "do not have a particular or mandatory format or ceremony for matrimony, only that there be a public declaration of voluntary agreement to be man and wife and some kind of ceremony. Just living together is not enough."

"Would having told Zaranaia that I cannot contemplate life without her and want her to be with me forever count?" asked the legate.

Replied Alban, "I think it might, if said publicly."

"How public is public?" asked Gaius.

"Two or three witnesses. Oh, call it two."

"There were two," Gaius said.

Alban smiled. "So, she converted after you were publicly married. This simplifies things. It also saves your pagan soul."

"How's that?"

"The apostle Paul wrote, in First Corinthians, that the unbelieving husband is made holy by the believing wife, and vice versa."

"Ah." Gaius asked, "If I may ask, why do you believe in Christianity?"

"There are several reasons," said Alban. "Very large among these are that it feels right and true to me, at a purely emotional level. But pure emotion is not, I would agree, the best way to determine truth and falsehood. But there is this: Christ performed miracles in the name of his Father, whom we call 'God.' He was crucified, died, and rose from the dead. You can scoff at this, of course. Me, in some other life? I might have scoffed. But the men who saw this went on to risk, embrace, and very often find—speaking of crucifixion and its terrors—lingering and unenviable deaths. Would they have done this had they not seen with their own eyes, heard with their own ears? I doubt it. And that is the unemotional, rational reason for my faith. They who had seen and heard believed what they had seen and heard, dedicated their lives to it, and testified to it by their martyrdoms."

"You have given me something to think about," said Gaius.

"And I," added Appius Calvus.

"How much for the wedding, then?" asked Gaius.

Alban smiled. "Oh, I wouldn't take a single *antoninianus* for it, Legate."

"Legate?" asked Calvus, "Sir, can you find your own way home to legionary base? I'd like to discuss something with Father Alban."

INTERLUDE

Londinium, Britannia, 406 A.D.

Lampadius' man, Bonitus, was less a spy than a clever and ruthless thug. He had some military background, as well. But, his chief had reasoned, a clever and ruthless thug with some military background might well be perfect for stirring up trouble in Britannia.

Bonitus, however, reasoned, *Gratianus is the* second *imperial usurper to arise in Britannia in the last few months. The earlier one, Marcus, an army officer, has already been killed by his own troops. I'm not at all sure how much more damage I can do here.*

In a fairly upscale-looking tavern and inn, where Bonitus was staying in Londinium, he asked the barkeep what was going on and what the future was likely to hold.

"What's been going on is that an *optio* in the local forces—goes by the name of Constantine—maneuvered the army, what's left of it, into electing Marcus emperor, then into getting rid of Marcus and raising Gratianus to the purple. Marcus was a soldier, but Gratianus is just a well-placed civilian, a bureaucrat, really."

"Any reason behind it?" asked Bonitus.

"Two different reasons," said the barkeep. "In the first place, none of the soldiers here have been paid in literally years. Why? Because all of the taxes raised here go to the Imperial Treasury, where a lot of sticky fingers take their cut, so they say, and what's left gets spent on barbarians."

Bonitus set his face in an expression of incredulity. "Well, surely this Marcus could have kept the taxes here to pay the army."

"Maybe he could have," said the barkeep, "but he didn't. So, since he couldn't pay them, soldiers and sailors, both, they got rid of him, at Constantine's urging, and replaced him with someone who understood something of finances and taxation.

"But the second problem—and mark my words—is that Gratianus doesn't understand the military or war. So Britannia is being raided by Picts, Saxons, and bloody Hibernians. And the 'emperor' hasn't a clue of what to do about any of it.

"I mean, the soldiers here may not be the best ever to serve the Empire, but Britannia is their home and the British their people. It eats their guts to see them being plundered and dragged off into slavery."

"I...see," said Bonitus. "And so?"

"And so Constantine, who *is* a soldier but not an officer, and scary smart to boot, is going to get the army to do away with Gratianus, raise him to the purple, and—remember that scary-smart part!—fix the taxation, fix the pay, expand the army, defend Britannia and maybe go on to take Gaul, Hispania, and even Italy."

"And you know all this because...?"

"Because he's one of my best...Why, there he is now. *Ave*, Constantine!"

CHAPTER TWENTY

The best swordsman in the world doesn't need to
fear the second-best swordsman in the world; no, the
person for him to be afraid of is some ignorant antago-
nist who has never had a sword in his hand before; he
doesn't do the thing he ought to do, and so the expert
isn't prepared for him; he does the thing he ought not
to do; and often it catches the expert out and ends him
on the spot.

—Marcus Binarius Clementius

Mogontiacum, 406 A.D.

Marcus Caelius had had the officers' mess and the centurions'
mess built side by side and with removable double partitions—
removable so they could have joint meetings, if necessary, and
double so that they could speak ill of, disparage, and generally
curse each other with no necessary ill feelings on either side.
For today's events, the partitions were gone and everyone above
the rank of *optio* was present, barring only one old centurion
who was down with his old case of malaria again. In that case,
the other centurion from his maniple stood in for him. Caelius,
too, was absent, but Gaius Pompeius had his proxy. Proxy? Yes,
because this was a voting matter and, although Gaius' one vote
outcounted all the rest combined, he thought it wise to bring the
rest on board. Even the centurions and *prefecti* of the cohorts
on guard along the Rhine, plus Pullo and *Medicus* ben Solomon

from his castle, had turned matters over to their most senior *optio* and raced to the legionary base to attend. Of those present, only Metilius, the first spear, and the veterinary centurion knew the subject of the meeting. Both had taken a fairly neutral stance on the subject matter.

Seeing everyone required was present, Metilius called them all to attention, then turned to face Gaius and announced, "All present or accounted for, sir."

"Very good. Take seats, please."

A lectern had been placed on one corner for the legate. He strode to it and put a waxen *cera* down, then opened it.

"Something has been bothering me since shortly after we were saved from the Germans. I can't say whether it predates our capture of our Scythian women or postdates it; I just can't remember, but it was about that time that I realized I just really didn't like slavery. I'd like you all to remember how pleased you were when I announced that your Scythian women were not slaves. I'd like you also to remember that I could have decided otherwise.

"Let me introduce to you now an exhibit. We shall call him Felix." At that, Centurion Decimus Vitelius made a come-here motion, inviting a very nervous veterinary slave named Felix into the mess. With another finger gesture Decimus directed Felix to walk up and stand by Gaius. Gingerly, a plainly terrified Felix made his way through the tables and chairs of the mess.

"Hello, Felix," Gaius began. "Good to see you again. Animals all doing well?"

"W-we-well enough, sir," the slave stuttered. "Th-th-though there's a donkey I'm concerned about."

"Calm down, Felix, nobody here is going to hurt you."

"Y-ye-yes, sir. If y-y-you say so, sir."

"Felix, tell me, how do you feel about the legion?"

Without hesitation or stutter, the slave answered, "Follow the eagle right up Pluto's arse, sir."

"And why is that, Felix?"

"Sir? Sir, the legion is my home. It's fed me and clothed me most of my life now. I have friends here, sir, and they're not all slaves, either. And then, too...well, I was being sent to the mines as a punishment for not letting my old master...well, sir, you know."

"I suspect I do."

"Yes, sir, just that. The legion saved me from that shame. I love the legion, sir. It's my..., my *family*."

"One last question, Felix: how old are you?"

"Thirty-two, sir. I think, sir. Been with the legion twenty years, sir."

"That's all, Felix, and thank you. After you leave, go see the barkeep in the troop mess and tell him I said to give you a cup of wine or a mug of beer on my ticket."

"Yes, sir! Thank you, sir!"

After Felix found his way out, Centurion Vitellius closed the door by which he'd come in.

"Centurion Vitellius," Gaius asked, "what's your opinion of Felix?"

"Well, you know it perfectly well, sir. Couldn't run the veterinary shop without him. Hardworking, smart, attentive... and you know he really loves the animals, too."

"Yes, I know. So, let me tell you, gentleman: I am going to free Felix, put him on salary, and enlist him as an auxiliary, still assigned to the veterinary hospital. Anyone have any problem with that?"

Nobody did, which, Gaius thought, *Bodes well for the basic humanity of the centurions of the legion.*

"Sir," said Faustus Metilius, "you didn't call us together to discuss the freeing of one state slave."

"No, Top, I didn't. Instead, I propose to free the lot."

Now *that* announcement got a certain reaction, not all of it positive.

"We've freed a lot of slaves, you know," Gaius said. "Remember all those Scythian slaves? You know, the ones, some of them blinded, who hold your horses when you dismount to fight? They were all slaves and yet we freed them, you and I and the legion. Indeed, we freed so many that I am sorely tempted to write to the current emperor asking that the Eighteenth get an honorary title, 'The Liberators.'

"*Medicus* Josephus, you have many slaves, don't you, working in the *valetudinarium*?"

"Several score, yes," Josephus answered. "They do everything from cleaning bandages to suturing wounds to helping men to and from the latrines."

"So, how many of you here have had to report to the hospital with a wound, or a fire in your bowels, or a fever? Hmmm...I can't see the ones who haven't. Let's try this, all hands down. Now, everyone who's never had to report to the medical establishment for any reason, please put up your hands. What's that? *Nobody?* You know, you all are some unlucky sons of bitches."

That got a mild round of laughter, as Gaius intended.

"But not as unlucky as the poor slaves, condemned to a life of hard labor for no crime they ever committed. And yet, and yet, you trust them with your health, don't you? You must have some faith in them.

"Tribune Rubelius, your quartermaster shop: do you depend on your slaves?"

"You know I do, sir."

"So, you must trust them?"

"Sure, sir, but I check the accounts, too."

"You 'check the accounts'? And this distinguishes them from any given legionary exactly how?"

"It doesn't, sir, not in the slightest."

"All right, then," said Gaius to the assembly. "I'm listening. Give me your objections."

One grizzled old centurion stood and announced himself, "Quintus Silvanus, sir, first-order centurion of the Twelfth Cohort. How do you know they'll stay? I mean, some of these slaves are, as you've pointed out, critical. And are we going to train any of them as infantry?"

"I don't know, Centurion. But I do know this: they are alone in the world except for us. Their families, if they ever had any, are all gone. Their hometowns are all changed beyond recognition. They hardly even speak the same language anymore. All their customs, all their gods, are all gone, except for here.

"Now, a few might leave and, tell you what, any of them who do I'll give twenty denarii into their hands from my own purse to give them a start in life. And I'll not lose a single *as*. Do you know why?"

There were a lot of shrugs and shaken heads.

"I'll tell you why: because I'll make a wager with as many of you as will take the chance that they'll be back, nine in ten of them. And I'll win most of those bets."

That got a few laughs and a lot more agreeing smirks and head nods.

"Now, as for training them as infantry—no, not generally. Oh, sure, maybe a couple. But you have got to catch them as young as the legion caught you and me. They're mostly too old now and far more valuable in the skills and arts they already know. Though we might work on giving them the ability to defend the camp in our absence. I'll talk that over later with the first spear and the first-order centurions.

"So, gentlemen, though we are not a democracy, in this case I will see a division. Those in favor of freeing our state slaves—no, not personal, just state; I lack authority to steal your personal property, though I am freeing my own—please stand and move to my right. Opposed, please stand and move to my left."

Gaius looked at the division, smiled broadly, and announced, "Right, then. Let me get back to my office and start writing that letter to the emperor about adding the honorific 'The Liberators' to our eagle."

A radiant Zaranaia was waiting for him, when Gaius returned to their quarters.

"I was listening from outside," she said. "Well, you never said I shouldn't or couldn't. And I am *so* proud of you. I mean, I always have been. But never before so much as now. Jesus would bless you.

"Before you write that letter to your emperor, come to bed. I want to bear another child from my hero, and the sooner we start on that, the better."

Via Agrippa, north of Lugdunum

Three weeks by my calculation, thought Marcus Caelius, *and the weather is already turning not just cold but bitter, with a fierce north wind. And we're not even that far north yet.*

The cold didn't seem to bother Tabiti in the slightest. She buttered her face, then put on a heavy shawl, women's trousers, fur-lined boots, and knit mittens, and wielded her whip over her dray team with the best of them.

I must be getting old, Caelius thought. *Cold I would have shrugged off as a young soldier I now feel in every joint in my body, from fingers to toes and everything in between.*

In the back of the wagon, shielded from the cold and chaperoned by her two younger sisters, Gailawera and they took Latin lessons from Eucherius and Gisco. A brazier mounted atop stone tile overcame the worst of the cold.

From inside the wagon came the sounds of Eucherius teaching them a Christian hymn, but in Latin. The girls all had very nice voices.

Fortunately, I didn't have to convert to marry Tabiti. Stilicho and his harridan wife twisted a few arms to make sure no questions were asked, and then it was done, with them standing in as witnesses.

Thing is, conversion is not that big a step, if I chose to. This new Nicene Catholic Church is my old pagan church, with the old gods dumped and a new God installed, along with a bevy of saints, two other persons in their Trinity, and a holy mother with a lot better disposition than old Juno had. Why, they even call the head of it "the Supreme Pontiff," the same as our old pontifex maximus. *Then there's the incense, some of the costuming ... and I understand that a good many of the churches in Rome are just our old temples. I could do it ... if only I could believe.*

Oh, well. Nice that that Paul fellow figured out that Tabiti saves me, in case I am wrong in my reluctance.

Though there was a charcoal brazier to warm the back of the wagon, and oil lamps to light the space, Tabiti did all her cooking outside, no matter the weather. Along with her Christian studies in Ravenna, she'd spent some time in Serena's kitchen, picking up the odd bit of Italian cookery. She'd also stocked up in Ravenna on every spice common to Italian cooking, and a few less common, plus honey and several amphorae of superior grade *garum*. On tonight's menu was a honeyed pork. The recipe called for a sucking piglet but those were quite scarce at the moment. Instead, she used salt pork from the barrel strapped to the outside of the wagon, soaking it overnight to remove most of the salt.

Bread ... She didn't have an oven for proper baking of bread, so she'd made the unleavened flat bread of her own people. It was considerably softer and more palatable than, say, legionary *bucellatum*. On wine she'd splurged a bit, with freeze-distilled Falernian, likewise bought in Ravenna, with the aid of Serena's chief cook.

For some reason, though they normally ate with Caelius' family, Gisco and Eucherius were both gone, as was Privatus.

"They are eating with Theodomir's family," Tabiti explained.

"I wanted us to have the wagon to ourselves for a change, at least for a few hours."

Caelius didn't question that; early forties or not she was a nice, enthusiastic playmate in the sack. He just gave her a wry smile and an upraised eyebrow. "Horny, are we?"

She smiled back. "Maybe some of that; I'm feeling unusually frisky of late, you know. But maybe something else, too. That's for later, though. Enjoy the wine and let me get you a plate of the pork and some bread to dip in it."

Winter-distilled Falernian flew out of Caelius' nose. After he finished choking, he blurted out, "You're *what*?!"

Tabiti just nodded while wearing a mysterious smile.

"But . . . how?"

"I'm not entirely sure," she replied, "but I think you must have had something to do with it."

"Well, yes, that . . . but I mean *how*?"

"It's not common," she said. "But it's not unheard of, either. Remember, my courses never stopped. And the women of my line tend to be fertile until they're almost fifty. So, yes, that."

Caelius took a very deep draught from his cup, refilled it, swallowed that, too, repeated that, and then reclined back onto the cushions. "There are worse things in life. Though I am at an age more suited to being a grandfather than a father."

"You will be a wonderful father," Tabiti assured him. "If we have a boy, to carry on your name, you make him stand tall and straight, and teach him to fight like a man. If it's a girl, she will wrap you around her finger far more thoroughly than I ever have. And you will love every minute of it."

"We had children, Dubnia and I," said Caelius. "You knew that. And, I suppose, I must have sixteenth-generation multi-great-grandchildren somewhere around Vetera. I wish I could have spent more time with my children, but duty and the legion always called. Maybe this time I'll finally take my retirement and get to actually spend some time with my children and, with a little luck and a little more enthusiasm, theirs."

"I had children, too," Tabiti said, "two boys and a girl. My husband had died fighting the Huns. My boys fell in battle with you Romans—no, don't apologize; they had their duty and you had yours. And at least they were not led to the river to have their throats cut like cattle. My girl is..."

Caelius howled with laughter when she told him.

Classis Germanica, *Mogontiacum*

Benedictus Candidus sweated despite the cold, helping his sailors move a new *lusoria* down the slipways and into the water.

Two dozen boats again soon, thought the naval prefect. *Two dozen and we'll finally be able to do our part keeping the barbarians on their side of the Rhine.*

Outside the harbor mouth two *lusoriae,* numbers IV and XI, were now on constant patrol, their crews clad in wool and leather against the cold and the spray, though there were easily undone ties to loosen the garments for when the rowing got heavy. Benedictus was still embarrassed by the fire raid and determined that nothing like it was ever going to happen again.

And I should have been able to prevent it in the first place. Damnit.

Within the next three days, four more *lusoriae* would join the fleet. Candidus could hardly wait.

By New Year's, in this year of Our Lord, 406, which is to say in a few days, we'll have complete control over the Rhine again. And if the embassy to Ravenna can come back with a couple of skilled shipwrights for larger warships, liburnians, *or maybe even* triremes, *we'll never again lose it.*

Generally speaking, the *lusoriae* were pretty easy to row, even against the Rhine's current. This is why, when the oar of one of the oarsmen on number XI struck a piece of ice, nobody was expecting it. It threw off that oarsman, which threw off that entire bank of oars, causing the boat to turn across the current in a way the steersman wasn't expecting. He had to fight to keep the boat steady. The commander of the *lusoria* called a halt to all rowing by having the oars lifted, then gave the commands to dip them once again, and recommence their slow stroke.

The surprise caused a hubbub that, were there any around, would have warned the enemy of the boat's presence.

"What the hell was wrong with you, Gummarus?" asked the boat's commander, crossly.

"My oar hit something, Chief, something floating on the surface. Sorry."

"A piece of wood?" asked the commander.

"Could have been. Or maybe wood with a little bit of iron on it. Pretty stiff, it felt, anyway."

"Well...watch yourself, Gummarus. You could have caused the boat to capsize."

"Do my best, sir. Sorry, sir."

Vandal camp, east bank of the Rhine

King Gunderic and his son, Godigisel, departed the camp, riding their horses. They rode to the southwest until they almost reached the bank along the long loop southeast of Mogontiacum, the same loop from which the king had launched the larger of the two waves of invasion across the Rhine some weeks before. A score of mounted guards followed them, insurance against the cross-river patrols the Romans had taken to launching. The boats used for that cross-river raid were drawn up atop the bank, partly to protect them from a retaliatory Roman fire raid, and partly because some portion of that long loop, with its sluggish current, had acquired a thin layer of ice. Gunderic didn't know much about boats, but he knew a good deal about ice, and how it could split vessels if it formed inside them. *If inside, why not outside?* So, at least, had the king reasoned.

Godigisel could walk, but he found the exercise excruciating. The javelin that had skewered one of his legs during the fire raid, had done damage none of the king's healers knew how to repair. The boy never complained, but the agony could be read on his face with every other step he took. To spare him that, Gunderic elected to ride this day, and every day he took the boy out.

But it's not as if riding doesn't use the muscles in the legs. Still, he keeps his face impassive. Such a good and brave lad.

"Father?"

"Yes, son?"

"What are we going to do? We have food enough for another month and a half, at the most. The game is all hunted out in this part of Germany. The Romans certainly won't sell us any; starvation is the cheapest way they have to get rid of us. And with spring their river fleet will be back to full strength and maybe more, if the scouts reports are to be believed.

"The Romans will probably cross when their patrols tell them that we're at our weakest, that the Alans' heavy horses have all perished to lack of grain. So, should we send emissaries to try to make peace with the Huns? It would be a peace of submission, but maybe they could at least feed us."

"They'd use us for spear fodder, son, then take our women as their concubines. There's no salvation for us with the Huns."

"Then what are we going to do, Father?"

The king hung his head in despair. After a long moment he said, "I confess; I just don't know. Every choice is bad. If we had enough boats to put the entire host in the water at once and swarm ashore on the other side, I'd try that. But we don't. If I could march south through the Alps, which maybe we should have done last summer, I'd try that. But those passes are closed and will remain that way until the last of us has starved. If I thought we could turn around and beat the Huns, I'd try that, too. But we were stronger when they drove us from our lands than we are now, while the Huns are stronger now than they were then. And to the north, while we beat them with the Alans' help, the Franks bled us white *and* killed your grandfather. I'd not care to try them again."

"It's all so damned foolish, Father. The Romans, allied to us, could stop the Huns. Why won't they trust us?"

"Ultimately, because they can't. We might say we want an alliance, and to help defend their empire, but what we really want and ultimately will insist upon is our own kingdom within the empire, under our own king and laws, and paying taxes to ourselves. We don't bring enough good, and do bring enough bad, for them to even consider it."

"We could give oaths," Godigisel insisted.

"Can we bind our great-great-grandchildren by those oaths, son? Think carefully before you answer."

Now it was the son's turn to bow his head. "No, nor even my sons, when I have them."

"And the Romans know this perfectly well.

"Wait here, son," said the king. Dismounting, he walked down to the bank of the river. On the way he spotted some of the Romans' hired Huns. For reasons he wasn't quite sure of, Gunderic raised one hand and waved at the presumed Huns. Stranger, still, they waved back.

"Well, why not, then?" the king muttered. "Just because we might find ourselves trying to kill each other tomorrow is no reason not to be polite today."

The ice didn't completely cover this great loop in the river. There were patches here and there, however. Gunderic stared at the patches long and hard, then returned to his son and the horses.

"I have an idea," said the king.

Mogontiacum

Appius Calvus shivered, despite his thick *sagum* and the woolen *udones* on his feet. The streets of the town were nearly empty, the people huddled indoors against the bitter weather. On diverse corners members of the garrison stood on watch, though the odds of thugs prowling the streets were rather low, given the cold.

The wind picked up speed, too, as it forced its way down the narrow streets. Under the wind and the cold, thin water deposited by the morning's rain had frozen, huddled in depressions and the lines of the cobblestones. More than once, Calvus had barely caught himself from slipping on the ice.

In his hands, Calvus clutched a tube of rolled-up sheets of his new paper, cut to be about four and a half feet long. Finally, he found himself at the door to the church, he entered without knocking and was disappointed to find the church nearly as cold as the outside. *At least the wind doesn't rule here*, he thought.

The glass on the small windows was not enough to illuminate the church to any appreciable degree.

"Alban?" he cried, and was rewarded by the door to the priest's humble quarters opening. The priest's simple brown robe nearly filled that door.

"Ah, Appius," Alban said. "It's good to see you again. I apologize for the temperature in the church; it heats up a good deal on its own when filled with my flock. And we also splurge to fill the hearths with wood on those days, too. But I just cannot afford it on normal days. In any case, please come in."

The *haruspex* hurried to the hoped-for warmth of the smaller room. "I have it or, rather, them."

"So soon?" asked Alban. "I confess, I am pleased but shocked."

The door closed, trapping the heat inside the priest's quarters. A small fire burned on a hearth. There were small skin-covered windows here, too, but Alban also had a number of lamps burning. It was enough to read by.

"And is that it?" Alban asked.

"It's a part of it," answered Calvus, "the first page. Setting the type is so time consuming that I printed off only that, enough to show proof of concept."

Hurriedly, Alban cleared away everything that had sat on the table: two scrolls, one lamp, a plate with some crumbs on it, and a half-filled cup. "Here, here, let me see!"

Calvus set down the tube of sheets of paper, released his grip, and let them unroll across the table. "Sixty-three copies of the first page of your book of Genesis."

Alban bent to look, his eyes glancing from one page to another. He lifted half the sheets to look at copies further down in the stack, then did the same to look at the very bottom page. He went from one to the other, his lips moving as he read, "*In principio creavit Deus cælum, et terram. Terra autem erat inanis et vacua, et tenebræ erant super faciem abyssi: et Spiritus Dei ferebatur super aquas. Dixitque Deus: Fiat lux. Et facta est lux. Et vidit Deus lucem quod esset bona: et divisit lucem a tenebris.*

"My God!" exclaimed the priest. "You did it, my pagan friend. It *works*. It's all the same, all easy to read, and all perfect. No scribal idiosyncrasies. No spelling errors..."

"Well, there is one I caught too late," Calvus admitted, "but only one. Look on the right middle, seventeen lines down."

"No, matter, better proofreading can fix that sort of thing. And we're going to need to find something for the scribes you've unemployed."

"So you will send it to the head of your church?" asked Calvus.

"Gleefully. May I have these to send, the entire sheaf?"

"Of course."

"Innocentius, the pope, is a highly capable man," said Alban. "He's only been pope for about five years, but in that time has done some marvels on behalf of the Church and the faith. I think he'll jump on this."

"And funding?" asked Calvus.

"Well, how, then, do you want to proceed? I can see a couple of ways. Were you also Catholic, I'd suggest a cost-plus basis, where you print, say, two hundred copies of each book of the

Bible and submit an invoice for your materials and workers and about ten percent for your effort and your invention..."

"Not mine, actually. I got the idea from someone who, I suppose, will never exist in this world, who would have lived in a place called 'Mainz,' wherever that is."

"God let you have the insight. He likely wants you to have the credit, as well."

Calvus shrugged. "If you say so."

"Another way, since you are a pagan, would be for you to get permission from the Church, and sell the copies directly to both clergy and laypersons. I think you could charge maybe as much as a solidus apiece for them."

"Is it necessary to become a Catholic to do the cost-plus system?"

"Maybe not. I can ask. Who knows? The Church is a financial organization, too; maybe one of the clerks will have a better idea."

"So," said Calvus, "these are yours. Also, printing these pretty much cleaned out the advance on my salary I talked the legate out of, plus the donations I was given, so..."

"I will ask for a grant for these, then, and for the Church to hire you on, on a cost-plus basis, to make at least two hundred copies, though I shall push for ten times as many. These"—Alban indicated the sheaf—"leave tonight."

"Excellent. Alban...I see dark days ahead for the Empire. Whether it was my—take your pick—visions or my travels, it was all bad news. From about now on."

"And you see," said the priest, "in contrast to that, I see bright things ahead. Over half your legion has converted, maybe as many as six in ten, and the rest are wavering. Their soldierly ability..."

"It is very high," interjected the *haruspex*.

"So I gather. Their ability as soldiers coupled to the true faith? I see a renewal and resurgence for the Empire and civilization such as we've never had before, even counting the crises of the third century. Speaking of which, since this coming Sunday is the last day of the year of our Lord, 406, your legate, at the insistent nagging of his lovely wife, has agreed to let me hold services for those of the legion who have converted, and their women, in the forum of the base. You should come and listen, for you, I sense, are of a good heart and might find something of value in it."

"I shall try, then."

Via Ausonius, ten miles north-northwest of Cruciniacum

There was a town nearby, with a road driven through the middle of it. Marcus Caelius, sitting atop his horse, didn't know the name of the place, and wasn't curious enough to find out.

Well, he thought, *it's really more of an* oppidum. *It's got something of that Celtic look about it, too.*

This close to Mogoniacum, he dispatched a Gaul to ride to the legionary base there and inform Gaius Pompeius of his approach, their numbers, and, *So it's on you, good legate, to figure out where we're going to put all these people. Oh, and they'll need rations for an initial three months, to boot.*

It was the promise of food for the Goths that had kept them pressing on. The roads, especially the good, metaled Roman roads, were so icebound, where not covered with fresh snow, that the horses had terrible trouble surmounting any hills encountered. It had frequently been necessary to use three teams, two of them off the road, to get a single wagon up the slope. In those cases, anything that could be done easily to lighten the load was done. Gothic women and Gothic children generally walked ahead while their wagons were being moved up the slopes.

And that takes a lot more than three times as much time. More like six or eight times longer, sometimes more. That's the price we pay, with our Roman roads. For saving material and saving labor by going as straight as an arrow, we sometimes lose time.

Caelius was pretty sure they'd not make much more progress before the sun went down.

"Theodomir?" he said.

"Here, Marcus."

"Send messengers. We'll laager where we are and continue tomorrow."

"Sound, I think. I'll take care of it."

Vandal camp, southeast of Mogontiacum

Godigisel rode into the camp breathlessly. He spurred his horse to race to his father's compound. Arriving, he flung himself off his horse, shouting, "Father! Father! It's happened."

"Slow down, son. You mean the river has frozen over?"

"Yes, Father, oh, yes, yes, yes! Your armsman, Oamer, got on his belly and slid out halfway, then came back."

"On his belly, you say? He didn't walk out?"

"Ummm . . . no, Father, he slid."

"Then we can't know if the ice will hold a standing man, let alone thirty thousand of them."

The boy looked crestfallen.

"No, no, son, cheer up; this is still good news. At this point, if we can't walk on it, it's time to chop some holes in the ice, pull up water, and pour it over the ice that already is in order to strengthen it. We begin tonight, right after moonset."

Ishkapaius lay upon his belly on the frozen ground overlooking the stream. He'd left the rest of his *turma* back a quarter of a mile, then come forward alone and on foot. The lack of a moon had helped him get to his listening post unobserved.

There was something going on below, or maybe several somethings. Occasionally he could hear Germanic voices, from his front, left, and right, all three. They never shouted . . . well, almost never; once he'd heard someone who seemed to be drowning. At least there was a distinct shout, the sound of splashing, some sounds of consternation, and then nothing. But, drowning or not, some numbers of them were doing something down there.

And I don't like it a bit. So push forward a little to maybe see better and take the chance of being caught or go back, find Centurion Vorenus, and report my suspicions? In this case, I think it's better to let him know that the barbarians are busy.

Carefully, the Scythian boy wriggled backward, snakelike, then, at some greater distance from the stream and when out of the concealing bushes, arose to a crouch and sought out his horse. He soothed the horse with his voice and a stroking hand, before mounting as quietly as humanly possible. Then, using his knees a good deal more than the reins, he directed his horse back to where his patrol waited.

"Something, yes, Centurion, but I don't know what," the boy reported. "Never really heard anything like it before. I was tempted to try to get closer, but I figured we were better off with you knowing that something seemed up, than with me knowing exactly what and getting caught."

Vorenus seemed tired, as one would expect of a man just awakened from a sound sleep. Even so, he was able to answer, "No, you did right, Ish. I'm going to send messengers to thin out the cavalry screen to one *turma* per maniple, and for the rest to assemble here. I want you and your *turma* to do the same thing north of here, then report to the legate and give him your suspicions. Then get back here. If there's to be a fight, I want you in on it."

"Sir," said the boy. "I'm on my way."

The king was one of the first men over; only a small guard of about one hundred and twenty men preceded him, and they didn't precede him by much.

In the darkness of the now moonless night, groups of Vandals and Suebi were led to the river's edge by guides. Once there, there were ropes laid along the ice to keep them on the generally right track. Initially, they went over in a marching mass. This caused the ice underfoot to creak ominously, so the command was given that some of them had learned in Roman service, "Route step, MARCH." At that point they got out of step and simply sauntered across, almost as if they were not warriors. Still, the ice creaked ominously. Word went back to spread out more. This helped.

Horses, except for the Alans' heavies, a much riskier proposition here on the ice, would come over after all the foot had crossed.

There were two reinforced routes, each, for the Vandals and Suebi. Two additional routes had been extra strongly reinforced with water for the very light Suebi and Vandal horse. The Alan king, Respendial, however, had refused to even consider bringing his heavy horse, at nearly a ton each in their armor, across on the bare ice.

Thus, Gunderic had directed that half a dozen raftlike sleds be constructed of split logs. The Alans' enormous, heavy, and heavily armored horses were brought across on these, a half dozen at a time, the rafts being pulled by teams of Vandals detailed to the purpose. Their heavily armored riders walked across beside the rafts, then took charge of their horses on the far bank. Each crossing took about fifteen or twenty minutes, meaning that the Alan heavy cavalry assembled on the other side at the rate of about eighteen to twenty men per hour. There was zero chance that all the heavies would get across by morning. Great good luck might see a tenth of that number across.

For the much lighter Vandal and Suebi horse, as well as the Alan light cavalry, they were simply walked across by their riders.

Legionary base, Mogontiacum

In all, what with the legionaries, the auxiliaries, and the nearly one-for-one representation of Scythian women, it was standing room only inside the forum of the legionary base. The children had been left behind with some of the other women because it was going to be hard enough to hear Father Alban as it was. All were bundled against the cold, which still poured down from the north on frozen wings of wind.

A very large cross had been erected, perhaps the first time in history that a Christian crucifix had been erected by men who had actually conducted a crucifixion. Most of them managed to keep their mouths shut over the issue, that it wasn't actually *done* that way.

Gaius Pompeius and Zaranaia stood very close to the platform for the priest. Gaius was not yet a convert, and knew better than to take communion, but he was willing to hear and to learn. Indeed, a good many of those gathered were not yet Christians but had come to placate their Christian women and maybe, just maybe, to convert, themselves, if they liked what they heard.

Prayers were said, some by the father alone and some by all the Christians present. Those, however, came after Father Alban had told not one but three jokes, all centered on elephants. There were also two readings from the Gospels, neither of them very long. Finally, it came time to bless the Eucharist. Actually dispensing it, individually, was obviously going to be impossible; one priest to administer perhaps ten or eleven thousand servings of the host was going to take days, not minutes or even hours.

I wish I could convert Calvus and then educate him and about a hundred other men of the legion, thought Alban. *Among other reasons for this, that we could turn them into deacons and then have a chance of administering the Eucharist in some kind of timely fashion. Lord, help this good to come to pass, please.*

Thus, Alban could not hope to give the Eucharist to each

man. Instead, he would do it only for himself until the deacon problem was solved.

While the priest was preparing the bread and wine, a teenaged boy, his eyes hard and fierce beyond his years, wound his way through the throng to the side of Gaius Pompeius opposite Zaranaia. The legate bent to hear what the boy had to say, then nodded and returned his attention to the priest. Half an hour later, another boy likewise came to the legate. At this the legate's eyes grew wide. He climbed the platform and spoke a few words to Alban.

Alban nodded, then rapidly finished his communion, taken on behalf of them all. The priest then stepped into the background.

Gaius stepped forth and announced, "The enemy are across the Rhine in vast numbers, ten miles south of here. When I release you, the legion is to be ready to ride to the south within the hour. Priest? Your blessings on the men?"

Heart pounding at the grim news, Alban again stepped forward. "You go forth to do battle not only for the Empire, but for the holy Catholic faith. Fear not, you will win; the Lord who called you forth from destruction four centuries ago is with you now. He didn't bring you here for no reason, but to save Rome and the faith. Neither should you fear death, for should you fall in defense of the faith, your soul will be translated straight to Heaven. Your families, for those who have them, will be cared for by the church and the legion."

At this, Alban made a sign of the cross with his hands, blessing the congregation and perhaps even those who might someday become members. He turned to Gaius and said, "Legate, they are yours."

"Men of the Eighteenth Legion: in one hour we ride."

INTERLUDE

Londinium, Britannia 406 A.D.

Bonitus purchased a jug of the best wine in the place, then went over and introduced himself to Constantine, requesting a private conversation. He led the soldier over to an empty table, distant enough from the roaring fire to keep from roasting alive.

"So, you are the clever man," said Bonitus, "who engineered getting the previous 'emperor,' Marcus, raised to the purple, and then arranged for Gratianus to replace the failed Marcus."

Bonitus was tactful enough to say "replaced" rather than "murdered."

"I don't know what you're talking about, friend," said Constantine. "The troops themselves raised Marcus, with no connivance from me, and then replaced him, because Marcus was too stupid and ignorant, both, to pay them. I'm just a simple soldier, and no party to these connivances."

"Yes, of course," said Bonitus, drily, leaving no doubt that he didn't believe of a word of Constantine's denial. "And how is Gratianus doing, then, with paying the troops?"

"Oh, he's paying them," said Constantine. "Paying them something, that is, with the promise of something more 'soon.' But that goes to the other problem: a fair bureaucrat Gratianus may be, but he's no soldier at all. The bloody barbarians are raiding us from every side except the one facing Gaul—Picts from the north, Saxons from the east, and Hibernians from the west.

463

"We used to be able to deal with them, and hurt the bastards badly enough for their temerity that few were willing to
risk it. But since that son of a bitch Stilicho dragged off most
of the troops, and failed to pay the rest, leading to a good deal
of desertion, we've been like a girl with her legs pried apart."

"So, when," asked Bonitus, "are the troops, in their righteous
anger, going to get rid of Gratianus?"

Constantine shrugged. "Hard to say, really. I gather that there's
a very large army of barbarians on the other side of the Rhine,
threatening to break into Gaul any day. If that happens, and even
the south of Britannia is opened up to raid, rape, and plunder,
then I would suggest that Gratianus' days would be numbered."

Bonitus read this to mean *I like having Gratianus on hand to
take the fall if the Empire reasserts itself, but if the Empire loses
Gaul, hence is in no position to punish Gratianus or myself, then
I will get rid of the incompetent son of a bitch and get myself
declared emperor.*

"Yes," said Bonitus, soothingly, "the people I represent, a
consortium of influential senators, suggested something like that
might happen. They will be most pleased to learn that there is an
astute and competent man here ready to take over from Gratianus,
at need. And that that man's name is Constantine."

"But what will you do if the barbarians don't get over the
Rhine and Gaul doesn't fall?"

"Exactly what I am doing now," answered Constantine. "Giving the civil authority—which I in no way had anything to do
with raising to the purple—the best advice I can, the better to
preserve this important piece of property for the true emperor."

"Most wise," agreed Bonitus. "Just out of curiosity, what would
it cost this consortium which I represent to get someone to get
rid of Gratianus anyway, and assume the purple himself?"

"Since I am certain no one is stupid enough to bare his neck
for the headsman in just this fashion *unless* Gaul is overrun,
there is no price great enough. However, if Gaul does fall, I won't
say that a few hundred talents of silver wouldn't go a long way
toward insuring that Britannia is retained and, who knows, even
Gaul recaptured. After that? Well, none can say.

"But it's funny, you know, how often people from Britannia
named Constantine tend to take over the Empire."

CHAPTER
TWENTY-ONE

Even Suetonius, in this critical moment, broke silence.
In spite of his reliance on the courage of the men, he
still blended exhortations and entreaty: "They must
treat with contempt the noise and empty menaces of
the barbarians: in the ranks opposite, more women
than soldiers meet the eye. Unwarlike and unarmed,
they would break immediately, when, taught by so
many defeats, they recognized once more the steel and
the valor of their conquerors. Even in a number of
legions, it was but a few men who decided the fate of
battles; and it would be an additional glory that they,
a handful of troops, were gathering the laurels of an
entire army. Only, keeping their order close, and, when
their javelins were discharged, employing shield-boss
and sword, let them steadily pile up the dead and forget
the thought of plunder: once the victory was gained, all
would be their own."

—Tacitus, *The Annals*, XIV, 36

Legionary base, Mogontiacum, 406 A.D.

The terrain model had long been set up in the *Praetorium*, updated
and improved daily for the last several months as new patrols
and survey teams brought in updated data.

Gaius Pompeius considered the terrain. *First and foremost is the Rhine, itself. Keep my left flank to it and that flank, at least, cannot be turned, because the Rhine hasn't frozen this far north.*

However, snuggle up to the Rhine and my right flank, even with the Palmyrene cavalry riding hard to reach us, and even with the German foederati, *the Gauls and whatever of the Scythian boys may survive their delaying action . . . even with all those my right flank may end up hanging in thin air.*

And that's another problem: attack or defend? It may be that, if I move south, I can meet the Vandals before they've had their entire force over, and smash them in detail. But that depends on which road they take or, indeed, whether they come cross-country. If I move south along the Rhine road, and they move west before moving north, we might miss each other and see them inside the town and at the granary before I know it. There's the very same kind of problem if I move to the west; they may come up the Rhine road to the same purpose and the same end. Except that then I've got both my flanks in the air, rather than just one.

The only place I can be fairly sure they're coming so that I cannot miss them is just about here.

But here it is possible that largish groups of them, big enough to take a large number of my cavalry to safely head off and delay while the rest of us catch up, would plunge into Gaul and ruin large swaths of it before we can destroy them.

And let's not pretend that those are the only options they have, either. They're a large army, probably about two and a half times the size of mine. They could split and the Vandals come up the Rhine road while the Suebi cut west, then north, the Alan cavalry in the middle to prevent us from separating them and defeating them in detail.

Can I use the cavalry—do I have enough of it—to more or less herd them toward me? No . . . no, I really don't. The initiative here is theirs and I'd be a fool not to recognize it.

So, how do I get it back? Maybe make a threatening move I'm not actually serious about. We're, all but the foederati, *mounted until we dismount for battle, but the legion has only a horse per man at this point and some spares. I don't want to wear out their horses before I have to. Only the cavalry has a string of horses per man, so it won't be worn out by making threatening gestures.*

Gaius' thoughts were interrupted by a knock on the open door to the command conference room. He looked up to see Tadmor, the prefect of the Palmyrene horse archers.

"Half my men are here with me," said the Palmyrene. "The others will be here within the hour. Where do you want us?"

Before Gaius could answer, the first spear walked through the open door. "The legion and the two cohorts of foot auxiliaries are ready to ride at your order, sir," Metilius announced. "Twelfth Cohort is packing their staff slings and fifty projectiles per man. The *foederati* are likewise ready to move—though, of course, on foot."

"Top, move the legion five miles due south." This would place them in the open, west of a north-northeast to south-southwest running ridge. He indicated the ridge with his right index finger. "I'll meet you and the legion in a bit."

"Sir." Metilius saluted, turned, and marched out. Already his facial scar was beginning to redden.

Gaius pointed to the northeast-southwest running ridge, southeast of the town. "Rubelius, you're in charge of the *foederati*. Bring them to take position along this ridge, facing to the southeast. Nothing fancy; simple shield wall on the high ground."

"Tadmor?"

"Sir?"

"If you wanted someone to go somewhere, would you herd them or bait them?"

The Palmyrene considered the question, then answered, "It depends. If they are many and strong you cannot herd them, hence must bait them. Only if they are relatively few and weak can you herd them."

"Very good. What I want you to do, then, is bait the enemy to come as directly north as possible towards Mogontiacum."

"Sir. I'll start south then, now, with half my *ala*. The others will catch up before it's too late."

"Again, very good. Go."

I wish Marcus Caelius were here to advise me, thought Gaius. *Metilius is good, of course, but it's not the same. Speaking of which . . .*

"Tribune Marianus?"

"Sir?" said Gnaeus Marianus.

"Get a half dozen guards for yourself from among the Gallic horse. Ride west. Find the *praefectus castrorum*. Tell him to hurry his Goths along, to leave the wagons behind in some defensible location with a minimal guard and force march every remaining man here. Tell him, additionally, that if the Vandals and their allies force us back to the defense of Mogontiacum I want him to hit them in their rear, but if they don't then I want the infantry to form up on our right to outflank the barbarians and their cavalry to report to me."

"On my way, sir." The officer hurried off at a canter, picking up those half dozen guards from Atrixtos on the way.

And hurry, Marcus.

A few prisoners taken in cross-river raids and then *vigorously* interrogated had seen Gunderic kept reasonably well informed of the forces opposite him. Oddly, none of them knew of any Huns in Roman employ up here along the Rhine, though there were rumors of the Roman general, Stilicho, keeping some on retainer down south in Italy.

So I don't know about those Huns we saw. Maybe Stilicho sent some north.

Gunderic stood on the riverbank between the ice path created for his own people and the cross-river sledding point made for the Alan cavalry, altogether too few of which had managed to make the crossing. This hadn't been helped a bit by the ice having cracked under one raft, sending both the footbound rider and his oversized, overarmored horse through the ice to their deaths.

Maybe two hundred of those ironheads on this side. Maybe. Well... best we can do; it's time to march. Maybe they'll get another hundred over now that it's daylight.

Ahead, to the west, the Vandal host was forming up under Gunderic's sons and the clans' own chieftains. Godigisel, though his father had tried to talk him out of it, had come across the agonizing three fourths of a mile of the ice road dismounted and leading his own horse.

Gunderic rode to where the columns that would form line of battle were waiting for the order to advance. They stretched between the shoulders of the Rhine loop, covering the two miles with Vandal infantry on the right, or north, Suebi infantry on the left, or south, and the Alans in the middle and behind, themselves flanked by the Vandal and Suebi cavalry.

At least twenty-two thousand of us here and a few thousand more still ready to cross. It's a risk, leaving only the rest of the

Alan heavies and maybe a thousand infantry to guard our laager, but it's a risk we have to take.

The king took a single look behind—the sun was up now—at the last groups crossing over and then rode east to the line of columns.

Those Huns were there, trading shots with the German skirmishers. The Huns seemed to be having the better of it. Indeed, the skirmishers mostly tried to stay behind their shields rather than risk the apparently certain and miserable death from even a light wound from one of their accursed arrows. Still, they were doing their duty, keeping those wicked little horse archers from getting close enough to the columns of lightly or unarmored infantry.

And that's the most I can expect of them, under the circumstances. I wonder if those little bastards realize they're doing me a service, keeping the Suebi—some of them, anyway—from striking off on their own until I can coax them into doing what I want done.

Gunderic posted himself in front of the cavalry. Pointing at the horse archers harassing his skirmishers he shouted, "Kill them!"

At a gallop, kicking up snow and even clods of frozen earth, the Germanic cavalry, but not the Alans, charged through the gaps between the groups of Vandals and Suebi, causing the horse archers to turn about and gallop off.

Then the king, himself, rode to the fore. He spread his arms and turned to the north. Immediately, the Suebi on the left began to march forward.

Atop his galloping steed, Vorenus turned in the saddle, risking a look behind. *Yes, the barbarian horse are keeping after us. I'm not worried about getting caught by them; we have plenty of spares and they don't.*

Around the centurion a swarm of the Scythian boys likewise sped to the west. They were all smiling or laughing, giving the distinct impression that they were having the time of their lives.

Don't they realize, wondered Vorenus, *that some of their friends were killed and wounded back there? Was I ever that young?*

Again Vorenus risked a look behind. *Ha! They're turning around and going back.*

"Turn around, boys, turn around! *Cornicines,* sound 'turn about.' Time to hit these fuckers in the ass."

Whooping, the Scythian boys turned about and began to close on the retreating barbarian horse. Soon bowstrings were twanging again, while arrows whistled through the air.

Realizing they couldn't continue to retreat a moment before the Huns were destroyed, again the barbarian cavalry turned west and charged, though this time they charged more slowly.

Vorenus gave the signal, which was echoed by a *cornicen*, to retreat. Again, the galloping boys easily outpaced the barbarian cavalry.

About four hundred of us, thought Vorenus, *and we're keeping four or five times that in barbarian cavalry out of play. I call that pretty nice work, if you can get it.*

If you tell Metilius to move three miles south and deploy, thought Gaius, *I can guarantee you that the men will dismount within twenty feet of three miles.*

Around and ahead of the legate, the legion was dismounting and forming up in a modified *acies triplex*. Four cohorts formed up in front, leaving spaces of cohort width between them. Behind those, five cohorts covered the gaps at some distance behind, or extended out to the flanks. In the third line two more cohorts covered the gaps between the outermost pairs of cohorts in the second line. The Twelfth Cohort plus the Rhodian-Thracian cohort of *auxilia* advanced past the first line in mixed groups of maniples and centuries. It would be their job to keep the enemy skirmishers back to a distance from which they could not annoy or tire the legion. The dozen pieces of light field artillery, the scorpions, were lined up near the center, at the rear.

The horse holders had taken the string of horses of their *contubernia* and assembled behind the second line, in the gaps left uncovered, but extending back for about five hundred feet.

Funny, thought Gaius, *though some of them are blind and most tend to be somewhat old, they* look *like a huge mass of cavalry.*

Gaius looked left. The *foederati* were not able to keep pace with the legion. Even if they'd been the legion's equals for disciplined marching, which they were not, they lacked horses. On the other hand, they did have the Rhine road to march upon, while the legion had been riding across a good deal of broken ground, so the *foederati* hadn't been *that* far behind in their progress.

Gaius looked left and saw them spreading out by the large

cohorts they called "legions" and moving to take up position on the military crest on the other side of the long ridge.

The legion's own cohort of German *auxilia* likewise mounted the ridge and disappeared over the crest. They could not bridge the gap between the legion and the *foederati*, no, but they could buy some time if the Vandals and their allies tried to punch through at the seams between the groups.

The final unit, the Gallic cavalry under Atrixtos, was held well back, behind some high ground between the legion and Mogontiacum. Gaius had a glimmering of an idea of what to do with them, but wasn't sure it would work. He also wasn't sure if he liked the idea on strictly moral grounds.

Which doesn't mean I won't order it, just that I won't like it if I do.

Satisfied that the first spear had the legion well in hand, Gaius pulled on his horse's reins to turn it to the left, then spurred it to a canter to join the German *auxilia*, the people with the best view to the south. A group of guards followed him.

"I *love* my job," exulted Tadmor, the prefect of the *ala* of Palmyrene horse archers.

The duties of a prefect of horse archers were somewhat limited. He set the direction. He gave initial orders. But once the *turmae* had closed to archery range, he generally kept back, accompanied by a couple of *cornicines* and a handful of guards, watching out for the time to sound recall or one of the few other general orders the *turmae* needed.

Tadmor's Palmyrenes, now with all of their *turmae* present on the field, were doing a fine job of maddening the Vandals and Suebi, though the Alans remained out of range.

I'm worried about those bastards, thought Tadmor. *Their heavies have no chance of catching us. Neither do the Vandals or Suebi, on their wretched excuses for horses. But the light Alan cav? They worry me.*

Maddening the enemy, as Tadmor had alluded to, to the legate, was largely a function of riding in, loosing a few arrows, inflicting some damage, hopefully, but some fear and anger, at a minimum, and then riding out again without being hurt. This would eventually piss off the enemy to the point where orders and discipline were largely forgotten, and they had only one thing on their mind, *revenge.*

And when they want nothing so much as revenge, they'll follow you to the ends of the Earth. That, or, as in this case, when they run into the wall of the legions.

Out in front, the *turmae* kept several hundred feet from the barbarians. Some rode in what is called a Cantabrian circle, though it was more like a Cantabrian narrow oval, wherein the cavalry rode around a given point on the ground, loosing their arrows at the point nearest their enemy, then riding out again while they nocked fresh arrows. This approach had several advantages, including but not limited to keeping the time of exposure to danger short, hence keeping up courage and morale, and presenting a very dispersed, moving target to any missile troops on the other side. It was especially useful against columns and lines of infantry.

On the other hand, it wears out the horses. Fortunately for us, that doesn't matter because we have lots of spares courtesy of the late Scythians.

Not that the Palmyrenes were invulnerable; in Tadmor's view several men had fallen and still more rode or were led away to get them to medical attention. It didn't worry him overmuch since: *We're hurting them a lot more than they're hurting us and, even were we not, we're still leading them toward the legion, while inflicting on them a good deal of disorder.*

West of Mogontiacum

Marcus had the Gothic cavalry and half the infantry, a total of about thirty-five hundred men, forming up in column on the road. Meanwhile, the families were circling the wagons but differently than they had in the first part of the journey.

"Are you sure about leaving half the infantry here, sir?" asked Privatus. The freedman sounded very dubious.

"Gaius Pompeius said 'minimal guard.' Well, what's a minimal guard for the families of unwashed barbarians—all right, that's not fair, the Goths are quite clean. But in any case, what's a minimal guard for them and what's a minimal guard for my wife, my *pregnant* wife, are two very different things.

"So, half the Gothic foot and a handful of cavalry stay right here. Fortunately, the number of food animals is at a low level, so the wagons can be formed into concentric circles. Otherwise, the numbers of men I could afford to leave would be totally inadequate to needs . . . especially with Alan cavalry possibly running loose. What the Hades; I can always tell him that the Goths wouldn't have come at all without adequate security being left for their families. Might even be true; I wouldn't want to stretch my authority until it breaks trying to find out, now, would I?"

"I suppose not, sir." Privatus still sounded very dubious.

"Plus, we're taking the youngest half and the cavalry. The older men would just slow us down."

"That *is* a superior excuse, sir."

"I'm very glad you think so, Privatus."

"*Praefectus Castrorum?*" It was a young man's voice, not quite finished changing. The sound of it filled Caelius with dread, which redoubled when he looked up to see a horse-borne, armored Eucherius, hanging a sword-bearing baldric over his right shoulder.

Oh, shit. Think quick, Caelius! You cannot risk this boy.

"Ah, Eucherius. Excellent! I was just about to send for you. I have a job, a job I wouldn't trust anyone else with."

"Yes, Prefect?"

"The battle rising to our east is right now formless. I have no idea what is happening there and I don't like that ignorance. I'm leaving Theodomir here with a handful of cavalry and half the infantry to guard the families, but the Goths are an argumentative and difficult lot. The Roman state has hired them, though, and if they won't listen to Theodomir they ought to listen to their paymasters. That's where you come in."

"Sir?"

"I want you to take command. Don't try to take control from Theodomir, just be there as the representative of the state, to back him up with the threat of withholding salaries."

"But I . . ." Eucherius hung his head.

"Yes, I know," said Caelius. "I even approve of your motives. But I need someone here I can trust to watch my wife and our unborn child. Can you name me someone better for that than yourself?"

Eucherius straightened. His face took on a determined look. "I'll do my best, Prefect."

"I know you will, son. I'm counting on it. Now go find Theodomir and tell him what I told you."

"That he's in charge and I am backup as the representative of the Roman state," Eucherius parroted.

"Exactly. Now do me a favor, would you?"

"Sir?"

"Before you see Theodomir, go find my wife and let her know what's going on."

The boy's face brightened up considerably, leaving Caelius to assume, *Aha! Gailawera is visiting my wife.* Eucherius turned and galloped off.

"That was well done, sir," said Privatus.

"I should hope so. Now get on your horse and find Theodomir, and quickly. Let him know exactly what transpired here. Please impress on him the need to flatter the boy, so he doesn't do something stupid."

South of Mogontiacum

Thancrat saw the legate and his party riding up. Nonetheless, he finished deploying his oversized cohort before turning matters over to his executive and reporting to Gaius Pompeius. There were gaps between each of the German *auxilia's* five maniples and still larger gaps between his flanks, the legion, and the pseudo-legions of German *foederati*. The men made themselves busy preparing to toss huge numbers of caltrops to their front and into the gaps. The caltrops sat in wooden boxes, for the nonce.

"Bad position I've put you in," said Gaius Pompeius.

"Might be, but equally might not. Men are not uniformly stupid so not many will be willing to risk getting between those gaps and being assailed by missiles from both flanks. Less still willing to be cut off. The way I see it, sir, I am a threat as much as a force.

"Now, if they do try to come through here, where my cohort stands, in large numbers, then I am so fucked we're going to have to come up with a new word; the cohort will have worn the old word out."

"How's morale?" asked Gaius.

"Actually pretty good. This cohort, while German, is unrelated to either the Vandals or the Suebi, and doesn't care much for either. We don't really even speak anything much resembling the same language anymore. The boys have been bored, too, with only one good fight since Varus. And having their terms of service commuted to match those of citizen legionaries, their pay matched, too, and becoming full-fledged citizens have given all of them a rosier outlook, in general.

"Then, too, we lost patrols on the other side and they're looking for a little revenge."

Thancrat stopped speaking for a moment, as if weighing his words carefully. "You've got a problem, though. In a little while, when the Palmyrenes succeed in leading the barbarians here, they're going to stop out of missile range. Then the *barritus* is going to start. It's a form of mental warfare, sir, as I am certain you've already figured out."

Gaius nodded.

"Well... it's mostly a volume thing. Volume measures morale. But it's also a sheer numbers thing. And, I'll tell you, twelve or fifteen thousand Vandals, or however many there really are, are a much bigger number than five or so thousand—what's that word they use now? *Foederati?*—right, five thousand *foederati*. And what *that* means is that the *foederati* will probably take to their heels when the Vandals get too close. Just the way it is."

"I see." And Gaius actually did see; the German was telling him his left flank was almost certain to collapse, and soon.

"Suggestions?" the legate asked.

"Two of them," Thancrat said. "One is move, oh, let's call it two cohorts of infantry up behind the *foederati* at the first sign the Vandals are going that way."

"As battlefield police and desertion control? Yes, I could see that. And the other?"

"Attack. Attack before the *barritus* can overwhelm the Germans to my left."

"How close will they come before they start the *barritus*?" the legate asked.

"Hard to say. Few hundred feet, maybe."

"I'm going to take part of your advice, then," said Gaius. "I'm going to move half the scorpions, plus a century each of archers and slingers, up here with you with orders to engage the barbarians the second they start their *barritus*. I'm also going to send Twelfth Cohort up behind the *foederati*. They can fuck with the *barritus*, hurt the barbarians on that side, and act as battlefield police."

"Going to leave you desperately short of missile troops on that flank," said Thancrat.

"I'll recycle the Palmyrene horse archers over to the right flank," said Gaius. "We'll be fine."

Gunderic cursed. "Of fucking *course* they have to take the bait. I need my damned light cavalry back."

Again, for the third time, he sent off a messenger to try to recall his light cavalry. This time he changed his message from "Break off and return" to "Tell him to split his force; send me half and keep half to dance with those Huns."

With a brisk nod, the messenger raced off on horseback.

An Alan rode up, the armor of his horse and his own making a terrible racket.

"Goar," said the king, in greeting, once the Alan had lifted the steel mask covering his face. The Alan lacked a beard, but had a rather expansive moustache.

"It will cost us some," said Goar, "but I think we need to pay that price to drive off those horse archers."

"Are you and your people willing to pay it?" asked Gunderic.

"You see me here, do you not?"

"Yes, and I thank you for that. The problem, though, is that almost all order is broken in the front and will not be reestablished until they see something that frightens them as much as those cavalry anger them. There's no way for you to get through without running down my men and the Suebi."

"Hmmm…maybe not," Goar agreed. "Tell you what, though: the Romans will not know that. We'll charge and stop short. If the Romans think we're coming through over the bodies of your men, maybe they'll bolt. That will give your clan chiefs a chance to reestablish order. That done, we can stay right behind them and dare the horse archers to keep it up."

"Let it be so," said the king.

"I will move up with everything I am allowed to take, heavy and light, both. Only one thing bothers me."

"What is that?" asked the king.

"All of those horse archers have a number of remounts. We have few, after all our travails, plus the lack of fodder in Germany. They can outlast us if this lasts a while."

"I know. I also know that we're already committed to an attack along these lines. If I try to wheel around to try to take the Romans in flank they'll see *my* exposed flank and attack. So those horse archers have probably done most of the work they were hired to do."

Tadmor saw the Alans' charge and also caught the hint of some of the enemy cavalry dancing with the Scythian boys returning to the enemy's main body.

"I don't know what they intend, but this is a little too chancy," he said, then told his *cornicines,* "Sound the recall."

The *cornicines* raised their horns and blared out the signal. The leaders of the *turmae* broke off their Cantabrian circles and began to lead their men northward at the gallop. Once Tadmor was sure they were all obeying—always an iffy question with every kind of cavalry; the whole breed was noted for pigheadedness—he turned his mount about and, followed by the *cornicines,* began to trot for the westernmost point of the Romans he could see, whom, from their shield markings, he made out to be the German light infantry *auxilia.*

Upon closer approach he saw the legate standing on his own two feet, one of his men holding his horse, and chatting with Maeonius, one of the senior decurions in Tadmor's command.

The Palmyrenes, quite properly, slowed their horses to a walk to pass lines, lest the infantry get the wrong idea. Tadmor and his little command party did likewise, passing through to the cheers of the infantry, rather than the sounds of panic.

Tadmor rode to Gaius Pompeius and likewise dismounted.

"Legate," he said.

"The was all well done, Prefect," said Gaius. "Your job isn't over, however." He indicated the centuries of archers and slingers moving to take up position on the right of the German light infantry, and then the Twelfth Cohort, staff slings over their shoulders, double-timing to get in behind the *foederati.* Down in the low ground, the scorpion crews were lashing their horses to a frenzy to get up the ridge. The lashing the horses received, however, was as nothing compared to the tongue-lashing administered to the crews by Quintus Junius Fulvius to keep them moving.

Said Gaius, "I want your men to rearm with arrows, then to go take up a supporting position on the right flank of the legion."

"Consider it done," answered the Palmyrene.

"Are your people all through?" asked Thancrat of the Palmyrene prefect.

"Yes."

"Great." Thancrat raised his voice to address the entire cohort. "Boys, start scattering the caltrops to your front and into the gaps."

From boxes at their feet, the German *auxilia* began to pull out four-pointed iron stars, by the thousands. These they flung as far forward as they could, up to about one hundred and twenty or even thirty feet in some cases, and densely enough to have a better than fair chance of taking out a horse by impaling one of their hooves. Others flung still more to fill in the gaps in the line.

West of Mogontiacum

In war, though Marcus Caelius, *everything takes twice as long and is twice as hard.*

The problem was that Caelius couldn't just go charging off with the cavalry. Neither could the infantry do without scouting. After all, who knew what parties of the barbarians had peeled off to ravage Gaul, who wouldn't mind a minor diversion to fight Goths and Romans. Hence, the cavalry had to move at the speed of the infantry, operationally, while tactically hurrying from place to place to scout out potential ambush positions or other clusters of rampaging barbarians.

And the Goths? *Well, they're really just mostly farmers who can fight. They would have been perfectly happy still doing that north of the Danube. So, while I could tell the legion to run all the way to a battle and expect them to do it and arrive as a still cohesive formations . . . the Goths? No, not so much. Even though I took only the youngest half, long distance running is not their forte. So we march no faster than the cavalry can make sure it's safe, and no faster than the slowest ten percent can make.*

South of Mogontiacum

The king put the respite from the missiles to good use. In both the Vandal host and that of their Suebi allies, to the west, clan columns veered to the right, forming a shield wall.

Romans we might not be, thought Gunderic, *but we've learned a good deal from them.*

As each column finished its evolution, drummers behind

them began a steady drone. The men in the ranks, also, lifted their shields to their mouths and began the *barritus*. The sound grew steadily louder, as more and more clans formed up and joined the chorus.

On the high ground ahead, the Romans—who were, in fact, likewise Vandals, Suebi, and the scions of still other Germanic tribes—began to answer with their own *barritus*. However, that sound couldn't even be heard above the near roar of the barbarians' chant. Meanwhile, the sound of the barbarians' *barritus* washed over the defenders like a tidal wave, drowning their confidence and morale.

Quintus Junius Fulvius, chief of artillery for the legion, sneered at the shield wall of barbarians and their reverberating war chant.

"Let's see how well they keep that bullshit up with bolts through their ranks."

Fulvius looked from left to right. Beside each scorpion the chief of the crew stood, one arm upraised, indicating readiness to loose their bolts. Their other hands grasped the cord that controlled the release mechanism. Fulvius raised his own arm, while shouting, "Prepare to loose...LOOSE!"

Almost as a single machine, the scorpions let fly. The range was extreme but, nonetheless, the bolts pierced shields to impale the men behind. In a couple of cases, the bolts managed to perforate the next men in line of flight, too.

The physical damage, except to those hit, was small. The damage to the *barritus*, however, was instant and significant. When another salvo hit, again the volume and consistency of the barbarian *barritus* dropped. Still more did it drop, even as the defenders arose, with the third, the fourth, the fifth, and the sixth volleys.

And then the barbarians started spontaneously moving back in an attempt to get out of range. Their *barritus,* for the moment, collapsed, even as the chorus coming from the hill on which stood the massed defenders, crested.

Fulvius called, "Cease fire. Cease fire." He then strode in front of his engines, deliberately out to where the Vandals could see him, spread his legs to shoulder width and crossed his arms in contempt.

✧   ✧   ✧

For the moment, at least, Gaius Pompeius could ignore the threat on his left and concentrate on the right. He wheeled his horse around and began a walk down the slope toward the legion, his guards and messengers following along. As he moved so, too, did the leading wave of the Suebi roll over the ridge to the southwest.

Gaius kept an eye on them and noticed that there were several minutes of hesitation on the part of each Suebi group as they crested the ridge and caught their first glimpse of a real, classical Roman legion, standing in good order and apparently completely unfazed by the barbarian horde. Those minutes of hesitation moved down the ridge to the southwest as still more groups of barbarians reached the top of the ridge.

More and more barbarians came over the ridge. Thought Gaius, *Jupiter, where did all those fucking barbarians come from?*

He also saw that their line was going to overlap the legion's. Nor was he entirely reassured by the very convincing stampede of the Palmyrene horse, galloping behind the legion to take up position on the right, while giving some very convincing cheers along the way.

As they reached that extreme right, the Palmyrenes took up position, until the Roman position overlapped that of the Suebi.

That's misleading, though, thought Gaius. *We extend past them, yes, but we cannot hold that long line with stationary cavalry like we can with infantry. Tadmor's going to have to stay mobile to keep us from being outflanked.*

Vorenus noted that roughly half of the barbarian cavalry facing his Scythian boys suddenly turned and left, while the other half held their position.

Is that enough for us to take them, head-on? No, not a chance. They still outnumber us enough to stomp us and, even at even numbers, if we let them get to close quarters they're too big and strong for the boys to deal with on anything like equal terms. We'll just have to keep up the arrow fire.

And pretty soon several hundred of them are going to discover they've been poisoned. Or that their horses have. Or both.

Gaius reached the center of the legion, relieving Metilius, who trotted off to take his position on the right front with the First

Cohort. From that center Gaius rode his horse at a walk, likewise to the right front. His purpose, however, was different from the first spear's. To achieve that purpose he trotted his horse around to the front center, right by but in front of the legionary eagle, beside which stood the first spear.

"Men of the First Cohort," Gaius began, pitching his voice to reach the hundred and forty or so feet to each flank. "Stand at...EASE. Now, listen up."

The legate waited a few moments for the men to settle down. "There's not a lot of time to talk but that's just fine. No doubt to your vast relief, I don't have a lot to say." This got Gaius a pretty good chuckle from the ranks. "And you don't need a lot.

"There is only this: whether you're a Christian or a pagan, one thing is obvious to all of us. This is that divine powers brought us here, to this time and place, to save the Empire. No one else could even hope to, but you, you who fought off the hordes of Arminius, who smashed the remnants of the Scythian horde and took their women for your own, you who marched across half the world to get here in time...you can do it. You can save the Empire. And you will.

"Now, we're not going to wait for them to crash against us. We're going to donate them your *plumbatae* and then we're going to hit them with your *pila*. And then, boys, it's out gladii and start cutting them up *on the attack*.

"First Spear Metilius?"

"Sir."

"The cohort is yours. Good luck to you all and the Divine watch over each and every one of you. Take charge."

"Sir." Metilius then turned about to face the cohort. "Men, give a cheer for the legion and the legate:"

"Hoorahhhh!"

With a wave, Gaius was off to give a few words to the next cohort in line.

Gunderic, having seen the terrible power and range of the Roman field artillery firsthand and on more than one occasion, kept his distance from the half dozen pieces he saw atop the ridge to the front. He'd also seen how those few scorpions had disrupted the *barritus* from his own Vandals, though he could hear it rising from the Suebi on his left, unseen on the other side of the ridge. He also heard some cheering that didn't sound remotely like the *barritus*.

Thought Gunderic, *The Suebi are going to do what the Suebi are going to do. What they're not going to do is take detailed orders from me. They have their own king, after all.*

The Alans are good folk; they'll at least cooperate, and pretty selflessly, too. I'd prefer them kept out of it until we have a hole we can exploit through. That place where the Roman artillery sits could be such a hole, but it looks too easy, so I'm not going to take that bait.

No...no. Fuck the barritus, *we're in pretty good order now. We march forward and just overwhelm those people on the high ground next to the river. It's our best chance. Then, when we've cleared them out of the way, we release the Alans and the rest of our cavalry, such as are not already tied up dancing with the Huns.*

The *vexillarius*, Mucius Tursidius, kept silent as the horde of barbarians broke over the ridge to his south. Tursidius stood in the front rank six spots to the left of the aquilifer, the eagle being in the hands of Titus Atidius Porcio. The entire party of aquilifer, imaginifer, and *vexillarius* stood centered in the First Cohort, with two very mean legionaries between each. It was the job of these legionaries to protect the standard-bearers who, after all, couldn't carry a shield. The *contubernia* behind those initial guards was likewise made up of unusually tough and skilled soldiers as, indeed, were the men in file behind the standard bearers, themselves.

Thought Tursidius, *If anybody in the cohort has to appear unperturbed, no matter what shows up looking to kill us, it's me. Oh, and the other standard-bearers and, of course, the legate and first spear.*

Well, no need to worry, anyway. One way or another, soon enough it will be over.

INTERLUDE

Portus Itius, Gaul, 406 A.D.

Thank God that's over, thought Bonitus, unsteadily walking down the gangplank to shore. Behind him he also left the overwhelming smell of human vomit, relic of the channel storm in which his ship had been caught. Some of that vomit was on the heavy cloak he wore.

Under ordinary circumstances, Bonitus would have used the official travel system, as a representative of the state. In this case, given that he was only the representative of one somewhat subversive senator, he thought it best to operate privately.

There was a small snack bar on the dock not far from the ship. Bonitus stood on the dock and signaled to one of the ship's crew to toss him down his bag. Naturally, the sailor was completely unaffected by the storm and stood a great deal more steadily than Bonitus himself.

Still swaying, Bonitus carried the bag and staggered to the snack bar. A doorman, well-dressed enough to suspect he was free, opened the door for him. Through the open door wafted the smell of some kind of fish stew, that, and baking or freshly baked bread.

Can I eat without hurling? wondered the man. *Well, maybe not just yet. A cup of wine, or maybe two, and some bread to settle my stomach and maybe then the stew.*

Still, an upset stomach is a small price to pay to coordinate matters to ultimately replace that barbarian Stilicho, and that thief

483

of air, Honorius. And this Constantine strikes me in every way as a better choice for emperor than either of those—smart, tough, and oh so sneaky. Plus a better soldier and a better politician, both. Another Aurelian, if you ask me, though one might hope he lasts longer than Aurelian. And, of course, Lampadius will ask me.

Also, of course, Lampadius doesn't confide in me, but he may have purple-tinged ambitions of his own. I wonder, will he decide to throw himself behind Constantine or will I be—again, thinking of Aurelian—sent to assassinate Constantine?

Time will tell.

CHAPTER TWENTY-TWO

The Roman order on the other hand is flexible: for
every Roman, once armed and on the field, is equally
well equipped for every place, time, or appearance of
the enemy. He is, moreover, quite ready and needs to
make no change, whether he is required to fight in the
main body, or in a detachment, or in a single maniple,
or even by himself. Therefore, as the individual members of the Roman force are so much more serviceable,
their plans are also much more often attended by success than those of others.

—Polybius, *Histories*, 18.32

South of Mogontiacum, 406 A.D.

The barbarians hadn't spent very much time on their *barritus*,
since the Romans neither answered it nor appeared to be, even
in the slightest, fazed by it. After a short time raising their own
morale, their chieftains ordered the mass forward. It looked a good
deal like an ancient Greek phalanx, the old-fashioned kind, from
before Philip of Macedon. The telling differences were that the
shields were thinner and lighter, and the enemy lacked almost all
semblance of armor in the rank and file. Even so, shields—even
if lighter—spears, and formation were all quite similar.

Just about time, thought Tursidius. *Just about . . .*

485

Metilius' earth-shattering voice rang out, "Readdyyy...LOOSE!"
...*now*.

The thing was, the rear ranks of the lead century could not
throw their *plumbatae* straight to their fronts. Neither did passing them forward make sense, as arms—arms soon to be needed
for sword work—would tire. Thus, while the four forward cohorts
threw four clouds of *plumbatae* high, across the space between
the forward four cohorts and the barbarian shield wall, the forward centuries of each maniple rotated men forward by ranks
to throw at low angle and directly.

The sound, at this distance, was much like that of large
hailstones hitting a tile roof. The damage to the barbarian front
ranks was minimal. Looking all the way from left to right, Tursidius saw fewer than fifty barbarians fall, and perhaps twice that
in wounded to some degree. And that was from approximately
eleven hundred missiles from all four forward cohorts, combined.

However, the ones thrown high had a lot more success, since
the barbarians had held their shields to their front against the
threat they could most readily see. The similar number of missiles thrown high and coming down on helmeted heads, mainly
unarmored shoulders, and some numbers of necks staggered the
enemy shield wall with a shock that emanated forward and back
from the center ranks.

Tursidius couldn't see well enough to count, but had the
impression that more than three hundred, and maybe as many
as five hundred, had been taken out by that half of the volley.

*Not necessarily dead, I know, but hurt enough not to be much
threat for now. And that's good, because the closer they get the
more obvious it becomes that those are some* big *bastards.*

Two more volleys of *plumbatae* followed in short order. It
was disappointing to see disappear the advantage of the missiles
coming down from on high, as the Germans behind the first
couple of lines very quickly learned to hold their shields overhead.

Maybe five hundred taken out, thought Tursidius, *or possibly
as many as seven hundred, though I wouldn't bet my next incre-
ment of pay on that. Beats getting slapped across the face with
a wet fish.*

"Readyyy...*PILA!*"

Whereas the three *plumbatae* per man had been held in a
kind of rack that had been added to the *scuta*, the *pila*, as was

traditional, had been held in the legionaries' left hands. These were quickly transferred to the right, gripped, and then held at an angle, awaiting the command.

Thought Tursidius, *Good thing Metilius is a master at this; it's always a tough call to gauge exactly when to throw the* pila *to get maximum effect, while still having enough time to draw the gladii.*

"First two ranks...ready!" shouted the first spear. "Wait for it...wait for it...LOOSE!"

That volley was absolutely deadly, penetrating the light German shields with ease and then driving past those a good foot and a half to pierce chests and abdomens. The German ranks staggered and came to a halt as men tripped and tried to climb over the dead and wounded fallen at their feet.

"Next two ranks...forward." This was accompanied by a whistle blast. After those Metilius ordered, "Next two." Everyone knew that all five or six ranks were to step forward. "Now...ready...LOOSE! Next two ranks...FORWARD!"

The noise coming from pierced Germans made it difficult for the men to hear Metilius, hence, he gave another whistle blast.

Two more sets of commands, only one of which called for loosing *pila*, saw the standard bearers to the front again. At that point, the first spear gave the command to draw gladii and then to, "CHAAARGE!"

Those leading four cohorts slammed into the German shield wall, now much the worse for wear, and began carving up the barbarians in front of them.

Not that it was all one-sided—Romans fell, too, or staggered or were helped to the rear with incapacitating wounds. Yet the ratio of death and damage favored the legion immensely.

The next five cohorts advanced calmly and at the walk to keep position relative to the forward line. Interestingly, as those five advanced, the barbarians in front of them automatically fell back, probably to keep as much distance as practical between themselves and those deadly *pila*. Inevitably, as those sections of the shield wall in the gaps between cohorts extended themselves, gaps likewise opened up in the shield wall. With a good deal more careful aiming than had been shown by the first line in the order of battle, the second line began sniping at the men exposed in those gaps with their *plumbatae*. Not too many fell to this, but they all became fatigued and fearful, the one reinforcing the other.

Gaius Pompeius and his little command group rode behind the central cohort of the second line of battle, just watching and judging. Especially was he watching and judging his right flank, where the Palmyrenes had managed to stymie most of the overlapping Suebi horde.

But not all of it. Fuckers are going to overlap us, anyway. Hmmm . . . Fifth Cohort sees it, too.

"Messenger!"

"Sir."

"Gallop to Tenth Cohort. They are to form up on the right of Fifth Cohort and prevent the enemy from overlapping us on that flank."

"Sir!" And the messenger was off with a flurry of his horse's tail.

Gunderic's horse's tail fluttered nervously. It was a fairly stupid beast, but not deaf. The sounds of the bolts from the Roman scorpions was strange to it. Moreover, troops marching uphill to beat the *foederati* awaiting them took many a bolt on their course. Between the *thwacks*, the whistling, and the screams from horribly wounded warriors, Gunderic thought the beast had every right to be nervous.

He leaned over and stroked the horse's neck, muttering soothingly, "Don't worry, old friend—but, just between you and me, I'm pretty nervous, too."

Next to Gunderic sat Respendial, king of the Alans.

"Are you sure you cannot take those artillery pieces?" asked the Vandal.

"No," said the Alan, "not sure. Pretty sure that the Romans have some kind of trick up there. Look too easy. Anything look too easy . . ."

"It probably isn't. Yeah, you're right. How about some arrow fire on their artillery?"

"Can do, sure?" agreed the Alan. "But ask self, is that the most important thing you can have us do? Think you need us for when you break Romans on our right flank. Don't think can do both. Sure cannot do both as well as just one thing. Now watch; Goar going in with fake attack with half my cavalry."

"Let's hope it works and they break," said Gunderic. Even as he spoke the Alan cavalry under Goar was shaking out from a column into a line. It did this maneuver at a walk. Once in line, the horsemen changed from a walk to a trot.

About the time they switched from a trot to a canter, a storm of rocks sailed out from the Roman line to meet them. The elevation of the Romans added a bit to the range. Before the first salvo of rocks had hit—or maybe they were bricks or some other kind of ceramic; Gunderic and Respendial couldn't be sure—another three sailed out, right over the heads of the *foederati* defenders.

The Alan cavalry's pseudo-attack dissolved into chaos as horses were struck, and injured right through their armor. And that was for the heavies; the Alan light cavalry took more serious injuries, some of those fatal to men or horses or both.

Then the bolt-firing scorpions pitched in, aiming especially for the heavies. After a few volleys from those, the Alan cavalry, heavy and light both, were racing for safety down the slope of the ridge.

"Well done, boys," called out Centurion Quintus Silvanus, amidst the appreciative cheers of the *foederati* spread out slightly lower on the slope of the ridge. "Now put it on their infantry."

The Vandals storming up the slope reacted quickly, most of the rear ranks raising their shields overhead to ward off the plunging half-pound projectiles. A great many shields were damaged, but not very many of the attackers.

I may have made a mistake, thought Silvanus. *No, I did make a mistake. Those cavalry weren't going to ride right over their own infantry. They were supposed to panic the* foederati *here. Using the staff slings on them warned the barbarian foot about what was coming. So they were not taken by surprise.*

Best I spread the men out to prevent desertions. Because this is about to get hard for the foederati.

"Those slings, or whatever they are, are amazing," said Gunderic to Respendial. "We've got to capture some and copy them."

"Win battle and we just take theirs," responded the Alan. "Lose and it won't much matter. And your foot have other problems."

The "other problems" were the archers and slingers in the center, making life miserable and uncertain for the Vandals on the left of the right flank.

"Can't you do something about those?" asked Gunderic, not for the first time.

"What you mean," said Respendial, "is can I trade the lives of some of my people to save some more of yours, at least long enough for yours to achieve something? And the answer to that is 'yes.' Actually, it's a happy 'yes,' because bastard Romans on those machines kill a fair number of my people, and we be very happy to pay them back in own coin."

Thancrat observed the approach of the Alan horse, heavy and light both, with dread. *They're going to try it, to ride right over us. And while the caltrops will help, they won't be enough.*

"Prepare to receive cavalry! Prepare to receive cavalry!"

This move involved the troops filling in gaps so as to present to the oncoming horses the appearance of a wall too tall to jump over, coupled to a forest of spears for the occasional horse either so stupid or so obedient that it would try to smash down a wall. The first two ranks got down on one knee, presenting their shields and spearpoints to the front. Subsequent ranks closed up their intervals to lend to the illusion.

Meanwhile Fulvius' scorpion crews worked double time to hit as many of the oncoming cavalry as possible. At first, they had a good deal of success. Then the Alan cavalry unslung their bows and began to spread out into somewhat narrow ovals.

"Oh, shit," said Fulvius. "Shields! Shields! Get behind cover!" The Roman artillery crews collected themselves and put their shields to the front in small groups. This allowed them to have shielding to their flanks, at least to some degree.

No sooner had Fulvius cowered behind his own *scutum* than an Alan arrow punched through it, in an upper quadrant, the point only stopping about an inch from the centurion's nose.

Fulvius looked at the point cross-eyed for a moment, then muttered, "Now that's what I'd call a powerful bow."

"No shit, Centurion," said the crewman just to Fulvius' right.

Another arrow came in, and then another. That last one penetrated the shield and then lodged itself in Fulvius' left forearm, passing through just above the bone. Blood began to run steadily across his arm before dripping to the ground.

Rather than cry out, the centurion contented himself with a steady stream of the most vile curses known to Latin, plus a few he'd picked up from the locals in Germany. Though he couldn't see it, the cursing brought smiles to such of his men as could hear him, the men passing the word, "Good old Fulvius—he's hit but as full of fight as ever."

Still cursing, Fulvius reached up with his right hand, snapped the arrowhead off, withdrew his arm, and then snapped off such of the shaft as had penetrated the *scutum*.

Fuck! If we try to man the scorpions we'll last about two shots each. But without our fire to the left, I'm not sure if the foederati *can hold. And the Rhodian slingers and Thracian archers are as pinned as we are...no help from them. Worse, if Thancrat tries to charge them they'll just pull back, surround his cohort, and shoot them to pieces, all to no gain to us beyond a couple of minutes of free shooting. Best I can say is that while they're shooting at us at least they're not shooting at anybody else.*

I really wouldn't mind, thought Thancrat, *if these fuckers would go shoot at someone else for a change.*

Though the German prefect hadn't taken a wound yet, there were no fewer than seven arrows sticking through the wood of his flat shield.

Thancrat smelled something odd. He sniffed more closely at the arrows sticking through his shield. *Hmmm...lard and beeswax. Helping the arrows penetrate more deeply? I think so. There's a trick our people could use.*

Another arrow sliced through the German's shield, stopping just shy of his hauberk.

Which might or might not have stopped it.

From Thancrat's right there came a heart-rending scream. He looked and saw one of his men, arrow sticking through his neck, grab the shaft and fall to the ground.

Must have looked over his shield. Stupid, stupid. Thancrat looked over his shield, then ducked down again.

Mucius Tursidius thought, *I wish that it were possible to both bear a standard and still use a shield.* At the moment of the wish he was involved in using his gladius to block one sword slash after a spear thrust, and then a spear thrust after a sword slash, with not a lot of time to recover between any of them.

His two guards, on the other hand, were busy with more offensive measures. At least half the attempts on Tursidius' life were foiled by counterthrusts from his guards' gladii and half the

rest by blocks from their shields. Some of those attempts ended
with a barbarian gurgling out his life on the frozen ground. Of
course, they weren't allowed to gurgle for long before their throats
were cut or their hearts sliced. Or, in one case, one of the guards
actually kicked a dying barbarian's head off his shoulders.

Mind, it took a number of kicks lubricated by a good deal
of rather personal cursing: "Stinking, unwashed barbarian." *Kick.*
"Nasty goat-buggering shit eater." *Kick.* "Motherfucker." *Kick.*
"Catamite." *Kick.*

The soldier behind Tursidius leaned forward and shouted
into his ear, "You need me to take that over for a bit, Mucius?"

"No...no, thanks. I'm good for a bit longer."

Then one of the barbarians got lucky. The aquilifer, Titus
Atidius Porcio, gave off a scream and began to fold himself
around the pole bearing the legion's eagle. Instantly, three
barbarians vied to get a grip on the pole. But, guts hanging
on the ground or not, Porcio was having none of that. With
strength leaving his hands, the aquilifer turned his entire body
into one big instrument for gripping. His guards didn't need to
be told, even though he did tell them, "Save the eagle, boys!
Save the eagle!"

They, and the three men behind, practically threw themselves
onto the Germans to save the legionary emblem. As it turned out,
three of those five had converted to Christianity at the behest
of their Scythian convert women. But for performance and guts,
none could have credited the Christians or the pagans with greater
devotion to the eagle or courage in securing it.

To Tursidius' right the imaginifer, Quintus, ordered, "Take
up our old emperor's likeness, Mucius, while I grab the eagle."

Tursidius looked behind himself and said to the legionary
there, "Take up my standard, and good luck to you."

Meanwhile, Porcio was helped and passed to the rear where a
horse-drawn ambulance awaited to whisk him to *Medicus* Josephus.

West of Mogontiacum

Marcus Caelius was livid inside. Had these been legionaries, he'd
have tongue-lashed them into a better, faster pace. But they were
not legionaries. And Goths were touchy.

So, paymaster or not, he ate at his own guts, terrified that the legion—*his* legion—might be lost without his thirty-five hundred Goths to help.

Somewhere off to the right there was a swirl of horse archers versus normal cavalry. Just who were the horse archers, Caelius couldn't know. Even if his eyes had been as strong as when he was young, the archers were still too far away.

Well, there are only two possibilities: the Palmyrenes and the Scythian boys. They're ... call it two miles away. That's a short journey by gallop. The infantry can keep marching while I hit whoever isn't a horse archer with these thousand Gothic horse. Beat them, then rejoin the infantry on the march. If it takes an hour I'd be surprised.

Caelius turned to the senior Goth present and said, "Take command of the infantry and keep marching east. Send me the cavalry. We're going to have a little fun."

"Just as well; I think I am a little old for 'fun.' Do try not to get my sons killed while you're having your fun."

"I can promise nothing except that I shall do my best."

The Goth rode off, shouting at the top of his lungs to gain the attention of the infantry. By dribs and drabs, clans and companies, the Gothic horse assembled on Caelius, shaking themselves into a line about a thousand feet across and sixty or so deep. One of Theodomir's sons, the next to eldest, Fredenandus, reported to Caelius as a translator.

"I've been listening to Gothic most every hour of every day," said the *praefectus castrorum*. "I think I've got enough to get by. Just stand by to correct me if I make any really ridiculous errors."

Then, raising his voice to full first-spear parade ground volume, he said, "Gentlemen, before you, you can see a battle raging between some horse archers—they will be Roman or Roman-allied—and a pack of Vandal or Suebi cavalry. I'm going to guess about seven or eight hundred of them. You have been, at Roman expense, fattened up from Roman granaries. As we passed through Augusta Trevorarum, you were partially rearmed at Roman expense. You have been paid, and well, at Roman expense. Now I want you to follow me to teach these fuckers a lesson they will never unlearn, to show that the treasure Rome has lavished on you was not wasted, and that you are truly men I think you are, men to be valued as allies of Rome.

"No time for questions now; just follow me."

The Goths didn't cheer; it wasn't that kind of prebattle speech. But heads nodded, chests swelled, and lances were raised. That was good enough.

Following Caelius, the column advanced at the canter. Halfway to the enemy cavalry, still swirling around in confusion, beset by those archers, the canter became a trot.

"Oh, shit," said Titus Vorenus, at the sudden apparition of a thousand strange and obviously barbarian cavalry materializing on his left flank. "We are so screwed. Just...*cornicen*?"

"Sir?"

"Blow break off and reca—No, wait. That man in the center...I'd swear he's Caelius, the camp prefect."

The *cornicen* strained to see. "I don't know the camp prefect at all well, sir, but that man in the center *is* wearing a helmet with a transverse crest. I think maybe it is him."

"Wooohooo!" Vorenus exulted. "Boys! Boys! We're going to finish off these bastards in the next ten minutes."

Closer and still closer came the Gothic cavalry to the scattered and disorganized swarm of Suebi horse. A few on their own right saw what was coming and tried to form a battle line to meet it. That lasted about three minutes as the gross disparity in numbers became obvious. Then they took to flight, shouting at their fellow tribesmen to run, run, run for their lives.

But the Goths' horses were fresh while the Suebi were winded and tired from playing games with the Scythian boys all morning. For that matter, the lack of fodder and grain had those horses in poor shape to begin with. The Suebi couldn't escape.

Two or three hundred of them went down to lances in their backs before most of the rest realized that it was better to die fighting than running like cowards. By ones and two, tens and twenties, the Suebi cavalry turned about and charged, as best their tired horses were able. Barring a few dozen who kept on running, the Suebi were crushed underfoot.

"Sir, I thank you," said Vorenus to Caelius. "That was well done and with perfect timing."

As they spoke, the Goths busied themselves with finishing off the wounded. The Scythian boys, too, replenished their quivers to some extent by ripping their barbed, poisoned arrows out of

Suebi bodies, men and horses, both. The horses, at least, had their throats cut before the arrows were withdrawn. Not all of the Suebi were so lucky.

"Never mind that," said Caelius. "What can you tell me of the battle ahead?"

"Nothing much," Vorenus admitted. "The *foederati* are lined up along the ridge south of the town. You know, sir; that ridge maybe five miles south of Mogontiacum. Last I saw, a great mass of barbarians, maybe twelve or fifteen thousand of them, maybe more, were moving on that line. The legion is closer to us but an even larger number of barbarians were moving on them."

South of Mogontiacum

The staff slings cracked behind even as heavy stones whirred overhead in a continuous onslaught. The effect on the enemy, however, was not great. Yes, their shields were often damaged or even wrecked. Yes, some went down with split skulls and smashed faces. Yes, too, some fell out of line with broken ribs, or collar-bones, or arms, or even legs. But in the main they pressed on.

"Can you hold them?" Rubelius asked Silvanus.

The senior centurion of Twelfth Cohort shook his head. "No, sir. If the *foederati* can't hold..."

"No, no, I *meant* the *foederati*, Centurion. Can you keep them from bolting?"

Silvanus considered this then, reluctantly, had to answer, "I just don't know. A civilized soldier, a legionary, would recognize that the threat of summary execution would keep his comrades on the line, and so would be more confident standing in line himself. But these *foederati* are definitely *not* civilized. They really settle their battles by who can make the most noise before the first blow is struck. Not soldiers at all, you see. Not used to our way of doing things. Don't have the mutual confidence our way of doing things brings."

"And so?" Rubelius prodded.

"And so," said Silvanus, "I think they'll break within ten minutes of the barbarians hitting them, that they'll plow into us and disorder us to the point we won't be able to hold them or the barbarians, and then we all collapse in a rout, with the Vandals sticking spears up our asses all the way to Mogontiacum."

"So, what do you recommend?"

Silvanus considered this, too. "I'd start pulling out now, trade this—admittedly strong—position for the chance to get them behind the walls of Mogontiacum. Above all, get them moving while they still have some order. Because once they lose that, they've got nothing."

"I can't do it," said Rubelius, feeling sick to his stomach. "We pull out and that leaves the legion hanging in the wind. Half the barbarians will chase us to the town while the other half, plus that cavalry, turn west and envelop the legion. No, I just can't do it."

"Then, sir, I'd suggest sending a messenger to Gaius Pompeius, telling him that he's got maybe half an hour, more likely twenty minutes, to gain a decision on his flank before he's going to have to deal with twice as many barbarians coming at him from all sides. I'd also think about ordering these *foederati* so that we can make some semblance of a fighting retreat back to, inevitably, the walls of Mogontiacum."

Rubelius asked, "How many men do you think, to hold the walls of the town? I'm assuming the stay-behinds in the legionary base can hold it."

"Eight hundred men on the walls could hold it against this lot for a month," was the centurion's learned judgment.

"I think so, too, so here's what we're going to do: We'll send the leftmost group of *foederati*—I can't quite bring myself to call them a legion—back to the town. The rest of us will wheel back to form a line more parallel to the line than perpendicular to it. That secures the town—well enough, anyway—and guards the legion's flank. Most importantly, it keeps us out of reach of the barbarians for a little while longer."

Rubelius' face acquired a sudden look of horror. "Oh, wait. Shit, that won't work either. The Alan cavalry will come pouring through the gap we leave, outflank us, outflank the legion, and then the massacre begins. No, we've no choice—we stand here and fight."

Silvanus nodded. He'd known from the day he'd first enlisted that it might come to this. *And what the Hades, I've had a pretty good life.*

"Then, sir, I suggest going and making the best speech you can to the *foederati*. I would not suggest overburdening your speech with any great degree of truth."

✧　　✧　　✧

Truth time, thought Gaius Pompeius. *Let's see if the barbarians facing the gaps between the cohorts of the first line of battle—Suebi, I am certain they're Suebi, from the side knots—anyway, let's see how their morale really stands. They've been hanging back rather than charging through the gaps; I think their morale isn't that good.*

"*Cornicines.*"

"Ready, sir."

"Blow, in order, 'Second line of battle,' 'Prepare to attack,' and then 'Attack.'"

The chief *cornicen* repeated that back and, on confirmation, had his team sound the signals. Immediately, four of the five cohorts in the second line of battle—the one to the right being tied down by the Suebi who had tried to outflank the Roman line—gave off a mighty cheer and advanced against the Suebi who had been holding back out of effective missile range. The latter launched axes and javelins, along with some arrows, but the Romans, largely safe behind their solid *scuta*, were generally unimpressed. Calmly they advanced to *pilum* range.

There were still some *plumbatae* held in the carrying frames on the backs of the Roman shields, but most had been expended keeping the Suebi at their concave distance. *Pila* it would have to be.

Under the command of their own centurions, the legionaries of the first rank launched. The long iron shafts of the *pila* went right through the light German shields and then, in many cases, right into the heavy German bodies behind those shields. On command, another rank of legionaries, *pila* gripped in their throwing hands, advanced. Another volley of the heavy javelins flew. The legionaries of the second rank took special care to target Suebi whose shields hadn't been struck by the first volley.

Since the relatively well-armored noblemen of the Suebi had been in the first couple of ranks, the volleys of *pila* represented not just a physical problem, but a social disaster.

Seven or eight volleys, cohort strength depending, flew. And then, on the orders of their senior centurions, the cohorts drew *gladii* and charged.

Suebi, already demoralized and disordered by the volleys of *pila*, were thinking already of running when the leading edge of the chopping machine that was the second line of battle reached them. Using their shields as battering rams, the smaller Romans simply bowled over the larger Suebi by the score, then saw the rear ranks dip to put a sword in their guts or necks, or to slash their throats with an accompanying great spray of blood.

On the flanks of the cohorts, the senior centurions of the flank maniples directed the rear centuries to strike into the flanks of the Suebi facing the cohorts of first line of battle, transmitting a pair of shocks across the Suebi masses that knocked men off their feet and pressed the bulk of them so tightly that they could barely wield their swords, axes, and spears.

From the rear of the Suebi phalanx, men began to run away in a trickle.

"*Cornicines*, blow 'First line of battle,' 'Prepare to charge,' and then 'Charge.'"

"Yes, sir."

A messenger arrived, riding hard from the east. "Sir," he said to Gaius, "Tribune Rubelius sends that his force may hold half an hour, no longer and possibly less. And that was ten minutes ago. He suggests that you finish up here quickly and come to his aid."

"Fuck." Gaius glanced around for one of the other tribunes, serving as field staff. "You! Go round up the horse holders and get them to ride to behind the German *auxilia* under Thancrat. Let themselves be seen. Then bring them behind the *foederati* on the left. I want them seen there, too. Have the men cheer the entire way."

"A bluff, sir?" asked the tribune.

"Yes, a big bloody bluff. When that's done, find Atrixtos of the Gallic Auxiliary Cavalry and tell him to cross the river, pass through the fort, and start attacking and burning the barbarian camps. Now go!"

"Sir!" The tribune galloped off to the right flank rear to start the horse holders moving. He knew some of them were blind and not a one was a soldier, so a bluff was all it could be.

Gunderic kept his shield high; the Germans fighting for Rome yet retained some missile weapons, both heavy and light. In front of the king marched his own personal force of guards. On each side of him were a pair of *lurs*, four in all, ancient German horns. These sounded the attack, over and over and over, encouraging and driving the Vandal infantry into the relatively thin line of *foederati* along the ridge.

It was a madhouse up there, Gunderic saw, with shield pressed to shield and thousands of arms wielding thousands of spears overhand, striking down and forward, again and again, in the hope—it was never much more than a hope for any given thrust—of reaching something vital.

Though the Vandals had the numbers, the *foederati* had been armed and armored by Rome. Any well driven and lucky thrust by the latter would find blood. A similar thrust by the Vandals might or might not.

Even so, the weight of manpower and fatigue began to take a toll on the *foederati*. More and more of them found their sword and spear arms becoming just that little bit too slow to deflect the latest Vandal thrust, their shields just that little bit off.

No one would ever say the name of the first of the *foederati* to bolt. If they had known, they'd have deliberately forgotten it as a shame to his people. Nonetheless, there was a first one. He came from one of the rear ranks and hadn't come close to trading blows with anyone. But he dropped his spear, dropped his shield, and ran. Then, like a madman, he clawed his way through any of his comrades who stood in his way. His commander looked over his shoulder and saw the man running. The commander was about to call out to him to return to the fight when he also saw two of the well-armored Romans lunge out to intercept the deserter. The Romans asked no questions. Indeed, they said nothing. They just stabbed the deserter, twice, each, and let his corpse fall to the snow on the ground, his blood spreading to stain it red.

"That's the justice that awaits anyone so cowardly as to run," said the late deserter's commander. "The Romans will, quite properly, execute him on the spot. So fight hard, my fellows, and fear not. No one else is going to desert you. There's no point to it."

The commander said it, but his troops didn't believe. To stay in position meant certain death, the certain death they could see. To run, if only they ran in enough numbers, gave them a chance at life, at least for a little while. That one deserter, cut down by the Twelfth Cohort, was joined by an increasing number. Some even managed to get through.

INTERLUDE

Mogontiacum, 406 A.D.

Bonitus detoured, not too far from his intended route but just enough to get a feel for the capabilities of this bizarrely reborn legion from ancient times. Since the legion had interrupted and quite possibly canceled his employer's plans for Constantine, in Britannia, he was sure to want to know about them.

On the way to the town, Bonitus assembled a small sack of trade goods, higher-end knives, silver and bronze cups, *udones*, cloaks, spoons and the like, all things legionaries used. On arrival, he set them up in the town's forum and managed to sell out—*Made a tidy profit, too, didn't I?*—and then repaired to a nearby tavern where he found some of his recent customers. He bought a couple of jugs of decent local wine and sat himself down at a table with a quartet of them, one a centurion, plus three others. Their names, first names, were Gratianus, the centurion, and then Titus, Quintus, and Mucius.

"I have heard rumors, gentlemen," said Bonitus, "that I find very hard to credit. Oh, wait, please help yourself to the wine freely. I made a good enough profit, too, this trip that it's not likely to run out anytime soon."

Gratianus looked over their benefactor and announced, "You were a soldier, once."

"Indeed, I was. With Stilicho, up to about ten years ago, now. I pegged you four for the same. And the very core of my interest is, just where the Hell did you people come from?"

"That," said Gratianus, "is a long story, and a big question, the answer to which none of us really have. But what we know, we'll tell you..."

"Holy shit!" said Bonitus, once the Romans had finished the telling. "And there's that much difference between you and the men who make up the Empire's armies, now?"

"Night and day," said Gratianus. "Even we're surprised at the difference. None of these pussies could get through us, given secure flanks, not if they outnumbered us five to one or even ten to one. And none could stand against us, even if they stood atop the highest walls in the world. We are—and here I speak for every man in the legion—just shocked and sickened at how badly the army has deteriorated. 'Legions' without more than a handful of Romans or Italians in them. 'Legions' of under a thousand men. 'Legions' that can do one thing only, where we can do anything and everything."

Bonitus asked, "But what about horse archers and heavy cavalry?"

Answered Gratianus, "We beat—beat is *such* an understatement—we *exterminated* a whole tribe of horse archers and did it, more-over, on their own ground. And heavy cavalry? The next cavalry charge that doesn't fall apart when faced with a human wall and under a hail of *pila* will be the first. We're not impressed."

"But the Germanic soldiers..."

"Other than our cohort of *auxilia*," said Gratianus, "there are no Germanic 'soldiers.' Warriors? Yes, of course, they have those in plenty. But mere warriors are meat on the table for soldiers. And we, my friend, are *soldiers*."

CHAPTER
TWENTY-THREE

We are born into this time and must bravely follow the
path to the destined end. There is no other way. Our
duty is to hold on to the lost position, without hope,
without rescue, like that Roman soldier whose bones
were found in front of a door in Pompeii, who, during
the eruption of Vesuvius, died at his post because they
forgot to relieve him. That is greatness. That is what it
means to be a thoroughbred. The honorable end is the
one thing that cannot be taken from a man.
                    —Oswald Spengler, *Man and Technics*

Mogontiacum, 406 A.D.

Bat-Erdene had excellent vision. From the southern wall of
Mogontiacum, he had a pretty good view of the Roman defenders
and the Vandal horde as it rolled over the ridge. He kept up a
running commentary to his followers, the one hundred old hands
who had reenlisted with the legion as noncombatant scouts, plus
the four hundred and twenty new ones.

He shouted down from the wall how the Romans cut down
the first *foederati* deserter, but how it also didn't matter. "They're
starting to break now," he said, "all those hired warriors, and
our friends of the Twelfth Cohort have no chance of holding on
their own, as thin as they are."

"Should we help them?" asked one of the Argippaeans standing below. "*Can* we help them? If so, how? We cannot fight, it is our highest law."

"It is," Bat-Erdene shouted back. "But it is not our only law. Taking care of one's friends? That, too, is part of our law. I would see a show of hands—who is willing to throw some arrows to help some friends?"

Perhaps one hundred and fifty hands were raised.

"Go, now, then," said the prefect of the *Ala* of Argippaean Scouts. "Get your horses, your bows, and your quivers. Assemble below, outside this gate."

Those men instantly ran off, leaving the rest feeling deeply unmanly and ungrateful.

One of those shouted up to Bat-Erdene, "If the law forbids us from fighting, does it forbid us from bluffing?"

Bat-Erdene considered this briefly before answering, "You know, I don't think it does."

"Very good, then. If most of us cannot in good conscience fight, let us get our horses and our bows and our quivers and pretend to swell the ranks of those who will. Hurry, my friends!"

That's at least twenty of them, Silvanus thought, *twenty foederati we've had to execute to stop desertions. If they ever all bolt at once they'll just run right over us.*

Even as he thought it, the centurion saw two small groups of the Germans flee, one of two and one of three men. One of the latter actually managed to not only force his way through the Roman line, but to avoid the *pilum* thrown at his retreating back.

Silvanus heard a sound, much like rolling thunder, and thought, *Oh, shit, we're fucked.*

The source of the thought was the sudden noisy arrival of thousands upon thousands of horses. *The Gauls and the legionary cavalry between here and in the camp, waiting for orders. The Scythian boys are off to the east somewhere, if any of them are still alive; same for the Palmyrene horse archers. So those can only be enemy.*

"Blow to the cohort 'assemble on me,'" Silvanus told his *cornicen*. No sooner were the orders issued than the Twelfth gave up its long, thin line and began racing into the center. There, Silvanus directed his six centuries into a rectangle, facing outward.

The *foederati* to their front didn't figure out that their way to the rear was now unbarred. At least not yet, they hadn't.

Then the men on the mass of horses to Silvanus' west gave off a rousing cheer and began to form up in ranks.

"But those *can't* be ours," muttered Silvanus. "Or...Oh, hell, yes they can, even if they're not cavalry. Horses, yes; cavalry, no. And the Vandals aren't likely to know the difference, not yet they're not.

"Back into line, boys! Back into line."

A lone horseman rode off from the mass of horse holders pretending to be cavalry, heading for a point south of the fort. Silvanus thought it was one of the gentleman ranker tribunes.

As the centurion's eyes followed the presumptive tribune, he also saw something he'd never expected to see, let alone hear. This was a mass of the nonviolent, noncombatant Argippaean scouts, charging south, waving bows, and giving a decent simulacrum of Roman battle cries.

"What the fuck?"

Gunderic's men were on the far side of the ridge now, and he standing on the geographical crest. Victory was almost within his grasp as the weak pseudo-allies of Rome gave way before his warriors. And then he realized three things.

One was the mass of Roman cavalry, sitting and waiting on his left flank for him to advance and expose that flank.

I have some reserves; I could put a force to face that cavalry.

Another was the smaller mass of horse archers coming onto the field from the town where they'd apparently lain in wait.

We can handle those.

A third were some scraps of Suebi cavalry racing across the field, followed by several thousand, maybe even eight or nine thousand, Suebi infantry, all hotly pursued by what looked to be those Huns and a larger number of larger horse archers. The victory whoops of both came faintly to the king's ears.

We are fucked.

But the very worst was the sight of what looked to be hundreds, maybe as many as a thousand, white-headed cavalry, now emerging from the fort on the other side of the river and racing for the nearest of the camps of his alliance. Thin trails of smoke rising over the columns said that they intended to burn the camps and the wagons.

And how will my people, any of my people, survive this terribly hard winter without shelter? It is over. We are finished.

The appearance of something above four thousand of what Gunderic was pretty sure were Goths on that flank with the mass of cavalry waiting to pounce was what decided the king.

To his men carrying *lurs* near him, Gunderic said, "Blow the halt. Blow retreat. Blow assemble on me."

The oddest thing, to Gunderic's mind, *is that none of those cavalry nor even that new group of infantry are attacking as we pull back. I can understand the Germans fighting for Rome not pursuing, we've given them all they can take already. But I cannot understand the others. Perhaps the Romans have some reason for keeping us alive. At least, I can hope they do.*

The withdrawal over the ridge was done in about as good an order as one might hope for, given the relative lack of discipline among the Vandals. The Alan cavalry helped cover the retreat, pulling back by echelons and threatening anyone who got too close with being turned into pincushions.

Thank the gods for the Alans, thought Gunderic. *Best allies the Vandal people have ever had.*

Swinging around the southern flank of the Alans, Suebi fugitives came in a steady stream. Most retained their shields and spears, too, though all seemed to have lost their barbarian confidence.

"Godigisel?" asked the King.

"Yes, Father?"

"Go try to organize those Suebi to fall in and form a shield wall on our left. I know it will be hard, but it's probably their only chance for survival."

"I'll do my best, Father," said the boy, before spurring his horse to race to intercept the disordered horse of Suebi.

Then, behind the mass of fleeing Suebi, Gunderic saw something no one had been privileged to see in centuries: a classic Roman legion of the Principate, conducting a very leisurely pursuit, in good order. The legion marched east, killing any Suebi who had fallen behind their panicked fellows.

By the time Gaius Pompeius and the Eighteenth Legion made their appearance to the southwest, smoke was rising from half a dozen encampments on the eastern side of the Rhine. The

Vandals had also managed to form a half perimeter, with their backs to this unfrozen part of the river. What looked to be a few thousand Suebi had joined them. The Alan cavalry, heavy and light both, were in the center of that perimeter.

From the Roman left to the Roman right around the barbarian perimeter, were the *foederati*, then Thancrat's German *auxilia*, with Jovis' missile cohort nearby. Behind the *foederati* was the Twelfth Cohort, their staff slings on prominent display over their shoulders.

To Thancrat's right was the legion, or at least eleven cohorts of it. These stretched almost all the way to the river. To their right, and stretching the rest of the way, were the Palmyrenes. Behind those Germans were the Goths in their shield wall, with their thousand-odd cavalry split to the flanks.

The *Ala* of Scythian Cadets was busy at the place where the barbarians had crossed, wiping out the crossing guards and the parties that had dragged the sleds and the Alan heavy horse across.

Once he was certain that all roads of escape were blocked, Gaius Pompeius rode forward, accompanied by a few guards. "I would speak with kings Gunderic, Hermeric, and Respendial, if they live, or their successors otherwise. I will give a short time to find them and send them forth. They must come out unarmed. If they are not forthcoming, I will recommence the slaughter and none of you, not one, will survive. Who then, will care for your families who are seeing their shelter burned down around them? Look behind you to see if I lie."

More than a few—indeed, nearly all of the survivors of the barbarian horde—did look behind and did see the now thick smoke rising over the frozen landscape.

Gaius felt a familiar presence to his left. Without even looking, he said, "About fucking time, *Praefectus Castrorum*."

"Isn't it just, son, isn't it just?"

"What's this 'son' shit?" asked the legate. "I've never been in any doubt who's the brains of this outfit but—"

"Now, that's a funny story," said Marcus Caelius. "I'll let you in on the joke in a bit. Oh, and that reminds me..." Caelius reached into a haversack and pulled out a letter, the seals to which were already broken. At Gaius' suspicious glance, the camp prefect said, "Well, I had to know what was in it, you see, so I could lose it while crossing a river or swamp if I thought it was not to the good."

"Yes, of course," answered the legate, drily. "So, what does it say?"

"It appoints you as *dux Germanicorum* and awards you full power to defend and settle matters along and across the Rhine. Also some powers in Gaul. It further directs you to look into destroying the rebellion in Britannia whenever it may look feasible without compromising the defense along the Rhine."

"Does it indeed? Well, not bad for a not yet wet-behind-the-ears child, shivering in Germany."

"Not bad at all, son, not bad at all."

I'd love to know, thought Gaius, *just what is behind that smile he's sporting.*

That knowledge would have to wait as the barbarian ranks split and three kings, each armored but unarmed, emerged. One of these was not on horseback but was borne on a litter carried by six of his men. The three wore no helmets, allowing Gaius and Caelius to see Gunderic and Respendial on horseback.

So I assume that's Hermeric on the litter. This was confirmed when the litter was placed on the ground and five of its six bearers turned about to return to their ranks. The one who remained announced himself as "Cimberius, younger brother and successor of Hermeric, who lies stricken before you."

Remarkable, thought Marcus Caelius. *The boy is the spitting image of Flavus.*

"I can have my surgeons look at him," offered Gaius. "They're very skilled."

"No point, Roman," said Hermeric, from his litter. "Unless they've a way to put me out of my misery."

"They do, actually," said Gaius.

"Then send me."

Gaius remembered that he understood Latin well enough, but spoke very little. He looked at Gunderic, who shook his head sorrowfully and said, "He's too badly hurt. Not just one but two of those accursed arrows loosed by your hired Huns in his body and his guts laid open from a sword's bite."

Gaius kept his face impassive while wondering, *Huns? What Huns? Ohhh, those "Huns."*

Gaius and Marcus Caelius both sniffed the air. *Oh, yeah, plenty of shit on the wind. He's a goner.*

"Before we begin," said Gunderic, "please stop your men from burning our camps. Our women and children don't deserve to freeze while they starve."

Gaius turned around and barked an order and a message. A messenger began racing north, toward the bridge, to call off Atrixtos and his hounds. The message sent was to stop burning the camps...for now.

Head slightly tilted, the legate said to the barbarians, "In a few minutes you are going to turn over command to your seconds, then follow me to my base. Cimberius, you can take your brother's place; there's no need to put him through the suffering of movement. We need to talk. Note that I have not ordered you to have your men lay down their arms. However, they look rather hungry and I will not feed them until they do turn over their arms. *All* their arms."

Gunderic explained what the legate had said to Respendial. The Alan responded by tossing his bow to the ground, followed by his quiver, his sword, his shield, and his lance. Gunderic did much the same, less the bow and quiver, as did Cimberius. The latter was about to take the sword laid upon the litter with his brother when Gaius said, "No, he can't do any harm with it. I'd rather he kept his sword until you may inherit it."

Cimberius bent and whispered a translation to Hermeric, who said, "Thank you," in Latin, again, but very weakly, in reply.

Gaius then said, with no great degree of harshness, "Now go tell your men to pass their arms and shields to their front where my men will collect them. Once you have that well started, return here so that we can go to our fort to discuss weighty matters."

"If our men give up their arms, they will be defenseless," Gunderic said.

"If they *don't* give up their arms they are still defenseless and also dead," Gaius retorted. "But if they do, they will be defenseless and fed, rather than dead, and probably sheltered, too, if they're quick about it.

"Look, I have no taste for massacre. You're a lot safer—a LOT—without them than you are with them."

Gunderic translated the exchange to Respendial who nodded sadly. Cimberius needed no translation. All three, now disarmed, turned about and went to explain the realities of life to their followers. Gaius believed that several hundred of those followers had to be killed, and were, to get all to comply. While they were waiting, Rubelius rode over, leading a score of wagons.

"I turned over command to Silvanus," said the tribune. "My best guess was that you would need me here a lot more than you needed me there."

"And the wagons?"

"Arrows, sling bullets, ceramic bullets for the staff slings, and bolts for the scorpions."

"Very good, Junius," said the legate. "What I want, first and foremost, is for the weapons to be collected from those men and stored somewhere not easy for them to reach. When that's done I want them fed: half a loaf of bread per man, plus some cheese and sausage, whatever's most available. Maybe a dollop of butter each, too. Plan on delivering a similar amount and menu tomorrow. After their first feeding, and once they're disarmed, I want a camp built to hold them under guard. Finally, they'll all freeze to death tonight in the open so I want tents—yes, our tents—set up for them. No firewood, though. I'm not sure they'll understand how flammable those oiled and waxed tents are."

The two barbarian kings and one heir apparent returned. Behind them, piles of sword and spears, shields, too, were growing.

"We are ready now, Roman," said Gunderic.

There were sufficient guest quarters in the *Praetorium*. These were nothing lavish, a bed or two, a stool, wash stand and bowl, pitcher, and a brazier for keeping off the cold. Those last weren't usually necessary, as the hypocaust would heat both floors more or less well.

Into those quarters were packed the six heads of the *foederati* "legions," the six Gothic clan chiefs, Gunderic, Respendial, and Cimberius. Matters had to wait several days while the paramount chief of the Franks—there really was no single king as of yet—Chlodio, as well as a half dozen other prominent Franks, were fetched by *lusoriae*, from farther north.

The Goths and *foederati*, as befitted allies, had the run of the base and the town. So, too, would the Franks have the same freedom. The three barbarian chiefs had similar privileges, but were required to be accompanied by three guards each whenever they ventured from the *Praetorium*.

All three of those kings—for, indeed, Hermeric took a fatal

dose of *opos* shortly after the surrender—were taken to the prison camp established by Rubelius to see to their men and their welfare. None were precisely happy, but they were in tents erected by the legion, and they were being fed an approximately adequate ration.

Wagons rumbling across the stone bridge over the Rhine said that food, too, was being sent to the families stuck on the other side. It was not enough to build up a stockpile, but it was almost enough to keep bodies and souls together.

"Almost" was the key word there. As the legate had told Rubelius, "I want them to be just about completely destitute of food, in case peace negotiations break down, so we can take the lot captive without much in the way of objections."

The already captured warriors—there were some, notably Alans, who remained free on the eastern side of the Rhine—were surrounded by those chevaux-de-frise, which had been carried on the Scythian wagons and used to keep off wolves from the herds inside the wagon laager on the long march from the east. In addition, a ditch had been laboriously scraped out of the frozen earth, with the resultant *agger* palisaded and mounted with towers. Inside the ditch various obstacles reinforced the new camp's prime purpose, to keep barbarians in rather than out.

In the tents, meant to hold about five thousand men, the barbarians were *ut in vasculo sardinae*, with but a single blanket each.

"But at least we're neither dead nor starving, boys," seemed the common sentiment. "And let's hope it stays that way."

Gaius Pompeius and Marcus Caelius talked late into the night, many nights. The boy, Eucherius, was sometimes included because he understood the way his father's mind worked.

"If you could send my father a legion like the one you have," said the boy, "I think he'd be happy to send his Visigothic 'allies' packing, probably after delivering a good sound spanking."

"But how do we do that?" asked Gaius. "We've only the one in the world."

"Might not be that hard, son." said Caelius, "After all, we are overstrength. But we'd have to make some changes."

"Like what?"

"Like partially revert to the old-style legion," said the camp prefect. "Oh, no, not entirely. The maniples were just too small to stand up to a horde of barbarians that weren't afraid to penetrate through the gaps in the line of battle and just swamp them from every side. We learned that at Arausio, before the second consulship of Gaius Marius. So we probably need to stick with cohorts. We're also going to have to promote some people from lower positions. The cohort is much better for this than a collection of maniples is, because it puts new centurions under older and more experienced ones who can train them.

"However, while we use the *acies triplex*, we don't use it the same way or for the same reasons as they did before the Marian reforms. Back then, the *triarii*'s function was battlefield police, to prevent desertion by summary execution. They hardly ever actually fought and when they did, it was in circumstances either very dire or very advantageous, as in hitting a phalanx from the rear at Cynoscephelae.

"And remember, the armies that win are the armies that desert least and last. That was necessary for those citizen soldier armies, but not so necessary for professionals like us, long serving with tremendous cohesion. If we expand, whether it's by adding the men of those new 'legions' to our cohorts, or by recruiting locally, we're going to be somewhat—or maybe a lot—closer, in terms of human material, to the legions of the republic than we are to ourselves as we are right now."

Gaius could more or less see that, and said so.

"So I'd suggest," continued Caelius, "keeping ten cohorts, still, but making an *acies triplex* with two of the cohorts half strength and composed of our older troops, with the prime mission of stopping desertion. The other two lines of battle can be four cohorts each, with First Cohort staying extra powerful. That would be...let me think..."

"Four thousand, six hundred and forty men," Eucherius piped in. "Not counting the cavalry. Or the slaves."

"I'll take this young man's word for it," said Caelius. The camp prefect's eyebrow was raised in surprise.

"However, young man," said Gaius Pompeius, not without a touch of self-satisfaction, "*our* legion has no slaves. As we've developed there are several hundred freedman noncombatants. So far, that's working well enough that I don't think we'd want to have any more slaves in it."

Caelius continued, "So we'd do it by taking nine hundred and sixty of our older soldiers and centurions and making them *triarii*, with some slight bump in pay. Then we find ninety-four centurions, which means also promoting some *optios* and maybe even a couple from the ranks. We give them each about thirty-five or forty men, from which they pick their own *optios* and *contubernia* leaders. Then we add in forty or forty-five men from wherever, train them like madmen for six months and, behold, we've got two probably pretty good legions, if not so good as ours. We've a good mix of *auxilia* so would want to do something similar there. Hmmm...I wonder where we can get archers and slingers to serve as mercenaries, these days. Eucherius?"

"The Balearic Islands, still, sir, for slingers. I understand you can get some very good archers in Britannia."

"Stout lad, thanks. But—and this is a huge but—the old republican legion's soldiers were barely paid. We must pay ours, and well. That means a tax base in our hands, not the Empire's. And that is going to be a problem, son?"

"All right," said Gaius, "that's about the fiftieth time you've called me 'son,' where you never did before. What's with that?"

"Ask your lovely Scythian wife," was all Caelius would say. "Anything else would spoil the joke. Son."

"Well, you never asked me, then, did you?" asked Zaranaia. "Indeed, nobody asked me just what the relationship was to the woman in the mess section that I got taken out of the prison camp early? I said 'family' and they are family.

"She's my aunt, my father's sister, and the boy and girls who joined her are my cousins. I didn't include my mother because she'd found a place where she was happy and taken care of with Marcus."

Gaius could barely repress a laugh. "Who is, apparently, now my father-in-law. Well, he thinks calling me 'son' is funny. But I've a trick for him, too."

With the arrival of the Franks, the "Conference for the Final Settlement of Germany" could begin. It took place in the centurions' mess, the officers' mess being too small for the purpose. The centurions ate in the officers' mess, in shifts, rather than in their usual place.

The various dignitaries had come with aides-de-camp, but Gaius had limited these to one per man. Those, and the extras, were billeted in an unused barracks on the north side of the base. Rubelius had arranged for one of the taverns near the gate from the base to the town to feed them, on a cost-plus system, issuing each man a certificate to present to the tavern keeper. The tribune had found that presenting actual money, and not some bronze that had had a bit of silver waved over it at some point, got him a better deal than even the official exchange rate. The Scythian women of the mess catered for the conference attendees.

Beer was available in the conference room. "Wine?" the legate had directed. "Wine is for toasting after success. If we have success."

Gaius Pompeius began by having each man in attendance introduce himself, stating his name, his patronymic, where appropriate, and his tribe. Language turned out to be no problem, as everyone but Respendial spoke fair classical or vulgate Latin, and even the Alan could understand enough of it.

"And I am Gaius Pompeius," the legate had begun, after the last of the Germanics had finished. "This is my second, Marcus Caelius, also known as 'Dad.'"

Though the other attendees were not in on the joke, they found it funny for other reasons.

"To my left is my tribune quartermaster, Junius Rubelius. You can thank him for the beer and the food. Behind me is Gisco, my personal secretary. Gisco will be keeping the minutes of the conference. Also behind me is Father Alban, a Catholic priest, who will ask for a benediction on our behalf and on behalf of this conference. And Goths? No complaining; looking from the outside in, the difference between you and the Catholics is trivial—no, it's *meaningless*—however large it looms in each of your minds. Father?"

Gaius stepped back from the lectern at which he'd been standing, making way for the priest. The latter raised his hands to Heaven, blessed the food and drink, the hypocaust, the lanterns, the furniture, and the people, then asked, "And Heavenly Father, please see fit to give us a solution to our problems, one that keeps as much blood as possible inside the bodies that need it."

While the priest was invoking the Almighty, Marcus Caelius made some not entirely successful effort to keep the grin off his face. "Took you long enough," he whispered.

"Well, it wasn't that obvious now, really, was it? My Zaranaia doesn't look like her mother. The Scythians didn't have a complex naming system, like we do, that would have given me a clue. And they both had reasons to be quiet about it. Dad."

Caelius' grin suppression failed completely as Gaius returned to the job at hand.

"Let me explain the problem, as best I understand it," said Gaius, retaking his place at the same lectern. "In the first place, many of you have Huns on your tails and they are bad news incarnate. Anyone object to that classification? Anyone? Ah, good.

"So, many of you—not all, but many—want a piece of the Empire to settle down on, which piece would pay taxes to you but not to the Empire. In lieu of taxes you would pledge to send your warriors to fight for the Empire both on the frontier and against rebels and usurpers. Is this a fair statement?"

Said Gunderic, "It's what we wanted, but you refused us. Are you changing your mind now?"

"No," Gaius replied. "It's a bad deal for us and a terrible precedent. Inside the Empire you may not come as tribes. Your warriors would never be our soldiers. Ultimately, it's a poor deal for you, too, as our people would hate you as new and intolerant masters, hence could be counted on to rise up against you.

"This is not to say that there is no room for you inside the Empire. We've had plagues, civil war, other natural and man-made disasters. There is farmland lying fallow, a lot of it. But if you came in, it would be as individual families, to be settled on individual farms, and *none* of you would be allowed to live within five miles of another."

"And be at the complete mercy of the Empire!" exclaimed Gunderic. "I don't think so."

"That may be," said Gaius, "but we've bought a few more than a thousand abandoned farms in Gaul and, if I must, I will put the question to your men individually. If they elect to take the farms, they'll sign a mortgage and pay not only what we paid for them, but pay with interest, and with taxes to the Empire. And if not, well, we'll settle our own veterans on those farms."

Said Gunderic, "The great and mighty Empire of yours has conquered many lands, peoples, and kingdoms, and made of them Romans like yourself. Why should we be different?"

"So, you want us," asked Caelius, "to settle you on land, then attack you, conquer you, burn your temples, loot your towns, rape your wives and daughters, and break your hearts? What's that? No, you don't. Then the example is nonparallel. You would not become us."

Marcus Caelius and Theodomir had spent a good few days talking out and planning what came next. The Goth stood, was recognized by Gaius, and asked, "Can you settle the Vandals, the Suebi, the Alans, and us Goths on the eastern side of the Rhine and defend us from the Huns there?"

"We've had pretty good success against horse archers," answered Gaius, "so we probably could but for one huge problem." He cast his eyes about the room. "Has anyone here not heard the name Arminius'? Or Varus? Right; I thought those would ring some bells.

"We cannot trust you. Not will not—*cannot.* The troops would mutiny at the first word of something like that. Every man in the legion has been through that and we didn't care for it a bit the first time. Never again."

"Is there no surety we could give?" asked Theodomir. "No treaty we could sign?"

"We had a treaty with Arminius' Cherusci," observed Caelius, drily. "Didn't do the men of the Seventeenth and Nineteenth Legions a bit of good."

"Germany has changed, you know," said Gunderic. "You were, I understand, caught in an ambush in the worst possible terrain. Some of that still exists, of course, but the great forests of the Germany you knew seem mostly to have fallen to the axe and the plow. You would be safer now."

"Germany has changed," agreed Gaius, with a deep nod. "But have you? I mean, it was not so very long ago—indeed, not long at all—that you were trying to get a foothold over the Rhine so that you could rape, kill, pillage, and burn to your heart's content."

Gunderic's face reddened with embarrassment, not anger. "We needed food to live. I won't deny that there would have been some raping, burning, and killing had we succeeded. In what war have these things not been present? But those were not our goals."

"What," asked Father Alban, from behind Gaius and Caelius, "if the Vandals, Suebi, and Alans became Christian? Assuming, of course, that they would consider it to save their people from the Huns."

"It might help," said Gaius, "but not enough. And speaking of burning, there are farmsteads and villages on this side of the Rhine that your raiders burnt out."

Gunderic looked at both Respendial and Cimberius. Each nodded, knowing what was in his mind. "We would volunteer our own labor to rebuild what we destroyed. Give animals from our own herds."

Gaius raised an eyebrow. "Ah, but how will you unrape the women and girls your men had their way with?"

"We cannot," admitted the Vandal king. "I wish we could. If I knew who they were, I'd order them executed in some shameful way. Since I cannot, I will offer monetary damages. Rome prides herself on her body of law; does Rome have no law allowing the payment of monetary damages for personal outrages?"

"We do. There are a few hundred victims, and a like number who were killed. On their behalf and under the authority granted me by the Empire, I would accept ten *minae* of silver for every woman and girl raped, and twenty for each civilian killed. Can you pay this?"

"Those prices are too high," said the Vandal.

"No matter," said Gaius, "for those are the prices. Can you pay them?"

The Vandal was silent for a moment, then conferred with the Suebi, whose men were about equally guilty. They came to some agreement.

"We can," Gunderic agreed. "It will hurt, as perhaps it should, but we can."

"Very good. But we are still stuck with the original problem: you need to fend off the Huns, or to have someone do it for you, and we cannot let you stay on this side of the Rhine."

"Hostages?" offered Theodomir. "We Goths, if you settled us east of the Rhine on good land, and vowed to help us keep it, would give a son from every branch of every noble family as surety."

"Two children," said Caelius, "one of whom could be a daughter."

"Two children," Theodomir agreed, "though it is a hard condition. Will you feed and clothe them, educate them, and give them shelter?"

"We would," said Gaius. "But one tribe with us cannot defeat the Huns when they come. It would take every tribe working together with the legion for that. So Vandals, Suebi, Alans, will you match the Goths' offer?"

Respendial said something that Gunderic translated as, "You hold the whip; do we have any choice?"

Tactfully, Gaius didn't address that. Instead he turned around as if to make sure Gisco had recorded the agreement. Satisfied that the Phoenician had, he turned back to the assembly, saying, "Be sure of it, we will hold your children in good care, but if any tribe should betray us as Arminius and the Cherusci did, we will cut the little bastards' throats, the boys, and sell the girls into brothels. Do you still agree?"

The Franks, led by Chlodio, suddenly stood in obvious outrage. "We agree to none of this."

Gaius held up a pacifying hand. "You Franks fought bravely and well to honor your part of the alliance. We need no surety from you."

Mollified, the delegation of Franks sat back down.

"That said, if we set up a school system for the sons and daughters of the Goths, Suebi, Vandals, and Alans, it would be churlish of us not to open it up to your children, as well. And *that* being said, it would be very suspicious of you not to want to take advantage of it."

The Franks may have been mollified, but that last had some implications they weren't sure they understood yet and were pretty sure that they didn't like at all.

"Now, having set something of a framework for further talks, Rome will, at this time and for a time, withdraw to allow the Germanic tribes and the Alans to discuss what they'd like to see in their relations with the Empire. Gentlemen, enjoy your lunch."

Theodomir was the Roman's agent in place inside the mess. He went to the table where the Franks had gathered, with his son, Fredenandus, acting as his aide.

"What do you make of all this?" the Goth asked Chlodio.

"Frankly, I don't," answered the paramount chief of the Franks. "I don't know what the Romans want. I don't know what anybody wants except for us, and we want mostly to be left alone on the land we took and the land the Romans ceded to us.

"What do *you* think they want?"

Said Theodomir, "I got to know their second-in-command,

Marcus Caelius, quite well on the march here. And he knows the Roman commander, Legate and *Dux Germanicorum* Gaius Pompeius rather well. He told me of the plan they had at one time, which was to let the Vandals, Alans, and Suebi starve to death, then cross and enslave the survivors, move the existing German farmers out into those farms the *dux* mentioned, and turn Germany into a wasteland that could not support the Huns for a day.

"He also told me that Gaius Pompeius *hated* that plan, but couldn't think of anything better that would secure the Roman Empire."

"I could understand why he hated it," said the Frank. "The Romans can be a rough bunch, but they don't usually like waste except in cases of extreme hatred. They prefer to leave places in a position to pay taxes and provide troops. Besides, I don't have the sense that they hate even the Vandals."

"They're too professional," Theodomir said, "as a general rule, to hate. Caelius told me once that 'hate clouds judgment.' It's a lot like love, that way, I suppose."

"Well," said Chlodio, "if I don't know what the Romans want, I can tell you what I'd want...or would like, anyway. That would be a lot more land. But that land could only come at Roman expense or from the east. And since the battles with the Vandals and Alans, we really don't have the men to expand east."

"Less still the west, my friend, since this new-old legion arrived from the past. Have you ever even imagined troops like that?"

"I may have had a nightmare once," the Frank said.

That raised a chuckle from Theodomir. More seriously, he said, "That sparks a thought: the Romans could lead the way in, taking more land for you to the east. But that said, they've got such bad memories of that part of Germany that they'd probably demand some 'sureties' from even such good and faithful allies as the Franks."

"If they'd help us take more land to the east, then we'd probably be willing to give hostages."

"Hmmm...a question: Are the Frankish lands inside or outside the Empire?"

Replied Chlodio, "Half and half...or rather less than half. That is to say that half our lands are west of the Rhine and half east. But while the lands west are inside the Empire, we pay no taxes, beyond a sort of token gift to the emperor, while the lands to the east are outside the Empire and there we pay no taxes and pay no attention, either."

"If they helped you carve out a bigger homeland, they might want a lot more than that. Would the Franks be willing to give up their land west of the Rhine?"

"If they tripled our lands overall, I think we would."

"Would they be willing to pay taxes? I am presupposing here that the Empire extended a guarantee to defend you in your new possessions. And I am also presupposing that the taxes you would have to pay would be enough to help defray the costs of keeping troops here but not to pay for solid gold chamber pots for the emperor."

"Depends on the rate. What does it cost to keep a legion somewhere?"

"I am guessing here, but something in the range of thirteen to fourteen hundred pounds of gold a year. Might go as high as sixteen hundred."

"Now *that*," said Chlodio, "is an amazing amount of gold. We could maybe provide two hundred, once we had farms in production. But fourteen hundred? That's way beyond our ability to squeeze out of our people. And even for that two hundred, half would have to be in kind—grain, meat, cheese, and such."

"We might be able to come up with the same," said Theodomir. "Surely not more than that, but then...Hmmm?"

"Yes?" asked the Frank.

"Well, if you Franks, and we Goths, and the Vandals, Alans, and Suebi could each come up with—I am speaking roughly here; surely amounts would be based on population and land—but say one hundred pounds of gold each and one hundred pounds of gold worth of food and other goods, each...well, that would pay for most of the legion to help us expand and help us defend against the Huns. Who are, if the chiefs of the horde are to be believed, coming.

"I think we have the beginnings of a plan, here. Let's go interrupt the barbarians, shall we?" asked Theodomir.

"We don't need Roman help conquering new lands," said Gunderic. "We're already sitting on a very large piece of Germany, and have enserfed the farmers already there. What we need, assuming we cannot get into the Empire, is defense against the Huns. As I have made clear many times."

Theodomir agreed with this, but then asked, "And you said you would be willing to give noble hostages, a lot of them, to get that help. But troops like the Romans must be paid. Would you be willing to pay to keep them here?"

"We Suebi would be willing to pay," said Cimberius, "for we faced this legion in battle and know just how frightful they are. But we'd need time to get our new farms running."

"How long?" asked Theodomir.

"Maybe two years. We and the rest have picked that part of Germany bare."

"We'd need two years, as well," said Gunderic.

Respendial shook his head. Through Gunderic he said, "I think that for the Alans, no amount of time would be sufficient. We are nomads and herders, not farmers. I doubt a one of us knows at which end of a plow the horse goes. I certainly don't."

"Hmmm... that sparks a thought," said Theodomir. "What's the land to the east like?"

"Traveling east from here," said Gunderic, "for about two hundred miles there are interspersed villages, farms, and forests, with the villages and farms getting fewer and the forests thicker with each mile. Past those there are mountains and other rough ground. Past those are open steppes."

"Who can move faster?" asked Theodomir. "Alans or Huns?"

"Well," said Respendial, "the fox is running for a meal while the rabbit is running for his life."

"So, let's suppose that the Romans helped carve out homelands for Franks, Goths, Vandals, and Suebi, all to the east, but left the grasslands further east to the Alans. The Huns show up and you and your people run like Hell, driving your herds and carrying your families, for safety in the west. The legion marches to where you tell them the Huns are coming from. All the allies gather under the Romans and meet the Huns. Win or lose, we'll bleed them so badly as to break their hearts and send them off. But with the legion and ourselves, and Alan cavalry to go with the Roman cavalry, I don't think we lose."

Respendial was silent for a long moment, thinking, *And the Alans then have the trade routes to the land of silk and opos.*

"There aren't going to be enough Alans for that. One of my

sub-chiefs, Goar, has already said he intends to take up with the Romans as allies, and take nearly half my people with him."

"Why would he do that?" asked Cimberius.

"Because the Roman legion terrified him," answered Respendial. "And Goar was never a man to frighten easily."

"Even with half," said Theodomir, "your population will grow with your herds. You'll fill up that strip quickly enough and then go looking for more grasslands to the east. In the interim, you take on patrolling against the Huns."

"It could be done," agreed the Alan.

"You know," said Cimberius, "if we're going to have Roman troops among us, if we're going to be dependent on them for our defense, if we're going to be paying taxes to them, is there any difference between that and being inside the Empire and part of it?"

"No," said Theodomir, simply. "Shall we petition to be admitted as imperial subjects, consistent with the requirements we've laid out today?"

"Aye," said Chlodio. "Aye … aye … aye," said the chiefs of the horde. And finally, "Aye, I think so, too," said Theodomir.

"But we need to hold out for as near to equivalent noble rank as we are entitled to," said the Vandal. "Otherwise, the Empire will not respect us."

POSTSCRIPT

Mogontiacum, 408 A.D.

There were three genuine legions now, Seventeenth, Eighteenth, and Nineteenth. There were also no eagles left in the Temple of Mars Ultor. The real ones had been returned to the reconstituted legions, whose members had almost uniformly wept over that much longed for return. The false eagle of the Eighteenth had been brought to Mogontiacum and urinated on by every man in the Eighteenth not in the hospital—and a collection of urine from them had been taken up and the eagle dipped in it—before being melted down and turned into much debased antoniniani. The pissing ceremony had taken days. Each man, while pissing, had uttered the sentence written on a sign over the false eagle, "Up your ass, Arminius."

The Nineteenth, under Rubelius, with a much-recovered Sattius as camp prefect, and Silvanus as first spear, was now down in Italy, with Stilicho, showing Alaric's Visigoths that the world had changed. In exchange, the Visigoths from the wreckage of the army of Radagaisius, once serving Stilicho, had been sent to Gaius Pompeius, for the conquest of *Germania*.

One of the two legions at Mogontiacum awaited the order to march east.

But whence had come the recruits, the roughly seventeen thousand recruits, to fill up three legions and sundry *auxilia*? Appius Calvus deserved much of the credit for that. Using wood cuts, thousands of recruiting posters—"Rome Wants You for the Conquest of Germany"—had been made and then gone out, accompanied by recruiting agents from the Eighteenth, to Italy, Gaul, Britannia, both Spains, Hither and Further, plus the Balearics, and western North Africa. Good pay was promised, as was good equipment, and the best training in the known world. Enough recruits had poured in to fill up the legions and the now citizen *auxilia*, with the legion's recruiting agents being able to be a bit choosy about who they'd accept.

The dozen additional tribunes needed, and half a dozen new prefects of the *auxilia*, plus a hundred and five would-be centurions, all well recommended from the very highest sources, had arrived in the usual Roman way, by appointment and recommendation, without qualifications. The Empire might be long in the tooth, but this never changed: nepotism and corruption were not flaws in the system, they *were* the system.

However, the legion had made one rather large change. Instead of simply being allowed to take their posts, the new tribunes and prefects, in three times the numbers required, had been subjected to a rather severe course in sheer soldiery under one Marcus Caelius Lemonius, assisted by one Faustus Metilius, until two out of three had quit and gone home. Only once that hard core had been obtained were the tribunes given over to the now very experienced tribunes of the Eighteenth for more professional training. The would-be centurions continued their instruction under Caelius until he had judged them fit for duty. One of the surviving candidates had even come up with a song, which became the theme song for the lot, entitled, "Caelius' School for Boys."

Seventeenth would be left behind, to secure the Rhine and the families and, of course, the hostages, in case everything went to crap. The rest of the army—Eighteenth Legion with two unusually large cohorts and three *alae* of auxiliaries, ten thousand Visigothic infantry and two thousand cavalry, a like number of Suebi, a slightly greater number of Vandal infantry, and about a thousand Vandal cavalry, plus a thousand Alan heavy cavalry and four thousand light—were ready to march and, indeed, were already placed on the eastern bank of the Rhine, barring the Alans who were scouting farther to the east. With the arrival of the Franks, five thousand foot and a thousand horse, the campaign could commence.

The purposes of that campaign? It was to secure *Germania* and points east for the Empire and its client kingdoms of Franks, Vandals, Suebi, Visigoths, and Alans.

Everything was ready, down to the soles of the *caligae*. Gaius Pompeius, surrounded by his staff and subordinate commanders, sat atop his horse, on a piece of high ground overlooking Pullo's castle, ready to give the order to march. Outside the eastern gate of the castle, the eagle of the legion was just emerging, borne by Mucius Tursidius. Drums beat while brass instruments played a martial air.

From the east, up a dirt trade road the Romans had never gotten around to paving, a small band of horsemen flogged their horses into a lather, racing for the Romans. These horsemen pulled up at one of the wagon laagers to either side of the road. After a brief moment, they turned to Gaius Pompeius and raced up the hill.

Breathless and filthy, Gaius thought that they'd not bathed and probably not eaten or slept much in the last couple of weeks. One of the horseman made a hand gesture that Gaius took to be a kind of Alan salute, then passed over a sealed cylinder. Gaius broke the seal and withdrew, then read a rolled-up message contained therein.

Lips pursed, face darkened and troubled, Gaius announced, simply, "The Huns are here."

POSTSCRIPT II

The two-member decapodal alien scout team had taken a personal interest in the progress and welfare of the creatures they had saved, whenever their busy schedule allowed. The time for their mission now being short, they looked in one last time on the dirt-bound creatures below. Those creatures, now in vastly greater numbers, were moving east.

"I took them for some kind of insects," sang Sweetasthescentofglowblossoms, or just "Blossom," to her mate, Red. "They're more than that, though, aren't they?"

She and Red followed the current progress of the group she'd once taken to be insects via reconnaissance skimmers and ground crawlers, tiny to the point of invisible. Those orderly lines, moving briskly in the direction of the rising sun, would never have been maintained by mere insects.

Red, officially known as Seetheredglowofmorning, answered, "It was those hard shells that fooled you, love...fooled me, as well, so don't be embarrassed. Turns out they're not part of their bodies, but a close-fitting artificial bit of covering. We might have figured that out if we were a species given to wearing anything beyond a bit of jewelry. Since we're not..."

Blossom clicked her beak in agreement. In a song both sad and worried, she mused, "I wonder what will become of them."

"Well," said Red, "everything we've seen says that, even if not murdered by shaggy creatures of the same basic species, these are a relatively short-lived folk. We cannot return for several dozen z)p$#la^ths, at the soonest. Maybe we could put in with

527

headquarters to come back after our next mission and see how they're doing."

"Oh, could we?" Blossom trilled. "That would be wonderful. Please ask."

"For you, love, I surely will. Now, are you ready to leave?"

"As I'll ever be," she sang in reply.

Red's tentacles became a blur as he tapped controls to activate navigation protocols long since prepared. "Perch, Blossom," he commanded, and, once he saw she was safely seated, he reached out a single tentacle.

When he pressed the button, their reconnaissance ship winked out of reality with a flash that would have been visible on the planet below, except that the shine of the local sun overwhelmed it.

APPENDIX A: GLOSSARY

ab urbe condita: Also written as AUC. "From the founding of the city." To convert our dates to theirs add seven hundred and fifty-three.

acies duplex: Double line of battle.

acies triplex: Triple line of battle, a standard Roman formation which, by the time of Julius Caesar meant four cohorts in the first line, with spaces between them of about cohort width, three in the second, covering those spaces, and three in the third, covering the same distance across as the first line but not covering open spaces. Light and especially missile troops—javelin men, slingers, and archers—could sally forth from those spaces and fall back to shelter behind the forward cohorts. Generally speaking, First Cohort, which was stronger than the others, nearly twice as strong, would be forward and on the right flank. This would be especially useful to keep their enemies from exploiting the seams between legions.

agger: The wall around a Roman camp, earthen for a marching camp, often stone for a more permanent one. Can also refer to the linear mound on which a road is constructed, presumably to elevate it above wetlands.

ala, -ae: Wing, as in a wing or wings of cavalry.

Albis: Roman name for the Elbe River.

Aliso: A Roman fort and town probably around Haltern am See, Germany, about thirty miles east of the Rhine.

Altrebatæ: Arras, France.

Ambiani: Amiens, France.

amicus, amici: Latin for "friend."

Angrivari: A Germanic tribe.

animus: Soul or spirit, as used herein, but with a great many more meanings in Latin, to wit: the mind, the rational soul in man, intellect, consciousness, will, intention, courage, spirit, sensibility, feeling, passion, pride, vehemence, wrath, etc., the breath, life, soul. As used: *anima ad animum*, spirit to spirit. I commend to the reader a particular song by one Anne Lister entitled "Vindolanda."

antoninianus, -i: A unit of currency equivalent to two denarii, but in practice, by the fourth century it took twenty-five antoniniani to equal a single denarius of the first century.

aqua regia: A mix of nitric and hydrochloric acids. Will dissolve gold when mixed together, although neither one will dissolve gold alone.

aquilifer: The legionary selected to carry the legion's eagle. One cannot help but suspect that these were some tough mothers. In battle they could be expected to earn their double pay...for the several years past.

Argentoratum, Argentoratus: Strasbourg, France.

Argippaeans: A people mentioned by Herodotus as living north of the Scythians and being not only pacifistic, themselves, but also immune to attacks by others. To the extent it is admitted they might have existed, modern scholars seem to think they were some sort of Mongolians. I have, based partly on Herodotus' description, written them as a sort of horse-riding, nomadic, pacifist Chatham Islanders...before the Maori showed up.

arhaan: Argippaean word for oats.

as, asses: Roman coin, generally of bronze, worth one tenth of a denarius.

atrium: A reception room in a Roman *domus*, generally with a pool for collecting rainwater and an opening above to admit rain and light.

Augusta Praetoria: Aosta, Italy.

Augusta Trevorarum: Trier, Germany.

Augustodunum: Autun, France.

auxilia: Auxiliary. About half of the Roman Army of the period around 9 A.D. was composed of foreign troops who served for pay and eventual citizenship. They made up the bulk of the specialist units, light infantry, cavalry, thrusting spear-armed infantry, and the like.

ave (pronounced ah-weigh): Hail.

ave atque vale: Hail and farewell.

balteus: A baldric used for carrying a gladius, q.v.

barritus: A Germanic war cry or war chant. We don't know what it sounded like. Then again, it's only rather recently that we figured out what the rebel yell sounded like.

beat: A measure of time the aliens who use it have not yet given to mankind. Our best guess is that it is about ninety seconds, but this could be wildly off.

Bingium: Bingen, Germany.

Bononia: Bologna, Italy.

Borysthenes: Dnepr River.

braccae: Trousers, generally Gaulish in origin, though others wore them. They could run from just below the knee all the way to the ankle. The colder the local winters, the longer and heavier they were.

bucellatum, -i: Basically hardtack, and generally made by the legionaries, themselves.

caligae: Hobnailed boots made from strips of leather sewn to a built-up sole.

capulus, -i: Hilt of a sword.

Castellum Mattiacorum (aka Pullo's Castle): A strong fortress on the east side of the Rhine, guarding the bridge from Mogontiacum.

castrum, castra: Camp or fort.

cera: Short form for a wax writing tablet.

cippi: Sharpened stakes, possibly fire hardened, dug into the ground, especially in ditches and pits, aimed towards the enemy.

classis: Fleet.

Classis Germanica: German Fleet or Rhine Fleet. The collection of generally quite light warships that patrolled the Rhine.

clepsydra: Water clock. Note that it is unclear whether or not hourglasses existed in 9 A.D., but there is no doubt that clepsydrae existed well before that.

cognomen: Which is to say, family, or last name. See praenomen.

Colonia: Formally "Colonia Claudia Ara Agrippinensium." Cologne, Germany.

Colonia Copia Felix Munatia: A city in Gaul, later known as Lugdunum, and still later as Lyons.

compluvium: An opening in the roof over an atrium that admitted both rainwater and light.

Confluentes: Koblenz, Germany.

congius, -i: Roman liquid measure, approximately .86 gallon.

"Conscribe te militem in legionibus. Pervagere orbem terrarium. Inveni terras externas. Conosce miros peregrinos. Eviscere eos." Join the legions; see the world; travel to foreign parts; meet interesting and exotic people; and eviscerate them. H/T Philip Matyszak.

contubernium, -ia: A Roman squad; at full strength, eight men who tented, lived, marched, and cooked together. I do not believe they were given two slaves as servants.

cornu, cornua: One of several brass musical instruments, also used for signaling.

cornicen, cornicines: A junior noncom in the legions who carried and played a cornu. Often held additional administrative duties.

Cruciniacum: Bad Kreuznach, Germany.

Danapris: Dnepr River.

Danubius: Danube River. The writer doubts many people couldn't figure that one out on their own, but one never knows.

decurion: Leader of a turma, or platoon, of cavalry.

decanus: Leader of a *contubernium* of *auxilia*.

"De gustibus non disputandum": Latin saying, more or less, "There is no accounting for taste."

denarius, denarii: A Roman coin, in Augustan times weighing about 3.9 grams of almost pure silver.

dominus: Lord or master or chief or boss.

domus: A Roman house.

double pace: Five feet. A Roman mile—from *mille*, meaning a thousand—is one thousand double paces of a legionary.

epityrum: A kind of olive-based relish. For a more thorough explanation visit *Tasting History with Max Miller* on YouTube; that, or buy the book, like I did.

eques, equites: Knight. A member of the equestrian order, one step below patricians and above plebians.

ergtil: An alien measure of time mankind has no clue to, except that it appears to be considerably longer than a beat.

Euxine: The Black Sea.

extraordinarii: Allied or auxiliary troops picked for special missions, point guard, rear guard, wherever the danger was great and the need for unusual skill or bravery was greatest.

fabrica, -ae: Arms factory.

Falernian: A high-end Italian wine, much prized by Romans, generally. It came from grapes grown on the slopes of a particular bit of high ground, Mount Falernus, generally south of Rome. It is widely believed that the modern wine, Falerno del Massico, is the nearest thing to ancient Falernian. Massico is the modern name for Falernus. There is a theory that Falernian may have been freeze-distilled to increase its alcohol component to about forty percent. Imagine all the methanol that got left behind in the drink, if so.

Felix: A name that also means "Happy."

fenestra, -ae: Window, though the Romans didn't use much glass for windows at this time.

fibula, -ae: A sort of large safety pin for closing clothing and especially cloaks.

flagellum: A particularly nasty Roman whip, quite capable of taking off large chunks of meat and skin with each stroke.

focale, focalia: Neck scarf.

foederatus, -i: In theory, allies, but in practice barbarian tribes to whom the Romans ceded land, especially along the borders, apparently on the twin theory that *these* barbarians aren't as bad as *those* barbarians and that they would reliably fight for Rome. In practice just out for themselves and their own, and in good part responsible for the eventual collapse of the Empire.

"Forget that town; it doesn't exist": Look up the Bielefeld conspiracy.

foss: Ditch, in Latin, *fossa*, and especially the ditch dug nightly around a marching camp. There were other ditches and, especially, some permanent defensive ditches. See, for example, the Fosse Way, in England. The spoil from the foss became the *agger*, or wall, around the camp.

framea: Germanic spear, effective at both short- and long-ranged combat, but not generally effective at piercing the Roman *scutum* or *lorica*.

"Friends and Allies": Independent states that had treaties with Rome.

furca, furcae: The pole to which a legionary's marching pack was attached.

Furor Teutonicus: A Latin phrase, "Teutonic Fury"—a reminder of the peculiar ferocity of the Teutons but also the Germans more generally, in the attack.

galea: A Roman helmet.

garum: A Roman fermented fish sauce, perhaps something like nuoc mam. Max Miller's channel, *Tasting History*, on YouTube, has one episode on him making some.

Gaul: More or less modern France with Belgium attached. Inhabited by Celtic peoples. There was also a Cisalpine Gaul, which was northern Italy.

Genua: Genoa.

ger, gerud: Yurts.

Germania: Should be obvious but maybe not: Germany.

Germania Inferior: Lower Germany, as in lower in height. More or less northern Germany, to include the areas on the Rhine.

Germania Superior: Upper Germany, as in higher in height. More or less southern Germany, to include the areas on the Rhine.

gladius, gladii: Also *gladius Hispanica*. The short sword that was the standard arm of the classical legionary. Though any sword is also a gladius.

glans, glandes: Sling bullet, includes both lead and ceramic and possibly rocks.

gratias: Thanks.

groma: Surveying instrument.

gromaticus, -i: Surveyors.

haruspex, haruspices: A diviner who was guided by studying the entrails and organs, especially the livers, of sacrificial animals.

hastatus posterior: Junior centurion of each cohort except the first.

Hispania: Also should be obvious but, just in case, Spain and Portugal. The latter was also referred to as Lusitania, more or less; a little bit less in the south and a little bit more in the northeast.

horreum, -ea: Granary.

hypocaust: The Roman system for below the floor heating. Fires were built in chambers that emptied out into channels and hollow spaces under the building. These heated the floor and the floor heated the rooms.

imaginifer: A position somewhat like that of the aquilifer, except that the imaginifer bore a standard showing the likeness of the emperor.

impedimenta: The baggage train of a legion or army.

impluvium: A pool in an atrium that collected rainwater. Unseen filtration systems tended to purify the water thus collected, cooling it as well. The *impluvium* could also be used for evaporative cooling.

"In principio creavit Deus cælum, et terram": "In the beginning God created Heaven and Earth." Just go read the beginning of the Book of Genesis.

intervallum: The space between the wall of the camp or fort and the beginning of the tents or barracks. It is said to have been a standard two hundred feet in depth, sufficient, with legionary artillery and attached slingers and bowmen keeping an enemy back, to keep any enemy from attacking the tents or barracks with fire.

jugerum, -a: Measure of land area, about .623 acre.

kestros (or *kestrophendone*): A dart propelled by a sling or the sling itself.

lectus, -i: An old-fashioned dining couch.

legate: Also *legatus*, the commander of the legion.

libra, -ae: Roman pound, about 11.6 ounces.

liburnian: A light warship with a top speed under both sail and oar, in a fair wind, of about fourteen knots. Which is, you know, pretty good. *Liburnians* typically carried about forty-four rowers, four sailors, and sixteen marines.

lilia: "Lillies," camouflaged pits with sharpened stakes at the bottom.

limitanei: Borderers. These were often legionary in origin, or from the *auxilia*, whose ancestors had proven either prone to rebellion or too easily manipulated by local commanders with a hankering after the purple. Progressively reduced in size by the habit of taking detachments—vexillations—from them to form ad hoc field armies, as well as some form of organizational reductions in strength, eventually they found themselves as unpaid local militia. In the period of the novel they are still professional soldiers, paid—albeit less than legionaries had been—but no longer capable of the feats of the classical legions.

linothorax, -es: Body armor made up of multiple layers of linen, glued or sewn together. Surprisingly tough and effective against the weapons of the day, though better steels and sharper edges much reduced the effectiveness.

Londinium: London.

lorica: Roman body armor. It came in several varieties, one of which, the one made of bands of iron, we don't know the actual name of but call it "segmentata" anyway. The others were *lorica hamata*, basically mail, aka "chain mail," for a common usage, and *lorica squamata*, fish scale. There some other variants but those are the big three.

lucerna, lucernae: Oil lamp.

Lugdunum: Lyon, France.

Lupia: Lippe River.

lur: An ancient Germanic wind instrument, generally made of bronze.

mansio: A government-funded rest stop on a major road. It would provide food and accommodations, perhaps also a change of horses, for official business. In the author's suspicion, they probably also served to support the official mails. It was also often possible to get laid at privately run *cauponae*, usually situated near a *mansio*.

Matisco: Macon, France.

medicus, medici: Physician.

medicus veterinarius, or just *veterinarius*: Just what one might expect, the veterinary.

meretrix, -trices: Prostitute. Another word for the same thing is *lupa, lupae*, which is also the word for she-wolf. This actually lends some credence to the myth that Romulus and Remus were nursed by a *lupa*, no?

mina, -ae: Another word for pound, but this one, originating likely in Sumeria, was usually about twenty-five percent heavier than our pound, whereas the Roman was about twenty-five percent lighter.

metator, -ores: Those who measure the layout of the camps and forts of the legions, with the *gromatici* (surveyors).

Mirabile visu: Wonderful to behold.

modius, -ii: Roman measure, about 8.7 liters.

Moenis: Main River, which flows into the Rhine near Mogontia-cum.

Mogontiacum: Mainz, Germany.

Morini: Gallic for "sea folk," sailors, a *Belgic* coastal tribe dwelling in the modern Pas-de-Calais.

Murmuring Rock: The Lorelei.

navis lusoria, naves lusoriae: Dancing ship or playful ship. No, not ballroom dancing. Think maneuverable.

Nemausus: Town in Gaul; modern Nimes.

Nemetæ: Speyer, Germany.

ngek, ngekud: Cattle, more specifically, domesticated aurochs.

"No man ever steps in the same river twice...": This isn't exactly what Heraclitus said, but conveys the sense of the thing better than a straight translation of the original.

Novempopulania: A province of western Gaul in the third, fourth, and fifth centuries A.D.

"O tempora, O mores": "Oh, the times, oh, the customs." It is a kind of reverse Roman lament for "the good old days."

oppidum: A village or town, generally fortified, generally on a hilltop, and generally Celtic.

opos: Juice of the opium poppy.

optio: Second-in-command of a century but also the centurion's administrative assistant. Appointed by the centurion.

Pannonia: A Roman province, the borders of which defy easy description, in part because those borders changed frequently and in part because they don't correspond well with any modern borders, encompassing parts of seven states. So, in general terms Pannonia was south of the Danube, east of northeastern Italy, north of the former Yugoslavia, and included western Hungary. If that doesn't work look it up on Wikipedia. Pannonia was the site of a substantial anti-Roman rebellion prior to the events of 9 AD.

patibulum, -a: The crosspiece for crucifixion.

phalerae: Decorations for bravery, if multiple, attached to a leather harness, arrayed across the chest.

pilum, pila: A more or less heavy Roman javelin. Each legionary carried two or, perhaps exceptionally, three. Effective range perhaps fifty feet, though it could penetrate shields and armor at that range. They had pyramidal heads that were difficult to extract from, say, a shield. Ones recovered seem to have bent.

Pisae: Pisa, Italy.

Placentia: Piacenza, Italy.

plumbata, -ae: A weighted projectile weapon, much smaller than a *pilum*, and capable of being thrown two to three hundred feet.

pluteus, -ei: A kind of moveable protective screen, used during sieges. ·

porta: Gate, in general, but as used here, a gate of a legionary camp or fortress. Each gate, of which there were generally four, had its own name, based on the street that led to it and its position relative to the *Praetorium*. They were the Porta Principalis Sinestra and Dextra, the Porta Praetoria, and the Porta Decumana. A Roman soldier would have taken one look at the orientation of the *Praetorium* and known which street was which and which gate was which.

Portus Itius: A Roman port, Gaul, on the English Channel, or more specifically the Pas-de-Calais. We don't actually know where it was—the likely candidates are Wissant, Saint-Omer, and Boulogne-sur-Mer.

praefectus: Most of the *auxilia* were commanded by *praefecti*, who were usually Roman citizens and sometimes local aristocracy from among the same area as the auxiliaries were recruited.

praefectus castrorum: Camp prefect, a former senior centurion, and, at least usually, a former first spear centurion. While one would normally expect these to be first class soldiers, the record is that Ceionius was not. The camp prefects seem to have undertaken, as with many British late-entry officers, a quartermaster function. They were very senior within a legion, outranking everyone but the legate in command and the senatorial class tribune, the *tribunus laticlavius*.

praefectus classis: Commander of a fleet.

praenomen: Given, which is to say first, name. See *cognomen*.

primus pilus: First spear. The senior centurion of the legion, commanding the first century of the first cohort. I have chosen to give him the informal address, based on American military usage, of "Top."

principia: Camp headquarters. Very often, on the march, these are the same as the *Praetorium*. In more permanent camps, the legate will have his quarters nearby but separate.

proskynesis: Bowing down before a ruler, the one doing proskynesis going all the way to his belly on the floor

pugio, pugiones: Dagger. Every legionary carried one. It served as a backup weapon as well as a utility knife.

Pullo's Castle (aka Castellum Mattiacorum): A strong fortress on the east bank of the Rhine. Guards the bridge from Mogontiacum.

"Quintili Vare, legiones redde!": "Quintilius Varus, give me back my legions."

Raha: Scythian word for the Volga River, meaning "the wetness." Borrowed by the Argippaeans.

Remorum: Rheims.

Romanes eunt domus / Romani ite domum: See Monty Python, *Life of Brian*.

Romanus, -i: Roman person or people.

sacramentum: Oath.

sagittarius, -ii: Archer and horse archer.

sagum, saga: A heavy wool cloak, replete with lanolin, generally associated with the military, hence with war.

sarcina, sarcinae: The legionary's marching pack.

savillum: A flattish cheesecake sweetened with honey and sprinkled with poppy seeds.

scorpion: A torsion-powered, very large crossbow. Crew served, it could still be operated by one man, if necessary.

scutum, scuta: Shield. Look to Appendix C for a discussion on why I don't think it was generally held one-handed.

Septentrio: The Seven Plow Oxen, also known to us as the Big Dipper.

signaculum: A Latin word for a sign or seal produced by a stamp or signet ring. For military purposes, however, the term "dog tag" is more accurate. It was worn inside a small leather pouch carried on a cord about the neck.

signum: Standard.

signifer, -i: Standard bearer.

silphium: A plant, possibly extinct though possibly recently rediscovered in Turkey, with a wide variety of uses ranging from birth control to treatment of a fever.

Skolotoi: Scythians.

soleae ferreae: Iron sandals. The Romans did protect their horses' hooves, but not with shoes, nailed on. Rather they used leather straps to hold them in place. Also known as hipposandals.

sotto voce: Speaking quietly, as if not to be heard. Under one's breath.

spatha, spathae: Roman long sword.

spinae: Spurs. But in siege and countersiege work, heavy logs about a foot long from which hooked pieces of iron sprouted.

spintria, -ae: Tokens depicting erotic acts. There is considerable argument about what the tokens represented—perhaps bathhouse locker room tokens, especially for people without letters or numbers who would still be able to identify a particular sex act to retrieve their clothing, gaming pieces, or actually exchangeable in a brothel for the sexual act they depict. My use here may or may not be anachronistic.

stirps, stirpes: The upright part of crucifixes.

subarmalis: A padded sleeveless jacket worn under the *lorica*. It would prevent or reduce blunt trauma and probably provide a bit of standoff for arrows that might get through.

sudis, sudes: The stakes carried by the legionaries and used to build the palisade atop the *agger* surrounding the camp.

taberna: A private inn or tavern on a road.

tabernaculum, tabernacula: Tent.

tabula cerata: A reusable wax covered writing tablet. Often called a *cera*—or "wax"—for short.

Tempestas: Roman goddess of storms and sudden changes in the weather.

Temple of Mars Ultor: A sanctuary dedicated to Mars.

tenaci: The actual part of the hilt of a sword that is gripped by the hand.

tesserarius: A very junior noncom, roughly equivalent to a corporal. His pay was one and a half times that of a simple legionary, but was really worth more because the deduction for rations was the same as a common legionary's. *Tesserarii* were responsible for standing the night's watch and presumably a certain amount of record-keeping.

testudo: Tortoise formation, a formation of overlapping shields that gave considerable protection to the legionaries inside and from all sides at the cost of much reduction in speed.

Ticinum: Pavia, Italy.

tormentum, -a: Roman artillery. Modern reconstructions indicate that a *tormentum* could throw an eight-pound shot about five hundred meters. These were, according to Ammianus Marcellinus, later called *onagers*.

Tornacum: Tournai, Belgium.

triarii: The third line of battle under the old republican manipular legion. The *triarii* were the old soldiers, very experienced, and organized in half-strength centuries and maniples. They rarely—not never, just rarely—fought. Their primary function was to keep the forward maniples from disintegrating by being there to summarily execute deserters. In the classic, professional legions of the Principate, there seems to have been reduced need for that kind of battlefield policing, so the cohorts that composed the third line of battle were useful for battle, and used in battle, as a general rule.

tribune laticlavius: There were six tribunes in a legion. Five came from the equestrian class and the sixth, the *tribune laticlavius*, or broad-striped tribune, from the senatorial class. That

tribune was second-in-command of a legion. He could generally be identified by a broad purple stripe on his tunic and a
purple cloak.

triclinium, triclinia: Upper-class Romans ate lying on one side, on
couches designed for the purpose.

turma, turmae: Platoon of cavalry, thirty men at full strength.

udones: Socks.

"ut in vasculo sardinae": Latin for "like sardines in a vessel," or in
our parlance, "like sardines in a can."

Vae Victis: "Woe to the vanquished."

valetudinarium: Hospital.

Vangionum: Worms, as in the city.

vermis, -es: Maggot or worm. As used here, maggot.

Vetera: A Roman fort near what is now Xanten, Germany.

vexillation: A detachment from a legion. Gaius Pompeius Proculus' use here may be inaccurate, but is sound on moral
grounds.

vexillarius: Standard-bearer.

vexillum: A banner, generally mounted to a crosspiece that, in
turn, was mounted on a bearable pole, serving as the standard
for a unit of the Roman Army.

via: Road.

Via Aurelia: Aurelian Road, a metaled public highway that
roughly paralleled the western Italian coast between Pisa and
Rome.

Via Ausonius: Ausonian Way, the road from Augusta Treverorum
to Mogontiacum. Not clear to me that this was ever an official
name.

Viadris: Oder River.

Visurgis: Weser River, Germany.

vitis: Vine staff, badge of office, along with the transverse crest of
his helmet, of a centurion.

Wolf attacks: Be it noted that, in 1439, a pack of wolves entered Paris and, getting all the way to Notre Dame Square, managed to kill forty or more people.

yob, *yobud*: Some proto-Mongolian word for stirrups. Yes, pure authorial fancy; we really don't know.

zingfurging: A game popular with a particular extraterrestrial species, involving catching large predatory fish by means of cast javelins attached to lines.

z)p$#la^ths: Nearest possible English pronunciation: Ziplaths. A measure of the passage of time in base 12. Without knowing the time it takes for Red and Blossom's world to make one complete orbit around its sun, we cannot know how long this is.

znarg: A measure of distance the aliens who use it have not yet given to mankind.

APPENDIX B: DRAMATIS PERSONAE

(historical in **bold**)

Agilulf: Cherusci, second-in-command to Flavus.

Ajax: Thracian archer, second-in-command to Zalmoxis.

Alban: A Christian priest, active around Mogontiacum, in the early fifth century. Not much is known about his life, and there are many conflicting theories about both his life and his death.

Sextus Albinus: First-order centurion of Second Cohort, Legio XIIX.

Alodia: Wife of the Gothic cavalryman Theodomir.

Ankhbatar: Argippaean scout.

Arminius: German princeling, Roman equestrian. Brother to Flavus. Enticed three legions under Quintilius Varus into a trap and destroyed most of them. Aka Hermann, though we really don't know his German name.

Artames: Scythian scout.

Atrixtos, son of Cotilus: Latin name, Attius Julianus. Chief of the cohort of Gallic auxiliary cavalry, attached to Legio XIIX.

Bat-Erdene: Argippaean scout, signed on to the legion as a non-combatant mercenary, leader of the other Argippaean scouts who took the emperor's denarius.

Berchar: Frankish warrior and negotiator.

Lucius Caedicius: Camp prefect of the Roman Fortress at Aliso.

Appius Calvus: *Haruspex* (diviner and taker of omens), seconded to Legio XIIX.

Aulus Camillus: First-order centurion commanding the Ninth Cohort.

Benedictus Candidus: Commander of the fleet based at Mogontia-cum.

Ceionius: *Praefectus castrorum* of Legio XIIX, lost his nerve and was killed in the Varian Disaster.

Gilbert Keith (G.K.) Chesterton: Writer, thinker, also known as "the apostle of common sense."

Cimberius: Younger brother and heir apparent of Hermeric, King of the Suebi.

Lucius Eggius: *Praefectus castrorum* of Legio XIX, KIA in the Varian Disaster. Reported to be a fine and brave soldier.

Eucherius: Son of General Stilicho, in our timeline executed by order of Honorius.

Cornelius Eustachius: An *optio* in Pullo's cohort of reenlisted veterans.

Felix: State slave in the veterinary department.

Firmus: A soldier in Pullo's cohort.

Flavus: Germanic princeling, Roman equestrian, brother to Arminius but utterly loyal to Rome.

Fredenandus: Son of the Gothic cavalryman Theodomir and his wife, Alodia.

Quintus Junius Fulvius: First-order centurion of First Cohort, Legio XIIX, chief of the light artillery.

Caius Gabinius: Centurion of Legio XIIX, commander of Mucius Tursidius.

Faustus Gabinius: Centurion and a nephew of Caius Gabinius.

Gailawera: Daughter of the Gothic cavalryman Theodomir and his wife, Alodia.

Gnaeus Gallus: First-order centurion of Seventh Cohort, Legio XIIX.

Gisco: Polyglot Phoenician secretary to the legate of Legio XIIX and occasional diplomat and trade representative.

Goar: Another leader of the Alans.

Godigisel: Youngest son of Gunderic, *not* the crown prince.

Gummarus: An oarsman on Lusoria XI.

Gunderic: Son of Godigisel, King of the Vandals.

Hermagoras: Chief of the Rhodian slinger *auxilia*.

Hermann: Arminius. We don't know his birth name, so Hermann will have to do.

Hermeric: King of the Suebi.

Honorius: Emperor of the Western Empire, born 386 A.D.

Ishkapaius: Scythian auxiliary cadet, commands the first maniple of the Fifth *Ala* of *Auxilia*, Scythica.

Jerome: Catholic, Eastern Orthodox, Anglican, and Lutheran saint.

Samuel Josephus: Jewish doctor, trained in Alexandria, attached to Legio XIIX.

Horatius Jovis: Equestrian prefect, commander of the mixed cohort of Thracian archers and Rhodian slingers.

Hrodebert, son of Sigifurd: A Germanic warrior in the service of Rome. Also known as Rodius Sigius or Rod.

Hrodulf: Very young Germanic warrior.

Rudyard Kipling (aka **Gigger**): English poet, journalist, and novelist.

Kunibert: Germanic warrior.

Lampadius: A Roman senator of considerable personal courage.

Leimeie: More properly *Princess* Leimeie, a young Scythian girl, who cares for several apparently orphaned children.

Marcus Caelius Lemonius: First spear centurion of the 18th Legion, later *praefectus castrorum*.

Leonidas: Palmyrene horse archer, killed by Scythians.

Justus Liberius: An arrogant messenger from the Imperial Court.

Gnaeus Marianus: One of the former gentleman rankers promoted to tribune.

Maeonius: A decurion of the Palmyrene horse archers.

Metrovius: Commander of the castle across the Rhine from Mogontiacum.

Faustus Metilius: First-order centurion, becomes *primus pilus* vice Marcus Caelius.

Aelius Nerva: A centurion detailed from his usual cohort to help train the Fifth Scythian Auxiliaries.

Constantine XI Palaiologos: Last emperor of the Eastern Roman Empire.

Ovidius Paulus: A centurion detailed from his usual cohort to help train the Fifth Scythian Auxiliaries.

Galla Placidia: Daughter, granddaughter, wife, and mother of emperors. In our timeline, a power in her own right, though also sometimes a pawn.

Privatus: Freedman to Marcus Caelius.

Titus Atidius Porcio: A soldier of the Eighteenth Legion, later promoted to aquilifer for the legion.

Anicius Petronius Probus: A Roman consul in 406 A.D.

Gaius Pompeius Proculus: Junior tribune, later legate, of Legio XIIX.

Lucius Pullo: *Optio* and then junior centurion in Legio XIIX. Great-grandson of both Lucius Vorenus and Titus Pullo. Cousin of Titus Vorenus.

Qadan: Paramount chief of the Argippaeans.

Respendial: King or chief of the Alans—I have chosen to make him the king—who joined with the Vandals.

Junius Rubelius: Gentleman ranker, equestrian legionary. Later promoted to *optio*, then to junior grade tribune.

Publius Rufinus: A centurion detailed from his usual cohort to help train the Fifth Scythian Auxiliaries.

Sextus Sattius: First-order centurion of Legio XIX, later detached to the Agricultural Department for a rest.

Serena: Wife of Stilicho and niece and adopted daughter of Theodosius I.

Sigigastiz: Germanic warrior, cousin to Flavus, KIA at the Varian Disaster.

Quintus Silvanus: First-order centurion of the Legio XVII, later transferred to command the cohort of refugees from Legio XIX, which became the Twelfth Cohort and acquired additional skills with the staff sling.

Seetheredglowofmorning: Red, for short. Scoutmaster of *Exploratory Spacecraft 67(&%#@*.

Skyles: Scythian scout.

Ruvaine ben Aharon ben Solomon: Surgeon at the Castle, aka Pullo's castle, across the bridge on the east bank of the Rhine opposite Mogontiacum.

Suero: Germanic warrior.

Sweetasthescentofglowblossoms: Blossom, for short. Mate to Seetheredglowofmorning.

Gratianus Claudius Taurinus: Aquilifer (eagle bearer) of Legio XIIX, later a centurion.

Tabiti: Scythian mistress, later wife, to Marcus Caelius. Her name means "the flaming one."

Tadmor: Leader of the Palmyrene horse archer auxiliaries.

Taurou: Second-in-command of the wing of Gallic auxiliary cavalry, under Atrixtos.

Thancrat: German in the service of Rome. Third commander of the German auxiliary cohort, after Flavus and Agilulf.

Theodomir: A Gothic cavalry officer.

Thiaminus: Freedman to Marcus Caelius.

Mucius Tursidius: Injured legionary, saved from amputation by maggot therapy. Later awarded the Civic Crown and made a tesserarius and standard bearer.

Christianus Vibianus: Prefect in command of the east bank castle, at the end of the bridge leading from Colonia.

Beatus Vitalianus: Quartermaster of the fort on the eastern end of the Mogontiacum bridge.

Decimus Vitelius: Centurion in charge of veterinary services. Proponent of maggot therapy.

Titus Vorenus: *Optio* and then junior centurion in Legio XIIX. Great-grandson of both Lucius Vorenus and Titus Pullo. Cousin of Lucius Pullo.

Waldalenus: Latinized Frank in command of the highly reduced forces at, and the fortress of, Vetera.

Wulfila: Gothic chieftain and negotiator.

Zalmoxis: Chief of the Thracian archer *auxilia*.

Zaranaia: Scythian captive girl, mistress to Gaius Pompeius. Her name comes from a word meaning "golden."

Zaya: Argippaean meretrix.

APPENDIX C:
THE SCUTUM

(What follows is a synthesis of a lengthy email discussion I had with the best historian of the Roman Army, living or dead, Adrian Goldsworthy. I commend to the reader both his nonfiction and his fiction. Note that these conclusions are mine, not necessarily Adrian's.)

As all right-thinking people know, the Roman shield, the *scutum*, was in battle held by a single hand and used as much for an offensive weapon as the gladius and *pilum*.

Sorry, no, I don't believe it. I think the scutum was routinely held by a two-point method, with the forearm feeding through a band, partially or all the way to the crook of the elbow, and probably some kind of flexible handgrip, rope or leather.

Why not? Why don't I believe it? What kind of arrogance and affrontery causes me to say that I disagree? There are three reasons, actually: common sense and reason, indirect written evidence, and direct epigraphic evidence.

To take the first point, common sense and reason, first, a one-handed grip is simply a lousy grip. An opponent can get more leverage by engaging the side of the shield than the user can at the single point in the center. A one-handed grip is also a tiring grip; no, no, don't talk about training here, equal amounts of training still make a two-point grip less tiring than a one-handed grip. Moreover, it is not necessary to use a one-handed grip still to be able to punch with the shield. Yes, range shortens with a two-point grip, but a lunge and a punch is still plenty.

The indirect written evidence concerns those writers who addressed the *testudo*. Allegedly, per Cassius Dio, *Roman History*, 30.1, to test the *testudo*, men would walk on it, would march over it, would ride horses upon it, and even drive carts on it. Here, however, is the problem: picture a single-handed central grip. A centurion walks along atop the *testudo*; what happens when he steps near the edge? Unsupported, it gives way and we have one very unhappy centurion, vine staff in hand, beating the poor legionary responsible.

So let's say that our legionaries don't just use their one-handed grip; they use their heads, too. Well, if so, they're really not using their heads because a two-point grip *still* cannot support a man walking on the edges. We still have that thoroughly annoyed centurion with his vine staff.

No, it takes three points to provide a strong and steady platform. Hence our legionaries can place one hand or fist away from the central grip and provide a solid platform, no?

No, in that case one side of the *scutum* is stable, but a foot or hoof or cartwheel on the other side is coming through.

And then there is the epigraphic evidence for a double grip. Look first to the famous bas relief of the Praetorians from the

FIGURE 1:
Bas relief of the Praetorians from the Arch of Claudius on display in the Louvre.

Arch of Claudius that is on display in the Louvre (figure 1). If one measures by eye any scutum from the Praetorian relief, it becomes obvious that, if a one-handed grip is being used there, that grip is below the center of mass of the shield. This would put gravity to work against the bearer, making the shield completely unwieldy and uncontrollable. Conversely, if there is a one-handed grip, and that grip is at or above the center of mass of the shield, the bearers would find it extremely awkward—I'm not sure it would even be doable—to hold the shields as close to their bodies as those shields are in the carvings. However, if they are using a more typical grip, with their arms threaded through a half loop or belt and their hands gripping a hand-hold, then the carvings make perfect sense and everything is where it should be.

Now go look closely below at the carvings looted from the Arch of Marcus Aurelius, for reuse on the Arch of Constantine (figure 2). Now look at the elbows of the two legionaries with their backs to the view. Yes, right there, in plain view, are straps near the elbows and nowhere near the hands.

The sculptor could have done that, just went with something old like the strap and grip for a Greek *aspis* he was familiar with. Conversely, though, he got the three different kinds of

FIGURE 2:
Arch of Marcus Aurelius carvings, reused on the Arch of Constantine.

FIGURE 3:
Detail of two soldiers with shields on the Ahenobarbus monument in the Louvre.

lorica portrayed pretty much right. That's enough accuracy to give him a presumption of accuracy on the *scuta*.

Note that there is, or at least could be, other epigraphic information that shows single point grips. With some, too, it is very hard to tell as the *scuta* are somewhat miniaturized to give predominance to the human illustrations. That said, the Ahenobarbus monument, also in the Louvre (figure 3), shows two soldiers with shields. One is consistent with either method. The other clearly shows the soldier holding his *scutum* one-handed, by a horizontal grip. But—and it is a very large but—that second soldier also appears to be resting his on the ground. So, why not use the two-point grip when needed to fight and have a one-handed grip for saving your strength by resting it on the ground when not actually engaged in close combat?

The monument of Aemilius Paullus from the Battle of Pydna (figure 4) doesn't tell us much. We have depictions of Roman

FIGURE 4:
Detail of the monument of Aemilius Paullus from the Battle of Pydna.

soldiers employing *scuta*, but they're generally just impossible. In one case we see a one-handed grip, but it's below the center of mass of the shield, hence utterly uncontrollable, unless there's a strap there, which there might be, given the carving around the elbow. Even if there is a strap in that carving, though, the position of the forearm relative to the shield is absurd.

Another part of the Paullus monument, not shown here, is no better, except that we cannot see the upper part of the forearm. And it, too, shows an impossible orientation of shield to arm, with or without an arm strap and two point grip.

Thus, we can probably say in all fairness that the epigraphic evidence is somewhat mixed. That still leaves us with the preposterousness of forming a *testudo* without using a two-point grip and either head or hand for the third point, and the fact that a one-point grip is simply a lousy grip.

Ah, but what about the two Roman-era shields archeology has, so far, found, the Dura shield and the Fayum shield? The latter is so heavy that one doubts it was intended for normal use, but may have been more of a pavise, rested on the ground or the floor of a parapet and intended only to ward off missiles, thus holdable one-handed. The Dura shield was crushed and flat when found, and is missing pieces. It may never have been completed. I don't think we can infer much from it.

All that having been said, there is a problem with straps that none of the sculpture I'm aware of addresses. Unless there is either a shock pad by the elbow or a horizontal bar against which the arm would rest, a blow to the shield is likely going to deliver almost all its force to the elbow. That would not only *hurt*, but might—given that it's the elbow—make the shield impossible to hold. I have no answer to this except to suggest that there likely was such a shock pad, or a bar, or both. Probably both.

In addition, there actually *is* a reason for a very temporary one-handed grip. Remember that the *pilum* could penetrate most shields to drive the point into the meat beyond. One way to defeat this would be to push the scutum out as far as possible, so far that either the point would not reach meat or, if it did, would not be able to penetrate very deeply before the shaft of the *pilum* was stopped by the wood of the shield. For most Roman v. barbarian fights this probably wouldn't matter. But for the all too frequent civil wars? Then it would be *pilum* against *scutum* and one would desperately want as much stand off as possible. Interestingly, the metal boss in front of the *scutum* also tends to support this idea, insofar as it would give extra protection to the hand and arm holding the shield at arm's length, in case a particularly well-aimed *pilum* hit near center of mass of the shield.

Recovery from the one-handed, outthrust grip to the better arm-loop grip probably took a good deal of practice.

Photos in this appendix used by permission of the photographers as identified below.
Link for CC-BY-4.0: https://creativecommons.org/licenses/by/4.0/

Figure 1, "Relief des Prétoriens," photo by Jean-Pol Grandmont (CC BY-SA 4.0) via WikiCommons, https://upload.wikimedia.org/wikipedia/commons/d/dd/0_Relief_des_Prétoriens_-_LL_398_-_Louvre_(1).JPG

Figure 2, "Address of emperor to soldiers (adlocutio)," photo by Sergey Sosnovskiy (CC BY-SA 4.0) ancientrome.ru/art/artworken/img.htm?id=2819

Figure 3, "Sacrifice scene during a census," photo by Jastrow (2007), public domain, upload.wikimedia.org/wikipedia/commons/9/9a/Altar_Domitius_Ahenobarbus_Louvre_n3.jpg

Figure 4, "Center of relief on Aemilius Paulus monument at Delphi," photo by Colin Whiting (CC BY-SA 4.0), upload.wikimedia.org/wikipedia/commons/8/8c/Pydna_relief.jpg

Appendix D: Field Sanitation

> I grow old ever learning many things.
>
> —Pliny

One of the joys of writing is research. Well, for me it is. Another is figuring out solutions to problems that would be practical for your characters, or which may have been known at the time, but have been lost to the mists.

So I ran into a mention that the Romans placed their latrines next to their kitchens. I am skeptical and consider it quite impossible for a marching camp, which had no kitchens except *maybe* for the seven officers and one late-entry officer per legion and possibly a centurions' mess. Neither of those would have been near the latrines because a) latrines smell unpleasant and nobody would be eating near them who had a choice . . . and they had a choice, and b) they'd have been centrally located while the latrines would have been between the tents and walls of the camp.

The troops? They detailed one man per squad—maybe by rotation, maybe by selection—who was a good cook, to do the grinding of the flour, the baking of the biscuits, and any meat and or vegetable dish. But kitchens on the march? No.

But, yes, the latrines would have been inside the camp because, outside the walls, life was a very uncertain proposition.

Still, what to do about flies? They had methods for poisonous bait for flies, generally involving hellebore and arsenic, also various concoctions of sulfur and olive or olive oil or olive oil lees. But, ya know, contemplate the sheer volume of shit produced daily by 5,000 to 8,000 men and a bunch of asses, mules, horses, and oxen and I just don't see the legion carrying enough. And fire, in the absence of gasoline or a lot of wood...nah.

The answer, I think, lies in the life cycle of the fly, where it can take anywhere from nine days to six months for the maggots to turn into flies. This was something the Romans could have figured out from simple observation.

So, for a marching camp for a force continually on the march, don't worry about it; you'll be long gone before the first maggot gets its wings. You're there for a day, maybe a few. You dig a latrine, the flies lay their eggs, and then you fill the latrine before you move on, leaving the maggots to turn into flies so far down only Satan will be annoyed by them.

Ah, but what if you have to stay there for a while, even though it is a marching camp or in siege lines? Similarly, you open the latrine, use it for a week, in a warm climate, or until it's mainly filled in, in a cold climate, then finish filling it in, and dig another one just like it. (Engineer attitude check: This place sucks. Now knock it down and build another one just like it...)

It's worth remembering, too, that it wasn't until about sixteen hundred years *after* the fall of the Empire that armies were able to replicate their success in defeating disease in the field.

Appendix E:
So where did the
barbarians cross
the Rhine?

Neither I nor anyone can say for sure. Nonetheless, I'd bet even money that it was where I've said it was, for the reasons implied and stated. However, where I said it was may not be entirely clear from the reader's point of view. Moreover, a modern map of the area around Mainz can and probably does give a very misleading picture of the shape of the Rhine in 406. I mean, I only even noticed the anomaly in trying to figure out if a peninsula a mile or so east of modern Oppenheim had been an island in antiquity (it had). A German would surely have known this right off, but I've only visited and been stationed there; I didn't grow up there.

So, gentle reader, go to Google and dig up the map of the Rhine near Mainz—Mogontiacum in our story. Go south, from old Mainz, about fifteen miles to a spot between Guntersblum and Ludwigshoehe. Now trace to the east to the Rhine River. Look beyond the river and see the grand loop labeled "Stockstadt-Erfelder Altrhein."

That *was* the Rhine up until 1828/1829. The line between the shoulders of the loop had been excavated, so that the next spring melt forced all the water that had once filled that loop to pass through the current course of the Rhine, cutting a deeper channel and leaving the Altrhein as a nearly still backwater.

Before that reconfiguration, the waters would have been relatively still and slow, and probably relatively shallow, as well, compared to the Rhine of today or its main course, back then. This would allow freezing to take place before the rest of the Rhine froze, thus giving as little advance warning as possible to what was probably a small force of Roman defenders.

Just because they were barbarians, it doesn't follow that the Vandals, Suebi, and Alans were stupid. If I can see the potential, so could they.